SWAN'S CHANCE

SWAN'S CHANCE

Celeste De Blasis

BANTAM BOOKS
TORONTO • NEW YORK • LONDON • SYDNEY • AUCKLAND

Bantam Books are published by Bantam Books, Inc. Its trademark, consisting
of the words "Bantam Books" and the portrayal of a rooster, is Registered in
the United States Patent and Trademark Office and in other countries. Marca
Registrada. Bantam Books, Inc., 666 Fifth Avenue, New York, New York
10103.

*To Jane Berkey, Linda Grey,
Anna Slavick, and Louis Wolfe—
agent, editor, proofreader, and publisher—
with thanks for restoring
my joy in the work.*

Notes
and
Acknowledgments

⟅⟆⟅⟆

As noted in *Wild Swan*, Thoroughbred is capitalized on purpose. And the man's name "St. John" is pronounced "Sinjin," with the stress on the first syllable, in this book (in England, the name may also be pronounced "Sinjon," with the emphasis on the second syllable). The nickname is "Sinje."

I do my utmost to establish historical accuracy in my novels. However, in the case of the Seneca Falls Convention of July, 1848, I have altered one detail. By most accounts, there was very little warning before the meeting was held. But the longing to improve the status of women predated the convention by years, and so I hope I can be forgiven for adding a few weeks of prior knowledge.

Though I consulted myriad sources, including thousands of pages of pre-Civil War newspapers, the best account of Thoroughbred horse racing in the nineteenth century remains Hervey's two-volume work, *Racing in America*, published by the Jockey Club, New York.

I owe particular thanks to strangers who took time from their demanding schedules to answer my queries. In addition to those people mentioned in *Wild Swan*, I would like to add William H. Anderson of the Jockey Club, New York, Ruby Woodard of the Recorded Sound Division of the Library of Congress, and Sandra Roff of the New York Historical Society, and Donald Kennon of the United States Capital Historical Society. And the Maryland Historical Society in Baltimore, Maryland, and the

Vicksburg Historical Society in Mississippi were very helpful when I needed confirmation of certain Civil War events and dates.

But I am most grateful to my parents, Jean and Ray De Blasis, and to a host of special people: Eric Auest, Barbara Caldwell, Joseph and Donna Campbell, Betty Coon, Craig Corder, Clint and Susan Dailey, Michael Edgar, Bonnie and Pete McRae, Fred and Mae Nassif, Nancy Nielson, Pat and Eddie O'Brien, Bob Paluzzi, Owen Pollard, Alice Sauls, Tony and Ernie Sgro, and Vivian Wright. All remained patient and kind while I traveled more than a century away from them.

Celeste N. De Blasis
July 1984

I've a picture, time-discolored, hanging on my chamber wall,
Taken from an old oil painting that to memory will recall

Years from now the ancient legends of those races run of old,
When the winters were of silver and the summer-times of gold,

On a race-track in the southlands, where those flying feet once trod,
That has blossomed out in gravestones, that has rippled up in sod.

from "Lexington: A Fragment"
by Richard L. Cary, Jr.

BOOK
ONE

Chapter 1

Alexandria Carrington Falconer knew better than most the perils of mixing past and present. And yet, this day would see it done when Hugh Bettingdon and his wife Angelica, the Duke and Duchess of Almont, arrived at Wild Swan. Alex had never met his wife, and she had not seen Hugh since the day sixteen years ago when she, St. John, and the children—the twins, Flora and Blaine, and Morgan and Nigel—had sailed away from Gravesend, England, bound for a new life in America. But when Hugh saw her again, saw her with her husband Rane and with their son Morgan and daughter Gweneth, he would know.

When Hugh had written to say that he and his wife were coming to the United States and would like to visit the Falconers, Alex could have refused. Briefly she had considered making some excuse that would keep the Bettingdons away without offending their feelings. Though Rane had not pressed the point, she knew he would have preferred she do just that. But she could not. She was proud of what she had made of her life in Maryland, proud of her husband and children. And beyond that there was part of her that wanted Hugh, who had been such a kind and supportive friend in England, to approve the choices she had made.

She was too restless with waiting to remain in the house, and she went outside, savoring the immediate welcome of the sunlight.

Spring was fully on the land, and Alex viewed the burgeoning acres of Wild Swan as if they were newly created. In a sense they were, for her, because she had just returned to the farm after being away for weeks while attending various horse races in Virginia and the Carolinas.

The fields, pastures, orchards, flower beds, and the herb gardens, which provided many of the ingredients Alex used in brewing her healing simples, were flourishing with the fierce energy of the season. And the air was alive with the sound of livestock from poultry to the red Devon cattle to the Thoroughbreds—the exquisite horses bred for speed and endurance, the aristocracy of their blood showing in every sleek, strong line.

The horses were the heart of Wild Swan, the reason that Alex and her first husband, St. John Carrington, had purchased the estate, rundown then, renamed it, and worked so hard to renew the fertility of the land. Hers had been the dream of a new life in a new land; his had been the dream of a stable of horses fit to compete in the most demanding races. They had merged their separate visions into one, and had transformed the dream into the reality of Wild Swan.

They had not done it alone. In England they had had the help of Alex's grandmother, Virginia Thaine, who had sold a treasured wood of oak trees in order that Alex and St. John might have the money for passage to America and for beginning a new life there. And in Maryland friends and employees had helped the Carringtons, first in the establishment of the Wild Swan Tavern in Annapolis, which had been the Carringtons' first business in America, and then in their move to the land that lay nearly equidistant, about sixteen miles, from Annapolis to the southeast and Washington to the southwest.

Alex smiled as she watched her daughter with Samson. Though Gwenny would not be four until the fall, she had long since learned that one of the most interesting places to be was with Samson, who was endlessly patient with children as long as they obeyed his basic dictates about taking care around the horses. Samson and his wife had much to do with the smooth functioning of the farm.

Even though it was a familiar sight, Alex never ceased to be touched by the sight of the huge black man trailed by the children of Wild Swan. Slavery had left its fearsome marks on him; his dark brown skin was scarred on wrists, ankles, back, and right cheek, and part of his right earlobe and a lower front tooth were missing. But Samson possessed the most unblemished heart and soul Alex had ever encountered.

He had come to Wild Swan as a fugitive slave. Legally, he was still a fugitive, and worse, a murderer. Though Samson had fled from his owner under the threat of maiming or death, he had planned to return to

Georgia to free his wife and his two children. But his owner had come to Wild Swan, drawn there by interest in the famous horses, and Samson had confronted him a little way from the farm, begging him to release his family. In a rage, the slave owner had not only refused, but had attacked Samson with his riding crop and threatened Alex as well for her part in sheltering a runaway slave.

It had happened very quickly, but Alex could still see it all unfolding before her, slowly, as Samson dragged the man from his horse and bashed his head in. She had witnessed the killing and her own fear. She and Samson had stared at each other over the chasm of the worst Southern fear—a black man had killed a white man. And then she had remembered that this was the same man who had been training the horses and guarding the children with infinite tenderness since the day he had asked for a job at Wild Swan.

Alex had devised the plan to make the authorities view the incident as an accident, and she had begged Samson to remain at Wild Swan. And here he had stayed even after he had learned that his family had died of fever shortly after Samson had fled the plantation. Alex's housekeeper Della had helped him weather the crippling blow of that truth, and he had married her. Della, half black and half white, the product of a white owner's love for his slave, was a beautiful, highly educated, and freed woman who had had no intention of falling in love with the untutored slave Samson had been on his arrival at Wild Swan, but her heart had not heeded her mind's reluctance, and Alex did not know a couple, black or white, more closely bound by love than Samson and Della. Nor could she imagine Wild Swan without them. In addition to doing the cooking, Della ran the household while Samson was the undisputed authority in the stables. It was an arrangement that allowed Alex to leave the farm for extended periods of time without fear that everything would be in disarray when she returned.

Samson eyed her keenly as she came near, taking note of the fact that she wore her riding habit.

"Mebbe you an' Swan be needin' a liddle runnin' fo' de spirit. Mista Rane an' de company dat's comin', dey come you worry or not," he observed.

"You know me too well," Alex said ruefully. "And you are absolutely right—I will feel better for a run on Swan."

"Me too!" Gwenny chirped, and Alex mentally adjusted the speed of the ride to accommodate taking Gwenny before her on the saddle.

But Samson came to her rescue, pulling a sad face and complaining to Gwenny, "You goin' leave me here wid all dis work to do by myself?"

Gwenny looked pensive for a moment, torn by wanting to do both, but then she said to her mother, "I better stay here 'cuz Samson needs me to help 'im."

Alex hid her smile, greeting this announcement with the solemnity the child expected though she was aware that Gwenny's decision had been influenced by the fact that her brother Blaine had given her a ride earlier in the day. "Maybe if you and Samson get very warm while you work, Della could be persuaded to give you something cold to drink," she suggested, and Gwenny nodded her head in vigorous endorsement of the idea.

The big chestnut stallion danced a little in anticipation of being taken out for a ride, but he quieted immediately at a few words from Alex.

Though everyone called him "Swan," his full name was Wild Swan. He had come with the Carringtons to America when he was a newborn foal at his mother's side. His mother, the lame mare Leda, had been bred to another stallion after the birth of Wild Swan and had given birth to a filly, Black Swan, in the United States. It was not only the connection with the mythical legend of Leda and the Swan, but also Alex's love for the wild swans of England that had led to the naming of the Swan line as well as the farm and before that the Wild Swan Tavern. Leda had been the foundation mare of the stables, producing a string of fine race horses, and Swan had been a racing giant in his day. Even more, he continued to command high stud fees, in addition to producing champions for Alex's stable through his breeding to mares outside his own bloodline.

Alex reminded herself that she had much to be grateful for from Hugh Bettingdon. Though Wild Swan's sire had been a different stallion, Black Swan's had been a prize horse in Hugh's stable and the breeding to Leda had been a parting gift to the Carringtons.

Mounted on Swan, Alex felt immediately more peaceful and in control. However badly or well the reunion with Hugh went, this was her reality. This land and these prize animals provided not only financial security but strength for her spirit, too, and while, with the exception of Gwenny, the children's lives were centered in Baltimore now as was Rane's with his business at the Jennings-Falconer shipyard, Wild Swan was still the heartland of the family.

She looked back as she rode away. Though the buildings were from the last century, everything was in perfect repair from the dependencies—the smokehouse, springhouse, laundry, necessary, and others—to the brick stables, wooden barns, and the separate buildings that allowed the staff to live their own lives. And dominating the scene was the main house, a five-part design in rosy brick with the central two-story block flanked by "hyphens," covered passages that connected the two side wings to the rest. It could not match the vast dimensions of Hugh's country estate, but the house had a feeling of airy space, and because it was no more than two rooms wide front to back and had large windows and doors, the air circulated and kept the temperature bearable even on the hottest days of summer, though winter heating from the fireplaces was sometimes a problem when the weather was severe.

Alex shivered a little thinking of cuddling close to Rane on a cold night—or on a warm night, for that matter. He had journeyed to North Carolina to be with her at one of the race meetings, but still, they had been apart for long days.

Swan sidled impatiently, and Alex laughed. "Sorry, my pet. Did you feel my attention wandering from your magnificent self?"

She guided him through fields and woodland, letting him cover the ground with his long swift stride when the footing was good, keeping him safely reined over rough terrain, and generally enjoying the feeling of being attuned to the big beast. Spring flowers and bird song gladdened the day. Alex's spirits rose even higher when she heard the voices as she turned for home.

"I thought I might meet you in my travels," she called to her three sons as they came into view.

Though her voice was casual, her heart overflowed at the sight of the three young men riding so gracefully on Thoroughbreds from her stable. Blaine was twenty-one this year, Morgan nineteen, and Nigel seventeen, and Alex was convinced there could be no more handsome or satisfactory sons anywhere. Sometimes she felt a quick sorrow that none of them had chosen the Thoroughbreds as their work, but the sorrow was far less than the pride she felt for their choices.

Blaine was establishing a law practice that was already the envy of older men; Morgan, with his passion for ships and the sea, worked at the shipyard; Nigel would begin medical school in Philadelphia in the fall and was currently completing his general education and spending his free time working with Dr. Benjamin in Baltimore.

Despite the busy lives the boys had in the city, they had not shown the slightest reluctance in complying with their mother's request that they meet her at Wild Swan on her return from the races. Without asking for details, they knew she was anxious about the English visitors, and if their presence at Wild Swan could ease their mother's way, they were more than happy to be here.

As Nigel had said to his brothers, "We hardly ever have a chance to do something for her. It's usually the other way around."

With Gwenny back at the house, it would have taken only Flora, Blaine's twin, to complete the family, but Blaine confessed his failure to persuade her to come with them.

"I think she is afraid Carlton would decide to follow her out here, and God knows how uncomfortable that would be," he had said bitterly.

Alex had known that whichever twin married first, it would be hard on the other, but Flora's marriage to Carlton Fitzhubert III in the previous year had made the situation far worse than Alex had imagined. The marriage was a disaster. Carlton was good-looking, and possessed a surface charm that had been more than adequate to the task of courting Flora, but after the wedding he had rapidly proved himself a wastrel. He drank and gambled to excess, and Alex suspected that he had other vices too. However, far from running home to ease her lot, Flora's response had been to cut herself off more and more from her family. It saddened them all but was hardest on Blaine. And because he had been harsh and accurate in his judgment of Carlton even before the couple married, Flora welcomed his interference even less after the marriage.

Studying Blaine now, Alex saw that being at Wild Swan and out with his brothers had already eased much of the tension from his face. He caught her look and smiled at her, looking for an instant so much like his father St. John that Alex's heart twisted. The twins were her sister's children by St. John, but Alex had had their care from so early in their infancy, when she herself had been little more than a child, that she thought of them as no less her own than the children she had carried in her womb.

"Everything seems better and less complicated when I'm here," Blaine said, and then he added, "I'm not sure, but I think I remember the duke and that he was quite kind to us in England."

"He was," Alex agreed, and inwardly she hoped that kindness could withstand the truth. "Did you ride over to Brookhaven?" she asked, deliberately changing the subject.

Morgan answered for the three of them, and his voice was aggrieved. "Yes, but when we asked Sam to come riding with us, she claimed she was too busy."

"It's probably true," Nigel pointed out peaceably. "Her stepmother doesn't turn her hand to anything but gossip, and her father has never seemed very handy around the place. Sam is the one who really runs Brookhaven."

Morgan was not mollified. "I know that! But we're not here in the country that often anymore. You'd think she could at least find the time for a ride."

What he meant was that Sam should have been able to find the time to spend with him, but his brothers hid their grins and forbore pointing it out.

Samantha Elise Sheldon-Burke had been part of their lives since she had first wandered into Wild Swan as a grubby eight-year-old. But Morgan had been her special friend from the first day. The problem was that Sam was no longer a child and wanted Morgan to see her as a woman, while Morgan, though at nineteen a year older than she, did not want the complications of readjusting his view of her and continued to treat her in the old way.

Alex sympathized with both of them, for she and Rane had suffered the same situation, in reverse, when they were young: Rane had recognized his love for her as a woman long before she had been willing to leave childhood behind. But she knew that interference in the case of Morgan and Sam could only do harm though she allowed herself to suggest, "Perhaps I can persuade Sam to visit while the Bettingdons are here; I would like her to meet them." If Hugh and I are not at war, she added silently.

She and her sons continued to talk about a variety of subjects as they rode in, but their conversation died abruptly as they drew close to the buildings and saw that Rane had just arrived with the Bettingdons.

Alex was hardly aware that Samson and the other stablehands had come out to take the horses as she and her sons dismounted. All her attention was focused on her husband and the Bettingdons.

Over six feet tall, broad of shoulder and showing none of the thickening in the middle that came to so many men of his age, Rane still had the power to steal Alex's breath away. His dark hair had faint streaks of silver beginning at the temples, and his eyes were startlingly green in his tanned face. His features were boldly drawn from firmly molded chin to the strong sculpture of jaw, brow and nose. At forty-one, he was a man in every sense and in the prime of his life. And Alex knew him too well to miss the tension in him. As they mirrored each other in appearance, so too did they reflect each other's feelings. Her heart sank a little; she had hoped that he and Hugh would have established some easy, common ground by the time they arrived at Wild Swan. It was why she had convinced Rane to meet the Bettingdons in Baltimore and escort them to her at Wild Swan.

It was not that Rane was being rude, but she saw the restraint and wariness in his expression before the light and the love flowed into his eyes as he looked at her.

Beside her husband, Angelica Bettingdon so forgot her usually impeccable manners as to breathe, "My heavens, they are so alike!" and although she knew she was staring, she could not stop.

Alexandria was a beautiful woman, tall and slender. Her heavy dark hair was swept back from her face and crowned by her riding hat, but a few wayward curls had escaped to brush the high-boned cheeks. Her nose was straight, with slightly flared nostrils over a generous mouth, but her most arresting features were her huge green eyes framed by thick black lashes under arching brows. Her eyes had a little tilt at the outer corners which, added to the soft golden glow of her skin, made her at once earthy and exotic. Her vitality was so enormously compelling that although she was dressed in a fashionable riding habit, it was as if she was so essentially female, outward trappings were of no moment.

Angelica had raised no demur about the visit, but she had dreaded coming face to face with Alexandria Carrington-Falconer. Angelica knew her husband loved her; their marriage had been for love, not for social position nor any other necessity. And if Hugh had wanted a wife solely to provide him with an heir, he would have chosen a younger woman, for Angelica had been past the first bloom when they met, and the two children they had produced had surprised and delighted both of them. Their life together had made Angelica happier than she had ever thought to be, and she had never had the slightest cause to doubt Hugh's fidelity. Yet, the strange soft look that came into his eyes whenever this woman was mentioned had always made Angelica feel threatened. But now the fear vanished. She could almost feel the river of energy flowing around the Falconers and through them from one to the other. Alex and Rane were a pair on such an elemental level, she could not imagine anyone coming between them.

Her smile was warm as she was introduced to Alex and the Falconer sons, and when Alex addressed her as "Your Grace," Angelica said, "Please, no titles here. My name is Angelica," and the two women exchanged looks of mutual approval.

Indeed, Alex felt as if she had found an unexpected ally in Hugh's wife. While Hugh was forty-seven, the same age St. John would have been this year, Alex guessed Angelica to be closer to her own age of thirty-six. She was slightly built with fine features. Her hair was dark gold, her skin fair, and her eyes saved her from looking the perfect patrician beauty. Framed by dark lashes, they were an odd deep gray with scarcely a touch of blue, the irises defined by deeper gray rings. They were wise, kind eyes that somehow reminded Alex of her grandmother's, though Virginia's had been very dark.

Alex hoped that the flurry of greetings was covering her nervousness at facing Hugh again. Aside from a few more lines on his face and a little gray in his hair, he was just as she remembered him—tall, dark-haired, black-eyed, a well-built man and self-assured. She steeled herself to meet his eyes squarely.

"Welcome to Wild Swan, Hugh," she said softly, and for a moment the comfort of old friendship blossomed between them.

And then Gwenny catapulted from the house and into her father's arms. Almost instantly Alex saw the flare of discovery in Hugh's eyes as they flickered from Gwenny to Rane to Morgan to herself.

She did not flinch from the accusation in his eyes, but she felt a welling sadness. He was reacting exactly as she had feared he would. She could feel his withdrawal, and suddenly he was very much the duke, aloof and removed from the scene around him. It reminded her of how he had behaved toward her when he had first met her, before he had learned she was not like her sister Florence, St. John's first wife.

"You have done very well here," he said. "The land is obviously prosperous and the horses are magnificent." The stiffness in his tone stripped the words of their generosity, but Alex acknowledged the surface meaning with a dutiful thank-you.

She could hardly bear to look at Hugh's wife, fearful of the change she would see there also, but Angelica's brief frown was not for her but for Hugh. And Alex was grateful that Rane seemed distracted by Gwenny's claim on his attentions, though Blaine wore a slightly puzzled expression, as if this reserved Hugh was not the man he remembered from England.

For her part, Angelica restrained herself until she and Hugh had been shown their room and left alone to wash and dress for supper. Then she said, "How can you be so rude when your friend Alexandria has greeted you with such warmth?"

"You don't understand!" he snapped. "It's there for all to see. Blaine has his father's vivid blue eyes, though his hair is not as pale as St. John's was. And Nigel looks as he should, too, the blend of Alex and St. John giving him those blue-green eyes and the dark brown hair. But Morgan and Gweneth are obviously Rane Falconer's children. I could not know that in England because there was no Gweneth. Morgan was only a small child when the Carringtons left, and I had never met Rane Falconer. I thought Morgan was simply a testament to the strength of the Thaine blood Alex carries. But now I know. Though the girl's skin is fair and Morgan's golden, they can be no less than full brother and sister with their green eyes, dark hair, and a thousand other things in common."

"Alex and Rane look nearly as much alike," Angelica pointed out, "and they are, you told me, only distantly related. So perhaps the Thaine blood is as you first thought, strong enough to dominate from only one side."

"Your sweet reason will not serve here," Hugh said. "It is not only the children; it was in Alex's eyes. She was daring me to—"

"To what?" Angelica asked with mocking calm. "To betray her, to rail at her, to condemn her? My lord Duke, I love you, but you are being an insufferable boor about this. You have no right to pass judgment here."

"St. John Carrington was my friend. And I trusted Alex. Now I see that she made a cuckold of her husband." He ground the words out and his face was dark with rage at being played the fool, but Angelica was far more afraid of seeing him act unjustly than of his temper.

"It is not your business. And from all you have told me before, Alexandria saved your friend's life when he would have died of his wound from Waterloo and gave him new hope. But she adores Rane Falconer; that is clear for anyone to see. If she was with him before it must have been agony to let him go from her."

"If she did," Hugh muttered, but even in the turmoil of his suspicions, he could not believe that Alex had led a double life for long while she was with St. John. He was as miserable as he was angry, and he didn't want to look too closely at why Alexandria's behavior so many years ago should so wound him now.

"My dear husband, perhaps it would be better if we did not stay with the Falconers after all," Angelica suggested.

Hugh heard the sorrow that underlay the words. He knew how much his wife had looked forward to staying put for a while after the trip from England and the journey down the coast from New York where he had conducted business. And ruefully he acknowledged to himself that Alexandria's old magic was still working—Angelica was already a good way toward being charmed by her.

"No, we will stay, at least for a time. And I promise I will be civil."

Angelica had to be content with this, but she knew that Hugh's idea of civility could be markedly lacking in warmth.

Alex was only too aware of this lack when they gathered for supper. She knew that Rane and their sons were wondering why she and St. John had ever been fond of this very aloof Englishman. Angelica did her best to instill life into the conversation, asking questions and relating her first impressions of America, a commentary which was much more tolerant than that given by many English visitors. But it was hard going with Hugh observing it all with cold obsidian eyes, and Alex was infinitely relieved when the evening was over and she was at last alone with Rane.

"Just hold me for a moment," she murmured, leaning against him, and he wrapped his arms around her, tempering the desire that flooded through him at having her within his reach after so many days without her.

"Your duke is behaving quite well, considering how hard it must be for him to see me in his friend's place," Rane said, striving to be fair.

And seeing that you had been in St. John's place before, as well, Alex added to herself. She did not want trouble between the men, and so she made no attempt to explain that the Hugh Rane was seeing was not the real man at all.

Rane tilted her head up and kissed her, and Alex opened her mouth to the invasion of his tongue, tasting his mouth in turn, letting the sweet rising warmth ease the tensions of the day. And suddenly she needed him desperately, needed him to banish Hugh's cold judgment.

She rubbed sinuously against his hard body, and Rane loosed the leash on his own passion as they undressed each other and tumbled on the bed, breathing in each other's scent and tasting the salt and sweat of heated flesh.

They had been apart too long to go slowly. When Rane loomed over her, she tilted her hips to meet his thrust and took the hard fullness of him deep, sighing his name.

Rane moved in her, savoring the warm, pulsing welcome and the long sleek lines of her as she moved to celebrate his body and her own. No other woman had ever delighted him as Alex did, and he acknowledged it to be as much a matter of heart and mind as of the flesh, even as his passion drove him to completion inside her.

Still harbored in her warmth, he rolled to his side, taking her with him, holding her close. "My love, my love," he whispered, "no matter how busy my days are when you are gone, nothing is complete until you are with me again."

She rubbed her cheek against the dark fur on his chest and felt the comforting thump of his heart. "It frightens me sometimes," she confessed softly, "to know how much I need you. I cannot imagine this earth without you. You worry about me when I am gone, but often you are far out to sea, and that is more dangerous than any of my travels."

"When I am at sea, I give her all my attention, and I do not tell her how much I love my wife. The sea knows no cause to be jealous on my account."

He was teasing, but Alex could hear the underlying seriousness; as rational as Rane was, he had his share of superstitions regarding the sea.

He left her briefly to snuff the candles the servants had left burning for them, and when he settled down again, he expected Alex to go right to sleep, but instead he could feel the lingering tension in her. His hands found the tight cords in her neck and shoulders and massaged them.

"This is your life, here at Wild Swan, and with me. It does not matter what the duke thinks." Rane's voice was gentle, but there was a thread of steel in it. He had been battling his jealousy ever since he had begun to suspect how much the visit of the Bettingdons meant to Alex, and the jealousy was still there, lurking in the back of his mind, even though he knew he had a depth of love from Alex that no one else, including St. John Carrington, had ever had. But he would never be completely comfortable with the fact of her past life with St. John, and he did not want this visitor from the past to have any power over her.

"You are my life," Alex said, and finally she relaxed against him.

But in the next few days, Rane discovered that Alex was fully at ease only when she was alone with him. In her role of hostess she was too brittle, too anxious to please. Accustomed as he was to the confidence she usually brought to so many tasks, it made his heart ache to see her so vulnerable. And he began to observe Hugh Bettingdon more closely and to understand the cause of Alex's hurt.

It no longer mattered that Rane had not known Hugh before; he began to see the deliberate coldness the man was displaying toward Alex. Hugh's own wife was a good measure of it because she was so obviously distressed at her husband's behavior and tried so diligently to smooth the way. Above all else, Rane had come to realize that Alex would never have felt friendship for such a rigid man as Hugh seemed to be.

Once he realized that Hugh's attitude was deliberate, it was all he could do to control his temper. His overwhelming instinct was to punch the man in the mouth and send him packing, but he knew that would never do because it would hurt Alex more than Hugh.

He cautioned himself to patience, and when he thought he could control his anger he sought Hugh out. "You and I have matters to discuss," he said without preamble, and had the satisfaction of seeing that the duke was taken aback by this direct approach. "Will you hear me out?" Rane asked.

Slowly Hugh nodded, feeling not only the strength of the man before him, but also his own guilt; Alex's patient sorrow in face of his treatment of her had begun to wear on his conscience.

"You are making my wife miserable, but she will not defend herself to you," Rane said bluntly. "And she should not. But I will not have you thinking ill of her; your good opinion means too much to her."

Hugh kept silent, wanting to hear what the other man had to say, wanting to understand.

"She cared for St. John even when she was a child. He was a special friend. And she was wise enough even at thirteen to see that her sister and St. John would make each other very unhappy. She told St. John that, and her sister overheard it and reported it to their mother. Virginia Thaine, Alex's grandmother, brought Alex to us in Devon because we were related and because she wanted Alex to be in a loving home. I am sure you know that Alex's mother did not love her, and her father was not strong enough to show his love. When Florence died after producing the twins and St. John went off to fight against Napoleon, Alex was summoned home. My poor love, she thought her mother had at last realized both need and love for her, but Margaret Thaine only wanted someone to care for Flora and Blaine and someone to blame for Florence's death."

He drew a deep shuddering breath. "She was not quite fifteen when she left us to return to Gravesend, but I already loved her and not as a cousin. The Thaine blood is strong; the green eyes and dark hair show up again and again through the generations, but Alex and I have nothing closer than great-great-great-great-grandparents in common. I gave her time, as much as I could bear, and then I went to Kent to claim her. I found her mother not only to the twins, but to a daughter of her own. I believed her married to St. John; I did not know that marriage law in England forbade St. John's marriage to his dead wife's sister. Alex was only sixteen, but she was fully a woman, and I loved her even more than I had before. She would not term it so, but I seduced her. She made no complaint against St. John then or ever after. Even now I do not know the full story. I only know that she was desperately unhappy when I came to her at Gravesend. She would not leave St. John nor take the children without word from him. I believe she thought he would tell her to go. But he never did."

He held Hugh's eyes with his own. "I had no word from Alex nor did I see her again until we came face to face in Annapolis four years later. I did not know about Morgan until I saw him there. Call it chance or fate —whatever you will—but Alex and I did not plan the emigration to America in concert. And by the time we met again, I was miserably married to a madwoman who eventually took her own life while Alex was fast bound to St. John Carrington, bound to him by love. I swear to you that that love never faltered, not even after St. John was crippled by the rogue horse. Alex and I did not love anew until a year after St. John died. She did everything she could to keep him alive. Even when others said he would be better off dead because he would never walk or ride again, Alex fought to keep him with her. And though I doubt you will believe this, I mourned his death. Whatever he had been before, St. John was a fine man by the end of his life—a good husband, a good father, a good friend."

Hugh still found it disconcerting to see this masculine version of Alex, but the strength and honesty of the man were too tangible for him to ignore. "I do believe you," he said, and he thought of how odd it was that he and this man should hold pieces to the same puzzle.

Hugh remembered too clearly how St. John had treated Alex at that unhappy time. Disinherited by his family on his marriage to Florence, further condemned for his association with Alex after her sister's death, and bitter at the necessity of having to adjust to the loss of his arm, amputated after the Battle of Waterloo, St. John had eased his own dark humors by taking out his frustrations on Alex, treating her as if she were a mistress soon to be cast off. So obvious had St. John been in his abuse and Alex in her misery that Hugh had made a calculated offer, telling St. John that he would take Alex under his own protection, since his friend had so obviously tired of her. He had meant to shake St. John out of his selfishness, and he had succeeded; St. John and Alex had been much happier together thereafter, St. John having realized with the threat of losing her how much Alex meant to him, how much he loved her.

But though Hugh had accomplished his goal, he had also lost, for he had begun seriously to consider what it would be like to be Alex's lover and to lavish her with gifts and care. He had even pictured her as his duchess. Instead he had had to be content with his role as friend to Alex and St. John and godfather to their children. He was perfectly content with Angelica, but she had not been in his life then, and seeing Alex again had reminded him of how strong the attraction had once been. The shock of discovering, through the proof of the children Morgan and Gweneth, that while he himself had desired her, Alex had been the lover of this Rane Falconer, was deep and personal. But now Hugh understood that it was by his intervention that St. John had reclaimed Alex—had he not interfered it was quite possible that St. John would have foolishly abandoned her, thus setting her free to marry Rane years ago in England.

It was a strangely humbling perception. While Hugh liked to control his own destiny, he did not like the idea of having such a hand in the course of other people's lives. He had no intention of telling Rane what his part had been. Rane had been extremely civil to the Bettingdons since he had met them in Baltimore, but Hugh did not mistake the tightly controlled power. In defense of Alex, this man would willingly inflict grievous harm, and Hugh did not think Rane would easily forgive him if he knew that he had offered for Alex, even though it had been years ago.

Instead he broke the uneasy silence between them by saying, "St. John was a fortunate man, and so are you. This place, the children, the horses—everything shows the strength and grace of Alex's loving."

For an instant, Rane was tempted to demand that the duke tell him all he knew of Alex's years with St. John in Gravesend—he had seen the bemused look of memory in Hugh's dark eyes—but then he thought better of it. He and the duke had been taking each other's measure since they first met, and he did not doubt that Hugh kept his own counsel. Beyond that, Rane reminded himself that Alex's years with St. John Carrington belonged to her. They could not be altered or erased by any means, and knowing more about them would not ease the old jealousy.

"Of course you need not tell me," Hugh said, "but does Morgan know?" The question was so gently asked that Rane could not take offense.

"I promised Alex I would never tell him. He was very fond of St. John. But I think he knows. He is not blind; he can see how alike he and Gwenny are, though he has said nothing to his mother or to me. Perhaps he does not want confirmation of the truth." Rane's voice was steady, but his eyes were sad.

Hugh thought how he would hate it if he were somehow prevented from claiming his son Christopher for his own. And yet, already he had witnessed how evenhanded Rane was in the affection he showed to all the children. He found his reservations giving way to admiration.

"I apologize," he said forthrightly. "And I must confess that behaving in such a beastly fashion has given me no pleasure at all. But it was not only a matter of being offensively judgmental, it was something more, something I can only hope you will understand. I think every man, if he is fortunate, meets a woman at some time in his life who becomes for him the epitome of everything he wants to find. Though Alexandria would never want to play such a role, I fear I cast her in it and demanded that she act it exactly as I wished. I do not even demand so much from my wife."

"I do understand," Rane said. "The only difference in our situations is that where first I worshiped so have I married. I have loved Alex for a very long time, and there is nothing I would find in a woman that she does not possess."

Rane debated inwardly for a moment, and then he added, "Alex made every attempt to keep the fact of Morgan's parentage from St. John, and St. John was a wonderful father to Morgan. He never gave Alex any sign that he doubted he had fathered the boy. But I think he knew. Before he died, he asked me to take care of Alex, and for an instant, it was as if he could see into my very soul."

"Then he knew that she would be safe and well-loved after he was gone," Hugh said, and he put out his hand. The two men sealed their pact with a firm handshake.

"To Alexandria," Hugh offered as if it was a toast. "And now if you will permit, I would seek her out and try to heal the wound I have caused."

Watching the duke walk away, Rane found that he now understood completely why this particular friendship mattered so much to Alex.

Alex sensed the change in Hugh's attitude before he spoke. Even the way he carried himself was less rigid, and his eyes were bright with the warmth and intelligence she remembered.

"Can you forgive the unforgivable?" he asked, taking one of her hands in both of his. "I am as ashamed as I have ever been in my life. My wife called me an insufferable boor, and that is too kind. I have no right to make any judgment about you or your husband, but were I called upon to make one now I would say that you share as much love as heaven allows and deservedly so—the two of you have weathered much together."

Much to Hugh's distress, the tears welled in Alex's green eyes and overflowed, but she hastened to reassure him.

"It is only that I am so glad you understand. I could not bear to think our friendship had ended because of my love for Rane. But oh, Hugh, I beg you to believe that I did love Sinje; I loved him very, very much."

"I do believe you. If your husband is gracious enough to admit that love, how could I doubt it? And in England I was witness to how happy you made St. John; I should never have forgotten that."

Alex's heart rejoiced not only in the reconciliation, but in the knowledge that Rane had engineered it, despite the fact that his own interests might have been better served had a final break come between her and this reminder of her past.

Her face was radiant as she looked up at Hugh. "Welcome to Wild Swan," she said, robbing the past days of all their bitterness.

Chapter

2

In the ensuing days, Alex basked in Hugh's approval, and Rane could not blame her. Hugh at his most charming was charming indeed, and his enthusiasm for Wild Swan was genuine, particularly in regard to the horses. Beyond their beauty, Hugh was impressed by the calm of the hot-blooded Thoroughbreds. It was not that they were above a sudden start now and then, or brief displays of temper, but overall they were extremely well-mannered animals. And there was no doubt that affectionate, patient handling had much to do with it. Whenever Alex approached one of them, she was greeted with friendly whickers of welcome and a head outstretched for a pat or a rub on a particularly sensitive spot.

In addition to the younger animals, Hugh saw the foundation mares, the chestnut Leda, now twenty-four years old, and Mab's Maid, "Mabbie," a bay of twenty-three. Their days as brood mares were over, and both showed signs of age in whitened muzzles, slightly swayed backs, and hollows near the eyes. But as in the case of women who age gracefully, it was easy to imagine their former beauty.

Hugh drew a sharp breath and then let it out in a long, low whistle of appreciation as he watched Wild Swan running in his paddock. When last he had seen him, Swan had been a mere foal at his mother's side, but now, at sixteen, he was magnificent. His chestnut coat glinted with dark red fire, and though he had not been entered in a race for years, he was still as powerfully muscled as if he were ready to step onto a course and fly ahead of all contenders at the first beat of the drum. In him ran the blood of such notable horses as Herod, Eclipse, and Matchem. His head was beautifully sculpted, and his large dark eyes watched the approach of his visitors with interest.

He came to the fence, and Alex offered him oats which he lipped off her flat palm. "You are a greedy boy," she crooned, and he answered with a comfortable rumble of sound.

Hugh was impressed as well by the nine-year-old black stallion, Magic Swan, born of Mabbie by Bay Swan, one of Leda's colts. Hugh favored black horses, and this one was superb.

"Sinje was always very clear about not investing the horses with more intelligence than their nature warrants, and that is not a great deal. But, I confess, I have difficulty believing they are all so stupid. Often I am sure that Swan and Magic understand everything—a silly fancy, I know."

"Oh, I don't know. One of my trainers told me that he had finally solved the mystery. He claims that horses aren't stupid at all, that in fact they are highly intelligent and simply have nothing to say to creatures as imbecilic as man."

They laughed together and felt the harmony of an old and tested friendship, and though they did not feel a need to articulate it, they were both grateful to their spouses for allowing them to indulge their shared interest in Thoroughbreds without interruption.

"He's so pleased to see the blood of one of his stallions carried on in your wife's horses through Black Swan, you would think he was viewing his own grandchildren," Angelica observed ruefully, and Rane grinned.

"I know precisely what you mean. When Alex has to sell one of the horses, even though it be for good cause, it is as if she is selling one of the children."

Rane found that he enjoyed Angelica's company very much, for she was intelligent, observant, and as forceful in her own quiet way as his own wife was. But he was surprised by her next words.

"I envy you and Alexandria, and even your children," she said and then hurried on when she saw Rane's apprehension. "Oh, no, I don't mean to say that I am not perfectly happy with Hugh, for I am. It is just that your lives are so much freer than ours. Your sons have chosen what they will do; our son Christopher may study what he likes and will have the funds to indulge his fancies, but he will be the next duke and take on all the duties that entails, no matter what his heart and mind might have liked to make of his life. Our daughter Amelia will have a little more freedom, but not that much, for she will inherit a considerable fortune, and that will necessitate great care in choosing a husband. And though we have competent and loyal servants, I would not call them friends. I believe they care more about their social standing amongst each other and in comparison to the staffs of other establishments than they do about the fortunes of the Bettingdons. Here at Wild Swan, it is quite different. There is an informality I envy, and yet the work gets done as efficiently."

Rane did not dispute her because he knew the truth of her observation. He thought not only of Samson and Della and their sons, but of Cassie and Ned Mathers and of Polly and Calvin Brown and their two daughters. Free blacks, Cassie and her sister Polly had worked for Alex since they were very young and had married at Wild Swan. And he thought of the Barlows, Jed and Mabel and their brood of children. Though they were white, they worked in harmony with the blacks and were openly appreciative of their good fortune. Before coming here, the Barlows had barely survived as tenant farmers raising scrawny, undernourished children with little hope for a better life. But at Wild Swan, Jed had gained his own importance in handling the horses, while his sons learned to be jockeys or horse trainers, and Mabel had her own place as part of the household staff. And neither Jed nor Mabel harbored any resentment about working under the direction of Samson and Della. Hard workers though the Barlows were, they were not the sort to take the initiative.

"It is not that usual a situation, even in this country," Rane pointed out. "It is Alex's doing. There have been no slaves here since Alex and St. John purchased the land and Alex has always insisted that blacks and whites work together or they do not work here at all. Though this is a border state, and thus different from the states further south, in most places where blacks and whites work together, the blacks are slaves under the domination of the whites."

"It is very hard, isn't it?" Angelica asked softly, responding to the troubled look in his eyes.

Rane nodded. "Even when one is not directly involved in slavery, the guilt is shared. Though my partner, Caleb Jennings, and I try not to sell our ships to slavers, middlemen often do the buying, so it has happened. We build fast ships, and men who are trying to run illegal cargoes of slaves need all the speed they can get."

Angelica knew that while slavery was legal in the Southern states and slaves could be sold from one of those states to another, the importation of foreign slaves was against the law. She repressed a shiver though the day was warm. It seemed particularly evil that slavery should exist in this green and fertile land.

"Someday there will be a reckoning and our children or their children will pay the price," Rane said, and Angelica was suddenly glad that her children were growing up in England despite all the restrictions of their lives.

Though the Bettingdons preferred that no special fuss be made over their visit, it was inevitable that news of their presence at Wild Swan would spread. People came calling, some of them eager to extend an American welcome to the English visitors, others motivated by curiosity about the nobility.

Hugh and Angelica were gracious though their tempers were tested by those who peered at them as if they were animals in a menagerie. However, their patience thinned noticeably with the advent of the Sheldon-Burkes.

Samantha was part of the Falconers' lives and always welcome, but her father and stepmother seldom set foot on the property. Though this stepmother was more sociable than the last one, she and the Falconers did not share the same friends. "Horse traders and boat merchants," Violet Sheldon-Burke called them. She aimed higher, preferring the company of statesmen (she would not call them "politicians") and people who had great wealth and did little for it. But she had a network of spies who would have done any government proud, and her penchant for gossip was fueled by frequent trips to Baltimore, Washington, and Georgetown.

Today's visit was solely for the purpose of meeting the duke and duchess she had heard were staying at Wild Swan.

Mr. Sheldon-Burke looked acutely uncomfortable, but Sam was utterly miserable, her eyes red-rimmed as if she had been weeping, her face pale and drawn, completely unlike her normally vivacious self.

"We just had to come bid you welcome to our fair state," Violet gushed. "And if your schedule permits, we would be pleased to plan some outing at Brookhaven."

Angelica could hear the unspoken, "to show you off to all of our friends." Her gaze was purposely vague and aloof as she acknowledged the woman, but when she turned to Samantha, her demeanor was entirely different, not only because she saw how worriedly Alex was regarding the girl, but because her own heart was touched by the grief she saw in Samantha's face.

"I am pleased to meet you," she said gently. "The Falconers are so fond of you, I feel as if I already know you." She turned her head partway, only marginally acknowledging Violet once again. "How proud you must be of such a lovely young woman."

It was a social cut performed so masterfully that Violet, not even sure she had been insulted, was helpless to do anything in retaliation. After all, how could one object to praise for one's child—at the moment, the distinction of stepchild did not seem as vital as it usually was. But she was still exceedingly cross at Samantha for the gloomy aspect she was presenting to the visitors.

"She is lovely when she wishes to be," Violet said, "but she has no sense about some matters. She is pouting because we sold some slaves who were favorites of hers, though a useless bunch they were."

Sam had long since learned that the best weapon against her stepmother was silence, but she could not bear the injustice of this. "They were not useless! They worked very hard for us at Brookhaven. And now they will not even be together. You sold Livy and Jeremiah's son away from them; they will be in one place, he in another, and they are a family! You sold them south though they were Maryland born!"

"Your father sold them, not I," Violet said coolly.

"Because you told him to!" Sam's voice rose to a shriek of rage, and then she bit her lip, savaging it in an attempt to control her emotions.

"We really didn't need them any more, and I couldn't find a buyer to take them all. Livy wasn't respectful to your stepmother, and . . ." Mr. Sheldon-Burke's whining voice died away while his eyes shifted into some middle distance where he did not have to meet anyone's gaze.

Alex felt physically ill as the full import of the news dawned on her. She knew who the slaves were. They had always been devoted to Sam. She could imagine how galling it had been for Violet to observe the slaves' devotion to someone other than herself. Her horrible revenge must seem sweet indeed; Violet Sheldon-Burke was that sort of woman. But she was by no means a good judge of character; she had obviously thought that people in the Bettingdons' exalted position would condone this disposition of servants as property. Hugh's and Angelica's faces proved her wrong as they regarded her with identical expressions of incredulity mixed with contempt.

It was Rane who broke the tense silence that gripped them all. "Our friends will not be able to visit Brookhaven," he said flatly. "They are accompanying us to Baltimore to the races."

Under the circumstances there was no use in pretending that the Sheldon-Burkes' visit was proceeding in the normal way. Alex did not suggest that her neighbors stay for refreshment, and Mr. Sheldon-Burke finally roused himself enough to mumble that they had to be getting along.

But Alex could not bear for Sam to leave in such a state. "Sam, the boys are still here and they so wanted to spend more time with you," she said. "Please stay with us, at least for tonight. They should be back in time for supper."

Whatever objections Violet intended to raise died under the force of Alex's clear green gaze. And Sam was too hurt and weary to refuse shelter at Wild Swan.

She watched her parents out of sight, and then the tears began— trickling down her cheeks in a steady stream. "It is my fault," she sobbed. "I run Brookhaven very efficiently, so efficiently that we can manage with fewer slaves. My father did not consult me at all; he just sold them. They were taken away early this morning."

"It is not your fault!" Alex objected fiercely. "It is all your step-mother's doing, just as you said." She put her arms around Sam, hating to see her so broken and vulnerable. She thought, as she had countless times, of how wasted the girl was on her unappreciative family and wished that Sam might never have to return to Brookhaven at all.

Though it was the middle of the day, she put Sam to bed, holding her hand until, exhausted by her grief, she fell asleep as if she were eight years old again instead of eighteen.

Alex took a deep breath and squared her shoulders before she faced the Bettingdons. She found them looking no less stunned than before, and Rane's face was taut with continuing anger.

"How is Samantha?" Angelica asked immediately.

"She's sleeping, poor love. It is so unjust! She virtually runs Brookhaven and does it well, but still her father bends to her stepmother's every whim, and this was a particularly cruel one. The lot of these slaves further south may be much harsher because of what they have known here. Sam was raised with slavery, but she supports it no more than we do and always tries to ease the way of the slaves at Brookhaven." She closed her eyes for an instant, and then opened them again to face Hugh and Angelica directly.

"A brief passage with strangers, but it was sufficient, wasn't it? Now you can see the serpent in this paradise quite clearly. And it is an insidious beast of vast reach. One becomes involved without intending to. Sinje and I, for all our determination not to, became part of it. Before we trained our own jockeys, we hired other people's slave jockeys to ride for us. In order to race our horses, we had to, but that does not make it right. We were never truly sure the jockeys got to keep the money we paid them, though their owners assured us such would be the case. Racing here is a Southern sport, despite events at the Union Course on Long Island and some other Northern courses."

She twisted her hands together in an involuntary gesture of frustration. "I am still part of slavery. I have more than a few friends who are slave owners, and when I visit them, their slaves serve me as they serve their masters. And I am witness to what slavery is doing to the South. It corrupts everything. It has frozen a whole society in amber. It is bad enough here, but this is a border state. It is much worse further south. Tasks that free men working for wages could finish in no time barely get done at all because slowing the work is one way slaves can make a constant protest against their lot. Indolence is everywhere, among blacks and whites. Too many whites are so accustomed to having their every desire served by another, they have lost the power to act for themselves. Even those who own no slaves aspire to be free of work; idleness is the mark of a gentleman. The South lags behind in education, in manufacturing, in so many vital ways. Even what they do best is not well done. Cotton and tobacco exhaust the land, and too often slaves must be sold away to places where there is more need for them, just as those from Brookhaven were sold today. With more acres being planted in such regions as Mississippi, Louisiana, and the Republic of Texas, it seems it will never end. And now the House of Representatives has passed a gag rule to prevent discussion of antislavery petitions. It shows how powerful the Southerners are when allied with Northern proslavery forces."

Her words were all the more powerful for having been spoken with deadly calm. But her eyes glittered emerald green in her white face, and Rane knew before he took one of her hands in both of his that her skin would be icy cold. "Sweetling, as much as you wish it, you cannot slay all the dragons on earth. There is no place I know where absolute justice holds sway."

Alex could hear St. John saying the same thing years ago.

"Rane is right," Hugh agreed, "and so are you. Slavery is so pervasive that, in a sense, it even exists in England where it has been against the law for decades. Cotton mills are important to England. The conditions in some are hideous, but I have prided myself on providing the best possible conditions for the workers. They are well housed, fairly paid, and I do not own them. But the cotton comes from the hands of slaves in this country. That surely makes me as much a part of slavery as you have ever been. But though I realize it is of no immediate comfort, certainly slavery will be outlawed in this country as it was in England."

For a moment Hugh felt as if he was drowning in Alex's eyes. Her voice was the ancient mourning song of women across the ages. "At what cost will it end? Many women I know in the South abhor the condition of the slaves, and yet those women depend on the comfort those slaves provide. When I first came here, there were some people who were vehement in their avowal of the right to own slaves, but many more spoke as if it were understood that slavery would eventually end, if not for ethical reasons, then because the land was weary and slaves were becoming a burden. But now with the increased need of them in the new lands, there is a different idea rising, an ugly reasoning that says there is moral rectitude in the owning of slaves, that even God wills that whites should be supreme over blacks, who can never be more than children in need of guidance. Proslavery feelings are not confined to the South; Abolitionists have been attacked in the North. And yet, by virtue of the fact that large factories and small farms, not plantations, exist in the North and slaves are held in the South, there is more and more sectional rivalry and division. It seems less and less one country. It is too easy to imagine that one region will go to war against the other, just as the countries of Europe have for centuries. The cost—how then shall we count it? I have seen what war can do. I do not want to measure it again in the maimed or dead bodies of my sons or of grandsons yet unborn."

Angelica heard the echo of Rane's voice saying, "Someday there will be a reckoning, and our children or their children will pay the price." Her hand stole into Hugh's, and she was grateful for the reassurance of his touch.

The tension was not eased when the boys discovered that Sam was staying with them and why. Morgan was particularly distraught, making his mother thankful that he had not been there to witness the confrontation with the Sheldon-Burkes. She was not sure he would have restrained himself from doing violence to one or both of Sam's parents.

"Be sensible!" Alex demanded. "Sam needs comforting, not more anger. She's suffered enough of that on her own."

Alex could still see Sam as she had been at first sight ten years ago. She had been a grubby, badly dressed child that day, but even then she had shown signs of the beauty she now possessed. Her brown hair was alive with golden highlights, her eyes were a lively mixture of green, gold and brown, and her even features were enhanced by a full, rosy mouth.

Beneath her surface beauty, Sam possessed admirable strength and resilience tempered by a warm heart. It was well that she was so, for her home life would have quenched a lesser spirit. Her father did not mean to be cruel, but through his self-indulgence, he was. He was the sort of man who could not bear the unmarried state. When Sam's mother had died, he had married Lydia, a woman from tidewater Virginia. She had provided him with two more children and had had no room in her life for the child of the previous marriage.

When Alex and St. John had discovered the little girl on their property, they had gone to the Sheldon-Burkes to request permission for Sam to continue to spend her days at Wild Swan whenever possible, even to taking lessons with their children. The permission had been easily given, and Sam had become part of the Carrington family, sharing the bad as well as the good times.

Alex had loved Sam on sight, recognizing in the small, disheveled and yet forthright figure a kindred spirit. The very fact that the child was allowed to wander so far with no supervision was proof of how little attention she received at home, and everything Alex had subsequently learned had underscored the parental neglect. With her own ineffectual father and unloving mother, Alex had had firsthand knowledge of how desolate a child could feel. And as Alex's grandmother had extended the love lacking at home, so Alex had offered her own love to Sam. And Sam had given it back in endless ways since that first day. But the time she spent with the family had been drastically curtailed for the past two years.

When Lydia died, Sam had willingly taken over the managing of her father's household. Indeed, she had been glad to be of use to him, mistaking expediency for love. But last year, with the end of the mourning period, her father had found Violet, another version of Lydia. Violet was a rather faded beauty from Savannah who, though she was blond in contrast to the dark-haired Lydia, had the same hard, self-serving nature beneath the soft surface. She liked Sam no better than Lydia had, but rather than casting her aside, she made good use of her, leaving her in charge of the household and conveniently banishing the two younger children to schools in Virginia for most of the year.

Sam even had a hand in the management of the land. Her father had started in the right direction some years before by realizing that tobacco could no longer be raised on the exhausted acres and that the earth must be enriched and turned to other purposes, mainly grains and garden crops. But marriage seemed to be the only activity Mr. Sheldon-Burke could carry to fruition. It was now largely due to Sam that the fortunes of Brookhaven were improving as she put to use the lessons she had learned at Wild Swan.

Sam and Morgan belonged together; the thought rose unbidden in Alex's mind. As the evening progressed, she saw that, though he was obviously distressed by Sam's sorrow, Morgan was still keeping his distance, acting the part of doting older brother rather than lover. But in this instance, Sam was so in need of love on any level that she forgot to mask her feelings as she usually did and gazed at Morgan with open adoration.

Nigel, always sensitive to other people's feelings, murmured to his mother, "It kind of hurts to watch Sam loving Morgan so much, doesn't it?" He did his best to divert Sam's mind from her troubles by describing one of the cases of Dr. Benjamin, the physician he worked for when he was not in school.

"The woman was so ill that she lapsed into a coma and for four days and nights, she didn't move at all. Dr. Benjamin was sure she was going to die, but he let her be rather than plaguing her with drastic measures. And on the fifth day, she awakened all of a sudden, looked right at her husband and asked, 'Samuel, did I burn the roast?' You see, that's the task she was about before she fell ill. She wasn't aware at all of the time that had passed."

"Well, did she?" Morgan inquired, keeping his face straight.

"Did she what?" Nigel asked, still lost in the wonder of the woman's recovery.

"Burn the roast, of course," Morgan said, and Blaine added, "If I were trying the case of the burnt roast, I do think that being unconscious for four days—oh, yes, and four nights—would prove a more than adequate defense for a crispy carcass."

"Such small minds," Nigel chided them, but he joined in the laughter and was pleased to see that Sam was smiling.

Morgan's enthusiasm was all for the new ship launched from the Jennings-Falconer yard. The *Lady of Kent* was a Baltimore clipper, a type popular for years, but this one was built to surpass even her fastest predecessors.

"Sam, you'll have to come aboard! She sings when she sails, truly she does! She cuts through the water and rides on the wind as if she were made of magic instead of timber."

Even his brothers were silent before his awe, and it was Morgan who poked fun at himself. "I think I'm in love."

If Sam wished the words were directed at herself, she gave no sign of it, but continued to relax in the lively atmosphere that was so different from her own home, saying, "I would like to sail on her one day."

"Love is the only way to feel about a ship like her," Rane said. "She's as demanding as she is beautiful. Because she's to carry more sail, the crew will have to spend longer hours aloft to keep her properly rigged. A lengthy voyage on her will mean very hard work, for all the ease in the look of her."

Watching Rane's face, Alex smiled to herself. His family had been smugglers—free traders as they preferred to name it—in Devon. They had run precious cargoes of tea, silk, spirits, and other luxury goods past the lurking revenue cutters, and Alex knew that whenever Rane thought of speed in ships, he thought too of the excitement of free trading. And when he was thinking of it, his face looked as young and intense to her as it had on the first day she had met him. Her gaze shifted to Morgan and then to Gwenny—living proof that her own youth and Rane's had passed to their offspring.

Gwenny, who treasured the special privilege of being allowed to stay up with the adults, had finally begun to lose her battle to remain awake. Blaine picked her up and settled down again with her in his lap. With a contented sigh, she fell asleep as the conversation swirled around her.

All three of her brothers doted on Gweneth, but Blaine and the little girl seemed to have a special bond. Her blood tie was closer to Morgan; the choice of her heart was Blaine. Alex sometimes thought that it was because Blaine had been born with a twin sister and had some deep instinctive patience with the role of brother to a female.

Angelica blinked back sudden tears and confessed, "Seeing her all curled up like that makes me miss my children quite dreadfully, though I know I shall call them scamps within hours of being with them again."

She and Hugh proceeded to tell shamelessly exaggerated stories of their offspring's crimes and set everyone to laughing again.

"Christopher is so agile that keeping him in sight is a task requiring not only diligence but swift legs," Hugh said. "He once went missing for more than an hour though the cook swore he had been right there and had then simply vanished. Of course, it could have been quite serious, but as it developed, he had climbed up and tumbled into a flour barrel. When he reappeared, he was dusted white head to toe and terrified the staff until they realized he was not a ghost."

Sam laughed aloud at the image conjured by Hugh, and everyone felt the evening was a success when it ended with Sam showing soft color in her cheeks and more life in her eyes than she had since her arrival at Wild Swan. But Alex knew that nothing would change the fact that, back at Brookhaven, Sam would find the slaves who had also been her friends and protectors gone forever. Often she wondered how Sam could bear the endless hurts, large and small, inflicted on her by her father and stepmother. Alex wished she could persuade Sam to make her home with the Falconers, but she knew it was out of the question. And she was not even successful in convincing her to accompany them to Baltimore.

Sam was preparing to leave the next morning when Alex asked her, and Morgan added his own urging, saying, "Do come with us, Sam. We'll take you out on the *Lady of Kent.*"

"Thank you, but no," Sam said. "I was in such a state yesterday, I almost did not come to Wild Swan. But somewhere inside I knew I would find comfort here; I always do. And now I must go back to Brookhaven. The other slaves are very upset."

Morgan rode with Sam but he could feel the closeness of the

previous night slipping away as Sam withdrew from him. It annoyed him, but he could think of no simple way to breach the barrier.

"You will come to us if you need us, won't you?" he asked, though part of him wanted to replace the "us" with "me."

"I always have," Sam replied. "Your family has ever been generous with their love."

"It isn't like that!" Morgan protested, angered by her response. "They love you because of yourself, not as some sort of charity or favor. And you have been like a daughter to my mother."

And a sister to you, Sam finished silently. With quiet dignity she bade him farewell as they approached the buildings of Brookhaven.

Chapter

3

The bustle of the city engulfed them as soon as they arrived in Baltimore. The Falconer sons went back to their jobs, and Alex was grateful that Rane and the Bettingdons had grown to be such good friends, for she was distracted by the upcoming races and it helped to have Rane take charge of their guests.

For his part, Rane enjoyed showing Hugh and Angelica the city and the shipyard. He took them by carriage to see various sights, including the shot towers, which, for all their lofty presence, served only for dropping splatters of molten metal from the top into water at the bottom, the force of the fall and the impact forming them into round bits of shot. He showed them newly built churches, busy shops, and spreading residential neighborhoods, but he did not pretend to be totally sanguine.

"We are getting a fair share of immigrants from England and Europe, as well as a share of the current prosperity, so there is some expansion, but I am sure you can see it is not the same as New York. For much of this century, Maryland has been losing her trade to the North. The Erie Canal gave New York access to the biggest Western markets, and New York already had the advantage of being just that much closer by sea to England. That city has naturally become the major clearing house for trade from Liverpool and elsewhere in England. Baltimore is in the odd position of being not quite Southern, not quite Northern, even as this state is. But there has been increased trade in fresh produce from the interior, as well as exterior traffic with the West Indies, since Britain lifted the restrictions on foreign shipping six years ago. So it goes along quite well at the moment, but I fear that if this prosperity does end suddenly, the city will be harder hit than New York and others."

Hugh was an astute businessman and aware of the risks the Jennings-Falconer yard was taking in building ever swifter ships in such a mercurial financial climate, for the vessels sacrificed cargo space with each increment of added speed, and that meant that their mainstay would have to be luxury goods—spices, tea, coffee, silks, and the like.

"Perhaps it is possible for the good times to continue," Hugh ventured, after Rane had named the price being asked for a city lot, "but logic would have an end to it somewhere. It reminds me of the speculation that went on during the war with France. After such a fever, there always seems to be a chill when everything falls."

"Unfortunately, you are correct," Rane said. "And we have the added problem of the country's banking policy. President Jackson's attack on the Bank of the United States was vicious and thorough, and yet he built nothing in its place. He attacked Mr. Biddle, one of the directors of the bank, as if there was a holy war. Biddle embodied all the president hates, the power of the so-called elite. While it is true that Biddle was a powerful man and associated with others of like fortune and temperament, I find it difficult to imagine men of humble mien and ambition rising to such positions in the financial world. It seemed to demand a certain pride and ruthlessness. And for all his protests of interest in the simple farmer, President Jackson is anyone's match in both of those categories."

The United States had never established a monetary system as standardized as England's, and many problems had arisen because of that. Bank notes accepted in one region might not be honored in another, and because of the distances to market and other factors implicit in such a big country, terms of credit were often so extended that delays in payment complicated trade at every turn. The Bank of the United States had offered at least a measure of stability in its handling of government deposits. But its charter had been due to run out this year, and far from being willing to let it serve its allotted time, President Jackson had moved to destroy it prior to that, using his power to withdraw those government deposits and put them in state banks, his "pet banks," thus decentralizing that system and finance in general. There were rumors that Biddle might indeed have been guilty of malfeasance, but even more obvious had been Jackson's determination to pursue his personal vendetta against Biddle, no matter what the cost.

"It's no excuse for what the president did," Rane said, "but greed must surely be counted one of our worst liabilities. Everyone wants to get the highest price without giving thought to how that increases his own cost. I am as guilty as anyone else; I want the best price possible for the ships I sell and the cargoes I transport."

"The problems are not confined to this country," Hugh said, and his dark eyes were intent and grim. "England and the United States are closely bound now in trade; what affects you affects us as well. We need your cotton for our mills, and you still need our manufactured goods despite the growth of factories in your Northern states. And greed is as rife at home as it is here. Englishmen are no more proof against foolish risks of capital than Americans."

He paused, and suddenly he looked embarrassed, an unusual state for a man of his confidence. "Having now witnessed how much a part of this country you and Alexandria are, I feel somewhat traitorous in my purpose for this trip. I did not come just to deliver the horses to the buyer in New York and to renew an old friendship. For some years I have had investments in America, among them factory shares in the North and some cotton shares in the South. It is my intention to sell all, either to American buyers or to countrymen on my return to England. I do not doubt the great wealth of this country, and I believe that ultimately her financial status will be as vast as her acres, but nonetheless, at present, I feel it more prudent to concentrate my interests at home."

Couched in the most courtly terms, it was an indication that Hugh hoped the Falconers would tread carefully in the hazardous financial waters of their adopted country. It was not condescending, but rather caring, and Rane responded genially. "It is useful to have your opinion. Sometimes it is difficult to have a clear view when one is too close to the subject. My partner, Caleb Jennings, and I do worry a good deal about the current situation. We have contracts on ships to be built in the future and for long-term payments on ships already built. If too many of these ventures fail, we stand to lose much of what we have worked for. And yet, it seems that to do business at all, one must accept precarious terms."

The Bettingdons had been told the story of Caleb Jennings's vital place in the Falconers' lives and were intrigued to meet the man. Caleb had been an escapee from the prison on Dartmoor where both Americans and Frenchmen had been held as prisoners of war during what the Americans had termed "The War of 1812", though the English had disdained to name the action against the Americans. Alex had discovered Caleb in the cave used for storing smuggled goods near Clovelly in Devon. Only a few years older than Rane, Caleb had lost his ship and all but one of his crew to the British Navy while he was engaged in running goods past the blockade to France. And after the last crewman had died at Dartmoor, Caleb had wanted nothing more than to go home. His longing had made him eloquent as he had described the rolling green country of Maryland and the great salt bay called the Chesapeake.

Rane and Alex had risked much, had in fact committed treason in getting Caleb safely aboard an Irish free-trading vessel that had in turn allowed Caleb to travel home through the tobacco-trading connections Ireland had with Baltimore and other United States cities. But Caleb had left behind him the vision of his homeland, a vision vivid enough to pull Rane across the Atlantic when he lost hope that Alex would be his; vivid enough to give hope to Alex for a new life with St. John and their surviving children after they had suffered the death of their little girl, Christiana. Though neither Rane nor Alex had contacted Caleb before coming to America, in each case the ties had been quickly renewed on arrival in Maryland and had grown stronger by the year. Caleb and his family had sponsored their English friends when many Americans were openly hostile to the British.

Hugh and Angelica were impressed by the skillful and efficient work being done at the Jennings-Falconer yard and by the contentment evident in the men who were employed there. But Caleb was a shock.

He was a handsome man, very tall and lean, with golden brown hair frosted with silver in contrast to his dark eyes. But the Bettingdons had expected a man as vital as the role he had played in the Falconers' lives. They met instead someone so unfocused and retiring as to appear frail.

Angelica's kind heart was immediately engaged, and though she listened attentively to talk about the new ship, the *Lady of Kent*, and noted the pride in Rane's voice as he described the improved inner fittings that had been designed by Morgan, she declined to go aboard.

"If Morgan and Mr. Jennings don't mind, I shall stay ashore while the two of you scramble over the ship. Truly, I am not dressed for it. But, Rane, watch my husband carefully. If the ship would fit in his pocket, he'd steal her away from you."

"That I would," Hugh agreed with a grin. "Even though I know the future lies in steam, and the signs of it are everywhere in England, no smoke-belching monster will ever have the same place in my heart as good stout sails on the wind."

When Hugh and Rane had gone aboard the *Lady of Kent,* Angelica turned to Morgan and Caleb. "Now gentlemen, if you would be so obliging, I would like to see your models and plans for future vessels." She hid her smile at Morgan's start of surprise while noting that Mr. Jennings did not seem to find her request unusual. But try as she might, she could not draw him out nor coax a smile from him. He was implacably polite, but nothing more, as if it took all his concentration simply to keep his mind on the matter at hand. And she noticed that Morgan treated him not only with respect, but with a special gentleness.

"That is one of the saddest men I have ever met," Angelica said as she, Hugh, and Rane were heading back to the Falconers' Baltimore house.

Rane's own face was somber as he agreed. "He is indeed a sorrowful man, but he was not always thus. Four years ago he suffered grievous losses in the epidemic of Asian cholera. He lost not only his parents but also his wife Penelope and their unborn child. My parents and my sister-in-law Barbara died of the disease in England and Alex and I lost many friends, but Pen was the center of Caleb's life. She was a lovely woman. We all miss her terribly, but for Caleb, it was as if the heart went out of his world with her death. His two sisters survived, but they are long married and live distant, separate lives in New York. I am quite sure that Caleb would have ended his own life were it not for his three children. He is a devoted father, but the thing they need most from him is his own joy in living, and that he cannot give them. We all hope he will heal and find life worth living again, but when I think of how I would view my life and the world did I know that Alex would never share either again, I wonder that Caleb continues at life at all."

Hugh's hand closed tightly over Angelica's; it was the dark injustice they dreaded most of all—that having found such happiness, one would then lose the other to the random mockery of death

Rane found himself anxious to see Alex, and he was relieved to find that she was home, outside with Gwenny in the kitchen garden. As her grandmother had before her, Alex always wore gloves and a hat to shield her from the sun when she gardened, but they were her only concessions to vanity. She was kneeling in the earth with a broad smear of it on one cheek, and she was patiently showing their little girl how to thin seedlings.

For a moment Rane watched them unobserved, and he was filled with unutterable contentment and at the same time the peculiar sorrow that comes from looking on something at once exquisite and ephemeral. And then the mood was broken as Gwenny caught sight of him. She immediately abandoned her work and ran to him, and he swooped her up in his arms, ignoring her dirty hands and laughing. "You smell just like your mother, spicy and flowery."

Alex sat back on her haunches. "I think I'll take that as a compliment since you didn't mention the smell of mud. Where are our guests?"

"I believe I wearied them with too much of Baltimore in one day. They've gone to their rooms to rest but will join us at supper."

He set Gwenny down and seated himself beside Alex among the plants. Gweneth wandered off, drawing a smile from her parents as they followed her progress from one plant to the next. She touched only the ones she knew, concentrating mightily on remembering their names and saying them aloud: "Parsie, sage, rosy mary, and minutes." The words trailed back to them.

Alex giggled at Rane's puzzled look. "Minutes means thyme. It's her private joke. She was not impressed when I showed her the different spellings." Her expression sobered as she continued to gaze at the child.

"Flora?" Rane asked, and Alex nodded. "I went to see her today. She is so nervous and unhappy! But she wants to sort it out on her own. If she has a chance. Carlton is absent so much, it will be a wonder if Flora can make him stay put long enough to talk to him about anything important." She shredded a sprig of lavender in her hands. "I hope she divorces him!"

"It is unjust, isn't it? If Flora does divorce him, she will be seen not only as improper, but also as a dangerous woman, no matter the cause of the marriage's end," Rane said angrily.

"Anything is better than staying in a failed marriage." Her eyes held his. "How very lucky you and I are!"

"Luck and some work," Rane corrected judiciously, but his expression was alight with love as he kissed her.

"Mama loves Papa," Gweneth announced, having circled back to them. She clapped her chubby hands together gleefully, and the three of them were laughing as they went inside.

Rane had had the Baltimore house built after his marriage to Alex, and his thoughtfulness showed in many ways, for not only was there ample room for the family but he had had elaborate stables built as well so that Alex could keep her horses and grooms there when she was in the city for race meetings. And Rane had hired Horst and Gerda Koller to run the household. They were as steady and strong as their square, sturdy forms looked. German immigrants, the middle-aged couple worshiped in their own way, spoke their own language to each other and little in any language to anyone else except the children, on whom they doted.

As soon as she was inside, Gwenny ran to Gerda for the cookies and milk the cook offered.

"Base bribery," Rane muttered with a smile.

"And completely to our advantage," Alex answered. "Gerda will keep her busy for the rest of the afternoon."

Within moments after they had reached their chamber, Horst and a maid appeared with hot bathwater, Gerda having anticipated the Falconers' wishes without being told.

"You were inspired the day you hired the Kollers," Alex told Rane as she eased into the bath. Rane got in with her, proving not for the first time that there had been a reason for purchasing such a large tub, though the islands of his knees always amused Alex.

"You might miss some spots if I don't help," he said, plucking the bath sponge from her hand and beginning to move it in slow circles over her. Then all coherent thought fled as Rane got out of the tub and lifted her out.

They were nearly late for supper, but the Bettingdons were not much before them, and Angelica looked as contented as Alex. Seeing this, Rane winked slyly at Alex, and it was all she could do to maintain even a semblance of dignity. Fortunately for both couples, the talk from Morgan, Blaine, and Nigel, all about the next day's races, provided a needed diversion.

The meeting had already begun this day, but the event had been for three-year-olds and had no entrants from Wild Swan. However, the second day would feature a race of two-mile heats, and Puck was entered in that, with his stablemates competing in the two following days in the three- and four-mile events.

"Have you informed Puck that he's liable to be living elsewhere if he doesn't mind his manners?" Morgan asked his mother.

"First I would have to explain to him what manners are," she retorted wryly. "Naming him for a mischievous sprite wasn't the best idea."

In the previous races of this spring season, Alex had taken three horses south. Dreamer, a seven-year-old mare, had beaten all comers at four miles; Wizard, a five-year-old stallion, had won more than he lost at three miles; but the six-year-old stallion Puck had been wholly unpredictable, sometimes running like the wind, and other times plodding like a plow horse.

When Hugh had first seen Dreamer and Wizard, he had smiled as if they were old friends, recognizing the look of his own line in them because their dam was Black Swan, the result of the breeding of one of Hugh's favorite stallions to Leda in England. Black Swan had done well in her own racing career and continued as a brood mare to throw lovely black foals. Dreamer and Wizard were brother and sister, sired by Oberon. Oberon was out of Mabbie, and his sire had been a son of the legendary Sir Archy.

Hugh knew of Sir Archy, not only from his own interest in race horses everywhere, but also because he had had news now and then from the Carringtons. Born in 1805, by Diomed, an imported English stallion, and Castianira, an old blind mare, Sir Archy and his get had dominated American racing for most of the century. Not only had the horse possessed great speed and endurance, which he passed to his offspring, but because of the uneasy relations and sometimes outright war with England, English imports had been almost nonexistent for more than thirty years. Only now was new blood coming in from that source. Thus Sir Archy had dominated by both talent and luck.

Hugh was fascinated by the legendary horse, particularly now that he had seen the strength and beauty the stallion had added to Alex's stable. "You saw him, did you not?" he asked.

"I did," Alex said, "though by that time he was quite old. But he was still magnificent. This country mourned him greatly when he died three years ago in North Carolina. It was peculiar; Sir Charles, his most favored son, died at almost the same hour in Virginia, though he was only seventeen years old to his sire's twenty-eight."

"The crosses must be getting very close with so much of his influence," Hugh commented.

"They are. It's the main reason so many horses are being imported now despite the huge prices. Puck has Sir Archy blood from both sire and dam, and he is too easily excited, even by normal handling. It interferes with his racing to the degree that I have nearly determined to sell him. Some owners have bred even more closely than this, but I don't approve. I think there is too much chance of producing a concentration of the worst traits as well as the best." She ignored the fond and conspiratorial looks her husband and sons exchanged—they knew how much she hated selling any of her horses. "Puck has never lost a race on lack of merit, only from temper."

"Perhaps he will be in good spirits tomorrow," Hugh suggested.

But it was not to be. From the moment Alex saw Puck, she doubted he was going to cooperate. She asked Jim Barlow if he would prefer not to ride him this day, but Jim was as reluctant as she to scratch a race and insisted there was still every chance that Puck would settle down.

When Alex heard Blaine's barely stifled, "God damn!" beside her and followed his gaze, she saw that the horse was not going to be the only problem that day.

Flora and her husband Carlton Fitzhubert III were making their way through the crowd. Their progress was slow because Carlton stopped often to display the full force of his charm to various acquaintances, most particularly women who were there on the arms of their own escorts, a circumstance that did not lessen their beaming response to Carlton.

Carlton was undeniably handsome. He was tall, well built, and when he doffed his hat his hair gleamed bright red gold in the sun, and his eyes were a deep blue. He was saved from too much beauty by the imperfections a childhood riding accident had inflicted on his otherwise even features. The little scar bisecting one eyebrow and the slight bump on the bridge of his nose gave false evidence of character where none existed.

He was not a stupid man, and was capable of flashes of humor and wit which could be quite entertaining, but all his energy was concentrated on his own pleasure. The only child of a prosperous merchant, he had been indulged since infancy and seemed incapable of understanding that his were not the only needs to be met. Though he was thirty years old, he seemed perfectly happy in the role of a rather naughty but charming schoolboy.

Flora, with her own vivid blue eyes and her wealth of golden brown hair framing delicate features, completed the picture of the elegant young couple. But to her family, the signs of strain were unmistakable.

In recent months, Flora had buried her practical, thoughtful side under the guise of a vapid, social butterfly. Even now, as she moved through the crowd at her husband's side, her movements were small and fluttery, her smile brittle, and when she reached the Falconer group and was introduced to Hugh and Angelica, her nervous greeting to them was more like that of a very young girl than of a woman with married status. And she kept darting glances at her husband as if she feared he would do something to embarrass them both.

"Good day, Mother Carrington-Falconer," Carlton said, and Alex was sure the smile she attempted looked the grimace it was. She hated it when he called her that, but she did not think he meant to be insulting and so had never asked him to desist.

"I hope Puck is at his best today; I've wagered a good sum on him," Carlton announced, and now Alex did not try to cover her dismay.

"And I hope you are jesting. Puck is not a sure winner on the best of days, and this is far from one of his best days."

"Idiot," Blaine muttered and then subsided at a look from his twin.

If Carlton heard the imprecation, he gave no sign. "Oh, I'm very lucky," he insisted airily.

But despite Jim Barlow's excellent riding, Puck refused to cooperate. There was no doubt of his speed; he took the first heat with no effort, but he went straight downhill from there. During the cooling out period between the first and second heats, he worked himself into a white lather, though he was kept at a slow walk. And in the second heat, he nearly bolted through the rail, losing the heat in the process.

Alex resisted the impulse to give in to poor sportsmanship and withdraw him from the third heat; instead, she gritted her teeth and watched him sulk and run a poor third in a field of six horses, the race going to a five-year-old bay stallion, Somerville, who won two out of three heats.

Her children refrained from commenting on the race, except for Gwenny who remarked innocently, "Poor Puck, he didn't do so good."

"No, he didn't," Alex agreed, disgusted. For a brief moment, she saw Carlton's pleasant facade falter as his face pulled into harsh lines of worry, and she wondered how much he had lost, but then his smile was back in place and in the next moment he and Flora bade a quick good-bye and left the family group. Flora cast one look back at her family, but then she went on with her husband.

"I assure you, you haven't seen the best of Wild Swan's stables today," Alex told the Bettingdons, shifting her attention away from her daughter's seemingly insoluble problems.

"I beg to differ," Hugh said. "In a way we have. In spite of Puck's fractiousness, your jockey rode him very well, your stableman handled him calmly, and the horse obviously has great speed even if he is unwilling to use it."

Alex knew he meant every word; he was too good a horseman to perjure himself for flattery. "Thank you. But the credit belongs to Samson. You've seen him work, and he is the one who saw the potential and trained the Barlow brothers—Jim, Georgy, and Tad. The younger boys, Billy, who is twelve, and Bobby, who is eight, showed early signs that they were going to grow bigger and taller than jockey size, but Samson and I think they'll be good at schooling the horses if not at riding them."

"Miz Falconer, hello there!"

Alex's eyes narrowed at the approach of a big man who should have had better taste than to wear an ornately patterned waistcoat over his bulging middle.

Angelica also studied the man, thinking that this was the sort of American she could do without. He was from the first instant overly hearty and loud. Angelica was interested to note that while Rane's face was no more welcoming than his wife's, he let her handle the encounter.

Deliberately Alex introduced the Bettingdons as the Duke and Duchess of Almont, and seeing the game, Hugh donned his haughtiest expression. Charles William Frederick Hugh Bettingdon looked about as friendly as a stone cliff.

Angelica had a difficult time controlling her amusement. Mr. Granger was visibly torn between the urge to assert his American equality and the impulse to bow to the aristocrats.

But not even the awkwardness of intruding on the Falconers and their guests could sway the man from his intent. "I heard you've had trouble with that horse before that. I'll give you a good price for 'im."

"For what purpose?" Alex asked.

"Why, to race 'im, of course. I don't mind tellin' you, he jus' needs a firmer hand, an' he'll run like he ought to, with none of that foolin' around."

"Mr. Granger, I am going to do you a favor. I am going to refuse to sell Puck to you. You don't mean 'a firmer hand'; you mean mishandling with whip and spurs. All your sort of discipline would do to Puck is to make him completely unmanageable. He is high-tempered enough as it is. Good day." She stared at him coldly, and whatever he had opened his mouth to say was left unsaid, though his anger was apparent as he stalked off.

"Forgive me," Alex said to Angelica and Hugh. "My behavior was nearly as uncivil as his. But I cannot bear men like that. He will beat a horse to death rather than admit that the animal is not up to a race. Happily, there are only a few of his kind; most find it far too expensive to be abusive or careless of their horses."

Another man approached. He had been observing them from the sidelines, and it was immediately apparent that he was not at all like Mr. Granger. Alex's voice was cordial as she greeted him.

"Mr. Challing, your mare ran very well today. If she shows such promise now as a three-year-old, she should be magnificent in another year or so."

Mr. Challing was a slender man of less than medium height, but he seemed to feel no disadvantage in finding himself in the company of those with more physical presence than his own. Unlike Mr. Granger, he was at ease without being overly familiar. He acknowledged the introductions to the Falconers' guests—this time "Mr. and Mrs. Bettingdon"—and then came right to the point.

"I too would like to purchase Puck, but I have no intention of racing him. If after all your good attentions, he still will not behave, I have no illusions that my trainer could make him perform any more creditably. But it is a shame to waste the good blood he has. I have two English imports and two native-born mares that are not of Sir Archy's blood. I think Puck would make an admirable addition to my stud. I believe with patience and care he can be bred without injury to himself or the mares." He offered a fair price for the horse, neither too high nor too low, and Alex's smile was wide as she offered him her hand.

"You have a bargain, Mr. Challing. I know how well-run your stables are, and I wish you luck with the new addition."

He agreed to take delivery of the horse at the close of the present meeting, as well as to arrange payment by then, and both buyer and seller were satisfied. His purpose having been business, Mr. Challing did not intrude any longer on their party but gracefully bade them good day and departed.

"Thank heavens for that! The child will have a good home," Rane teased, and Alex made no attempt to hide her relief.

"Indeed he will. Mr. Challing has a fine farm in Pennsylvania. And though that state has had on-again, off-again regulations against racing, Mr. Challing has maintained good horses for years. He brings them south for bigger races or when racing is prohibited in his own state."

Hugh and Angelica had learned even more than before about the Falconer marriage in the past moments, and they were impressed. Alex was clearly well established amongst the racing fraternity; both of the buyers had come to her, not her husband. And more, Rane had kept strictly out of the transaction, his restraint a sure indication of his belief not only in Alex's competence, but also in her right to run this part of her life by herself.

The next day they shared the excitement of seeing the five-year-old Wizard win the Proprietor's Purse of $500 by taking the first two three-mile heats in succession, thus qualifying for the two-out-of-three victory without having to run a third heat. The race gave Hugh special pleasure: one of Wizard's grandsires had been his own stallion. He felt that pleasure even more keenly the next day. This was the fourth and final day of the meeting and featured the premier event—the four-mile heats, two heats needed for victory.

Georgy Barlow had ridden Wizard, but Jim Barlow was back in the saddle this day on seven-year-old Dreamer, full sister to Wizard.

The first heat broke very fast, too fast for the sustained effort needed in additional heats. Hugh applauded Jim's control of Dreamer. The mare was fast and more than willing, and she was bred to win races. She would gladly have stretched herself out to keep well in front, but her jockey kept her back, letting a big chestnut colt take the first heat. With less than an hour's rest, the horses were back on the course, and this time Jim's strategy was proven wise. The colt who had run so fast previously began to falter, and Dreamer left him and the other two horses behind in the final mile and sailed over the finish line well ahead of them.

As a special treat, Caleb Jennings's children, the nineteen-year-old John in firm charge of his fifteen-year-old sister Liza and his ten-year-old brother Blake, had been allowed to join the Falconer party, and there was great excitement as they watched Dreamer run.

The only person who did not seem to share this was Alex. Her face was still, her eyes intent as she watched the racing, and in the rest periods she left the party to check on the horse and jockey. Hugh knew exactly how she felt. It was agony to watch a prized animal in such a contest, no matter what the outcome. Despite instructions to one's jockey, and knowledge of both rider and horse, every race was different, and there was no more helpless feeling than having to watch from the sidelines.

Hugh was not alone in his observations. While Alex was gone the second time, Rane said, "If she could, she would be riding in Jim's place. And she could do it. She's one hell of a rider. It was the only condition I asked before we were married—that she never race again. Of course, she would never have been allowed to race at a formal meeting such as this one, thank God, but she managed to race a heat in a match race, and she took the horses out on practice runs at Wild Swan. She was nearly killed when one of the horses broke a leg at full speed." The old pain was fresh in his eyes as he remembered. "I could not have married her had she not promised she would never race again. But I do understand how it must be for her to watch this and know she will never again feel that particular excitement and power."

Hugh shuddered at the risk she had taken. "For the sake of those who love her, it's well for her to do without those sensations."

The two men felt a deepening of their friendship in that moment of perfect understanding.

There was perfection too in the way Dreamer ran the third heat. One of the competitors had dropped out, unable to continue the arduous contest, and the other two ranged against Dreamer showed more signs of distress than she. Dreamer was all business for this third heat. Her stride was long and ground-eating, and she ran brilliantly, finding that last burst of speed to take her away from the others to the finish, winning the Jockey Club Purse of $1000 without having to run additional heats. She had set no records, but she had done very well, running all the heats in under eight and a half minutes.

The spectators roared their approval; Alexandria Carrington Falconer, the Englishwoman, was a legend to many of them, and Dreamer was a fine piece of horseflesh.

"My heavens! What bottom!" Angelica exclaimed, surprising both herself and her husband. Her cheeks suddenly showed a fiery blush.

Hugh gave a shout of laughter, and then they were all laughing together in relief and excitement.

"Bottom indeed!" Hugh said when he'd gotten his breath back. "It must be seen to be believed. I'm not sure I could have borne it had it gone on for more heats. I'll admit it, I'm glad my horses do not face such distances!"

Finally able to relax, Alex was once more aware of the conversation, and she nodded in agreement with Hugh. "It was a tremendous shock to Sinje and me to discover what racing meant in this country. The first time I watched Swan run the distance over and over again, I thought my heart would break for him."

Racing in England had for decades been concentrating more and more on dashes at fractional distances, the emphasis being on greater speed and less endurance than that required of American horses. On a practical level, it allowed for many races in one day, and thus for more betting, which was legal and increasingly organized in England. Betting remained officially illegal in America, though it was part of every race meeting.

There were other differences too. American courses were invariably circular or oval in deference to the democratic idea that the spectators ought to be able to see the whole race, while in England many races were still run on the straight. Handicapping by weights was accepted practice in England now, but in America, it was still regarded by many as suspect and too vulnerable to fraud; weight by age was the rule here. On the other hand, timekeeping was an American obsession and one that Hugh found particularly characteristic.

"It doesn't surprise me at all," he said. "With all the hurry I've seen in this country, it makes sense that people would want to know how many minutes and seconds their horses have taken to win a race." He looked suddenly uncomfortable, as if he'd said too much, but Alex hastened to reassure him.

"It is silly. After all, the point is to win the race. And I've never been able to understand how a measure of time can mean very much when the conditions of the courses vary so with care and weather. There are endless squabbles over the records from one course to the next and one region to the other. In some Southern states they will use the May first birthdate instead of January first, and they use lighter weights, thus some of their times are extraordinarily fast. It's quite convenient if one happens to enter horses there. It's possible to have a horse with a true January birthdate—and we breed for that—classed as a year younger and carrying a lighter weight for the first four months of the year."

The press of people who wished to offer congratulations ended further conversation, and Rane helped Alex make her way through the crowd to congratulate Jim Barlow and to receive the prize.

Dreamer was cooling out nicely, none the worse for wear, but Alex felt tears prick her own eyes even as she noticed the suspicious moisture in Jim's.

"Well done, no one could have ridden her better," she praised him, and then she turned to her family to explain the well of emotion.

"Only Samson, Jim and I knew it, but today was Dreamer's last race. She's done a splendid job for us, and now it's time for her to begin producing foals as fine as she is." She went to the mare and stroked the velvety muzzle. "You've taken the prize, my lovely Dreamer," she said as if the animal could understand, and the mare blew softly and made little snuffling sounds, familiar with the scent of Alex and the sound of her voice.

Everyone knew that the horses belonged to Alex and that she had full charge of them, and most good horsemen dealt directly with Alex, but it made the officials more comfortable to pretend Rane was the owner. The various jockey club memberships were in his name, and when he was with her, he accepted the prizes. When he did not accompany her, the prizes were given to her either in his name or, where his name was not entered in the jockey clubs, in the name of friendly horse owners who arranged for her horses to enter their jockey club races.

Alex had long since decided it was useless to be angry over this situation and had allowed it to amuse her instead, so that in fact she sometimes had a difficult time restraining her mirth when she watched Rane solemnly pretending that Thoroughbreds and racecourses were his consuming passions. Today she saw he was having trouble too, and she saw the cause—Hugh and Angelica had donned their most proper expressions as defense against their own smiles. They could not have looked more solemn had they been garbed in velvet and ermine and attending the coronation of a king. Alex's sorrow at knowing Dreamer would never perform for the crowds again passed in the wake of the Bettingdons' performance. Despite Puck's misbehavior, it had been an enjoyable race meeting, and Alex, wrapped in the warmth of family and friends, felt content. Yet she could not help but wish that Caleb and Flora, each so troubled, could have shared that warmth.

Chapter

4

Before she left Baltimore, Alex had an uncomfortable meeting with her daughter. At first she was glad that Flora had sought her out, but it was not an easy encounter.

Flora fussed about, talking about the weather, new dress styles, anything as long as it was meaningless, until finally Alex could bear it no longer.

"My dear, I am prepared to listen to this nonsense if you insist, but I am sure it was not your purpose for coming here. You are nervous and upset all the time these days. There must be something your father and I can do to help."

Flora's nervous hands fluttered to a stop, and then she lashed out. "I am surprised you noticed, your damn horses keep you so busy!"

Alex studied her daughter for a long moment. "I don't think I deserve that," she said carefully, "but if I do, then I am sorry. I would hate to think that you have ever believed that anything on earth could be more important to me than the welfare of my family. And in any case, I am here now, and I do not want to fight with you."

Flora's face crumpled then, and the tears started to roll down her cheeks. "I didn't mean that, Mother, I didn't! I just wanted to make you hurt as much as I do. Oh, God, why did you let me marry Carlton? I know you don't like him. And now I don't either. He's a worthless fool!"

Understanding the confused mixture of anger and grief, Alex went to her, cradling her against her body as if Flora were small again and could be protected from all harm. But she knew it was no longer true. "Lovey, I have a story to tell you. I should have told you long ago, I suppose. But it just didn't seem necessary." She could feel Flora listening intently as she related the story of her attempt to persuade St. John that marriage with Florence wouldn't work and of her exile to Devon.

"In the end I was proved correct; Florence and Sinje did make each other miserable. But I was wrong, too. No one has the right to interfere like that in other people's lives. If I had been successful, you and Blaine would never have been born, and what a tragedy that would have been! And sometimes matches one would never think workable go along quite nicely while seemingly perfect marriages flounder. Perhaps I should have said more about Carlton. But I was afraid. I didn't want to repeat old sins."

Flora nestled closer for an instant, but then she pulled away. "Am I like my—like her?"

Alex's heart skipped a beat. She was glad Flora could not easily call Florence her mother. She had been very careful not to malign Florence beyond saying she had not gotten on well with St. John. But Flora sensed more, perhaps from some note in Alex's voice, perhaps simply because she could not imagine anyone not being able to get along with her beloved father. Alex had hoped to avoid this situation forever—there had never seemed a need to speak of Florence because Alex had been mother to the twins from their early infancy—but now it was upon her. Too clearly the reality of her sister came back to her across the years.

She took a deep breath and committed herself. "No, you are nothing at all like your mother except that you are beautiful, but even that has more of Sinje in it than my sister. Florence was not a happy person, and she made others unhappy too."

She knew it was the right answer when she heard Flora's sigh of relief and then the painful words. "Lately I've wondered. I've wondered about everything. I was beginning to think that maybe she explains it, that maybe I'm just like her. And I imagined she was much worse than you have described.

"My brothers are all good at something. But I'm not. I thought I would make a great success at my marriage, and that would show everyone, myself most of all." She stopped, swallowing hard to regain control of her quavering voice.

"It's far from a success; it's a disaster. I hardly even see Carlton any more, so busy is he with his gambling, drinking, and, I expect, whoring. I've tried to talk to him about it, but the only result has been horrible rows. Even his family has lost patience with him and with me. They thought that when he married me he would grow up and become responsible; instead he has just gotten worse. His parents are threatening to cut him off entirely because he wastes the money they give him within days of the quarter's beginning, and our legitimate bills remain unpaid. I am embarrassed to face some of the tradesmen. That's why I came today, to borrow money. I swear to you I've learned to curb my own extravagance, but it's no use. Carlton far outspends what I can save. And I am sure there are unpaid gaming debts and such of which I know nothing."

"Has he spent what we settled on you?" Alex asked, and Flora nodded. "A lot of it went into our house. It made sense then. Carlton said most of his money was tied up in investments that would be worth much more later. I believed him." All the bitterness of her disillusionment was in those three words.

Alex made a supreme effort to be measured in her response. "It is possible that he will yet grow up. Perhaps he has found marriage much more of a change than he thought it would be, and he's making a last attempt to avoid responsibility. I fear he has always been too much indulged. Perhaps he will come around and begin to behave himself. But it is also possible that he cannot or will not change. There are some men who never grow up; I know more than a few from the race meetings. They spend all their time and their money on wagers, spirits, and women. It is a ruinous life. Flora, you made a solemn vow when you married, but you are not obligated to destroy yourself at Carlton's whim."

"'Divorce?" Flora whispered.

"I know it would be difficult, and the rumormongers would find you fair game for a time," Alex admitted. "But eventually they would find other prey. Rane, your brothers and I would all stand by you. But it is a decision only you can make. And if you still love your husband, it is no answer at all."

Flora looked away, nervously clasping and unclasping her hands. "Love? I don't know. I thought I loved him, and sometimes I still do. He can be very charming. But nothing seems to work, not even . . . I thought . . . the way you explained . . . the way it seems between you and Rane and with my father and you before. . . ." Her voice trailed away in embarrassment, and her face was alternately flushed and pale.

Alex took her daughter's hand and held it gently in her own. "It is nothing to be ashamed of. I had hoped I'd taught you that. Your body belongs to you, even though you are married, and you have the right to want pleasure, not pain, in your relations with your husband. But sometimes it takes a while and a good deal of patience for a man and a woman to learn the rhythm together. It is possible if you are both willing to try. It is a much more serious problem if you no longer love him or he you. I think for women, particularly, the body experiences little of value if the heart and the mind are not involved."

"I just don't know any more." Now Flora sounded more weary than anything else, as if she hadn't the energy to consider her problems any longer.

"We're going to take the Bettingdons to Annapolis to see the Bateses, but then we'll be at Wild Swan. Why don't you come out? It would be good for you to get away for a while."

"I don't think so. It would be too much like running away. I still know I have to sort this out by myself even though I'm not doing a very good job of it. And Blaine might be at Wild Swan too. I've been horrid to him lately; I'm not sure I can face him again until I've come to a decision."

"It will never be easy for you and Blaine to share each other with outsiders, but you must never think Blaine wants anything less than your happiness," Alex reminded her.

"But don't you see? I can't talk to him about this! It would only make things worse. And as calm as Blaine is, I fear he might come to blows with Carlton."

"Unfortunately, I must concede your point. But do consider coming out to us. Blaine will keep his peace if you do not wish to confide in him." Inwardly Alex resolved to make that true if Blaine showed signs of not restraining himself, but she doubted that Flora would join them in any case.

She loaned Flora the money, but she wished she could do more for her. "I hate to leave you in such a state; I wish I could make it easier for you, but I can't, not any more," she told her daughter. "However, I want you to remember that you are not only a beautiful woman, you are also a very intelligent one. Don't make the mistake of thinking of yourself as nothing more than Carlton's wife."

At least Flora looked more thoughtful and more resolved than she had for a long time when she left the house. But Alex still hoped she would reconsider and seek refuge at Wild Swan for a while.

Alex enjoyed the diversion of going to Annapolis, for she still had tender feelings for the town where she and St. John had made their start in America.

Though Annapolis had lost its bid to be the nation's capital in the last century, it was both the capital of the state and the governmental seat of Anne Arundel county. Its halcyon days had passed with the richness of the soil of Maryland's tobacco lands, and its harbor had silted up, making it difficult for large vessels to land there, while Baltimore possessed a deep water approach to its docks and had lured trade away. Annapolis had a quiet, shabby air of neglect, but it was still a lovely little city with its streets fanning out from the two circular drives which were named Church and State for the functions of the buildings on the respective sites. It boasted many fine houses in the same five-part style of the house at Wild Swan and intricate gardens, though some of these showed want of care. Its streets had such names as Cornhill and Fleet, taken directly from street names in London, and it was altogether more English than Baltimore, which was more a product of the present century and was attracting myriad immigrants.

They went to the Wild Swan tavern, the first business the Carringtons had started when they arrived in Maryland. Alex was able to laugh now at the memory of how angry St. John had been at the very suggestion of such a venture, though it had not been amusing at the time.

"He was furious," she recalled. "He didn't fancy himself as a publican, but he actually got to be quite a skilled host. And I'll claim credit too. Della and I worked very hard to provide the best food in Annapolis, and weary politicians soon learned they could eat and discuss their affairs without having them repeated to all and sundry. And Mavis and Timothy have kept up the reputation and enhanced it. Mavis is known as one of the best cooks in the state."

Mavis and Timothy Bates were the main reason for the Annapolis visit. They had worked for the Carringtons in England and had come to America not because they yearned for the new land, but because they could not imagine that Alex and St. John could do without them. They had been so essential in those early days, Alex suspected they had been right. But when the Carringtons had purchased the acres of Wild Swan, the Bateses had stayed at the tavern in Annapolis. The only problem with the situation was that over the years it had become both feasible and sensible that the Bateses should own the Annapolis business and no longer have to share the profits with anyone.

It was a stone wall Alex had at last ceased to assault. No amount of logical argument could sway them. They did not want to own the tavern. They knew Alex would never sell it away from them, and they wanted things to continue just as they were.

There was great pleasure on both sides when Hugh and the

Bateses greeted each other for the first time in sixteen years and Hugh introduced Angelica to them.

Hugh was amazed by how little they had changed. Tim was still the same tough little man; his hard childhood in London's slums having made him look older in youth, it now seemed only just that he should look the same, as if he had aged to a certain point early on and was not going to age further. Mavis had added a bit more to her plump figure, but the round brown eyes set in the broad country face and framed by soft brown hair were the same. And despite their years in America, they remained true to their origins in their insistence on addressing the duke and duchess as "Your Grace." It was only when Angelica added her pleas to the others that Mavis and Timothy even agreed to share the evening meal with them rather than waiting on the table.

"Please, you are old friends of my husband's. I shall feel so very uncomfortable if you will not join us."

The Bateses were as susceptible to her charm as everyone else, but it took them half the meal to relax.

Alex watched Rane anxiously at first, because much of the conversation was perforce of the days when she had been with St. John—indeed they had been married in Annapolis, there being no law against their union in this country—but she was relieved that though Rane said little, he appeared to be at ease. She knew he would never be wholly comfortable with reminiscences of St. John; it was enough that he no longer perceived any threat from Hugh. And she knew it helped that Tim and Mavis were fond of Rane for his own sake. They had been very loyal to St. John, but with their practical, earthy view of life they had more than accepted Rane's place in Alex's life—they had approved it wholeheartedly, not wanting her to mourn forever for her dead husband and understanding that the bond between Alex and Rane was one that stretched back into the past, just as it was destined to reach into the future.

When they finally arrived back at Wild Swan, Alex was touched when Angelica exclaimed, "I feel as if I'm coming home!" and the women shared the thought of how satisfying it would be if they lived closer together and could nurture their friendship with more time together.

Alex loved the altered rhythm of life at Wild Swan in the summer. Though there would be plenty to do, with various crops of fruit, vegetables, and grain ripening in their turn, there was yet a sense of freedom. Horace Whittleby, the tutor for the children of the farm, spent the summers traveling to various cities to indulge himself in lectures, plays, and musical recitals, and thus the children were set free. They liked their lessons with Mr. Whittleby, but he as much as Alex and Rane saw the need for a break. And it was the same with the horses; they were allowed a lighter training regimen in the heat until it was time to bring to peak condition those who would race in the fall. It was a break for Alex, too, between the spring and autumn racing schedules, and since Rane and the children spent as much time as they could at the farm during the summer, they were more a family than at any other time except Christmas.

Though she knew they would be on their way soon, Alex was glad that the Bettingdons had an opportunity to savor Wild Swan at the beginning of the honeyed days of summer, and she was grateful that her sons made the effort to spend more time at the farm before the Bettingdons left. They were so big, healthy, and exuberant, they generated their own hurricane of energy.

They arrived full of the news of the just-run John Bascombe–Post Boy match. The results of the May 31 race at the Union Course on Long Island had traveled swiftly by rider, coach, and rail, the interest in North versus South matches being keen even among those who normally took little notice of horse races. And though Alex's sons had chosen careers apart from the racing world, they had been raised in that world and followed news of it out of their own enthusiasm as well as for their mother's sake.

"Can you imagine?" Morgan said. "John Bascombe had already walked over five hundred miles to races all over the South before he came from Virginia to Long Island, and that trip is nine hundred miles, half of which he walked and half he spent on one boat or another. And still he won! What a phenomenal performance! The South is vindicated for her past losses."

"I'm sure that is how it will be viewed," Alex said tartly, "but it is hardly accurate. In the most important sense, both John Bascombe and Post Boy are Southern horses; they're both grandsons of Sir Archy. And Post Boy's sire was Henry and his dam had almost the same blood as American Eclipse who, like Sir Archy, had Diomed's blood. So which is North and which South is a matter of opinion." For a moment she was back at the race course on that May day in 1823 when she had discovered that St. John had risked Leda, Swan, and Black Swan on the nine-year-old Eclipse against the four-year-old Henry in the first North-South match. It had seemed impossible, but the older horse had won, and St. John had been a winner as well, collecting the $5000 that had allowed them to make the first payment on the acres they had rechristened Wild Swan.

Nigel's voice broke into her thoughts. "Some reports have more than twenty thousand people attending the race. What a crowd it must have been!"

"Are you sure there were that many people?" Morgan asked. "That's an awful lot to crowd into one racecourse."

"Of course I wasn't there," Nigel began and then caught himself as he saw the gleam in his brother's eyes. "Honestly, Morgan, if you don't learn to pay more attention to detail yourself, you are going to sail into some odd ports."

"I'd say that evens the score," Blaine offered in his best judicial manner.

Hugh enjoyed the byplay, but he was more interested in further information regarding the North-South races. "I should think you would have been approached to enter one of your horses," he said to Alex. "They are by every measure among the finest in the land."

"I have been asked, but I've refused on the ground that Maryland is neither wholly Northern nor wholly Southern. It is a transparent excuse, but it has been accepted. I don't really know how I feel about the matches. They are exciting, but the division of loyalty between North and South is disquieting. Perhaps it is a way to express it harmlessly, but then again, perhaps it only emphasizes the rivalry between regions. I am at once attracted and repelled by such contests, but I am certain about one thing —I do not want my horses put to such use."

Put in that light, it was a point of view Hugh could readily understand. He turned his attention to Morgan. "You said the horse, John Bascombe, walked or was on board ship for all that distance. Tell me, is there any talk of using the railways for transporting horses? It's been suggested in England, though I don't know of anyone who has done it."

"It's being done in rare instances, but it is not only very expensive, it is also hazardous. It's quite a different proposition to load a horse rather than a person onto a train, and there aren't enough connecting lines to make it very practical yet." Morgan kept abreast of developments on the railroads, not because he particularly liked them, but because he viewed them as a possible threat to coastal shipping. "If mother has her way, the railroads will cease operation altogether," he added with a grin.

Alex could not prevent the blush that colored her cheeks. It was a standing joke that, while she was willing to ride the fastest horses, her one ride on a railroad had terrified her.

"I detested every minute of it," she admitted. "I am hopelessly old-fashioned. I expected to catch fire from the sparks and burn to a crisp at any moment. I hated the noise, the soot, and even the motion. No wonder they are allowed only to the outskirts of cities. There will have to be great improvement before I trust my horses to them."

"I like 'em," Gwenny announced. "When I'm big, I'm goin' on one. Blaine's gonna take me." She fixed her brother with the intensity of her gaze. "You pwomised."

"Promised, 'rrrrr'," Blaine corrected automatically. "And yes, I did. When you're bigger."

"Better you than I," Alex muttered. She knew the railroads were bound to be part of her children's lives, but she intended to avoid the machines as much as possible.

When Caleb and Flora arrived late in the evening, Alex's first thought was that her happiness was complete because they had both decided to visit after all. But in the next instant, she knew that something was terribly wrong.

Caleb's face was tired and set, and Flora looked so white and ill, it seemed she could not have remained upright without Caleb's strong arm around her.

Her name was an anxious exclamation from her twin, and only then did some flicker of life show in her wide, blank eyes. Blaine went to her, and Caleb stepped away, letting him take charge of his sister.

"Take her into the library and give her a glass of brandy," Caleb ordered. "Alex will be along in a moment."

No one questioned his authority, least of all Flora, who moved like a mechanical toy with Blaine's support.

Gwenny, worn out from the exciting day, had succumbed to sleep earlier and been put to bed, so there was no reason for Caleb to censor his news. "There's no easy way to tell you what happened. Carlton was killed on the dueling ground at Bladenburg outside of Washington. It was over a woman, another man's mistress. Thank God the man who brought the news to Baltimore had the sense to come looking for you, Rane, at the shipyard before he told Flora. I went to her instead. She hasn't wept, nor has she said a word since she got the news."

"What about Carlton's parents?" Rane asked.

"They've been told," Caleb said grimly. "The messenger went to them first, thinking they would be of comfort to the widow. Far from it; according to him, Mrs. Fitzhubert immediately began to shriek that it was all Flora's fault."

"That bitch!" Alex snarled, and then she went to Flora, hearing Rane's "Call me if you need me," trailing behind her.

Blaine was talking to Flora in a low, soothing voice; Flora was making no response whatsoever. An untouched goblet of brandy was on the table beside her.

Blaine looked up at Alex's entry. "What happened? I can't get her to tell me. It's got to be something to do with that swine—"

"Don't," Alex cut him off. "Go join the others, please. They will tell you what has happened. And ask Della if she would bring us a pot of tea."

He was obviously reluctant to leave his twin, but he felt helpless, so he did as his mother bade him.

Flora did not resist when Alex took her hands in her own, but her skin was cold and clammy to her touch. Alex spoke to her softly as if awakening her from sleep.

"Flora, love, I know what you're thinking, truly I do. You think it is somehow your fault. But it's not." She felt the hands twitch in her own, and she held onto them. "Because you were considering ending your marriage has nothing to do with Carlton's death. Nothing. He was dueling over another woman. Do you hear me? He wanted another man's mistress."

Flora shook her head dazedly, not in negation, but as if she were coming up from under water. Alex knew then that both Caleb and the messenger had spared her the reason for the duel, mistakenly assuming it was in her best interest.

Alex picked up the glass of brandy. "Will you take a little of this now? It will warm you."

Flora turned her head away. "No! Carlton reeked of it too often these past months." Her first words were rusty, but Alex heard the anger as well as the grief and was glad of it.

"Flora, he was your husband. You have a right to mourn him for the waste of a young life, for how unnecessary his death was. But you have a right to your anger too. He treated you shamefully and damaged your marriage beyond repair." She could almost see the words registering one by one.

Flora turned to her and then burrowed against her when Alex

opened her arms. "After the races, we fought about money, about us, about everything." The low, dreary sobbing tore at Alex's heart far more than wild hysteria would have.

Flora did not notice when Della brought the tea, but when her sobs diminished and her mother offered her a cup, she drank it greedily, without noticing that Alex had added sugar. Normally, Flora hated sweet tea.

"I'm so sleepy," she sighed finally, her eyelids drooping.

Alex led her upstairs and put her to bed. Stroking the fair hair back from her daughter's face, she crooned, "Sleep now, darling. We're all here. You're safe at Wild Swan."

Flora fell asleep almost instantly, a soft pink coloring her cheeks and her skin much warmer to the touch than it had been.

Only when she was sure that Flora was sleeping deeply did Alex return to the others.

"How is she?" Blaine asked anxiously.

"Sleeping peacefully and looking better than you do at the moment," his mother replied.

She listened to the babble. It was natural in such a situation for everyone to review again and again every bit of information and to hunger for more; human drama had its own compulsion. Caleb was patiently repeating what he knew, though he did not have all the details. No, it did not seem there was to be any arrest made for the duel, but, yes, it was likely that the story would spread far and wide—such scandal usually did —that was one of the reasons he had spirited Flora away to Wild Swan. No, he did not see how Flora could help with any funeral arrangements, considering the Fitzhuberts' attitude.

At a lull in the conversation, Alex said, "We can and we will talk this to death. But please, don't tell Flora that Carlton deserved it. It is one thing to say it was not her fault, another to say it served him right. No one deserves to die so young and so violently."

"I do understand what you're saying," Blaine conceded. "But it's hard to make my heart believe it. Carlton was a bastard. It was only a matter of time before something like this happened."

"Exactly so," Rane said, "but your sister chose to marry him. She will have to live with that failure for the rest of her life."

Alex appreciated his support. She turned her attention to the Bettingdons. "I am so sorry this has happened; I would have wished that nothing mar your visit to Wild Swan."

Angelica answered for both her husband and herself. "But don't you see, that you all feel comfortable enough to be so open in our presence in the midst of this crisis is most flattering to us; it makes us feel as if we are part of your family. And that is a very good thing to be, even for a short time."

" 'Your Grace' is a title well earned by you, Angelica," Rane said.

The next day Rane and Caleb returned to Baltimore, but the boys remained at Wild Swan, ostensibly to finish out the days as they had planned, but in truth it was in case their sister needed them.

Sam's arrival gave them a good measure of how fast the story of the duel was traveling.

"I'm so sorry. Is Flora here, and what can I do to help?" were her first words to Alex.

"Caleb brought her home, bless him. She's still abed. Sleep is the best medicine for her right now. Poor love, nothing can make this easy for her, but at least she's away from the wagging tongues of the gossips. Speaking of which, how did you hear?"

Sam grimaced in distaste. "The usual way. My stepmother, for all her indolence, invests a great deal of energy in keeping abreast of the current scandals—Oh, dear! I might have chosen a better term."

"But hardly a more accurate one," Alex assured her.

"Well, in any case, one of her friends dropped by this morning, all the way from Washington, mind you. The woman must have left before first light. I don't know who had the greatest pleasure—the woman for bringing the news to Violet before anyone else had or Violet for being the first to tell me."

"Sam, I am sorry! Things have been all at sixes and sevens; I should have sent someone to tell you," Alex apologized.

"I didn't mean that! Honestly, perhaps I ought to go home again. I came here to offer my help, and instead, I keep putting my foot in my mouth."

Suddenly they were both laughing. Sam was always like a breath of fresh air, and Alex felt her own burden eased by the girl's presence.

Morgan discovered them at that moment. "What a welcome sound that is in this house!" he exclaimed as he gave Sam a brotherly hug.

For an instant, Sam's face was so alight with love, Alex thought Morgan must be stone blind not to see it, and then the light was gone, and Sam greeted Morgan easily in return, but she also stepped away from him. A frown of annoyance creased Morgan's brow and then disappeared.

"Want to go for a ride?" Morgan asked.

Sam shook her head. "No, thank you. I've come to see Flora."

"She's probably still asleep," he pointed out reasonably. "You can see her when we get back."

"No," Sam's voice was still polite, but it was also firm. "Some other time."

"We're seldom in the same place any more," Morgan complained.

"That's true," Sam agreed equably. "But I still won't go riding with you right now. Maybe later."

At that moment, Sam was all woman, and Morgan was the pettish child.

"Go on upstairs and look in on Flora," Alex instructed. "She may be awake again. But I warn you, she is feeling so sad and guilty, she's not making much sense. I've tried to convince her that she's not at fault, but I haven't been very successful. She doesn't believe it for more than a few minutes at a time. Maybe you will be able to reach her."

Sam found Flora sitting up in bed, her eyes wide open and staring off into space. Though she was not weeping at the moment, her face was blotched, and the skin around her eyes looked swollen and bruised. Her hair fell in wild disarray around her face.

"Flora, it's Sam," she called as she went to her. She sat on the bed and put her arms around her.

Flora shuddered once, and then she wailed, "Oh, Sam, I've made such a botch of everything!"

"I should think it was Carlton who did that," Sam said, her practicality undiminished even in this crisis. "He wasn't your child, you know. You married him to be his wife, not his mother."

"You don't understand," Flora accused flatly. "I wasn't a good wife to him. I—I couldn't even stand to have him touch me these past months."

The image rose unbidden in Sam's mind—Morgan touching her not in that brotherly way, but as a man touches a woman. She could not imagine finding his touch repulsive.

"Flora, I admit I don't know as much about it as you do; I am still a virgin, but I vow the basics are the same for everyone. You're warm and loving, and you married Carlton in good faith. If you did not find pleasure together, surely it was as much his fault as yours, probably more because I doubt he was a virgin."

Though Flora said nothing, Sam could feel her listening. She left her for a moment and found a brush among the toilet articles Alex had laid out for her daughter. She returned and began brushing Flora's hair with long, slow strokes.

"He never did this," Flora said suddenly. "I always wished he would brush my hair, touch me gently just to touch me, not because he wanted to possess my body. But he never touched me unless he wanted to take me. And it was always so swift, muddled, and untidy, I never liked it. I—My God, what am I thinking of to tell you these things?"

"Of yourself, which is exactly right at the moment," Sam assured her. "I may not be married, but I am not entirely ignorant."

"No, you're not. You're entirely sensible." For the first time Flora smiled. It was wavery, but genuine. But then it disappeared as she contemplated reality again. "I suppose I must go to Baltimore and make arrangements for—"

"Your family will tell you if there is anything you have to do. I think you ought to concentrate on getting dressed and going outside. It's a beautiful day."

"More beautiful here than at Brookhaven?" Flora asked gently, her attention finally focusing completely on Sam.

"Always," Sam answered promptly, and Flora was able to think of how lucky she herself was. Even in her current disgrace, for so she thought of it, she had a warm and loving family to support her. Suddenly she felt much more able to cope.

"You've been a wonderful help," she told Sam, not explaining that it was the other's situation rather than any words she'd said that had bolstered her sagging courage. "Please stay at least the night," she pled. "We'll send a message to Brookhaven, and you can borrow any of my clothes you need. Even in the rush to get here, Caleb made sure I didn't arrive without luggage, bless him. Do stay, it will be as it was when we were little girls."

Sam's stammered protests met with no patience from Flora whose will could be formidable under any circumstance. Flora felt no qualms about using her own need to make Sam tarry because it was for Sam's good. Morgan was here, and so here was where Sam belonged.

Flora had not discussed it with her siblings, not even with Blaine, but she suspected Morgan must be the only one who didn't see how much Sam adored him. Even though her own match had ended in disaster rather than love, it was no reason for Morgan and Sam to meet the same fate. Flora felt quite pleased with the generosity of her own feelings; life with Carlton had begun to make her feel dark and niggardly inside.

But whatever her high-minded motives, Flora was too aware not to see that Sam served as a buffer when they came downstairs together. Sam had not spent much time with the family lately, and so there were a host of questions to be asked, and everyone was relieved to have something other than Carlton's death to talk about.

And as always Sam wanted to see how all the crops were doing, how the horses were faring. Flora found herself enjoying the rounds. The sun was warm, and Wild Swan was humming with life that pushed her own darkness back. It didn't even matter that she was receiving sympathetic looks and low, murmured words from the staff; even here Sam helped to ease the way, not letting awkward silences develop.

Until Morgan came riding up. Flora could almost see Sam shrinking into herself like a snail withdrawing into its shell. It was startling; Sam was so steady and outgoing. But then Flora remembered how Sam had been when she'd first come to Wild Swan. She'd been game for anything, but she'd also been very wary until she'd learned that her welcome was assured.

Morgan wasn't behaving much better, acting curiously aloof and unlike himself.

Flora felt immeasurably older than both of them, and she was tempted to tell them bluntly to stop acting so foolishly. But inwardly she conceded that she was not the best authority on relationships between men and women, and so she held her peace and pretended to notice nothing unusual. Most of all, she tried to listen to them, to anyone outside of herself.

Regret, disgust, outright horror—her inner thoughts contained them all. And the worst was the contemplation of Carlton's dead body. She had not seen it; she hoped she would not. But the horrid vision of it was there just the same. "Shot very near the heart"—that was what the man had said. There must have been an ocean of blood, pumping until his life was gone. Once she had thought she loved that body as well as the man inside. Too vividly she could see Carlton's strongly muscled limbs— even in his dissipation he had remained fit, his vanity allowing no less— and his thick red-gold hair with its tendency to curl on his brow above his blue eyes. She had thought they would have beautiful children, children with golden-red hair and deep blue eyes. She could not decide now whether she was glad or sorry that she had not conceived. A child would have been proof that she had at least done something right; but it would have been his child, and a lasting connection with his parents.

She faded in and out of her surroundings, sometimes aware of what was going on around her and sometimes lost in her own thoughts. Sam stayed close by, serving as a reference point, demanding nothing of her. For Sam, it was enough that Flora had come out of her room.

With profound admiration, Alex observed Sam's careful shepherding of Flora. Conversation at supper was erratic, skipping from spurts of nervous verbiage to uncomfortable lapses into silence. They did not have the advantage of remembering the deceased fondly so that reminiscences could flow with laughter and tears. But Sam gallantly jumped in when she could, her agile mind producing one subject after another. And then Morgan began to speak in counterpoint, picking up the thread of conversation when Sam faltered. It was as intricate and melodic as a piece of music, but Alex knew they were unaware of what they were doing.

Alex missed Rane desperately that night. He and Caleb had gone to Baltimore to see if there was anything they could do in spite of the Fitzhuberts' attitude toward Flora. During the day Alex had been able to concentrate on all the work that must go on at Wild Swan no matter what happened, and on Flora, but alone in the wide bed, all she could think of was her husband. Somehow the knowledge that Flora's marriage had gone so wrong made her own harmony with Rane even more precious.

He and Caleb returned two days later. Between them they had taken care of everything they could for Flora, even to bringing her additional clothing.

"It was just as well she wasn't there," Rane told Alex when they were alone. The Fitzhuberts are still in no mood to be reasonable. They've focused all their hurt and anger on Flora. According to them, their son's death is entirely her fault."

The funeral had already taken place, a rather shabby affair arranged in haste which did nothing to mitigate the scandal. The gossips would soon have other bones to chew, but at the moment, the lurid details of the duel were amusing an avid audience.

"Flora seems much better. How is she really doing?" Rane asked.

"Very well on the surface, though I know it will take her a long while to find true peace. Poor darling, the problem is obvious. There's nothing nice or sensible about what happened. It's hideous. Someday Flora will have to accept that. Some things can't be rectified even in memory." She explained how helpful Sam had been, and then she gazed thoughtfully at Rane. "I'm very pleased, but how did you persuade Caleb to return with you?"

Rane looked puzzled. "Now that I think about it, I didn't persuade him. He helped me arrange everything, and it seemed perfectly natural for him to come back here. But it isn't natural at all, is it? At least not the way he's been since Pen died. It's much more like the Caleb we used to know. I expect he just had to reassure himself that Flora was all right. She was so stricken when he brought her here, anything would have been an improvement. After all, she did live with the Jenningses for months at a time when she and the other children were at school in Baltimore. But whatever the cause, even so grim a situation as this one, I rejoice in the change in him."

"And I rejoice in you, Mr. Falconer." She gave a tired sigh and leaned against him, working her hands under his shirt so she could feel the warm reality of him.

He rested his chin on top of her head and wrapped his arms around her, emphasizing how well they fit together.

They broke apart only long enough to undress, and then they lay down in bed together in the candlelight, resting on their sides to draw mutual comfort from the sight of each other.

"Even with all we've had to go through together, we are so fortunate. So many never find the other person who fits so well into their hearts. Poor Flora, what an ill-suited match that was," Rane said, and he felt Alex shiver. He ran his hand up and down her back, warming her. "What was that for?" he asked.

"Because even now, even after all this time, I am still shaken when I find my own thoughts and words coming from you. You are the mirror of my soul, of my mind, of my heart, as I am of yours. To love you is to love myself is to love you. I used to try to make it more sensible, but it no longer baffles me so much. Love for one is love for the other. It doesn't need to be separated."

Weariness forgotten, Alex pushed him to his back, and kneeling over him, she began to tease his body with tendrils of her long hair, feathering it through the springy curls of his chest and over his small nipples until they were as hard as pebbles, using her hair like a small brush to trace the muscular contours of his flat stomach and delighting in the quivering response she could see rippling his skin. Leaning over his groin, she let the heavy curtain of her hair fall over him, and she moved her head in slow circles until a long curl caught on his swelling manhood. Gently she pulled and released, pulled and released.

"Alex, you witch!" he gasped, but though he could easily overpower her, he held himself still, savoring the exquisite torture until he could bear no more and lifted her up to straddle him and then let her down, slowly impaling her on his staff, loving the wild sweet abandon of her face as much as the hot, tight fit of her flesh around him.

"Love for one is love for the other." The words sang in his mind until they were eclipsed by the driving rhythm of his body.

Chapter
5

Hugh's ship had long since docked in Baltimore, and though the Bettingdons were loath to leave Wild Swan, it was time for Hugh to be about his business further south.

Too often the departure of guests brought only relief and left profound weariness in its wake. But this was far from the case when it was time to bid farewell to Hugh and Angelica.

It was particularly difficult for the women, for in a very short time they had become close friends.

"If the weather is too warm for you, come back to us, and Hugh can collect you afterwards," Alex told Angelica, worried that the Englishwoman would find the humid heat unbearable.

"I expect we will be on the coast most of the time, and it is bound to be cooler there," Angelica assured her.

For the last days they had both avoided talking about the subject closest to their hearts. Since it was doubtful Alex would ever go back to England even for a visit, and because Hugh was selling off his American investments, it was equally unlikely that Angelica would return to America, there was little chance that the two women would see each other again.

It was too painful to face openly, so they approached it obliquely.

"If ever any of your children wish to know England, send them to us," Angelica said.

Alex hoped her voice would hold steady. "And if ever yours should want to see this country, we will welcome them."

Finally there was no more time. Alex was grateful for the bustle of the dock and the cries of the watermen. But her self-control nearly deserted her when she saw that both Hugh and Rane had suspiciously bright eyes as they shook hands in farewell. Hugh said something to Rane that won a grave nod in return, and then Hugh came to Alex.

"Live long and prosper, Alexandria. In all the world, you could not find a man who loves you more than your husband does." He kissed her gently on the forehead and turned away.

She moved to stand beside Rane, tucking her arm in his, comforted by his nearness as they watched the ship depart.

A week later, she shed all the tears she had held back at the parting.

Hugh had planned it very carefully so that his gift could not be refused. The horses had been stabled in Baltimore and then delivered on the specified date to Wild Swan.

The stallion was a six-year-old, and his coat was glossy true black, the color Hugh favored over all others. His name was Fortune, and he was not of the same bloodlines as the stallion that had been bred to Leda in England. He was perfect for breeding to both Leda's and Mabbie's lines.

Alex could hear Hugh's voice as she read the letter that was delivered with the horse:

Fortune's bloodlines, enclosed herein, will tell you what you need to know of his sire and dam. And you will see by his racing record that he did well as a two- and three-year-old.

He was then fouled by another horse and injured his right foreleg. It healed well, but I do not think he should be raced again. I rested him for a year and then bred him last year. It is too early to know what his progeny will have of him, but it is to be hoped that both his speed and his endurance will be passed on to them. You see, he is a bit like Leda, not quite sound and in need of a kind stable.

All of this tells you about the horse, but not about why he is now yours. I can hear you protesting that the gift is too much. I would remind you that I am godfather to your sons. In the normal course of events, you would not be thousands of miles away, and I would have many responsibilities toward your children. I still stand ready to provide anything they require that is in my power to give. Your care of them is and always has been exemplary. And as things are, I can foresee little chance of proving the truth of my promise and so must content myself with this gift. I can imagine no better way to provide for your sons than to benefit you.

With love, Hugh.

Alex was not fooled by the protestations of Fortune's imperfections; he was by all English standards a horse of enormous value, just the sort that was being imported now into the United States at great cost. The tears poured down her cheeks, and when Rane came out from Baltimore a few days later, she still wasn't able to tell him of the gift without weeping anew.

Rane thought how wise Hugh was. If he had presented the horse upon his arrival, Alex would have been overwhelmed and embarrassed, and Rane knew he himself would have found reason for jealousy.

Della claimed that Samson was acting as if he had been presented with a new child. "If I'd known that was what he wanted, I would have saved myself a lot of trouble and bought him two colts instead of bearing Malachi and Jotham," she said, but her expression was fond.

Summer was a busy season at Wild Swan, with ripening crops going to market in the cities, but it was happy too, as if the plenty of the land spilled over to people's spirits.

Rane did not have to ask Alex how Flora was; he could see the change for the better in her. Her face had lost its pallor, and her eyes no longer looked so haunted.

At first people had dropped by out of curiosity, the truer friends sending word that they were available should the Falconers need them, but respecting the family's privacy. And as the days passed, other scandals took the place of the duel.

"She is fine here for now," Alex told Rane, "but I expect her to want to go back to Baltimore soon. She prefers living in the city, and she does have friends there. She will have to face everyone eventually."

Flora's house was in the process of being sold to pay Carlton's debts. It still made her parents angry to think of it, but she was adamant. "It's not because the Fitzhuberts think I ought to be responsible; it is because I think so," she insisted. "We were married, and what was mine was his as well as the reverse." There was a new maturity about her that could only be to the good.

Rane was not at all dismayed by the idea of her returning to their Baltimore house. "She can be a civilizing influence on Morgan, Blaine, and me."

"Don't expect miracles," Alex cautioned him. She suspected Flora would not stay very long in her parents' house in the city. She was accustomed now to having her own establishment, and though she might like the security of the family again for a while, it would not last forever. Alex decided not to borrow trouble; time enough to worry about it when it happened.

In the meantime, Sam came over as often as she could, and the Jenningses spent as much time as they could steal from their lives in the city. It was particularly pleasing to see Caleb so often. It was as if Flora's rude loss had shaken him out of his preoccupation with his own. Every time they saw him, he seemed more like the Caleb they had known years ago. He even looked younger. And as a result, his children were feeling more secure and less burdened.

It seemed that happiness was not confined to Wild Swan, for Alex received a letter from her brother Boston announcing his marriage.

Five years older than she, and the only one of her siblings who had been concerned about her in her childhood, Boston would always have a special place in her heart. He had lost his young wife in England and had traveled to America with the Carringtons. He had remained in Maryland for a while, but then he had begun his travels which had taken him all over the continent. At first, Alex had found his absence hard to accept because she knew that part of the reason he had gone had been his discovery of her liaison with Rane whom Boston had not seen before the two met in Annapolis. But gradually she had come to understand that, even without that goad, Boston carried the blood of adventure that had sent generations of Thaine men to challenge the sea, though this Thaine spent that energy in exploring the land. She had learned to live without hearing from him for months at a time and to regard any news he sent as a special gift. But she had long since ceased to hope he would marry again, and had resigned herself to the idea of his being alone for the rest of his life.

"My heavens!" she exclaimed as she read the letter. "His wife is an Indian! Or at least partly so." She read further. "She's part Scot and part Cherokee. She's thirty years old, a schoolteacher among the Cherokee, and her name is Rachel McDonel Thaine."

The dazed look in her eyes drew a smile from Rane. "Trust Boston. He hasn't done the expected since he arrived in this country," he said.

"He met her in the Indian territory out west, but they're in Georgia now—that's where she was raised—and they're coming here this summer! I can scarcely wait!" Clutching the letter to her breast, Alex whirled around as if she were a young girl again, but suddenly she stopped and her face was grave.

"I just thought, the Indian Removal Policy—it concerns the Cherokee as well as other tribes. No wonder they have been out west." She wrinkled her brow, trying to recall anything she had ever heard about these particular Indians. "I think they have resisted the policy, but I am woefully ignorant of the details. It makes me feel guilty. I can worry about slavery because I see it all around us, but the Indians' loss of their lands seems as if it is happening in a different country."

Rane nodded. "And the worst of it is that it seems so inevitable. There is even some justification for the claim that it is in the best interest of the Indians because they are endangered wherever the white man covets their lands, and thus must be moved to safer places."

"That's a nasty piece of sophistry, inevitable or not," Alex said in disgust.

It was Blaine who had more knowledge of the Cherokee through his legal training. "They are losing, but they have tried every means to keep their lands in Georgia." He went on to explain that the Cherokee had relinquished certain of their lands to Georgia by treaty in 1791 in return for recognition as a nation with their own laws and for a guarantee of the remainder of their territory. But Georgia in turn ceded her Western lands to the government in 1802, and with less land began to feel less charitable toward the Indians. Then, in 1829, gold was discovered on the Cherokee property. "They haven't really had a chance since then, because settlers started pouring in," Blaine said. "It's gone back and forth in the courts. Four years ago, Chief Justice John Marshall held in a particular case that the Cherokee are a nation under the protection of the United States. But Georgia ignored the decision and President Jackson refused to enforce it. The result has been that the Indians have no legal recourse and are being subjected to dispossession as whites move in and take everything. Some of the Cherokee leaders have accepted that the Western resettlement is bound to come, while others have continued to resist, and that has made the Indians bitter against each other." Blaine's voice was grim. "It's the sort of situation that makes it difficult to believe in the legal system in which I labor."

There was nothing Alex could do for the Indians in Georgia, but she was resolved that Boston's wife would feel so welcome at Wild Swan that she would know it as a refuge always open to her.

Boston and Rachel arrived the second week of August, and within twenty-four hours, Alex's resolve had faltered. Warmth offered to Rachel was frozen by her implacable politeness. She used it as a weapon, and Alex could find no way to get past her guard.

Rachel was a lovely woman with honey-colored eyes and deep chestnut hair. Her features were strong and even, her skin a dusky rose. The irony was that she looked no more Indian than Alex, and yet she obviously felt wholly so.

Nothing could dim Alex's pleasure in seeing Boston again, and his joy in seeing her was no less. His green eyes were vivid in his tanned face, and his golden brown hair drew light around his face. The same age as Rane, he was no less powerful a man, and when Alex thought of their past in England, she could hardly connect him with the slender and diffident young man he had been.

When he first saw her, he hugged her boisterously, but even then there had been a warning about Rachel, a softly murmured, "Give her time."

Alex quickly came to wish quite desperately that Rane was there, but he was at sea on a coastal trading run and not due back until the following week. Out of cowardice, she nearly sent word for her sons to come immediately, but she restrained herself enough to limit the message to the news that their uncle had arrived with his wife and would be pleased to see them when they could find the time to make the trip.

There was no way she could take Boston and Rachel to Baltimore. Rachel was so tense, even in the gentle surroundings of Wild Swan, Alex shuddered to imagine how she would be in the city.

Boston was watchful and protective of his wife, with the result that Alex hardly had a chance to talk to him alone until the second day.

"It's not going very well, is it?" Boston asked ruefully.

"It's going very badly," Alex replied bluntly. "What in the world does she think is going to happen to her here?"

"It's not here, it's everywhere. I met her father, though not her, years ago in Georgia. He's a forthright Scot who married a Cherokee maiden and never regretted his decision. He has a great deal of respect for the Cherokee, and Rachel was raised among them. Now everything is being stolen from them in Georgia. Rachel has had one shock after another, and it's left her bruised and angry. She and her father made the long trip west to the Indian territory in order to see what it was really like. They were appalled. Compared to their green land in Georgia, it is bleak beyond belief. I know; I was there.

"I met Rachel's father again and her for the first time. The three of us came back east together. I'm glad I persuaded her to marry me before we reached Georgia; I'm not sure I would have been able to after we arrived there. Her Indian grandfather was still doing fairly well when Rachel had last seen him, but when she saw him again his livestock had been confiscated and his fine house. From a once strong, proud leader, he has been reduced to a withered old man waiting to die. And her father is ailing now too. Rachel has become more Indian because of them. And I can't blame her."

He was so sad, Alex stiffened her determination to get past Rachel's wall of defiance, but she made no headway.

When she offered to show Rachel the horses, Rachel said flatly, "My grandfather used to have fine horses, but they were taken from him. You will excuse me if I do not wish to see yours." And then she walked away.

Unfortunately Gwenny, after careful study, was moved to comment, "You don't look like no Indian, or least not like I 'spected 'em to look."

It was said in perfect innocence; Gwenny had never been taught to hate or fear Indians and only knew that they were the people who had been in America first and had a different way of life in some places.

"More's the pity," Rachel said, and though Gwenny didn't know what she meant, she knew that the lady wasn't being very nice, and she avoided her thereafter.

Flora, angry that Rachel couldn't be friendly even to Gwenny, gave up any attempt to communicate with the woman.

The staff was delighted to see Boston again, but in no time at all they were very sorry for him and wished his bride had stayed in Georgia.

Rane and the boys arrived home to find Alex looking wild-eyed and worn from the tension. Though the boys were impressed initially by Rachel's beauty, they soon saw the cause of their mother's distress. They were nonplussed, unaccustomed to having their friendly overtures so thoroughly rebuffed.

"She didn't even smile at Nigel," Morgan muttered to Blaine. "And no one can be mean to him. It's like kicking a puppy."

"Well, it must be hard to have such terrible things happening to your people," Blaine pointed out, but neither of them was convinced that that excused such behavior as Rachel's. After all, she was married to their Uncle Boston, and that made her their aunt.

"Don't tell her that," Morgan said. "It might be the final straw."

Rane alone was not paralyzed by Rachel's behavior. He observed it long enough to see what effect it was having on Alex and to notice that Gwenny shied away from the woman at every opportunity. He didn't need to see any more. He was no more willing to abide Rachel's behavior than he had been to allow Hugh to hurt Alex. It took some time and maneuvering, because Rachel seldom left Boston's side, but finally Rane managed to waylay her.

"Mrs. Thaine, for my sake I don't care how you behave, but I will not tolerate your rudeness to my wife," he said without preamble. "Boston is very dear to her, and they see each other so seldom, it is wicked of you to make the visit so uncomfortable. I do not blame you for being angry about what is happening to the Cherokee; it is wrong. But it is not happening here. Look around you. This is a tiny corner of the world that my wife has made safe for all. Blacks work with whites, and no one is enslaved or dispossessed.

"Boston says you are a schoolteacher. I hope to God you do not teach children to hate as much as you do. I cannot think of a more useless lesson."

She blinked at him, her mouth open in shock. He expected her to gather her wits and snap at him. Instead, huge tears gathered in her eyes and rolled down her cheeks.

"Oh, damn," she swore softly. "I thought if I stayed angry enough, I would not do this." And then she began to sob like a bereft child.

Rane was completely disarmed. He hesitated and then put his arms around her, patting her back. "There, there, at least talk about it," he said gently.

It took a while; he had to sort the words out of the weeping. He was shaken by the picture she painted. Her mother had died when she was quite young, and her grandmother not long after, but her grandfather and assorted uncles and aunts had been generous in their love for the little girl and later the young woman. They were hardworking, prosperous people. Rachel had grown up proud of her Cherokee blood. Even when she had seen things beginning to change, she had been unable to believe that a people and a way of life such as hers could be so coldheartedly destroyed. But now she knew it was so, and her grief and rage were boundless. Everything her Indian family had worked for was being threatened, but more than that was her conviction that her grandfather would never survive the journey west.

"We will have to go, and it will be soon. Even John Ross, the chieftain who has fought so hard against the move, is beginning to accept that there is no choice. He too is part Scot." She pulled away from Rane and looked up at him. "Don't you see? Though I grew up as both a white and an Indian, now I have no choice. I have become all Indian because my heart cannot bear what the whites are doing."

"What of Boston? He is white." His voice was gentle.

The soft look in Rachel's eyes told much about how she loved her husband. "He isn't, you know. Boston is part of the land, part of everything he has seen. Boston is a witness to all the changes good and bad, but he is unchangeable. He is the one thing I trust. It is why I married him and not another. He is the one constant in my world. Even my father is not as he once was. He fears the future as much as my grandfather now."

"Be certain that Boston knows how you feel," Rane said. "I am sure even he has need of reassurance now and then."

Rane's talk with Rachel made all the difference. Now no one at Wild Swan had any difficulty in understanding why Boston had married her. But it was not an easy time. Listening to her recount what was being done to the Cherokee was painful.

"The worst irony is that the Cherokee became more white than the whites in an effort to live beside them. We adopted the white ways of government, of ownership of property, of houses and clothing. We have a written alphabet, a constitution which the women as well as the men voted for, and in some cases, regrettably, slaves are kept, though they do not all stay so, because the children of many have married Cherokee and are free. None of it is enough. We are still Indians. But now we have property to love, and the United States government will not protect us as new white settlers move in and take what they covet."

Alex, watching Boston with Rachel, understood why he had not taken his wife to task for her earlier behavior. He had loved his young wife Dora in England and had mourned her deeply when she died. But he had not been capable then of the depth of feeling he had for Rachel. What she was suffering on behalf of her people, he too was suffering. Alex knew that when the Cherokee went west, Boston and Rachel would go with them. She knew there would be nothing easy about the migration, but the couple had more strength together than most to face whatever lay before them.

She felt a new ease with Boston. The past no longer mattered. They had both chosen the directions of their lives and were set on their separate paths. And yet, their love for each other was stronger than it had ever been.

"So, little sister, you are flourishing and so am I. I never forget that it is because of you that I found a new life in this country."

"I thank you for the accolade, but in truth, you have enough of the Thaines' adventuring blood so that I think you would have wandered, no matter what."

They made a trip to Baltimore after all, and to Annapolis, but Alex did not press Boston and Rachel to stay longer when they decided it was time for them to depart. Rachel had good cause to be worried about her grandfather, and having been gone from him for so long during the western trip, she wanted to spend as much time as possible with him now.

"Auntie Rachel, you come back an' see me again, won't you?" Gwenny asked in the last moments before the Thaines left. Her face puckered against the impulse to cry. Her first impression of her Aunt Rachel had undergone a radical change since Rachel had relinquished her anger and had made deliberate attempts to woo her niece's favor.

"If I can, I will," Rachel said, not wanting to promise what she could not guarantee.

"I'm glad to have you for my sister," Alex told her. "You are always welcome here."

"It means a great deal to know that you and Wild Swan exist, steady and true, while all else changes," Rachel said, and it was more than enough.

Alex and Boston clung together for a moment and then let each other go.

It was far harder for Alex to see Nigel off to Philadelphia in September, and she admitted as much to Rane.

"It's irrational. I know he's mature for his age and no child any longer, but I still feel as if I'm sending a little boy off into the wide, wide world."

"Nigel was the baby for a long time," Rane pointed out. "It's only natural for you to feel that way. As a matter of fact, I have found myself giving him advice at every turn, most of it unsolicited."

Nigel alone remained calm. He was looking forward to his studies, and the hardest part for him had come when he had first told his mother of his decision to study medicine, for he knew how contemptuous she was of the violent methods most physicians employed to treat their patients, harming as many or more than they helped. His mother's methods of healing, learned from her grandmother, were far more gentle, depending as they did on common sense and time-tested herbal remedies.

But she had reminded him of the respect she had for Dr. Alastair Cameron, a longtime friend of the family.

"You know I trust Alastair. He saved my life when Winter Swan fell on me. And I assume you have learned from me as well as from him," she had pointed out. "Do you think that a few years of formal training are going to turn you into some kind of blistering, bloodletting, purging monster? If so, then you certainly cannot go to Philadelphia. But if you intend to take your good sense with you and keep it by you, I can think of nothing you are better fitted for than the healing of the sick."

He had been so glad of her response, he had had to struggle against tears. And he accepted all the current fussing by his family as an expression of love, even allowing his brothers to counsel him.

Morgan amused himself when he heard his voice telling Nigel to "avoid the kind of women I like." "Oh, hell!" he said finally, "Have a good time and don't study too hard."

Fall always brought a rearrangement of their lives as the race meetings began again. But at least Alex did not have to worry about leaving Gwenny at Wild Swan. If anything, the little girl got too much loving attention rather than too little. Della mothered her, as did all the other women on the place. Samson had infinite patience with her, and Horace Whittleby had returned to resume lessons for all the children on the farm.

Now nearing forty, he was a colorless, reserved, narrow-faced little man with bowed legs. His hair was less by the year and his nose more beaky beneath his spectacles. But he was a gifted teacher, transformed to a bell-voiced orator when he was expounding on the subjects he loved. Alex and St. John had found him in Annapolis where he had been working both as a private tutor and as a clerk for various governmental officials. At first he had come out to Wild Swan only during the week, but over the years his life had shifted so that now he lived at Wild Swan except in summer, when classes were suspended and he went traveling. Always, he seemed pleased to return to the children and the farm.

He had never married and did not seem to feel the lack. His books were his life and the children, both black and white, were his family. His only demand was that they pay attention and do the best they could. The only prejudice he had was his continuing dislike of horses. He had not liked them when he had first begun to work for the Carringtons, and he did not like them now. He rode poorly and as seldom as possible, despite his years of observing fine horsemanship at Wild Swan. It was an endearing peculiarity.

This year it was not her younger daughter but her elder whom Alex feared to leave. Flora seemed more her old self by the day, but there was a restlessness about her, and Alex worried that if she were not present to give Flora tasks to keep her busy, the girl would brood too much.

In the end it was Flora who solved the problem herself.

"I'm going back to Baltimore, if no one objects," she announced calmly. "I've hidden myself away for long enough."

She was relieved to discover her family was in complete agreement.

"What did you think we had planned, that you should be buried in the country for the rest of your life?" her twin teased, and Alex was pleased to see that they were at ease with each other again.

With that settled, Alex was able to turn her energies to preparations for her departure for the races. In actuality, she had little to do. Samson had the horses ready and their grooms too, and the maids Cassie and Polly were superbly efficient in organizing Alex's clothing.

Cassie had begun accompanying Alex as maid and companion when after St. John's crippling accident Alex had had to go to the races without her husband, and she took great pride in this special aspect of her job. She had had no intention of giving up her privileged position for the sake of any man, even Ned, whom she had loved enough to marry. Knowing her intention before they married, Ned had accepted it. But under

Samson's tutelage, Ned had worked very hard to prove himself a good horse handler that he might go with Cassie, and now he was a part of the caravan.

Alex did not approach the fall racing season with false hopes. Wizard would do well enough at three miles, and Swan's Scion would do his best at four miles. But despite being Wild Swan's son, he was not as good as Swan had been in his racing days. Sorceress, a full sister to Dreamer, was a better horse, but she had come up lame in a practice run in August and was still not fit enough to race. Swan Princess, a three-year-old daughter of Black Swan by Oberon, was entered in short races in order to test her mettle. Though she had done well on the practice track at Wild Swan, such performances did not always carry over to a formal racecourse.

It was not that Alex was ashamed of any of the horses. They were all well-schooled, well-bred animals. But Wild Swan was one of the premier racehorse stables in the country, and that meant spectacular results were expected whenever its Thoroughbreds appeared on the track. It was a reputation worth having in spite of the demands it made, for it guaranteed top stud fees and high prices for the horses sold from the farm.

By the time Alex and her entourage departed, the nip of fall was in the air. She loved the season, but it also brought a tinge of sadness. Rane felt it as well.

"It is probably from old superstitions of the earth dying," he said as he held her the night before she left.

"My love, you are surely lively enough," Alex said, snuggling closer to him, her mood shifting to the immediate pleasure of his warmth and the caresses he lavished on her as if to imprint himself on her body for the days she would be without him.

"I never truly leave you," she whispered. "The children are in your care, and thus I am with you as well."

Chapter

6

Though he had come to them late, Rane took his duties as a father very seriously, but he realized there was little he could do for the older children except to be there when they needed him and offer the best advice he could when they asked for it.

During Flora's first weeks back in Baltimore, he escorted her to some of the city's finest restaurants and generally made it known that she was in no disgrace and that anyone who thought she was would answer to him. More specifically, he called on the Fitzhuberts and told them flatly that if they did not treat Flora with the utmost respect, he would make sure everyone knew just how worthless their son had been. They took him at his word, and in any case, many people had known what Carlton had been like—he had never hidden his vices—and did not hold Flora responsible. The duel was stale news now.

It did not surprise Rane when Flora approached him about finding a house of her own.

"I feel ungrateful asking," she admitted. "I don't have any money, and I haven't any idea of how to earn it at the moment, but I'm used to having my own domain, and I . . ." Her voice trailed off.

Rane hastened to reassure her. "Your mother and I discussed it before she left. We do understand. It's difficult to go back to being a child after one has been an adult. We will rent or buy the house for you. But there are some conditions. You must have a housekeeper who lives on the premises. It's for your safety as much as for your reputation. And I would hope you won't rush into this but give yourself time to find a good property."

Flora, having expected opposition, was stunned by this generosity. She blinked at him, her eyes momentarily filling with tears, and then she gave an unladylike whoop of joy and hugged him. "We're so lucky that Mother fell in love with you!"

Rane was very pleased by her reaction.

Though Blaine tried not to show it when Flora shared her news with him and Morgan that night at supper, he was not happy about his twin's plan. And he was still brooding about it on the following day.

He had a lot on his mind, but Flora was his main concern. He wasn't at all sure it was a good idea for her to set up her own household again, though he could understand why she wished to. Despite their best efforts, he knew that he, Morgan, and Rane were overprotective of her.

Blaine could feel Flora's restlessness as if it were his own, but there was more to it than that, more than the change in her circumstances. Often these days she was so far away, one had to be very insistent to get her attention. And yet, it was not the same dark humor that had haunted her in the weeks right after Carlton's death. Whatever her reverie was, it gave her an air of suppressed excitement as well as trepidation. Blaine very much feared that Flora was contemplating something that she knew would startle them all, something beyond living in her own house, but for the life of him, he could not figure out what it was.

In truth, Blaine was restless too. June Stinson, a young woman with whom he had spent considerable time over the past weeks, was beginning to lose her attraction. They had quickly exhausted topics about which June knew anything, and Blaine had discovered that her blond beauty paled after a time, supported as it was by such a flimsy foundation. He thought that if he had to attend one more musical evening or lecture with her, he would go mad, not that June would notice unless in his ravings he mussed her hair. June attended such gatherings to be seen, not to be informed. Morgan was undoubtedly right in his cynical contention that respectable girls were rarely worth the bother of courting.

Nor, perhaps, were some clients.

Blaine was having difficulty with the client he was on his way to see, Mrs. Podringham, a wealthy old woman whose current determination was that a favorite nephew receive everything after her death. Unlike many of his colleagues, Blaine believed in clear language in legal documents, but Mrs. Podringham did not agree that straightforward English was adequate to her needs. In addition, she changed her will frequently, using it as a weapon against her family. Her husband had left her a great sum of money, and the chief pleasure she derived from it was holding it out like a carrot to a mule, to first one and then another relative. Blaine thought her family deserved the treatment since they were willing to tolerate it in hopes of inheriting, but he wished he wasn't involved.

Inwardly he chided himself; young lawyers in the process of establishing a practice had no business being so petty. Rather, he knew he should be grateful for the variety of clients he already had. He blamed his foul temper on the unpleasant weather. It was unseasonably cold for an October day. The wind had an icy edge to it, and now it was beginning to rain again. He hugged the packet of papers to his chest as an added buffer against the chill and wished he'd worn a hat in spite of the wind.

He barely restrained an oath as he jumped out of the way of waste water splashed from the street by a passing coach. It did not improve his temper to know that the occupants of the vehicle were undoubtedly warmer than he.

Up ahead, the carriage pulled to the side of the road, and as Blaine strode past, he turned his head in idle curiosity as the door opened.

It happened so fast, he didn't know how he managed to drop his papers and catch the body that fell out of the carriage, automatically shifting it to a comfortable position.

Her bonnet had fallen off and soft black curls were coming loose. Her eyes were as blue as his own and heavily lashed under dark brows. Her nose had a light tilt, and her mouth was disconcertingly ripe in an otherwise impish face.

Aside from one gasp of surprise as she fell, she was taking the whole incident with remarkable calm, not struggling, just lying in his arms gazing up at him while a smile began to shape that remarkable mouth. A few drops of rain sparkled on her fair skin.

"My goodness, you are quick!" she complimented him, and he felt her gurgle of laughter as much as he heard it.

Suddenly he was aware that his papers lay in the dirt; they had spilled partially out of their covering when they had fallen. Large drops of rain were splattering on them. A resigned-looking woman was emerging from the vehicle now, her plain garments a clear indication of her status as chaperone. And the coachman was standing helplessly by, obviously unsure what to do.

Blaine felt ridiculous. The girl's blue eyes were dancing with mischief and amusement as if she were a spectator at a play and was waiting to see what the script called for next. Blaine had no idea why he had not put her down immediately; now it seemed as if he had been holding her for much too long.

With none of his usual grace, he set her jerkily on her feet and glowered at her. She was tiny and had to tip her head back to look up at him.

"My, my, you are a grumpy sort of person, aren't you?" she teased and laughed again.

"I trust you suffered no hurt," he said stiffly.

"Only to my pride. You look as if you'd rather have caught a flying pig than me. But I do thank you for saving me from my own folly." The image of a pig flying invited him to laugh with her, but he was still feeling as if he had somehow made a fool of himself. His sense of humor seemed to have deserted him.

She noted the lack. Her smile faded, and she shook her head sadly. "Thank you again, and good day." With that she disappeared into a nearby bookshop, her companion bringing up the rear with the somewhat bedraggled bonnet retrieved from the street.

Without being aware of his actions, Blaine gathered up his papers, brushing ineffectually at the spreading blotches and then giving up and stacking them together again. He was well along the street with the rain dripping down his face before he realized that he hadn't asked the girl's name. Somehow it seemed important, and he stopped in midstride, hesitating for a long moment before he went on. Better to maintain anonymity on both sides after such a silly incident.

But he found that as he talked to Mrs. Podringham, commencing with a lengthy apology for the state of her documents and a promise that they would be recopied for her final signature, his mind kept drifting to a pair of very blue eyes. Blue eyes alight with humor and intelligence. And the dowager's voice droned over him as he wondered what it would be like to kiss that mouth.

"My nephew is the only one in the whole family who appreciates me. The others are only after my money. But I'll teach them a thing or two. Mr. Carrington! Are you listening? You've a most peculiar expression on your face."

Blaine wrenched himself back to the present, and with great effort he managed to concentrate on the will for the rest of the meeting.

He retraced his steps and hesitated before the bookshop. The carriage was, of course, gone. But it occurred to him that he could go into the shop, describe the girl, and ask if the proprietor knew her name. He couldn't do it; it seemed as foolish an action as his earlier performance.

But in the ensuing days, he found himself seeing her face over and over and at the oddest times. One moment he was perfectly aware of his surroundings, and in the next he was holding her in his arms in the rain. So small, but curved in all the right places—he was sure of it though she had been warmly dressed and he had held her for only a few moments.

He had been logical and measured since he was very young; he did not like this erratic behavior, but he seemed powerless to stop it.

"Blaine, let us know when you're home, and we'll come to visit," Morgan teased one night at supper. "I would not have thought that Miss Stinson could have such an effect."

Blaine blinked at him owlishly for a moment, finally focusing on what his brother was saying. "You should talk!" he snapped. "You probably don't even know the names of most of your women; they come and go so quickly."

Morgan could not have been more surprised had a rabbit attacked him with bared teeth; even more than Nigel, Blaine was the peacemaker in the family. Morgan stared at his older brother with wonder, but his apology was genuine. "Sorry, none of my business."

"I'm just preoccupied with a client," Blaine lied gruffly and proceeded to give what he hoped was a convincing recitation of the widow's machinations. "And from what I can judge, the nephew may well be the worst of the lot. Actually, I don't suppose I should worry; my client will undoubtedly change her will again shortly."

If Rane or Morgan was still skeptical, neither of them made a point of it, and none of the men noticed that Flora had taken no part at all in the exchange.

After a succession of absent-minded days and dream-haunted nights, Blaine decided the only sensible course was to return to the bookshop, learn the girl's name, and seek her out. He was certain that reality would end the wild flight his imagination had taken.

He was stunned to discover that the bookshop owner could not or would not tell him about the girl.

"But you must remember her!" Blaine insisted. "She has very black hair and very blue eyes. She came in with her maid last week when it was raining. She'd lost her bonnet; her maid was carrying it." He stopped abruptly, realizing he was babbling and not reassuring the man at all. He took a deep breath and tried again. "Pray believe me. I have no wish to harm the young woman, only to meet her. My father, or rather my stepfather, is Rane Falconer of the Jennings-Falconer shipyard, and I am an attorney-at-law. I'm quite respectable, even though I mightn't seem so."

"Knowing who you are, sir, does not tell me who she was," the man told him calmly. He was small, round, and elderly, and his eyes peered myopically through spectacles. Blaine realized with a sinking feeling that even with the glasses, the man probably saw little except for print held extremely close. And yet, there was intelligence and integrity in the scholarly face, and there was little chance he would betray the privacy of his customers.

As a last resort, Blaine took out his card and handed it to the man. "Please, if she comes in again, at least give her this."

The man took the card, but his gaze was eloquent—what well-bred young woman would seek out a strange man? Introductions were far more formal and scrutinized than that.

Blaine was growing quite angry with the unknown young woman. She had made him self-conscious and awkward from the first moment. And he was still behaving foolishly over her. It would be just as well if he did not see her again. His rational mind told him that, and still he passed the bookshop at every opportunity and looked for her everywhere else too.

And in the midst of his own preoccupation, it suddenly occurred to him that Flora was behaving much the same way. She was not wearing mourning for Carlton; she had decided that was too hypocritical considering the way he had died. She was a beautiful woman, and there was a legion of young swains who wanted to comfort her in her bereavement, but she hardly seemed to notice their gifts of chocolates and flowers and was quite careful not to favor one man over another. As far as Blaine could tell, Flora spent as much time in the familiar surroundings of the Jenningses' home as she did with any of her suitors. But he wondered if she were secretly favoring any of them.

Blaine found himself wishing, childishly, that his mother was home. She had a way of finding solutions to difficult problems. But she was not due back until the end of November. Rane had twice made trips to meet her, once in Virginia, once in North Carolina, and he'd brought back the news that Wild Swan's horses were doing well at the fall meetings. Blaine dismissed the idea of talking to Rane about his own problem or what he suspected about Flora; Rane had more important matters to concern himself with.

This night Blaine found June Stinson's company particularly annoying. He knew he should have stopped seeing her long since, out of fairness to her and himself. They were attending a reading grandiloquently entitled, "Great Poetry of the Ages." But the reader's voice was more tinny than resonant, and Blaine could not concentrate from one line to the next. June was craning her neck, her head swiveling constantly as she surveyed the audience to see which of her friends was there. She liked having it recorded that she was with Blaine Carrington. Blaine did not flatter himself; it had little to do with him as an individual; it was more a matter of his social acceptability.

He shifted restlessly in his seat, fighting a sudden overwhelming urge to sleep. The past days and nights had taken their toll, and the room was overly warm. He gave up the struggle and leaned back, letting his head fall to the side. But sleep did not steal upon him gently. It pounced on him so abruptly, his body shifted sideways like a sack of meal, jolting his head and neck. He yelped in surprise and just barely saved himself from toppling out of his chair.

The titters that swept around him told him there was no hope his near disaster had gone unnoticed.

"I am completely mortified!" June snapped.

He looked away from her, glancing down the row in the opposite direction, and for a moment, he thought his heart would stop. The blue-eyed girl was there, and she had obviously seen everything. One delicate, gloved hand covered her mouth in an effort to smother her mirth, but her whole body was shaking. With devastating clarity, Blaine could see the color that suffused her face, and the tears that stood in her eyes as she fought the hilarity sweeping through her. The elderly gentleman who sat beside her was making fluttering motions, obviously thinking the girl was having some sort of coughing fit.

Blue eyes met blue eyes, and Blaine glared. It was too much! He didn't even know her name, and yet this was the second time she had made him feel a complete buffoon. He wished there was no lighting in the hall; he felt as if he were stark naked.

Far from inhibiting her, his glowering expression increased her amusement. Though several people separated them, Blaine could hear the noise she made; she sounded like a kitten sneezing.

He gathered the tattered remnants of his dignity about him and sat rigidly erect through the rest of the performance. But every now and then he heard little eruptions of sound from the girl as laughter seized her again. He no longer had any desire to know who she was; he just wanted to leave the scene of his latest debacle and never see her again.

It was not to be. It seemed to him that June insisted on stopping to talk to everyone, as if paying him back for causing her embarrassment.

And then the moment was upon him. Suddenly she was in front of him, the old man with her.

"Uncle, this man saved me from a very bad fall from the carriage some time ago, and I never got the chance to thank him properly." Her eyes dared Blaine to contradict this version of the incident.

"Always going too fast, my dear. I have cautioned you again and again," the old man said, but his look was at once so vague and indulgent that Blaine doubted his admonitions to his niece were ever very severe.

The man put his hand out. "I do thank you for rescuing her. I am Virgil Winslow."

"And I'm Philly Winslow," the girl supplied helpfully.

Blaine offered his own name grudgingly and introduced June, all the while eyeing the girl with acute disfavor. He wondered what kind of mockery this was. Obviously she knew about Wild Swan's horses, but he was shocked she would call herself a filly in front of her uncle.

The light went out of her eyes as she studied him. "I am sorry I laughed tonight," she apologized dutifully. "I truly tried not to, but that just made it worse."

She took Mr. Winslow's arm. "Come, Uncle, we mustn't detain Mr. Carrington or Miss Stinson further."

"Philomena, you are rushing again," the old man chided as they walked away.

"Philomena? Philly!" Blaine groaned audibly as he made the translation. "June, please wait here for me. I'll be right back." He left her before she could protest, but he could feel her eyes boring holes in his back. It didn't matter. He brushed by people without acknowledging their greetings, intent only on stopping the Winslows.

"Philly!" he called as he saw her nearing the exit.

She stopped and her uncle with her. Her look was inquiring but neither as merry nor as open as it had been before his last rudeness.

"Please forgive me. It was your name, you see. 'Philly.' I thought you were saying filly with an 'f'. I thought it was a jest about the horses at Wild Swan. You see, my mother raises racehorses. Oh, God, I'm babbling again, just as I did when I asked the bookshop proprietor who you were. He wouldn't tell me. I have given you no proof to support this contention, but I ask you to take it on faith that I am not usually such an idiot." He took a deep breath and decided a full confession was the only course open to him. "Perhaps you have some strange power, at least over me. I seem to fall apart in your presence."

It was understandable that Philly had had some difficulty understanding the first part of Blaine's explanation, but then the words had fallen into place, and by the time he finished it was all perfectly clear.

She tried to keep it back, but it was impossible. Her heart was singing with relief that she had not misjudged this tall, fair young man, and his confusion over her name coupled with her uncle's muttered, "I've told you that nicknames are a nuisance," finished her. The laughter bubbled up inside her and overflowed.

She expected him to stalk away, but this time, his own sense of humor revived, and he joined her, his laughter a deep, hearty sound that drew the notice of people around them. But Blaine was not aware of them; he saw nothing but the way Philly's eyes shone, inviting him into a world where laughter colored the days.

"We are drawing quite a lot of attention," Virgil muttered uneasily. He would suffer almost anything for Philly's happiness, but being the cynosure of all eyes was his idea of a nightmare.

"And Miss Stinson is bearing down on us," Philly croaked and was off again.

Though Virgil Winslow spent most of his days in contemplation of subjects far from everyday concerns, he was, in moments of need, capable of practical action. "We would be pleased to have you call on us," he told Blaine hurriedly, and gave him their address. And with that, he bustled a still giggling Philly out into the night.

Blaine turned to face June's ire, but even when she began berating him in a low, furious whisper, he could not wipe the silly grin off his face.

"You have publicly humiliated me, first during the reading and now, chasing after that—that person, and then braying like a donkey."

"I wouldn't blame you if you said 'ass,' " Blaine offered obligingly. Philly affected him like strong wine; he still felt giddy though she was out of sight.

June looked angry enough to slap his face, and he finally had the sense to try to pull himself together. It was not her fault that he had been struck by lightning in the form of Philomena Winslow. June might not be his idea of the most desirable woman, but she didn't deserve to be treated so cavalierly.

"I don't suppose it would help if I offered my apologies?" he asked.

"No, it would not!" June said. "Not unless you can tell me that you do not plan to see her again." He watched with detached interest as she curbed her temper and essayed a smile. "If you will promise that, I'll pretend this evening never happened."

He stared at her, wondering if he had ever heard her really laugh or had ever seen her smile spontaneously with no calculation as to its effect. But she was not so dim as he thought; she perceived the threat of Philly.

Slowly he shook his head. "I am sorry, but I cannot promise it." He wanted to explain that he had been bewitched by Philly from his first sight of her. But he did not think that explanation would make June feel any better.

"Do you think you can manage to take me home?" Her voice was ice.

He escorted her to her house and tried to look apologetic, but he felt more embarrassment than regret. And when he was finally on his own way home, he felt as lighthearted as he ever had in his life. He had been invited to call on the Winslows. It was all that mattered.

Blaine resisted the impulse to tell his siblings about Philly; the feelings he had were all too new and confused to share.

He could hardly wait until the following afternoon. It took all his willpower to fix his attention on his clients, but at last he was on the Winslow doorstep.

Maybe she wasn't home. Maybe her uncle hadn't really meant for him to call on them so soon. Maybe she wasn't as compelling as he thought. Misgivings assailed him until the door swung open, answered by Philly herself.

"I'm so glad you've come so soon! I couldn't have borne it if you'd waited days and days!" Her smile of welcome was as forthright as her words. All Blaine's doubts vanished. And to his profound gratitude, his former awkwardness in her presence also disappeared.

The afternoon was pure enchantment for Blaine.

The Winslow house was in a state of beguiling untidiness. Books and papers were stacked on most surfaces. It was, Philly explained, Mrs. Miller's day off. Mrs. Miller was cook, housekeeper, and chaperone, and she had obviously long since resigned herself to the chaotic state of the house.

The tea Philly served was lukewarm and brackish, but it tasted ambrosial to Blaine. And Philly's uncle might have been a benevolent philosopher from the ancient world. Mr. Winslow was delighted that their young visitor was capable of intelligent conversation, and he happily introduced one subject after another.

In addition to utopian ideas for the spirit, Mr. Winslow had great plans for a perpetual motion machine, a flying machine, and various other exotic engines. And he had been writing his history of the world for decades.

Blaine was more interested in the family history. Virgil and his brother, Pindar, Philly's father, were the result of a marriage between a scholarly older man and a young heiress, the only child of a shipping magnate.

"It must have been considered a very odd match when they married, but my grandparents never regretted a thing," Philly said proudly. "I never met my grandfather, but I knew my grandmother when I was quite young. I remember her telling me that she hardly knew how to read when she married, but her husband taught her. She considered that more of a treasure than all the money her family had."

Pindar and Virgil had been raised to view education as the most precious commodity on earth, and both had been of a scholarly bent, though Philly's father had been more adventuresome than Virgil. He and Philly's mother had perished abroad in a fire, and their little girl, who had been left with her uncle, simply stayed on. The Winslows had originally been from New England, and then from New York, but Virgil had moved with Philly to Baltimore some ten years before just because he liked the Chesapeake Bay.

It seemed to Blaine a perfect life. The inheritance from his mother had allowed Virgil to pursue his studies and to provide his niece with a comfortable life. It did not trouble Blaine that Philly evinced no noticeable domestic skills; she had been raised to be a scholar, not a kitchen maid, and Blaine was dazzled by the quickness of her wit.

The hours slipped by far too quickly for him as they discussed one thing after another, from the upcoming presidential election to the best bookshops in Baltimore.

"The proprietor of that bookshop does know me," Philly told Blaine. "But obviously he thought you quite deranged. He never gave me your card or told me you had inquired after me. Very protective is Mr. Deats."

"Every young knight ought to slay at least one dragon. Deats the Dragon, it will serve," Virgil said.

Blaine found his days filled with joy now that Philly was part of them. He wanted to know what had happened to her in every minute of her nineteen years before she had met him. He spent every moment he could with her. Sometimes they went to lectures or musical recitals, but more often they strolled around the city when they managed to have time together during the daylight hours, or spent the evenings at the Winslows' house.

Blaine quickly grew fond of Virgil and enjoyed the time he spent in the old man's presence. In his sixties, Mr. Winslow was one of the most benevolent human beings Blaine had ever met, and though he was abstracted most of the time, he also possessed a quick eye. Blaine discussed legal cases with him, giving the details though not the names of the clients involved, and invariably he found that Virgil had sound advice to offer.

Blaine did not press Philly for passionate kisses or illicit touching in the shadows. It was not that he did not desire her physically, for he did, sometimes so much that his whole body ached for her, but he had a sense of timelessness about their relationship, as if they were so suited to each other that nothing could come between them. And Blaine was too sensitive to Philly to mistake her innocence regarding lovemaking, for all her boldness of mind and spirit.

He was quite certain she knew the basics, for her uncle was no prude and considered all subjects fit for study. But practical experience was another matter altogether, and Blaine knew Philly had none of that. The few times he kissed her had been sweet but by no means expert on her part. Blaine had reason to be grateful for Rane's insistence that loving was an art to be carefully learned and practiced. When the time came, Blaine had every intention of teaching Philly the pleasures of the flesh. Until then he would be cautious.

He was cautious too about introducing her to his family. He knew that Morgan in particular was suspicious of his abstraction, but Blaine just wasn't ready to share his newfound feelings of romance or to be teased. However, he spoke freely about his family, albeit unknowingly he left a great deal out. His description of his mother's horse business left Philly with the mental image of a strapping outdoorswoman with a long, equine face, and she pictured Rane as a cross between a swaggering sea captain and a well-padded merchant. She no more than Blaine wanted to rush the first encounter.

But gradually a plan formed in Blaine's mind. He couldn't put off the introduction forever; he had every intention of marrying Philly, and that meant that she and Virgil would become part of the Carrington-

Falconers and vice versa. He decided he would begin by inviting them to dine at the Baltimore house as a prelude to having them spend Christmas at Wild Swan.

He gave himself away when he told Rane about the supper guests.

"She is very special company, I take it?" Rane asked, hiding his smile as well as he could; Blaine glowed at the mere mention of Philomena Winslow.

Flora took one look at Philly and Blaine together and knew that her twin was caught for all time. Her first reaction was a savage stab of jealousy. Even when she didn't need his counsel, she had always been aware that Blaine was there for her. But once he had a wife, it would never be the same again. Now she knew how he had felt when she married.

She caught the look in the girl's eyes and felt instantly ashamed. Philly was neither defiant nor possessive, but rather anxious that Blaine's sister would reject her. Flora could almost hear her pleading for understanding.

Flora smiled warmly and said, "No wonder my brother has been so deliriously happy lately; I didn't think it could be because of any of his cases."

Philly's little sigh of relief was audible.

Morgan suffered no conflicting feelings; he thought Blaine was a lucky man, and he said so, causing a soft blush to color Philly's cheeks.

It wasn't long before Philly was enjoying herself, and she could see that her uncle was content as well. Blaine's family amused and intrigued her. It was interesting to note the resemblance between Rane and Morgan though Rane was Morgan's stepfather. Blaine had described the Thaine look and the persistence of it, but Philly hadn't expected it to be so strong. And Rane certainly bore no similarity to the mental image she had drawn of him.

But what mattered most to her was that everyone was bright, witty, well educated, and urbane. Philly had few prejudices, but she did find it difficult to be with the dull-minded. In that situation she was apt to say the wrong thing and draw blank looks from every quarter. Even worse was to find something amusing when no one else did.

There was certainly no lack of humor in Blaine's family. He recounted the story of his first meetings with Philly so engagingly, Philly was as tickled as the rest of his audience.

"At the reading, well, that was not exactly my fault. I swear that sleep leapt upon me, giving me no quarter, nearly felling me from my chair. And then I heard unholy mirth down the row, and there was Philly." When he went on to explain his confusion with her name, they laughed harder, and Rane remembered explaining to Alex, "R-a-n-e, not r-a-i-n," and wished she was with them now. He could not wait for her to meet Philomena.

Chapter

7

Alex arrived home at the end of November, weary to the bone. But when Rane came out to the farm and told her about Blaine's new friend, she was prepared to go to Baltimore to meet her.

"No, I think Blaine's plan to bring her here for the holidays is best. If you make a special trip, she might be intimidated. You are, after all, Blaine's mother."

"You make me sound like a harpy!"

"A fiercely exotic, mythical creature, not a harpy." Rane nibbled at her earlobe, and they were both glad she was home.

Though he had to make a few trips to Baltimore, Rane had arranged to spend most of December at Wild Swan. It was a slower shipping time than other seasons, and so Caleb would not be overburdened and would even be able to spend Christmas with them. Rane enjoyed being part of the preparations for the festivities, especially because Gwenny was still young enough to be in a state of constant excitement. Her green eyes glowed, and she was a whirl of energy from morning until night. For Rane, watching her was like seeing a part of Alex's childhood that he had missed.

And then suddenly Wild Swan was filled with visitors, including all the Jenningses and Nigel, home from Philadelphia. Sam had been coming over from Brookhaven as often as she could since Alex had returned, and Alex pressed her to continue her visits, though she doubted that she would now that Morgan was home. Secretly, Alex hoped that Morgan, seeing how happy Blaine was with Philly, would begin to long for the same closeness with Sam.

That Blaine and Philly were perfectly suited was abundantly clear. Alex could see it from her first sight of the two together. Despite Rane's glowing report, it was a relief to see for herself that Philly was everything she could want for her son. After Flora's disastrous marriage, Alex had feared Blaine might make an equally unwise choice, but Philly was exactly the leavening he needed in his sober life. She was equally pleased by Philly's uncle. Alex knew only too well that relatives could make a great difference in a couple's life, and it was a blessing that there was no cause for conflict on either side.

She was amused as well as relieved. Virgil Winslow and Horace Whittleby had quickly discovered they were kindred souls and had embarked on what promised to be an endless series of chess games and discussions of a great variety of subjects.

"I would never have thought Horace believed in perpetual motion," Alex told Rane with a smile.

"I'm not sure he does, but Virgil can be very convincing in his quiet way." He paused thoughtfully. "I'm convinced too, of a miracle. I've been almost afraid to mention it, but it seems that the old Caleb is really back to stay. Have you noticed how—how—"

"Alive?" Alex supplied helpfully.

Rane nodded. "Exactly. It started when he rescued Flora last summer, and he's just gotten better and better ever since. Perhaps her trouble made him see things differently."

"Whatever the cause, I am glad to see the change," Alex said.

There was so much catching up to do, the exchange of stories and information kept the conversation lively. Nigel was enjoying every minute of his medical studies, though he assured his mother that his common sense was still functioning. When Dr. Cameron visited from Annapolis, he and Nigel had a grand time vigorously but amicably debating new courses of treatment.

Alastair Cameron was a compassionate physician who believed no more than Alex in the dire treatments too many doctors used. In his early forties, Alastair was just under six feet tall with craggy features, freckles, reddish hair gradually fading to gray, and crow's-feet radiating from the corners of his mouth and his deep blue eyes. American-born of Scottish immigrant parents, he had taken his training in Edinburgh and a faint burr still softened his speech in times of stress.

By his own admission, Alastair had been "born rumpled." A new suit of clothes seemed to sag the minute he put it on, and even his horse and buggy looked in need of tailoring. But he was as fanatical as Alex on the matter of cleanliness in his medical practice, both of them perceiving filth to be one of the worst enemies of the sick.

Listening to him talking to Nigel, Alex thought she could not have hoped for a better mentor for her son.

And then Alex took center stage when the family demanded complete race results.

She pulled a long face. "Scion did his best, and sometimes it was good enough, but he lost three four-mile races, so he can hardly be hailed as a hero. Wizard was more consistent. He's comfortable at three miles and was only beaten once there. But when we tried him at four miles, he begrudged the extra distance and let an inferior horse beat him." She tried to keep her sad expression intact, but her exultation broke through as she saw the filly's races in her mind's eye. "Swan Princess was spectacular!" she crowed. "At only three years old she has it all—speed, bottom, and the manners of a champion. In two or three years, she will be a four-miler! I'm sure of it!"

"No wonder Samson looks so proud," Morgan said. "Princess is one of his favorites."

Philly tried to follow all this, but it was a foreign language to her. She hoped no one noticed, but she rather feared they did, or at least Alex did. More than once she felt the intensity of that green gaze on her, and though she detected no animosity, it still made her nervous. Alex made her feel hopelessly gauche.

The woman had been a shock to Philly, even more different from what she had expected than Rane had been. Here was no horse-faced matron, but an elegant beauty who seemed to know how to do everything in the world. Alex and Rane together seemed a single force of such vitality; Philly felt like a feeble spark indeed and cowardly besides. She was relieved when the topic shifted away from the horses; so far she had avoided riding, but she didn't see how she could manage that indefinitely at Wild Swan.

Flora, who now had her own house, captured everyone's attention when she announced that she had been taking pupils and teaching them various subjects.

Her family stared at her in wonder for a moment, and then Blaine said, "Well done! I wondered what secret you'd been keeping."

"I don't want to be completely useless," Flora explained. She looked at her parents. "I'm not earning enough to be independent, but maybe someday I will. I want you both to know how much I appreciate having a house of my own."

Rane and Alex were at once stunned and proud of the action their daughter had taken, and Flora was pressed for details of her new enterprise.

Only Philly noticed the quick look Flora and Caleb had exchanged at Blaine's mention of a secret. She did not mistake the warmth and intensity of that glance. She was glad for them; they fit into this setting, and despite the discrepancy in their ages, she thought they could fit together as well. As for herself and Blaine, her doubts were multiplying by the day.

Philly's distress did not go unnoticed. In spite of the constant whirl of activity, Alex observed the girl with growing dismay. She was still as pleasant and as anxious to please as she had been on her first day at Wild Swan, but something was desperately wrong. It was as if her special inner light was dimming. Her laughter was no longer as free, and when she thought no one was paying attention to her, she watched Blaine with profound sorrow shadowing her eyes.

Alex considered talking to Mr. Winslow, but the old man was spending his days happily debating the classics with Horace Whittleby, and she was quite sure Philly had done her best to hide her feelings from her uncle. And reluctantly she gave up the idea of talking to Philly herself; the young woman was nervous enough around her without such a confrontation. She decided Flora might be the key.

"What do you think of Philly?" she asked her daughter.

Flora smiled. "I wanted to scratch her eyes out when I first met her. Pure jealousy. I knew right away that Blaine was serious about her. And then when I took a closer look, I could understand why. She's not only bright, funny, and beautiful, she adores him. I give Blaine into her keeping with my blessing."

Alex breathed a sigh of relief, then confided her fears as Flora listened.

Flora decided subtlety would not serve. She waited like a cat after a mouse and trapped Philly alone.

Philly smiled questioningly at her, but the expression was so timid, Flora's heart ached for her.

Flora's voice was gentle but to the point. "Somehow it's all gone wrong for you here. We've done something to frighten you. I know we can be overwhelming en masse, but you seem a brave soul, or at least you did. What is it? What's happened?"

"Oh, no! You've all been wonderful to me!" Philly protested, horrified that Blaine's sister had noticed her sagging spirits and was blaming herself and the rest of her family.

"Blaine is going to notice," Flora pointed out. "He's so much in love with you, he's floating somewhere above us all, and he thinks you are too. It's going to be a shock for him when he finds that, far from being there with him, you're getting ready to bolt out of his life entirely. Please, tell me why."

Philly gazed at Flora for a long moment, her heart breaking because his twin looked so much like Blaine. "I never thought much about marriage. When I considered it at all, I imagined someone very like my uncle, a quiet, studious man. I thought we would read and discuss books and ideas, and that's as far as the dream ever went. It seemed just as possible that I wouldn't marry at all. And then Blaine caught me that day when I tumbled out of the carriage, and I thought he was the most handsome man I had ever seen in my life. Adonis at the very least, even if he did look disapproving. But his eyes didn't look like that, and now I know he's as comely inside as out." She drew a small, hiccoughing breath. "But Flora, I swear to you, I won't marry him. I fear he is going to ask me, but I promise I will refuse."

Flora shook her head dazedly. "Why in heaven's name will you refuse?"

Now it was Philly who looked confused. "Surely you do not wish me for your brother's wife? I can't do anything your family does. I don't even know how to ride a horse, and to tell the truth, they frighten me. I've never cooked a meal. We've always had someone to do it, and I never interfered in the kitchen. I can't sew a straight seam. I've studied botany and planted a few flowers because I like them, but I've never raised fruits or vegetables. I can play a lute and sing ancient French and English ballads. I can read in several languages, and I'm good at mathematics. Don't you see? My Uncle Virgil raised me to be the scholarly son he never had, not a wife to someone like Blaine. I can't do anything you and your mother do! I didn't think about it before I came here and met your mother. Now it's all different."

Despite the tears gathering in Philly's eyes, Flora had to restrain her laughter; only blind panic could have made this girl think Flora was as competent as Alex. "My mother is like that; I think she was born knowing how to do everything, though she claims it was her grandmother Virginia who taught her. But there's not a thing you named you couldn't learn if you wanted to. And if you don't want to, you don't have to. Blaine isn't a poor farmer. He's a successful lawyer. He doesn't need you to milk cows; he needs you to just be you and to challenge his mind with yours. Most of all, he needs you to go on loving him. You belong together. And you make him laugh; you make him more lighthearted than I have ever known him to be. This is a gift I would have him keep all the days of his life."

"And so would I!" The exclamation startled both of them.

"Blaine, how long have you been listening?" Flora demanded.

"Long enough." The twins exchanged a look, and Flora was gone before Philly could stop her.

Philly blushed to the roots of her hair and then went deathly pale.

"Adonis, am I?" Blaine teased, and then when he saw her tears spill over, he gathered her into his arms. "Sweetheart, don't weep. I can't bear it. You are going to marry me, you know. If you don't, I shall go back to being that stuffy fellow who didn't know his own good fortune when it fell into his arms."

She started to murmur additional protests, and suddenly Blaine was struck by the thought that the happiness within his grasp might truly escape him. Philly was as strong-minded as anyone he knew; if she was truly determined to set herself on a course of self-sacrifice for his supposed good, she could do it.

He had courted her with great care, aware of her inexperience with men, but something snapped in him now as the fear of losing swept through him. He brought his mouth down on hers, kissing her hard as he molded his body against hers, trying to brand her with his flesh through her clothing.

Philly stiffened for an instant at the unexpected onslaught, and then she melted against him, giving herself up to the marvelous new sensations he was arousing in her. For the first time, her body completely dominated her mind.

She opened her mouth to Blaine's invading tongue and felt every inch of his muscled leanness as his body pressed against her softer curves. The hard bulge in his trousers left her in no doubt as to the strength of his desire, and she felt more powerful than she ever had in her life. This beautiful, beautiful man wanted her. Everything else would have to take second place to that.

Blaine wrenched his mouth away from hers, and they gasped, "I love you," in unison.

Philly didn't want to laugh, but she couldn't help it. It was partly nervousness, partly joy, and partly the image of how stunned everyone would be if they discovered her and Blaine—cautious, controlled Blaine—locked together.

Blaine felt the laughter shaking her small form before the sound poured out of her. For a moment, he wanted to curse the bad timing of it, but then a different impulse seized him. Philly's sense of humor was as sensuous as her kisses, an intrinsic part of her appeal. His own laughter was low and husky as they clung together.

"When will you marry me?" he asked as soon as he had the breath for it.

"Anytime you choose," she answered, but Blaine had only a brief instant to savor her capitulation before she gave a cry of dismay and pulled out of his arms. "Uncle Virgil! What will he do? I know he seems content in his own little world, but he's used to having me close by. I'm the only family he has."

"Not any more," Blaine said. "Of course he will live with us or we with him, whichever causes the least upheaval in his life. He has done a very good job of raising you, and I have no intention of rewarding him by abandoning him."

She looked at him in awe and with so much love, Blaine feared that he might be the one to shed tears next.

Philly found that when they faced the family, she was no longer cowed. Blaine was hers, and all the faces of his family reflected her own joy. She went to Flora first and hugged her.

"If you hadn't taken me in hand, I might have done something very foolish," she said, and her eyes were eloquent in her gratitude. Philly was fully aware of how important his twin's approval was to Blaine, whether he knew it or not.

"Mother put me up to it," Flora confessed with a smile.

"Blaine is a very fortunate man," Rane said, and Alex murmured, "Nothing on earth could please me more."

Philly wondered how she could have been frightened of this woman. But the best part of telling the news was to be able to assure her uncle that she was not deserting him.

Virgil offered his hand to Blaine. "Thank you, my boy. It is more than I would ever have hoped." Blaine saw the tears in the old man's eyes.

"Mother, you'd better tell the bees or else they might pour out in the cold and freeze their little wings off," Morgan teased after he'd given Philly a hearty kiss.

"She says she's not sure it's fact or fable, but it served her grandmother well, so she does it. The bees must be told all the important family news or else they'll fly away," he explained.

"I'd watch my tongue if I were you," Alex suggested. "You eat enough of the honey to account for a good deal of the bees' work."

Nigel, Sam and the Jenningses offered their heartfelt congratulations in turn, and Gwenny was entranced at the idea of having Philly as her new sister. In no time at all, the news had spread to every corner of Wild Swan.

Supper was a high-spirited celebration, and Philly wondered how she and her uncle had ever managed with only each other. It was as if Christmas had come to stay; each day was a gift of revelation of another facet of her new family.

When they were pressed for the wedding date, Blaine said, "I wish it could be New Year's Eve, but I know that's impossible."

"Why?" Philly asked. "If we just have a small, quiet family"—she savored the word—"ceremony, could we not do it then? I should feel so much more at ease if there was as little fuss as possible."

"Bless the woman!" Blaine's words were so enthusiastic, everyone was amused, but then Alex said, "There might be talk about your haste. Would you mind?"

Philly and Blaine grinned foolishly at each other. "Not enough to postpone the date," Philly said softly.

Since she believed in the utter rightness of the match, Alex did nothing to try to dissuade the young people. Conventional restrictions and considerations had caused nothing but misery in her own life; she did not want them to do the same to her children's lives. But she still wanted Philly to have a wedding to remember, and she immediately put her considerable energies to that purpose, enlisting the family, the staff at Wild Swan, and Sam, who could hardly refuse, and thus spent more time at the farm than she might have otherwise. It did not matter that they were celebrating Christmas, too; it just added to the festive air.

They were usually joined by close friends on New Year's Eve at Wild Swan in any case, and these, including Alastair Cameron, provided the perfect guests for the wedding. But Blaine and Philly were oblivious when they spoke their vows. Even the minister's voice seemed to come to them from far away. They were alone, pledging a lifetime of love to each other with the golden rings Blaine had purchased in Annapolis.

When Blaine kissed Philly he forgot that anyone was watching until he heard Gwenny's voice chirping, "They's kissin' just like Mama an' Papa!"

Only then did Philly laugh.

Chapter

8

The first few months of marriage were a revelation to Philly. Having given so little thought to marriage before she met Blaine, she was unencumbered by years of dreams and expectations. And the reality of it filled her with more joy than she had ever thought to experience.

She loved talking to him. He expected her to be informed and to voice her opinions. It was as if it had never occurred to him that women should be mentally subservient to men. And when she thought of his mother and his sister, she could understand his attitude.

She loved listening to him. He considered things so thoroughly and logically, he had a direct eloquence of speech that fascinated her.

She loved loving him. It was an unending wonder to her that a man and a woman could fit together with such physical perfection. As unversed as she was in their first days of lovemaking, still she was aware of how skilled he was, and she learned from him with unabashed eagerness. The taste, the scent, the different textures of him—everything about him enchanted her senses. The sound of his voice or the touch of his hand was enough to cause a tug of desire deep inside.

"With my body I thee worship." The words from the marriage ceremony meant far more to her now than they had on the day she had spoken them. His attention made her blossom. She discovered that the sensual part of her nature was as strong as the scholar in her, and through Blaine she learned that they were not exclusive, but rather complementary.

His family continued to be another gift from Blaine. When Rane brought Gwenny to Baltimore for a few days, the little girl was allowed to visit Philly, and the two of them had a grand time together. And Philly saw a good deal of Flora and gave thanks for their growing friendship, never losing sight of the importance of Flora to Blaine.

She was most touched by the messages from Alex; her mother-in-law never wrote to her children in Baltimore without including Philly. And though Philly hadn't made much progress in overcoming her apprehension regarding horses, at least those of Wild Swan were beginning to be familiar to her and their racing to be of interest.

Only one area of her marriage remained a source of discontent. She had cherished the foolish hope that somehow domestic skills would come to her by the simple virtue of being married. To her chagrin, nothing of the sort happened. Her attempts to cook special meals for her husband and her uncle were disasters, the meat, fowl, or fish invariably underdone or overcooked, the side dishes no better. The victims of her experiments never complained, but it wasn't hard to read the martyrdom in their faces. Even Virgil, who, like her, normally noticed little about what he ate, began to look apprehensive before he had so much as tasted her latest effort. Philly didn't dare invite the rest of the family to share such meals, though she did have them over for suppers prepared by Mrs. Miller, whose cooking had improved under Blaine's direction. Blaine had, by observation and a few questions here and there, ascertained that the Winslows' housekeeper was capable of doing a much better job than she had heretofore. She'd grown slovenly because her employers were so lenient and cared so little for the finer details of domestic arrangements. With Mr. Carrington there to notice what she did and praise her better offerings, Mrs. Miller had taken heart.

Though she was grateful for the results, it hardly helped Philly's pride to know that Blaine was more capable of running a household than she.

Even her sewing skills remained too far below average to be acceptable. Blaine soon learned to sew his own buttons back on as quickly as possible lest Philly beat him to the task and mangle it with loving ineptitude. He had not known previously that it was possible to sew a button on so tightly as to render it useless or so crookedly, despite marks left by the old threads, that the garment no longer closed properly.

These shortcomings amused Blaine rather than annoyed him, and in his kindliness he was blind to how much they mattered to his wife until he came home to find her weeping copiously over an evil-looking stew.

"It can't be that bad," he exclaimed, wrapping his arms around her. "Oh, Philly, please don't cry! You know I can't bear it."

"It is that bad!" she wailed. "Look at this disgusting concoction. I can't even make a stew. I can't cook or sew or do any of the things wives are supposed to do."

Blaine pulled back so he could see her face. "I thought we'd solved all that before we got married."

"Don't you see, that *was* before," she protested. "Now I am married, and I ought to be able to do these things."

Blaine thought fleetingly that he had caught the habit of laughing at inopportune times from his wife, but he couldn't help it. He suddenly understood her belief that domestic skills would attach themselves to her simply because of the change in her marital status, and it amused him to think her logical mind could be guilty of such illogic.

Her tears stopped as she glared at him, angry that he did not share her distress.

"Oh, sweetheart," he choked, struggling for control. "Do you think I ever would have married you if I'd thought it was going to change you? I married you because I love you as you are. Let Mrs. Miller and the daily take care of dust, stews, and buttons. I need you to warm my mind, my soul, my heart, and my body."

Her anger died abruptly, and she gazed at him with adoration. "You are so gallant," she purred.

Blaine picked her up. "Imagine that, you still fit perfectly in my arms, even after all your cooking," he teased. He carried her up to their bedchamber, and the stew was forgotten for hours. Neither of them worried about what Virgil might think; he had adapted very well to having her husband as well as his niece in the house.

But despite Blaine's assurances of her worth, Philly was no longer content to be so useless. After giving it considerable thought, she asked Flora if she might teach with her.

"I'm not ever going to be any good in the kitchen," she said. "But I think I would be quite passable as a teacher. That's something Uncle Virgil taught me a good deal about by his example. But if I don't do well, you can tell me so and that will be that."

Far from being reluctant about the idea, Flora was all for it. She had been thinking of expanding her list of pupils but needed help to do so, and she thought Philly would be perfect for the task.

Philly loved it from the first day. She had had little experience with children, but she treated them as her uncle had always treated her, as if they were interesting human beings despite lack of years and stature. They responded with wholehearted enthusiasm to "Mrs. Philly" and learned even when they thought they were playing.

What had begun as a matter of private tutoring rapidly grew into the "Carrington and Carrington Day School," Flora having taken back her maiden name. Flora's house was in a state of mild to serious disarray during the week, alive with the sounds of children, and she could not have been more pleased.

Efforts to build a credible public school system still faltered for lack of funds and other complications, and there was a great need for additional educational opportunities. Flora knew she and Philly were offering a valuable education for a reasonable fee. She felt useful, and compared to the futility of her days with Carlton, it was a glorious feeling indeed. Sometimes she wondered if things would have been different had she had her work when she was with him. But she suspected the situation would have been worse, not better. Carlton had not wanted a responsible wife; he had wanted a plaything. The good would have come had she been wise enough not to marry him at all.

Gradually she was learning to accept her past without guilt or regret and to look to the future with hope. And Caleb was helping her to do it. There were many difficulties, but this love was completely different from what she had felt for Carlton. This was deep, enduring, and kind. She and Carlton had never been kind enough to each other, not even in the beginning of their courtship. Nor had they been patient, and patience was a vital part of her life now. Sometimes she longed to confide in Sam or in Philly, but she resisted the impulse. Time enough when it was all out in the open. It never occurred to her that her sister-in-law already knew.

Philly had no intention of betraying her knowledge; it happened inadvertently. Blaine, having found love and marriage so pleasurable, was feeling expansive enough to want his twin to have the same happiness, and to that end, he began producing men he considered suitable to court her. They were so dull, Philly didn't blame Flora for being impatient with them. And when Blaine made William Blunden his next choice, Philly felt obliged to protest.

"You can't mean her to entertain such a stick! Honestly, the men you judge acceptable are such bores, I wonder how you've gotten to know them at all."

"William is a prosperous businessman and only ten years Flora's senior," Blaine said defensively.

"Has he a sense of humor, a sense of adventure, a sense of romance?" Philly demanded.

"Well, no, but he's settled and can give Flora security. I think she needs that after being married to Carlton."

"I think she needs the man she's got," Philly retorted, exasperation leading her astray.

Blaine stared at her. "And who is that?"

She clapped her hands over her mouth as if to take the words back. But it was too late. For a moment she considered a lie but knew it would never serve; Blaine would confront his sister if his wife wouldn't tell him.

"Flora and Caleb love each other. They're being very discreet about it, but it's easy to see when they look at each other. They are . . ." Her voice trailed away as she saw the blank disbelief on Blaine's face.

"You can't mean it!" he said harshly. "Caleb is old enough to be her father! Flora stayed in the Jenningses' house, lived with them as if she was their daughter while she went to school here. You're wrong!"

She could see rage superseding all else in him as he mentally reviewed the evidence despite himself, remembering how changed Caleb had been after he had taken Flora out to Wild Swan, recalling the secretive, restive air his sister had had about her for so long now.

Philly had expected surprise, but not this overwhelming anger. She had never seen him truly furious before, and her first impulse was to cower away from him, but she made herself stand her ground. "You're the one who is wrong, Blaine Carrington! I'm sorry I said anything about it. I didn't mean to. It's for Flora to tell you. But if you can't see how well-suited they are to each other, then you're blind. As a matter of fact they're far better suited than we are."

The flash of fear he had seen in her shocked him more than her defiant statement, and he tried to get a grip on his rage. But he could not adjust his mind to the idea of Flora and Caleb as lovers. "Better than we are?" His voice sounded tinny in his own ears.

"Of course, they have much in common, a whole lifetime. And if you decide that only so many years can be allowed between a man and a woman, you're going to have to make considerable changes in the world."

"I don't want to talk about it any more," he announced, still angry.

"Fair enough. But promise you won't talk to Flora about it either. Not until you've thought about it calmly for a long time."

She was relieved when he gave his word; she could not bear the idea of Flora being made miserable because of her too-ready words.

Blaine did not find his promise hard to keep. He found it difficult to be around Flora now, let alone to confront her. It seemed he had indeed been blind. She glowed at the mere mention of Caleb's name, and she was often at the Jenningses' house or Caleb was dropping by the school. Because of Philly's association with the school and Flora, it was impossible for Blaine to cut himself off from his sister without being obvious about it. He wondered how long it would take his mother to notice what was going on when she returned from the spring races further south to run her horses in Baltimore. Even in his confused state, he could see that Flora and Caleb had become less circumspect than they had been before.

The change did not come about swiftly in him, only the realization of it. He had no intention of letting his feelings about Flora and Caleb come between himself and Philly. He decided that after less than twenty-four hours of coolness between them following their argument. It was unnerving to discover that he could not hope to win any war with her as he could not even stand to engage in a battle. He hoped this wasn't apparent to her, and then he decided that Philly was no more capable of hostilities than he; she had responded immediately to his first overture of renewed warmth.

And it was Philly who was responsible for the change in Blaine's attitude regarding his sister.

As they lay in bed one night in the afterglow of loving, Philly took his hand and placed it on her abdomen.

"I don't know for sure, and I haven't talked to anyone yet. But I think I am pregnant. We should have a child in October," she said and felt Blaine's hand jump on her skin. "Is it all right?" she asked anxiously when he said nothing.

"All right? My darling, it is far more than that!" He drew her against him and wrapped himself around her as if he would shield her from everything in the world. "It is wonderful, joyful, and frightening all at the same time. Do you feel well? Should we be doing something special? Should we have made love?"

Philly giggled. "I feel very well. And for someone whose mother is a healer, you are very ignorant, more so even than I. I am absolutely sure that as long as I am healthy and happy, the baby will be too."

"Midwifery isn't my mother's specialty," Blaine pointed out self-righteously and laughed with her, so glad to be alive and in love with his wife, he felt as if he would explode.

He lay awake for a long time after Philly had fallen asleep in his arms, and he thought of many things. He thought of how odd it was that now he would be a father. He thought of what a good father St. John had been to him, of what a good father Rane still was. He hoped he would display the same patience and wisdom. He thought of how happy he would be with a healthy child, no matter whether it was a girl or a boy, but he also admitted to himself that he would very much like to have a daughter just like Philly.

Most of all, he thought of how lucky it had been that he had walked down that street on that day so that Philly could fall into his arms. It came to him that the odds against finding someone to love so much were vast. Not that it wasn't possible to find someone to be quite contented with, but that was not the same as what he felt every time he looked at Philly. He thought of Flora and of how miserable her first choice had made her. And suddenly there was room in him for everyone in the world to seek joy as he or she would, and most particularly his twin, in any way it could be managed. He found that the pain and revulsion he had felt at the idea of Flora and Caleb's loving each other had vanished.

He nearly awakened Philly to tell her so, but then a tender smile curved his mouth as he listened to her even breathing. She needed her rest now, his love, the mother of his child.

When he told her the next morning, her approval showed on her face before she said a word. But she would not tell him what he ought to do next.

"She's your twin. It's up to you to decide whether or not to talk to her about Caleb," she insisted.

When he came to it, Blaine found it a far simpler task than he had expected. He told Flora about the coming child, and while she was still contemplating the prospect of being an aunt, he added, "I would like everybody to be as happy as I am, particularly you, sister mine, with Caleb or whomever else you might choose."

There was only relief, not denial or anger in her expression. "We haven't been careful enough lately, or at least I haven't," she admitted ruefully. "Caleb is better at hiding what he feels than I. I can scarcely look at him without wanting to proclaim my love to the world."

"I know how you feel," Blaine agreed. "Philly has exactly that effect on me."

"Did you hate the idea of Caleb and me when you first thought of us together?" Flora asked timidly.

Blaine was tempted to lie but thought better of it. "Yes, I did. It was a new way of thinking of the two of you. Philly told me in no uncertain terms that I was being blind and stupid, and she was right."

Flora sighed. "I'm so glad both of you are on our side, but it isn't going to be easy. I can hardly bear to think of what Mother and Father will say."

"They'll come around. I know they will. They want your happiness as much as I do."

But Flora's trepidation did not ease. "There are also Caleb's children to consider."

"But they've always liked you. It isn't as if you are a stranger to them," Blaine pointed out.

"That's just the problem, isn't it? They are accustomed to me as a friend, almost as a sister, but a stepmother is quite another matter. I don't want to take Penelope's place; I could never do that. But I'm not sure they'll understand."

"They will have to learn to understand it," Blaine said firmly, though inwardly he was thinking of what a hellish atmosphere the three young Jenningses could create for his sister and their father if they so chose.

"I don't fully understand it myself," she admitted, and her face was so vulnerable and full of love, Blaine had no doubt of the depth of her feeling for Caleb.

"It has been so strange," she mused. "I've known Caleb nearly all my life. And he belongs to another generation. I was so sad for him when Pen died, but I certainly didn't think of him as a man without a woman, as naive as that sounds. But then when he came to tell me about Carlton and to take me to Wild Swan, my view of him began to change. At first I told myself it was only because he had helped me during a crisis. But it wasn't that at all. Once I had seen him as a man, not as a friend of my parents or the father of my friends, I couldn't see him the old way any more. He is such a strong, intelligent man with so much humor and tenderness to give. And I want it all." Her voice strengthened. "And I want to give him everything I can to make him truly happy again. I know Penelope will always be part of his life, just as our real father will always be part of Mother's life. But that doesn't mean he should have to mourn forever. Mother and Rane are very happy together, and I plan to be so with Caleb."

"You don't have to convince me," Blaine protested gently. "Remember, I'm already on your side."

Flora's smile was wistful. "I know. I think I'm just practicing what I will say to the others. But for now, there is nothing to say to anyone. Poor Caleb, he still feels very guilty about this. And he wants his children to have more time to adjust."

"At least you can trust me not to introduce you to any more 'suitable' men."

"Thank heavens for that!" Flora exclaimed. "They really have been dreadful."

"So my wife told me," Blaine said, and they laughed together, as close to each other as they had ever been.

Flora agreed to keep the baby a secret from the rest of the family until Alex was home, and they looked forward to seeing how she would react to being a grandmother.

"She wasn't very strict with us; I'd guess she will be even more indulgent with grandchildren," Blaine ventured.

"You can be firm with them and let Mother teach them what an interesting, joyful place the world can be," Flora suggested.

Nothing could dim Alex's excitement and Rane's when they learned of the coming child. But outside of that small circle of celebration, the world seemed to be collapsing around them.

The financial house of cards was beginning to fall just as they had all feared it would. And the major cause was overspeculation in Western lands.

In the previous summer, President Jackson had issued the Specie Circular, which required that the Treasury accept only gold or silver or bank notes based on these payments for public lands. Jackson had intended that this measure would inhibit the decline in the value of paper currency. This decline had stemmed from the unbridled printing of paper money by Western banks after Jackson's withdrawal of federal funds from the Bank of the United States and his depositing of those same funds in

Western as well as other "pet" banks. Much of the buying of Western lands had been done with this paper money with such unstable value.

There were other destabilizing factors. Imports had exceeded exports in the past years. States had incurred enormous debts as they financed the building of canals and railroads as well as the chartering of new banks. And England, with whom the United States now had such a close trade relationship, was suffering her own financial crisis. This in turn caused many British creditors to call in their loans and shorten credit. At the same time, crop failures made it more difficult for American farmers to purchase what they needed. All of this served to unbalance the already precarious structure of credit and payment.

Then on May 10, New York banks suspended specie payment, and there was every indication that other banks in the country would follow suit. In no time at all, the prices of food and other necessities soared, and news came of factories shutting down in the North, causing widespread unemployment. And in the South, the value of land and slaves was falling.

President Van Buren, Jackson's personal choice as his successor, could hardly be blamed. Past problems had culminated in crisis.

Neither Caleb nor the Falconers had indulged in wild speculation in land or transportation shares, but that did not insure their financial safety. They were bound, as was all the business community, to the same shocks of shortened credit and worthless bank notes.

Horse prices and race prizes seemed in no immediate danger of decline because the sport was still, for the most part, the province of the very wealthy, but Alex had no doubt that changes would come here too if the financial depression went on for long. And she could not see how the situation could be quickly eased when it was the product of years of overspeculation.

Her immediate concern was for Rane, Caleb, and the shipyard. The effects on their business swiftly became apparent. Cargoes for coastal trading decreased as merchants failed and purchasing power declined. And worse, commissions to build new ships began to disappear as the buyers found themselves stripped of their wealth by bad investments and bad bank notes.

Slowly the shipyard ground to a halt. The brightly colored chalk lines on the black floor of the mold loft began to fade as no new patterns were drawn for various parts of ships.

Those fading lines haunted Alex most of all. They were the tracings of Rane's and Caleb's dreams for better, swifter ships. They were the dreams and livelihoods, too, for the skilled designer and the other craftsmen employed there, and for Morgan. Rane and Caleb were determined that none should lose their jobs and were letting no one go. But that situation could not continue forever. And the employees were not the sort of men who would suffer charity that would ruin the company they worked for.

Despite the fact that the best racing had moved further south, Alex took her horses only as far as Virginia in the fall of 1837. Her excuse was that she wanted to be close to Philly for the birth of the child, but in fact, she was as concerned about Rane as she was about her daughter-in-law.

Rane did not complain to Alex about the growing problems at the yard, but she did not need his words to know the truth. Even had she been ignorant of the national crisis, his face would have told her of his own. Too much of the time he looked tired and careworn—and hopeless, something that worried Alex most of all. She knew he was perfectly aware that with the produce and solvency of Wild Swan, it was not a matter of the family starving. If the shipyard went under, the Falconers would still be far better off than most. Even Nigel's education was assured, as there was still money from a trust that St. John's grandmother had given him. Long ago Alex and St. John had earmarked the money for the children's education, and the proceeds from it would always be for them or their children. It was not a huge amount, but over the years it had been adequately managed and reinvested.

It was not a matter of survival, but it was no less vital. It was a matter of Rane's pride. He had worked hard to be a success in his adopted country, and now everything was threatened.

She and Rane kept separate ledgers on their ventures, but they kept funds in common for such things as the purchase of Flora's house, anything that concerned any of the children or the two of them together. It had never caused any conflict before, but Alex could see it was going to now. Rane had adjusted very well to her pursuit of her own work with the racehorses, but she knew that, regardless of how hard he might try to convince himself, he would never be able to believe that it was all right for her to support the family for a while without his help. That she had done so after St. John died and before she married Rane would make no difference to him. He was feeling even more protective of the family with his first grandchild on the way. In some aspects, Rane was very old-fashioned. And Alex loved that as much as anything else about him.

Rane's spirits lifted for a time along with everyone else's when Philly gave birth to Larissa in October.

For all her small size, Philly had an easy time of it. She had not resumed teaching at the school in September, but there were fewer pupils anyway, due to the bad financial climate, and when Flora needed assistance, Virgil filled in. Philly had kept active with long walks and had followed all of Alex's other instructions in the weeks preceding the birth, eating sensibly and generally treating her condition as normal rather than as an illness, as too many women now did.

She had been enthusiastic about the whole adventure of being pregnant. She might not be any use at domestic chores, but she had conceived Blaine's child, and that was best of all. She had loved the feeling of the baby stirring inside her, and even the burgeoning of her tiny figure had not dismayed her. Instinctively she had felt that her body would adjust well to childbearing. But she had never suspected how beautiful the child would be.

From the day she was born, Larissa was an enchantress, so perfectly formed and so alive, it was some time before Philly could believe she was not some sort of magical illusion. Blaine was no help in this, as he considered his daughter nothing short of a miracle. Philly loved to watch him as he held the baby, his face inexpressibly tender. It was he who insisted on the name "Larissa," which in Latin means cheerful or laughing. He chose it, he said, "that she might be like her mother." The name seemed prophetic, as Larissa seldom cried, reserving that for what her Uncle Morgan termed "dire emergencies such as famine or flood."

Alex found it more than a little odd to be a grandmother, and she confessed as much to Rane. "I've realized that it isn't at all like being a mother. When I hold Larissa, I think of all the secrets and stories I want to tell her, but I don't feel as if I have to mold her into a responsible citizen. Let her parents do that. My own grandmother makes more sense by the day. Though she taught me much, she always made me feel she loved me just the way I was."

"She was remarkably wise and so are you," Rane said. "But you don't look the least like a grandmother. You look like a certain young girl I met years ago in Clovelly."

He held her close and hoped she did not feel the desperation of his touch. She was the one sane sweetness in a world that no longer made sense. No matter how he and Caleb did the calculations, they could not make the figures come out right. He thought of the one contract that had recently been paid in full, and he heard his own harsh laughter, though he had not meant the sound to escape.

He answered Alex's question before she asked it. "I was thinking of the irony of my being involved in building a revenue cutter. She's a lovely ship, to be sure, and the government is pleased with her, but I keep wondering if there is some moral lesson in the free trader building his own doom."

Alex remembered how they had laughed together when the contract had first been awarded to the Jennings-Falconer yard. The federal government had discovered that its own facilities were not adequate to the task of building enough revenue cutters for the customs service, and so had given the work to a handful of private shipyards, most of it being done in ports north of Maryland. It had been a measure of their reputation that Caleb and Rane had received the commission. But at the time, it had simply been added work for the yard, not the last thin wall between survival and disaster. And Rane's amusement had been genuine.

"You know the cutters are most often employed in stopping slavers. You detest that trade as much as anyone." Her voice was sharper than she intended it to be because she could not bear the note of defeat in his voice. He wasn't really talking about the ship; he was talking about the days when he had been young and had believed that anything was possible. He was feeling diminished and beaten, and she could not bear it.

She wrapped her arms around him and felt him shudder once before he was still. She wanted to make love to him and did not dare; if the worry and weariness that enshrouded him made him unable to respond, it would be the final blow.

She held him without demand, as if he were a child in need of comfort. She spoke of common everyday things, of the horses' progress, of the people at Wild Swan, and of Gwenny's response to Larissa. "She's not at all sure she likes this new addition to the family. I've spoken to Blaine about it. Gwenny has always adored him, and he is going to make a special effort to make her understand that Larissa hasn't taken her place in his heart."

She kept her voice soft and even, but as she felt him relax in sleep, a plan was forming in her mind. Her first impulse was to thrust it away and never think of it again, but once conceived, it took root and began to grow.

Chapter

9

Day by day, Alex's idea took on more concrete shape in her mind.

Philly and Blaine were all right because, regrettable as it was, the more trouble there was, the more people needed lawyers. And they would make sure that Virgil Winslow was taken care of. Alex did not know whether any of his investments had been seriously affected by the bank and business closures; he certainly gave no indication of disquiet.

Nigel's suggestion that he quit school in Philadelphia had been quickly denied, and Alex had pointed out that the money for education had long ago been put aside.

Flora was getting on well enough with the pupils she had left, her house was paid for, and Alex made sure she did not want for money to pay her bills when things got a little tight.

Morgan's fortunes were more closely tied to his father's, and as the days passed, he suffered the same growing depression as he watched the business disappear despite all their efforts to keep it intact. Like his father, he was well suited to standing his ground and fighting, but now there was no visible enemy, just the steady erosion of the business in the failure of investors to meet their obligations, in the diminishing cargoes, and in the dearth of new orders for ships.

Seeing Morgan so downcast made Alex more determined than ever to pursue her course. Anything was better than to watch Rane's and Morgan's self-confidence worn away day by day by circumstances beyond their control.

In late November, Alex wrote to Allen Ralston in Virginia, stating her plan precisely and making sure he would understand that she would not contemplate a loan, and that this business was private even from her husband.

The next step was to speak to Samson, but she waited until Christmas was over, not wanting to spoil the season for him.

Watching Rane's behavior during what had always been a festive time at Wild Swan stiffened her resolve. He was kind and attentive to the children, he sang the carols in his beautiful deep voice, and he even made love attentively to Alex, but the sorrow lurking under the surface never abated. And she could see the same in Caleb, as if the gains of joy he had made were slipping away again. She was too preoccupied to notice how anxiously Flora watched Caleb.

Nothing made it easier to tell Samson. She handed him the list of horses, and she made herself face him squarely as she said, "We are going to sell them."

He read the list, and then he stared at her, knowing nothing so dire could be in jest. "Wizard, Robin Goodfellow, Scion." Slowly he said the names of his beloved charges until he got to Magic. His face contorted in pain. "Not ma Magic, not dat boy! Della an' me an' de res' a' de people, we all gib you what we gots—"

She reached out and gripped his arm. "Please, no more. All of you will stay here; no one will lose his job or his savings. We are keeping nearly as many horses as we are selling. There will still be mares brought here to breed to Swan and the other stallions, and the mares we have left will give us new foals. Wild Swan's day will come again. But in the meantime, I need a great deal of money, and I need it quickly. Rane and Caleb will lose the shipyard, or, at the very least, most of what they have worked for if something isn't done. And I have thought of how to do it. I've asked Mr. Ralston to organize the sale for me. As you can see, I've established the lowest price acceptable for each horse. The buyers will have to bid above these prices to acquire the horses. And I trust Allen to invite only people you and I would judge to be acceptable owners. Magic is Allen's reward for organizing this for me. He will have to pay a fortune for him, but if he wants him, I'll entertain no other bids on Magic. I ask that you don't tell anyone else about the sale yet; time enough for them to be as sad as you and I are now." Her voice quavered as she finished.

"Mista Rane, he know 'bout dis?" Samson asked gruffly.

"No. He would never let me do it," she replied. "He believes that what is his is mine, but what is mine is not his. I don't agree with that." She knew she had Samson there. His and Della's marriage was very much a matter of mutual support.

Samson closed his eyes for a moment and swallowed hard. And then he said, "Dem hosses be lookin' fine as paint when dat sale comes. Dem men pay an' smile at de same time seein' dem so fine."

"Thank you, Samson. Somehow we'll survive this. And I know you will not be able to keep the secret from Della for too long. Tell her when you must." She left him abruptly, afraid that both of them would cry if they spent another minute discussing the sale. They would just have to mourn inwardly and adjust so that they could make a smooth business of it when the time came.

Had Rane not been so distracted by his own problems, he would have noticed Alex's strange moods, which varied from a brittle facade of joy when she was with the family to weary pensiveness in quieter moments. She knew what she was doing was right, but she also knew that nothing could soften the pain that would come on the day the horses were sold. Not even the flocks of wild swans passing overhead from their winter quarters on Chesapeake Bay gave her the customary comfort.

Allen Ralston's reply had been swift. He agreed to contact the other buyers, just as Alex had hoped he would. Allen owned a Virginia estate called Windower, and he was wealthy, sophisticated, and astute in everything but his choice of horseflesh. He loved beautiful horses, but he had no talent for picking winners. It was a sense he lacked, and it rendered him incapable of building a stable of champions from unproven horses. If Allen had a winning horse, it most often was because he had paid a high price for a known quantity.

Times were so unsettled, Alex's family accepted with little comment her decision to forgo the 1838 spring racing season, aside from May races in Washington and Baltimore.

"You know I always prefer you to be with me," Rane said. "But are you sure this is what you wish to do? We are, I admit, in some distress at the yard, but we will manage, and having you stay home to worry about it won't help."

The words made sense enough, but the tone of his voice betrayed his relief that she would not be traveling away from him.

"I don't plan to sit in Baltimore and fret. There will be more than enough at Wild Swan to keep me busy with the breeding season beginning and new foals on the way. Of course, I just might manage a few trips to the city to see my granddaughter and my husband too," she teased, but her heart was breaking for the uncertainty in him. His protest had been no more than a token; he did not question her further.

It was Sam who suspected something was very wrong.

"I don't know what's going on," she said bluntly, "but if I can help, please allow me to. So much of what is good in my life has come from you and this place; surely there must be some way for me to give something back."

Alex was suddenly perilously close to tears, but she managed to say, "My dear, you do that just by being yourself." And by being kind to my thickheaded son, she added silently. She had seen that Sam was unable to maintain her aloofness toward Morgan now that he, like Rane and Caleb, was so worried about the future of the yard and shipping business. His smile wasn't so ready these days, and he looked older and more like his father than ever. In response, Sam had once more slipped into the role of faithful handmaiden. She came more often to Wild Swan, and if Morgan was there and needed a riding companion, or a chess opponent, or another pair of hands to complete a task, Sam played her old familiar part without demur. And Morgan accepted it as his due.

As much as she loved him, Alex was sorely tempted to give him a good shaking, but she was forced to concede that it was still a matter of Morgan and Sam's coming to their own agreement.

Even the traditional celebration of New Year's Eve brought little relief from the financial woes, as little else was discussed by the guests at Wild Swan. Alex could hear the desperation that made wishes for a happy 1838 sound more like prayers. Even those who were still solvent were beginning to see that few would escape a protracted depression.

"I have more patients with indeterminate symptoms," Alastair Cameron grumbled. "Makes me feel damn helpless."

"I know," Alex agreed. "I have people coming to me for herbs and potions, and I know what they would really like is some charm to make their lives come right again. It's horrid to realize how much economics has to do with one's well-being. So much for humans as spiritual creatures."

"Speaking of well-being, thank you for the hospitality you offered my friends. They were greatly refreshed and able to travel on to their destination."

Even though they were out of earshot of anyone else, they did not speak openly of the latest group of escaped slaves who had passed through on their way north. Alastair was much more active in helping fugitive slaves on their way, but Wild Swan served as a refuge when it was needed, and gradually Alex had become more involved, ministering to the sick among the escapees as well as offering them food and shelter. She knew the risks; it was against the law to aid them. But the slaves were so threadbare and terrified, and yet at the same time brave enough to run for freedom, she could not turn them away. The employees at Wild Swan did not discuss it, and Alex trusted them all to keep the secret. Only Della had ever lodged a complaint, and her concern was deep and personal. She never lost the fear that slave catchers would come and take Samson away. But even with her misgivings, she never refused to prepare the food for the night visitors, and more than once she had helped Alex tend to them.

Alastair watched Alex's eyes search restlessly until she caught sight of Rane talking to one of the guests; no subject was compelling enough to take her mind off her husband for long.

"He and Caleb will be all right," Alastair said gently. "I know things must be hard now for them, but they are both too hardworking and talented for it all to be lost."

"You're correct. It won't be lost," she replied, and Alastair heard the resolution in her voice and wondered at the fierceness of it. But he did not question her. He had long since learned that Alex told what she wished and kept her own counsel on the rest. Deliberately he brought up another topic.

"Lissa is an extraordinarily beautiful baby," he said, using the baby's nickname, and he was rewarded by Alex's smile.

"She is that, in addition to being intelligent, charming, and a host of other things, including just a trifle spoilt. The only problem we've had is in assuring Gwenny that the baby is not taking her place. Philly's been very good about it, enlisting Gwenny's help in caring for Lissa." Her eyes were fond as she looked at Blaine and his wife. Tonight was the anniversary of their marriage, and they looked even more entranced with each other now than they had been then.

"We have a great deal to be thankful for," she reminded Rane softly as they listened to the mantel clock chime in the new year. She thought of Boston and Rachel. The Cherokees' time in Georgia was running out quickly now. It made Wild Swan seem more a haven than ever.

"I know we do," he said, and when they finally went to bed, he made love to her as if there were no problems at all facing them. She was grateful for the respite, brief as it was.

Things grew more complicated when Rane asked her to accompany him on a trip to New York, planned in February. It was a desperately unlikely chance, but Rane hoped he might be able to persuade a group of moneymen there to finance the shipyard. He wanted Alex with him, not only as company, but also because he knew she could charm even the most cold-eyed businessman.

Alex could not go. His absence could not have been more fortuitous because the horse buyers would come while he was gone. But she could hardly bear his disappointment.

"I don't understand," he said. "Even though I'm going for business, if you went with me, we would have some time to ourselves. We have little enough of that, God knows."

"I'm sorry, truly I am. But there is so much to do here, and Gwenny needs more attention now that Larissa has arrived in the family." The excuses sounded thin even in her own ears, and she looked away from his gaze as she saw the look in his eyes.

"Gwenny is doing very well regarding the baby," he observed slowly. "And the farm is well taken care of when you go to the races, so why not now? I know I haven't been the best company lately, but I swear you would have my attention on the trip."

The pleading note in his voice was nearly her undoing, but she shook her head. "Maybe later in the spring?" she offered.

"Maybe," he said, but Alex could see that he was not comforted by the idea. And the worst of it was that he would have been angry had he known the reason she was going to remain at Wild Swan.

Rane knew her too well not to suspect something was going on, but she did not confide in him, and though they both tried to pretend nothing was amiss, feelings were decidedly cool between them in the days before he departed. He found less cause to go out to Wild Swan, and she spent little time in the city. Rane's hurt withdrawal produced matching sorrow in her but no way to bridge the gap. She had never thought there would be such distance between them, and more than once she questioned the wisdom of her actions, but she was committed to the sale.

She went to Baltimore to be with Rane right before he left, and it was a difficult visit. At first he thought she had changed her mind, and when he found she had not, he cloaked his disappointment in aloofness until their last night together.

Alex could feel his tenseness, his muscles coiled as tightly as hers. And then wordlessly he began to make love to her. He knew her body well. He was methodical, and he used his knowledge to evoke a response from her. But everything he did bordered on violence. His teeth raked her tender nipples and scored the satin over her hipbones. His hands pulled a little too much at her hair and ran over her body hard enough so that his calluses scraped her skin. His fingers probed roughly between her legs.

She started to murmur a protest, but his mouth ground against hers, stopping the words. Still she cried out when he entered her, thrusting deep before her body was fully ready for him.

Her cry stopped him for a moment, and in that instant, she knew his desperation, hurt, and anger as if they were hers. Her body opened to him, and she met his violence with her own, scratching, biting, and writhing against him until both of them were lost in the sea of sensation that washed over them.

"Are you all right?" Rane's voice was husky and broken in the darkness.

Alex traced the shape of his face with one hand. "Yes. I love you, Rane Falconer."

"I know there is no other man. And I think all is well with the children. Nor do I know of any problem at Wild Swan—" He stopped talking as a new thought occurred to him. Alex had looked tired and preoccupied for a long time now. His hands sought her in the darkness, now gentle and questing, confirming the changes; she had lost weight she could ill afford to lose. He damned himself for having been so preoccupied with his own problems that he had not noticed until now.

"You are not—you're not ill?" He could scarcely force the words out.

"No, love, I swear I am not!" she hastened to reassure him. He sounded so terrified she felt more guilty than ever for not telling him what was bothering her.

Rane gathered her close. "You know where I'll be staying in New York. Send word if you need me."

"I will," she agreed, knowing she would not call on him, nor any of the men, including her sons.

Before she returned to Wild Swan, Alex saw Rane off on his journey to New York, her smile in place and her eyes dry, and inwardly she hoped she would never have to keep another secret from him as long as she lived.

As the day of the horsemen's arrival approached, Alex found herself entertaining wild thoughts. Maybe Rane would return early to announce that the New York bankers had decided to back the shipyard in grand style—she knew how unlikely that was even as she considered it. Maybe a huge snowstorm would blanket the roads, postponing the sale, and giving her horses a reprieve. Maybe Allen Ralston would send word that the buyers were not coming after all.

But the weather held fair, and Ralston and the others arrived. Alex hoped they would pay no attention to the long faces at Wild Swan. She had finally told the rest of the staff about the impending sale.

"It's too bad you and my husband aren't given to strong drink," Della said. "It might make you both feel better, at least for a while."

Della made Alex's favorite dishes and clucked over her failure to do more than taste them, and Alex was grateful for the motherly fussing even if it didn't restore her appetite.

She appreciated Sam's support, too. She simply appeared on the day before the visitors arrived. She took one look at the frantic activity on the farm and asked, "What can I do?"

"You can help me play hostess," Alex replied, and she explained what was going on.

Sam did not question the necessity of the sale. As far as she was concerned, Alex could do no wrong. Alex found such unqualified acceptance balm to her soul, and she was glad to have the young woman beside her.

Though he had summoned the buyers, Allen Ralston was not as calm about it. "There is still time for you to cancel the auction," he told her. "I would just as soon your husband did not come after me with murder in his eye for my part in this."

"The horses are mine!" she snapped and was instantly contrite. "Forgive me. I will never be able to thank you adequately for arranging this. But I would be a liar were I to tell you that it is easy to know that so many of the horses will be gone forever from here in a few days. Please just believe that it is necessary."

"My dear Alex, I have never doubted your courage, nor in the end, your good sense." His smile was wry. "It will be as you wish."

After St. John had died, and knowing Rane Falconer only as Alex's cousin and a married man besides, Allen had asked Alex to marry him. They did not speak of it, but it was always between them, and because of Allen's innate gallantry, it was a tribute to a special feeling he had had for her rather than a cause for embarrassment.

"Would you at least consider keeping Magic Swan? Your race on him and his riderless run are legendary, and his get are beginning to prove themselves more than worthy on the tracks."

"No. Either you buy him at the price specified, or I will allow the others to bid on him. I am doing you no favor, as I am asking a king's ransom for him." Her voice was firm.

"Then consider him sold." He recognized the strength of her will and his own chance as well; no racehorse owner in his right mind would pass up the opportunity to buy the famous stallion. There were many who would beggar themselves for the horse.

The men Allen had summoned for the private sale were an impressive lot in the racing world. There was an agent for William R. Johnson, known as the "Napoleon of the Turf," the man who had organized the North-South matches. Two more were from southern Maryland, three were noted horsemen from Virginia, three were from North Carolina, four from South Carolina, two from Georgia, and three were agents representing Louisiana buyers. The market in Louisiana for good horses was extremely strong due to the addition of the Eclipse Course opened the year before and the Metairie Course scheduled to open this spring. New Orleans was rapidly becoming known for the most luxurious of all racecourses in the United States.

From the North, there were two buyers from New York State as well as Mr. Challing from Pennsylvania. And most of the men brought handlers and grooms with them. Though Allen stayed at Wild Swan, the others found lodgings elsewhere so that no favoritism could be charged. However, all were well-fed and catered to during their visits to the farm.

Allen had been honest when he had chosen the field of buyers. He had told them he was acting on Mrs. Carrington Falconer's behalf, that the prices would be high as befit some of the best horses in the country, and that there would be more buyers than horses. Nearly all his summonses had borne fruit; the men had not quailed at any of the conditions. A major sale at Wild Swan was not to be missed. When foreign imports were bringing so much more than domestic stock, it was a measure of the fame of Wild Swan's horses that this sale was so attractive.

For the first two days, no bids were entertained. The buyers were shown the horses and allowed to check them over at their leisure. With Samson's advice, Alex had prepared a detailed inventory of the strengths and weaknesses of each animal as well as a record including the training routines that had been employed, the feeding schedules, and the remedies that had been used for any illnesses or injuries. The buyers were impressed by this, seeing it as an act of good faith on Alex's part, and it made them more anxious than ever to purchase her stock.

On the third day, the bidding began. Allen officiated, and despite his misgivings about the sale, he could not help but be pleased for Alex by the results. Even the youngest animals went for good money.

As hard as it was for him to do so, Samson kept well in the background. Even after all these years, there was still a chance someone might suspect his papers were forged and decide to seize him as a fugitive slave. Alex was glad she did not have to face him while the horses were being looked over. She was determined not to weep in front of these men, but she doubted she could keep to her resolve if she had the grief in Samson's face constantly before her.

She studied the men while they studied her horses. She was relieved to see that not one of them, not even the agents for buyers who were not present, handled the Thoroughbreds with anything but calm and gentle authority. Allen had chosen well.

One of the Virginians, Justin Sinclair, intrigued Alex. He was tall and fair, and the graceful competence he had in the saddle reminded her more than a little of St. John's style. Beyond that, she noticed him because he had noticed Samantha. He was openly smitten with the girl, paying subtle court to her at every opportunity, though he was careful not to press her too hard with his attentions. He was in his late twenties, and Allen Ralston gave him high marks for good character and industry.

Justin had inherited his lands from his father, his parents having died when he was in his late teens. His father had been a progressive man with an interest in new methods of farming and much else, and Justin was like him. The acres of his plantation were well-nurtured and turned to other crops besides ground-exhausting tobacco, racehorses being an addition of the past few years. Justin had spent considerable time in the North and had been to Europe as well, and thus he did not suffer from the insularity of plantation life. He was witty, urbane, and he showed a genuine interest in other people. Allen laughingly claimed that at least half the marriageable girls in Virginia, plus those in contiguous states, had their caps set for the popular bachelor, though no one wore his ring yet.

"That may change, though," he said to Alex, nodding toward the spot where Justin stood in animated conversation with Sam. "I've never seen him so taken."

Alex's heart sank at this confirmation of her observations. Allen was a shrewd judge of men if not of horses, and she had no reason to doubt the validity of his praise for Mr. Sinclair. In other circumstances, she would consider a young woman fortunate to be courted by such a man. But not Sam, Morgan's Sam. Alex had feared all along this would happen, but she had also hoped it would not until Morgan was more ready to see Sam as a woman rather than his childhood companion.

She was briefly tempted to treat Justin coldly in an effort to make

Sam doubt his charm, but she could not do it. Justin was just too nice a man, and Sam deserved the best, even were it not to be Morgan.

Watching the two together was another sorrow to add to the hours. She was sure that if Justin had anything to say about it, Sam would be living in Virginia in the not too distant future. Sam and the horses, all of them gone to live in other places—it seemed unbearable, but Alex kept smiling, kept portraying the gracious hostess.

Besides Magic, the stallions, Dark Swan and Swan's Scion, both eight-year-olds, and Robin Goodfellow and Wizard, both seven-year-olds, were sold. Two mares, ten-year-old Fire Swan and eight-year-old Sorceress, both with newly born foals at their sides, brought extremely high prices. Among the younger horses sold were foals born in the past three years to Fire Swan, Taney, and Black Swan.

Alex had sold a few of the colts from these mares before, but never had she so depleted their lines. She was keeping the five-year-old Swan Princess, out of Black Swan, and Ember, a three-year-old daughter of Fire Swan and an English stallion owned by another farm. Taney, who had produced two colts by Swan and could be bred to him again, would remain. Taney had not borne a colt this year, but Alex was sure the fourteen-year-old mare would produce at least one or two more before her days as a brood mare were over. In addition, the month before Black Swan had produced a filly, Alchemy, by Oberon.

Alex tried to comfort herself with the thought of what remained rather than contemplating the horses who were leaving—bays, browns, blacks, and chestnuts, coats gleaming and sculpted bodies held proudly, they departed with their new owners. She forced them out of focus in her mind, made them into a blur of color and sound, made herself forget the countless hours she and others had spent in tending their hurts, schooling them, admiring and loving them for the exquisite animals they were.

The spell of indifference was broken by Magic's departure. The son of two bays, Mabbie and Bay Swan, the black of Magic's coat showed rich undertones of mahogany as he grew older. He was eleven years old this year, and even his hooves gleamed from the care Samson had lavished on him.

Alex could still see Samson's face the day ten years before when he had run in and hurried her and St. John outside to watch the impromptu race Magic and other colts were running on the practice track. And she could still feel the enormous power of the stallion beneath her when she had run the first heat of the match race on him. How capably he had won the second heat on his own, running as if he were being ridden with great skill by a ghost jockey!

She could see herself in her widow's black at the National Colt Stakes in May, 1830. They had entered Magic in his birth year of 1827. It had been St. John's dying wish that she take the colt to the race as planned. Despite having been fouled by the winning horse, Magic had run well enough to place second.

With this horse, more than with any of the others, Alex admitted to herself that she was selling part of St. John's dream so that Rane's dreams might be saved.

All the horses were accustomed to being handled by the people of Wild Swan, and when they left the farm, Alex was usually with them. They were too well trained to fight leaving under different circumstances, but they knew things were not the same this time, and nervous, questioning whickers came from them as they left. Alex managed to ignore the sad chorus of the others, but Magic's uncertainty tore at her.

When Allen's groom led Magic out, the horse looked around alertly as if searching for familiar figures in his landscape.

She went to him and rubbed under his jaw. He blew softly, and rested his head against her shoulder, and then when she stepped away from him, he whinnied, a plaintive little sound mourning the loss of attention.

Allen was already mounted on his saddle horse, and he watched this exchange intently. "It is not too late. Magic can stay here," he said.

Alex looked up at him. "He goes with you. You've paid a good price for him. It was the condition of the auction. I needed to sell the horses, and I could never have gotten so much for them without your help. I will always be grateful."

"Magic will receive the best care at Windower," Allen promised, and he thought if he didn't leave immediately, he would weep.

Alex maintained her own control until they were out of sight, and then it overwhelmed her, the sad faces of the Barlow boys who had ridden the races of the older horses and had looked forward to those of the younger ones, the sad faces everywhere at Wild Swan. The empty spaces in the paddocks and barns were too obvious. And even worse was the diminution of sound. The remaining horses were unnaturally quiet, breaking the silence only occasionally with nervous calls, as if they already missed their stablemates.

Alex made her way blindly into one of the barns and then wished she hadn't. Samson was slumped on a pile of straw, and he was crying, his vast shoulders heaving with his sobs. To see the huge man so hurt was the final blow.

Alex knelt down beside him and grasped his broad hands with her own slender fingers. "I had to do it, Samson, I had to! Rane will never get the money he and Caleb need. I cannot let them lose everything when I can prevent it. I think even Sinje would understand. And we still have Swan, Fortune, Black Swan, Taney, Dreamer—" She choked on her own tears and was unable to go on. She bent over in spasms of grief.

Samson freed one of his hands from hers and clumsily patted her shoulder. "It be fine, it be fine," he murmured, trying to give comfort where none was possible.

Sam backed out of the barn before she betrayed her presence. She had been looking for Alex to see if there was anything more she could do, but she decided that adding her own tears to those of the pair in the barn would be of no help. She was not only upset by the sale of the horses, she was also unsettled by the departure of Justin Sinclair. He had vowed to return to visit her, but she didn't know whether to believe him or not, or even if she wanted to see him again. He had startled her out of her normal routine. For the first time in her life, she had found herself attracted to a man other than Morgan. She felt as if she was being disloyal, and yet the realistic part of her was growing to accept that Morgan would never look on her as other than a little sister. She wanted a husband and children of her own someday. Justin was certainly everything most women wanted in a man, everything, in fact, that she wanted—only she wanted it from Morgan.

"Damn," she muttered, wiping angrily at her tears.

"What in the hell has happened here?" Morgan's voice cracked over her like a whiplash.

The emotional upheavals of the past days caught up with her at the sound. "Don't you dare snap at me, Morgan!" she yelled. "And you'd better not be rude to your mother, either. We've all had about all we can stand."

Though he lived in the city now, Morgan was still attuned to life on the farm, and when he had ridden in, he had known at once that something was seriously amiss. Horses were not where they were supposed to be, and there had seemed to be no people at all until he'd caught sight of Sam. That she was crying had added to his alarm, and fear had sharpened his voice. It still coursed through him as he dismounted and put his arms around her, but his words were gentler now.

"What is it, little one? Is someone ill? Has one of the horses been injured?"

For a moment, Sam leaned against him, sobbing too hard to speak, but then she got control of herself. It was an automatic response. Morgan was in need of answers, and Morgan's needs came before hers. Haltingly she explained about the sale, and she finished by telling him what she had witnessed in the barn.

"Give them some time," she said. "They are both so sad. The horses are like children to both of them."

Morgan was so stunned, at first he could find no words. Her need for money must have been very great for his mother to sell her beloved horses. But he knew the mortgage was long since paid on Wild Swan and that the land had more than paid its way for years under his mother's careful management. And then he knew without doubt that the money was for Rane and himself, not Wild Swan.

He closed his eyes. "Oh, my God," he said slowly. "Father is going to be furious."

"Why? She has torn her heart out for him!"

"That is just the point. Father doesn't want her to do that; he wants to be her security, not the other way around."

"Then he's a fool. The woman has as much right to sacrifice to preserve the security of a marriage as the man has. If that isn't understood by both, then there isn't much hope the marriage will survive."

It gave Morgan an odd start to hear Sam speaking so passionately about how a marriage should be, but before he had a chance to explore this further, she had turned on her heel with a curt, "I must go home now."

"I'll escort you to Brookhaven and then return here. No one expected me anyway," Morgan called after her.

She spun around. "No. You're needed here. This has been upsetting for everyone, and though Mr. Whittleby has kept the children busy, I am sure they are as distraught as the rest of us. Gwenny will be glad to see you. And I want to be alone." She meant it. Morgan made her feel too many things at once. And she wanted to feel nothing at all right now. Justin's fair image and Morgan's darkness danced together crazily in her mind.

Morgan helped her with her mount, trying all the while to think of something to say to break the chill that surrounded them, but he had not managed it by the time she rode off.

He went in search of his little sister, but he found himself wishing that Sam was beside him to ease the way through this troubled time at Wild Swan.

Chapter

10

Alex knew Morgan's shock over what she had done was nothing compared to what his father's would be. But she did not wait for Rane to return to Baltimore before she delivered the money to the shipyard. She took it to Caleb, with Jed and Jim Barlow helping to guard the treasure she carried.

Morgan also accompanied the party back to the city, but he did not go into the shipyard with his mother. He had promised not to interfere, and he intended to keep his promise. He had felt badly enough about being after the fact in his visit to Wild Swan, because his father had specifically told him to go out and check on Alex. Logic told Morgan that there was nothing he could have done to prevent his mother's action, but he still felt guilty.

Caleb's desk told its own story; it was far too bare in contrast to the stacks of figures and rolled plans that had covered it in the past. But Caleb continued to come to the yard out of sense of duty and because he could not bear idle days at home. Alex felt more sure of her action than ever.

Caleb's face brightened at the sight of her, and his grin broadened as he studied her face. "You look as if you are about to explode with a secret. What is it, have you a new champion?"

Alex opened the leather bag she carried, spilling gold and silver coins on his desk. "This is only a very small part of it; two Barlows are waiting outside with the rest."

When she named the total, Caleb's eyes widened in shock. "What have you done, turned highwaywoman?"

"I sold some of the horses. It is done; there is no going back. The money is for you and Rane, for the shipyard. I hope it is enough so you can keep building ships, and when times are better, you can sell them. You cannot refuse me, not after all the help you gave Sinje and me when we arrived in this country. I do not need the money, and I would not have sold the horses for any cause less than this."

She had expected him to be surprised and to refuse at first, but his reaction went beyond that. He looked stricken; the healthy color faded from his face and his eyes were haunted.

"Caleb, you needn't take it so hard! I've kept the best of the breeding stock. I haven't done any lasting damage to my stable."

But his mood did not lighten. "Does Rane know?"

"No, he doesn't. He will simply have to accept it, as you will." Unnerved by Caleb's behavior, she spoke defiantly.

Caleb knew as well as she that Rane would not get the backing they needed in New York, knew that Alex's offer was salvation for them. He knew she had acted out of love for her husband and, in a different sense, love for himself, and that he could do her no greater injury than to refuse her gift. His hand trembled as he touched the coins.

"All was paid in specie; we have had enough of worthless bank notes," Alex said, continuing to watch him intently.

Finally Caleb got a grip on himself. "It is a measure of my distress that I will accept this from you, but only as a loan. Someday, it will be repaid. I accept it now because, without it, the shipyard will fail entirely. Rane and I have worked hard; we want not only to be secure in ourselves, we wish to leave something to our children. You have made that possible." He lifted her hand to his lips and kissed it. "Thank you, Alex."

She had no doubt that his gratitude was genuine, but she could feel the weight on his spirit. Pen had been a very independent sort of woman, though she had not run her own business. It just wasn't like Caleb to resent the help because it came from a woman. He might have misgivings about what she had done, but not this despair.

"If I see Rane before you do, I will tell him what you have done for us," Caleb said gravely, but both of them were aware that the confrontation would be between Alex and Rane.

The Barlows would give the rest of the money to Caleb, and Alex had instructed them to leave her horse at the Baltimore house before they returned to Wild Swan. As soon as she left Caleb's office, she went in search of Blaine. He was busy with a client, and she waited patiently until he was through.

Calmly she told him what she had done, including the presentation of the money to Caleb and his reaction.

"You and Philly see quite a bit of Caleb; would you hazard a guess as to why he reacted the way he did?"

Blaine was visibly shaken by what she had told him. The idea of so many of the horses being gone from Wild Swan gave him a strange, empty feeling. But he understood the depth of her love for Rane in the action, and he understood Caleb's feelings, too. For a long moment he debated whether or not to tell her the truth, and then he decided the avoidance of it would cause more harm than good.

"This is not my secret to tell," he began, "but I think it is time you know, for their sakes as well as your own. Caleb and Flora are in love. They would have announced it by now had it not been for all of this financial trouble. Caleb has been very worried about losing the business and has felt unable to offer any kind of future to Flora. You must see how he felt when you gave him the money. Both of them have been concerned all along about what you and Father would think. What an exquisitely painful irony it must have been for Caleb to see the money that would make his future secure once more coming from your hands."

Alex stared at him. "Caleb and Flora?" Her mouth was so dry, she could scarcely force the words out. "You must be mistaken. He is older than Rane."

"It doesn't matter. He is an intelligent, patient, and kind man. I could not choose anyone better for my sister. I did not see that at first, but Philly made me understand."

Alex's stomach lurched as the image came to her with horrifying clarity—Caleb looming over Flora and sinking into her young flesh. Caleb who had been like another father to Flora.

"I know what you're thinking about," Blaine said gently. "And it isn't fair. I am sure you do not think of a man taking a woman when you look at me and Philly or, indeed, at anyone else. You are only thinking about it now because you are shocked by the match. I know because I thought the same thing for the same reason."

"Not another word!" she snapped. "I don't wish to speak of it further."

As she left his office, it was galling to note that his expression was that of a parent saddened by the behavior of a stubborn child.

She walked for a long time, ignoring the curious looks she received, an unaccompanied woman in her smart riding habit. Her expression was so fierce, no one accosted her.

She had thought raising children was complicated enough, but she was finding that suffering their adulthood was harder. Caleb and Flora— Caleb was of her own generation, not Flora's. Caleb was her friend and Rane's, not the children's. Even as she considered him in that light, she knew the selfishness and the jealousy of it.

She stopped so suddenly, another pedestrian nearly bumped into her. What right did she think she had to decide whom Caleb should or should not love? She wondered if she had unconsciously hoped he would mourn Penelope forever. Oh, let him regain some of his old good humor, and yet let him not truly desire another woman to share his life. And surely not Flora.

She walked on, thinking of her daughter, so flighty on one hand but capable of the practicality that had enabled her to start her school. If Caleb had not been so entwined in their lives, Alex had to admit she would probably have welcomed him as a suitor for Flora's hand with few qualms, in spite of the age difference.

Life offered no guarantees. And with the risks of childbirth, many younger wives predeceased older husbands. And Flora was not, after all, Caleb's daughter, no matter that she had once resided in the Jenningses' home.

If she thought of it without prejudice, it was just as Blaine had claimed; there could not be a better man for Flora.

She wondered if her blindness had been deliberate. Caleb had begun to come alive the very day he had brought Flora out to Wild Swan after Carlton had died in the duel. She and Rane had noticed the change in him, but not the cause.

It occurred to her that Rane would be more accepting of this than she. She had always been more possessive of the friendship with Caleb than Rane was.

And finally she thought of how ungenerous she was to begrudge anyone else happiness when she had found it with not one, but two good men.

She was exhausted when she arrived on the doorstep of the Winslow house.

Philly gave a shriek of joy at the sight of her mother-in-law. "We've been so worried!" she exclaimed. "Uncle Virgil, Blaine, and Morgan are out looking for you, but they'll be coming in within the hour. You look as if you need a strong cup of tea and something to eat, at the very least."

It was nice to be fussed over, and the refreshments Philly offered tasted so delicious, Alex knew how truly tired and hungry she was. And it was good to be able to tell Philly about her change of heart. She felt so contented, she fell asleep in a comfortable chair by the fire. The next thing she knew Blaine was calling to her.

She blinked and looked up, bringing his face and Morgan's behind him into focus with effort, still feeling warm and relaxed. "If you say you are proud of me, as if I were six years old, I might strike you," she told Blaine.

"I had no intention of saying any such thing. I was going to tell you that if you ever give me a scare like that again, I will declare myself an orphan."

"I am going back to Wild Swan tomorrow, but I will visit Flora first," Alex said.

His grin was wide with relief and joy, and he looked so much like St. John, Alex's heart turned over.

Philly had resumed teaching at the school, taking Larissa with her each day, and Virgil continued to conduct occasional classes, so Flora was not alone with her students when Alex arrived the next day.

Having no warning of her mother's mission, Flora greeted her with a smile. "Are you checking on your children while Father is in New York?"

"I didn't mean to, but it turned out that way," Alex told her. "I know about you and Caleb."

The instant defensiveness on Flora's face was proof of her dread.

Alex hastened to reassure her. "Don't worry, you are an adult, and you don't need my approval, but I am here to give it in case it will make things easier for you."

Flora's mouth formed a perfect "O" of surprise and she sat down abruptly, listening as Alex explained what had happened.

Flora sprang up and threw her arms around her mother. "I can't tell you how much I've feared having you find out," she sobbed. "I love Caleb so much, but I could not bear the idea of losing your love or Father's, or of destroying your friendship with Caleb. It seemed so complicated and impossible, I can hardly believe it is so simple after all. Even Caleb's children don't seem so great an obstacle now."

Alex had no intention of ever telling Flora how complicated it had been in her own mind at first. "My darling girl," she said. "There is nothing you could ever do that would cost you my love or Rane's. Nothing. Our love for you is immutable, everlasting. I want you to know that as well as you know the beat of your own heart."

She felt closer to Flora than she ever had before, and she found herself beginning to look forward to the celebration of Flora's marriage rather than just accepting it. But she cautioned her against pressing Caleb too hard. "I would let him tell Rane, if I were you, or both of you together, though I don't think your Father will have any objection to your marriage. But it may take some time before Caleb wants to tell his children."

Flora smiled at her. "If you're trying to tell me that I am more impetuous than Caleb, it is something I already know."

Alex left a note with Flora for Caleb. It read: "You have my blessing. Make each other happy. Both of you deserve no less. Love, Alex."

She would have returned to Wild Swan with a light heart had it not been for the fact that she still had to face Rane when he returned. The thought of that made the days pass very slowly. It didn't lift her sagging spirits to see the somber faces at Wild Swan and to miss Magic and the other horses at every turn. and to know that this was the first time she had ever dreaded Rane's homecoming.

He rode in looking as dangerous as a storm on the bay. His eyes were green slits, and his face was lined with bitter weariness from the fruitless days in New York. His hands flexed as he faced her, but he did not touch her, fearing his own capacity for violence.

"How could you do it? I feel like a kept man. I have never interfered with Wild Swan; how dare you take over my business?" He was shaking with rage.

"I have not taken anything over. I merely offered help so that you could continue your work and not feel kept. Would you allow me to lose all this if you could prevent it?" She didn't want to fight with him, she wanted to curl into his arms.

Her calm reply infuriated him further. "It isn't like that! Every man has a right to succeed or fail on his own. Now I will never know whether or not I could have managed. The ships will never belong to me and Caleb again, never!"

"What of the men who work for you and need their jobs more than ever? What of the crews who will sail on your safe, swift ships? And Caleb, what of him? What of everyone else?" She thought she was shouting, but her voice was no more than a thin thread of sound. She had dreaded this so much, somewhere along the way she had lost the energy to do battle. And though she thought he was wrong, she could understand his attitude; it was exactly what she had feared. Yet, she could not apologize. The words would not come. Magic and the others were gone because of her love for Rane. Somehow it would demean their going to apologize.

She stared at him dully. "We seem to have reached an impasse. I feel in need of fresh air. I will return later." She turned on her heel and left him there, and though it was late in the day, she rode out on Black Swan. She tried to empty her mind, but she could not banish Rane's image. They were too close, too close to fight well.

Rane was feeling the same way. He had arrived full of righteous anger, but it had been crumbling away by the minute. Wild Swan was her domain, nurtured by her hands, her heart, and her mind, and much of it was missing now for his sake. Suddenly he wondered what life would really be like without her, and it did not help when Gwenny greeted him with, "Now Mama won't be so sad any more!" Her faith in his ability to make Alex happy simply by appearing pierced him to the bone.

And still there was part of him that wanted Alex to admit she had been wrong to interfere in such a profound way.

He felt so restless and unsettled that he thought he might ride out after her. He left Gwenny with Della and went to get his horse.

"Mista Rane, I gots to say dis."

Samson's firm voice startled Rane into immobility.

"Mebbe white folks' marriage be diffent, but doan seem so befo' wid you an' Miss Alex, seem jus' like Della an' me. What I gots be fo' Della, what she gots be fo' me. Dat way, we bof gots mo' dan we gots alone. Miss Alex, she sell dem hosses fo' you, an' it be like sellin' part a' her spirit, 'specially dat Magic, he go way back in her heart. But Miss Alex, she sell 'im. Doan seem right you be mad fo' dat."

Samson's eyes were full not of anger, but of patient sorrow. He had no illusions about the risk he had just taken. To lecture Mr. Falconer on his behavior was to risk all the security he had ever had at Wild Swan.

Rane was humbled and not a little awed. He had never doubted that in a moment of danger Samson would gladly risk his life for Alex or the children, but somehow this quiet insistence that Alex be treated more fairly by her husband was an act of even greater bravery.

"Samson, I promise you, she will not suffer at my hands," he said, and he saw the huge shoulders relax.

In the next instant, both men froze in rigid attention as Black Swan came in without her rider.

"God, no!" Rane screamed as the horrific vision of Alex lying somewhere with a broken neck possessed him. He saw her as she had been after the fall from Winter Swan when she had nearly bled to death.

Rane was sprinting toward the pasture before he knew he was moving.

The big bay hunter was dead. Alex had known it at first glance. He lay on his side with his legs outstretched, all the marks of age showing more than they ever had while he lived. He was very old and had not been ridden for several years but had been treated like an honored campaigner. He had been put out to pasture on fair days, kept in his own stall when the days were too chill, and fed, groomed, and generally cosseted. He had been St. John's riding horse in England and in Maryland until the fateful day when St. John had replaced him with the demon Vulcan.

Alex had known that Sir Arthur would not last much longer, but to find him dead on this day was too much. She discovered she had not shed all her tears in the barn with Samson. She crumpled down beside Sir Arthur and rested her head against the cold, unforgiving flesh of his neck and abandoned herself to the sobs that racked her.

She wept for far more than the loss of a beloved pet. She wept for her grandmother, for her daughter Christiana buried in England, for the unnamed baby girl lost in this country, and for St. John. And under it all lay the grim fear that when the horses had left Wild Swan, the love Rane had for her had gone with them.

Strong arms lifted and cradled her. She felt the frantic pounding of Rane's heart as he held her against him.

In that instant of fearing her mortally injured or already dead, the priorities of Rane's life had radically rearranged themselves. He no longer cared if the shipyard went under or went on; he didn't care whether there were a hundred horses or none at all at Wild Swan; nothing on earth was as important as the fact that Alex was alive and whole in his arms.

He heard the echo of her pathetic sobbing voice saying, "I'm so sorry, Sinje, so sorry. Magic, oh, my lovely Magic," and he wondered if she was injured after all. Only now did he realize how it must have been for her to sell so much of St. John's legacy to aid himself.

Rane had not noticed Samson motioning away Tad Barlow and the others who had been drawn to the scene. There was no one else in Rane's universe except Alex.

"Sweetling, I love you," he crooned. "I've loved you longer than half my life, and I will love you until the last second of the last day of it and beyond if that is possible. Nothing, no one else matters as much, certainly not the damn shipyard. It's good that it will survive, but without you, I would not. When Black Swan came in without you, I died."

She touched his face. "She was frightened by the smell of death," she explained huskily. Her mind was working very slowly but it was dawning on her that the rapid beat of his heart had been caused by fear for her and that his anger had been eclipsed by his love. She looked back down at Sir Arthur.

"There is nothing you can do for him now. Samson will see that he is buried," Rane told her gently, and she did not struggle when he led her out of the field and back to the house.

She was very sleepy in the aftermath of the emotional storm, and Rane did not try to keep her awake. He stripped off her clothes and bathed her with a cloth before he tucked her into bed.

When Alex awakened the next morning, the first thing she saw was Rane. He was propped on an elbow, looking down at her, and the anxiety in his expression told her that the upheaval of the previous day had been no nightmare.

She stared into his eyes for a long moment, and then very deliberately, she rose up and planted her mouth firmly on his, telling him without words that all was healed between them.

Rane's response was to make love to her with such sweet, slow delicacy that she was writhing with need by the time he came into her. It was a perfect counterpoint to the violence of their union on the night before he had left for New York.

"I can almost understand why some couples fight in order to be able to heal the breach like this," Alex murmured afterward.

" 'Almost' won't do. I hate fighting with you!" His voice changed, softened and trembled. "Alex, thank you for sacrificing the horses for my sake."

"You are welcome," she replied with the same directness.

And then inexplicably, Rane was laughing. Their bed shook with the force of it, and it took him some time to control himself enough to explain.

"Poor Caleb, all these months he's borne the secret of his love for Flora and has dreaded our reaction. But you apparently gave your blessing, and when he told me of his plans, I scarcely listened. You were all I could think about. I believe I wished him joy with Flora. Only now can I see his face clearly—he looked like a man who had been battering his head against a wall only to have someone open a door. He fell right through. I expect he's still wondering what happened."

Alex laughed with him at the image until both of them were lying flat on the bed, comfortably weary. "It will be good for both of them, won't it?" she asked, trying to be responsible despite the drunken joy she felt.

"It will be as good as they make it," Rane answered. "And I think that will be fine indeed. The twins have looked for each other in a way, and the search is ended. Blaine has married someone as joyful as Flora can be, and now Flora will marry someone who can be as serious as Blaine. It's not exactly the same, I know, but close enough."

"You are a very wise man."

"To match my wise woman," he said, calling her by the old country name for one who heals the sick with herbs and simples.

Flora and Caleb were married at Wild Swan in March. Only the family, including Nigel who came from Philadelphia, and Sam, Dr. Cameron, and the Bateses attended. The couple wanted a minimum of fuss, particularly for the sake of Caleb's children. The two boys were adjusting well enough, but seventeen-year-old Liza was not as sure she approved. Liza was a bright, kind girl, but it was not easy for her to see Flora, whom she had always regarded as an older sister, become her stepmother.

Alex was proud of the way Flora was handling her new stepdaughter. Even when Liza was sulky, Flora went out of her way to make sure she felt included in whatever was going on, and she had enlisted her aid in planning the wedding. Liza had found it increasingly difficult to maintain her pose of disapproval and aloofness. Flora was making no attempt to step into Penelope's shoes. She knew that that was an impossibility, and she wanted the children to know it too. Her role would be different.

She let them know in every way she could that she was still their friend and there as such whenever they needed her. Even the youngest, Blake, was, at twelve, too old to welcome too much mothering from Flora.

But the children could not fail to see that Flora was making their father extremely happy, and that went a long way toward aiding the adjustment. Nor did they mind that their ties would be even closer to Wild Swan now than before; they were all fond of the farm and the people there.

Caleb was so transformed, it was all Rane and Alex could do to hide their amusement. It was not that he would ever forget Pen. He had loved her dearly, and they had produced three fine children together. But he had come to accept that he had mourned long enough, and that another chance at happiness had been offered to him, no matter how unlikely the circumstance. Flora danced through his days, beautiful as the first rays of the morning sun after long darkness. And she looked at him with such open love and longing, he felt more alive than he had since Pen died.

He was sure many would judge him an aging roué. He might have done so himself had he not known what he gave Flora in return for her gifts to him. Flora's exquisite blond beauty made many think she could not possibly have problems or doubts in spite of the disastrous end to her first marriage. Caleb knew better. Carlton had been a bad mistake and had shaken her faith in herself as a woman.

Caleb believed in Flora, in her intelligence, in her heart, in her ability to manage and to survive. And he was proud of her. Proud of how she had handled the disaster of her first marriage, proud of her efforts to establish her school. And constantly, steadily, he was communicating his belief and pride to her.

That Rane and Alex approved of his marriage to their daughter was all the blessing he needed, but he repeated his vows with grave intent.

Alex thought the couple looked splendid, Caleb so tall and lean with his intense dark eyes and golden brown hair only lightly touched with gray, and Flora standing so fair and shining beside him, her blue eyes brimming with love when she looked up at him.

Spring was coming, and the first soft breath of it caressed them all. The children were prospering; the shipyard and Wild Swan were safe, and new champions would be born of the remaining horses.

Such utter contentment was rare even in the happiest of lives, and Alex and Rane savored every moment of it, Rane even going with Alex to tell the bees the news, though this was not his favorite chore.

"Three more children to go," Rane teased. "Of course, no man on earth will be good enough for Gwenny, so I may send her to a nunnery."

"I think she might have some objection to that," Alex replied.

"And if only Morgan would wake up and take a good look at Sam, there would be one less to fret about. I refuse to worry at all about Nigel. I expect him to make a sensible choice when the time comes, just as he has with everything else in his life since he was a small child." She paused, gazing at Rane. "I'm not sure any of us tell you often enough, but I hope you never doubt that we know how fortunate we are in you, I for a husband, they for a father."

Rane's throat was suddenly so tight, he had to swallow hard before he could speak. "When you look at me like that, sweetling, you don't have to say anything at all."

Chapter 11

It became more and more apparent that it was going to take a long time for the country to regain financial health. Some banks were resuming specie payment, but there was no guarantee of how long that would last, and it did nothing to resurrect failed businesses.

Alex was grateful that her family was doing so much better than most, and she planned a limited racing schedule to underscore her own survival.

She took Swan Princess and the three-year-old Ember to both the Kendall and the Central Course races at Baltimore in May. Ember triumphed in the mile heats of the Maryland Jockey Club Races at the Central Course, and Swan Princess took the three-mile heats there and the four-mile-heat race at the earlier Kendall Course meeting.

Taking the horses to those races was Alex's way of saying that Wild Swan still had champions even if their numbers were decreased. Though the day would undoubtedly come, she was relieved that none of the Thoroughbreds she had sold were in the field against her entries. She was also glad that, as far as she knew, all the horses she had sold were healthy and well cared for. In February, a trainload of prize animals en route to Charleston, South Carolina, had suffered injury and death when the train had wrecked and burned. Each small car had carried only one horse and a groom, else the toll might have been worse. It made Alex more resistant than ever to the idea of transporting her handlers and horses by rail. A van pulled by teams of post horses, a recent British innovation, was scarcely more appealing, since most of the racing in the United States was in the South where roads were generally execrable.

Frequently Alex wondered if she could cope with the changes, small or large, that came day by day at a rate that seemed much faster than in the past. Progress seemed to hurt so many in its path. The news from Boston and Rachel in Georgia was all bad. The Cherokee attempts to resist removal from their lands had failed. By May, only two thousand of the Eastern Cherokee had gone, and so General Winfield Scott, along with reinforcements of artillery, cavalry, and infantry, was ordered to take command of the troops already in the Cherokee region. He had the authority to ask the governors of adjoining states for as many as four thousand volunteers and militia. The result was a force of seven thousand soldiers empowered to remove fifteen thousand Cherokee.

Though white settlers had been taking their land and possessions for years and subjecting them to constant harassment, nothing had prepared the Indians for what happened now. Families were snatched from their homes and marched to stockades, too often looking back to see their frame houses burning to the ground. Many of them had no time to pack even the most basic of their possessions. Greedy whites waited to seize the farm lands and the livestock, and many blacks were taken as well, a particular agony as many were free and married to Cherokee or were part Indian and part black, the children of such marriages. A drought had bedeviled the region for some time, and it added to the misery of summer imprisonment.

Not all white voices of outrage were silenced. Missionaries continued to protest the treatment, and even some of Scott's soldiers were conscience-stricken. They had arrived expecting to find savages and had found instead a highly cultured people and beautiful Indian maidens, many with as much or more white blood than Indian, which added to the soldiers' confusion.

But the voices raised against the removal were faint compared to the determination of the state of Georgia to take the lands. Neighboring states with their residual Cherokee populations cooperated with Georgia. The Indians could not hope to win.

It was happening to, or had already happened to, other civilized

Eastern tribes—the Choctaw in Mississippi, the Creek in Alabama, the Chickasaw in Alabama and Mississippi, and the Seminole in Florida—but to Alex and the rest of the family, it was personalized in the plight of Boston and Rachel.

At first Alex was determined to go to them, to lend moral support, if nothing else, but Boston wrote specifically asking that she not; he knew his sister well despite the separation of years. He did not flinch from describing the horrific turn of events, but he added:

> *I beg you not to come. Rachel asks it as well. There is nothing you can do for us. We would rather remember you as safe and well at Wild Swan than have you here with us. Rachel's pride in her heritage has carried her this far, and it will carry her on. But it would be very hard for her to have you see her people as they are now.*

Alex bowed to the couple's wishes, but after spending futile days in worry and sorrow, she determined a course that channeled her energy at least in a small way. She gathered together everything she could think of that might aid Boston and the others on the trip west. Calomel, opium, and various other drugs and herbal remedies were carefully labeled and packed. The finest blankets, light and yet warm, were folded into the smallest possible packets as protection against the cold that would surely find them if their departure was delayed until fall or winter. Parcels of the highest grade sugar, salt, coffee, tea, and chocolate were prepared, as well as dried fruit and cured meat. A small kit of surgical instruments for emergencies and a more homely sewing kit were included. And Alex was determined to include gold and silver coins, too. She trusted Boston would not refuse them in this dire situation.

The next problem was in how to make sure Boston and Rachel received the goods. Rane volunteered, but Morgan asked that he might go instead.

"If you go, it wouldn't be much different from Mother going to Georgia, and Uncle asked her not to," Morgan pointed out. "But it's more than that. I want to see for myself." He did not want to admit that it was also a matter of not wanting his parents to be apart any more than they had to be. They had gone through a bad patch over the horse sale, and Morgan thought it better that they be together as much as possible now.

He was so quietly insistent, his parents finally agreed, with the condition that he take a few chosen men with him. Rane made sure the men were not only mentally capable but physically quick as well. It was not that he did not trust Morgan, it was the violence in Georgia that he mistrusted. Though Morgan was physically imposing and mentally astute, he was, after all, only twenty-one years old.

Weeks later when he returned, he looked a good deal older than that.

"What I witnessed will stay with me forever," he told them. "The Cherokee are, above all else, bewildered that such a thing could happen to them in this republic. They are not cattle, to be herded and sold at will. They are a civilized nation of human beings. Rachel is typical, not rare, in their society. But now they are stripped of all they own and will be forced into exile. It is a tragic crime!"

He swallowed hard against the constriction in his throat. "Uncle Boston and Aunt Rachel are as well as they can be under the circumstances, but her father and her grandfather are failing. The grandfather particularly is so old and frail now, and there are other relatives to worry about, too. Uncle told me that he will do his best to make them agree to voluntary leaving because that should improve conditions for them. But I doubt they will agree. The Cherokee are proud; even now they are quietly resisting by making the government move them. Uncle has managed to retain some money and possessions, but he and Rachel were very grateful for what you sent to them. The government payment for their lands won't begin to cover all the costs of resettlement of some five thousand families."

He handed Alex a note from her brother: "Bless you for your practicality. Everything you sent will ease our way. We will think of you and be comforted," it read in part, and Alex did not try to stop the tears that rolled down her cheeks.

Morgan had found his parents and Gwenny in Baltimore, and though their praise for a job well done meant much to him, he still felt restless and heavyhearted. He decided to go out to Wild Swan for a few days, not even admitting to himself that it was Sam he missed, not the quiet acres of the farm.

Though Alex made no comment to her son, she was not fooled. "It was bound to happen," she told Rane, "but I'm sorry for Morgan's sake that it has to be now. I think Justin Sinclair is going to be an unpleasant surprise."

Justin had come to visit Sam at Brookhaven a week before, and showed every evidence of planning to stay for some time longer. He had given good warning of his visit, and Alex had seen Sam go from feeling some reluctance to actually looking forward to seeing Justin again.

Alex couldn't blame her. Morgan had given Sam no sign he would ever see her in a romantic way, and it was undoubtedly balm to her spirit to have a man like Justin showing so much interest.

Morgan managed to spend an entire day at Wild Swan before he faced his true reason for being out in the country. The next morning he rode over to Brookhaven.

It was a rude shock to be informed that Sam was already out riding with Mr. Sinclair and was not expected back for some time. The avid gleam in Sam's stepmother's eyes and the relish with which she told him of Sam's whereabouts alerted Morgan to the fact that Mrs. Sheldon-Burke had high hopes for this Mr. Sinclair and her stepdaughter. But he felt no more than a passing annoyance. He could not imagine Sam approving of anyone Violet liked.

He knew Sam's favorite riding trails, and he set off, feeling no compunction about seeking the others out. He wanted to see Sam, and see her he would.

He intercepted them on a tree-shadowed path. Previously, he had dismissed Mr. Sinclair; now Morgan's feelings underwent a radical change. He would have been blind and stupid had he not felt the impact of the man—handsome, self-assured, well-dressed, and with a laudable seat on his Thoroughbred mount.

After her first start of surprise at the sight of him, Sam made the introductions calmly.

"I would recognize you easily," Justin said. "You have the look of your mother, a most impressive woman. I am relieved that Fire Swan is flourishing in my stable; I wouldn't be able to show my face in these parts if anything happened to that mare."

"Justin was one of the buyers who came to the sale at Wild Swan," Sam supplied, noting Morgan's blank look.

Justin's manner was easygoing and friendly; Morgan hoped he seemed the same, though he didn't feel that way inside. Several things were occurring to him at once, and he didn't like any of them. Sam had met this man at Wild Swan, yet no one had told him about it. Mr. Sinclair owned one of Alex's prize horses, and Morgan wished he didn't have that particular tie to Wild Swan and to Sam. And the man had not said, "Oh, yes, Sam has told me about you." Nor did Sam give any indication now that she was uncomfortable at having the two men meet. She was playing no flirtatious game with either of them; she was her usual straightforward self. And as such, she was immensely appealing. That bothered Morgan most of all.

He felt as if he were seeing Sam through Justin Sinclair's eyes, and it was a disconcerting view. He wondered if her hair had always had such vibrant golden-red strands mixed with the brown and if her eyes had always been such a light-filled combination of green, brown, and gold and so large.

Sam was a beautiful woman. It jolted him to acknowledge it. When in the hell had it happened? He could still see the grubby little girl in ragged smocks. How had this creature taken her place without his noticing the transformation until it was accomplished?

Sam saw his dazed expression and mistook the cause. "Was it very bad in Georgia?" she asked softly.

That steadied him, and briefly, grimly, he told her of the conditions he had found there.

"Your poor uncle and aunt! What an awful situation, and no easy way out," Sam said.

Justin made no attempt to gloss over the subject. "There are things happening in our country now that will forever dim its light."

"Do you own slaves?" Morgan could hardly believe the belligerent rudeness in his own voice and wished desperately that he could take the challenge back. He could see the shock in Sam's face.

But Justin answered calmly. "No. My father began to free them in his time, and I finished the task. The people at Greyoaks are paid for their labor."

"I apologize," Morgan managed to say, but he thought, "I'm sorry you're here at all." Justin made Sam appear different, and he made Morgan feel young and gauche.

"No offense taken," Justin assured him, and there was a gleam of understanding humor in his eyes.

It did not add to Morgan's confidence to know that Justin saw right through him and was amused rather than threatened. He bade the couple good day rather stiffly. Sam did not ask how long he would be at Wild Swan, and he returned immediately to Baltimore, finding he did not want to stay in the country without Sam's company.

He sought his mother immediately when he reached the city. With barely a greeting, he growled, "Who is Justin Sinclair?"

Alex raised an eyebrow at his abrupt manner, but obligingly she told him what she knew about Justin. Morgan's anger pleased her. At last he was seeing Sam as she was, fully grown and attractive.

"Do you have to make him sound such a paragon?" he protested.

"That is exactly what he seems to be. And Allen Ralston judges him so. One can hardly ask for a better character reference than that."

"Well, as long as Sam is safe with him," Morgan grumbled, retreating back into his brotherly role.

Alex nearly swore aloud.

With plans for new ships going forward, due to the money Alex had given the yard, and with coastal shipping improving somewhat, Morgan had no lack of work to fill his hours. Yet, he still found himself brooding over Sam. It was, he told himself, ludicrous to do so. Sam was the companion of his youth, not a woman he desired. In order to prove that to himself, he increased his social pursuits so that he was scarcely ever home before late and often not then. He found particular enjoyment in the arms of a voluptuous redhead named Rose. She wasn't the sort of woman he would bring home to meet his parents, but that wasn't what he required of her. Nor did she demand anything of him aside from a good time and his talents in bed. It was, he reminded himself, the only kind of affair he wanted in his life at this time. He shied away from admitting to himself that by thinking in these terms, he was already considering the role Sam would play in a man's life as that of wife, never less.

Believing he had convinced himself that what Sam did was no concern of his and vice versa, Morgan discovered how wrong he was when he ran into Sam one evening in Baltimore. Rose was on his arm, and Sam was on Justin's when the two couples came face to face outside a popular restaurant.

Morgan was so shocked to see Sam in this circumstance that for a moment he could think of nothing to say, though his first impulse was to scold her for being out at night with a man and no chaperone, a clear indication of her parents' approval of Justin Sinclair. He wondered what awful friends of Violet's they were staying with.

For her part, Sam was as frozen in place as Morgan, and her face was curiously still, her eyes unreadable in the fading light.

It was Justin who made the introductions, waiting patiently for

Morgan to supply Rose's name and then saying, "We've just finished dining. The food was very good."

Nothing in his demeanor betrayed any judgment of Rose, and Sam, recovering, was equally polite. It was Morgan who felt decidedly uncomfortable. He was relieved when Justin tipped his hat and led Sam away.

"Aren't they grand, those friends of yours," Rose said. "Nice enough, though, and a handsome couple."

Morgan just barely resisted telling her to shut up, and in the ensuing days the image of Sam and Justin standing there in the twilight haunted him. Finally he decided he had to go to Brookhaven to see Sam. He wasn't quite sure what he would say to her, but somehow he wanted to explain that Rose wasn't that important to him. He hoped Justin would not still be there.

Justin was not there, but neither was Sam. She and her stepmother had gone to visit the Sinclair plantation in Virginia.

It was a circumstance Morgan had not even considered. It was the first time since he had met her that Sam had been completely out of his reach. It made him feel physically ill to think about it, as if the center of his world had dropped away, leaving him unbalanced.

Once again he returned to Baltimore and threw himself into his work, not confiding in anyone, trying to sort out his feelings for once and for all. He honestly didn't know whether his possessiveness was simply a result of having had Sam as a special part of his childhood for so many years, or whether it was because he wanted her to be an equally special part of his adult life. One thing he did know—Rose was less and less appealing, and as kindly as he could, he extricated himself from the affair.

He welcomed any business that took him away from Baltimore, particularly the trading voyages, because he felt more at peace on the deck of a ship than he ever did on land. And gradually he became convinced he was right in judging himself unready for the commitment of marriage to any woman. He was glad that Blaine and Philly and Flora and Caleb were so happy, but he did not envy them the ties that bound them to each other.

He was in Philadelphia when Sam returned to Brookhaven at the end of November.

When Sam sought her out at Wild Swan, Alex knew immediately that it was no casual visit. Sam was uncharacteristically nervous, knotting and unknotting her hands and chattering inconsequentially until she brought herself up short and took a deep breath.

Raising her eyes to Alex's, she said, "Justin Sinclair has asked me to marry him. He is a fascinating and honorable man, and Greyoaks is lovely. I could be very happy there with him. I want a husband, a home, and children of my own. But . . ." she hesitated and then squared her shoulders. "I'm sure it's no secret. I have loved Morgan for a very long time, first as a little girl, and then as a woman. I tried not to, but it happened anyway. I've dreamed that one day he would suddenly see me in a new way and love me, too. But it is not going to happen, is it?"

Alex wished desperately that she had something reassuring to tell her, but nothing less than the truth would do for Sam. "I don't know. Morgan is my son, and I love him dearly, but I do not know what plans, if any, he has for marriage and a family. He loves ships and the sea, and perhaps they are enough for him now, perhaps they always will be. I have hoped that you would be his choice to wed. I could not choose any other young woman I would rather have for my daughter-in-law, but it is not my choice. And I do not want you to lose a chance for happiness because of Morgan. But are you sure you love Justin enough to be his wife?"

Sam nodded slowly. "It took me a while to understand. I've known Morgan for so long, there is a special feeling there that I can't expect to have for anyone else. I love Justin in a different way, but it is no less valid. I asked myself if I would be glad to wake up beside him ten years from now, and the answer is yes. He's very astute. Though I said nothing about it, he realized there was something more than old friendship in my feeling for Morgan, but when I explained, he understood. There's a girl, Cissy Peters, who lives on the plantation next to Greyoaks. She and Justin are a lot like Morgan and me. They have known each other for years and thought they might be in love. But the feeling changed, and now they are just good friends."

Very calmly she stated, "I will be marrying Justin in the spring. He is coming back to Brookhaven next week. I promised I would give him my answer then. The week after that there will be a party to announce our engagement." Sam made a face. "My stepmother made that plan should I accept Justin's offer. And actually, it is not a bad idea. I would like Justin to meet my friends, and that means the Carringtons, the Falconers, and the Jenningses. I hope all of you will come. Will Nigel be back by then?"

Alex was less calm than Sam. Her mind was hopping about like a rabbit and with about the same lack of intelligence. The plans that would take Sam away from Morgan forever were crystallizing far too fast for her, and yet she couldn't think of anything useful to do about it. She could hardly send word to Morgan that Sam was accepting a marriage offer and he'd better do his best to prevent it; Morgan had made no move in that direction on his own, and it was not his mother's place to urge him to do so. In the same way, because she wanted Sam's happiness, she had no right to ask her to delay the decision. What she had to do was to let go. She reminded herself that, no matter what the similarities, Morgan and Sam were not the same people as she and Rane.

"I believe Nigel will be home in time for the celebration of your engagement. And I hope it goes without saying that whatever help you may need from Wild Swan for the party is here for the asking." Alex hoped she was smiling; it felt more like a grimace.

Sam studied her for a moment, and then she put her arms around Alex and rested her head for an instant against her shoulder. "It will be hard, not living close to you any more. I could not have asked for more love had you been my own mother."

Both of them were wiping away tears when Sam left. Alex felt in dire need of a confidante and went to find Della. As much friend as employee, Della could be counted on to offer sensible counsel.

But in this case, Della heard Alex out in growing dismay and had no advice to offer. "I hope Morgan enjoys his extended boyhood, because he's lost a good woman," she observed tartly. "I hate to admit it, but I liked Mr. Sinclair. I think he'll take good care of Sam." Her beautiful brown face softened. "It makes me more grateful than ever that I have Samson."

It made Alex wish that Rane was at Wild Swan or that she was with him in the city, but with Christmas approaching, there were many preparations to be made, so she kept to her schedule and sent a message to Rane asking him to tell the children about the party at Brookhaven that they might not miss it. They were due at Wild Swan around that time anyway, and Rane had planned to arrive a little before that.

To Alex's joy, he showed up days earlier, taking, he informed her, just enough time to deliver the message about the party before setting out. "I thought you might need a shoulder to cry on."

"At least to lean on," she said, suiting the action to the words and resting against him for a moment, savoring the reassuring strength of him as he wrapped his arms around her.

Brookhaven was ablaze with lights, and the beaming faces of Sam's parents were proof of how much they approved of the match. Sam was serenely beautiful in a gown of deep amber silk that brought out the gold and red in her hair and the green-gold in her eyes. Beside her, Justin was strikingly handsome and at his ease, greeting people as he was introduced to them.

No expense had been spared. Tables overflowed with a great bounty of food and drink, and musicians played both formal and country dances. Alex could not forbear noting the irony of it—there was generosity toward Sam only now that she would be leaving. It was easy to see her stepmother's hand at work. Alex wondered if Sam's father had yet considered how he would manage his acres once his capable daughter had departed.

Alex accepted the compliments about her children with real pleasure. They did look handsome tonight. She was especially proud of the graceful confidence with which Flora carried herself; marriage to Caleb had made a noticeable difference in her. And Alex was amused by the attention Nigel was receiving from the unmarried girls.

"In his quiet way, he's quite effective," Rane said with a smile, as aware as his wife of what was going on.

Alex was waltzing in his arms when she breathed, "Oh, dear lord," and nearly overset them. Rane swung around so he could see whatever it was that had caught Alex's eye, and then he too froze.

Morgan had swept into the room travel-stained and wild-eyed. "Sam, you can't marry him!" His enraged bellow spread silence in its wake. Even the musicians stopped playing.

"We've got to stop him!" Alex whispered desperately, taking a step in her son's direction.

"No. This is his show, foolhardy or not." Rane's hand on her arm held her firmly in place.

Morgan didn't notice his parents or his siblings; he had eyes only for Sam and for the man who had been dancing with her and who stood beside her now. He had ridden into Wild Swan in the dark, expecting to find his family there and had instead been told by Samson that they were all, with the exception of the sleeping Gwenny, at Brookhaven for Miss Sam's engagement party.

Everything he had been running from caught up with him then. He hadn't any clear idea of what he was going to do, but he knew he could not let another man claim Sam for his own.

It was still the single idea in his mind as he stared at her. "Sam, you can't," he repeated, softly this time. "You've belonged to me since you were eight years old. You still do. Samantha Elisa Sheldon-Burke, I love you. I want to marry you."

Sam showed no reaction. She could not believe this was happening. She had been relieved not to have to face Morgan this night; it had been all she could do to feign regret when she had learned he was still in Philadelphia. His words made no sense to her. She had relinquished the idea of spending her life with Morgan and had begun to look forward to her days with Justin with real joy. Morgan's declaration was like some unintelligible echo from the past.

Justin alone was not immobilized. He stepped forward to confront Morgan. "Mr. Carrington, you are out of order. I suggest you leave."

The calm patience in Sinclair's voice infuriated Morgan. Too clearly he could see the man taking Sam away, possessing her. Morgan had never felt such a primitive urge to strike out, and his fury made him clumsy.

As Morgan swung at him, Justin sidestepped and delivered a stunning blow, every graceful line showing that he was no stranger to the art of boxing. Morgan crumpled slowly to the floor.

Again Alex started forward, and even as Rane restrained his wife, Sam's cry rang out, just the single word—Morgan!—and then she sank down beside him in a billow of amber silk and pillowed his head in her lap.

"You crazy man! Whatever possessed you? Are you all right? Morgan, say something!" She was as oblivious to her surroundings as Morgan had been.

Blearily, Morgan looked up at her. "Will you marry me?" His words were muffled because his jaw was already swelling, but Sam understood him.

She doubted he was truly ready for marriage yet. But she did not doubt the love she saw shining in his green eyes. She felt as if she'd awakened from a long sleep. She could not fathom how she had ever thought she could love any man except Morgan. It simply wasn't possible.

"I'll marry you," she said, and she leaned over to kiss the unbruised side of his mouth.

Violet Sheldon-Burke had had enough and slipped gratefully into a faint, which did her no harm, as two gallants standing close by caught her before she hit the floor.

Alex wished she could do the same thing, but instead she slipped out of Rane's hold and went to Justin. "You don't deserve any of this," she told him quietly, ignoring Sam and Morgan. "I hope my son will be able to make her as happy as you would have. He will have to work hard to do that."

"Thank you for the kind words, Mrs. Falconer, but you are wrong. In a way, I do deserve it. I knew there was something between them; I knew it in the way he looked at her and in the way Samantha returned that look, no matter how unaware they both were, no matter what Samantha said. And I saw that from nothing more than brief meetings. But I chose to ignore it. I took the risk. I tried to get in the way of something that began long before I came here and will continue long after I'm gone. And that perfect blow was probably the most foolish action I've ever taken. Had I landed on the floor, she might not have seen things so clearly. I might still have had a chance to steal her away and make her forget." He smiled at both Alex and Rane, who had moved to stand beside her, but his eyes were bleak.

Chapter

12

Sam spent Christmas at Wild Swan. Her stepmother suffered the vapors at the mere sight of her, though the condition had been somewhat improved by the assurance that Morgan really did intend to marry Sam. Sam was sorry that her half brother and half sister had to spend the holiday at Brookhaven, but they spent so much of their time away at school, they were not very close to Sam in any case.

Alex experienced a sort of giddy hysteria whenever she thought of the chaotic end to the engagement party. If the truth were known, most of the guests had thought the finale very romantic and far more interesting than what they had expected. Sam claimed she was not likely to forget how Morgan had proposed.

The worst of it was not the gossip that made the rounds after the party—the Carrington offspring were, through Flora and now Morgan, acquiring quite a reputation for interesting marriages—but rather the unfairness to Justin.

Morgan had had the decency to go to the man and tell him everything start to finish about the dilemma he had faced in understanding Sam's changing role in his life, but he doubted that it had done much good. Justin had been gracious because he was a gracious man in all things, but the fact remained that he had lost the woman he loved, and nothing could mitigate that loss.

If Morgan had had his way entirely, he and Sam would have been married immediately, but Sam was adamant. She needed no time to reconsider, but she wanted Morgan to do just that.

"You asked me to marry you because I was going to marry Justin. Otherwise, you might have waited a long time; you might not have asked at all. I want to make sure it is not just because you felt threatened by him," she told him honestly. "And I want you to know that I won't ever be as—ah, as tempting as that woman Rose."

Morgan winced. "God, what an ill-fated meeting that was!"

Sam was not deterred. "I am glad you see me as a woman now; I've wanted it for a long time. But I don't want you to go too far and see changes that haven't happened and never will. I'm still Sam, grown up, but still much the same inside. I don't want you to wake up someday and find that that is not enough."

"That is exactly why I love you," he insisted. "And the same can be said of me—I'm just Morgan. Will that be enough for you?"

The look she gave him was enough to convince him.

They talked endlessly of where they would live, of how they would order their lives. Morgan was determined that Sam should have her own house in Baltimore; as far as he was concerned, she had been displaced too often at Brookhaven by her two stepmothers. Though he had suffered the lean times in the shipyard, and in spite of his liking for a good time, Morgan had not been profligate with his earnings. He was glad now that he had inherited some of his mother's practicality regarding money. He had enough saved to give himself and Sam a creditable start. But he understood her reluctance to give up all ties to Brookhaven. He agreed with her opinion that Violet would settle down and that her father would need his daughter's help again. Sam had quietly run much of Brookhaven for so long, despite her youth, it was not a place she could easily abandon.

"Work at Brookhaven, but sleep at Wild Swan when we're out in the country," Morgan insisted, thinking of how awful it would be to have to spend too much time under the Sheldon-Burkes' roof.

"I'll sleep wherever you are," Sam said, her voice low and husky, and Morgan wondered how he was going to survive the agony of waiting until the spring to wed her.

Christmas took on a special meaning for all the family, not only because of Morgan and Sam, but also because Philly was expecting another baby.

Blaine said, "Of course, the first thing I want is a healthy child, but I would also like another girl. I find Larissa more charming by the day, and she thinks I'm wonderful, bless her. She's marvelous for my vanity. I'm not at all sure I'd cope as well with a boy."

Philly appreciated his unorthodox view, as she knew too many men could think of nothing but a son to carry on for them.

The happiness at Wild Swan was made more precious by the family's concern for Boston and Rachel, who had finally headed west with one of the emigrating parties in October, various groups having left in October and November after the drought had broken in Georgia and Tennessee.

Boston had promised he would write and give them an account of the journey once their destination was reached. Alex knew he wanted to spare her the pain of constant reports carried back, but even without letters from her brother, enough news filtered back east in newspapers and by word of mouth to make it clear that the trek, which would come to be known as the Trail of Tears, was taking an awful toll of the Indians.

"I know it is of little comfort, but it does seem that there is a pattern here," Rane told her. "As Boston has become the most American of us, so it is hardly strange that he should be a participant in the darkness as well as the light of this country's great passion for change. By the time he is an old man, he will be more of a witness to the nation's virtues and sins than most who were born here."

Rane was wrong; there was a good measure of comfort in his words. Not only had he made it seem as if Boston was part of a much larger canvas of history than the life of one man could provide, but also his reference to Boston as an old man subtly eased Alex's fears that her brother would succumb to the hazards of the forced march.

She was fully aware of how much she had to be thankful for as she saw the new year of 1839 in with her husband and children and the extended family of Philly, Mr. Winslow, Caleb, his children, and close friends.

There was additional cause for gratitude in January and early February as Taney, Dreamer, and Black Swan gave birth to healthy foals— Fairy Swan, a chestnut filly, Fortuna, a black filly, and Swan's Chance, a black colt. Though Swan Song had been bred, she had not conceived. Alex and Samson did not feel too badly about it; they knew how lucky they were to have such a fine crop from other mares.

Alex named the colt with a good deal of emotion and great hope. His dam, Black Swan, was now eighteen years old, and this would be her last foal. She had done her work well over the years and would not be bred again. For her last chance to produce another champion, she had been bred to Fortune, the gift stallion from Hugh Bettingdon.

Fortune and chance—they had so much to do with producing winning horses, no matter how carefully and rationally the breeding had been planned. But when Alex, after anxiously attending Black Swan during the birthing, first saw Swan's Chance, she knew in her bones that he was destined for greatness. It was an instinctual response to something in the animal that went beyond his long-legged beauty. St. John had had the same ability to judge horseflesh, and it had rarely failed either him or her.

If Swan's Chance could be shielded from illness and accident, he would indeed be a new chance for Wild Swan to prove itself the seat of champions, despite the fact that the best stables were now concentrated much further south and to the west in Kentucky.

Alex took Swan Princess and Ember to a few spring meetings in Maryland and Virginia just to keep Wild Swan's name alive, but her greatest pleasure came from watching the new foals grow stronger by the day. All of their breeding told them to run, and run they did, clumsily and erratically at first, but with increasing confidence as they grew accustomed to their long legs.

Alex felt as full of life as they, as if she could race the wind and win. She and Rane had weathered a hard time and were prospering. She felt gloriously alive and sensitized to everything and everyone around her. And feeling thus, she could not miss the changes in Morgan.

He seemed older and steadier, as if the journey to Georgia and then the near-loss of Sam had wrought a transformation. It was not that the quick restlessness so typical of him was gone, but it was tempered. He was more given to pensiveness than he had ever been before. It was clear he adored Sam and that he had no lingering qualms about marrying her.

His occasional air of distraction came from something else, and Alex suspected the cause strongly enough to discuss it with Rane.

"I think he is going to ask about his parentage. Don't ask me how I know that, but I can feel him debating how to approach the subject, and I have seen him studying us with an odd look when he thinks he's unobserved. Do you think we ought to talk to him before he comes to us?"

"No, I think it ought to be at his instigation," Rane said slowly. "I know how much he loved St. John, and he has a right to maintain the belief that St. John was his father if he wishes to do so. I promised you I would never tell Morgan the truth, and I will keep that promise even to the point of lying, if you wish it."

Alex shook her head. "Don't do that, don't lie to him, if he asks. I thought the day would never come when I would want him to know, but I find that is no longer true. As he has a right to the fiction if he does not question us, so he has the right to the truth if he does. He is about to start his own family. Perhaps he needs to know exactly where he came from in order to do that."

Rane knew it was more an act of courage for her to face this than it was for him. It was unjust, but nevertheless true that greater virtue was expected of one's mother than of one's father. Despite the love Morgan had for his mother, it was possible that confirmation of adultery would forever change the way he felt about her.

Even though he was forewarned, Rane still felt the jump of his heart when Morgan finally asked him.

He and Morgan were having dinner together, both of them bemoaning the fact that Alex and Sam were out in the country rather than in Baltimore, when Morgan said calmly, "I've put this off long enough. Are you my father?"

"Yes, I am," Rane answered with the same simplicity.

They looked at each other across the table, and Rane thought, My God, what a fine young man he has become! He had lived with the knowledge of his paternity ever since his first sight of Morgan in Annapolis nineteen years before, but somehow this encounter was releasing a well of emotion so strong, it was all he could do to control his response. He clenched his hands together so tightly that pain shot through his fingers, steadying him.

"I want you to know how it was," he said, and strangely he did not have to search for words. He found that memories of how Alex had looked when he first saw her and of how she had grown to be part of his heart and soul before she had left Clovelly flowed easily into words to give their son. It was more difficult to explain how sad and neglected Alex had been in the early part of her time with St. John, but Rane got through it as gently as he could, not wanting to launch an attack on a man Morgan had dearly loved. Rane was not so sparing of himself, taking full responsibility for his affair with Alex.

"She was still so young and so vulnerable; I took advantage of her love for me, and I used my love for her as a weapon to have my way. I would have taken her away, but she would not go. She would not leave the twins or St. John. She did not believe he loved her then. I did not know, but she wasn't legally bound by marriage to him at the time because the marriage could not be sanctioned in England. But she would not abandon him. Your mother has always thought more of the well-being of others than of her own. I did not know of your existence until I saw you in Annapolis." He paused, remembering his first sight of Morgan. He was unaware of how tender his expression was.

"Your mother and I made every effort not to betray ourselves to St. John, and after he died, I promised her I would not claim you as my son to his cost." He had no intention of telling Morgan that he suspected St. John had known after all; that was a secret Morgan did not need to know. He searched his son's face but saw no condemnation there.

"I have known for a very long time," Morgan said. "Even before Gwenny was born, I knew, and she confirmed it; we look so much alike. And even in the beginning, I did not think that Mother had done anything wrong. I am not sure I can explain it clearly, but there is a rightness about Mother, a kindness and tolerance that go so deep, it is not possible to think of her doing something evil. She is a healer, a giver of life. But she knows the killing herbs, too. I am very glad she saw fit to bear me even though she knew it might not have been St. John who fathered me."

He drew a deep breath. "I might never have asked, but getting ready to marry Sam has made me want to have things in order. I am very fortunate. St. John was a wonderful father to me, but so have you been. Blaine and Nigel bear his name; I would like to bear yours. I would like Sam to become Mrs. Falconer."

Rane was not aware that his tears were overflowing until he saw that Morgan's eyes were also wet. "Nothing on earth could honor me more," he said. He hesitated for a moment, regaining control of himself. "I know your mother will understand, but what of your brothers and Flora?"

"With your permission, I will explain. But I don't think it is necessary. They are not blind. I think they have known as well as I have. And they love and respect Mother and you no less than I." Suddenly he laughed. "What a complicated family we are! It is a good thing no distinction has ever been made between natural and stepchildren. It would have muddled things entirely."

They laughed together, relieving the tension, but Rane was thinking how easy it was to give love while underestimating the capacity for love in return. He thought of how he and Alex had worried about Morgan's reaction should he discover the truth. He and Alex had been so concerned with protecting the children, and all along the children had been protecting them. He was, however, not sorry that he and Morgan had not had their exchange of truth earlier; he realized that Morgan had needed to confirm it in his own time. Above all else, he was joyful that at long last Alex could stop worrying about the secret she had kept so long.

Only after he lay down to sleep that night did Morgan realize how important it had been to him that his father not deny the truth, not even for a second. He felt drunk with relief and infinitely peaceful. Rane's acknowledgment had somehow reinforced Morgan's feelings about himself as a man. For the first time in his life, he needed to know that worth intimately that he might bring the best of himself to Sam. Everything revolved around her now.

When he told her that she would be Mrs. Falconer rather than Mrs. Carrington, she reacted exactly as he had hoped she would. There was no shock, only acceptance, and humor, too. "I don't care if I become Mrs. Threadneedle, or Treacle, or Pie-Eater, as long as you are the mister."

Because of the increasing sensuality Sam displayed, Morgan found it more and more difficult to school himself to patience. She was perfectly willing to kiss him and to melt against him when he put his arms around her, and it made him determined to protect her from himself. She trusted him so absolutely, he knew she would let him make love to her before the wedding date, if that was what he demanded.

When the day of their wedding dawned, Morgan felt none of the legendary reluctance of bridegrooms; he could scarcely wait for the vows to be spoken. And from the time he saw Sam dressed in white satin, he saw no one else. When she put her hand in his, it was warm and steady, and her face glowed with happiness and complete confidence in the step she was taking.

Alex touched the gold circlet of swans at her throat, the necklace given to her by Rane for Christmas in Clovelly all those years ago, and she prayed that Sam and her son would find the same happiness she and Rane had found. Rane saw the gesture and captured her hand in his own, and together they shared the pride of hearing their son called "Morgan Falconer."

Sam's stepmother had sensibly decided that the wedding could be used to make up for the disaster of the abortive engagement party, and so Brookhaven was once again offering lavish food and drink to many guests. For her own sake, she made no point of the name change.

Sam had a hard time controlling her amusement when she observed Morgan trying to curb his impatience as he greeted everyone and listened to endlessly repeated wishes for a happy life with his bride.

Finally, she whispered to him, "I think we could be excused now. After all, we don't want to arrive in Annapolis too late."

They had decided to spend their honeymoon at the tavern. Mavis and Timothy were overjoyed at the prospect of offering their hospitality to the couple, and Morgan and Sam had thought the quiet, familiar town would be a perfect place to spend their first days together, away from the bustle of Wild Swan or Baltimore. Their clothing had been sent ahead, and Mr. Sheldon-Burke's carriage would take them there, so all Sam had to do was to don a cloak to protect her wedding gown from the road dust.

In the flurry of good-byes, her sisters-in-law each hugged her in turn. Flora said, "He adores you. Be happy," and Philly, her pregnancy obvious now but not slowing her down a bit, added, "I highly recommend marrying into this family. All sorts of wonderful things happen." She patted her growing belly, her eyes alight.

Seeing how happy Philly and Flora both were in their marriages had made Sam even more eager to marry Morgan, but she was glad they had waited until this fine spring day. She could feel the difference in Morgan. He had acquired a new air of authority. Ruefully she thought he was going to need it. She had no illusions about herself; she could be both stubborn and willful when she felt the need. Morgan had not taken a docile wife this day.

"You look very thoughtful," he said as they bowled along in the carriage. "Are you having doubts?"

"Actually I was feeling sorry for you," she said virtuously. "You've taken on a handful, you know. I can't make any promises about behaving properly all the time."

"Thank heavens for that!" Morgan exclaimed. "And remember, I've had a lot of practice in dealing with you. You won't find me climbing any more trees just because you dare me to."

They chuckled over the shared memory, though Sam had been terrified at the time. Because she had been lighter than he, the tree she had climbed and dared him to climb had expelled him with a broken branch. And his arm had broken too. She had been sure she was directly responsible and that her beloved Morgan was going to die. But Alex had told her that Morgan would be all right and that he should have had the sense not to climb the frail tree, dare or no. Sam hoped she would bring the same calm reasonableness to motherhood.

She felt a warm rush of pleasure at the thought of all she and Morgan already shared in common memories and of all the sharing yet to come, including the children who would be part of both of them.

Mavis and Tim greeted them with open arms but left them alone as soon as they had shown them to the spacious room prepared for them. Candles had been lighted against the descending night, a fire burned merrily on the hearth, and a selection of cheese, meat, bread, fruit, and wine had been laid out for them.

But neither Morgan nor Sam had any appetite for food. As soon as the door closed, Morgan took his bride in his arms and kissed her so thoroughly that she sagged against him as her knees gave way. Her cloak dropped to the floor, and Morgan picked her up in his arms and settled into a chair with her in his lap. He cradled her against him, just savoring the knowledge that she was his now, his until death.

"I do love you so," he murmured, and he kissed her again.

Sam had wanted him to love her for so long, she felt no shyness at all with him when he helped her out of the wedding finery and stripped off his own.

The silken nightgown lying across the bed was cast aside as Morgan put Sam down on the white sheets.

"Oh, Sam, I never knew," he breathed. "Even after all these years, I didn't know. You are exquisite!" His eyes burned bright jade as he gazed on her nakedness. He had loved and wanted her, and he had come to know she was beautiful, but until this instant he had not known the full extent of the transformation from gawky child into lovely woman or of his passion for her.

As long as they both lived, no other man would ever look on this creamy white body with its long slender limbs and rose-crowned breasts;

no other man would drive himself home in the warmth of her; no other man would receive the look of endlessly trusting love that he saw in her hazel eyes.

He touched her all over, wanting her body to learn pleasure from his hands, his mouth, from all of his flesh. She felt softer than the finest silk; the taste of her was salt and sweet and the essence of clean, young skin. The perfume of her was heady and warmed him all over.

She moved beneath his caresses, her little purring sounds changing to pleading, "Morgan, I want, I want . . ." She tossed her head from side to side in need, not knowing the exact feeling her body was searching for, only knowing there was something more than the ripples of heat spreading through her, something she would only discover with his full possession of her.

Morgan wanted to go slowly, wanted the taking of her to be as painless as possible. His fingers found the warm moisture and probed gently to prepare his way. She arched against his hand and breathed his name as he teased the tight bud of her desire, and watching her face, he thrust slowly into her, gasping at the tightness that closed around him.

She did not cry out in protest, and his own desire made him interpret her expression as pleasure. He felt the barrier of her maidenhead, and he tried to ease through it. But it was much more resistant than he had expected. And suddenly the slow tempo was unbearable. The mindless driving need to thrust hard seized him. He lifted her hips as his own drove forward. The membrane tore, and Sam whimpered. But Morgan was aware only of his own sensations. Even with the maidenhead breached, the passage was still so tight, he felt as much pain as pleasure. He could hear his own groans of effort as he drove on to completion, finally shuddering in relief.

Only then was he aware of what he had done to Sam. Her face was bleached white in stark lines of agony, and tears trickled from the corners of her eyes. Tears from Sam, who cried for other people's pain, not her own—they told him how much he had hurt her.

He withdrew and froze at the sight of her blood. He had known it was to be expected with a virgin, but the reality shocked him. It slipped from her mixed with his semen, staining the sheet.

"My God, sweetheart! I didn't mean to hurt you so!" He gathered her trembling form into his arms, rocking her to the rhythm of his own grief, hot tears searing his cheeks and mingling with hers.

It took him a moment to understand her muffled words, and then he recognized them as, "I am so angry!"

Sam squirmed out of his hold and cupped his ravaged face in her hands. "I'm not angry with you. It wasn't your fault. I know what care you took with me. And I liked it. I liked it all until you were inside of me. Don't you see, it isn't fair that it hurt like that! Women should be able to go out and gain experience just as you and your brothers did, so the wedding night wouldn't be like this."

He was touched and amused at the same time. "Sam, sweet Sam, I would not claim that this is an experience I would want to repeat. But I am glad it was I and not someone else. I assure you a man's virginity is much easier to lose; it is just as well you did not experiment."

He laid her back down on the bed, and she settled against the sheet with a little sigh. With a damp cloth he gently sponged the blood from her thighs and the tangle of soft, golden brown hair. The bleeding seemed to have stopped, but he was still worried.

"Are you all right?" he asked. "Or should I fetch Mavis?"

"I'm fine, just sleepy," she assured him, and it was the truth. The acute pain had ceased with his withdrawal, and now all she felt was a dull ache. She reached her hand up to him. "Lie down beside me. I think we've both worked hard enough for one wedding night."

Morgan gave thanks for the undiminished love in her eyes. He snuffed the candles and lay down beside her in the darkness. He thought she was asleep until she said, "Don't get any ideas about easing yourself with other women, especially with Rose the Redhead. My body will learn to accommodate yours, and then what music there will be!"

Carefully he put his arms around her. "I love you."

"I never truly loved anyone else but you," she answered.

In the ensuing days, Morgan saw the proof of it. Sam was a woman beautiful enough to draw masculine attention wherever she went, but her concentration was so wholly on her husband, she didn't notice other men. It made Morgan feel as if he'd been crowned king of the world. And it made him want to protect her from every hurt, including his love.

It was Sam who moved enticingly against him in their bed several nights after he had taken her virginity.

"Sam? Are you—"

His question was cut off by her ready answer. "I am fine now. I want you to love me again. I want to learn how."

His laugh was shaky as he felt her hands beginning to stroke his body. "You know quite enough now to test my control. But I couldn't bear to hurt you again."

"You won't," she said confidently. "I am no longer a virgin; I'm an old married woman now."

"Not old, not old at all," Morgan said, touching her in turn, running his hands over the sleek young curves.

His fear of causing her pain made him infinitely slow to take her, and by the time he entered her, she was moaning not in hurt but in need, and her body was open and ready for him. Her cries grew high-pitched and primitive as he thrust in and out with long, sure strokes, and he felt her body convulse and shudder with the force of her response. Still he rode her, bringing her wave after wave of pleasure until he seated himself deep and found his own release.

When she could finally breathe and think normally again, Sam thought that never, ever would lovemaking have been like this with Justin. But she did not say it aloud. Instead she kissed Morgan gently and said, "Thank you, my love." And then she fell asleep, causing Morgan to smile with great tenderness.

When they returned to Wild Swan and then to Baltimore, no one needed to ask how they felt about married life; they glowed with the joy of it.

Alex decided that the older one got, the more mixed the joys and sorrows of life became. On the one hand, all her children were flourishing and her grandchildren as well. Philly had given birth to another girl, Phoebe, in June. And this time Gwenny was quite ready to welcome another member of the family, though Larissa wasn't convinced she wanted a sister.

And yet there was sorrow too. A letter came from Alex's brother Paris, bearing the news that Margaret Thaine had died. Alex and Boston's communications with the family left in Gravesend had dwindled to little more than duty notes once their father and grandmother had died, and the lines from Paris were nothing more than a brief, cold announcement.

The savagery of her own grief shocked Alex until she realized she was not weeping over the death of her mother but over the final loss of her own hope. Somewhere inside she had harbored the fantasy that someday, somehow, she and her mother would be reconciled, that the woman who had never cared for her would assure her that love had come at last. Now it would never happen.

Rane, having been generously loved by both of his parents, could not fully comprehend the depth of her hurt, but he believed it existed and had seen the damage the wound had done to Alex in various times of her life. He was endlessly patient with her grief, and he lavished love on her that she might realize she did not need it from Margaret Thaine.

He was beside her as well when Boston's letter came.

On foot, in wagons, and in intolerably cramped flatboats, the Cherokee had gone west. Measles, cholera, and a host of other virulent plagues had traveled with them and strewn the way with the weeping and the dead.

In spite of Boston's efforts to ease the way for them, by the time he, Rachel, and her family had reached the Indian Territory in March, her father, grandfather, and several other people who were kin to her were dead. The Cherokee had not been hardened bushmen, but rather civilized people accustomed to fresh food and clean living conditions. The salt pork which had been the government's main offering on the journey and the crowded conditions had hastened the spread of disease, but broken hearts had as much to do with graves left in the wake of the Indians' passage.

It had not been enough to change the course of history, but all along the way there had been evidence that not all white witnesses were without conscience. Missionaries who had traveled with their Indian congregations had done their best to minister to their physical as well as spiritual needs. And townspeople and farmers had turned out to offer food and clothing and to protest the injustice of the forced migration.

Boston wrote:

So little against the great tide of greed and bigotry, and yet enough so that even Rachel, who has lost so much, cannot wholly condemn the species.

It is hard to write the words—Rachel is with child. I am at once elated and terrified. I find that even after all these years, the memory of Dora's death is too clear. Rachel tells me it is not the same, and I must believe her or go mad. In this she is very much one of the Ani-yun-wiya, "Real People," as the Cherokee name themselves. She sees our child as a gift to ease the sorrow of the long journey and the death that stalked us.

Already Rachel has begun to teach again as she did in Georgia. Somehow, we will survive here. Rachel's people, now my people as well, will build anew.

"It is the best there can be," Rane told Alex. "That any joy at all can come from a tragedy of such magnitude is perhaps a miracle."

It came to her then that the capacity for pure joy with no perception of threatening shadows was a function of youth, ignorance, or lack of experience. As one grew older, the obligations and connections to other people broadened, as did the possibilities of sorrow and loss. But the contrasts between bitter and sweet, grief and joy were also heightened, making the experiences of both pain and pleasure more profound than they could ever be for the young. The depth and passion of the love she and Rane now shared would have been impossible in their youth.

A new decade was almost upon them, and the country seemed to be growing more restless and complicated by the year. More immigrants were finding their way to the United States, and yet internally, the problem of slavery made the newcomers seeking work unwelcome or useless in a large part of the country. Financial storms made those dependent on wages vulnerable to sudden disaster and starvation, while at the same time vast new areas, ruthlessly cleared of their native populations, were opening up, beckoning those who would risk a plow on the rich earth. And always there was the promise of new life in this still new land, no matter what the obstacles.

It was at once confusing and exhilarating, and Alex would not have lived anywhere else in the world. With Rane beside her, she felt as if she could face anything life had to offer.

"What are you thinking?" he asked.

"That you content me, Rane Falconer. That you give me courage when I would fear, and joy when I would weep. There is no hazard I cannot face as long as you are beside me."

He enfolded her in his arms, too filled with love to speak, trusting her to know his heart by the mute testimony of his touch.

BOOK
TWO

Chapter 13

~~~~

Wild Swan, Prince George's County, Maryland, 1844

"Push, Sam, you're nearly there," Alex coaxed, trying to keep the worry out of her voice. This was Sam's second child, but the delivery had been as long and hard as when Seth was born three years before. Now, as then, Sam endured while Morgan fell apart. He was outside the room, in Blaine's custody. Alex had found it was easier for Sam if her husband was allowed in only at intervals; otherwise Sam worried too much about him rather than concentrating on the task at hand.

Morgan wanted to throw his head back and howl against the primitive terror clawing inside him. He knew Sam was dying. She had nearly died the last time. He would have stopped their family with Seth had he had his choice, but Sam wanted more children, and she was seductive as well as persistent. Rage mixed with his fear; how could she risk anything that would take her away from him?

"Dr. Cameron is just downstairs if he's needed, and Mother and the midwife are with Sam. She'll be all right, you know," Blaine offered. "Mother would tell you if Sam was in danger." He wasn't sure she would, but it seemed the thing to say. "You'll be able to go to Sam again in a minute."

Morgan regarded his brother with near hatred. "You haven't any experience with this. Philly produces babies as easily as a rabbit."

Blaine knew his brother was nearly crazy with worry, but even so, he found the slur on Philly hard to forgive. "My three daughters are not rabbits, nor is my wife," he said coldly.

A scream froze them both in place.

Alex came out just long enough to grab Morgan by the arm. "Your child is being born. You can fight with your brother later."

Morgan welcomed the feeling of Sam's nails digging into his hands as she strained to expel the baby from her body. Her face was contorted with the effort, her hair plastered to her skull with sweat, and the strength of her hands gave him proof that she was still very much alive.

Adam Magnus Falconer was a perfectly formed baby, and, even wet and red, he looked exquisite to Morgan. Morgan was hardly aware of his mother and the midwife as they deftly continued to minister to Sam and the baby, not leaving the room until both mother and child were clean and comfortable.

Sam was so weary, she could scarcely keep her eyes open once she had seen that her new son was complete, but she stayed awake long enough to hear Morgan murmur, "I love you more than my life," and she believed him; the toll of his hours of worry for her was etched on his face.

Alex was weary, too. "I feel every day of my forty-four years," she confessed to Rane, inexpressibly glad that he and Blaine, as well as Morgan, were here at Wild Swan for Sam's lying-in. "I feel an old grandmother indeed. Sam just isn't built for easy childbearing. It frightens me as much as it does Morgan, though I hope I don't show it as much as he."

"You don't," Rane assured her, massaging her stiff shoulders. "You seem as calm and serene as any grandmother could hope to be." He kissed the tip of her nose. "But I would prove how young you are if I did not wish to go and greet my new grandson. This is surely a fertile place, children and foals abound!"

Alex smiled at the truth of his statement as she watched him leave the room. Blaine and Philly's three daughters—Larissa, Phoebe, and Anthea, seven, five, and two—were with Philly in Baltimore, and Seth St. John Falconer, Morgan and Sam's sturdy three-year-old, was with Flora and Caleb. But there were children aplenty at Wild Swan. Polly and Calvin's two daughters were flourishing, though Polly's sister Cassie had never had any children and didn't seem to feel the lack. Three of the five Barlow sons were married and had four children among them, Jim with two sons having the lion's share, while Georgy and Tad each had a daughter. Alex never ceased to be amused by the fact that Jim and Georgy, both such small men, had married girls much taller and broader than themselves.

Della and Samson's sons were growing apace, sure to develop the stature of their parents. Della claimed that she was just as glad she had not had a daughter, as the poor child might have inherited her father's massive form, and then where would she have been?

Other workers at Wild Swan also had children, so Horace Whittleby's responsibilities as a tutor had increased over the years, and he had slipped from behind his cool facade long enough to confess that the added duties kept him mentally alert, though Alex could not imagine him ever being less than that.

But there was sorrow mixed with the joy. Though Caleb was perfectly content with his children from his previous marriage and, in fact, had dreaded that he might lose Flora were she to conceive, Flora wanted desperately to give him a child and was beginning to lose hope. Alex kept her opinion to herself, but it was difficult not to draw a parallel with Florence, Flora's natural mother; though Florence had borne much of the responsibility for not wanting to recover, still her death had been connected to the birth of the twins, and Alex never wanted to discover that daughter was like mother in this.

Nigel. Alex was accustomed now to feeling pain every time she thought of him, but she could not yet understand how he could have become entangled with such a dreadful woman as Piety Thurgood. As Philly had once remarked, the name alone should have been enough to warn him.

Nigel had brought the woman home as his wife three years previously, and nothing had been right between him and his family since. That Nigel, the kindest of all the children, should have fallen for Piety's machinations had stunned them all.

The situation seemed clear to everyone except Nigel. Five years older than the newly fledged doctor, Piety had been leading a drab, pinched life, barely earning enough as a seamstress to support herself and her two sons. She had met Nigel when one of the boys had been injured, and Nigel had treated him. And she had gone after Nigel with singleminded purpose. The widow had seemed so brave and yet frail, so in need of a protector for herself and her children. Nigel had fallen quite blindly into the trap, led astray by his kind heart, and marriage to Piety had seemed the natural conclusion.

Alex knew with bitter clarity why Piety had wanted to be married before Nigel brought her to Wild Swan.

Piety was attractive enough to look at, with a trim figure and soft brown hair framing even features and big brown eyes. Her eyes were deceptive. She was rather shortsighted but refused to wear spectacles, and thus her eyes had the wide innocence of myopia. But there was no innocence in Piety. She was cold, self-serving, and hypocritical. While claiming to be a Christian, she was devoid of kindness and extremely intolerant. She condemned drinking, gambling, horseracing, and all manner of pleasure, while finding a rightness in slavery, because, she claimed, the Bible established the inferiority of the black race and bade servants to obey their masters. She adhered to the beliefs of the more radical evangelical movements, and when she happened to be at Wild Swan on a Sunday, she invariably made the day miserably embarrassing for everyone by insisting on praying for their souls in a loud voice wherever she found more than two people. The inhabitants of Wild Swan had learned to scatter widely when Piety was in the vicinity on the first day of the week.

Though of the finest cloth, her clothes were severe and plain, and she made it a point to show her displeasure over the rich colors Alex, Sam, Philly, and Flora preferred. Often it was not a matter of words; Piety had a host of mannerisms—a certain tilt of her head, the narrowing of her mouth and eyes, a disdainful sniff—with which to express her self-righteous judgments.

"It's like being followed around by a particularly noisome insect," Sam had observed, thoroughly out of patience with her sister-in-law.

They all treated Piety as if she were a bad joke that had been played on Nigel and the rest of the family, but Alex knew it was much more serious than that. Piety was draining the joy away from Nigel as surely as if she had tapped his veins with a lancet. He had decided to remain in Philadelphia. He might have done so anyway, but now he had no choice. He could not bring his family back to Baltimore to be in daily contact with his siblings, their spouses, and Rane, or with Alex when she was there.

Nigel never said a word against his wife; he considered himself the fool of the piece and did not complain about the sorrow his action had brought him. He maintained his own feeling of worth by calculated defiance, but only in matters that were of great importance to him—his medical practice and his daughter.

He had only *one* criterion for the patients he treated, and that was that they need him. The color of their skin, country of origin, religious or political beliefs made no difference to him. It did, however, make a difference to many of the more affluent people who might have come to him because of his growing reputation as a fine healer. Many did not want to be treated by a physician who was so undiscriminating in his choice of patients. This did not trouble him, but it drove Piety wild; her idea of being a doctor's wife included genteel visits with people of high social standing, not involvement with the diseases of poverty. But Nigel stood firm.

He was firm too about his daughter Virginia. She had been conceived on Nigel's and Piety's wedding night or shortly thereafter, for Nigel had soon found that Piety considered sex an unpleasant duty. Nigel had no interest in lying with a woman who had such an attitude about it, and he soon learned that he could not change her mind. He was thankful that Piety had not destroyed the child in her womb; in this the Bible had served him with its injunction to be fruitful, though to Piety, one child by Nigel was enough. She felt overtaxed enough by having borne two to her previous husband.

From the day of her birth, Virginia delighted him, and now he could see clear traces of the Thaine blood in her. Her eyes were grass green and her hair a gilded brown. There was Carrington in her too, in the fineness of her features. Nigel hoped no sign of Piety would ever show in Virginia.

At first he had thought he could be father to Piety's sons, Mark and Matthew. But he soon discovered that though they were only three and five when he married their mother, they were already beyond his influence. What he had taken for shyness was oppression visited on their spirits by their mother from the moment they had been born. Anything that gave pleasure was sinful. Life was a matter of duty and suffering that only ended with death followed by the great reward of admission to Paradise. To Piety, Paradise was some vaguely realized place whose main attraction was that only the chosen few would be admitted; certainly no blacks, Catholics, Jews, or other undesirables would be there.

Nigel had known people existed who believed so harshly, but his own family was so tolerant and so essentially joyful, he had not really understood the extent of the darkness in some minds and hearts. Mark and Matthew he could not help—no matter how hard he tried, they remained locked away from him—but he was determined that Virginia should not succumb to the same malady of the soul. His first defiance had been in choosing his great-grandmother's name for her. Virginia Thaine's free thinking and tolerant ways were legendary in the family; he chose her name as a talisman for his daughter, though Piety would have called her

Chastity. And in his choosing of her name, it was as if his daughter had become wholly his; Piety showed her little attention.

Nigel had never spoken about these things with his mother, but Alex was painfully aware of the state of his life. She loved him too much to misread him. She wished he would divorce his wife, but she doubted he ever would. Part of Nigel's charm was his steadfast loyalty. And she knew he would never desert little Virginia.

She was still thinking about her youngest son when she and Rane retired for the night.

It had been a long siege for all of them. Sam's labor had lasted for more than twenty-four hours. But now both mother and child were doing well enough so that Dr. Cameron and the midwife had both been able to depart. Alastair's last prescription had been that everyone get some rest.

With the house settled down for the night, the doctor's suggestion was even more appealing now than when he had made it, but Alex's mind refused to rest despite the exhaustion of her body.

Rane, having worried about Sam nearly as much as Morgan had, was more than ready to sleep, but Alex's tossing and turning made it impossible.

"Too tired to sleep?" he asked, and though his voice was patient, Alex was instantly contrite. "I'm sorry. I didn't mean to keep you awake. It's just that I keep thinking of Nigel."

Rane drew her against him spoon fashion, comforting her with his warmth. "It's natural to think of him on a day like this one when all of the family except him has shared in some way in the birth of Adam—Jim Barlow will have reached Philly, Flora, and Caleb by now with the news. But there isn't anything we can do for Nigel, not as long as he's married to that woman. I think it shows a great forbearance that we allow her here at all. Lord knows, she does not deserve any sort of welcome! I suppose we ought to be grateful; three fine marriages out of four is not a bad record." He paused and then added, "Of course, if and when Gwenny marries, it will be another fine choice."

Alex giggled, shaking against him. "Or else you will run the man off with a gun."

"At the very least," he agreed promptly. "You are very calm about it. You have no idea what worries I have now that Gwenny is growing up so quickly. I know what men are like!"

Still laughing, Alex turned in his arms so she could kiss him. "I know what men are like too, and I hope Gwenny finds one just like you."

She loved him for countless reasons, but one of the most important was his involvement with the children; she had seen too many men who had little interest in their offspring, let alone stepchildren, as the twins and Nigel were. "Tell me about your other woman," she said, snuggling against him.

He chuckled, for the "other woman" was the new ship being built at the yard. After years of dreaming, he and Caleb were at last seeing the dawn of the swiftest ships ever to sail the seas.

The final impetus had come from the so-called "Opium War" in China, whereby China had lost her attempt to rid herself of British smuggling of opium, the drug being wisely forbidden by the Emperor. The British Navy and the Royal Marines prevailed against the Chinese after the Chinese had tried to stop the trade by seizing and dumping a fortune in opium. The resultant treaty, signed in 1842, had given the island of Hong Kong to the British and had opened five "treaty ports"—Amoy, Foochow, Ningpo, Shanghai and Canton—to the outside world. Though England had favored-nation status, traders from other countries could also bring their families with them now to live in these cities, and they could deal more directly than before with the Chinese government. Various nations were gradually establishing their own consulates to aid this process. It was an enormous change from the old system of access to China—through one severely restricted strip of land along the Pearl River and the Chinese agents who had served as intermediaries. That the root cause of the change in Chinese policy had been their failed but justifiable attempt to resist the importation of a dangerous drug into their culture was seldom contemplated. The fact was that the luxury trade had opened up for the West. Tea, silk, gingerroot, jade, bronzes, porcelains—the list went on and on.

But China was far away, and tea and other goods were not improved by long storage in damp holds. The freshest and least-damaged cargo would command the highest prices, and the fastest ships would be the most valuable in the China trade.

The *Liza Gwen*, named by Caleb and Rane for their daughters, was one hundred fifty-nine feet long but only about thirty-two feet wide. With her shallow draft, sharp bow, and tall masts built to carry a great expanse of sail, she was the culmination of years of planning. There were many who said she would never make it out of the bay, let alone to China, but Rane and Caleb remained confident. They had not designed her alone but had hired a talented Scotsman, Iain McCord, to help them. And their craftsmen had put their own loyalty and dedication into the work.

Rane and Caleb planned to sell shares in the ship. Though this would lessen the risks as well as the rewards, they would retain, with Alex, more than fifty percent of the ownership. At first Alex had protested the idea that she own part of it, but the men had prevailed by insisting that without the money she had lent to the yard, the *Liza Gwen* would never have been built at all. They stressed "lent" and had made payments to her, never having accepted the money as a gift. Rane had also been quick to point out that he did not expect her to sell her share in the ship to anyone else. And Alex had to admit it was exciting to know that she owned part of a ship destined to sail to such exotic ports.

"The *Liza Gwen* is nearly finished. Shall we sail away on her maiden voyage to China?" Rane asked her now, and for an instant she contemplated the idea, thinking of leaving all the problems of children, horses, and land behind. But then she sighed. "No, I think not. My voyage to America was enough for me." She hesitated and then asked, "And for you? Is this enough for you, or would you truly like to go to China? Six or seven months away at best if the *Liza Gwen* sails as swiftly as you think she might." She swallowed hard, thinking of how she missed him when he was gone on much shorter voyages or she was away at the races. "I would not like it, but if it is something you wish to do, then you must."

Rane's answer was to kiss her soundly, and then he murmured, "And be without this for all those months? I am too old and settled."

"Settled?" Alex asked huskily, her hands running lightly over his lean back and tight buttocks, circling forward to cup the heavy sac and stroke the hardening staff of his sex. "Old?" she whispered, moving her head to tongue his flat nipples, and both of them forgot how tired they had been but a short time before.

Rane paid tribute to her in turn, touching every curve and hollow in wonder that something so familiar as her body was to him could be forever new. And when he entered her, he thought of how long she had been wild voyaging as well as safe harbor for him.

Alex was still glowing from Rane's loving as she went about her duties the next day, and as she held her new grandson, she found herself feeling more peaceful about the changes in her own body. She had always hoped to bear another child for Rane, but gradually she had come to accept that it was not to be. She knew that some women did have babies even so late in their lives, but she was certain she would not be one of them. Already there were changes signaling the end of her childbearing years. And though she knew it was foolish, she had begun to question whether or not she would still be as attractive to Rane. The lavish attention he had showered on her the night before had reminded her that fathering children had never been his goal when he lay with her; his intention had always been simply to love her.

Looking down at Adam's tiny, sleep-clenched face, she was flooded with contentment. Quite distinctly she could hear her grandmother reminding her that there was a season for everything on earth. Strange how the words from the Bible could have been a song when spoken by Virginia Thaine but were a curse when invoked by Piety.

Her own time for sheltering children in her womb was past. Now it was time for the next generation to be producing descendants of their own. Even Gwenny was, at nearly twelve years old, competent in the care of infants and very pleased that Sam had already allowed her to hold Adam. Soon Gwenny would begin the monthly courses that would mark her crossing from child to woman. And Alex hoped that she would eventually make a good choice of the man to whom she would give the gift of herself.

The next day the rest of the family arrived from Baltimore, causing complete confusion until everyone was settled. Larissa and Phoebe both wanted to hold their new cousin as if he were a doll, and they had to be convinced that he was a bit too fragile for such treatment. After a brief look at Adam, two-year-old Anthea decided he wasn't nearly as interesting as the kitchen cat. Three-year-old Seth was puzzled and more than a little suspicious of the new addition to his family. His parents both made a great fuss over him, but it was going to take a while before he was willing to give up his position as only child to Sam and Morgan.

Alex went out of her way to spend extra time with Seth. It wasn't difficult; she found him a fascinating child. He had the look of both of his parents in the hazel eyes of his mother and the dark hair of his father, and the combination was evident in his personality, too. Morgan's headlong flight into life was part of Seth; he had never shown the slightest timidity when he was learning to crawl and then to walk but had gone at the greatest possible speed, even after painful encounters with furniture and the floor. But he had some of his mother's reasoned directness, too, often asking questions that gave clear indication that he had thought about something at length and wanted to settle the matter.

Several days after he had arrived with the others at Wild Swan, he interrupted his reading lesson with Alex to propose a solution to the problem as he saw it.

"Gamma," he said, twisting around in her lap so he could look up at her, "when we goes back to Balamore, you keeps Adam here?"

"I'm afraid I can't do that," she told him, fighting a smile. "You see, Adam is your brother, and he belongs with your mother and father just as much as you do."

Seth's lower lip stuck out mutinously. "Doan want 'im!" he insisted. "He smells bad an' makes noises."

Alex hugged him. "So did you when you were that little. Just think, before long, he'll be big enough for you to play with, and he'll need an older brother to watch out for him, so you'll have an important job then."

Seth thought this over for a while, but he was still not convinced. "Mebbe Aunt Philly'll take 'im," he muttered, but at least he settled down again for the story Alex was reading and obligingly pointed out the letters and words he knew.

Alex loved him all the more for the fact that though he did not like the idea of having to share with the new baby, he made no attempt to harm him nor did he throw temper tantrums to gain attention. Such violence was foreign to his nature. He would retaliate when pushed too far by one of his cousins, but he did not initiate trouble. Among the grandchildren, Phoebe was far more apt to do that, seeming to feel obligated to defend her territory as middle child. When Phoebe dug her heels in, she was nearly immovable. Alex could foresee that whatever Phoebe chose to do in the future would be thoroughly done indeed, and she hoped Phoebe would find something that would demand all of her energies.

But at the moment, Alex was more worried about Flora than she was about any of the grandchildren. Flora had been genuinely warm in her congratulations to Morgan and Sam, but Alex had seen her face as she held Adam. The sorrow there had been so profound, she longed to ease it. But she had no simple palliative to offer, and so she did not press Flora to speak of her problem, not until Della came to her.

"Flora flew past me toward the herb garden. She didn't see me, she was crying so hard," Della reported. "I don't expect there's anything to be done, but I hate to see her like that. It must be harder with each new child in the family."

Alex sighed. "With all of the things herbs and other plants can do, there is not a potion I know of that can safely make a fertile woman infertile or an infertile woman fertile, only noxious brews that can kill a babe in the womb and often the mother as well."

She found Flora standing in the garden. She was making no sound, but tears were rolling down her cheeks. Alex put her arms around her. "Lovey, I am so sorry. I wish there was something I could do for you, but there isn't."

Flora turned her face into her mother's shoulder and sobbed, "I want so much to give Caleb a child! I love his and Penelope's children, I do, but I want a baby to suckle at my breast. God, I can feel it when I watch Sam with Adam."

She pulled away, scrubbing angrily at her tears. "Blake is eighteen this year and will marry soon enough. With John and Liza both having children of their own now, I am already a grandmother, or at least a stepgrandmother. Do you realize how odd that is? I do not begrudge them their happiness, but I want to share the same kind of joy with Caleb."

"It may still happen," Alex said, torn between her wish to see Flora obtain her heart's desire and her fear of the risk.

"I know it will not," Flora said. "I cannot tell you how I know, but I do."

Alex did not dispute this; sometimes there was no gainsaying that sure internal knowledge. "Have you spoken to Caleb about how you feel?" she asked, half expecting that her daughter might protest that her husband, being a man, did not understand. But instead, Flora's face softened.

"We have talked about it, and he has been honest with me. He would welcome a child were I to conceive, but he would rather not worry about me bearing one. He could not be more understanding and loving than he is; I don't regret a single day of our marriage. I know I should be grateful for what I have, and I am. But my desire for a child is almost something apart from him."

Absentmindedly she stripped some leaves from a bayberry bush and rubbed the fragrance from them as she sought the words to frame her thoughts. "It is as if the only measure for a woman is her ability to produce children, as if nothing else she could ever do could equal that. Caleb does not think that, but still it is a pervasive idea. Too often I believe it myself, and feel as if I will never be complete and worthy. Yet, in my mind, I know such thinking is wrong. A man is not judged by his ability to father children, but by what he accomplishes in his work. And I have begun to see that it should be the same for women, but that it will never be until we are granted more rights and take on more duties outside our homes. How can one be a responsible citizen if one possesses so few rights under the law and cannot even cast a vote for or against those who would govern us? The women in this family are exceptions, and the men, too, because you have taught us all that a woman can conduct a business as well as a man. But most women are little better than slaves."

Flora's voice remained even, but there was an undercurrent of passion that told Alex her daughter had considered the subject of women's rights closely. Flora was not alone; more and more women and some men, most of them New Englanders, were speaking out on the subject—and being vilified for their efforts.

Alex thought of how far Flora had come from the heedless girl who had rushed blindly into marriage with Carlton Fitzhubert.

"I am very, very proud of you," she told her daughter. "Your school, your marriage to Caleb, yourself—they are all worthy. You have become a splendid woman, and I agree with all you have said about women in general. But I would caution you to move carefully in your support for the rights of women lest you damage the reputation of your school. It is a bitter truth, but truth nonetheless: we live in a country that allows the buying and selling of human beings, a country that forced Rachel's people from their legally owned lands. So many have no rights, I fear it will be a very long time before the power is shared justly. You must remember that what you already do every day is important. Every child, male or female, you lead away from ignorance is a vote cast for future justice."

"If ever you should wish a new career, you could go on the lecture circuit to encourage women to take pride in themselves," Flora said with a smile, but then she sobered again. "Slavery. It is the fire that will burn us all, isn't it? Some time ago Blaine told me he was glad that he and Philly did not seem destined to have sons; he sees war coming. I do not want to believe it, but it seems as if the unity of the country grows ever more fragile."

Though the day was warm, Alex shivered. The continuing westward expansion and the admission of new states brought the constant problem of balancing slave lands against free lands in order to prevent ascendancy of either proslavery or antislavery forces. And the country was becoming increasingly divided. There was little talk any more from slave states about freeing their slaves; the everexpanding cotton fields of the new Southwest demanded vast armies of workers. And as the abolitionists slowly gained strength and respect in the North, the South was turning inward on itself, and more and more openly claims were being made for the basic rightness of slavery.

"Many good men share Blaine's fear and have worked tirelessly to keep the peace; God willing, they will continue to do so and to succeed," Alex said. "And this country is still the dream of many, else the immigrants would not be coming by the thousands."

"Indeed, there are streets in Baltimore where I could swear I am in Germany and others where it must be Ireland," Flora agreed. "The Irish, they are so wretched. When I think of their lot, I am ashamed to have any complaint at all. Most of them have come from decades of poverty, and though their lives are hard here, they seem to hold to the belief that things will get better."

"Perhaps any change is better than what they knew at home," Alex suggested.

She thought of how different the passage across the ocean was for these new immigrants. She and her family had been treated with courtesy aboard the small, privately owned *Paul and Sarah*, but now people were packed into the holds of large steamers and sailing vessels with no view to comfort or health. Too many died on the way. Already weakened by impoverished lives at home, the rigors of days in a damp, crowded, disease-infested hold finished them, and they never saw the promised land.

"If I ever try to tell you that it was harder to be alive when I was young, don't believe it. Life is far more complicated now."

"That may be," Flora said, "but you have a way of sorting things out and making them seem less complicated." And then she added, "Please, don't tell Caleb that I wept; he is too kind."

Observing Caleb later, Alex realized that he didn't have to be told; he was so close to Flora's heart, he knew when she was troubled. But Caleb was a wise man and did not press his wife to confide in him. Instead he wrapped her in his love until her blue eyes glowed when she looked at him, and the shadows of her sorrow lightened.

Alex wished they could all stay at Wild Swan, but the press of their lives was in Baltimore, and she went along for the launching of the *Liza Gwen*.

The ship had been towed to another yard for rigging, and she was a splendid sight with her canvas displayed as the lines and sheets were tested.

Alex went on board with Morgan, Caleb, and Rane, and when she tilted her head back to look up at the masts, she felt as if she were spiraling away in space and had to look down again.

"It's enough to make you lose your bearings," Caleb chuckled beside her, holding her arm until he was sure she was steady on her feet. "And to think the crew will have to climb the rigging and spend hours aloft!" He shuddered. "I'm sure I would plunge from my perch only too quickly."

"Not I," Alex said. "If I ever got up there in the first place, I would hold on so tightly, someone would have to come and pry me loose."

Her eyes studied first Rane and then Morgan, so comfortable in this environment that was alien to her. They were standing a little distance apart, each engaged in his own conversation with a workman, but they were so alike in the way they stood, even in the way their heads tilted and their strong hands emphasized their words, that Alex felt an overwhelming flood of love at the sight of them.

Rane felt the sound as much as he heard it, a discord in the hiss of lines and snap of canvas as each was tested. He jerked his head up and saw the loose spar falling, slowed by the tangle of sail but still coming down. Everything was moving swiftly and slowly at the same time. Even as he opened his mouth to shout at Morgan, he realized the futility of it and launched himself at his son, crashing into him, sending Morgan and the other man sprawling. He felt a slash of fire across the back of his head and his shoulders and then nothing at all.

Alex reached Rane before Morgan or anyone else understood what had happened. She clawed at the spar that lay across him as if it were a living beast, not even aware of the snarling coming from deep in her throat. She had actually lifted it by the time the men moved to help her. They tossed the heavy wood away and then stood frozen, uncertain what to do next. Morgan had regained his footing, and his face reflected his dawning horror as he began to comprehend the risk his father had taken for him. His only coherent thought was that if Rane was dead, nothing would ever make sense again.

Alex's own heart was pounding so loudly, at first she could not determine whether Rane's pulse still beat. "You cannot be dead, you cannot. I won't let it be so, I won't!" She muttered variations of the words without knowing she was speaking. And then she found the rhythm of life in Rane's neck, the beat light and racing, but blessedly there.

Rane heard someone groaning and stopped the sound when he realized he was making it. The deck was hard beneath him, and he wondered why he was lying face down on it. Then he remembered the lethal timber falling toward Morgan, and he moved sharply, his son's name ending in a cry as murderous pain shot through his skull and back. He closed his eyes again and lay breathing in shallow gasps, waiting for the agony to ease, infinitely glad that he could hear Morgan's voice saying that he wasn't injured.

"Love, don't try to move again, please!" Alex pled. "One of the men has gone for Dr. Benjamin. I want his help."

The darkness closed in again, and he welcomed it.

The next time he was fully conscious, he found himself in his own bed. He felt awful, but he was alive, and he remembered that Morgan was, too. Alex's face swam into focus as she leaned over him. He drew a harsh breath at the sight of her face in the candlelight; it looked like a skull, so tightly did the skin seem stretched over her bones, so big and sunken were her eyes. And then he understood.

"Alex, it is not the same." His throat was so dry, it was difficult to get the words out, but he persevered. "It is not as it was with St. John. I can move everything; I can feel everything. I know who I am, where I am, and who you are. And I love you."

She managed to give him a drink of water before the violent tremors swept over her and the tears came. "You saved our s-s-son. You did it with—without even thinking. But I have thought—Oh, God, Rane, I could not choose! It was worse than when Sinje was hurt; it was worse. And I could not choose between you and Morgan!"

Despite the lingering haziness in his mind, he did not mistake the profundity of what she was saying. She was fiercely maternal. He knew she would gladly die to save any of her children. But she would not give his life for them. Her admission touched him deeply.

"You do not have to choose, sweetling," he said.

His voice was so tender, Alex cried harder. She never wanted to live through the past hours again. She and Dr. Benjamin had bound the broken right shoulder, but the head injury was another matter. Dr. Benjamin had been unable to tell her any more than she already knew, which was to keep Rane warm and quiet and to wait.

She had feared he would never open his eyes to sanity again. She had had visions of him lying in a coma until he slipped away. And the wildly evil thought had intruded that she might, by a simple wish, reverse time and change what had happened, sacrifice her son in place of her husband. A question of her willingness; a vivid, waking nightmare now dispelled by Rane.

She leaned over and kissed him and then straightened. "I know your head must ache abominably and your shoulder too, but Morgan needs to see that you are all right. I drove everyone away. They're all waiting downstairs for some word."

When Rane opened his eyes again, Morgan was standing beside the bed, looking nearly as worn as his mother. Rane studied him for a moment and then managed a grin. "I feel as if I am at my own wake. I assure you that while I have felt better in my life, I am not dying. You can stop looking so guilty. You had nothing to do with what happened, and I know you would have done the same had our positions been reversed."

Fear of losing control of his emotions made Morgan's voice gruff. "I thought I knew before today what you mean to me, to the others, and most of all to Mother. But I didn't. I didn't really know until after the accident. If something happened to you now, we couldn't . . . we wouldn't . . ." He drew a deep, shuddering breath and tried again. "Nothing would ever be right for any of us again, but most of all for Mother. We all think of her as being so strong. But you are a great part of her strength. Whatever risks you take, you must remember that. What happens to you, happens to her, to all of us."

Rane stretched out his left hand, offering it to his son. "Thank you," he said, and both of them had tears in their eyes.

Rane had known of the children's acceptance and surely of Alex's love, but he had been far more aware of what they gave him—all the warmth and joy of belonging to a family after the cold, desperate years with his first wife Claire and her demons—than of what he gave them in return Though his body was battered, his heart soared

Chapter

14

Alex had sent for Nigel before Rane regained consciousness, and even when she knew Rane was going to be all right, she made no attempt to prevent Nigel from making the trip. Not only would it be nearly impossible to intercept him, but she wanted an excuse to see him. Worry about him was never far from her mind.

He arrived to find his stepfather pale but recovering and determined not to be coddled.

"He's a terrible patient," Alex complained. "He insists he can have a headache standing up as well as he can lying down."

Diffidently Nigel asked if he might examine Rane just to put his own mind at rest.

"Don't worry. You haven't roused my professional jealousy," Alex assured him. "I would appreciate another opinion."

Nigel looked so earnest and concerned, Rane acceded to his wish, and Nigel was able to give a good report to Alex. "Of course, he's trying to do too much too soon. Head injuries take time to heal, and his shoulder can't be comfortable, but he's a very fit man and should be as good as new before too long."

Alex thought of how much Nigel's competence and gentleness must mean to his patients, and her pride in him was immense, but the toll his life was taking on him was too visible. It was not just a matter of the worry he had felt as he traveled to Baltimore; he looked years older than twenty-five. His blue-green eyes were darkly circled and his skin, which had always had a golden cast, was gray.

"And what of you, Dr. Carrington, how do you fare?" she asked softly.

For a moment, the bleakness of his life with Piety showed in his eyes, but then he shrugged. "I am well. It is only that there are so many who are sick and in need of comfort. Particularly the children. Hunger makes them so prone to disease. I find it difficult to accept how little I can do."

"That way lies despair," Alex chided. "I know it is hard, but try to remember how many you have healed." She ruffled his dark brown hair, not even conscious of the old maternal gesture. "And unless you take care of yourself, there will be many more who will need help and will have no one to turn to."

She could not bring herself to ask after Piety; she had no interest in the woman, and Nigel knew it. But his daughter was a safe topic, and the minute she mentioned her name, his eyes brightened.

"Virginia is a marvelous child, though I admit I am prejudiced in her favor. She is so clever, despite her lack of years. Don't fear she will forget you; I speak of you so often to her and of the rest of the family." He did not have to tell his mother how much his wife resented this practice. "I must warn you, however, that she has decided her name is 'Gincie.' "

"Gincie? What sort of name is that?"

"Her own version of Virginia. Lord knows how she arrived at it, but she is immovable. If one calls her Virginia, she points to herself and says, 'I Gincie' quite firmly. So Gincie it is."

Nigel stayed long enough to witness the launching of the *Liza Gwen*. It was a moving sight for all of them and for the huge crowd gathered to witness it as the ship was towed out and set free, flying the house flag—a golden falcon and the letter "J" on a crimson ground. Strong male voices joined in a chantey to set the pace of their work:

> A Yankee ship came down the river,
> Blow, boys, blow,
> A Yankee ship came down the river,
> Blow, boys, bonny boys, blow.

> And how do you know she's a Yankee clipper?
> Blow, boys, blow,
> Oh, how do you know she's a Yankee clipper?
> Blow, boys, bonny boys, blow.

> The stars and bars they flew behind her,
> The stars and bars they flew behind her.

The ship rode like a great white bird, and Rane murmured, "She's almost as graceful as one of your swans."

He was torn; he was glad to be alive and with his family, but part of him, despite his assurances to Alex to the contrary, longed to be sailing away on the *Liza Gwen*. His right arm was still bound to keep his shoulder immobile, and he chafed at the restriction and understood more clearly how St. John had felt managing all those years with only one arm. He glanced at Sam, standing with the baby Adam in her arms and Seth holding on to her skirt, and he reminded himself that her role was harder than his. Morgan was going partway on this first voyage, and it could not be easy for Sam to watch him sail away on this innovative craft.

The ship would not be arriving in China at the optimum time for taking on the highest grade tea, but there would be teas of less, though passable, quality to buy as well as the silks, firecrackers, porcelain and other Chinese goods which were increasingly popular with American buyers. This maiden voyage was to test the ship on the trip east around the Cape of Good Hope at the southern tip of Africa to China. For the first days, the *Liza Gwen* would stay fairly close to the American coastline in case of trouble, and Morgan would be aboard.

Rane was less worried about his son than he might have been. He had faith in the seaworthiness of the ship, though he was just superstitious enough to resist the impulse to proclaim it aloud and tempt fate. From captain to first mate to the lowest crew member, every man had been carefully chosen for his experience in deep water sailing. They might be rough and multinational, speaking a polyglot, but they were as fit as the ship. After the accident with the spar, everything had been checked and rechecked, and nothing had been found wanting.

It was a grand adventure for Morgan, and Rane was suddenly able to wish him the joy of it without a trace of envy. Alex's hand had crept into his free left hand, warm and comforting, her fingers curled around his. It reminded him that the hardest voyage in his life had already been accomplished in his long loving and final winning of Alex.

"Honestly! Even my lawyer husband longs to be aboard that ship!" Philly exclaimed. "Don't deny it, Blaine. I can feel it." She forestalled his protest and won a reluctant grin from him. "You men, I think you're mad to want to be aboard a wallowing ship for months on end."

"The *Liza Gwen* doesn't wallow," Nigel protested, and he sounded so much like the old, precise Nigel, they all laughed.

Alex tried to persuade Nigel to stay long enough for a visit to Wild Swan, but he refused, insisting politely but firmly that he had family and professional obligations in Philadelphia.

"Then come for Christmas," she urged.

"It would mean bringing my family."

"I know. Does Piety pray harder at Christmas?" she asked wryly and immediately wished she hadn't.

To her relief, Nigel did not take offense. "Piety's prayers aren't seasonal; they're continuous. I think she fears someone else will capture the ear of God if she doesn't keep up her chatter."

Never before had Nigel displayed such ironic humor about his wife, and Alex was encouraged by it. Perhaps he could learn to distance himself from his marriage.

"Divorce is not the end of the world, though it might seem so," she ventured even as she had to Flora, and she knew instantly that she had overstepped her bounds.

Nigel's face was suddenly cold and shuttered. "Piety would never let me have my child. It is not that she wants her, but she knows I do. And for spite, she would make sure I never saw my little girl again. I could not bear that."

"Of course you could not! I am sorry; it is not my business. I am clumsy when I interfere."

Nigel kissed her on the cheek. "No apology necessary. I know your concern comes from your love."

Alex considered Nigel's situation long after he had departed, and she found herself wishing he had not grown into such an honorable man. It occurred to her that he could simply take his daughter and disappear. His skills as a physician would assure him of a living wherever he might go. She knew he would never do it.

As she watched the energetic play of the children during the summer at Wild Swan, she was more resolved than ever that Virginia—mentally she corrected herself, Gincie—would be part of it before long.

As she had done with her own children, Alex taught her grandchildren all manner of practical skills as soon as they could understand what was required of them. She was particularly pleased that Larissa was very interested in herbs and flowers and was quick to remember what she had been told about each one. And she was proud of Gweneth, who got along so well with her young nieces and nephews.

"If ever anyone was born for mothering, it is our Gwenny," Rane observed. "She manages the whole brood as if they were no trouble at all."

"Ah, but mothering requires fathering," Alex teased.

"Don't remind me! It's hard enough to see her growing up by the day," Rane groaned.

"It is for me as well," Alex said, all levity gone. "I think it is time for her to go to Baltimore to school. I thought I might talk to Flora about it. Of course, Gwenny can live at our house; Mrs. Koller will keep a good eye on her. But I want Flora to be involved, too. It's not that you aren't a good father," she amended hastily. "You are, but I think you deal more calmly with sons than with daughters."

"I'll concede the point. I also detect a certain deviousness, though for good reason, in your plan. I suspect you intend that Flora will feel that she has at least one chick to mother, even if it is her sister."

Alex regarded him anxiously. "There are so many years between them, don't you think it will work? Or is it too obvious?"

"Obvious or not, it will work because Flora is very fond of her little sister. And it will work for me also," he noted, "because I know that with Gwenny in the city with the others, you will spend even more time there."

Alex shook her head in mock despair. "After all this time, how can you think that anyone, even our daughter, could draw me more strongly than you do?"

Rane thought if the day ever came when Alex no longer had the power to make his pulse race at unexpected times, he would know he was dead.

Sam rather thought she *was* dead. She paid attention to her two sons and to the other children. She made herself useful at Wild Swan and rode over to Brookhaven to work there, too, because even living in Baltimore, she was still very involved in making Brookhaven run smoothly. Outwardly she was serene and smiling. But inside she felt curiously numb, as if the most vital part of her had ceased to exist—the vital part that was Morgan.

She had felt this emptiness before when he had been gone on one of the ships, but never to this degree. The *Liza Gwen* was something else entirely. Morgan had been afire with enthusiasm for her since the first plans were drawn, and there had been no question that he would go on the maiden voyage once Rane had been hurt. Sam had wasted no energy in futile protest. She had known since the beginning of her marriage that her greatest competition for Morgan's affections was ships and the sea. And this sleek vessel with her black hull and soaring white sails was the most formidable rival yet.

She could scarcely bear to see the other couples together, most of all Rane and Alex; they were so close to each other, it made Morgan seem even further out of reach. Morgan was her weakness. She was strong enough to have made an attempt to banish him from her life when she had been prepared to marry Justin. But in the end, it had all come back to Morgan, and in the years of their marriage, she felt as if she had lost more and more of herself in him. She had not intended that to happen. She had intended to love him and to remain at the same time separate and complete.

Now it seemed as if she had not been so since the first day she had met him, as if he had begun to absorb her into himself even then. It was not that the same thing didn't happen to other happily married couples; she could see that it did. But it seemed to work both ways for them, each taking in and becoming part of the other. That did not seem true in the case of herself and Morgan. She wondered if it was a family trait; her father had a habit of so completely disappearing into his marriages that it was difficult to find him.

But nothing could suppress the rush of joy she felt when Morgan arrived at Wild Swan weeks after he had sailed away. He looked so tanned and fit, so alive, her body responded instantly as he gave her an exuberant hug before greeting his sons and the rest of the family.

His enthusiasm for the *Liza Gwen* was immeasurable. "It is as close to flying as I shall ever come," he declared. "The trip back on a lesser ship seemed as slow as walking. The *Liza Gwen* performed in every way we could hope. Of course, there are problems, just as we foresaw. The sails take constant tending. When the ship is in colder waters, it is going to be demanding work for the crew to stay aloft to do the work required."

The Jennings-Falconer yard had been building leaner ships for years, but the *Liza Gwen* was the most radical yet, and Rane showered Morgan with technical questions.

Sam watched the two men, her expression carefully schooled to show nothing except interest. Rane and Morgan were so alike, but there was one great difference—Rane's days of wandering far were over.

Morgan found it difficult to think coherently about anything, even the ship, when he looked at Sam, so he studiously avoided gazing at her as he spoke to his father. His body felt as if it had been deprived of the comfort of Sam for years, and indeed it had been a long time as they had not yet resumed lovemaking after the birth of Adam when Morgan had sailed away. When he stole glances at Sam, he couldn't tell whether she was thinking the same thing; she could be circumspect when she wished. He hoped her desire was kindling behind her polite facade.

Suddenly he wanted very much to be alone with his wife, and he was grateful when his mother smoothly suggested that he must be tired from traveling and that an early night was in order, adding that she would take charge of the boys except for Adam's feedings, which only Sam could accomplish.

Morgan watched Sam nursing Adam, and so great was his own need, he found the scene more erotic than tender. The tiny mouth of his son suckling at Sam's blue-veined breast caused his own mouth to hunger for her, his groin to tighten. He had been too long without her, and he cautioned himself to go slowly.

But when he held her in his arms at last, all thoughts of restraint fled. The warmth of her body, the scent of her, the candlelight dancing golden in her eyes and hair—the sheer desirability of her swept over him, making his blood pound until all he knew was the driving need to possess her.

For a dangerous instant, Sam was swept by rage so deep it eclipsed her own desire. How dare he come at her like a rutting stag when all it was was an overflow of his lust for the damned ship! He had hardly noticed her all evening, and now his face was hardplaned, his eyes nearly blind with the demands of his body.

"Oh, God!" he moaned. "I could not even look at you tonight for fear of disgracing myself! Sam, my sweet Sam, I've missed you so!" His hands stripped away her robe and stroked down her body as he bent his head to nuzzle her breasts, licking and sucking in a rhythm completely different from the nursing of their son.

Sam's resistance vanished. It was not impersonal after all. He wanted her, not just any woman, to slake his lust. The *Liza Gwen* could not compete with her here. Her body yielded to him as the sense of her own power flooded back into her.

She drew his head up and kissed him deeply, probing his mouth with her tongue, melting against him, and running her hands down his back to the flex of his buttocks.

Morgan lifted her easily, put her on the bed, and rid himself of his own clothing without being aware of it, conscious of nothing but Sam's response. Normally no matter how willing she was, her body required patient coaxing to be made ready for him. But tonight she urged his entry as soon as he lay down with her, and his heavily engorged sex found her hot and slick and open for him.

He sank into her and stopped, trembling in his effort to maintain control of his body. But Sam moved against him urgently, her nails biting into his taut flanks.

"Don't wait!" she gasped, and he lost himself at her command, crying his passion aloud as his thrusting was met by her muscles stroking him inside of her until their voices joined in a song more compelling than any ever sung by sea siren.

"What happened?" he asked, dazed, when he had the energy to speak.

"I think it is fairly obvious—I missed you," Sam purred, and their laughter was shared as their passion had been. But inwardly Sam was resolved that she would make sure that no ship, no far port, nothing would hold his heart and soul and body as she did, as he held hers.

Chapter 15

Throughout the summer, the work of training the horses for fall racing had gone on, but nothing was quite the same as it had been in the previous decade. The Panic of 1837 had gradually made itself felt in the racing world.

After years of expansion, races in Virginia and Maryland (long known as the "racehorse region") were being eclipsed by events much further south and to the west; overall there were fewer race meetings in the country year by year; and no region was unaffected. The values of purses and prizes were diminishing. For a time there had been so many races that there weren't enough good horses to fill the fields in all of them, but now there was an overabundance of fine horseflesh. The rash of expensive imports in the thirties had led to overpriced stud fees and foals, and those prices were toppling.

Paradoxically, the horse sale that had hurt Alex so much at the time had turned out to be fortunate for Wild Swan. The sale had dispersed the bloodlines and allowed the fame of the stable to spread further than it would have done otherwise. More than once in the past years, Alex had found her horses racing against their own blood, and when her own lost to the challengers she did not mind as much as she would have had the horses been descended from animals other than Wild Swan's. And because her horses had been known as among the finest in the land for so long, her business did not suffer as much as many others did.

But still there were changes and adjustments to be made. Though Wild Swan, Oberon, Bay Swan, and Fortune were consistently listed among America's leading sires because of the quality of their get, not as many mares were brought to them as in better days. Glencoe, one of the English stallions imported in the last decade, and others of his high quality and repute were suffering the same fate. It was not only a matter of less revenue from stud fees, it also meant that the bloodlines were not being perpetuated in as many animals. Though some did not approve, Alex counterbalanced some of this lack by offering her stallions to breed half-bred mares as well as Thoroughbreds. The desired result of such unions was not racehorses—the pedigrees of such colts would not allow admission to race meetings even if the speed was there—but improved saddle horses. With so many people going west, there was always a market for good horses.

At first, Samson had not approved of this expanded business. He was terribly bigoted when it came to his charges. He believed Wild Swan's horses were the best in the world, and he did not want the stallions bred to inferior mares.

"Dem mares pass on ugly faces an' bad habits, ma boys gets de blame," he protested stubbornly.

"Your 'boys' won't have nearly enough work to do if we don't make them available to a wider selection of mares," she retorted. "And they have some bad habits of their own to pass along."

He'd looked as though she'd insulted one of his sons when she'd said that, but he'd adjusted to the new program.

Wild Swan produced enough fruit, vegetables, nursery stock, and dairy products to do quite well without the horses, but there was no question in Alex's mind about the importance of the Thoroughbreds.

They remained the heart of the dream for which the land had been purchased in the first place. And racing was still what they did best.

She had continued to take them to race meetings in Maryland, Virginia, North and South Carolina, but it was becoming more and more important to go further south. Though Charleston still had some of the old luster, New Orleans had more.

Alex had attended the races at the Metairie Course in March of the previous year, and been impressed by the condition of the track itself and by the festivities attendant on the races. There was even a ladies' stand, complete with a parlor for added comfort. And there were two other courses there as well, the Eclipse and the Louisiana, though they seemed to be fading a little.

There was some truth to the contention that the record times posted in New Orleans were due to the use, except in special cases, of the weight-for-age handicapping coupled with the May 1 birthdate. This allowed horses foaled in the early months of their birth years to be classed and handicapped as a year or more younger than their actual ages for spring races when they were old enough to compete.

But there was more to the New Orleans speed records. The continually moist ground of the area provided a nearly perfect climate for a resilient, fast surface, except when extremely heavy weather oversaturated the soil.

The major problem with taking Wild Swan's horses to New Orleans had nothing to do with jockey club regulations. The horses were of such stature now, they were welcomed anywhere. Because they added status to any event, ways were always found to accommodate Alex's entries. The difficulty lay in the distance. Under the best of circumstances, it took more than two weeks to ship the horses by water, and with time allowed for them to recover from the voyage, a trip to New Orleans and back required a minimum of six weeks and would usually mean two months or so.

Lexington, Kentucky, another place where racing continued to be of high caliber despite financial setbacks, was only half as far away as New Orleans, but it meant taking the horses overland, making them walk most of the way or trusting them to various rail lines part of the way, something Alex was still loath to do. Accidents and fires occurred too often for her peace of mind, as did explosions on the steamboats that plied the Mississippi, other great rivers, and the sea. She had shipped horses down the coast on these boats a few times, but she had not lost her reluctance to do so.

Sometimes Alex envied Hugh Bettingdon, with whom she corresponded regularly. His stable continued to produce winners for Epsom, Newmarket, Doncaster, and other famous courses. Hugh did not have to worry whether this or that race would be held; they met their schedules like well-wound clocks. And, compared to the vast spread of meetings in the United States, the distances to travel in England were negligible. Hugh had long been urging Alex to find an agent she could trust to take her horses to various races. She knew his suggestion was a valid one, but still she had not acted on it.

Her and Samson's methods of training horses were far more patient and kind than those employed by most, and she was horrified by the idea of hiring someone who might abuse or push the horses too hard once they were out of her sight. To have that happen even once would be too much. And she was further worried about what Samson's reaction might be to such an addition to the staff.

Samson was in charge of the horses. Only her word was above his, and she could not remember a time when she had disagreed with him over a training or feeding schedule. He was phenomenal in his ability to coax the very best from each animal. But Samson was truly safe only at Wild Swan.

More than a decade had passed since Samson had killed his owner, but the fact remained that his papers were forged. He was still a fugitive slave, and a murderer besides. Even free blacks were being stolen to be sold as slaves in the Deep South; how much more vulnerable Samson would be in such a situation. Alex knew that had she asked him to go with her to the races in recent years, he would have gone, but she had no intention of ever putting him to that test. No contest on earth was worth that risk. It was enough that he had remained at Wild Swan rather than having gone on to Canada.

Under Samson's tutelage, Jed Barlow had grown to be very competent with the horses and was vital help on the racing circuit. But he was not the sort of man to put himself forward. He remained self-effacing and satisfied to work under someone else's orders. Alex knew he would be horrified were she to put him in charge and send him off without her. And his sons were like him.

She was accustomed to taking the horses to the race tracks herself, and even with the increased distances to travel, she would just have to manage.

But she began to doubt her ability to do so when Jed was injured in Baltimore. They had done well in races in Virginia and Washington City in September and the beginning of October, but things fell apart at the mid-October meeting at the Kendall Course. Heavy rain had turned the track into a quagmire. The three-year-old Swan Sprite, by Swan out of Taney, ran badly, though mud had not seemed to bother her before. Sprite, a graceful chestnut, was usually even-tempered, but on this day she was in a fractious mood, suffering from what the journalists of the sport would delicately call "female disorders." Alex would have put it more bluntly—Sprite was longing to be mating with a stallion, not competing in a race.

Even after Sprite had been walked and cooled out, she was still dancing about and tossing her head, and when Jed took her from the groom, she went crazy, rearing up and throwing Jed against a fence before he knew what was happening. Sprite was instantly overpowered by other hands, but Alex had eyes only for Jed.

He was chagrined and apologetic, but he was also hurt. Sprite had dislocated Jed's shoulder, and he had bruised his back badly on the fence. He kept insisting he would be all right, but Alex was firm.

"You will rest a few days at the house, and then you will go home to Wild Swan." She refused to listen to his protests, insisting that with two of his sons and two handlers, she had more than enough help. But she knew it would mean closer attention from her, for the remaining men were even less likely than Jed to take the initiative. Her regret was that she would not be able to spend as much time with her children and grandchildren as she had planned on this visit.

She confessed as much to Rane that evening. "At least you're here," she said, settling against him gratefully, weary after the long day.

"You could forfeit," he suggested gently, and felt her body stiffen in protest before she voiced it.

"I could not. We are racing little enough these days, and my horses run as long as they are able. Though if I'd been more alert, I might have withdrawn Sprite today before the race—her mind was not on business."

Neither is mine, Rane thought, but he forbore to make the point. He knew Alex would not refuse him if he wanted to make love, but he knew as well that what she really needed was just to be held and given refuge until she fell asleep.

"Day by day, that's the best anyone can do, my love," he murmured, and he felt sleep steal over her.

When Alex awakened in the morning, Rane had already left for the shipyard, but the effects of the sweetly sheltered rest he had given her lingered, and she felt prepared to face the day as she dressed hurriedly in preparation to go back to the racecourse. She took the time to eat a hurried breakfast with Gwenny before her daughter had to be off to school, and she was pleased to listen to Gwenny's enthusiastic chatter about the friends she had made and her favorite subjects at school. Flora figured largely in the spate of words—"Flora says," "Flora took me to see . . ."—and Alex was reassured that her plan was working. Gweneth was enjoying life in Baltimore, and Flora was doing well as older sister and substitute mother.

Alex was on the point of leaving when Mrs. Koller announced that someone wanted to see her. The housekeeper's guttural mutterings gave clear indication of what she thought of people who came without prior appointment to bother Mrs. Falconer.

"It's all right, Gerda," Alex soothed her. "I can take a little time. Did he say what he wanted?"

"Ja, is about your horses," Gerda answered shortly; she had never adjusted to Alex having her own business, and racehorses at that.

Padraic Joyce was a slender man of medium height with dark hair and deep blue eyes. Alex judged him to be in his thirties, though it was difficult to tell. His fair skin was weathered and further marked by bitterness. His pose of affability was surely no more than skin deep. His eyes remained hard and watchful when his mouth smiled.

And even his smile faded when Alex introduced herself as the owner of the Wild Swan horses. He looked around suspiciously as if he suspected Mrs. Koller had played some jest on him by bringing him before the Englishwoman.

It was clear that it mattered to him that she was English; he had stiffened as soon as she spoke.

"The horses are yours?" he asked incredulously, and his Irish brogue rolled the words.

"Yes, they are." She said it quietly, but her green eyes snapped with impatience at having the old doubt confronting her again after all these years.

Mr. Joyce seemed to recollect that he had come to ask for something, and he made an effort to appear politely subservient, but his tension showed in his hands that twisted his cap over and over.

"I want ta' work yer horses." All efforts to the contrary, it came out as a demand rather than a request.

Alex raised an eyebrow and regarded him coolly. "You have a unique way of asking for employment, Mr. Joyce. You have in a few brief seconds made it clear that you do not care either for the English or for the idea of a woman owning racehorses. Have you any other complaints to make? I have a busy day ahead and was just on my way out."

"Pride, stiff-necked, un-raisonible pride, t'will be the death a' me!" The brogue was even thicker now, but Alex could see beyond his hostility for the first time.

"I've heard about yer horses, and I've seen them. They're foine beasts. And I heard you had a man hurt yesterday. I know horses. I know racehorses best. I've trained them since I was a young lad in Ireland."

"Jed Barlow, the man who was hurt, will be back at work before very long. And my head trainer is out at the farm. I was not looking for another horseman, at least not permanently," Alex explained slowly, wondering why she was considering giving this difficult man even temporary work.

"Try me, Mrs. Falconer. See how I get on with the beasts and then decide." Again it was more of an order than a request, though he tried to make it the latter.

Despite his attitude, he had two factors in his favor, though he couldn't know anything about them. His accent reminded her of Sean O'Leary, the captain of the *Silkie Wife*, the ship that had taken Caleb away from England and to eventual safety. And as Samson had appeared just when Alex had needed a new trainer, so it seemed Padraic Joyce had arrived at an opportune time.

She felt a little chill, wholly pleasurable, run up her spine when she saw him with the horses. Whatever his shortcomings with the human race, he was wonderful with Thoroughbreds. St. John had had the touch, Samson had it, so did she, and now this strange man showed his possession of it. Nothing could equal its value in training. The animals could be asked for obedience and speed and would give it in far greater measure than if they were handled by someone without that magic.

Even fretful Sprite quieted under Padraic's gentle words and hands, and two days later, on the final day of the meeting, Alex could have sworn that the five-year-old Swan's Chance won the four-mile heats because Padraic asked him to. Swan's Chance ran brilliantly, distancing one opponent in the first heat and the second in the second heat so that he won the race and the Jockey Club Purse of $400 in only two heats.

The second race of that same day was for three-year-olds, and Sprite ran as if she had never had her mind on anything else, redeeming herself for her bad behavior earlier in the week.

After the day's events were over, Alex approached Padraic. "You are every bit as good with the horses as you claim," she told him forthrightly. "And I would like you to join the staff at Wild Swan. But I must tell you again that I already have a head trainer. No one will ever supplant him. You could never be more than second man. You must consider whether or not that would suit you." She felt no obligation to explain anything about Samson; the old habit of protecting him was very strong.

Though his face was shuttered again, Alex knew the man was struggling with his self-confessed pride; being second did not come easily to him.

"I'll take the job," he said curtly, and she had to remind herself how good he was with the horses; she was not hiring him for his manners with his fellow human beings. At least his lack of ease in that department made it easier for her to pose a blunt question.

"Mr. Joyce, for your way with horses, I would risk almost anything on my own account, but many people live at Wild Swan, and I am responsible for their welfare. If you are wanted by the authorities or in any sort of trouble, I should like to know about it now."

He studied her for a long moment, as if debating how much to tell her, and then he shrugged. "There's not a soul in the world lookin' fer Padraic Joyce. Born the wrong side a' the blanket I was, with an English lord fer a father and an Irish housemaid fer a mither, an old story in the old sod. Nither a' them were lookin' fer me then, and they'd have ta journey back from the grave ta be lookin' now. And I niver married. I couldn't marry up, and I wouldn't marry down," he stated flatly. As he talked, Alex gleaned a vivid picture of his life.

His father's idea of largess had been to allow his illegitimate son to learn how to read and how to handle the highly bred racing stock that the boy might have a trade in the horse country of Ireland. The nobleman's generosity had not extended to legal acknowledgment, though his fathering of the child on Maire Joyce was commonly known. Maire had died of a fever when her son was quite young—Padraic scarcely recalled what she looked like—and the Englishman had gradually lost his wealth in Ireland by unwise and unlucky gambling and had in turn demanded rents that rose so high, his tenants lived on the brink of starvation, eating little else except potatoes for much of the year because other crops had to be sold to pay the rents. There had been some talk of the man returning to England, but he had broken his neck in a fall from his favorite horse two years ago. His long-suffering wife and his legitimate children had sold what was left of the estate, including the horses, and had gone back to England, leaving Padraic and the others who had been part of the land to fend for themselves on the exhausted soil. Finally Padraic had fled from the sight of dire poverty stripping the flesh from the bones of everyone he knew and the few he loved.

The only time his eyes had lightened during the grim recital had been when he mentioned the Curragh—the wondrous grassland of Ireland where horses had long grown sleek and swift on the bounty of the land, a land that provided less well for the people on it.

"Is that enough information fer you, Mrs. Falconer?"

She met his gaze squarely. "More than enough. I do not doubt that you will find this difficult to believe, but I understand your bitterness quite well. My first husband, St. John Carrington, was disinherited by his family, and they did more than their share of foolish gambling. He loved their land and their horses, but all was denied him because he married down, first my sister and then me. I am English, but I have no more love for that kind of cruelty than you do."

His smile was brief but genuine, and it transformed his face, making him look years younger and quite appealing. It made Alex sad for him that he should so mind his parentage.

"I think we'll be dealin' well togither, Mrs. Falconer," he said, and this time the tone of his voice was respectful and cordial.

It went badly from the moment Samson and Padraic were introduced to each other. Alex had expected it would be awkward, but it was far worse than that.

The Irishman bristled as if he'd been dealt a mortal insult, and Samson was suddenly a figure carved in stone. Not since her first sight of him had she seen the black man's face so devoid of expression. It struck her that this must have been exactly how he had presented himself to his master. It was a slave's face, betraying nothing of the inner man.

The idiocy of prejudice having such sway swept over Alex, and she was so furious, it took her a moment to gain enough control to speak.

"Samson, your position is unchanged. You are in charge of the horses of Wild Swan. Mr. Joyce, think very carefully before you stalk off. If you leave, I promise you will never work with one of my horses, not as long as you live, and you will never find better anywhere." She drew a deep shuddering breath. "You are both fools! It makes no difference on a racecourse whether a horse is chestnut, black, bay, or any other color. The only thing that makes a difference is the animal's ability to run. It is the same with human beings. And the two of you are more alike than different. You both know how to school a horse to run without killing himself or his jockey. You both know how to do it without breaking the animal's spirit or abusing his body while you train him. And training racehorses is what both of you want to do above all other work. That is far more important than the fact that one of you was born in Ireland and one in this country or that one of you is white, one black. If you can't see that, I pity you." She turned on her heel and left them staring after her.

By the next day, Della was hardly speaking to her, and Alex did not have the patience to bear that. "You and Samson are like family to me. How dare you think I would do anything to diminish Samson's position here? But he cannot go to the racecourses with me, and Jed Barlow is not a man to take charge. And, damn it, sometimes I need someone to take the burden from me, if only for a little while." To her horror, tears began to run down her cheeks.

Della's resentment melted away in face of Alex's distress. "Good lord, I am sorry!" she apologized. "I'm a practical, logical woman about everything except that husband of mine. About him I have no sense whatsoever. And for all his great size, I am as protective as if he were a small babe."

Alex essayed a watery smile. "I am much the same about Rane. But it is important to me that Padraic and Samson find a way to work together. They are both so skilled; there would be no better team of trainers anywhere. Do you think they can manage it?"

"I don't know. Right now they're circling each other like two bad-tempered dogs." She paused, and when she spoke again, her voice was sad. "Just as you say, they are more alike than not. There is a part of Samson that despises his brothers who are slaves as much as he loves them. I know that part because I have it too. It shames me, but it is there. The bowing and smiling—even if it all ended today, it would take more time than we will ever see to wash away the sickness of it. I don't know anything about this Mr. Joyce, but I wonder if he feels the same way about his people.

Everyone knows how poor and uneducated most of the new Irish immigrants are. Perhaps Mr. Joyce hates the low place the Irish have here and hates them for putting up with it even while he pities them. So there they are, the two of them so proud and so afraid they'll be like the most desperate of their kind if either man has power over the other."

Alex was sure that Della had found the heart of the matter. She watched the two men closely in the next days. Though Padraic hadn't left, and he and Samson hadn't come to blows, she couldn't see much progress. Their postures around each other remained stiff. The only time either relaxed was in the actual working with the horses. Samson was reluctant to have the Irishman anywhere near them, but even filled with resentment, he could not deny the calming effect Padraic had on them. And Padraic, seeing the same skill in the black man, gritted his teeth and did as he was told when he was set to mucking out stalls and forking hay. These were jobs that would, in other establishments, be done by someone of lower rank than his. But Padraic's anger eased when he noticed that Samson lent a hand even with the lowest chores when extra help was needed. Samson's lesson was clear—everyone at Wild Swan was expected to work for the good of the farm without thought of personal consequence.

Under the circumstances, Alex did not think she could take the Irishman with her to the racecourses. Nor would she allow Jed Barlow to go. He was still moving so gingerly, she did not want to risk any further injury to his back. Cassie's husband Ned was competent enough with direction, but the burden of it all would be hers. It made her even more impatient with Samson and Padraic, but there was nothing to be done until they made their own truce, if they ever did.

She thought all hope of that gone one morning when she heard the voices of the two men outside Della's kitchen. They were discussing the pros and cons of close inbreeding, but the talk seemed to be degenerating.

"You damned black ape!" Padraic swore. "If you don't take a chance on mixin' the line deep, you'll niver get that foine burnin' sort a' beast."

"You tatta eata, do it dat way, an' you gets crazy hosses mo' offen den not."

"Táirnge derg sa teanga, a dúirt é!"

"None a' dat talk! I gots no African to gib back fo' dat."

Alex had been prepared to fly out the door at the first insult, but Della's hand had stayed her, and Della had motioned for silence. And

Alex was beginning to understand why. Despite the imprecations, the tone was amicable.

"What is a 'tatta eata'?" she whispered.

"Potato-eater," Della explained with a grin. "But as for what Mr. Joyce said, I have no translation; I believe it is some sort of curse in Gaelic. Their way may be a little unorthodox, but they seem to be working things out. I think you can take Mr. Joyce with you when you leave tomorrow."

Samson, never one to shirk his responsibilities, came to tell her the same thing that afternoon. "I should a' knowed you doan put nobuddy bad wid de hosses. Dat Irish, he be almos' good as me wid 'em." The twinkle in his black eyes belied the boast.

"Almost. But no one will ever be quite as skillful as you," she said firmly.

Padraic was invaluable on the trip, proving himself possessed of exactly the degree of initiative Alex required of him without being combative about her decisions. But he was not so peaceable about everything, as one of the hands from a rival stable learned. The man kept muttering about the Irish coming in and breeding like vermin and taking everyone else's jobs. Padraic stood it for a while, and then he challenged the man and finished him off with a savage display of fighting skill.

When Alex heard about it, her overwhelming feeling was relief that both Padraic and the other man were all right, though the Irishman was more than a little battered. However, Padraic obviously felt she was sure to make some judgment against the fight and him, for he came to her with a good measure of defiance.

"I suppose you'll be tellin' me there was anither way," he said.

"No," she replied. "I have no intention of telling you anything of the sort. You are an intelligent man. I presume that had there been another way, you would have found it. However, I would prefer that this not be an everyday occurrence."

"The man was English," he ventured, still not believing that his employer could be taking this so calmly.

Alex shrugged. "I do not love or hate all English or Irish or Americans. That is the way wars begin, and I do not approve of wars." Suddenly she sounded so much like her grandmother to her own ears, she nearly laughed aloud. "Tell me, please, Mr. Joyce, what does this mean?" She tried to repeat the Gaelic curse she had heard, making no attempt to hide her smile. And as far as she was from the correct pronunciation, Padraic knew what she was referring to.

Even his weathered skin showed the blush, and a smile illuminated his face. "It's glad I am that I didn't say worse. It means 'a red nail on the tongue that said it!' "

"It has more authority in Gaelic," Alex told him solemnly, and then they were both laughing.

Padraic shook his head ruefully. "It used ta be I wasn't carin' much fer me Irish blood, nor much fer the English, come to that. But since I've come ta this country, I find I'm more and more Irish. Even the Gaelic I wouldn't speak, unless I had ta back there, has its uses here."

"I do understand," Alex said. "I've been in the country for twenty-four years, more years than I spent in England, and yet many still call me 'The Englishwoman.' And my brother Boston, who has traveled all over America and has married into the Cherokee, writes that his old nickname of 'English Boston' is still used in some quarters. I've given up trying to sort it out. Some days I feel completely American, some days completely English, and on some, a little of both. I leave it to my children and their children to feel wholly American all the time. If these feelings weren't common to most immigrants, there wouldn't be whole sections of American cities now where little American English is spoken."

"And where there's little likin' one group fer the next." Padraic was once more somber.

"That too," Alex conceded. "But again, the children will change that. They will be Americans, and the old ways that set their parents apart will mean less to them."

"It's full a' hope you are, Mrs. Falconer."

"Sometimes it's the only way to be, Mr. Joyce."

He hesitated a moment, and then he said, " 'Padraic' or 'Irish,' if you don't mind. Samson calls me 'Irish,' and I find it doesn't bite like I thought it would."

"Padraic or Irish, so it will be," Alex agreed, and she did not mistake the importance of his gesture. It was a step toward becoming more a part of Wild Swan, and she was glad of it.

They lost a few races, and one of them was to a son of Wild Swan, another to a daughter of Fortune. Padraic felt as Alex did, that it was all in the family and thus less of a loss to be so beaten. But no horse could come close to Swan's Chance in the four-mile heats. He made this test of endurance and speed look easy, often distancing his opponents in the first or second heat and thereby making it less work to win.

"It's demoralizing. Even when we buy your stock away from you, you continue to produce winners."

Alex turned from watching Swan's Chance being exercised to find Allen Ralston beside her. They greeted each other with mutual delight. But she felt a moment's discomfiture when she saw that Justin Sinclair was also there, standing back politely. She had seen him several times in the past years, but she had never ceased to feel a pang at the sight of him. It wasn't really her fault that her son had made such a mess of the engagement party, but having always wanted Morgan and Sam to be together, she felt as if she shared in the blame for Justin's heartbreak. That it had affected Justin deeply, she had no doubt. Though he was far too sophisticated to betray himself easily, his eyes always became more intent when Sam was mentioned, and on occasion he had asked outright for news, cloaking the hunger to know about her in the mannerly inclusion of her husband's name in the request.

This time there was news of Justin himself, and Allen proffered it smoothly. "You must congratulate Justin. He married Madlen Chartier, a lovely girl, early this year, and now they are expecting their first child."

Alex did not have to manufacture her enthusiasm; she felt the burden of sorrow for Justin leave her at Allen's words, and the smile she turned on Justin was radiant. "Your wife is a very fortunate woman."

"Though the truth is quite the other way around, I will tell Maddy that I have reliable testimony to her good luck given before a witness," Justin replied, and then he added, "She is very like Samantha in some ways—she is full of life and capable besides—but she is not a substitute for Samantha. Maddy is very much her own woman, and I love her for that."

"Sam will be happy for you."

"I know she will," he said, and then he took his leave of them so that the old friends could talk.

Alex watched him walk away. "I hope my son never forgets that Sam gave up a very special man for his sake."

"One thing has nothing to do with the other," Allen insisted gently. "Morgan and Sam belong together, no matter what problems they may have in future. Anyone who came between them was bound to suffer for it."

Alex knew he was speaking as much about herself and Rane as he was about Morgan and Sam, and she thought how gracious in spirit Allen was to have remained such a true friend after she had refused his offer of marriage. He was, at fifty, a trim figure of a man with a sense of humor and humanity that ran deep, but despite his sterling qualities, Alex had never felt the slightest passion for him. It was no lack on Allen's part; it was because Rane had filled her life for a very long time.

They talked about a variety of subjects, including the health and breeding record of Magic Swan.

Magic was a topic Alex didn't really want to think about and yet could not ignore. Of all the horses she had sold, Magic remained the one she missed most of all. She knew he had a good home at Allen's Windower plantation, and despite the setbacks in the racing world, fine mares were brought to Magic every year. But she could still hear his plaintive cry as he was led away.

Allen was lavish in his praise of the seventeen-year-old stallion, but there was an odd light in his eyes as he talked, and it worried Alex.

"Are you sure he is all right?" she asked anxiously.

"Of course he is," Allen exclaimed. "I wouldn't dare lie to you about him!"

She had to believe his fervor, and she reminded herself that the one time she had seen Magic at Windower since the sale, the stallion had been in fine condition. But it had not been easy to see him and leave him. She could have sworn Magic remembered her and that there was sorrow in the big dark eyes as she left him—a silly notion.

"I've heard some very good things about your Irishman," Allen said, changing the subject. "So good, in fact, that I may try to steal him away from you. I thought I ought to warn you."

"You can try, and you may succeed if you offer him the job of head trainer, but I don't think so."

"Don't tell me—you've given him some potion that makes it impossible for him to hear offers from other stables."

Heads turned at Alex's merry peal of laughter caused by Allen's exaggerated expression of dismay. "It's nothing I've done; it's the horses. He's got the eye for them, and he knows how good my animals are." She tried not to sound too smug.

"Well, if he knows that, I don't think I'll bother to make a fool of myself," Allen said gloomily.

"No, please do make your offer," Alex said, suddenly serious. "It's difficult to explain. He's a complicated man, proud and yet with doubts about himself. If you wouldn't mind, I would like him to know, even at the risk of losing him, that some other stable would be willing to pay for his talent."

Allen threw up his hands in surrender. "No wonder I can't steal your employees. I can offer them good pay and good living quarters, but I can't mother them. However, for your sake, I will humiliate myself by allowing the Irishman to reject my generous offer."

"You are a prince among men," Alex said, and the lavish praise was more in truth than jest.

She did not ask Padraic about the job offer, and he did not volunteer any information, but on the journey home, he was much more relaxed and confident than when they had set out. He was even easy enough with the company to offer Irish ballads to help pass the time.

As beautiful Kitty one morning was tripping,
With a pitcher of milk from the fair of Coleraine,
When she saw me she stumbled, the pitcher it tumbled,
And all the sweet butter water'd the plain.
"Oh, what shall I do now? 'Twas looking at you now!
Sure, sure, such a pitcher I'll ne'er meet again!
'Twas the pride of my dairy; O Barney McCleary,
You're sent as a plague to the girls of Coleraine.

As Alex listened to his lovely tenor voice singing the song with just the right note of mischief, she thought of what a waste it was for a man as gifted as Padraic Joyce to be so full of bitterness about the unchangeable circumstance of his birth. And she hoped that, with time, Wild Swan would lighten the darkness in his soul.

Chapter

16

Alex had hoped that the Christmas festivities at Wild Swan would be joyful enough to offset the presence of Piety. The Falconers, Carringtons, and Jenningses had every reason to celebrate. Children and grandchildren were all healthy; the various businesses were doing well; and the *Liza Gwen* had returned from China, out and back in record time. The cargo of tea, silk, and other exotic goods, available just before Christmas, had sold immediately.

The house was filled to overflowing, and the conversation was lively. There was speculation about what Mr. Morse's new telegraph would mean and a sense of pride because the first message had been sent from Washington, D.C., to Baltimore. The first American edition of Alexandre Dumas's *The Three Musketeers* and a book written the previous year but only now growing popular, *A Christmas Carol*, by the English writer, Mr. Dickens, were given approval, though Virgil pointed out that after the spiteful things Dickens had written about Americans after his visit in 1842, it was a wonder he was still published in America at all. The recent election of James K. Polk and the summer signing of a treaty at Canton establishing the status of Americans in China were discussed, as well as the continuing work of England and the United States to agree on the border between the United States and Canada without resorting to battle. The Polk election slogan had been "Fifty-Four Forty or Fight," referring to the Oregon border and demanding that it be set at 54° 40', though the English wanted it further south. There was general agreement that, though Texas was independent, it should not be annexed as a territory without the approval of the Mexican government.

General agreement except for Piety. Her malignant spirit settled in their midst, waiting to unravel the harmony and joy of the occasion.

"Why should those ignorant Papists have anything to say about what our government does?" Piety sniffed, having already declared that foreign novels, indeed novels of any sort, were evil and that trade with the heathen Chinese could bring nothing but disaster to those who engaged in it.

The rest of the family had been doing their best to ignore her, but it was hard going.

"Piety, one very practical reason to ask Mexico is that she might take enough offense to fight back with guns," Blaine pointed out reasonably.

Piety bristled even more. "Surely you don't think those decadent people could fight against our soldiers!"

"I do," Blaine returned.

But Sam had had enough. Though her sons were very young, any thought of war struck at her heart. "Tell me, Piety, did you join in the riots against the Catholics, the Papists as you say, in Philadelphia? It must be a terrible trial to you to know how many people of different beliefs reside in your own city."

Everyone, even Morgan, froze at the slow venom dripping from Sam's voice, and Piety was as taken aback as the rest of them, obviously unaccustomed to being challenged with her own weapons. She rose from her seat at the table and checked, waiting for Nigel to exit with her.

"You go on," Nigel said quietly. "I'll join you later." Only his eyes betrayed what this piece of defiance cost him.

Piety gaped at him and flounced out of the room.

Sam broke the silence that followed Piety's exit. "I am sorry for your sake, Nigel," she muttered, "but not for any other. Your wife is a most unpleasant woman."

Nigel had nothing to say to this, and the general chatter resumed, but it was nervous and lacked heart.

Alex waylaid Nigel before he went up to the room he shared with his wife.

"I thought it might work with so many of us gathered, but I was wrong. I am sorry. I know it is making everything more difficult for you. But I am glad to have a little time with my granddaughter." That much was true, though she hated the way Piety treated the child, demanding rigid behavior no two-year-old could possibly manage. Alex feared for the future of her granddaughter, but she was heartened by the streak of defiance that showed now and again. Young as she was, Gincie had a sense of herself and did not like being too harshly suppressed. It was harder to witness the baffled sorrow that sometimes pulled the little mouth down and made the eyes too big in her small face when she looked for approval from her mother and did not receive it. And it was hardly reassuring to see what lifeless puppets Piety had made of her sons. They kept themselves aloof from the other children at Wild Swan and did not seem to know how to play. Praying aloud with their mother seemed to be all they knew well.

"It may seem otherwise, but I am not sorry we came," Nigel said. "I want Gincie to know what a happy family is like. I want her to know you and Wild Swan." He paused, and when he continued, his voice was low and weary. "I do not like the way Piety behaves. I don't like her lack of charity and humor. I don't approve of what she believes, of her self-righteousness. But added to that long list is the fact that I pity her. Her parents raised her to believe God would descend at any moment to smite the wicked and save the few. It is so deeply ingrained in her, she cannot escape from it nor see the full horror of such a belief."

Alex drew his head down and kissed him on the forehead in benediction and watched him walk away. That Nigel pitied his wife gave Piety a terrible hold over him; that Nigel's tender heart should be the destruction of him seemed profoundly unjust.

"She is worse than my mother was," Alex told Rane as they lay together in the shared warmth of their bodies. "I never thought I would say that of anyone, but Piety is so single-minded in her dedication to making sure no corner of joy escapes her crushing spirit. At least my mother could be distracted with luxuries that allowed her to pamper herself. I'd like to pour a good bottle of French brandy down Piety's throat or suffocate her in a length of velvet, just to see if there would be change."

Her humor was too grim for laughter, and Rane was no more capable than she of making light of the situation. "Claire at least had an excuse. She was mad. But there is an awful sanity in Piety; she knows quite well what she is doing. Perhaps it will go easier now that Sam has taken a stand. This is a strong family. If Piety pushes too hard, she is going to be pushed in turn."

It was a measure of his distress over Piety's behavior that he would mention Claire, and Alex hoped desperately that he was correct in predicting Piety would be less aggressive.

It was a short-lived hope. Piety's first victim the next day was Caleb. "Though there are many precedents for it in the Bible, still it must present certain problems to be married to a woman so much younger than yourself," she remarked, as casually as if she were commenting on the weather. "But I'm sure your years of experience allow you to guide Flora."

Caleb was suddenly very much a Jennings, with years of wealth and social prominence behind him. "I do not guide my wife. I love her, and to my eternal gratitude, she loves me. It is enough for both of us."

Flora was not so restrained. She looked as if she wanted to throttle Piety, but instead she chose to taunt her on her own ground. "So you enjoy the love stories in the Bible. I believe Boaz was some years older than Ruth:

> And it came to pass at midnight that the man was afraid
> and turned himself; and, behold, a woman lay at his feet.
> And he said, Who art thou? and she answered, I am
>   Ruth, thine
> handmaid; spread therefore thy skirt over thine
> handmaid; for thou art a near kinsman.
> And he said, Blessed be thou of the Lord, my daughter;
> for thou hast shewed more kindness in the latter end
>   than
> at the beginning, inasmuch as thou followedst not
> young men, whether poor or rich."

Despite her anger, Flora's voice was melodious as she quoted the story, and still letter perfect, she went on.

"Or perhaps the Song of Solomon is more to your taste?:

> Thy two breasts are like two young roes that are twins
> which feed among the lilies . . .
> Thy lips, O my spouse, drop as the honeycomb; honey
> and milk are under thy tongue; and the smell of thy
> garden is like the smell of Lebanon . . ."

She spoke the words softly as if to Caleb alone, but her bright blue eyes watched the blood mount in Piety's face.

"Sister-in-law, you would be wise to remember that you have fallen into a den of lions, not a flock of sheep, and you are no Daniel. The only thing staying us is our love for Nigel." Flora still did not raise her voice, but the threat was all the more powerful for the quietness.

Alex was relieved that Nigel was not present to witness this latest clash, and that she herself had not entered the fray; Flora had done very well on her own. Piety blinked rapidly and shifted uncomfortably in her chair, taking new stock of this adversary.

Finally she murmured, "Evil-doers can twist the words of God."

"Indeed they can," Flora retorted. "You seem to have more than a little experience in that direction."

Piety subsided, unwilling to duel any longer with Flora's clever tongue.

Caleb caught Alex's eyes, and they shared the unspoken thought—pride in Flora, but also a sense of incredulous despair because Nigel had to live with this woman whom the rest of them could not easily tolerate for even a limited time.

Like a contagion, Piety seemed to be everywhere at once. Quelled at one point, she erupted at another. From the first time she heard Padraic's brogue, she embarked on a series of lectures about the dangers of the Irish Catholics being allowed into the country. It did no good to point out that whatever Padraic's religion was, he had made no point of it, and it was his own business. To Piety, religion was the only business.

Rather than showing any anger, however, Padraic countered Piety's hostility by casting soulful looks her way every time he had the chance, and he embroidered the performance by singing, very low, an endless variety of questionable songs. Della, who had heard some of them and had an account of others from Samson, could hardly contain her mirth as she told Alex.

"I never knew there were so many lewd verses in the world!" She wiped tears of laughter from her eyes.

But Piety herself was not amusing. Thwarted at every point by the adults at Wild Swan, she turned her malevolence on the children, constantly carping at her sons and her daughter to sit up straight, wash their hands, be quiet, and a host of other commands, most often needless, because the children were usually subdued in her presence and leery of the quick slaps she administered to hands and bottoms. Nigel did his best to run interference for them, but he could not watch his wife every minute.

Alex was not surprised at her own restraint; she was well aware of the enormous fury building inside of her and the necessity of controlling it. She didn't think she could find a middle ground. She felt physically violent toward the woman. In her mind's eye she could see herself wrapping her hands around Piety's neck and not letting go until the last pulse was stilled.

She was not alone; she knew her daughters and daughters-in-law shared the same impulses. And Philly added, "I wouldn't leave my girls alone with her for all the tea in China." Alex noticed that the Jennings grandchildren were also kept out of Piety's way by their watchful parents.

In spite of their efforts to gain control of Piety, by Christmas Eve she had effectively destroyed the perfect ease they had all hoped to enjoy for the holiday. Everyone was on edge from wondering what Piety would do next; at the same time, they were trying to make the most of the gathering.

Though the children had been fed most of their meals apart from the adults, on Christmas Eve all the generations were together for supper, table space supplemented by trestles with boards laid over them, those in turn covered with linen to disguise the rough arrangements. Alastair Cameron had joined them, and Mavis and Timothy were there too; but, adhering to their old ways, the Bateses had politely refused to sit down with the family and preferred to be in the kitchen with Della and the rest of the staff.

"Virginia, wipe your mouth!" Piety's voice hissed through the babble of sound.

Gincie was seated in a special chair, one of several that had been lovingly made by Samson over the years so that the smallest children could, when the occasion called for it, eat with the adults at the dining table. The little girl had been enjoying herself until her mother interrupted her. Her blond-brown curls were tousled around her face and a smear of berry preserves decorated her chin. At the command, she turned her head to look at her mother, who was separated from her by one of Gincie's stepbrothers. And then she looked back at the bit of bread and jam still clutched in her hand. She was clearly puzzled by the logistics of wiping her mouth while still eating, and, deciding that finishing the treat was the better course, she popped the bread into her mouth.

Without hesitating, Piety reached past her son and slapped Gincie across the mouth, causing the child to sputter and choke as her eyes filled with tears.

All hell broke loose. Nigel, who had been sitting further down the table, shot out of his chair, but Alex beat him to Gincie, lifting the little girl out of her chair and holding her close, patting her back and coaxing her to drink a little water to help the bread go down. There were frightened whimpers from some of the other children. Even Horace Whittleby, who seldom showed his emotions, looked utterly horrified by Piety's casual violence.

"By God, there's an end to it!" Rane's voice roared over the assembly, silencing everyone. With the grace of a stalking beast, he moved to loom over Piety so that she had to crane her neck to see his face. "You will not so much as touch your children or anyone else's while you are here. Others far better qualified than you will tend to their needs. You will keep your wicked tongue to yourself. There will be no more of your shrewish utterances, not one word more! And you will not leave Wild Swan until Nigel is ready to go; he will keep Christmas with us. Disobey me and I will horsewhip you within an inch of your life. No one here would lift a finger to help you."

He was trembling with his rage, and Alex understood then that he had not interfered before because he shared her fear that he would do harm to Piety; he looked fully capable of killing her in front of everyone right now.

It seemed Piety had finally been vanquished. She looked terrified. Wrenching her gaze away from the hypnotic power of Rane's, she darted her eyes about the room as if seeking aid, and finding none—even her sons stared resolutely at their plates rather than at her—she bowed her head and sat absolutely still until Rane moved away from her. Then she bolted from the room, her chair toppling over behind her.

Blaine moved to Nigel's side and put a comforting hand on his arm. "I think you could use another glass of wine. Mother will take care of Gincie."

Nigel nodded dazedly, but before he accepted Blaine's offer, he went to Rane. "Thank you, Father," he said.

Rane, having suffered Claire's excesses for so many years, understood only too well the private hell of Nigel's life as well as the public humiliations. And he felt helpless because he could offer nothing more than his love. He couldn't find easy words. Briefly he gripped Nigel's shoulder, letting the warmth of his touch communicate his affection.

Alex was only marginally aware of what was going on around her. All her energy was concentrated on reassuring Gincie. "It's all right, it's all right now. You didn't do anything bad. I love you very much. There, sweetheart, there." She held the shivering child in her lap, stroking her hair and rubbing her back.

Finally the little girl shifted in Alex's hold and peered up at her. "I Gincie," she said in response to her mother calling her Virginia, though her lower lip still trembled. Her face was tear- and jam-stained, but she was so resolute that Alex felt her heart contract with a searing stab of love. She wanted to cherish this child forever, keep her safe from her mother's habitual cruelty. To accomplish that, she resolved she would even put up with Piety's presence at Wild Swan.

Determined not to let Piety's poison spread further, they went ahead with the Christmas Eve celebration, exchanging gifts and singing old carols. Alex was glad Nigel stayed with them instead of going to his wife. And he took special care to show his love for his daughter, who, worn out from the emotional upheaval, fell asleep in his arms before the evening was over.

Rane gave Alex a shimmering length of creamy silk embroidered with a rainbow of exotic birds and butterflies, and she was entranced by the gift, running her fingers over the work in awe at its intricacy.

"Is that all you think I got for you?" Rane asked, an odd light in his eye.

Alex regarded him in puzzlement. "It is a gift fit for an empress. My love has always been generous with me." She touched the golden swan necklace at her throat. "He gave this to me when he was scarcely more than a boy and I was a green, green girl."

Rane shook his head to dispel the illusion that they were alone when in truth they were surrounded by the family and friends. "You bewitch me," he murmured. "But I have some magic of my own for you. Come with me." He put out his hand and she took it.

He stopped only long enough for her to don a warm cloak against the chill of the winter night, and then he led her to the stallion barn. She went with him willingly, but she had no idea what he had to show her. Her confusion increased when she found that Samson and Padraic were waiting there with lanterns, both men looking inordinately pleased.

The graceful black head and neck stretched over the stall door, and the stallion whickered low in greeting.

"Happy Christmas, sweetling," Rane said.

Alex stood still, not believing the sight before her. And then she called, "Magic?" as if she expected him to vanish before her eyes.

Magic Swan blew softly and stretched his neck further, proving himself very real indeed.

Alex threw her arms around his neck and rubbed her cheek against his sleek coat. "Magic, beautiful boy, you're home!"

Six years before she had sold him, and she had never in her wildest dreams expected to have him back at the farm. She would not have asked Allen Ralston to sell Magic back to her; she had made a bargain, and as far as she was concerned, that had been an end to it. Now she understood the unease Allen had displayed when they had discussed the Thoroughbred. It must have been hard to keep the secret.

She left Magic to hug Rane in turn, ignoring their audience who slipped away unnoticed, having seen everything they wished in the blaze of joy on Alex's face.

"How did you persuade Allen? How did you think of this? Oh, he is a perfect gift. How . . ."

"One question at a time, and this first of all," Rane laughingly protested and kissed her.

"Actually, Allen Ralston is a very kind man, though I've not always been willing to concede that since he had the audacity to fall in love with you. Even though he bought Magic fairly, he's never felt wholly right about it. He knows how special this animal is to you. He also knew he could never persuade you directly to take the stallion back. I think he was rather relieved when I offered to buy Magic back. And don't look so worried; he made a substantial profit on the horse," Rane confessed ruefully.

Alex looked up at him through a blur of tears. Her stable did not need Magic for breeding; there were, given the falling market, enough good studs at Wild Swan to service all the mares brought to the place, a fact Rane knew well. But he had also known how fond she was of the stallion, how many memories were attached to him. And Rane had arranged it so all parties were satisfied. Allen had had six years of stud fees and the prestige of the stallion in his stable; now he had made a good profit on his investment.

"I do love you so much!" she managed shakily. She thought of the Christmas gifts she had given him—books, a new suit of clothes she had had tailored for him in Baltimore, a fine set of drafting tools—they had all seemed worthy, but his purchase of Magic dwarfed them. "I gave you so little," she mumbled.

"Children, grandchildren, a sense of belonging to a family, the salvation of the shipyard, and most of all yourself, not to mention a lordly selection of Christmas gifts—'so little'? I think not." He gave her a little shake and kissed her again.

Only then did she think to ask how he had managed to get Magic into the barn without her knowledge.

He chuckled. "Why do you think Della and everyone else kept you so busy in the house today? You keep such a close eye on your horses, it was a delicate operation even for an old free trader."

She found that most of the family and the people of Wild Swan had been in on the secret; only the smallest children had not been trusted to contain their excitement, and Piety had not been trusted at all.

Alex's obvious delight in the return of Magic went a long way toward restoring everyone's spirits, and allowing them to pretend Piety had not disrupted the evening, but Alex and Rane could hardly wait until everyone had settled down for the night. Filled to the rafters as the house was, they still had privacy in their bedchamber and their own plans for thanking each other. They shared a sigh of relief as the door shut the world out.

Disdaining a robe after she had shed her clothes, Alex draped the embroidered silk around herself and modeled it for Rane, moving with sinuous grace until he unwrapped her from the folds, murmuring, "I like the silk of your skin more than the silk of China."

"You are more like satin, rough satin," she replied, touching the shadowed skin of his cheek. She dropped her hand to the smooth skin of his buttocks. "But here you are silk." Her hand moved again to tangle in the fur of his chest. "And here velvet."

The Chinese silk was left in a brilliant swirl on the floor as Rane drew Alex down on the bed. They savored each other as if for the first and last time. Again and again they brought each other close to release, drawing back each time to prolong the pleasure until they could wait no longer.

Rane lifted Alex over him and brought her down on him, enjoying the abandon of her riding until the last moment when he shifted them both so that she lay under him, and the long spiral of anticipation exploded in a star stream of pleasure.

They were still not asleep but lazily touching each other when the bell rang.

At first Alex could not identify the sound, and then she could not believe it. Except for a few random tones caused by mischievous children, it had never been tolled in all her years at Wild Swan. The children had soon learned that the bell was serious business, and they were never, never to touch it. But its wild metallic notes were in dead earnest now and could only mean the worst disaster—fire.

They tumbled out of bed and into their clothing with little consciousness of what they were doing. Doors were slamming all over the house when they left their room.

Though there was no sign of smoke or flame, it was impossible to tell if the fire was in the house until they were outside, and then it was clear that the alarm was for the stallion barn.

The basic structure was brick, but the stalls, roof, and supporting timbers were of wood, and there was highly flammable straw and hay inside.

It was a scene from hell. A bucket brigade was already forming, but the flames had a head start, their glow lighting the night sky. The screams of the terrified horses rent the air.

Samson, Jed Barlow, and Padraic, swathed in wet horse blankets, were already braving the fire to lead the horses out.

Rane divined Alex's intention before she could break away from him. "No!" he shouted. "Let us do it!"

"They are my horses!" she shrieked. "They know me!" And she wrenched herself out of his grasp.

There was no time to argue further. Rane followed her.

Every adult and the older children seemed to be involved in trying to control the blaze. But the stallions, normally so well mannered, were in a frenzy of terror, and fit and heavily muscled as they were, it took more than one man to handle one horse.

Rane and Alex got Magic out, blindfolding him and wrestling his plunging body every step of the way while the heat of the fire beat at them. Only when they were outside did Alex realize that Morgan had been helping them with Magic.

She looked around frantically and saw the men had Fortune and Oberon out, but there was no sign of Bay Swan, Swan's Chance, or Wild Swan. The rescue teams went back into the inferno, and Bay Swan was saved without injury. But as they were dragging the last two stallions out, their luck failed. The roof beams started to give way, spilling a lethal hail of burning timber. Swan's Chance was struck on the side of his head and jerked up, toppling over and throwing Rane, Morgan, and Alex to the ground. They were up in the instant, not aware of their singed hair and skin, grappling with the thrashing horse until they got him up again and ran him out of the barn.

The horror of the next moments would stay with Alex until the day she died. Screaming in agony, Wild Swan bolted out of the barn, his coat flaming, those who would have helped him helpless in face of his mad race. The stallion was crazed with pain and terror, scattering people in his wake and crashing into fences until he came to a shuddering stop and collapsed on the ground.

Alex knew it was too late even before she reached him and water and blankets were thrown over him. "Get a gun! Someone get a gun!" she screamed, and heedless of the stench of burned hair and flesh, she slipped to the ground and cradled the noble head.

Wild Swan did not struggle in her hold. Mortally injured, he simply lay there, his breath a rasping effort as his lungs filled with fluid.

"My lovely, lovely one. It's all right. You'll sleep, you'll sleep now." The tears poured down her cheeks.

When Rane tried to lift her away, she held on to Swan for a moment more and then let go. The shot rang out in the still darkness of Christmas morning.

The wailing rose from the black throats first, but white voices joined immediately, Padraic's keening a primitive call of rage and grief. It was as if a person had died, a tribute to the importance the stallion had had at the farm and to his singular magnificence.

Rane could see that Alex was close to complete shock; her tears had stopped abruptly, and her eyes had a strange glitter. But when he would have coaxed her into the house, she refused. "Not until everyone's burns are seen to," she said flatly, and the fact that Dr. Cameron and Nigel were already moving to treat the injured did not sway her from her purpose.

She spoke to everyone, thanking each of them for the valiant battle against the fire. As if it were all apart from her, she noted each expression, the men weeping as well as the women. Philly looked tiny cradled against Blaine, and Sam was clinging to Morgan as if afraid the fire would yet claim him. Mavis and Tim looked somehow old and crumpled; the gruesome death of the animal that had sailed across the sea with them from England had particular significance for them. The Barlows were huddled together, and Samson was standing with his arm around Della, his face a mask of hurt for the suffering of Swan, who had so long been in his charge. Nigel's face was sculpted in weariness as if he was too accustomed to seeing sorrow at every turn. Flora, Caleb, Virgil Winslow, and Horace Whittleby were standing together, Horace shaking his head as if he couldn't believe the scene before him. Cassie and Polly had taken charge of the children who had been roused by the noise, and Alex could hear their voices trying to soothe the youngsters. Her glance fell on Piety and noted that the woman looked as dazed as everyone else; apparently her dislike of racehorses and betting had not been enough to cushion the reality of the fire and its aftermath. No one was unmarked by the fire.

Alex, Nigel, and Alastair tended the animals as well as the humans and tried to be thankful that, aside from Swan, there were no other fatalities. None of the humans was seriously hurt, but Swan's Chance had a nasty wound across his right eye where the board had hit him. It was too early to be sure, but Alex feared he was going to lose the sight in that eye, if he hadn't already.

There had been no wind to carry the fire, and the temperature had not been low enough to have made getting water difficult. The stallion barn was the sole loss. From within the brick shell, there still came crackling and spitting noises, and little flurries of flame were doused as soon as they appeared.

With a wind or a freezing night, the losses would have been far greater. Alex tried to remind herself of that as she continued to move from one person to the next. And then the ugly and obvious question swam through her brain. How had the fire started? Everyone at Wild Swan was scrupulously careful with any source of fire around the barns; they all knew the dangers of smoldering hay and manure and of dry timbers. She remembered the lanterns Samson and Padraic had held when Rane had taken her to see Magic. She remembered that the lanterns had still been there, hanging on special hooks, and the men had been gone when she and Rane had left the barn. But she knew Samson, knew his meticulous eye to detail. She could not believe he would not have checked the barn once more after she and Rane had left it, particularly because he was as excited as she about the return of Magic. And in any case, the lanterns had been safely secured and should not have caused harm.

In the first faint light of dawn she caught sight of Padraic's face, and her heart twisted within her. He was standing apart staring at the ruins of the barn, and his face was rigidly set.

What did she truly know of him after all? She had thought she understood his inner anger and sorrow, but perhaps she was mistaken. Perhaps he had a streak of destructiveness that made him hit back at those who possessed more than he. Perhaps he had not adjusted to being second trainer. Perhaps above all it was a way to get back at Samson, who so loved the horses.

That stopped her train of thought and turned it around. No matter what else was true or false about the man, he loved fine horseflesh with a passion and tended it with complete devotion. No human quarrel would make him willing to destroy prize-winning animals.

She went to him, noticing he was cradling one burned hand in the other, having sought no help.

"Let me tend your hands," she said. "Burns are easily infected." As gently as she could, she cleansed his hands, applied ointment, and bandaged them lightly. Despite the care she took, she knew she must be causing him extreme pain, but he didn't seem aware of it. The planes of his face did not change, and his eyes burned with a peculiar fire, as if the flames of the night had settled there.

"You must not try to do any work until these are fully healed. Samson has a burn on his arm, but his hands are all right and Jed's and some of the others as well. They can do the work for those of you with injured hands."

His head shifted until he was gazing directly at her. He studied her closely, and then he said, "I don't know why on earth you'd be believin' me over one a' yer own, but the fire was no accident. T'was the bitch married ta yer youngest son. I don't care much fer Christmas—too many memories, good and bad. I was out in the night when I saw her. She was carryin' a lamp, one from the house, I'd wager. It is certain it was her. I followed her toward the house, wonderin' what she was about. I should've gone back the way she'd come instead. I hadn't seen her come out a' any a' the barns, but after she stole back inta the house, I looked back and saw the fire. I rang the bell, but t'was already too late. Too late fer that great foine stallion. T'would a' been better had the hag herself burnt."

Not for an instant did she doubt his account. She could see the truth in his eyes, could feel it radiating from his inner rage at what Piety had done.

Her own fury was so overpowering, she swayed on her feet as her mind replayed the sight of Piety on the outskirts of the fire fighters, Piety's dazed expression. Piety had set the fire but had not faced, even in her own mind, how dreadful it would be. All she had known was that it was a way to strike at the heart of Wild Swan, where she had been chastised for her behavior.

Padraic gripped her arm to steady her, fearing that she would faint. "I'll kill her fer you, I will. She's not fit ta live!" he said.

"No, she is not. Nor is she worth your life or mine." She was steady again, filled with purpose that blocked out all else.

Padraic resisted the impulse to retreat from the feral gleam in her eyes.

"I don't want you to tell anyone else what you saw, but I want you to write it down exactly as you remember it. I want to know I can count on you to swear to it. Will you do that?"

He nodded, though he still did not understand.

"If my husband or Samson finds out before Piety is gone from here, I would not trust what either of the men might do. I want my granddaughter, and blackmail will do nicely to take her away from Piety. Let Piety wonder who saw her, man or woman, one of the family, or one of the workers. Let her understand that she could be charged with arson at any moment."

"Yer son?" Padraic asked softly. He had seen how the man adored his little girl and had felt sorry for him for being cursed with such a shrew for a wife.

"What you cannot protect, you cannot keep. My son cannot be with his daughter enough to shield her from her mother. He has forfeited his rights as father to the child." Her voice was implacable.

She made it a point to go on speaking to one person after the other before she confronted Piety, making sure the woman could not ascertain that the witness was the Irishman. And the whole time she kept track of Piety, seeing that though she was offering no assistance to anyone, she was watching the scene avidly, her expression looking more self-satisfied by the minute. If she had had any remorse earlier, it had passed.

The sun kept rising, casting stark winter light on the smoldering barn, on the lifeless carcass of Swan, on the cold, soot-grimed faces of the people.

Alex glided toward Piety with sure steps, nothing showing on her face to betray her inner turmoil.

"A life for a life. That is what I want. Gincie is the price for my silence." Deliberately she used the little girl's name for herself. "Arson is punishable under the law. I have a witness to your stealth, to your crime. A reliable witness. He or she, I will not tell you which, will swear to your action. You have a choice. My silence, the silence of the witness, for Gincie, or I will bring charges."

"You wouldn't! The scandal—" In her shock at being accused, Piety did not immediately deny that she had started the fire. She recognized her mistake, but it was too late and her attempts to rectify it were futile. "I didn't—you can't prove—"

"You did, and I can prove it," Alex insisted relentlessly. "Don't waste my time or yours in lying. And never think that the threat of scandal will stay my hand. My family and I have weathered a good deal of it before; a little more will not finish us."

Piety's eyes darted frantically around the scene before her, seeking to look at anything other than her mother-in-law. But inexorably her gaze was pulled back to Alex. "Why? Why do you not just betray me? You might well take Virginia from me that way."

"Because someday Gincie will want to know about her mother, and I do not want to tell her that she was a convicted felon. If there is no other course, I will tell her, but I would prefer not. If you stand trial, it will be in the newspapers, and someday someone will mention it to Gincie." Alex let the truth beat at Piety, and she could almost see the woman's inner thoughts—the public humiliation of being in the dock.

"There are many who believe as I do that gambling is evil," Piety pointed out feebly.

"There are many more who love these horses and racing as much as I do," Alex retorted. "And they will see you, as I do, as a murderess. Wild Swan raced the wind in his day, and he sired a legion of fine horses. He was only twenty-four years old and in the prime of health. He could have sired many more champions in the coming years. Instead, you sentenced him to an agonizing death because you are a cruel, evil woman." Her voice trembled only slightly; the full grief of Swan's death was held at bay. "You are cruel to your children, to your husband, to everyone around you, and that could be easily proved. It might even be decided that you belong in a madhouse." She gloried in the growing fear in Piety's eyes.

"Nigel? What of him?" The words were hardly audible.

"I will not tell him what you did," Alex stated flatly, "though I cannot promise he will not know by his own intelligence. He will miss having Gincie in his home, but he will know she is safe from you. He may come and visit his daughter any time he so desires; you are never to come here again. You will sign a document to make this legal. Dr. Cameron will witness it. Choose, Piety, choose now, or I will proclaim your guilt and let come what may!"

The fear in Piety was full-blown now, but so was the twisting craft of her mind, and Alex watched its emergence with disgust.

Piety did not want her daughter except as a weapon against her husband and his family, and now that that weapon was blunted by what she had done, the worst that would befall her if she gave up the child was to be free of the burden. Free of the little green-eyed girl who looked too much like the woman who was accusing her now. And Nigel would mourn. Weak Nigel, who yet had the strength to keep close ties with this sinful family who felt themselves so superior to her. Even without her daughter binding him to her, she doubted he would divorce her, but she considered that eventuality, too. It was better than prison or a madhouse. And if he dared it, she would make sure he paid a high price. She suspected his mother would be willing to pay a good sum to ease the proceedings for divorce. In spite of Alex's iron self-control, Piety could feel the hatred seething inside of her, a hatred to match her own, and she thought how sweet it would be to bend it to her profit.

The two women stared at each other for a long moment. Then Piety said, "I will sign. Virginia is yours."

Chapter

17

Busy as a spider, Alex swiftly wove a tissue of half-lies and half-truths. She was aided by the numbing shock of everyone around her; she was the only one moving with single-minded purpose.

Rane had a burn on his forearm. Though he tried to ignore it, the throbbing set his teeth on edge. And it made him conscious that the ugly mark on the tender skin of Alex's neck must be just as sensitive, though she hardly seemed to know it was there. Every time he thought of her going into the burning barn, his stomach clenched. But Alex seemed to have no feeling about the danger all of them had been in, no lingering grief about Wild Swan or Swan's Chance, who had probably lost the sight in his right eye.

Rane was not fooled. He knew that Alex was up to something, concentrating her energies on whatever it was, and he knew that the toll of the fire would catch up with her. He waited, prepared to be there for her when she needed him. But when she told him that Gincie would stay on with them for a while after her parents returned to Philadelphia, he was taken completely by surprise.

"Of course I am glad for it, but I don't understand. However did you persuade that harridan to agree?"

"Piety doesn't love her daughter."

"No, but she knows you do, and I should think that would be enough to make her reluctant to leave the child with you for even a short time."

Not for a short time, forever, she thought, acknowledging to herself that Rane should have been party to the plan. But that could not be, not yet. "Don't think about it. Just be happy that Gincie will be with us," she said, trying unsuccessfully to keep the sharpness out of her voice.

Rane eyed her speculatively, but he did not press her further. It made sense that Nigel had, for his mother's sake, somehow prevailed on his wife with regard to the child, and that the prospect of having the little girl with them was what was keeping Alex from dwelling too deeply on the fire. It made sense, but he still felt as if a vital piece was missing. Alex was hiding something. Not for the first time, he wished that she did not try to carry so much on her own shoulders.

Far from playing the role Rane suspected, Nigel was the victim of the piece.

Granted the complicity she demanded from Piety, Alex had told Nigel that she and his wife had decided that it would be better for Gincie to live at Wild Swan for a while, as Piety found it hard to cope with her active daughter as well as her sons. She could not bring herself to tell him that the arrangement was to be permanent, and the startled look of pain that crossed his face when he first heard his daughter was not going home with him nearly undid Alex. She stiffened her resolve by picturing, in perfect detail, Piety's hand slashing across Gincie's face.

Nigel had no defense; he had witnessed too much of Piety's harshness, and despite his own loss, he could easily imagine Gincie growing sure and happy at Wild Swan. But he could not imagine his wife giving her permission.

When he pressed for more details about how she had persuaded Piety to agree to the plan, for an intolerably long space Alex fought the desire to tell him the truth. It was the obvious, seemingly easy way to end his marriage once and for all. And she couldn't do it.

"Deep down, Piety is a mother concerned for the welfare of her child." The lie nearly choked her, but she managed it.

Nigel searched his mother's face, but Alex kept her gaze steady on his. And she saw it, a flicker of horrified comprehension quickly denied. She wondered if he had known that Piety was absent from their bedroom when the fire started or if the trigger was more fundamental than that—the basic knowledge that only some sort of dire force would have persuaded Piety to leave Gincie at Wild Swan.

Nigel did not ask the question. And two days after the fire, he, his wife, and his stepsons left without Gincie.

"Gincie will miss you very much," Alex said to Nigel in parting. "I will make sure she does not forget you, but you must come to see her as often as you can." She hoped he would think of her words and come gradually to realize that Gincie was to be at Wild Swan for a long time and his life must adjust to include coming here to see her—unless he divorced Piety and made a new beginning with his daughter.

Work was begun immediately on rebuilding the stallion barn, there were chores aplenty for everyone, and Alex had the added job of trying to make Gincie's adjustment as painless as possible. The child was confused and frightened by the absence of her parents, even though she was surrounded by love on all sides. It was particularly hard to hear her sobbing for her "mama" who had treated her with so little kindness. She alternated between screaming tantrums and withdrawn silences, with brief periods of distracted pleasure in games or songs. And she clung fiercely to her grandmother, having decided that Alex was the most stable presence in this new and uncertain world.

Nigel's brothers, sisters, and sisters-in-law were all relieved that Gincie was out of her mother's clutches. Whatever speculation there was among them about the change, they kept it to themselves. Though Caleb's children and grandchildren had returned to Baltimore, and the Bateses and Dr. Cameron to Annapolis, the rest of the family, including Virgil Winslow, planned to remain at Wild Swan through New Year's Eve, and Alex was glad of the distraction they provided. In addition, Gweneth, with her boundless love for small children, had easily added Gincie to her list of charges. Though Gincie was reluctant to accept the substitute for too long, Gwenny's help allowed Alex to devote some time to other matters.

Alex was grateful that the demands gave her little time to think. The horrors of the fire, the screams of Swan, and the knowledge that Piety had deliberately caused the disaster, were gathered like dark clouds in the corner of her mind, waiting to roll over her consciousness the instant she ceased to hold them back.

Everyone did his best to feel festive on New Year's Eve, but it was a subdued evening at best, haunted by the events of the previous week. And the only outside guests—Dr. Cameron and the Bateses—were under the same cloud.

For the sake of the children, they had instituted the wassailing of the apple trees on New Year's Eve, a custom Alex had first encountered with Rane's family in Devon, though at Wild Swan they stretched the rules a bit and trooped out to the orchard long before midnight.

They hung little cakes on the trees, poured cider around the bases of them and sang:

> Here's to thee, old apple-tree
> Whence thou may'st bud and whence thou may'st blow
> And whence thou may'st bear apples enow!
> Hats full! Caps full!
> Bushel-bushel-sacks full
> And my pockets full too! Huzza!

Rane heard Alex's voice trail away beside him, and glancing at her, he saw her tears catching moonlight. Holding Gincie as he was, there was little he could do. But Alex felt his gaze.

"I'm all right," she whispered, though her unsteady voice belied the claim.

New Year's Eve was always a nostalgic time, but this night Alex found it particularly hard to control her emotions. Past and present seemed to rush in on her at such dizzying speed, everything was reduced to brightly colored pieces tumbling about in a child's kaleidoscope. St. John seemed at once very close and very far away, as did the lost children. And Swan was at the same time a newly born colt, with all the promise of races to come, and a heap of burned flesh.

Alex dug her fingernails into the palms of her hands and willed her mind to stop its mad tumble. And she managed to maintain a calm facade until toasts had been made to the new year and she was alone with Rane. Even then, she might have gone on with the pretense had he not been so tender.

"Now are you going to tell me what it is that has tried you so sorely?" he asked softly, drawing her into his arms. "I know it is something beyond the fire. I am not only here for the good times, you know. I married you for the bad as well."

"Swan," she gulped. "I cannot believe he is truly gone. It is different than it was with Leda and Mabbie. They were old and frail when they died, and they died peacefully." As the mares had been a year apart in age, so had they died. There had been no violence in either death, and though she had been sad, Alex had, having lost St. John's faithful gelding Sir Arthur in the same way, seen the approach of the end in both cases and had been prepared.

Rane held her, waiting, knowing there was more to it than this.

"Gincie is not here just for a visit. She is here for us to raise unless Nigel leaves Piety. I traded for her. I traded freedom from prosecution for her." She could feel the coiled stillness of Rane's waiting. She was no longer making the choice of what to tell him and what not; the words poured out.

"Piety set the fire. She did it on purpose. Padraic saw her. I made her sign a paper giving us custody of Gincie. I made her promise she would never come here again. Alastair knows; he served as witness."

Rane fought the blinding rage that filled his veins so instantaneously, he felt as if his heart would burst with it. Rage against Piety and against Alex for acting without him.

He put her away from him, and his eyes were green glass as he glared at her. "How could you do that without consulting me? How could you? We now have another child not just for a few weeks, but possibly until she is fully grown. And you have let a felon go free. How could you?"

She stared as if hypnotized at the pulsing vein in his neck, at his clenched fists. "Because of this," she whispered, sounding utterly defeated, "because I was afraid you would kill her. God knows I wanted to kill her myself, but I saw a way to get something from her, something I wanted—Gincie. Gincie is more important than putting Piety in jail. And I never want the child to have to bear the stigma of having a convict for her mother."

She looked so forlorn standing before him, remorse began to ease the pound of aggression in Rane's heart. She was completely justified in having thought he might have done grievous harm to Piety. She was completely justified in having shouldered the burden alone for the sake of the child, though he still didn't understand all her reasoning. He did understand, perhaps better than she, that much of what motivated her came from her bitter experience with her own mother.

He opened his arms again, not reaching for her but silently asking that she come to him of her own volition, and he sighed audibly in relief when she nestled against him once more.

"Poor love, you must indeed have feared there would be murder done before Piety left. I am not the only one who would have volunteered for the task had the truth been known. It is a measure of the Irishman's devotion to you that he has shown such restraint. But what of Nigel?"

"I am not sure I did the right thing, but I could not tell him. I wanted to, so that he would cast her off and be free of her forever. But I know our son too well. He is a man of great honor. He does not flinch from responsibility; it is one of the reasons he is such a fine physician. For all the ill she has brought him, Piety is his wife and the mother of his child and of those pathetic little boys. Had she been put on trial, Nigel would have felt obligated to stand by her, to stand against us. And I know he would have taken the blame for the fire and Swan's death on his own shoulders because he brought Piety here, because he did not understand the depth of her destructiveness and hate. His heart would have been torn into too many pieces ever to heal again. And the worst of it is that for all my efforts to protect him, I think he knows. Just for an instant I saw it in his eyes. But he did not ask. My hope is that he will, with Gincie here, come to realize that he needn't stay with Piety any longer." Rane felt the shudder that racked her body before she continued. "If I am wrong, then all I have done is to deepen his misery by depriving him of the joy of his daughter."

Rane moved his hands in slow patterns of reassurance across her back, much as she had comforted Gincie on Christmas Eve. "You did the best you could." In spite of knowing her as he did, he was stunned by the restraint she had shown in not telling Nigel the truth without thought of the subtle consequences. "And no matter how much we both care about Nigel, Gincie is more important right now because she is so defenseless. To have gotten her away from her mother by any stratagem was the most important concern. You will see; before long, she will be as joyful as the rest of our children."

It was his gentle acceptance of responsibility for Gincie that finished Alex's precarious self-control. The few tears she had shed earlier had been but a faint herald of this. She sobbed desolately, not only for her own pain, but for Nigel and for Swan, who had deserved so much better than the fiery death that had claimed him.

Rane held her until the storm was over, and then he put her to bed and lay beside her, considering all she had told him long after she had slipped into exhausted sleep.

She had not mentioned it even obliquely, but it suddenly occurred to him that his chastisement of Piety had certainly been as much to blame for her setting the fire as anything else. Perhaps she would have done it anyway, but he doubted it.

Taking great care not to awaken her, he kissed Alex on the cheek, needing to pay tribute even in the sleeping darkness to the generosity of her spirit.

The guilt he bore for not understanding what Piety was capable of he would bear alone. To tell Alex that he had made the connection would only add to her burden; what he suffered, she suffered, too.

The addition of Gincie to their lives wrought profound changes. Suddenly they were once again in the role of parents to a very young child. It was far different from their relationship with their other grandchildren who, though they enjoyed time with their grandparents, were the responsibility of their parents.

Alex knew she could not go to the races this season. Though Gincie was daily responding more openly to the love offered her, she still needed Alex to center her world.

Rather than forgo the races altogether, Alex sent the horses in Padraic's charge and with full confidence in him, she did not send him to insignificant meetings to test him; she sent him to the Metairie Course in New Orleans for the races at the beginning of April. It was not only that she thought Padraic capable of managing the horses and the men, it was also an extravagant gesture to tell the racing world that in spite of the recent trouble, Wild Swan was still fielding champions.

There had been mares scheduled to be bred to Swan, and Alex had had to notify the owners that this was no longer possible. Alex offered free stud service from one of the other stallions (now including Magic) to those mares booked to Swan if their owners still chose to bring them to the farm. A few had politely declined, but others were amenable to the offer in recognition of the fact that Wild Swan had more than one fine bloodline.

There would have been no way to keep the fire a secret even if Alex had wanted to, and she had no intention of trying. But it was hard not to be able to explain that arson rather than carelessness had caused the blaze. She would not have blamed horse owners for being reluctant to board their precious mares and colts at the farm, a necessary circumstance when the mares were bred to the stallions there. But to her gratification, she found that most of the owners, mindful of the excellent care their stock and their stablehands had received in past years, did not now express doubts about the safety of the facilities.

As a final gallant show, Swan's Chance was sent to New Orleans with the other horses.

Alex had been stunned when both Padraic and Samson pleaded the stallion's case. They admitted they had rigged blinders for him and found that with the vision in his left eye limited to the business before him, he did not seem to notice the lack of sight in his burned right eye.

"He's as fast as ivir he was before," Padraic claimed. "And he has the right ta prove he can still run and win."

"He used to dat blind eye now," Samson said. "He disremember what it be to look wid two eyes."

She was persuaded more by the collaboration between the two men than by their insistence on the horse's continuing talent, and she agreed on the condition that there be no question of racing him if he showed any sign of distress.

There was no problem with a late entry, as she had listed him among her entries before the fire, before Gincie had come to live at Wild Swan, when she had still thought she would take the horses to New Orleans herself.

With the *Liza Gwen* due to sail again and a new ship being built, Rane had to spend most of his time in Baltimore, but Alex stuck to her post at Wild Swan, acting as hostess to visiting horsemen, and preparing for the yearling sale in April.

The sale was something she had instituted in the past few years as racing opportunities diminished. Keeping only those colts she judged would be champions, she had begun to sell the rest on a regular basis. It was a gamble, because more than a few good horses did not show their potential until they were considerably older than a year, and so it was very possible that she would sell a future champion away from her own stable. It was part of what made the sales worthwhile to the horsemen who attended them, always more in number than the few yearlings offered. In addition, the buyers knew that even those colts Alexandria Carrington Falconer chose not to raise herself would, with few exceptior.s, be a cut above those available anywhere else.

Being home for spring provided Alex with a benefit beyond being able to oversee things at the farm; she managed, with the help of her children and their spouses in Baltimore, to plan a special birthday party for Rane, a party that included family and friends. Rane had expected Alex to come into the city for a simple family evening; the huge party at one of the city's finest hotels took him completely by surprise.

Caleb kept Rane late at the shipyard, and then with feigned casualness, though it was closely timed, Blaine and Morgan persuaded their father that it was their right as sons to take him to a favorite tavern for a toast to his birthday.

Rane protested that Alex expected him home on time since he was to be the guest of honor at supper that evening.

"Don't worry about it, Father, you know how it is when Flora and the others haven't seen Mother for a while. They'll have a thousand things to tell her and to ask. They won't miss us for a long while yet," Blaine assured him smoothly.

Morgan's part was to detour them as they left the tavern, which was conveniently close to the hotel, and he performed his role with devilish ease, choosing a stranger at random and waiting until the man had entered the hotel before he exclaimed, "Well, I'll be! I'm sure that was George Ellingby! I wonder what brings him to Baltimore?"

Ellingby, a New Yorker, was one of their chief investors in the new ship, and his name was guaranteed to make Rane tarry for a moment.

"It will only take a moment. Let's go see if it was he," Morgan urged. "And I'm sure Mother wouldn't mind another guest, not when he's such an important client."

The next thing Rane knew, he was being escorted into a room filled with people assembled in his honor. "Silver-tongued confidence men, I won't ever trust either of you again," he muttered to his sons, but in fact he enjoyed the evening, especially dancing with Alex to the music of the orchestra she had hired.

"You are a minx!" he whispered as he guided her in the gliding steps of a waltz.

"Ummm, I know, and such a clever one! Of course, it helped to have the children assist in the plotting." She looked up at him, at his dark hair still only lightly touched with silver at the temples, at his steady green eyes and his weathered face, and she felt the strength radiating from his hard, fit body. "You are fifty years old, and you are more magnificent than I ever thought a man could be."

Rane missed a step and swore softly, "Be careful, wife, too much of that, and I'll disgrace us both." His eyes glowed.

However, in the early hours of the morning when they were finally home, Alex discovered that hers was not the only surprise.

With a smug grin, Rane handed her a letter. It was a confirmation of reservations for rooms at the Astor House in New York City beginning on May 8 and continuing for ten nights.

"We'll be sailing north on your real birthday. Sailing with a discreet crew." He kissed her on the sensitive hollow of her throat, just below the curving gold swans of the necklace. "And we will attend the Peytona-Fashion race in fine style on May tenth."

The significance of their dates in New York had begun to dawn on her even before he confirmed it. Another great North-South match race—she was as aware of it as was most of the country, but she had given up all thought of attending once Gincie had become part of their lives.

"Gincie—I can't leave her," she began, but Rane put a finger to her lips.

"Gincie is perfectly all right at Wild Swan tonight, and she will be fine while we are gone. She has aunts, uncles, and cousins here, and an army of people who love her at the farm, and she is not the same confused child she was at first. She is growing quite secure and independent. You know I would not suggest this trip if I thought it would harm her. But you need to get away for a while, and I need to be with you."

She could not refute his arguments because she knew he was right. And to be overprotective of Gincie would not help the child in the long run.

Suddenly Alex laughed. "I do worry too much about the children. I was worried that Gwenny would be hurt by not being included in your party. She is, after all, almost a young lady and a good deal older than her nieces and nephews. I asked her about it, prepared to allow her to come if it was important. It wasn't. She said, and I quote, 'Oh, no, everyone there will be so old!' She quickly realized that that might not have been the most diplomatic thing to say, but there wasn't any easy way out."

"Your soon-to-be forty-five years and my fifty, that adds up to nearly a century. There are some advantages to age. Think of all the ways we know to please each other now that we did not know in the beginning." He lazily nuzzled her breasts while she stroked his head.

"We can't really count all of those years," Alex pointed out judiciously. "After all, I didn't even meet you until I was thirteen and you were . . . Her voice trailed off as she realized that Rane had fallen sound asleep against her breast. Even when her body shook with barely contained laughter, he did not awaken.

Chapter

18

The days before they left for New York were very busy for Alex. Nigel arrived for a brief visit with his daughter, and in one way it was comforting, in another disquieting. As for the first, he was kind and matter-of-fact with Gincie, who greeted him with both joy and confusion, finding him at once familiar and strange. He did not press her to accept him too wholeheartedly, but rather played the part of a fond uncle. It was an approach precisely calculated to cause the least upset to his daughter without regard to his own cost.

He looked dreadful, more thin and worn than before, but he made no complaint. Alex wondered countless times if she should tell him about Piety's crime, and once again decided she would not. She had made a bargain with the woman, and beyond that, she still did not know what Nigel's reaction would be to the confirmation of what he surely suspected.

It was no comfort when Della commented, "He looks more like his father every time I see him."

Alex doubted that Della was conscious of the fact that the resemblance she was seeing was a similarity between St. John and Nigel when the former had been ill rather than when he had been in full health. Nigel had the same fine-honed look St. John had had in his last months. She reminded herself that there was good reason for Nigel to appear overtaxed, reason beyond his sad life with Piety.

The one area Alex and her son could talk about without strain was the treatment of the sick. And though he still had episodes of despair about patients he could not help, Nigel was content in the practice of medicine, and he and his mother discussed various cases with their old ease. Daily he learned the truth of what she had long since discovered and her grandmother before her—that the worst enemies of the body were poverty, despair, and ignorance, the first with its filth and hunger so often causing the second, while ignorance found victims everywhere.

"It is not," he noted, "that the wealthy cannot feel despair too, but it is far easier to alleviate if the belly isn't cramping as well, and if the mind has some sense, not, unfortunately, a common virtue these days."

They discussed the plethora of patent medicines that crowded the shelves of apothecary shops (or drugstores, as Americans called them), and were advertised in all manner of publications, and here too they were in agreement.

"Most of them are far from harmless," Nigel lamented. "They are full of opium and alcohol. No wonder people feel better when they take them; they are inebriated. But it is quite different when they try to stop dosing themselves. Then too many find themselves as addicted as any wastrel who ever patronized an opium den. Both opium and alcohol are beneficial with proper usage, but these brews are immoderate. And most of the people taking them are women." He shook his head. "Mother, there is so much we don't know about treating women's problems. Too many doctors simply prescribe opiates to cloak the symptoms without curing the cause. And the new simpering modesty some women think required of them aids nothing."

"I have watched it happen, but I am still amazed," Alex told him. "I am amazed that those who are newly rich think they must conform to some odd code of behavior in order to deserve their wealth. The women lace themselves so tightly, they can neither breathe nor move comfortably, and they do little of either for hours at a time, so it is no mystery why they fall ill. Recently I read an article that explained in the loftiest terms why horseback riding was dangerous to the physical well-being of women. In truth, the only thing dangerous about it is falling off, and that applies to men, too. There is far more peril in remaining immobile all day. Yet to become a silly, useless creature is to be desirable to men. Thank God my husband does not subscribe to that idea!"

Nigel smiled at that. "And I must thank the powers that be that most of my practice is among the poor. Though I find some spend too many pennies on Doctor So-and-So's lethal syrup and on cheap whiskey, at least they do not play games of fashion and are more sensible in their lives for all their deprivations."

For a moment, he was transported to the dank and narrow streets where most of his patients resided in Philadelphia. He felt the curious blend of contentment and power that came to him when he was ministering to them. It was not that he overestimated his ability to stay Death's advance; rather, it was a matter of knowing that he was willing and able to plant himself between his patient and the darkness to battle fiercely for the light.

He thought of Meggie Murphy and her infant daughter Mary. They both would have died at the birth had it not been for him. He had fought the long labor and the river of blood for hours until the boundaries between himself, the woman, and the unborn child had slipped away, and they had all become part of the same sacrament.

Meggie's life was hard, with a frail husband who was out of work more often than not, and her own earnings from taking in laundry were pitifully small, and perhaps little Mary would fare no better, but they were alive and joyful, the child's smile the image of her mother's, and Peadar Murphy was profoundly grateful not to have lost them.

Hesitantly, Nigel began to tell his mother about the Murphys, his confidence in the recital growing as he saw his own enthusiasm and interest reflected in her face. And then unbidden and unwelcome rose the image of Piety with her mouth pursed in disapproval of his work with the poor.

As he thought of his wife, the light dimmed in Nigel's eyes, and Alex knew where his mind had gone as clearly as if he had spoken the name of the woman aloud. She thought how terribly unjust it was that this strong, compassionate man her son had become should have such a damaging weakness—Nigel was incapable of dealing with unkindness; he would harm himself before he would risk an unpleasant confrontation with anyone.

Suddenly she remembered a particular incident between Nigel and Morgan. Blaine, Morgan, and Nigel had always gotten along very well, but they had also had their share of squabbles, brief skirmishes for dominance. Nigel had usually been at a disadvantage, not only because he was smaller than his older brothers, but because even then he had been reluctant to argue or indulge in aggression. But one day he had reacted so quickly to a taunt from Morgan that he had managed to punch him in the nose before Morgan had had a chance to defend himself.

Blaine had frankly cheered the event, telling Morgan that it served him right to have a bloody nose for picking on their little brother. But Nigel had been horrified, frozen in place with big tears trickling down his cheeks.

"Oh, come on. Blaine's right, I did deserve it," Morgan had chided Nigel, but Nigel had looked remorseful until the swelling caused by his blow had disappeared.

Yet not even to make Nigel less vulnerable, not even to change Gincie's lot, would Alex change the essential kindness of his nature.

"I am very, very proud of you," she said.

"Thank you," he replied gravely, his eyes betraying how much her praise meant to him. "You are never far from my thoughts when I am treating my patients. I had years to learn that healing is not the violence too many would make of it." He drew a deep breath. "The healing here is exactly what my daughter needs. Gincie is thriving. I will never regret that she is with you."

It was as close as he came to commenting directly about his sad home life. Alex was grateful for his words, but he left her feeling more unsettled than Gincie did. If she had her way, Piety would simply cease to exist. Wryly she admitted to herself that it was a good thing her life was too busy to allow much time for brooding.

Padraic, the other men, and the horses arrived home just before Alex and Rane left for New York.

Wild Swan's entries in the Metairie Course races had done extremely well, particularly Swan's Chance, who was on his way to becoming something of a legend for winning at four miles despite being blind in one eye.

Padraic was flushed with success, but he was also justifiably apprehensive, for he had, without authorization, bought a five-year-old mare with part of the winnings. Lucky Lady was a well-proportioned chestnut out of an American mare by the English import, Glencoe, and she was compatible as an outcross for the stallions of Wild Swan. Padraic had bought her for a reasonable price because she was, as Leda had been all those years ago, lame. She had been raced despite sore ankles after too hard a season, and there was little doubt that the damage to her right foreleg was permanent. She managed well enough at a slow pace, but great speed with a jockey on her back was beyond her now. The man who had sold her had, like many horse owners these days, more need for ready cash than for a lame mare, no matter what her breeding potential.

"I know I overstepped me bounds, and I'll work ta pay fer her meself out a' me wages if you decide ye're not wantin' her fer yer stable." His brogue was broad in his agitation, and his attitude much as it had been after the fight with the stablehand, with a good deal of defiance showing.

What he had done was no small matter. He had made not only an investment, but a bloodline decision without consulting Alex. She thought about it very carefully before she said anything at all. And her first jolt of surprise and anger quickly faded. He had made a good decision; she was as intrigued by the possibilities of the mare as he was. And he had shown the kind of initiative she had hoped to find in an agent.

"Well done, Padraic," she said. "But I leave it to you to explain the new acquisition to Samson."

The Irishman's relief showed in his wide smile. "There'll be no problem with him. Show him a lovely horse, and he's lost. And Lucky Lady, she's a lovely lass indeed. With a name like hers, she was meant fer Wild Swan."

Alex had to admit that with the stallion Fortune already in residence, Lucky Lady did seem a likely addition.

It both touched and saddened her to see how happy Gincie was that Padraic had returned. The Irishman had treated the little girl with great gentleness since the first, as if he had accepted some special responsibility for her because he had witnessed the perfidy of her mother and had something to do with Gincie's change of circumstances.

It was all to Gincie's good, but it was hard to ignore the fact that Padraic was taking a more important and immediate place in the little girl's life than her own father.

Alex knew that Rane was correct in his contention that Gincie would be well cared for in their absence, but it was still difficult to leave her knowing that it would be for more than a few nights.

"I'm sure you are more distressed than she," Rane chided as they boarded the ship in Baltimore. Alex reminded herself that to spoil Rane's enjoyment by fretting about Gincie would serve no good purpose. Having so decided, she found herself relaxing—sleeping far longer than her normal hours and indulging in pleasurable laziness even when she was awake.

"You see, you have corrupted me," she accused Rane, who nodded happily, making no secret of how pleased he was to see her so content.

It was such a peaceful voyage that the bustle of New York came as a shock, though not an unpleasant one. It was just another texture in this special time Rane and Alex were sharing with each other.

They had been at the Union Course, Long Island, for the Fashion-Boston race in 1842, a match many said was the best in the history of racing, in addition to being one of the best attended of the North-South contests. The Southern entry, Boston, by Timoleon, a son of Sir Archy, out of a sister of Tuckahoe, had been the favorite with a great sweep of victories behind him. The rare losses in his career had come not from lack of speed, but from his notoriously bad temper getting so out of hand that he could not be made to concentrate on the race.

But he had met his match in the little chestnut mare Fashion, out of Bonnets o' Blue (the mare who had beaten Magic Swan in the National Colt Stakes in 1830) by Trustee, an imported stallion. On her maternal side, Fashion shared Sir Archy blood with Boston and other great race-horses. But beyond the fame of her inheritance, she was a charmer in her own right. A dainty head and neck and long clean legs gave her a feminine look, and she also possessed a deep chest and well-muscled quarters to give her speed and endurance. She had not been broken until she was three years old, running her first race in the fall of her third year.

Alex had a special place in her heart for the mare. Fashion had, in the fall of her fourth year, run at Baltimore and had defeated Alex's entry in three-mile heats over a slippery course. It was not that Alex ever liked to lose a race, but Fashion was an extraordinary horse, as fine and true as any Alex had seen, and to lose to her was no dishonor. Many judged Fashion to be the greatest mare ever to race in America.

For this match between Peytona and Fashion, Fashion, again the Northern entry, was favored not only by the odds but in the hearts of many. So beloved was she that her likeness or her name appeared on everything from bonnets and gloves to such disparate items as molasses jugs, hotels, and racetracks. Rane presented Alex with a handkerchief painted with the little mare's image before they left for the track.

There had been numerous problems on the day of the Boston-Fashion match three years before. The crowd had been estimated from fifty to seventy thousand, and some people had never arrived at the course at all, due to a breakdown in train service and traffic jams on the road. Though there was a grandstand, the Falconers preferred to travel in a hired carriage and to park it on the infield.

Their foresight proved sensible; what they viewed as a sea of humanity would later be estimated at seventy to ninety thousand people. The South and Fulton ferries and the train service were filled to capacity for hours, and the race started an hour late, due to the time it took the special police force to clear the track.

Though Fashion was still favored by the odds at the start of the race, they had altered somewhat when the contrast between the two mares had been noted. Peytona looked enormous compared to Fashion and was obviously capable of longer strides. Her bloodlines were good—Giantess by Glencoe—and she was two years younger than Fashion. But prior to today, Fashion had been reported very fit, and she was known to be in a class by herself, so the age and structural differences had not been judged so important.

When the two mares appeared, the cheering of the crowd was deafening, and watching the horses, Alex gripped Rane's arm. Fashion, her chestnut coat now so liberally sprinkled with white hairs that she appeared to be a roan, was reacting badly to the noise, showing her fright in nervous starts and head tossing.

Alex craned her neck to see more clearly. She was sure she was not mistaken. Fashion was exhibiting the same kind of behavior Swan Sprite had at the races in Baltimore when she had done so poorly and injured Jed Barlow.

"She oughtn't to be raced today," Alex told Rane. "She's thinking of stallions, not running. No wonder she's distracted by everything that's going on around her."

Alex had no money bet on Fashion; she had decided she was nervous enough about the little mare's race without having money at risk. But the course brought back memories of the wager St. John had made on the Eclipse-Henry match in 1823. He had risked so much of their future without telling her; he had won enough for the first payment on the farm; and he had promised he would never take such a chance again. The course held memories for Rane as well because he and Claire had attended the race with the Carringtons and with Caleb and Pen.

Now, even with no financial stake in the outcome, Alex could feel her anxiety build for Fashion.

It took some time for the officials to make sure the track was clear. Peytona had the pole position. But due to the enormous crush of people, it was impossible to see more than glimpses of the race once the heat had begun. Peytona kept her inside position, and though Fashion tried, in the four miles she never managed to take the lead. Peytona ran like a machine.

The odds changed then, though many still seemed reluctant to bet against Fashion. Again there was a delay while the track was cleared, and then the horses were off again. Outbursts of wild approval marked Fashion's gains on the turns, but when the mares came down the home straight of the final mile, they were neck and neck until Peytona pulled ahead and won the second heat and thus the match. The Southerners roared their victory. This was the fifth of the great three- and four-mile North-South contests, and it was the deciding one, breaking the tie and putting the South ahead.

Despite the excitement of them, Alex had never lost her unease about these North-South races. But there was no denying the pleasure of seeing the best horses in the country race nor of denying the irony of such a spectacle attracting so vast a crowd in a time when racing was fading in so many parts of the country.

"Disappointed?" Rane asked.

"A little," she admitted. "I do think Fashion is wonderful. But Peytona is also a grand horse, and she deserved to win today. In any case, I have realized how nice it is to steal away with just my husband and no one else."

They didn't even mind the slow progress they made leaving the course with thousands of other spectators. Both of them knew how soon the press of their lives would catch up with them again, and they savored every moment. Rane had to attend some meetings of investors in the new ship, but Alex politely declined invitations from the racing fraternity for various dinners and celebrations, and feeling young and carefree, they gave themselves up to the attractions of the city, dining in fine restaurants, attending plays and musical performances, and generally enjoying the busy opulence of New York.

However, one show Alex did not enjoy was that of a minstrel troupe at one of the Bowery theaters. The display of white men, with their hands and face blackened and their mouths ringed in white, cavorting about in exaggerated poses, singing "darkie" songs and telling "darkie" jokes, seemed to her in the worst of taste. And the rigid line of Rane's jaw showed his agreement with her. They left long before the show was over.

"I don't know quite what I expected, but it wasn't that. How could anyone think such a demonstration amusing?" Alex asked in disgusted wonder.

"People are capable of the most appalling bad taste," Rane reminded her. "And perhaps there is something even more serious about laughing over such a spectacle. It does make slavery seem a friendly institution, doesn't it? All those nice blacks singing and dancing just like they do on the plantations. The North is no more ready to deal with the black man than the South is, for all the North claims more and more fervently that the South must abolish slavery."

It was a subject that always chilled them with the knowledge that the fundamental evil of slavery continued to eat away at the fabric of their adopted nation, and the balance of power between slave and free states grew more and more precarious to maintain.

"We can't solve it tonight," Rane pointed out gently, and Alex forced the subject from her mind, conscious of their need to make every moment of their vacation count.

Even with the distractions of the city, their strongest focus was on each other. They made voluptuous love to each other whenever they pleased without fear of interruption, their hotel suite becoming a secluded bower. And at those times, Alex felt more completely herself than she had in a long while. She was not then someone's mother or grandmother, but just Alex with the man she loved.

They continued to savor each other's company all the way back to Baltimore, and the glow lingered for days after that. Alex even felt a vicarious delight when she heard the news that on May 28, at Camden, New Jersey, Fashion had beaten Peytona for the $1000 Jockey Club Purse. It did not quite make up for the defeat at the Union Course, but it was close enough. The only sad note was that Peytona had shown ill effects from the big match that had hampered her at Camden and might keep her out of top form for some time. To glean every advantage, she had been fitted with very light plates for the big match, and the track had been hard and dry, particularly in the pole position she had held in the first heat. As a result, she had developed sore front feet and ankles. Alex knew that, had the mare been hers, she would not have been raced in such light shoes in the first place and would never have been required to run in pain.

And then Rane and horses and races and everything else ceased to have any meaning for Alex.

Nigel was dead. The messenger who came to Wild Swan swore it was so, though it took Alex an interminably long moment to believe it. And then it was as if all the light and joy that had ever been in her life with Rane or since the day she had been born was rushing toward a long tunnel of darkness.

She could never clearly recall what happened in the next hours. Samson picked her up in his massive arms and carried her in to Della. The two of them stayed with her while Padraic rode to Baltimore for Rane.

But Alex was unaware of anything except the sharp, steady repetition of the stranger's words in her brain.

Rane was stunned and heartbroken, but the instant he saw Alex, he knew his own grief must not overpower his ability to act. She looked as if she had shrunken in on herself in the short time since she had received the news, all confidence and competence gone. He took her in his arms and did not feel as if he were holding her at all; it was another woman who felt so angular and resistant.

They went to Philadelphia the fastest way, by train, and it was a measure of Alex's shock that she did not seem to notice that she was traveling in a manner that had heretofore terrified her. Rane had persuaded the children to remain in Baltimore, promising them that Nigel's body would be brought home for burial at Wild Swan, and he was glad now that none of the others were with them; Alex was enough to cope with.

In the shock of the first revelation, neither Alex nor Rane had thought to question why Piety was sharing the fact of Nigel's death with them; it would have been much more in character for her to have buried her husband hastily and then informed his parents. But once they confronted her, her motive was only too clear.

Piety did not want to bear the cost of the funeral or the burial. Rane understood it at once, and with a minimum of words agreed to her terms—in exchange for allowing her to do as she wished with the city funeral, they could take Nigel's body home afterward.

Alex did not seem to understand anything at all. Softly, hesitantly, she asked repeatedly for details, though the facts were few. Nigel had been treating an outbreak of fever in one of the poorest sections of the city and had succumbed to it himself.

"Niggers and Irish beggars, he would treat them. I warned him, the fool, the ridiculous fool!" Piety ranted.

Alex only gazed at her in bemusement, though Rane wanted to kill the woman. He was sorely tempted to denounce Piety for the fire at Wild Swan, but he resisted the impulse, knowing that that might well be the final straw for Alex to bring it out in the open now, after she had kept it from her son. Rane knew Alex's guilt was as profound as her grief, though she recognized neither now and was floating helplessly in some private, fog-shrouded world.

Piety obviously relished the role of grieving widow. No small funeral would do for her ambitions, and she was even willing to let Nigel's poor patients attend to swell the numbers. Rane found some comfort in the results of this, for he could see the genuine grief in face after worn face, young and old, no matter what travesty Piety would have made of the day.

The preacher ranted endlessly about the trials and tribulations of this earthly life, the eternal fire awaiting sinners, and the Paradise reserved for the Chosen. He even went so far as to express some doubts about the deceased's chances of entering heaven since Nigel had not testified publicly to the presence of Christ in his life, but he added that good works might have made up for the lack.

To keep from commanding that the proceedings cease, Rane conducted his own inner service for Nigel, thinking, "You were such a good, kind man, my son, if there is a life hereafter, you deserve the very best of it."

His throat tightened, and he gripped Alex's hand more firmly, but she gave no sign she was aware of his presence or of where she was.

Observing Piety, Rane understood more than ever why Alex had been willing to go to such lengths to get Gincie. He wished he could take Piety's sons with him and teach them how to laugh and play as children should. They looked like two little old men in their dark clothes and somber faces. He shifted his gaze from them so that he would not have to think about them any more.

People who had loved and depended on Nigel wanted to give their condolences to his parents. Rane wondered how Alex could bear it. But he found he need not have worried. She accepted their words with calm dignity. Only he knew that empty little voice and the peculiar yellow-green of her eyes were nothing like his Alex.

Many tarried long enough to tell of specific incidents of Nigel's kindness and skill.

"My little girl was taken turrible sick, an' Doc Carrington he sat with her an' kept on doctorin' her 'til she came back from the dead."

"My husband, I feared to lose 'im, but Doc Carrington cured 'im."

The loving tributes went on and on, often accompanied by tears, but Alex shed none, not even when she met the Murphys Nigel had spoken about on his last visit home.

Piety could not stand what she viewed as Alex's self-possession, and just before the Falconers departed, she sidled up to Alex and hissed, "As much as his work, it was you who caused his death. You took his daughter away from him, and he spent even more time with his patients than before. God gave him a talent and he wasted it."

Alex simply stared at her as if she wasn't quite sure who Piety was, but Rane snarled, "What a foul piece of work you are! You and your hellish friend. Does he liven your cold flesh while he preaches to your soul? Just one more word, and I will see you in prison before the day is out. Nigel has no need of protection any longer, and Gincie can learn to live with the truth about you someday if she must."

Piety believed him and backed off, but she had gotten no satisfaction in any case with Alex acting so distant. Suddenly she just wanted them gone with Nigel's body. Nothing had worked out as she had planned in her marriage to Nigel Carrington. Her life was bound to be better with a man of God, a man who knew the responsibilities and privileges of being among the Chosen.

Rane watched her stalk away, and he wanted to be at the farm more than ever before.

When they finally stood beside the open grave at Wild Swan, Rane was thinking of Alex rather than the quietly dignified words so fitting for Nigel, being spoken by Alastair Cameron:

> Lord, when saw we thee an hungred, and fed thee? or
>   thirsty, and gave thee drink?
> When saw we thee a stranger, and took thee in? or
>   naked, and clothed thee?
> Or when saw we thee sick, or in prison, and came unto
>   thee?
> And the King shall answer and say unto them, Verily
> I say unto you, Inasmuch as ye have done it unto one of
>   the least of these my brethren,
> ye have done it unto me.

During the train journey home, Alex had not wept and had scarcely spoken, but the few times she had broken her silence, her comments had been random and eerie.

"He had very dirty fingernails," she said.

"Who?" Rane asked, having no idea of where her mind was leading her.

"That dreadful man who preached. He reminded me of a man Sinje knew. He came to our house in Gravesend, and he insulted me. But

Hugh took care of it." Her voice was low and rambling, lost in the past, and then it sharpened. "Is he on the train with us?"

"The minister? Of course not."

"No, I mean Nigel," she explained impatiently.

"His body is, but Nigel is gone," Rane said gently, feeling an icy wave over his spine. She sounded as if she thought Nigel was still alive.

"I know that," she insisted, but her voice was sly.

Now watching her as the first shower of earth rattled against the casket, Rane saw a last spark of light die in Alex's eyes.

Chapter

19

Alex knew that Nigel's sisters, his brothers, and Rane were devastated by the loss of him. And she knew that life had to go on. But she knew it all at a distance. There seemed to be layers and layers, not only between herself and the rest of the world, but between herself and herself. It was like having a fever and only being able to grasp reality in brief flashes.

She tried, she tried very hard to respond to everyone's needs. She spent extra time with Gincie, who, while not sure about what had happened, could not help but be affected by the mourning of the family. She was careful to give added attention to her other grandchildren, too. And when Samson and Padraic came to her with questions and plans for the fall racing season, she tried to concentrate, but too often even the names of the horses sounded unfamiliar, and she would catch herself thinking that she would see Swan proud and sleek running at his ease in the summer pastures and that everything would go back to a better time.

And then she would see Nigel as a child again, his face alight with the excitement of discovering that the nest he had been watching now had baby birds in it in place of the eggs; Nigel laughing at the antics of a new foal; Nigel asking Samson if the horses minded having their hooves trimmed and filed.

Image upon image of Nigel crowded Alex's mind until she scarcely knew who or where she was.

It was worst of all with Rane. When he turned to her for comfort and love, she wanted desperately to be fully involved with him, but though her body went through the motions of the old ritual and even responded to his touch, an essential part of her remained aloof, observing the love-making with cold pity, finding it an absurdly futile gesture against the darkness.

The darkness was all around her, waiting to fill every curve and hollow of her body and her soul. She knew Nigel's death had to be faced, but she could not do it. It was unthinkable that a man of so much compassion, skill, and promise could be so suddenly gone into the damp earth. It was worse than when the babies had died, worse than when St. John had died. It was a perversion of the whole rhythm of life that her son was dead while her own heart beat so strongly. And that she might have contributed to his death by keeping Gincie at Wild Swan and by not telling Nigel the truth about his wife's crime was so intolerable that she could not face the pain of it.

When he should have been closest to her, when he was making love to her, Rane felt Alex's distance most of all. Had he not experienced it, he would not have believed it possible. Even when her body received him, opened to him, even when she used all her skill to increase his pleasure, the essential Alex was not there. He knew it with chilling certainty when he looked into her eyes and saw nothing—not light, not joy, not even lust. At first there was anger mixed with his concern, and sometimes it made him rough in his loving, as if he could shock her out of the strange twilight she had entered with Nigel's death.

Then one morning he saw a bruise on her ribcage, a bruise he had made, and he was appalled. He leaned over and kissed it with infinite tenderness.

"I am so sorry, my love," he murmured.

She looked at him blankly, taking a moment, despite the kiss, to understand what he was apologizing for. "It doesn't matter, truly it doesn't," she said.

She looked so anxious, he wanted to weep, and the last of his anger died in his realization of how hard she was struggling to please everyone in spite of the disorienting burden of her grief. He resolved that he would be patient and would make sure that everyone else was, too. Trying to talk to her about Nigel was no use; she was far from ready for that. But he hoped that with time she would feel the love all around her and heal.

He tried to imagine what it would be like to have nurtured a child inside one's own body, struggled and risked all to give birth to it, and raised it to be the finest kind of human being, only to lose all to an untimely death, but he knew that whatever his mind could conjure was a pale shadow compared to the reality. And though he tried not to dwell on it, he knew that in addition to everything else, Alex had to be thinking that she had lost the last of her life with St. John when she had lost Nigel, the only child living of the three she had conceived with St. John.

The children mourned Nigel, but they went on with their lives, and they did not smother Alex with their demands or their love, but treated her with gentle compassion, trusting, as Rane did, that they would have the old Alex back eventually. Even Gweneth showed remarkable forbearance, considering that she was only thirteen. Flora was a great help in this; having served as a surrogate mother to Gwenny since the child had started attending school in Baltimore, she continued in the role more intensively, making sure her little sister never felt she was without a mentor.

In fact, Sam suffered more than Gwenny from Alex's vagueness. Even the news that Sam and Morgan were expecting another child in December seemed to have touched no more than the surface of Alex's consciousness, as if the pattern of generations no longer made sense to her. But underlying the appearance of indifference was Alex's primitive fear that if she concentrated her love too fiercely on Sam and the coming child, she would lose both of them as she had lost Nigel.

Outwardly, Sam maintained her usual calm poise about her advancing pregnancy, but inwardly she felt very cowardly. She wanted another child, but having had so much difficulty in giving birth previously, she could not help but be apprehensive. She did not want Morgan to know this—he managed to be terrified enough for her on his own—but she would have liked to confide in Alex, who, in other days, would have met the fear head-on with practical reassurances as well as understanding sympathy. But now, Sam did not think her mother-in-law could cope with any emotions other than her own. She gave thanks that she felt so well thus far, and sometimes she discussed her pregnancy with Philly, but it was not the same as having Alex vitally concerned. She hoped it would be all right in the end, since she was going to Wild Swan in November to await the birth of the baby in early December. At least that tradition was still in place, even if it had been a matter of automatic response on Alex's part and equally automatic assumptions from Rane and Morgan.

The hot humid days of summer slid into September. Though Alex had been consulted, Samson and Padraic had in truth made all the decisions about which races the horses of Wild Swan would enter. Padraic took a few horses to Broad Rock near Richmond, Virginia, to start the season in September and was particularly pleased by the performance of two three-year-olds, Royal Fortune, a black colt out of Swan Princess by Fortune, and Swan Dancer, a bay colt out of Taney by Wild Swan. Royal Fortune placed second in the sweepstakes for three-year-olds, and on the next day, Swan Dancer won that day's event for the same age category. It was particularly gratifying to see Wild Swan's son perform so well, as if the stallion's fiery death had not been so final after all. But though Padraic reminded himself that his job was to take the horses to the meetings and to win races with them and that he had done this, he also admitted to himself that he wished Alex had been present to see her horses run so well, wished the enthusiasm he had grown accustomed to in her was still there.

Nigel's death was common knowledge now, and Padraic was questioned closely about Alex's well-being by many of her friends in the racing world, not only owners and agents, but also jockeys, trainers, and stablehands. He gave all but one the same restrained account, telling them that Mrs. Falconer was doing as well as could be expected from such a grievous loss. The exception was Allen Ralston. Padraic recognized him as a very close and caring friend of the Falconers and could not put him off with the same brief words he had given to others.

"How is she really?" Allen asked. "I thought to go to Wild Swan to see for myself, but I decided it would be an imposition."

"Ye're kind ta be thinkin' that," Padraic told him. "On the outside she's well enough, but inside I fear 'tis anither matter altagither. She's gone away where no one can follow."

Allen considered how Rane must feel, and he was sorry for both Alex and her husband. "She's a very strong woman. Give her time, and she'll come back," he assured Padraic, hoping he was right. He supposed there was a limit to what anyone could endure, and lord knew Alex had had more than her share of grief.

For a moment, Padraic was tempted to confess what he knew about the fire. He carried his own guilt, though he wasn't sure what he could have accomplished had he publicly denounced Nigel's wife for her crime. He resisted the urge to share his secret with Mr. Ralston. What was done was done, and nothing good would come of confiding in anyone else.

He was heartened when he returned to Wild Swan and learned that Alex planned to attend the three-day meeting at Washington, D.C., beginning on the twentieth of October.

Alex went to the Washington Course out of a sense of duty, not pleasure. Even in her dazed state she had not lost sight of the fact that the business of the horses was hers and that she was expected to be visible at least part of the time. It was the way she had built the fame of her stable after St. John's death, and it continued to be important. She steeled herself to accept the condolences offered by one person after another and did her best to ease their awkwardness. And all the while it was as if she was watching someone else in her place.

But when she saw Swan Dancer win the $100 purse for all ages in mile heats, she felt the first start of joy she had experienced in months. He ran with all the graceful power of his sire, and she remembered how hopeful they had all been from the first day of the colt's life. Even then he had seemed quick and graceful despite his long, long legs, hence they had named him Dancer. She thought of Swan's Shadow, another colt out of Taney by Wild Swan. Taney, whose actual name was Titania, had proved fruitful in her last years of breeding, and Shadow had been born a year after Dancer. He was a chestnut like his sire, and at two years old looked even more the image of Swan than Dancer did. Wild Swan's blood went on, in the colts of the farm and in the many other horses he had sired on the outside mares brought to him.

As Gincie carried on for Nigel, as many who owed their lives to Nigel carried on in his place—the cycles of life and death were the same for man and beast, no matter who cried against the loss; the inevitability was strangely comforting to Alex.

Swan's Chance raced for the Citizens' Purse of $300 on the last day of the meet. It was three-mile heats open to all ages, with weights for ages and sex assigned as handicaps; Swan's Chance carried one hundred and eighteen pounds as a six-year-old stallion.

There was an appreciative murmur from the crowd when they saw the stallion led out on the course. Though some didn't believe a horse blind in one eye could run a good race, many more knew that Swan's Chance had already proven he could still run as swiftly as ever.

There were four other horses in the field, two other stallions, a mare, and a gelding. Swan's Chance broke clear of them by the second mile and kept his lead to the end of the first heat. But in the second heat, he was beaten by Old Kentucky and Patsey Anthony.

Alex was relieved to find the stallion in good condition when she went to see him after the second heat. Both Jim Barlow and Padraic were confident that the horse could still win.

"He jus' needs to pay attention more," Jim said. "An' I'll make sure he does."

Privately Padraic thought they'd already won, since Alex looked so bright-eyed and interested, though he hoped the stallion would take the purse for her.

Alex closed her eyes, unable to watch the finish as Chance lost the next heat in the final mile, but the race went on since no horse had won more than one heat. And in the fourth heat, Swan's Chance pulled ahead and stayed there to win the race with two heats out of four. Alex watched him all the way and did not realize until it was over that she had cheered aloud.

She wished Rane could have been with her instead of back with the moneymen in New York, for in that instant she realized how long it had been since she had shared anything with him except the weight of her mourning. He had not even suggested she travel north with him this time; he had known she would go.

She was emerging from the darkness, but she barely had time to savor the first rays of light back at Wild Swan before Caleb rode in in search of her.

She knew the instant she saw him that he had brought bad news; his face was a mask of worry. When he told her that Sam had been in labor when he left Baltimore, Alex's heart contracted with fear. Sam wasn't due for more than a month. She was supposed to have come to the farm in the next few days to await the delivery of her child. To give birth this early was hazardous for mother and child, even more so with Sam's past history of difficult labor.

Leaving Gincie in Della's care, Alex went with Caleb. Throughout the journey, all she could think of was that it simply wasn't possible that Nigel and Samantha would die in the same year. The fear of it had been lurking in the depths of her mind ever since she had learned of Sam's pregnancy. Now it came to the surface full-blown and hideously threatening.

When she first saw Sam, she breathed a sigh of relief, for it seemed her worry had been needless. Sam had produced another boy. He was small, but his breathing was clear and his heartbeat strong. And though the birth had been early and very fast, Sam did not seem to have suffered any lasting hurt from it. She was tired and content to sleep, but there was no hemorrhaging.

It was Flora who rekindled Alex's anxiety. She and Philly were taking care of Seth and Adam, as well as seeing to Sam's household, and they were relieved by Alex's arrival.

Flora described the sequence of events. The onslaught of Sam's labor had been so swift and severe, her housekeeper had done the best she could. Unable to find Dr. Benjamin, whom she knew Mrs. Falconer trusted, she had gotten a midwife. And in one sense, the midwife had done very well. The baby had been safely delivered by the time Philly, Blaine, Flora, and Caleb had been summoned.

"But, Mother, her hands, everything she was using, they just weren't clean! And it wasn't from Sam's delivery." Flora's face was drawn with disgust. "It was the kind of filth that comes from just not caring about it or understanding. Lord knows I absorbed a great deal less of your teaching than I should have, but I know how important you think cleanliness is. Or am I just finding something to fret about?" she asked, wanting to be reassured.

Alex shook her head. "Unfortunately you're not. But perhaps Sam will escape any ill effects. Damn! It is such a basic premise; I will never understand how anyone can believe that filth enhances medical treatment!"

Within twenty-four hours, Sam had all the signs of the dreaded puerperal fever. It began with her being mildly disoriented, not sure which day it was, one minute thinking Morgan was home and in the next understanding that he hadn't returned from his voyage south yet. But as her fever mounted, the intervals of lucidity vanished, and she alternated between lying in a stupor and twisting and turning in delirium.

A wet-nurse was found for the baby, and Alex ministered to Sam, using all the skill she could summon to keep the fever from burning her alive, knowing that if the infection continued to spread, there would be nothing she could do to stop it. Dr. Benjamin looked in on the patient but had nothing to recommend beyond the treatment already being given.

Morgan was due back any day from the south, and Rane from New York. Had Sam carried the baby to term, the plan would have worked perfectly, with Morgan returning in time to take Sam out to Wild Swan to await the birth. Now it was horrifyingly possible that he would arrive just in time to attend his wife's funeral.

Sam's fever sent her rambling over childhood. Almost all the memories involved Wild Swan and Morgan rather than Brookhaven and her own family, and that touched Alex unbearably—Morgan when Sam was a child, Morgan when she had grown to womanhood.

Once she opened her eyes and looked straight at Alex. "He isn't ever going to want me as a woman, is he? He's always going to think of me as a little sister. I will make Justin a good wife."

It sent chills down Alex's back to hear Sam speaking so clearly of another time.

"Sam, darling girl, Morgan will be home soon. I promise he loves you. He married you because he loves you."

But her words of reassurance didn't penetrate the place where Sam was. "Married?" she questioned softly and then closed her eyes as if too weary to make sense of the word.

"I lost Nigel. I won't lose you, Sam, I won't!" Alex held one of Sam's hands in a firm grip as if to anchor her to life.

Morgan came home like a harsh wind from the sea. Caleb had told him the news the moment he docked, and the shock of the announcement showed plainly on Morgan's face. His eyes were wild, his voice frantic as he called his wife's name.

Alex met him at the door of the bedroom. "She's very ill, but she's alive. And you have another son."

He hardly heard her, and she stepped aside to let him approach Sam's bed.

The only times in his life Morgan had felt physical fear had been when Sam was in labor—first with Seth and then Adam. Threats to his own safety had never caused more than an exhilarating race of his pulse to meet the challenge. But Sam in danger made him feel as if all courage had been drained from his body to leave him trembling like a child in the throes of a nightmare.

And this was worse than anything he had ever faced before; he knew that the minute he looked down at Sam's fever-flushed face, before he even touched the dry heat of her skin. He could feel her drifting. His Sam, who was so vitally alive that her mere presence in a room radiated a nearly tangible energy—now it was as if she was barely present.

"Oh, Sam, don't leave me!" He would have given anything to feel her fingers curl around his when he took her hand.

Seeking to help numb his despair with action, Alex enlisted his aid in caring for Sam, and tenderly he bathed his wife with cooling cloths and tried to make her swallow broth and medicines. And he talked to her, a constant litany of love.

Aside from a cursory glance at his new son, he ignored the baby, and Alex did not press him. Time enough for him to realize that this child was no less a gift to his life than the other two.

For Morgan, there was no world but Sam. He listened to her rambling fever dreams and recognized the source of most of the distorted images immediately, so bound were his own youthful memories with hers. And he concentrated fiercely on Sam in the present, seeking by force of will to keep her with him.

Sam's father came as summoned, but he offered nothing useful beyond handwringing and incoherent mutterings, and Morgan was glad when the man was firmly escorted from the sickroom by Alex.

Sam's eyes had been open off and on, but this time when they opened they had a peculiar intensity. "He loves her more than he loves me," she said flatly, and Morgan froze. He had been absolutely faithful to Sam since their marriage. He still noticed beautiful women, but they did not move him as his wife did, and the vow of fidelity had not been hard to keep. He wondered if Sam was remembering the redheaded Rose she had seen him with that night in Baltimore. He could not believe that after their years of sweet loving, Sam could, even in her fever, think he loved another woman.

She tried to struggle upright, and he held her down. "Please, sweetheart, please lie quietly," he begged.

She resisted his efforts for a moment more, and then lay still briefly before her hands began to pick restlessly at the bedclothes. "He loves her. I always knew, ships and the sea, I always knew. But I couldn't know about her, couldn't. She'll take him away, far away to China, without me. Great white sails, taking him away. Morgan, don't leave me!" she finished with a cry of sudden strength.

Not Rose or any other woman, but the *Liza Gwen* and distant ports, fears she had never betrayed until now, when she was helpless to prevent the truth from escaping.

With a sob, he buried his face against her neck. "If I go to China, you go with me. Other wives sail with their husbands, and you have always been a good sailor. Remember when Father took us out for the first time, when we were children? You and I were the best sailors of the lot. Sam, I love you more than the sea, more than ships, more than anything else on earth. You have no rivals. Sam, if you leave me, I'll never be whole again." He went on talking to his wife, forgetting that Alex was in the room.

There was no dramatic change to mark the turning point, but by dawn Alex knew Sam was going to live. Her fever was finally going down, and she was sleeping peacefully. She was pale, but that was preferable to the hectic flush that had colored her skin before.

Morgan was slumped half over the bed, his head still resting in the hollow of Sam's neck and shoulder. He was neither asleep nor awake, but somewhere in between, just enduring, empty of everything except the knowledge that her heart still beat.

Alex touched his back gently. "Morgan, she's going to be all right now. I'm sure of it." She felt him shudder under her hand, and then he drew back slowly and stared at Sam, absorbing the changes.

"Thank you, Mother, thank you for saving her life," he whispered brokenly.

Alex cradled his head against her breast for a moment and then she dropped a kiss on his soft hair. "It was you as much as the rest of us. You reminded her that she has much to live for. You will find that she heard a lot of what you said, though she couldn't tell you so."

Alex's own memory still held the words Rane had used to keep her with him when she had lain near death from her fall from Winter Swan.

"Then China it is," Morgan murmured, and the first note of joy was dawning in his voice.

Alex left him and went downstairs to relay the news. So filled was she with longing for Rane, when she first saw him, she thought he was an illusion. But he was real, and he was terrified that she was going to tell him Sam had died.

Flora was there with Caleb, taking their turns at the vigil while Philly and Blaine, with Gweneth's help, cared for their daughters and the two Falconer boys. Sam's father was there, too. Rane had just arrived, having received the news with his first step on land at the yard.

Alex saw all of them except Rane in a blur of profound fatigue. She heard her own voice as if at a distance, giving them the good news, and then Rane was sweeping her up in his arms. "One invalid is enough. I'm taking Alex home and putting her to bed," he announced.

"There are things I must—"

"Allow other people to do for you," he supplied smoothly. "Your children are very competent, and they will ask you if they need help. In the meantime, you are going to rest." His voice brooked no argument, and she was too tired to fight him.

He took her back to their own house and before he let her fall asleep, he ordered water for a bath, anticipating how grimy she must feel from her long hours of tending Sam and knowing she would sleep more soundly from the effects of the warm water.

In fact, she could barely stay awake once she was in the tub, and he bathed her as if she were a child and put her to bed. And he was there beside her when she cried out, caught in a nightmare about Nigel.

"Wake up, sweetling, wake up now. It's only a nightmare," he coaxed, gathering her into his arms.

Her voice was dazed. "I could see him so clearly, and he was ill. But I couldn't reach him, couldn't help him."

Rane winced at the hurt in her voice, and yet, he thought it was probably a good sign that her control was slipping enough to allow her son into her dreams. Her strange lack of focus, as if the guilt and agony of losing Nigel was so deeply buried in the center of her that she could not even acknowledge it, had frightened him far more than hysterical weeping would have. He had no way of knowing about the changes that had begun as she watched her horses race in Washington.

"I thought Sam was going to die, too," she said.

"But she didn't," Rane reminded her. "She is going to recover." He hesitated, searching for the right words. "Do you recall what you told me after Claire committed suicide? You told me that it was not my fault, that Claire's unhappiness came from inside herself. It took me a long while to believe that and sometimes I still feel guilty, still feel as if I might have found a way to make her happy. But when I am most honest with myself, I know that you were right, that we really have very little to do with how other people survive or fail to survive. It's true of Nigel as well. You gave him everything a mother can give to a child. You gave him love, a comfortable life, a fine education. But then he became a man and responsible for his own life. You did not choose Piety for him; he did that himself. And he chose to stay with her, even after he knew what sort of woman she was. She could only make him unhappy because he allowed it."

"I didn't tell him the truth about the fire. He might have left her then. And I took Gincie from him."

Her words were so harshly spoken, Rane felt the rasp of them in his own throat. "And he might not have left her," he countered. "Given the kind of man Nigel was, I doubt he would have. You made your decision knowing that. You prevented further violence at Wild Swan. You kept Gincie from bearing the stigma of a felonious mother, and you took her away from that woman who abused her viciously. Even though he missed her, Nigel knew Gincie was better off with us."

He held her more tightly, just on the edge of pain, willing her to concentrate on what he was saying. "Nigel did not swallow poison or open his veins. He died of disease. It is true that he was tired and overworked, and that that might have caused his failure to recover. But he did not take his own life. His commitment to his profession took it. It is a risk you have run as well. To deal with contagion is to be vulnerable to it. You cannot judge what he would have done had he had more time. I think he would have left Piety eventually, but I cannot swear to it. And you cannot know that anything would have changed had he been without Piety or with Gincie—you cannot! He was not a babe in your womb or a child at your skirt; he was a man when he died. You are not destiny for yourself or your children; you are just a human being living with the risks everyone lives with."

She heard echoes of her grandmother's words in Rane's, Virginia saying that the superstitions ringing round birth and death were to give the impression of control where none existed.

She wept then—slow, healing tears long overdue. There would always be some guilt; it was part of her now when she thought of Nigel, but acceptance was beginning. Acceptance that he was truly gone and that there was no way to change what had happened, no sure way to have changed it before it happened.

She fell asleep again, secure in Rane's warmth, and this time she slept peacefully until late the next morning, rousing to find Rane, fully dressed, smiling down at her.

"I've been to visit the children. Sam is doing fine, and even Morgan looks as if he'll survive." Rane kissed her. "I would have let you sleep longer, but I feared you would then be wakeful tonight. I brought you some breakfast."

"Such royal treatment; have you confused me with Queen Victoria?"

He pretended to study her closely. "No, you're too tall. And from what I've heard, the young queen would judge this highly improper "

"Maybe she would not if her German prince served her breakfast in her bed."

"I doubt that was part of his training."

They laughed over their own nonsense, and Alex felt more alive than she had in months as she arose and performed her morning ablutions, washing away the last traces of her long sleep. She accepted a cup of tea from the tray, but when Rane offered her a tempting morsel of food, she slowly shook her head. "Later. I can think of something I want more now," she murmured, and she opened her arms in invitation.

Despite the fact that he was dressed and ready for a day's work, Rane did not hesitate. He had begun to wonder if he would ever have the old Alex back, the Alex who had made love with the same energy and concentration she brought to everything, instead of the accommodating but elusive lover she had been these past months.

She had never looked more beautiful to him than she did now with her green eyes glowing, her dark hair tumbling about her face, her lips parted in anticipation of his mouth meeting hers. Even her body, such familiar territory to him, was changed, renewed somehow so that only now with the softening lines welcoming him could he recognize how rigidly she had been holding herself since Nigel's death.

He stripped off his clothes, catching fire from the pleasure of Alex's eyes as she watched him. And when he lay down with her, her hands traced what her eyes had approved.

He kissed her, and her mouth opened to his, her body pressed pliantly against his as if she would shape herself to his desire. They came together with all of their old fire and rhythm, and Rane's passion was immeasurably heightened by knowing he had Alex back again.

Their children showed admirable restraint when the couple finally arrived at Morgan's house, but it was soon evident to all of them that Alex was much more like her old self than the ghostly presence she had been since Nigel's death.

Alex recognized the change as clearly as they did. Her reawakening extended far beyond lovemaking with Rane. Sound, color, even the taste of food and the textures of everything she touched—sensations flooded over her, true and rich in comparison to the gray, blank world she had been inhabiting.

When, the next day, Morgan and Sam diffidently told her that they would like to name their new son Nigel Carrington Falconer, she gladly gave her consent, aware that what pleased her now would have appalled her before.

"You were right, Mother," Morgan told her once the matter of the name had been settled. "Sam did hear me. The first thing she said when she opened her eyes was that I promised her China." He cradled his tiny son in his arms. "And China it may be, but not until this little fellow is a bit older and a bit bigger."

Later Alex confided to Rane, "I thought I was traveling far when I left England to come to this country, and now my son speaks of going to China! It makes our voyages seem quite tame."

"Not at all," Rane objected. "When you set out and when I did, both of us sought to establish new lives. Morgan and Sam might go to China, but they will return to all that is familiar. You and I, we traveled far beyond that." He drew her close. "And it was worth every mile."

Chapter

20

By the time the new year of 1846 dawned, not only had Sam regained her strength, but the baby was flourishing despite his meager size at birth.

Alex felt as if she were somewhat like little Nigel, awakening each morning to learn more about an ever-expanding world. Where nothing had interested her for months on end, now everything did.

In October the Naval School had opened at Fort Severn in Annapolis. It was a consolidation of various schools from various ports, and other cities had wanted it located in their region, but little Annapolis had won. Alex was particularly glad of it for Timothy and Mavis's sake. They continued to make a good living from the tavern, but the addition of the school with its instructors and students could not help but enlarge their business.

The Jennings-Falconer yard was gaining a reputation for building the new China clippers, so much longer and leaner than the old Baltimore clippers. The yard had now produced two, and two more were being built, each vessel varying from the last as one innovation followed another.

Blaine's law practice was thriving, and Flora's school, while it catered to fewer and fewer wealthy students, was more than justifying its existence by the number of children in need it served. Philly managed to keep her hand in, in spite of the responsibility of her own children. She maintained that no place was more suitable for the amusement of children than a school that truly cared about enriching their minds. Virgil Winslow could also be found at the school on many days.

The number of race meetings continued to decrease, but Alex and her staff adjusted to it, sending horses to enough of those remaining to maintain the prominence of Wild Swan's name in order to guarantee buyers for the horses to be sold and mares for the stallions to breed. While it was true that the race purses were fewer and less plump, there was still a strong market for good horses, particularly for the push westward, and to that end, they bred more half-Thoroughbreds along with the purebreds. Though, try as she might, Alex could no longer keep as close a watch on the treatment her horses received after they were sold away from the farm, she did her best to make sure the buyers had good credentials, so much so that word spread that purchasing a horse from Mrs. Falconer was akin to applying for a job.

Informed of Nigel's death by Rane, Boston and Rachel had sent a letter full of love and grief. More than that, it contained some of Boston's memories of his nephew, just a few amusing stories, but enough to affect Alex profoundly, making her more aware than before of how much others besides herself had lost. And the loss was not confined to the immediate family. She came to understand that the Bateses and Della and Samson, who had all helped to care for Nigel when he was young, Dr. Cameron, who had guided him in his choice of medicine for a career, and many others, missed him deeply.

Alex noted in the passing months that she and young Nigel were not the only infants reaching out to the world; the country was doing its share of growing, and not always gently.

Though there were occasional angry flare-ups, relations with Great Britain were steadily improving through a series of agreements that were settling borders with Canada and various other matters of mutual interest without bloodshed, but relations with Mexico had gone rapidly downhill.

Diplomatic contact between the Americans and the Mexicans in the past ten years had been fraught with misunderstandings and blunders, but the 1845 annexation of Texas by the United States was the last straw; Mexico viewed it as an act of war, just as Blaine had once suggested they might.

President Polk, and others who were looking ahead to the acquisition of California and wished to manage it without bloodshed, had great hopes that John Slidell would triumph in his secret mission to secure California and New Mexico by purchase rather than aggression, while easing rancor over the Texas problem. Slidell's mission ceased to be secret when its failure was revealed in war.

Mexico refused to reopen diplomatic relations. President Polk ordered General Zachary Taylor to advance from Corpus Christi, Texas, to the Rio Grande in January, 1846. In short days, the first encounters with Mexican troops had occurred.

All this was made public on May 11 when the president submitted a war message to Congress. The message stated that war already existed, and had been started by Mexico on American soil. The outcome was a prompt declaration of war and plans for naval and military operations designed to force the Mexican government to settle with the United States.

The status of California also changed. A false rumor had a small army of Californios advancing on Sacramento. In response, Americans armed and organized themselves, enlisting the explorer, John Charles Frémont, to aid them, and through a ludicrous series of nonbattles, they created the Republic of California. The Californios were peaceful cattle ranchers far from Mexico, and had neither the means nor the will to defy the excitable and greedy Yankees.

It was not so with the army of Mexico and the United States forces; in battles between them blood was shed, and the American soldiers also suffered casualties from disease, a circumstance that caused Alex special pain. Many of the soldiers were so young, she hated to think of them suffering from infections that burned them with fever and sapped their vitality with violent dysentery, a more ignominious way to die than by bullet or saber. And Alex also had a selfish thought—a great relief that her grandsons were not old enough to be involved and neither of her surviving sons was a soldier or likely to be.

To Alex, the greatest tragedy of the Mexican War was that it was such a useless expenditure of young lives on both sides. The outcome was inevitable. The United States would expand clear to the Pacific and to the southwest, and would take as well those lands already settled by her citizens. Mexico was not strong or united enough to prevent it. Prevention would have been possible only had American settlers been denied access to the land decades before.

On September 17, 1847, General Winfield Scott hoisted the American flag over the palace in Mexico City. Though Mexico had refused to negotiate a peace previously, now the war was over, and the most pressing problem left to the Americans was to find in the disarray of Mexican politics a government powerful enough to enforce a treaty. On February 2, 1848, the treaty of Guadalupe Hidalgo, named for the town where it was completed, was signed. By its provisions, hostilities officially ceased and the United States agreed to pay $15 million for New Mexico and California.

Aside from some extra shipping contracts for the Jennings-Falconer line, the war had not directly affected either family, but they all knew that the aftereffects would. With so much new territory, the question of a balance between slave and free lands would undoubtedly be even more pressing than before. Frustratingly, there was little any one person could do except to hope that reasonable minds would prevail.

In many parts of the world, chaos, caused by nature and man, seemed the measure of the times. The Continent rumbled periodically with various political movements and revolutions, and England, for all the peace and prosperity that seemed to mark the reign of Queen Victoria for many, produced an ever-increasing number of desperate poor. The revision of the Poor Laws, and of the rates levied to care for the poor, had resulted in a system of workhouses and deprivation designed to shame people out of poverty. And while it might have caught the lazy here and there, the overall effect was to make life so intolerable for thousands in England that those who could, left.

Even worse off were the Irish. The poor there depended on the potato as their staple food, and in 1845 a potato disease reached the country. But in that season, some of the crop had already been dug, the yield was quite good, and not all counties were affected. It was hoped that the blight was only an isolated incident not to be repeated. Hope failed as a wet spring and humid summer gave way to the total failure of the 1846 potato crop. Though the blight did less damage in the following year, for many it was too late; they had either neglected to plant again or eaten their seed potatoes. And it was impossible to predict how long the cycle of blight would continue or how severe it would be.

The disasters on other shores brought shipload after shipload of refugees to America, and in many respects these were different from the immigrants of the decades before the forties, who had, for the most part, been skilled in some trade and had brought with them at least the minimal means to establish a new life. The new arrivals were far less well equipped, but they believed in the promise of America, and they joined the enclaves of their fellow countrymen determined to find a better life.

Alex suspected it was because of Padraic's place in their lives, but for whatever reason, she found the plight of the Irish the most appalling. Indeed, they seemed the most wretched of all, so many of them so gray-faced and emaciated when they arrived, it seemed a miracle they had survived the ocean crossing. Alex could not bear to think of those who had not, those who had ended their lives in the dank holds of overcrowded ships and had been cast overboard to sink beneath the waves forever.

It did not surprise Alex that of all her children, Flora cared the most about the miseries of the Irish she saw in Baltimore. It was not that the other children lacked compassion, it was just that Flora's heart seemed to have expanded year by year until it encompassed not only what she saw as injustices to women, but the troubles of every other downtrodden group, too. Alex often wondered whether Flora's limitless compassion stemmed from her inability to bear a child of her own or whether it was a part of her that would have emerged no matter what, despite the frivolity she had shown in her youth. In either case, the result was the same—Flora took in strays. She gave temporary employment where she could and looked for regular work for her own collection of refugees. She enlarged her school to include more poor children and illiterate adults also, determined that she would, by teaching them the basic skills of reading and arithmetic, enhance their chances for better jobs. The Jenningses' food bill reflected the feeding of many more than their small household, and Caleb learned that if he wanted Flora to wear a new dress, he had to give her the actual garment, else the money would be absorbed by one of her charitable projects.

Sometimes Alex worried about Flora's relationship with Caleb; he was an exceedingly kind man, but she worried that even his generosity and patience might be tested by Flora's myriad projects.

"Do you mind?" she asked him gently one night at a family gathering in the city as Flora argued passionately that basic provisions made for food, clothing, shelter, and education would be more than repaid by the improved citizenry they would produce. Blaine was countering her argument by pointing out that while he agreed with her sentiments, he could see no logical way to provide such things evenhandedly without setting up a system resembling serfdom in Russia, thereby negating the whole concept of a new, free life in America.

"Sometimes I do mind," Caleb admitted to Alex, "not because we cannot afford Flora's charities, but because she is so dedicated to them that I cannot help but be jealous. And then I remind myself that the people she helps are truly in need; hers is not an exercise designed to garner praise for herself. And further, I benefit as well as all the others do. Flora has learned so much about loving, I am humbled by what she knows. I loved her very much when we married; I love her so much more now."

Caleb's smile was so tender, Alex turned her attention back to the twins lest she cry.

"What were you thinking of when you were talking to Caleb this evening?" Rane asked her later, and he looked so anxious, she knew he had seen the threatening tears.

She traced his face with careful fingers, savoring the various textures of his skin. "Don't fret. I was thinking a little of Nigel, but more of the others and of how well they have turned out. Happy tears, I promise, though I felt some guilt. There is so much misery in so many places."

"Which you do your best to alleviate," he pointed out. "Fugitive slaves sheltered at Wild Swan and money to Flora for her starving Irish."

"How do you know about that?"

He had the grace to look sheepish. "Because I am no more proof against her pleas, even the silent ones, than you are. I only hope I have the strength to refuse to adopt a boatload of immigrants when Flora asks me to. I fear that will be her next plan."

"Even Flora isn't that radical," Alex said, laughing as she rested against his hard chest.

At this, the end of May, the 1848 spring racing season was over for her horses, and though summer brought the care and harvesting of one crop after another, it also brought Alex a feeling of release as if she had been set free in the pastures like the horses and out of the classroom like the children.

"When can you come out to Wild Swan?" she asked, thinking of her own plan to return to the farm on the morrow.

"Not for a fortnight, I regret to say." He stroked her hair with one hand while the other rubbed her back in the same rhythm.

"That will be all right as long as you don't forget how to do this,"

Alex said with a shiver of pleasure. "You can't hear it, but I'm purring like a cat."

"You feel like a cat, sleek and rippling under my hands."

Conscious of the nights to be without him, Alex made the best of this time with him, concentrating all her senses on him until she was as much him as herself and mutual pleasure wrapped them round.

Though she always missed Rane when he was not with her, she was never sorry to return to Wild Swan. And now more than ever, she looked forward to it as a peaceful island in the turmoil of the rest of the world. With the summer coming, the children and grandchildren would spend a good amount of time there.

But her image of peace was altered two days later by Padraic with Flora's connivance.

Alex had not discussed the horrible effects of the famine in Ireland with Padraic, but she did not doubt his pain. She suspected he spent time with the growing Irish community in Baltimore on his days off. Sometimes he returned from the city wearing the pleasantly weary look of a man who had indulged various appetites to his satisfaction, but more often he looked haunted, a strong man pursued by phantoms he could not fight. She thought of how hard it must be for him, torn as he was by both love and hate for the two sides of his heritage, to see so many of the Irish in even worse straits than he remembered from his homeland.

But the last thing she would have expected was Kathleen O'Reilly.

Kathleen was scarcely more than a child, though her eyes were decades older than her seventeen years—huge, deep blue eyes in a hunger-etched face framed by a ragged mop of red-brown curls. Her arms were sticks protruding from her patched dress. She looked at once bravely determined and scared to death, except when her gaze fell on Padraic—and then she looked so worshipful, it was embarrassing to witness.

That Padraic was embarrassed, there was no doubt. He was so ill at ease, Alex's amusement was nearly equal to her curiosity, but she waited patiently for his explanation.

He spat it out, as if he still couldn't believe his own actions. "She was tryin' ta sell herself on the street in Baltimore and doin' a bad job a' it ta be sure. Her family's just over and doin' poorly, ten a' them altagither, and her the oldest. I can't save them all, but I bought her."

"You what?" Alex asked.

"I bought her," Padraic repeated. "Paid her family more than she would've earned on the street fer a long while even was she better at the trade. Her name is Kathleen O'Reilly." He shook his head. "I don't know what I was about, but there 'tis. I took her ta Miss Flora, and she said she thought you might have a place fer her."

"I think I might," Alex agreed, and she guessed that Flora had matchmaking as much as a job on her mind.

"Kathleen took the bath Miss Flora offered, but she wouldn't take the dress," Padraic explained, not wanting Alex to think her daughter had been less than generous.

"I'll not be takin' charity. I'll be workin' fer what I have," Kathleen volunteered. Her voice quavered, but there was a stubborn set of pride to her small, pointed chin, and Alex liked her the better for it.

"Indeed you will," Alex said. "Everyone does his or her share at Wild Swan. I'll take you to Della, and she will instruct you in your duties and show you where you will sleep." And feed you, she added inwardly, her maternal instincts aroused by the emaciated appearance of the girl.

Kathleen's courage faltered, and her voice was very low as she confessed. "I niver served in a great house. Me mither's health was poorly 'til she died last year, an' I couldn't be spared, even was there work to be found an' there's precious little a' that in Ireland now. But I can learn!"

Kathleen was so obviously torn between the desire to tell the truth and yet not lose the job, Alex's heart went out to her.

"Don't worry," she said. "You will be taught what you need to know. And though I'm flattered by the description, this is not such a great house."

Della was no more able to resist the frail look of Kathleen, soon called "Katy," than Alex was, and immediately took her under her wing, pretending not to notice that the girl regarded her with something approaching superstitious awe—educated black women were not part of Katy's previous experience.

The only one who still felt uneasy about the new arrangement was Padraic. Taking responsibility for someone else was a new experience in his life, and he felt the need for further explanation, though Alex demanded none.

"It was thinkin' about the tatties that did it—believin' yer food is just waitin' ta be dug from the earth and findin' nuthin' but black slime. Times were hard enough when I was there, but not like that. Nuthin' but black slime ta feed the children." His face was gray and drawn at the image.

Oh, Irish, for all your cynicism, you have a soft, soft heart, Alex thought, and she did her best to reassure him. "You needn't worry about bringing Katy here. She is willing and has already proved herself quick to learn. She'll be every bit as good for Wild Swan as I hope the farm will be for her."

By the time Rane arrived at Wild Swan, Katy was beginning to show the first soft hint of improving health from fresh air and good food, though she would probably always be very dainty. And though her hands were as small as the rest of her, they were capable.

"Poor waif, she really has had to learn everything from the beginning. She didn't even know how to make a bed properly; linens were not part of her life before. And setting the table for a meal was like solving a puzzle for her. But show her something once, and she remembers."

When he'd heard the whole story of Katy's arrival, Rane's smile was rueful. "Well, Flora didn't send a boatload, but damn near, if the girl's family is involved."

"I don't think they will be. Della told me that Katy plans to share her wages with them, but not her life. She feels, justly, that her father took the money for her and that she belongs to Padraic."

"And how does the Irishman cope with that?"

"Better than you might expect. He's embarrassed, but he's also very patient with her. It must be an odd situation for him. He thinks of himself as an Irish-English bastard with more pride than sense, but Katy regards him as close to God. She lights up like a candle at the mere sight of him." She frowned thoughtfully. "The only immediate problem is Gincie. She and Padraic have a special relationship, and she's not very happy about having another female around to distract his attention from herself. But Katy's quick; she's noticed the situation and is going out of her way to be kind to Gincie. I marvel that, after having such a hard life and having to take care of no fewer than eight brothers and sisters and her father, she still has such a giving spirit. It occurred to me that she would be perfect to help Philly with the girls or Sam with the boys, but that would require sending her away from Padraic, so I'll just have to be content with having her help when the grandchildren are here."

"Pity Padraic, he hasn't a chance with both you and Flora planning his future."

"Pity Padraic indeed!" Alex retorted. "It can't be all bad to be worshiped like that. Shall I try it to determine whether or not you like it?" She widened her eyes and gazed at him with such youthful adoration, he warded her off in mock horror. "Spare me! I don't think my heart can stand it!"

Gweneth had come home with Rane, and would spend the summer at the farm. She was very fond of Gincie, and it was soon clear that her presence went a long way toward easing Gincie's jealousy of Katy. Katy herself took another big step in that direction by confessing to Gincie that she couldn't read and thought it wonderful that the little girl could.

Gincie came to Alex with this amazing piece of information. "Was she fibbin'?" she asked. "Everybody reads, don't they?"

"They certainly do not. Many, many people do not know how to read even the smallest word," Alex told her.

"Are they stupid? Is Katy stupid?" Gincie looked as if confirmation of this wouldn't entirely displease her.

"Katy is not the least bit stupid! But she's never been taught how to read. And I'd like to remind you, missy, that you weren't born knowing how to read either."

Gincie frowned in concentration, trying to remember when she had not known how to pick out letters and words. She had been taught from such an early age, first by her father and then by Alex and Horace Whittleby, it was difficult for her to recall being without the skill. And because she enjoyed books so much, it began to dawn on her how awful it would be to be unable to read.

Alex, understanding the play of expressions across her granddaughter's face, said, "Perhaps you and Gwenny could teach Katy her letters this summer, and then when Mr. Whittleby comes back, Katy can study with him."

Gincie thought it a grand suggestion and whirled off to find Gweneth. Alex considered Katy to be very clever to have made her confession to Gincie, thus giving the child a feeling of adult superiority with which to salve her wounded heart. Katy was a survivor of some subtlety, which was just as well; otherwise, she might not have lived to begin a new life in America.

Of Gwenny's willingness to enter into the scheme, Alex had no doubt. Gwenny was a natural for the task, and her admiration for and observance of Flora's and Philly's teaching methods had enhanced her skills over the years.

In her sixteenth year, Gweneth was a lovely young woman, though Alex recognized the vanity in that judgment since their daughter with her dark hair, green eyes, and lithe figure so closely resembled herself and Rane. But Gweneth's self-judgment was quite different. Given the general preference for the full-blown rose in women, Gwenny was resigned to the nonconformity of her own appearance. However, it didn't seem to trouble her. Nor did it trouble the young men who, in the past year, had been appearing in increasing numbers to pay awkward court to her. Gwenny treated them with patience, but she was as baffled as flattered by their attentions.

Rane had no such confusion. He was, despite his efforts to the contrary, not wholly reasonable about his daughter's suitors.

"She is always well chaperoned," Alex had pointed out. "And furthermore, Gwenny is very sensible and has strong ideas about what she wishes to do with her life. An early marriage is not part of the plan."

"But I know what those young men are planning and what kind of ideas they have!" Rane had protested, and he had been mightily displeased when Alex laughed.

"You of all people ought to know the truth of what I am saying," he persisted. "I was a young man once and remember . . ."

She put a hand over his mouth to stop the words. "Don't you dare compare yourself to the callow boys who are making eyes at Gwenny. And I was a married woman, not a schoolgirl. What we felt for each other even then—well, it was and is another thing entirely."

He accepted her logic with a grumble, but he had no intention of relaxing his vigilance, and he tried Flora's patience as well as Alex's with his repeated injunctions that they make sure no young man take liberties with Gwenny.

"I pity the man who finally asks for her hand," Flora told her mother. "Father is apt to slit his throat and drop him in the Chesapeake."

Rane, Alex knew, was relieved when Gwenny was at Wild Swan; he had not yet, it seemed, noticed that the countryside yielded its own crop of young men who suddenly found Wild Swan a likely place to come calling. And she hoped the myriad comings and goings of summer would keep him in ignorance; she didn't relish the picture of Rane pouncing on Gwenny's young friends.

Baltimore had become the site of various political conventions in recent years, and the family filtered out to Wild Swan when they could, anxious to avoid the congestion of the city. And usually they arrived in good spirits. But such was not the case with Caleb and Flora this time.

They wore similar expressions of sorrow and anger thinly disguised by bright, false smiles.

Alex was baffled. Having left them in a state of such understanding, she could not imagine what had caused the current rift, and when twenty-four hours passed with no information offered and no easing of tension, she could not bear it. Philly, Blaine, and Virgil were there too, with the girls, but if they noticed anything amiss, they made no comment. And at least they were genuinely relaxed and prepared to enjoy the farm.

"I'm usually not so fastidious," Philly said, "but electioneers spit everywhere! It's most unpleasant. I feel sorry for Sam having to stay in town."

Morgan was in charge of the shipyard while Caleb and Rane were away during this busy time for the business, and Sam was determined to stay with him until he could go with her to the country.

Still thinking of her older daughter, Alex nearly asked Philly outright if she knew what was troubling Flora and Caleb, but then she decided to go to the source. She chose to approach Caleb rather than her daughter.

"I'm being an interfering mother-in-law, and you may tell me to mind my own business, but I hope you won't," she told him. "I hate to see you and Flora with such a distance between you."

"There's soon to be more of a distance between us," Caleb complained, and then seeing Alex's face pale, he hastily added, "I mean in actual miles. Flora has announced that she is going to some women's meeting in New York State."

Alex studied him carefully. "Are you angry because she is going, or because she told you instead of asking?"

"The latter. I used 'announced' advisedly; there was no asking involved."

"I see. She told you, just as I presume you tell her when you are going away on business for the shipyard."

"It's not the same!" he barked, and then he winced as he reconsidered. "Well, it didn't seem the same at the time."

"But it is. Not long ago you told me how proud you are of Flora's capacity to love. Her commitment to and love of the idea of freedom for women is no less strong than other facets of her loving. Why does it make you so angry, so afraid?"

"I'm not afraid!" It was a near bellow, and Caleb heard the desperation in it as plainly as Alex did. "The hell I'm not," he muttered. "Trust you to make me realize it."

He rubbed his face wearily, admitting some hard facts to himself for the first time and searching for a way to explain them to Alex.

"I suppose it's always in my mind, though I have pretended it is not. I am old enough to be her father. I was when we married, and I still am, only now it matters more. I feel as if—as if," he swallowed hard, "I feel as if this trip is a sign that I don't satisfy her any more, as if she needs this to make up for the lack in her life."

Alex's heart contracted with pain, and she reached out to him, cradling one of his hands in both of hers. "Oh, my friend, how wrong you are! It is no wonder Flora looks so confused and hurt. Your doubts are all your own, not hers; I swear to you! Don't you see, she feels strong enough to be passionately committed to a host of causes precisely because she's strong in her love for you. You don't seem to have kept a very close count. She is a thirty-three-year-old woman who adores her husband more, I would say, than the day she married him. The gap between your ages is narrowing, not widening. And perhaps your interests should converge a bit more, too. Why don't you go to the meeting with her? I don't know as much about the subject as Flora does, but I know that there are prominent men who support the cause."

He was silent for a long moment, considering what she had told him, and then he smiled. "You may be an interfering mother-in-law whenever you wish; what I have complicated with my own insecurities, you have just made simple."

"It's always easier to be logical and objective about other people's problems," she said, and she hid her own smile; she could feel how anxious he was to seek out Flora and mend the breach between them. "I highly recommend a stay at the Astor House in New York City, if you have the time, and if your sisters will forgive you for not staying with one of them."

Caleb's two sisters were long married and residents of New York, and though the three of them were together very seldom, Julia and Peggy continued to believe their brother Caleb was as nearly perfect as a man could be. Even when he had written to them about his marriage to Flora, he had received only best wishes.

"I'll tell them I didn't want them to fight over us," he said, "though the truth is that it will be easier all around if they don't feel they have to entertain us every minute."

Alex understood what he meant; with so much time elapsing between visits and with their lives so separate, not even deep affection could totally relieve the strain of a reunion, and it was important that Caleb and Flora have time alone.

Alex liked the gleam in Caleb's eye as he went in search of his wife.

Flora regarded Caleb warily as he approached her. They had scarcely exchanged a civil word since she had told him her plan to travel north.

"I've just been speaking with your mother," he said.

"And what did she say?" She kept her voice carefully neutral, but she thought that she would not be able to bear it if Alex was set against her, too, in this matter.

"She said I was behaving like a fool, though she phrased it more politely than that." He went on to tell her, without faltering, why he had reacted so badly to her determination to travel to Seneca Falls. And then he asked, "Will you forgive me and permit me to go with you?"

Incredulity mixed with joy on Flora's beautiful face. "My dear husband! You are not the only fool. I am so accustomed to your strength, and depend on it so, I have taken away your right to be human and to have fears. It is particularly inexcusable because I champion the rights of the poor, of blacks, and of women. I am shortsighted indeed to have so misjudged you. I thought you did not want me to go because you had measured your indulgence and had reached the end of it—let her play at this but not too much, surely not as much as the meeting at Seneca Falls might indicate. Never once did I consider that you could doubt yourself or my love for you."

She wrapped her arms around him and rested her cheek against him, feeling the beat of his heart through the fine cambric of his shirt. "Until you, I thought tales of fulfillment between a man and a woman were lies, at least for me. I thought my body was incapable of feeling more than a vague enjoyment, and even that was rare in my first marriage. Yet, I married you anyway. I married you because I loved you in so many ways that that one did not seem important. I was prepared to content you as you wished. But I never dreamed how you would pleasure me." Her arms tightened convulsively around him, and then she pulled back so she could look up into his face.

"I do worry about the age difference between us, not because of the way you are now, but because you may die before I do," she confessed. The depth of her fear bleached her face and made her blue eyes shine with unshed tears. "Don't ever leave me, Caleb. Let me die first. I could not bear to be left here without you."

"Your mother suggests that a visit to the Astor House in New York City might not be amiss, a touch of luxury just for us," he said, but his smile was not quite steady. He kissed her hard as if to ward off thoughts of separation and death, but their mutual awareness of the threat drove both of them as they stole away to spend the rest of the day in their room. When they appeared for supper, Flora's mouth was deep rose to match the blush that stained her cheeks every time she glanced at her husband.

Alex noted the changes in both of them and had all she could do not to laugh aloud, particularly because Caleb looked dazed, more like a lovestruck boy than a man past middle age.

But he wore a far more sober expression when she asked him about the Seneca Falls convention.

"Flora and I had a fine time together; we do not get away often enough, I discovered," he said, wanting to reassure her about the continuing strength of his marriage to her daughter. "And we had a nice visit with my sisters, though Julie's husband is no less of an overbearing ass than he ever was. He reminded me of why I visit them so infrequently. And having been to the convention made me more aware of Kenneth's abysmal nature than ever."

He regarded Alex gravely. "That meeting in Seneca Falls will stay with me forever. I take you for granted. You, Flora, Philly, Sam—the women I am closest to. I took Pen and my mother for granted, too. I am accustomed to intelligent and capable women. But until now, I have not closely considered the legality of a woman's position, in spite of Flora's interest in the subject. It has been a shock to learn that a woman's status is truly only slightly less onerous than the position of a slave and that women are nearly as dependent on the good will or lack of it of their masters— husbands, fathers, or brothers though they may be. It makes no sense. Women who are entrusted by nature with the nurturing of children in the womb, and in so many cases by men with the safety and well-being of everyone from children to servants and everything from the food on the table to the pennies that mean the difference in countless families between surviving and not, these same women are not trusted to vote or hold public office or manage their own affairs. The franchise has been expanded to include many more white males, but everyone else is outside." He took a deep breath. "Suddenly I was so angry, I think I must have felt at least a little of what drove Mrs. Mott and Mrs. Cady Stanton and the others to organize the convention. They are dedicated women, but they control their fury well. I am not sure I would in their place. At first they did not want men allowed at the meeting, but in the end, not only were we admitted, but Mr. Mott was appointed chairman. He did well enough, but it is sad that none of the women had the confidence to preside."

Alex knew that the genesis of the convention had been the refusal of the World Anti-Slavery Convention in London in 1840 to admit several women delegates who had been sent by American antislavery societies. Mrs. Lucretia Mott had been among those women turned away, gender being the only reason.

"The worst of it is, for all the brave words, the determination to put forward a body of law that would give women reasonable control of their lives is doomed to failure. This is a country where a large section still believes one man is justified in owning another, and until slavery is resolved, there will not be enough energy devoted to the problems of women to change anything."

"I would like to think that you are wrong," Alex said softly. "I would like to think that there are many men like you, but I know that is not true. You are a rare human being, Caleb Jennings, and my daughter is fortunate to be your wife."

Caleb colored at the compliment. "Do not forget that Flora's vision opened my eyes."

Chapter

21

On January 24, 1848, gold had been discovered at a place called Sutter's Mill in Northern California, and the news, once it reached the East Coast, began to spread like cholera. Indeed, Alex regarded it with nearly the same degree of distaste. Heretofore sane men were suddenly talking of leaving everything to go searching for the metal.

"California would have to be made of solid gold to provide enough for everyone," she observed tartly and was dismayed to see a touch of the same avidity in Rane's eyes.

"Everyone won't find it," he said, "but a lucky few will. And what a feeling that will be—to pull raw wealth from the earth!" Noticing the look on her face, he hastened to add, "I have no intention of rushing off with a pick and shovel, but I think I know a way we can share in the gold. From what I've heard of California, it is a pastoral land and produces little except beef, tallow, and hides. If great numbers of people arrive there suddenly, they will need all manner of supplies, and if there truly is gold in any large amount, the prices will be high enough for goods offered—one can't eat gold. The swiftest ships will have a decided advantage in cargo runs, and we have swift ships."

By the end of the year, Rane was proven correct. President Polk observed that "the accounts of the abundance of gold in that territory are of such an extraordinary character as would scarcely command belief were they not corroborated by authentic reports," thus giving the gold strike official standing, and if that were not enough for the skeptics, there was a small chest of gold flakes and nuggets on display at the War Office in Washington.

Countless men were determined to go west, some by land but many by sea, a route which consumed two hundred days by conventional sailing ship, if the ship made very good time. The way could be made shorter if proper connections could be arranged to leave one ship in order to cross the Isthmus of Panama by land and then take another ship the rest of the way to California, rather than going clear around Cape Horn. But this route soon betrayed its hazards, as scores of would-be miners languished on the steamy, fever-infested shores of Panama, waiting on one side for guides to lead them across, waiting on the other for a vessel to take them aboard. Coastal craft did a brisk business, cramming every available space dangerously full of passengers.

By 1850, three Jennings-Falconer clippers were carrying cargo and a few passengers to San Francisco in California, making the trip in an average of one hundred ten to one hundred thirty days, a great saving of time over the old average. With eggs selling for a dollar apiece, and five dollars' worth of flour bringing fifty, the profits were astronomical.

From California, the clippers plied the Northern ports for furs and lumber to take to China, where they exchanged their cargo for tea, silk, and other exotic goods, before continuing west around the Cape of Good Hope to bring the cargo either to London or to the east coast of the

United States. Parliament had repealed the Navigation Laws the previous year, and now the English markets were open to American shippers, and the demand for fine tea was growing by the year, with premiums offered for first arrival of the best.

The extreme clippers did not have the cargo space of other vessels, but their great speed allowed them to deliver their goods ahead of other ships, thereby receiving higher prices, as Rane had foreseen. And though the winds might be unpredictable and storms hazardous, these did not present the same problems that refueling was for steamships attempting long distances. The most difficult problem the clipper captains faced was keeping their crews from jumping ship in order to go to the gold fields.

Rane and Caleb could do nothing about the conditions on the ships they had sold, but for the ones that flew their house flag, the ones in which they still owned all or the greatest percentage of shares, they made policies that stunned other shipowners. With increasing opportunities in factories and in western lands, the number of young men attracted to the hard life aboard ship had decreased dramatically in the past decade, making it difficult to recruit competent crews. Many who signed on were intent only on getting to the gold fields and knew nothing about duties at sea. And on too many ships, a good part of the crew had been "crimped" or kidnapped, drugged or knocked over the head in a waterfront tavern, not to regain consciousness until the ship to which they had been sold was far out to sea.

Rane and Caleb recognized a basic cause of much of the trouble was the fact that the average $12 monthly wage of a sailor could not compete with the $50 that even a clerk or a barkeep could earn every week in labor-starved San Francisco. Since their clippers were reaping enormous profits, recouping the cost of construction in as little as one voyage, the men saw no reason not to pay the crews extremely well in order to get the best men and keep them. They also subjected the captains to rigorous standards, hiring no one with a reputation for being overly harsh, though discipline was essential in the tight world of a ship. And taking on a "bucko" mate was strictly forbidden, such men being widely known for their habits of violence in controlling crews. The Jennings-Falconer crews were on the whole far more loyal and apt to stay with their ships than others, and as a final precaution, shore privileges were carefully controlled in San Francisco, with promise of a bonus at the end of the voyage easing the deprivation.

Alex loved to read the bills of lading, which listed everything from cloth and nails to metal pans for washing gravel to find gold. It reminded her pleasantly of her father. Though he had been ineffectual in his own home, in his business as a supplier for ships, he had been highly respected.

The people going to the gold fields were almost all male, most of them young bachelors, but many married men, too, who left their families in the East with promises to send for them or return to them as soon as the gold allowed. promises that too often would not be kept. And it was soon apparent that this growing male society did not have Puritanism at its heart.

Gamblers, women of easy virtue, and troupes of actors flocked after the miners. And horseracing was a natural development, particularly because California was a place of vast spaces where horses were an essential part of life. Fine stock brought in by the Spaniards had long flourished there. But that did not lessen the newcomers' determination to import racing stock as they knew it from home. By the beginning of 1850, Alex found her horses in greater demand than ever, though the number of race meetings in the East continued to decline.

The decline was due not only to lingering economic effects of the speculative markets and panics of the past years, but also to a much more ominous cause. What Thoroughbred racing there was on the Eastern seaboard was in the South, with Northern tracks given more and more to trotting horses. And never had the North and the South been so separate. The North had continued to grow more industrial by the year while the South kept to her old ways; the economic interests were vastly different in the two regions; and the crushing weight of slavery overshadowed all.

The South was becoming ever more adamant about the righteousness of owning slaves, more insistent that God and the natural order of things dictated that black men and women were destined to be under the domination of white masters. Much of the Southern stance was to counter the swelling voices of Abolitionists in the North. The majority of these reformers did not want to live beside or otherwise mix with blacks; their objections were made on purely moral grounds—slavery was so evil, it contaminated the whole country. Newspapers in their cause were openly published now and meetings held without the constant threat of reprisal, though the Abolitionists were still markedly unpopular in many quarters. And the flow of fugitive slaves continued, further infuriating the South.

Alastair Cameron was more involved than ever in helping the runaways continue north, and through him, Wild Swan continued to shelter them. Slave catchers were more in evidence than ever, and because of that, Alex had long since modified the old, rather haphazard way of hiding the slaves. Now there was a secret underground room beneath the rebuilt stallion barn. The room could be entered from inside the barn itself or from a tunnel that led some distance away from the barn to concealing trees and bushes. The stallions were constantly conditioned to accept the sounds of movement beneath them. It was a perfect ploy because few would ever suspect that such high-strung horses would adjust to such a situation. If slave catchers did enter the barn, they would see for themselves that they, not anyone else, had excited the horses from their relaxed state. That the horses would react badly to slave catchers, Alex had no doubt. The men were in the main unkempt ruffians who were so aggressive in their methods, the horses of Wild Swan, accustomed to gentle treatment, would surely react badly to their presence, though Alex hoped it would never come to that.

The admission of new states and territories was bringing all the trouble foreseen. The South wanted the new lands opened to slave owners; the North wanted slavery restricted or forbidden. One angry word led to another until suddenly the talk of secession was very real.

"All these years, I've dreaded this," Alex confided to Rane, "but now I don't know how I feel. I fear I would sell my soul to the Devil to avoid outright war. Some cowardly part of me whispers, 'Let the South go her own way. Let her be backward and slave-owning for the rest of eternity, as long as there is no war.' "

"You know that is impossible," Rane chided gently. "This country cannot tolerate such a division and survive. Other nations would be upon us like jackals. And the cotton, rice, and sugar cane, as well as a host of other crops, are vital to the wealth of all."

"Then what do you suggest, war to solve all the problems?" She could not keep the anger out of her voice, though it was not directed at Rane.

He answered patiently. "If I had the solution, I would be a very valuable man. The best we can hope is that reasonable minds continue to prevail as they have in the past."

Her face blanched and her expression was so odd, Rane put his arm around her, fearing she was going to faint. "What is it?"

"God forgive me," she whispered. "I just had the most dreadful thought. Quite coldly I considered that it might be better to have the war now rather than later, now while our grandsons are too young to march away and our sons are just old enough so at least they would not go with the first ranks. War is a young man's sport, after all." Her mouth twisted with the bitter words.

"No forgiveness is needed. You are only doing what you have always done—seeking to protect your own in any way you can. Perhaps war will never come." His voice lacked conviction, and he wrapped his arms around Alex, holding on to her for comfort as much as he was offering it in return.

When Congress had assembled in December of the past year, the members could not even agree on the election of the speaker. The Free Soilers held the balance of power and did not want to use it in agreement with either of the two major political parties. In the course of the seemingly endless balloting, violent words were exchanged. The Southerners feared that the principle of the Wilmot Proviso might be enacted into law. The Wilmot Proviso had been introduced in 1846 into the House of Representatives, where it had repeatedly passed only to be defeated in the Senate. It had been designed to insure that there would be no slavery in any part of the territory that might be acquired from Mexico during the war then in progress. The Free Soilers rallied around its provisions, but the Southerners wanted recognition of the Calhoun Doctrine instead, an assurance that under the Constitution all territories would be considered open to slavery.

In the South, talk of secession became more and more commonplace.

Henry Clay, a statesman of great repute, had retired, but he returned to the Senate when he saw how far out of hand the rivalry between North and South was getting. Though a slave holder himself, he did not wish the Union to dissolve, and he sought a conservative approach to ease the tension between the sections.

In January, 1850, he proposed a series of resolutions which were referred to a select committee of thirteen of which he was made chairman. Clay wanted above all else to prevent war.

On that account, Alex and everyone close to her were in complete agreement. Sometimes she wondered what the use of anything was if it was all to be swept away in war, but she forced herself to behave with grim logic. There were no longer regularly scheduled or well-attended races at either Baltimore or Washington, and she forfeited the entry fees she had posted in the South. She had no intention of having her horses located in what might well be the path of advancing armies. And as calmly as she could, she discussed further plans with Rane.

"If war comes, the armies will need good horses. I will not have my stable requisitioned for the cavalry of either side. My horses are as gallant as any on earth when they're used for the purpose of their breeding. But I won't have them abused by loutish soldiers nor run to the ground in fields of carnage. If war comes, I want the horses safely away."

Rane did not make light of her fears or her plan. Instead he agreed. "I've considered it, too, and I think it would be best if the stock was sent to Canada, perhaps to Nova Scotia. I still have contacts there from the lumber and fishing trade. It would hardly be the climate or the care the horses are accustomed to, but at least they would be safe from the abuses of war." As we will not be, as the farm will not be, he added silently to himself, knowing she was as aware of it as he. For the first time he wished that Wild Swan was located somewhere else. In any armed conflict between the North and the South, Washington would surely be a target since it was the capital city of the federal government. And Wild Swan was not nearly far enough away from that city.

"It is up to you," he continued, "but I would suggest that we wait until we know what Clay can or cannot accomplish. No state has seceded yet, and war has not been declared."

"Agreed," Alex said, torn between wanting the horses in a place of safety and yet dreading having them out of her control.

Clay was enlisting the help of some strong Union men, among them Daniel Webster, Henry S. Foote, Lewis Cass, and Stephen A. Douglas. These Southern and Northern interests were not bound together by good fellowship, but by the single determination to prevent war. Alex felt that if such an unlikely lot could work together, she could at least wait for the outcome of their labors.

In May, Clay and his committee recommended an omnibus bill, which included provisions for the territories as well as for abolition of the slave trade in the District of Columbia and an amendment to the Fugitive Slave Law of 1793. But though President Taylor wanted California admitted to the Union, he wanted no decision made about slavery or the prohibition of it in the territories of New Mexico and Utah until they were ready to come into the Union as states; therefore, he was a serious obstacle to passage of the statutes the committee was proposing.

The nation was in this precarious position when Padraic broke his own impasse and asked Katy to marry him.

"I hope he really wants to marry the girl," Della told Alex. "Honestly, I think Samson has more to do with this proposal than Padraic."

Della's face had the soft, luminous quality it always had when she talked about her husband, but there was a twist of rueful humor as well. "Samson's been acting as if he's the Irishman's or Katy's father. For weeks now he's been dropping hints that are as subtle as lead weights. 'Irish, I be thinkin' you make an honest woman a' dat Katy, it be betta fo' everybuddy.' 'Irish, nobuddy goin' love you mo' dan dat Katy, not neber.' 'Irish, I doan know fo' sure, but I think mebbe dat ol' Frank from down de road gots his eye on Katy,' " Della mimicked her husband perfectly. "He changes Frank to Joe or Mike or so and so, so that Padraic doesn't have a specific target in case he loses his temper, and he always makes it clear that the men are making calves' eyes at Katy, not the other way around. With all this talk of war, Samson seems to want everyone he knows to be settled and happy. Do you think he might be forcing Irish to do something he doesn't really wish to do?"

Alex giggled at the picture of Samson as a heavy-handed matchmaker and general patriarch of the staff at Wild Swan. When she regained control, she said, "I don't think anyone, even Samson, could force Padraic to do anything he doesn't want to do. He is a very self-possessed man. However, if the occasion arises, I will try to make certain that he's not marrying Katy for the wrong reasons."

Della was still convinced that her husband's campaign might have too much to do with the match, but she was satisfied that Alex was now in charge of the outcome. For her part, Alex could not imagine how she would approach Padraic on such a delicate matter.

As it turned out, he gave her the opening, coming to her to announce his intentions as if the news hadn't already spread to every corner of Wild Swan.

"I'll be marryin' Katy, and she'll be feelin' better about it if ye're given' yer approval," he announced, clearly wanting Alex's approval for himself, but not willing to admit it.

"Congratulations to both of you. Of course I wish you happiness," she said.

"We'll get on well enough. But it's that old Samson who's wantin' this most, been after me day and night he has."

"If that is really true, then you shouldn't marry Katy," Alex said quietly. "She deserves better than that. Remember when you told me that you couldn't marry up and you wouldn't marry down? If you think marrying Katy is marrying down, then neither of you will be happy." She could not help remembering that Padraic had come to Wild Swan already knowing how to read, write, and figure, plus a good deal more, while Katy had been completely untutored; perhaps her humble background still bothered him.

Padraic's eyes locked with hers, and then he ducked his head in an endearing gesture of embarrassment. "Marryin' Katy will be marryin' up fer me," he said, his voice gruff with emotion. "She's a dear lass and beautiful and bright as the sun at mornin'. Samson didn't say a single thing me own heart hasn't been sayin' all along. The honor's all mine, and I'll niver know why she said yes when I asked 'er."

"I do. She's adored you from the moment you saved her. I doubt she's seen any other man clearly since that day. I wish you years and years of joy together."

"I'll do me best to make Kathleen happy every day a' her life," he said, and it was a solemn vow.

Though Katy made no onerous duty of her faith, she was enough of a Roman Catholic to want to be married in that church, and so Padraic took her to Baltimore for the ceremony, and then the couple returned to Wild Swan for the celebration everyone helped to plan. Alex did not ask if Padraic had had to deal with Katy's family at the wedding, but she doubted that he had since he looked so happy; she didn't think he would have kept his temper with a father who would surely have gloated over the marriage after having sold his daughter to the man.

Even in their absorption with each other, the couple did not neglect Gincie, and Alex was touched by their thoughtfulness. Gincie had grown as fond of Katy as she was of Padraic, and she bustled about with all the confidence of a child who believes she has had a hand in arranging adult affairs.

"I knew they should get married," she told her grandmother. "Now they can be like you an' Grandpa an' everybody."

The joy of celebrating the marriage of Padraic and Katy was welcome in the tense time. And then there came reason for rejoicing on the national level as well, though there was guilt mixed with it because it had to do with death.

President Taylor succumbed to typhus in July.

"God knows it's a cruel thought," Rane admitted. "And I don't wish such a death on any man. But if by his death, the way is cleared to avoid war, then . . ."

"You needn't finish; I will be the voice you so often are for me. You didn't cause his death, any more than I did. God, or fate, or whatever, has intervened; now let it be for the country's good," Alex said fervently.

And it seemed that it was, because Taylor's successor, Millard Fillmore, was not set against Clay's proposals.

Because there was no cannonfire but only birdsong, the drone of bees, and the sounds of the horses and people working at Wild Swan, because there were no armies swarming over the land, that summer seemed particularly golden to Alex. Nothing was final yet, but war had not begun, and she was content to celebrate that fact alone.

Gwenny was home, but the rest of the family, though they had all spent some summer days at Wild Swan, were in Baltimore and would be filtering out to the farm again over the next week. Sam and her sons were due first, within the next few days, because Sam had duties at Brookhaven that brought her to the country, though she would have preferred to wait until Morgan could come with her. The general plan was that the whole family would spend as much of August as possible at Wild Swan, though Rane, Caleb, and Morgan would be available to their foreman should anything go amiss in the shipyard.

Alex and Della were planning menus for the coming horde when they both froze at the unusual sound of Katy's voice raised in shrill anger. Katy, for all the talk of Irish moods, did not often lose her temper, but she obviously had now.

"Herself's not expectin' th' likes a' you, an' I know that fer God's own truth! Take yer dirty self away. You've got no business here. I know all about you, I do, an' ye're not welcome. Piety—what a name that is for a she-divil like you!"

Somehow Alex knew even before she heard Piety's name. Though Katy might not know about the fire, she was well aware that Gincie's mother was a horrible woman; everybody at Wild Swan knew that except for Gincie.

The summer heat fled from Alex's body and left her cold to the bone. Della took a step as if she would shield her from any contact with Piety, but Alex shook her head. "No, it is I she's come to see, and see me she will." The same protective frenzy driving Katy rose in her. "Don't worry. I will make Piety sorry she ever came back."

Seeing the look on her employer's face, Della did not doubt that Alex was capable of dealing with Piety. It occurred to Della that if she ever saw that concentrated fury directed at her, she would run for the hills; until that moment she had not known that human eyes could turn cat yellow.

Katy withdrew from the battle at Della's gesture, as aware as Della of the force emanating from Alex.

Even Piety, never astute at judging other people's needs or emotions, checked momentarily as she confronted her adversary, but greed strengthened her resolve.

"I've come—" she began, but Alex cut her short. "I can imagine what you've come for, but we will discuss this in the privacy of the library, unless you wish my staff to witness it."

Piety glanced around, suddenly furtive at the thought that the witness to the fire might be in the vicinity. "I thought as much," Alex said curtly and led her toward the library.

She sat at her desk, fixing her eyes on the woman, not offering her a chair or anything else, simply waiting. And it came to her that Piety looked much as her own mother had looked the last time she had seen her, somehow withered by discontent as if the soul inside were sapping the body. Drab and pinch-mouthed, Piety was well on her way to becoming a truly ugly woman.

Piety looked around for a place to sit and then thought better of it, hoping to maintain an advantage by remaining upright.

"I don't want to be unreasonable," she began, "but circumstances force me to ask your assistance. I am lamentably short of funds and know you can afford to help me. A small price, for after all, you have Virginia."

"You are right. I have Gincie. And I have no intention of losing her. Why on earth should I pay you anything?" Alex's voice was silky soft, and her feline stare did not leave Piety's face.

Piety swallowed nervously but plowed ahead, determined to break Alex's control and gain the advantage. "So that I will go away without making a scandal or taking my daughter with me. We both know I don't want the brat and you do; that should be enough to settle this matter."

"It is, oh, indeed it is. I presume that sorry excuse for a man of God has not been able to provide as well as you thought he would. I wonder, is it he who has sent you, or is it your own venality?" The flicker in Piety's eyes told Alex it was the preacher who was behind this invasion. She gave a low laugh, devoid of humor. "He is as witless as you are. I know what you are thinking. You are thinking that the authorities would hardly have any interest now in a fire that happened years ago. You are thinking that you have gained something because you have only me to deal with now and not the courts. I wonder how much your paramour knows about your past?" She shrugged. "No matter, he deserves you in any case, I'm sure. You've told me how you think things should be; now I will tell you how they will be.

"You will leave here today, and this time you will not come back, not for any reason, not as long as you live. Because if you do, you will live a very short time. I will kill you or hire it done. You seem to have forgotten that protecting Nigel dictated much of what I did before. Nigel is dead. He no longer stands between me and you."

Alex's lethal calm began to penetrate Piety's defenses. "You wouldn't kill . . . you couldn't," she forced the words out through dry lips.

"I could and I would, and more than that, I find I would very much like to. I would like to know that you could never hurt anyone again." As Alex stood, Piety backed toward the door.

"You take care of niggers and Irish beggars here. What of my sons? Nigel always provided for them," Piety whined, trying a new tactic.

"You should have considered that before you drove Nigel to his grave. Nigel left you a creditable sum; I made no effort to interfere with your inheritance of it. As for your sons, the only hope for them would have been that they be taken from you at birth. And now I think you ought to consider your own health by leaving Wild Swan as swiftly as possible."

She advanced with slow deliberation, and Piety turned tail, the last of her defiance deserting her as the full depth of Alex's determination and hatred assailed her in waves.

Alex felt her heart jump as she saw that Mark and Matthew, Piety's two sons, were waiting for their mother in the hired carriage. At fourteen and twelve, they had more the look of their mother than before, both of them as grim-faced as if they never smiled. Piety said something to them, and they stared at Alex. The look in the younger one's eyes was flat, dull, but Mark glared at Alex with implacable hatred, much the same, she realized, as her own emotion toward Piety. She resisted the impulse to step back and made herself return Mark's stare until he looked away. She was more sure than ever that Piety's sons were far beyond her help, and she wanted them far, far away from Gincie.

She watched the carriage out of sight, and then she swayed, feeling the last of her energy ebbing away.

Della materialized beside her. "I am afraid you have a more serious problem than that woman; Gincie must have been listening outside the door. She came through the kitchen, and her face was as white as death."

Alex caught up with her granddaughter before Gincie had had time to climb her favorite pear tree in the orchard.

She wrapped her arms around the slender body, but Gincie suffered this no more than an instant before she pulled away violently.

"That horrible woman was my mother," she said flatly, not asking a question. "She hates everybody. Me an' Padraic an' Katy an' Della an' Samson an' everybody. You lied, you said she just had to go away."

Alex had always known that Gincie would ask for more details as she got older, and she had never pretended to be anything other than her grandmother. She had told her when she asked that her father Nigel had been a wonderful man who had died because he had fallen ill while being a good doctor to many sick people. But of Piety she had said as little as possible, though she had painted her in undeservedly humane colors when she had spoken of her. Gincie remembered very little of her life before she had come to Wild Swan, and Alex had always thought that whatever she needed to know could be gradually and kindly told. Now Piety's visit had changed everything.

"I didn't exactly lie," Alex protested. "I just did not tell you all of the truth because I didn't want you to be hurt." Though it was true, the reasoning sounded weak to her own ears, and it didn't seem to impress Gincie, either.

The eight-year-old had more vital things on her mind. "That was really my mother." She shuddered with disgust, still overwhelmed by the knowledge. "Will I grow up to be like her? or like those mean-looking boys? They are my brothers, aren't they?"

This was far worse than when Flora had feared she would be like her own mother, because Flora had never had to see Florence. The fear in Gincie's eyes tore at Alex's heart, and she gathered her close again. "They are your half-brothers, but you will not be like them or like your mother, not in a million years. Human beings do not always breed true. You know how it is with the horses; we can breed two swift horses together, and their offspring may yet be slow. Human beings are even more unpredictable than that. If you favor either of your parents, it is your father you are most like. And Nigel was a wonderful man. You are kind and intelligent, just as he was. Can you even imagine being as full of bad thoughts and feelings as that woman?" She could not bring herself to say "your mother," and she did not want Gincie to focus on her half-brothers, either in pity or dread. They were, after all, far too like their mother.

"Sometimes I don't do what I'm supposed to," Gincie ventured in a small voice, testing her moral rectitude. "And sometimes I do bad things. I did eat that gingerbread yesterday even when Della told me not to."

"Gincie, my dear child, no one is perfect! We all try to do the right thing all the time, or we ought to, but it just isn't possible. You are a very good girl, and I wouldn't want anything about you changed." She kissed her on the tip of her nose and made herself smile, though it was all she could do not to weep.

At last the tension began to drain out of the little girl. "I feel better now," she assured her grandmother, "but I still need to be in my thinking tree for a while."

"I can understand that," Alex said, and gave her a boost to help her up the first part of the tree, then waited until Gincie was safely ensconced above the world. Alex remembered how she herself had found a haven in various leafy bowers when she had been a child. And she remembered her unhappiness at home, too, and hoped Gincie would never feel that at Wild Swan. But she did not believe Gincie would forget the shock of this day.

She trudged back to the house feeling as if she were a thousand years old and knowing that the contentment she had felt this summer would not be restored until Rane returned. Briefly she considered going to Baltimore, but she rejected the idea. Gincie needed her and needed to be at the farm right now. And then she decided she had no valor left, and she sent a message to Rane:

Piety was here. I sent her away. Gincie overheard our conversation. She seems to be all right, but I am not. I need you.

She maintained rigid control, telling Gweneth what had happened when Gwenny returned from a ride to a neighboring farm, telling it in stark terms with no visible emotion and enlisting her daughter's aid in making sure Gincie felt particularly cherished. She kept the hard rein on herself until Rane arrived the next day, but as soon as they were alone, the last of her strength deserted her, and she fell into his arms, moaning, "I threatened to kill her, and I wanted to! I wanted to strangle her or beat her head in, anything, just as long as she was dead!"

He did not tell her that she hadn't really meant it or that Gincie was too young for any of it to matter. He just held her until she was able to understand that he was there for her and it was not graven in stone that she must be strong for everyone all the time.

Chapter

22

During September, the proposals of Clay's committee were enacted as five statutes with President Fillmore's approval. A territorial government was established for Utah, and a popular sovereignty clause provided that any state or states that might be formed out of this land would be admitted as free or slave, depending on what their constitutions should provide. The same provision regarding slavery was applied to a territorial act for New Mexico, and the conflict between Texas and the federal government over the Santa Fe region was resolved by directing payment to Texas in return for the cession of the disputed area to a new territory. California was admitted as the thirty-first state in the Union with slavery forbidden under her constitution. The slave trade, but not slavery, was abolished in the District of Columbia. And the Fugitive Slave Act amended the original 1793 statute.

Even having known that some compromise must be made between Northern and Southern interests did not prepare the Falconers for the provisions of the Fugitive Slave Act—nothing could lessen the impact of the terrible words.

Alex woke up screaming in the night, caught in the grip of a hellish vision of Della, Samson, and their sons being taken away while she stood rooted, unable to help them.

"Hush, now, hush, sweetling," Rane soothed her after she had gasped out the nightmare. "It hasn't happened, and it won't."

"I must tell everyone what I have decided. I am a coward not to have done so already."

"I will tell them, if you wish," he offered, but she refused. "No, it is my task, but I would very much like you to be beside me."

They were in Baltimore, but they returned to Wild Swan, and Rane held Alex's hand tightly as she spoke to the assembled staff.

"I know you have all been discussing the new Fugitive Slave Act. I have found it difficult to think of anything else. The provisions are very specific. Special commissioners are being appointed to add to the numbers of officials who can issue a certificate of arrest. It is the law. At no trial or hearing will the testimony of an alleged fugitive be admitted as evidence, nor will any fugitive claiming to be a freeman have the right to a trial by jury. It is the law. Federal marshals and deputy marshals are now liable for the full value of a fugitive who escapes their custody, and those marshals are empowered to summon aid from any bystanders. It is the law. Any person who willfully hinders the arrest of a fugitive or aids in his rescue or escape will be subject, not only to severe civil damages, but to a thousand-dollar fine and imprisonment. *It is the law.*" Though her voice was not loud, it seemed to echo on the windless autumn air. Her audience was deathly still, all concentrated on Alex as if she would yet tell them there was some way around this terrible new burden.

"All of you know that fugitive slaves are harbored here from time to time; all of you have kept the secret well for years, and I could not love you more for it than I do, but now the risks are higher, the penalties more severe. I have thought of what I must do, but you must make your own decisions. I cannot deny refuge to the fugitives, not even to make Wild Swan safer for the rest of us. In the North there is already talk of passing laws designed to foil the new statutes, but this is Maryland, a slave state on the border between North and South. I expect the law will be enforced here to its full extent. If any of you wish to leave, I will not blame you. I will do everything I can to find employment for you elsewhere. You do not have to decide right now. Be honest with yourselves and with each other, and do not be ashamed to tell me if you wish to go."

High and sweet, the wobbling challenge of a colt was met by the full-throated trumpeting of a mature stallion. One of the red Devon cattle lowed, a comfortable sound that seemed to say horses weren't to be listened to. The October day was warm but bore the first hints of cold around the edges, and the air had the definitive seasonal smell of wood smoke mixed with dying leaves. The beauty of the day made the oppressive provisions of the new law seem even more obscene. The humans remained silent, painfully aware of the contrast. And then Katy spoke, startling them all.

"Me skin isn't black, so I'm not runnin' th' risk a' being carted off by th' slave catchers. An' I can't be speakin' fer any a' th' rest a' you, black or white. But fer meself, I want ta stay right here an' go on helpin' those poor wretches. I know what it is ta be sold, though Our Lady blessed me that day an' brought Padraic ta me. Still an' all, no one person should sell anither. I say ta hell with th' law! A law that makes us do evil things should be no law a' tol." Her face was quite pink when she finished, but her chin was raised defiantly, her dark blue eyes alight with the fire of her convictions.

Padraic looked as if he was going to explode with pride, but all he said was, "I guess I'll be stayin', bein' as me wife'll be livin' here."

The courage and humor of the Irish couple eased the tension. No one had any intention of leaving Wild Swan. Alex was particularly touched by Della's quietly spoken, "We would not even consider leaving you or Wild Swan," because she knew Della had always had reservations about the sheltering of fugitive slaves due to her fear that it would somehow prove dangerous to Samson, revealing him for the escaped slave he was.

When Alex decided she ought to go to Annapolis to tell Alastair of their resolve, Rane proposed that they spend the night at the Bateses'.

Alex complied readily, feeling the same need to retreat from the emotional toll the past weeks had taken.

Alastair was deeply moved by their pledge to continue working for the cause he held dear; it did not seem to occur to him that he himself had risked all far more often than they.

But with Mavis and Tim, aside from a mutual acknowledgment that the new Fugitive Slave Act was going to be difficult to live with, the talk was all of the children, the grandchildren, and of the thriving business of the tavern. The Naval School, now called the United States Naval Academy, had indeed increased business, for many of the faculty had found the tavern a reliable place for good food and drink, and the midshipmen, when they were permitted and had the funds, frequented it, too, and recommended it to family and friends who visited the town.

"If Gwenny lived 'ere, dere'd be a trail o' dem young fellows leadin' to 'er door," Mavis said, Kent still sounding in her voice despite thirty years away from England. "She be yur image as a lass, dat she be," she told Alex.

"There is already a line of young men leading to Gwenny in Baltimore, and to Wild Swan, too," Rane grumbled.

They all laughed at his disgruntled expression, but Alex gave him high marks for patience, since he had obviously noticed the youthful swains at Wild Swan, after all, but had done nothing drastic.

"Gwenny's very clever," Alex said. "She's kind to all the young men in such an evenhanded fashion, none is favored above the others, and all are kept at a careful distance. She hasn't met anyone yet who can touch her deeply."

"I'll flay anyone who tries that," Rane muttered, deliberately provoking another round of laughter at his expense.

But later when they were alone, Alex asked, "You really won't stand in Gwenny's way when she falls in love, will you?"

"Not as long as the man loves her, appreciates her mind as well as her body, doesn't gamble or drink too much, and can be faithful," he replied, and Alex had to concede that none of the conditions was unreasonable.

They spent more time together that fall than usual because of Alex's lack of racing commitments. While it seemed that war had been averted, there were still many in the North and the South who did not like the new statutes, the one side chafing against the Fugitive Slave Act in particular, and the other believing slavery was not well enough protected or extended. Alex had decided that if the peace held, the spring racing season of the next year would be soon enough to compete again.

She clung to Rane as the one unchanging force in a changing world. Things seemed to be moving too fast, literally and figuratively. An American steamer made the trip from Liverpool to New York in only ten days, four and a half hours, and railroads seemed to be sending their tentacles everywhere.

"You should like the modern mania for speed," Rane teased. "After all, you are built like your Thoroughbreds, long and lean."

Alex made a face at him. "I am not at all sure being compared to a horse, even to the finest among them, is a compliment."

"It was well meant," he protested with a grin. "I was thinking of my part as stallion to your mare."

Alex laughed. "You have a glib tongue." She rolled her eyes. "And thank goodness for it!" But even under the easy banter, she clung to the strength of him to counter her insecurities.

There was sorrow as well as joy that season, for Virgil Winslow died quietly in his sleep. He was old and had been growing frail in the past two years, but it was hard nonetheless to be without his gentle presence. Perhaps the finest tribute to him came from Horace Whittleby. The little tutor had respected the old man deeply, and enjoyed their discussions and chess games, but he took the news of Virgil's death and attended the funeral with his usual reserve. However, when Philly gave him the collection of rare old books and the fine chess set Virgil had specifically designated for him, Horace cried like a child, apologizing all the while for his loss of control.

"It's all right," Philly told him. "Uncle Virgil was very fond of your company. The talks you had with him helped keep his mind young even when his body was failing."

And hardly had they buried Virgil when Alex received letters from Boston and Rachel that left her unsure whether to mourn or rejoice, though her overriding feeling was shock.

Boston wrote that he, his wife, and son would be leaving for California in the early spring. Boston's letter was matter-of-fact; they had not entirely lost their minds, for they did not intend to dig for gold but rather to open a shop or establish a farm in a place they understood to have plenty of good land. He had left it to Rachel to explain their reasons for leaving the Indian territory:

> *Dear Alex and Rane,*
>
> *I wanted to write separately so that you would know that this change in our circumstances has my full approval.*
>
> *The part of me that is Cherokee will be so forever. But I have learned since coming to this desolate land that anger and defiance, while they might sometimes serve a good purpose, can also wear the heart away. And grieving that never ceases turns the spirit to stone. This territory will never be my home; it will never be more than a place the government chose to hide its shame and my people.*
>
> *I am not as strong as I once believed. Boston is strong, the strongest man I know. For my sake, he gave up his own blood ties and became a Cherokee. Now it is time for me to*

become a white woman. I do not mean to say that I am
without guilt for this decision, but reason reminds me that,
in truth, I am white as well as Indian, as is our son Caton.

I know there will be perils in our new life, but there is
promise as well.

Even so far from Wild Swan, I can feel you wishing us well!

Love, Rachel.

Boston was fifty-five years old, the same age as Rane, and it stunned Alex that he would even consider beginning a new life. But the more calmly she made herself think about it, the better the idea seemed.

"Do you suppose Boston would like to be my representative for the horses in California? It would be a much more direct way of selling them. They could go by ship or even overland with a good agent, but the final disposition of them would be in Boston's hands. The prices they would fetch would mean more for my accounts than I gain by selling them to a middleman."

Rane's eyes began to kindle with the same light of speculation. "And if Boston was in San Francisco or close by, he could serve as an agent for our ships as well. I know that doing business with one's relatives is not always the best plan, but I would trust Boston with my life."

"I shall write to Boston and Rachel immediately and hope the letter will find them before they depart," Alex said, her face alight with excitement.

"We mustn't get our hopes up too high," Rane cautioned. "I would not blame Boston if he prefers not to work for us, for that is what it would be. It would be understandable if his pride prevented his acceptance despite our enthusiasm."

"In the case of other men, I would agree, but Boston has both the dreamer and the clerk in his character, and his pride is not a touchy thing. In his quiet way, Boston is as sure of himself as any man I know."

Contrary to Rane's misgivings, Alex was proven right. Her letter got through in time, and Boston and Rachel professed themselves glad to have a more specific plan in mind. Far from being reluctant, Boston even suggested the new enterprise be called "Wild Swan West" in order that there be no doubt where the horses came from. Rane and Caleb obligingly pronounced it a grand idea, and the Falconers and Jenningses celebrated together with enough French champagne to make everyone giddy by the end of the evening. Though they all knew it would be well into 1852 before the new business could be fully organized, they all felt as if it had been fully accomplished upon the arrival of Boston's letter of acceptance.

Though war would have changed all their plans for the new venture, as time passed they grew more confident that peace would hold, at least for a while. The Southern Rights Party was formed to agitate for proslavery forces, and in the North, the states began to enact "personal liberty laws" to foil the Fugitive Slave Act. In February 1851, there was what proved to be only the first in a series of mob rescues of fugitive slaves being returned to the South. In the Boston case, the slave Shadrach escaped to Canada, but in other cases in other cities, the outcome was not always so fortunate for the slaves. The Southern Rights movement and the counterweight of the Abolitionists made the peace fragile. But as 1851 gave way to 1852, it became increasingly clear that the statutes, now being lumped together as the "Compromise of 1850," were gaining gradual acceptance for the sake of preventing war.

Alex resumed a racing schedule at Southern courses, but she could not help noticing that many conversations came to an abrupt halt when she approached. Old acquaintances were still cordial, but they knew her views on slavery and did not wish to discuss the subject in her presence. It was, in one sense, a courtesy to her, though it had the effect of making her feel the outsider.

She had no doubt that one of the main topics of infuriated debate was *Uncle Tom's Cabin or Life Among the Lowly* by Mrs. Stowe. First published as a serial in an Abolitionist paper, the Washington *National Era*, it was now being issued as a book, and everyone seemed to have already read it, to have heard the gist of the plot from someone else, or to be planning on purchasing a copy of the novel as soon as possible.

Never had the cruelty of slavery been described in such a riveting way. The high melodrama of the book captured audiences in a way dry, moral treatises never could. Simon Legree, Uncle Tom, and Little Eva were becoming common household names. And there seemed to be no middle reaction to the novel. Slave-owning Southerners loathed it, claiming that its harsh portrayal of slavery was designed to strip them of their property and their honor as well, while Northern admirers of the book saw it as a moral indictment of a system that was corrupting the whole country —they pointed out that the wicked Simon Legree was a Yankee in the novel—and as a warning that the "peculiar institution" must not be allowed to continue.

On closer consideration, Alex decided it was just as well that none of the Southerners had attempted to discuss the story with her. There were subjects that were simply too volatile to allow an amiable exchange of ideas by opposing sides, and slavery was surely one of them.

She never lost sight of the fact that the tragedy of slavery was not confined to a novelist's imagination but was the daily lot of thousands of people who, solely because of their skin color, were condemned to be owned like livestock. And the pain of it sharpened at one of the Virginia race meetings.

The encounter was brief and wholly unexpected, but the memory of it etched deep. It was the second day of the races, and she was watching the early morning exercising of her horses and others, making mental notes about the fitness of various animals.

She recognized the young black man who came to stand beside her as one of the grooms belonging to a well-known horse owner from North Carolina. Her assumption that he was there just to watch the horses was quickly dispelled.

"Please doan look at me, ma'am," he whispered, and she froze.

"Everybuddy know you doan hold none wid slavery. You takes me north, please, you takes me? Den I works fo' you long as you wants."

Her skin was instantly bathed in icy sweat. She could smell his fear and her own. And for a long moment, she wanted to do as he asked, take him away, free him, reward him for his enormous courage in approaching her. Then sanity returned, and her body hurt with the pain of it.

"I can't do it! God help me, I cannot! Stealing slaves is a crime, and I have no means to get you away without discovery." Her mind started to work more rapidly. "But I will try to buy you, I promise I will. And then I could legally grant your freedom further north."

"He woan sell me, but I thanks you." The soft, sad words, no anger, just hopeless sorrow struck her like blows. And his despair became more deeply her own when his master, as the slave had foretold, refused to sell him.

She made a generous offer for the young man, saying that she had seen how well he handled horses and wanted him to work for her.

"Why should I sell a valuable slave to you, Mrs. Falconer?" the owner asked coolly. "I know your reputation; you do not own slaves, and you don't think anyone else ought to own 'em either. My people are well treated. But people like you make 'em discontented. If I sold Roscoe to you, the others would know that he was goin' north to be free. Only trouble would come from it."

Alex had to concede that under the circumstances, the man was being as polite as could be expected, but still she had to fight the urge to scream at him that it was being denied freedom that made slaves discontented. She had failed utterly in her mission. She could only hope that the man would not suspect that his slave had approached her first. Suddenly, she longed to be home where she could look at black and white faces and know that all the people were free.

Chapter

23

Before Alex had left for the races, she had received a letter from Hugh and Angelica Bettingdon asking if their son Christopher might visit the Falconers for the coming summer. Though there had long been an open invitation between the two families should any of their offspring want to visit across the Atlantic, Alex nearly refused the request.

She had no objection to Christopher; she assumed any child of Hugh and Angelica would be a delight. It was the state of the country that distressed her. She dreaded having the boy see how the nation was caught in the web of slavery. It was the old dilemma of feeling English around Americans and American in the presence of the English. And it was as if the nation were an odd and ailing member of the family, someone who needed to be sheltered and cared for away from the unsympathetic eyes of strangers.

And then Alex reminded herself that the Bettingdons were very aware of the problems and injustices that existed in their own country and in America. Christopher would one day be the Duke of Almont; it was even more important for him than for most to understand the pain of those less fortunate than he. Rane had agreed without hesitation to the visit, and so they had both extended their welcome, and Christopher was due early in June. From the moment of his arrival, he put her and everyone else at ease.

Hugh and Angelica had produced a fine son. Christopher looked so much like the Hugh of years ago—so young, tall, and dark with strong features—that Alex felt her heart give a queer little jump, and the past was for an instant clearer than the present. But Angelica had left her mark on her son too. His eyes, rather than being nearly black like his father's, were a silvery gray with a dark ring around the iris. And his demeanor was less forbidding than Hugh's had been when Hugh was a young man, though there was a certain reserve in addition to bright intelligence in Christopher's eyes.

His manners were faultless, neither too lordly nor too hearty, though he was already Earl of Claverly, having inherited one of his father's lesser titles, and he possessed that most useful of all social charms, the ability to make each person he encountered feel unique and worthy. He even managed to do it in the confusion of the family party held in his honor on his first night in Baltimore.

It amused Alex to listen to the contrast in accents. Her own children, by blood as English as Christopher, sounded utterly American compared to him. And then her amusement faded as she witnessed an extraordinary thing.

Gweneth walked into the room, and she and Christopher were introduced. The words they exchanged were commonplace. But nothing else about the meeting was. Alex felt the world stop for the two of them, and she saw the shock of recognition that widened the gray eyes and the green for a timeless instant.

Alex glanced nervously at Rane and then the rest of the family, but no one else seemed to have noticed anything out of the ordinary. Still she knew she was not mistaken. So had she and Rane looked at each other the first time they had met, though neither had known for a long time, and she longer than he, what it had meant. It was as simple and as complex as finding the other half of one's self even when there had been no intention to search.

Alex had every hope that Gweneth would be happily married someday; she was not the sort of mother who wanted to keep a child too closely tied to her. She wanted her daughter to know the joys as well as the sorrows of sharing her life with the man of her choice, though in light of Gwenny's independent spirit, she had also considered the possibility that her daughter might choose a life without marriage. She had been prepared to accept that, too.

What she had never considered was that Gwenny might marry an Englishman and go to live in England. Christopher's destiny was set. He would be the next Duke of Almont, one of the most powerful lords in the land. He had been raised from the cradle to know his duties, responsibilities, and privileges. There was no question of him throwing it all away for love, no matter how much his heart might wish it. His wife, even were she American born, would have to become an Englishwoman.

She was dismayed by the idea, but the depth of her negative reaction dismayed her almost as much. Most mothers would be beside themselves with delight at the prospect of a daughter marrying a genuine English lord, particularly since there had been a plague of bogus nobles invading the country for the past two decades in search of rich American wives.

She chided herself for her flight of fancy. Gweneth and Christopher had just met; it was surely foolish to speculate about any relationship between them, let alone marriage. But the memory of the look they had exchanged lingered.

In the days that followed, Alex knew she had not been mistaken.

Gweneth had planned to spend most of the summer in the city because she had many friends there, particularly a young lawyer, John Russell, who had recently sparked a little more interest than her other admirers. And there were lectures, libraries, and a host of other attractions she had wanted to be near. But now the city and John Russell seemed to have lost their fascination for her. She announced her change of plans with elaborate casualness, but the real reason was clear to Alex—Christopher was going to spend the summer at Wild Swan; therefore, that is where Gwenny wanted to be.

They rode together, and she introduced him to everyone who came to visit the farm. They played chess and draughts when summer rain kept them inside. They argued amiably over the merits of various books and political ideas. Together they lent a hand to whatever chores were in the offing, and Christopher soon showed himself no stranger to hard work. They were constantly together, but they did nothing improper. Even when he was teasing her, Christopher treated Gweneth with the utmost respect. Alex was not sure her daughter would have exercised the same restraint if given a choice, but Christopher set the rules of their courtship, and Gwenny, usually so fiercely independent, complied.

That it was a courtship, Alex had no doubt, though the rest of the family took longer to come to the same conclusion. And when Rane finally noticed what was going on, his reaction was not what she expected.

"I do believe Gwenny and young Bettingdon have developed a liking for each other. I hope so, for then I could cease to worry about her," Rane said.

Alex stared at him. "Have you lost your mind? After all this time of worrying about every young man who has come within a half mile of Gwenny, you are now prepared to let Christopher come very much closer?"

"I never meant our daughter to live a celibate life," Rane observed with amusement. "I simply do not want her to make a mistake as Flora did with her first marriage. Christopher is a fine young fellow. I trust him to do her no hurt." He studied Alex's face, and his amusement was eclipsed by a frown. "Why ever are you looking so grim? You have cautioned me all along that Gwenny was a sensible girl who would make a wise choice. Why have you suddenly lost faith in her?"

His logic made her more angry. "Christopher will be the next Duke of Almont, for God's sake! Gwenny has no place in that progression. She's American born and bred."

"So she is," Rane agreed softly, and his eyes were speculative. "And you are not thinking of her at all, at least not directly. You are thinking of Florence and St. John all those years ago. You are thinking of the rejection of his family and of all the misery your sister and St. John put each other through. For shame! You have no right to judge Hugh and Angelica so harshly. You know them; you know how sensible and kind they are. And you know how much they love you. Do you truly believe they would find Gweneth unworthy of their son? I should think they would be as happy about it as I am."

It didn't make her feel any better to know that he was right. But irrational as it was, beyond the memories of St. John's family's rejection of Florence and herself, she dreaded the idea of Gwenny going to England to make a life there; it seemed as if it would be a reversal of everything she herself had fought to establish.

It was as if she had spoken aloud; Rane read her easily.

"Don't think it," he warned gently, but there was a thread of steel in his voice. "It is not your life; it is hers. And if you reject her choice of Christopher, she is going to have to choose between the two of you. If you bring her to that, both you and Gwenny will lose, no matter what choice she makes."

Afraid of what she might say, she stalked away from him, and he let her go. She was glad they were at the farm; it allowed her to ride out on Magic, giving the old stallion the exercise he still craved while she worked off her own temper. And finally she was able to see the humorous irony of the situation. Her own mother had been frantic for Florence to marry St. John, wanting the titled connection far more than she wanted the couple's happiness. And there she was, acting much like her mother, though in the reverse, wanting no official connection with dukes and the established order in England. She imagined herself explaining to Hugh that while she was perfectly willing to be his friend, she did not think his family was suitable marriage material. And she imagined his reaction to that!

She started to laugh, startling Magic, and finally she had to rein the horse to a stop until her mirth had run its course. She stopped again on her way home, this time to pick a bouquet of multihued summer wildflowers, though there were many blooms in her gardens at Wild Swan.

As soon as she got home, she sought out Rane and gave him the flowers and a kiss. "For being so wise and patient."

She soon had cause to be thankful to Rane for having made her exhaust her temper and see reason without inflicting her disapproval on the young couple. Gweneth and Christopher's affection for each other began to register at last on one member of the family after another, and the staff of Wild Swan, having seen them together so much, began to treat them as if they had always been together, asking where the other was if one of them appeared alone. Gweneth and Christopher realized that the time had come to admit their plans openly and appeal for approval, though both of them knew they would proceed without it were it withheld for some unfathomable reason.

Because Gwenny had no intention of being a spectator in her own life, she and Christopher approached her parents together.

"Mr. and Mrs. Falconer, Gweneth and I would like your permission to marry." Christopher's voice was strong and calm. He knew he could provide well for his wife, and his nervousness had come when he had asked Gweneth to marry him. Even being fairly certain of her had not kept him from breathing a sigh of relief when she had answered without coyness or hesitation, "Of course I will. I cannot imagine living without you now." Having that assurance from her had left him feeling sublimely confident about the interview with her parents. To Alex, he appeared to be more than ever like his father.

"We want nothing more or less than Gweneth's happiness," Rane said. "And you seem well able to insure that; my daughter has done little except smile since your arrival." Gwenny's laughter rippled through the room at this, and she blushed, earning a fond look from Christopher.

"However, I feel obliged to ask for your word in regard to prior commitments. I trust there is no young woman waiting in England with the expectation of becoming your wife?"

Christopher did not take offense at the question; most men in his position had marriages arranged for them, often from the cradle, so that suitable matches could be made between great houses. "Not only is there no woman waiting, sir," he replied, "but I told my mother before I left that she had better adjust to my being a bachelor forever. She laughed at me, for good reason, it now appears. But how was I to know? The last gathering I attended that was designed to present the latest crop of eligible young women was a disaster for me. I fell asleep in the library and missed most of the party. I hadn't met Gweneth then, you see, and I had no idea of how it would feel to love someone as I love her."

The direct eloquence of his explanation touched both Alex and Rane, but still Alex felt obliged to ask, "And what of your parents? Even though they surely expect you to marry, that does not mean they will be pleased with your choice. I am very proud of my daughter, but she has no title and she is an American. Despite a long-standing friendship with them, I am not at all certain they will be pleased by this match."

"But I am," Christopher insisted. "Long ago, they told me that for good or ill a great deal of my life was set without my volition, but that the choice of the woman who would share it would be entirely mine. I expect that in addition to being happy about my choice of Gweneth, they will be relieved that I have not acted in defiance and presented them with an actress or a dancer." His grin was so endearing, for an instant Alex felt the full power of his appeal and knew why Gwenny had fallen so quickly and completely in love with him.

Rane glanced at Alex, and she nodded in agreement.

"Then you have our blessing, as long as your parents truly have no objections," Rane said, and Gwenny threw her arms around his neck. "Thank you, Father, thank you!" she cried, giving him a kiss before she went to her mother to thank her, too. Christopher contented himself with more restrained thanks and a handshake.

But though she knew it would make no difference, Alex still felt obligated to make one more attempt to ascertain that Gweneth had no illusions about what her new life would bring. It took some doing, since Gwenny was so much in Christopher's company, but Alex finally managed to speak to her alone.

Gwenny eyed her apprehensively before she even spoke, and Alex was reminded of how carefully she had to tread.

"I'm not going to forbid the marriage," she said, "but I do worry. Have you truly thought of how changed your life will be? The independence you have known in your life here will not exist there for you. You will be among the highest ladies in the land, and you will be expected to behave in a very circumscribed way or else run the risk of being declared eccentric and of earning censure for Christopher and his family. And what of your plans to teach?"

"Mother, it is not as if I have a choice," Gweneth said quietly. "I have not had one since I first saw Christopher. It was as if it was always meant to be, as if nothing else could ever be more important than being with him. I know that a certain standard of behavior will be expected of me, but I do not plan to become a meek woman. According to Christopher, there is much need of reform in England, and remember, Mary Wollstonecraft began asking for rights for women there before this century even began. I will not be alone in my views. And Christopher already has estates of his own to manage and will have more and more responsibilities as time passes. Thanks to you and to Flora, I am well educated enough to be of help to him in many ways." Her earnest expression dissolved in a smile. "Oh, Mother, surely you cannot think I will become either a timid little mouse or a useless creature clothed in lace!"

The humorous extreme of the image was irresistible, and Alex had to laugh with her daughter. And at that moment, she felt her opposition to the match begin to dissipate. Gweneth was the same intelligent, sensible human being she had always been, despite her romance with the Englishman.

"Just consider," Gwenny coaxed, "I might have fallen in love with a gold miner heading for California or a sailor on his way to some savage port at the other end of the world. After all, England is one of the most civilized nations on earth, so at least you need not fear that I will be off in a jungle somewhere fending off hostile natives and wild beasts."

Alex laughed harder, thinking of England's placid countryside dotted with fat cattle and sheep and of otters, hedgehogs, and robins—

though England had her wild sweeps of moor and rugged coastline, it was not the same as the raw power of much of the United States. "I concede the point," she said.

Christopher immediately sent word to his parents of his plans, though he was quite sure they already suspected since he had written in glowing terms about Gweneth. But he and Gweneth set their wedding for early December rather than rushing the ceremony, despite their eager anticipation of life together.

Christopher said he wanted to extend his stay and delay the wedding in order to learn more about his future wife's country.

Gweneth agreed it was a good idea for his reasons and for her own. She did not expect opposition from Hugh and Angelica, but she wanted to give them time to adjust to the idea of the marriage. And as for the ceremony itself, she wanted to be married at Wild Swan, and she wanted the guests limited to family and close friends.

"No matter how we try to control it, I expect there will be all manner of functions to attend once we are in England. Christopher is, after all, a most eligible man, and many will want to see what sort of wild woman he has married in America." Pride for her husband-to-be was plain in her words.

But Alex soon discovered that while all the reasons they had presented were valid, their true motivation was to allow her to get to know Christopher better. Though he had been with them for the whole summer, it was nonetheless different to know he would be Gweneth's husband, and he sensed Alex's residual reluctance, despite her sanction of the match.

The young couple accompanied Alex and the horses to race meetings in Virginia and the Carolinas. Gweneth was a superb rider and knew as much about the horses as any of the children, but her experience of the courses was limited, so it was as much an adventure for her as it was for Christopher. And while the races might be shabby affairs compared to the glory they had once had, Christopher showed every sign of being fascinated by both the horses and the spectators.

He was already establishing his own stable of racehorses and was as keen a horseman as his father, but he professed nothing but admiration for the American horses, and he lost his natural reserve enough to yell quite loudly for Fire Dancer, the three-year-old chestnut by Swan Dancer out of Ember, when the filly won in mile heats at Broad Rock. He was visibly disappointed when their four-year-old filly lost, and Alex felt as if she were a little in love with Christopher herself when she watched his reaction to four-mile heats raced and won by Lucky Chance, the five-year-old stallion out of Lucky Lady by Swan's Chance. He was glad that Wild Swan's entry had won, but his empathy for the horses made it difficult for him to witness the strain of the heroic distance race. She remembered very clearly how dismayed she had been when she had seen her first four-mile race, and she felt closer to Christopher than ever before and more reassured—any man who could feel such tenderness toward a dumb animal must surely be capable of the same toward his own species.

Day by day Alex learned what a genuinely fine man her future son-in-law was. He was even-tempered but capable of quick and chilling anger for good cause—a horse handled too roughly, overt rudeness, or deprecating remarks about England were among those things that could rouse his ire. He had a subtle wit and a slightly skewed view of the world that allowed him more patience and humor than most, but he was deadly serious about the duty and justice he owed those who were and would be dependent on him.

Alex's sole objection to him—that he was English and would live forever in England—lost substance day by day. Even Padraic, who had a less than good opinion of English nobles, had been won over by Christopher.

"He's a Thoroughbred, that one," Padraic declared. "Foine blood and bones and no foolishness about him a' tol."

Alex had also discovered that Flora, who might have been expected to oppose the marriage since she had had much to do with her sister's independent attitudes, was in favor of it. "I'm so glad I have Caleb by my side; how could I wish Gwenny to have less than the joy I've known?" Flora asked.

The one reservation Alex had had about Christopher's journey to the races had been that it would expose him more fully to the horrors of slavery, as they would be going to places where it was more in evidence than in Maryland.

But as well as the other things he was, Christopher was perceptive, and when Alex did not broach the subject, he did. "Mrs. Falconer, I do not condone slavery any more than you do. I think it is despicable, and I regret that America has not put an end to it long since. But this nation is not the only one guilty of wrongdoing. Every country has facets of its character that would be better gone. England's handling of the famine in Ireland has been shockingly inept. Thousands upon thousands of people died who might have been spared, had England but made a concerted effort to feed them. Instead, shipments of Indian cornmeal were sent late, tightly controlled, and too often sold rather than freely given. It was as if the greater the numbers who came to the grain depots, the more the government decided it could not cope, and the more miserly it became. And though the legal union was to have made the Irish equal to the English, that is not at all how they were treated when they began to starve. It is not how they are treated now. There are too many, even in the highest positions in government, who think it is an efficient act of nature for famine to thin the Irish population and do not want to interfere with the process. Tell me, would you judge that less evil than the buying and selling of slaves in this country?" Though he did not raise his voice, it vibrated with the passion of his convictions, and his eyes were dark and wounded with the knowledge of suffering on such a vast scale.

Alex remembered a passing mention in one of Angelica's letters to an Irish relief fund Hugh had been organizing some four or five years before, and she had no doubt that the Bettingdons had done more than their share to alleviate the tragedy, even as she and the others at Wild Swan tried to help the plight of the fugitive slaves by maintaining a "station" on the Underground Railroad.

At her age or at Christopher's, it was never an easy lesson to learn how to temper moral outrage and action with acceptance in order that one did not become a humorless fanatic doing more harm than good. Not for the first time, she was struck by how mature Christopher was for his age. Gwenny was getting the best of both worlds—a man of her own age physically with the tempered inner wisdom of someone much older.

Upon returning to Wild Swan in mid-November, Alex found Rane waiting for her. "Permission for the marriage has arrived from England," he announced, and his smile was so broad, she wondered if he had had doubts he had not shared with her. But then she understood as Hugh, Angelica, and Christopher's sister Amelia emerged from the house. Alex was so stunned that, for a moment, she showed no reaction at all. Then pandemonium prevailed as her joyful welcome was added to Christopher's greetings to his family.

"Oh, this American trip has been good for you!" Angelica told her son. "Not only do you look extremely fit, you have found a beautiful bride." Without hesitation, she took Gweneth's hands in her own and kissed the girl on the cheek. "I don't have to ask if you love my son; it shows on your face and on his. Thank you, my dear."

Christopher's sister, who looked very like him though redefined in a delicately feminine form, was a little shy but no less warm in her welcome of her future sister-in-law, and Hugh followed suit, as relaxed as Alex had ever seen him.

Only then did she know how much she had dreaded his disapproval of the match, and she soon realized that the Bettingdons had made the trip by steam packet for precisely that reason—that no doubt might mar their son's wedding.

"Surely you could not have believed we would be anything but pleased?" Hugh said softly. "I already know from Christopher's letters that Gweneth has changed him for the better. Not, of course, that he hasn't been all we could wish for in a son since the day he was born," he added hastily. "But there's more joy in him now, more joy in the present, more hope for the future. Those are the only gifts worth giving to one's beloved. And don't worry, Alexandria, we will take good care of her. It won't be the same as it was with St. John's family; we are not the Carringtons."

"Thank God for that!" Alex breathed, and they both smiled, the anguish of old memories blunted until the remembered pleasure was stronger than the pain.

The time rushed past in a flurry of preparations for the wedding and exchanges of information about what the past years had brought. Hugh was much at court and had a great respect for England's diminutive queen, and everyone pressed him for details.

"Personally she is not one I would ever feel comfortable with; she is rather forbidding and can be as sharp as a sword to anyone who has fallen out of favor. But she loves the country as fiercely as any monarch ever has and wants the best for her people. And the Prince Consort is proving himself to be a most intelligent and thoughtful man. We are in good hands and prospering, though there are still far too many who have too little." He heaved a little sigh. "I begin to think that that will be the state of affairs forever, now that the machines have come to change the ways of working beyond recognition."

"Sometimes I wonder if America might not be better off with a crowned head," Alex admitted. "Politics here continue to confound me. The parties are ever changing and ever more ominous. Now there are those who want free soil, those who want slavery, and those who want every foreign-born person—by which they mean everyone who came one generation after they themselves arrived, and Irish Catholics in particular

—banished. The past few presidents have not seemed to be men cut of fine enough cloth to serve in so important an office, and the Congress has degenerated to uncouth bellowing on the floor of the House. It is slavery. There are other problems, other divisions, but slavery is the heart of it. We are running aground on it. The compromises made two years ago prevented outright war, but for how long? That is a question no one can answer, and it has made the country very nervous indeed."

She took a deep breath, trying to shake off the fear. "Everything is such a tangle now, but I swear it is yet a magnificent country."

"Countries are not born easily," Angelica said. "Remember that England has had her own bitter civil war and encounters with foreign governments. It may be of no comfort, but perhaps nations must be tempered by fire just as fine metal is."

In that fire my children and their children might perish—the thought crept unbidden into Alex's mind, and she thrust it away, vowing not to dwell on such horror in the midst of such joy.

And joy there was on Gweneth's wedding day. The December sky was clear, deep blue, and, as if in blessing, a flight of swans passed overhead. Allen Ralston had come up from Virginia, but the other guests were limited to the Bateses, Caleb's children and grandchildren, Alastair Cameron, a few close friends from Baltimore and neighboring farms, Sam's parents (invited only, Sam had observed, because it was easier than facing the ire of her stepmother should she be excluded), and the people of Wild Swan.

It was strange, but only as she watched Gweneth marrying Christopher did Alex become aware of the marks of time on Hugh, Angelica, Rane, and herself. She had not really noticed the additional gray hairs and lines on the Bettingdons when she had first seen them, but now she did. And looking down at her hand resting on Rane's, she saw the faint tracery of lines beginning to etch her skin and the weathered roughness of Rane's capable fingers. She was not dismayed. They had all—Caleb, the Bateses, Alastair, and Allen, too—dealt honorably with their lives, with time, and it was only fitting that there be marks of the passage from one year to the next. Suddenly the image of her grandmother's face as she had last seen it was very clear—the dark, fiercely tender eyes so bright in the noble, aged face. She thought that any beauty Virginia Thaine had had as a young woman could not have compared to the beauty she had earned by the time her life was coming to an end.

Her silent prayer for Gweneth and Christopher was that they have time to grow old and beautiful together. Her hand closed tightly around Rane's, and he looked at her questioningly, the question disappearing as he read the answer in her eyes. For a moment they were the only people in the universe.

Hugh caught the look they exchanged, and smiled to himself. It was his own secret pleasure to note that the emeralds around Gweneth's neck, part of her bride gift, were the same stones he had envisioned around Alexandria's neck so long ago when he had offered to take her under his protection, away from St. John. He had done it to make St. John realize how shabbily he was treating her, but he had meant it all the same. Now he could not imagine another woman in Angelica's place any more than he could imagine Alexandria choosing any other man over Rane. But there was a marvelous completeness in seeing Gweneth in the emeralds, in knowing the intertwining tendrils of the years had resulted in this marriage between the two families.

Alex's gift to the couple was a fine two-year-old filly by Swan's Shadow out of Dreamer, the shared grandparents giving the horse the blood of Mabbie, Sir Archy, and Leda from both sides, something of Wild Swan's history to take with them. And Rane's gift was a generous settlement for Gweneth that she might never feel dependent no matter how wealthy a family she was marrying into. From Rane there was also the legacy of his family, his brothers and their families still in the West Country. They would be there, warm and loving, should Gwenny ever need them.

Alex had been blunt about her own family, too easily envisioning her brothers trying to use Gweneth to further a profitable business connection with the powerful Duke of Almont.

"My grandmother and my father were worth knowing; I am sorry you never met them. But my brothers, Paris and Rome, are nothing like your Uncle Boston. You owe them nothing, and I would advise you to ignore their existence."

"How could I want anything to do with anyone who was unkind to you?" Gweneth replied, and Alex's anxiety eased in face of her daughter's serene strength.

"You will have to consider coming to England now, if only for a short visit, though we would have you stay for as long as possible," Hugh told her as the Bettingdons prepared to leave the farm to travel to New York where they would take a steam packet to Liverpool.

Alex glanced at Gweneth, who was saying good-bye to her siblings, their spouses and children. In spite of the sorrow of farewell, she was glowing with contentment. She and Christopher had chosen to spend their wedding night at Wild Swan, and this morning, Gwenny had whispered to Alex, "Oh, Mother, Christopher is such a lovely man!" and she had looked so starry-eyed, Alex had known that Christopher had been as patient, kind, and skilled in initiating Gweneth in the rites of lovemaking as he was in everything else. In all probability, there would be grandchildren born in England before too long.

She turned back to Hugh. "I will not make any promises; there is still part of me that never wants to return to England for any reason, but I expect I will after all."

There was that heart-stopping moment of grief when Alex saw Gweneth out of sight and understood again how her grandmother had felt when she had seen Alex sail away from Gravesend, but the sorrow eased. There was a good chance she would go to England to see Gweneth, despite the hesitation she had expressed to Hugh. And for now, Rane was beside her, and the rest of the family.

Then Morgan said, "My God! I just realized our little sister is already a 'lady' and will someday be a duchess! Sam, I don't care what you say, I won't wear satin knee breeches when we go to visit her."

They all laughed at the image of Morgan so attired and the idea of Sam, who cared so little about fuss and frill, pressuring him to wear such garments.

But Rane and Alex exchanged a rueful glance. How easily this generation spoke of traveling great distances! For both of them remembered what an irrevocable decision coming to America had been.

BOOK
THREE

Chapter 24

Wild Swan, Prince George's County, Maryland, 1857

A baby wailed fretfully, and it sounded as loud as a gunshot on the muggy air of the June night.

"Hush dat chile!" The order was given in a growly whisper before Alex could say anything.

There were nine of them tonight—three men, two women, three children, including the baby and two toddlers, and their guide, a stout black woman who was leading the fugitives north. Alex had met the woman before. Her name was Harriet Tubman, and there was a price on her head in the South. Gaining her own freedom from slavery in Maryland had not been enough for her; she had returned again and again to help others escape not only from Maryland, but from states further south. She carried a huge pistol; slaves who set out with her did not turn back. There was a brooding, mystical aura about Harriet Tubman, as though she believed the hand of God had selected her for her mission. Alex did not feel any warmth from her or for her, but she respected her.

There had been little warning of the slaves' coming tonight. Scarcely more than half an hour before their arrival, a young Quaker, son of other agents on the Underground Railroad, had ridden in to say that the first destination of the slaves might be under surveillance, and that Dr. Cameron was diverting the slaves to the farm. But the inhabitants of Wild Swan were accustomed to the night visits by now, and work went smoothly. In the room beneath the stallions, there were food and drink, water for washing, and medical supplies.

And concealed in the darkness, Padraic, Samson, and Jed Barlow would be watching for pursuit, ready to challenge any who followed the slaves. The men were armed. This had become an increasingly dangerous game, as more and more slaves fled from the South and more and more of their owners sent slave catchers after them, expecting the government, by the terms of the Compromise of 1850, to support them in their efforts to reclaim their property. Personal Liberty Laws had been passed in some Northern states to assist Abolitionists in protecting the fugitives, but this was a slave state, quite a different circumstance.

They did not plan to have a gun battle with slave catchers, but rather to plead ignorance and stall them for long enough to allow the fugitives either to leave or to be warned to maintain absolute silence in the hideaway.

Trusting the men to keep a keen watch, Alex went about the business of seeing to the little party's needs, with Katy and Gincie assisting her. She was relieved to find that there were no grievous wounds, though the slaves were footsore, hungry, and, most of all, terrified, their eyes as wary as those of wild creatures caught in a trap.

Alex did not blame them. She could barely imagine the depth of fear they must suffer when one wrong step could lead to mauling by dogs, beating, mutilation, or death. And she could only admire the vast and desperate courage it required to set out on this journey, most of them hardly knowing how to follow the North Star, let alone anything about the world that existed beyond the plantations where they had been held. The more she learned of them, the more she respected Samson for his escape all those years ago.

Della still had reservations about sheltering the slaves at Wild Swan, though that did not prevent her from preparing the best food for the night visitors. However, it was Katy and Gincie who worked most closely with the escapees. Katy had never lost her horror of the idea of one person having the power to sell another, and having been among the poorest of the poor, she was not dismayed by the condition of the runaways, but rather determined to alleviate their suffering, her soft Irish lilt soothing even the most abject of them.

Gincie's motives were more complex.

Though every child had ups and downs in the growing process, Alex worried about Gincie far more than she did about her other grandchildren. The others had their passions and enthusiasms, but Gincie was two people. One of them was a perfectly normal fifteen-year-old girl, at one moment a child, in the next a woman, the usual mixture at that age. The other part of her was wholly adult and burned with a white-hot flame. It was as if her mother's fanaticism existed in her but was transmuted into a completely different form. Where Piety had been sanctimonious and self-serving, Gincie could not stand to see suffering in others and would go to any length to alleviate it.

Gincie had absorbed Alex's healing skills from the time she was very young, and Alex was amazed at the calm care the youngster was able to give in emergencies. Blood spurting from a cut, skin burning from fever —Gincie approached such situations with a serene competence that would have been admirable in a woman twice her age. And it allowed her to claim the privilege of remaining with the refugees to tend to their needs.

With her grass-green eyes, honey-brown hair, and her finely etched features reminiscent of St. John Carrington, she gave the appearance of fragility. It was an illusion. The slender body was capable of great endurance, the hands of reining the most spirited horse, and the head poised on the graceful neck contained a mind as bright and stubborn as any Alex had ever encountered. Gincie was normally easy to get along with, but when she set her mind on something, it was as good as done. And step by step, she had involved herself in the work of Wild Swan as a station on the Underground Railroad.

She had obediently attended school in Baltimore these past years, but her holidays and the summers were spent at the farm, despite invitations from her cousins to spend more time in the city. It did not seem to matter to her that the fugitive slave traffic was very irregular, so much so that weeks might pass before the secret room was used. What mattered was what she could do when the slaves were there.

And because her granddaughter's cause was just and her care so tender, Alex was left without a good argument against it. At Gincie's age, Alex herself had had no more talent for the frivolous than her granddaughter.

Inwardly she sighed, but by not protesting she tacitly gave Gincie permission to stay with Katy and the fugitives for the rest of the night. Tomorrow work would proceed as usual at Wild Swan, and if there was no sign of pursuit, the slaves would go on at nightfall.

Though there was ventilation in the secret room, provided by the outside passage and by well-concealed air pipes running to the surface in the shadows of the barn, it was a relief to emerge into the night air. The heat had finally dissipated somewhat, and she welcomed the slight chill.

Fergus, a disreputable black and tan hound belonging to Padraic, greeted Alex with a soft ruffle of sound as she approached his master. The Irishman claimed that the dog was capable of feats of great bravery, but the twinkle in his eye when he said it made Alex hope they never had to put Fergus to the test. At least Fergus was well enough trained to accept the presence of strangers quietly when he was so commanded.

"Not a sign a' anyone followin'," Padraic reported with satisfaction. "But we'll keep watch."

She found the same steady confidence from Jed and Samson, but she could feel the currents swirling beneath Samson's impassive exterior. She knew how difficult it was for him to witness the misery of those fleeing from slavery, and more, it conjured the old ghosts of his first family, of the wife and sons who had died after he escaped.

She reached out and pressed his hand for a moment and then went on into the house. Not only was Della still there, but she was in a frenzy of cooking.

"Everything is all right, and your food is much appreciated," Alex told her. "Really, you ought to sleep now; it's been a long day."

"Time enough to sleep when the people have moved on," Della retorted, and then her voice softened in confession. "You know how it is with me; I just can't relax when the fugitives are here." She paused. "It's not only that I fear for Samson, there are other things, things I haven't wanted to face. Every time they're here, they take him back to that first woman and his sons by her. And in the deepest part of myself there is more, there is shame that I share blood with these half wild, ignorant people."

Her last words trailed off miserably, and Alex wished she weren't so tired; she wanted to choose the right words, knowing how much the admissions had cost Della. And she was startled by the parallel train of her own thoughts regarding Samson's reaction to the slaves.

She took a deep breath, and the silence stretched between them as she searched for a way to begin, rejecting lies and denials as useless.

"I'm sure he does remember his first family at times like these," she agreed. "Just as I remember St. John, Christiana, Nigel, and even the little girl I never saw. They are part of me and always will be. But Rane and my living children, they are the spirit of my days; they are what make my life real and valuable. I am absolutely sure it is the same for Samson.

You and your sons—you are those he loves above all others in the world, living or dead. And as for the other, Della, you are not responsible for the whole black or the whole white race. Your thoughts may not be the most charitable, but they are valid. You have nothing in common with an unlettered slave except that you are both human beings. I don't know why it is expected that all blacks must be the same, and that the measure of the whole must be the least educated. That is not the measure applied to whites. And it is education, more than anything else, that separates people. Who can say what those people in the barn would be like had they had the advantages of learning and freedom? Perhaps the children will have the chance their parents were denied." She thought how ill-suited she herself would have been for the role of wife to some untutored young farmer or laborer in Kent. To live without books—it was a horrid idea.

She sighed wearily, rubbing her eyes. Whatever sleep she managed this night would not be enough, while Gincie might well stay up until dawn and would be fine if she got no more than a short nap during the day. Alex felt distressingly old and wished Rane were there to convince her otherwise.

Della set a cup of tea before her with a soft, "Thank you," and then poured a cup for herself and sat down. "I feel old, too," she said, as if Alex had spoken aloud. "Everything now seems so . . . so extreme, as if all of the middle ground has crumbled away, as if there's no balance and everything is going to fall."

Alex nodded and cradled the warmth of the teacup, feeling as if a sudden frost had invaded the mild summer night. Della was correct. Alex could not remember a time in her life when things had seemed so extreme to her.

While women like Flora struggled valiantly to make the need for women's rights a common cause, the ideal woman was pictured as a tiny-mouthed, big-eyed creature with billowing bust and arms, but tiny hands, feet, and waist, and a brain even smaller than these. Though some women were speaking out on the subject of controlling their own bodies so that they might not spend so much time in poor health from too many pregnancies, Alex was shocked by the number of young women who were completely ignorant of their own anatomy and viewed their natural female cycles with fear and loathing. More women came to her now asking for potions to ease their "vapors," and more often than not, they were either suffering from the debilitating effects of bearing one child after another, or bored to the point of madness, and sometimes both causes came together. But the point of their lives seemed to be to prove affluence by uselessness. And some men were taking on a different shape in this same pursuit, allowing their bellies to swell their suits as if they felt impelled to prove physically that they were ample providers. Alex remembered how her grandmother had deplored such gluttony in some of her newly wealthy patients decades ago.

She thought of the trim athleticism of her family, and of Rane in particular, and was glad of it. And she thought of the women; there wasn't a lazy, self-indulgent one in the lot, and her grandchildren had been raised much more in the tradition of a time earlier in the century, in the freedom her grandmother had allowed her. And she took some comfort in reminding herself that on many farms and in the wilder country of the Western frontiers, life was still much more sensibly lived, albeit with more hardship.

Business had its share of immoderation. Reasonable expansion was one thing, but the preference was for wild speculation, particularly in lands touched by the spreading railroads. It was as if no lessons had been learned in the financial panics of the past.

But the excesses of behavior gripping the country affected far more than the prosperous. As Della said, there seemed no middle ground left; everything became an occasion for upheaval. Political conventions in various cities too frequently led to brawls in the streets, and on that score, Baltimore had had more than its share, with gangs of bullies whose sole purpose at election time was to intimidate foreign-born citizens either to vote for certain candidates or to abstain from voting altogether. Many of these thugs belonged to the Native American or "Know-Nothing" Party, the nickname stemming from their standard answer to questions about their secret regulations. And there were other dedicated radicals in parties whose main cause was proslavery, as in the case of the Southern Democrats, or free soil, as in the case of the fledgling Republican Party.

This was the most extreme situation of all—the proslavery versus the antislavery forces, particularly the Abolitionists. There were many people who fell between these views, people who were not sure how to solve the country's ills, but they did not raise their voices so loudly or command the same attention. Attracting far more notice were such incidents as last year's attack on Senator Sumner of Massachusetts by Representative Brooks of South Carolina. Sumner had been verbally violent against slavery and its supporters for years. Brooks, feeling the honor of the South and of his uncle, a senator from South Carolina, had been impugned by one of

Sumner's most accusatory speeches, had beaten Sumner nearly to death with a cane. The senator's chair was still empty as the long months of his convalescence stretched on.

It was becoming increasingly evident that the Compromise of 1850 had solved nothing. Alex pictured the country as an enormous volcano shifting and rumbling with the seething fire just below the surface, ready to explode with the slightest shift of earth.

Indeed, Kansas, the subject of the Sumner speech which had so angered Brooks, had been in the grip of erupting violence ever since the Kansas-Nebraska Act of 1854. This act had decreed that Kansas and Nebraska be organized as territories, and all states and territories formed therefrom would operate under the principle of popular sovereignty in deciding whether or not slavery would exist within their borders. The act had superseded the old Missouri Compromise, which had prohibited slavery north of the line 36 degrees, 30 minutes. Though it had been assumed that, with more people in the North, more Northerners than Southerners would emigrate to the territories, which would make them free, the reality had been a huge influx of settlers from both North and South. "Bleeding Kansas" was now common and accurate usage as the civil war raged on between the opposing forces, each side spilling blood in the effort to gain control of the Kansas legislature. The savagery in Kansas was but a small warning of what a full civil war, North against South, would be. Yet, despite the death and destruction in Kansas, the rest of the nation was not ready to take heed.

The racing world reflected the general malaise. Although there was continuing talk about how fitting it would be to have a National Jockey Club located in the capital, almost everyone knew it would not be established. Fewer and fewer Southerners would bring their horses as far north as Washington any more, so leery were they of having the slaves in their entourages spirited away to freedom. The last racing event to have drawn a big crowd, including Rane and Alex, had been the second Lexington-Lecomte match, won by Lexington in New Orleans in April 1855.

Even the careers of these two horses had generated controversy; a small war waged in the sporting journals. Both horses had been sired by Boston, who had been by Timoleon, one of Sir Archy's most illustrious sons. But some people heatedly claimed that Boston had been an inferior horse, and that his bloodline should not be perpetuated. Others had resented the two for breaking cherished records held by old favorites and had denigrated the record-keeping and the lighter Southern weights used at the Metairie Course. And still others had divided into camps favoring one or the other of Boston's offspring, and had hurled accusations of unfair matches, not enough matches, and so forth.

On the surface, the division of people into Lecomte and Lexington camps had been petty and ridiculous, but underneath, the current seemed more ominous to Alex. It was as if the need for dissension was so pervasive, it was seeping into every aspect of life.

More than ever, Alex felt she was entering a foreign country when she traveled south to the races. The upper-class Southerners seemed to be growing daily more insular, more disdainful of the Yankees to the north, and more defiantly addicted to the indolent, fanciful life slavery allowed them. And, as always, Maryland was balanced precariously between the two cultures, uncomfortably containing elements of both, though inclining more toward the South than the North.

The Dred Scott decision, handed down in March, had grievously heightened tensions. Dred Scott was a slave who had been taken by his master from the slave state of Missouri into free territory established by the Missouri Compromise, and then back into Missouri. Eleven years before, the slave had sued for his freedom on the basis of his period of residence in free territory. The case had finally worked its way to the highest court in the land, but far from siding with him, the United States Supreme Court had ruled that not only was he still a slave, an "ordinary article of merchandise," but that Congress had no power to limit the expansion of slavery, and that the Missouri Compromise had been unconstitutional. In addition, three justices stated that no Negro, clearly being of an inferior race, could ever be a citizen of the United States.

The South was jubilant over the decision; antislavery forces in the North were enraged. Above all else, Alex was terrified. She hated the decision as much as any fire-breathing antislavery New England preacher, but she hated the prospect of war even more, and it seemed only too possible that this might be the quake that would set it off.

She shook herself sharply, forcing the vision from her mind. "I fear we cannot solve the problems of the world tonight," she said. "And I for one am too weary to try. Will you not get some sleep as well?"

"In a while," Della replied. "I have some cooking to finish. It makes me feel peaceful to begin a task and finish it. There are too many things now that seem to run on forever without solutions. Samson says my cooking tastes better when I've put my worry into it." Her smile was at once fond and sad.

Alex found her bed particularly cold and empty without Rane, and she lay awake, even though her body cried out for rest. In the early hours of the dawn, she heard Gincie come in, and only then did she sleep for a few brief hours. But at least the slaves got safely away the next night, and a few days later, Alastair brought the news that Mrs. Tubman and her charges had made it to free soil without loss.

"Of course, they won't be truly safe unless they go on to Canada," he remarked grimly. "But at least they are not still in bondage in a slave state."

Alastair's face became more craggy and lived-in by the year, as if at the end of his life he would be a rocky part of the landscape rather than an old man, but the deep blue of his eyes still reflected his concern for his fellow creatures.

"You do so much," Alex reminded him, "and you have for a very long time. You must allow yourself some contentment from that."

Never comfortable with compliments, Alastair shifted uneasily and changed the subject to questions about the family, especially about young Nigel, who had recently announced his intention to become a physician like the uncle for whom he had been named.

"By God, I think the boy will do well. He's been skilled at binding up birds' broken wings and children's scraped knees for some time now."

"He might change his mind," Alex warned with a laugh. "He's only twelve years old. A year ago he wanted to be a lawyer like his uncle Blaine and before that a sailor or a shipwright like his father. You might do better to look to Anthea to carry on the tradition."

Alastair winced visibly. "I keep hoping she will give up that idea. She has read every medical text I own, and I have no doubt that she would make a fine physician, but I tremble to think of the obstacles she would face. She would most assuredly have to go to Europe to receive her training, and even there she would not be welcome. And if she did achieve a degree, she would still have to battle every prejudice when she came home. Female doctors are as rare as roses in winter and appreciated a great deal less."

"If she and every other woman who wants to practice medicine wait until it is easily done, it will never be done at all," Alex said, though she shared his misgivings. "I ask only one thing of my grandchildren, that they not squander whatever talents they possess."

"Is that all?" Alastair asked wryly.

Alex told him as much as she knew of the family summer plans.

Though it was not always possible, he tried not to use Wild Swan too often when most of the family was there. It was not that they were disapproving of the activity; it was simply a matter of decreasing the risk and confusion. Spring and fall did not present the same traffic problems.

Alex was even more delighted than usual to see Rane when he came to Wild Swan. He had been in Philadelphia on business, and that seemed so much further away than Baltimore, more than the actual miles.

He felt her mouth quiver under his as he kissed her in greeting, and he held her very close for an instant before releasing her. But he did not ask what was wrong. She would tell him if something untoward had occurred. He doubted that it had. It was much more likely that another human cargo had passed through Wild Swan. He knew that Alex had to help the fugitives—her conscience would allow no less—but it took a toll of her, more than she was aware of. And he knew it was not fear for herself, but for Gincie and the others at the farm.

"Did all go well in Philadelphia?" she managed, though in truth she did not want to discuss business; she wanted to go on basking in the security of his arms as if she were sixteen instead of nearly sixty.

"Well enough, though the investors wanted more generous terms of credit than we were prepared to give them. In the end we compromised, but they gave more than we. They're hungry to have the ships." He paused, eyeing her boldly. "And I'm hungry to have you."

Even after so many years, she blushed at being caught out in her own desire, and he grinned, touching a hand to her warm cheek.

"The day you cease to delight me will be the beginning of my senility," he said.

She helped him to bathe, and when he seemed about to fall asleep under her ministrations, she nipped his earlobe, growling in mock anger, "I have things other than sleep in mind for you."

His arms snaked out and pulled her, clothes and all, into the tub on top of him, and her startled yelp gave way to laughter as she admitted she deserved it.

When at last they tumbled on the bed together, the warmth of the summer day and of their own bodies enveloped them in a languorous wave. They made love slowly, stretching out their enjoyment with the practice and knowledge of long years together. And when they were at rest again, Alex ran her hands idly over Rane's chest, tangling her fingers in the grizzled hair and tracing the contours of bone and muscle. Sometimes it surprised her to see the gray hairs among the dark. Strong, enduring, life-giving—and as vulnerable as anyone else. The sorrow swept through her so suddenly, she was helpless against the onslaught, and the tears welled and fell without her volition.

"Most of the time I keep it at bay," she sobbed, "but I am so afraid! I can feel it coming. I can almost see it, like a great thunderhead on the horizon. And I am reacting with all of the control of a child afraid of the dark."

He cradled her against his chest and stroked her back. "No, you are behaving exactly like the woman you have always been; the woman who would do anything to protect those she loves. It is no wonder that the prospect of war is hard for you to bear." He felt her shudder at the word, but he went on. "It has not started. And our children and grandchildren are all doing well. It seems to me that the best we can do is what we have always done, which is to carry on." He forbore to mention that her wild swings of mood seemed a common affliction; even in Philadelphia, a far more decorous city than New York, he had seen a reckless surface gaiety underlain by nervous dread, very much the atmosphere that gripped nations on the eve of war.

When the children and grandchildren arrived, Alex tried to banish all thoughts of war from her mind, but it was difficult. Her children were as loath to mention it as she, but the grandchildren were not so inhibited.

"I don't see any reason why I have to be able to do arithmetic if I'm going to be a soldier or fighting from a ship in the navy," thirteen-year-old Adam protested.

"All the more reason to know mathematics," his sixteen-year-old brother Seth replied. "If you are going to fire anything larger than a pistol or a musket, you've got to be able to calculate angles and distances for the trajectory."

"I think war is stupid," Nigel announced. "I have thought a lot about it, and it doesn't make any sense. Men marching back and forth, shooting at each other—that's stupid!" There was passionate conviction in the twelve-year-old's judgment.

"It's not!" Adam was not about to let his younger brother tarnish the glorious image he was seeing of himself in uniform.

Seth was long accustomed to serving as peacemaker. "War or no war isn't something either one of you is going to decide, so I'd suggest you both just keep on with your studies. Whatever happens, it won't hurt to know more than you do now."

Alex overheard this conversation in one of the barns where the boys lay sprawled in the straw, seeking the coolness of the shadows after hours in the hot sun. Her first impulse had been to announce her presence and end all talk of war. Instead, she backed away, chilled to the bone to hear her grandsons behind her; she spun around to find Sam there. Neither of them spoke until they were outside.

"I came to ask them if they'd like to come to the kitchen for something cool to drink," Sam explained, her voice sounding faint. "Morgan and I have discussed this, and we know there is no sense in forbidding such talk. Boys will always talk of being warriors. I remember planning to slay a few dragons myself. But it was all make-believe then. This is not. I have always been proud of my sons, proud I could bear them for Morgan and myself. God help me, now I wish I had borne daughters like Philly! It will be hard enough on the women left behind, but they will not fall in battle." Her voice dropped even lower. "I almost wish the war would start today. Surely my sons are still young enough so that I could keep them by me."

Alex put her arms around Sam and held her. Sam's dread was beyond the comfort of idle words, and Alex was fighting her own horrifying vision of grandsons lying sprawled, not in the welcome shadows of the barn, but in the mocking sun of a battlefield, their beautiful faces slack in death: Seth with his strong, slender body, his dark hair and hazel eyes, his perfect blending of Sam and Morgan; Adam with his chestnut hair, green eyes, and broad build; and Nigel with the Thaine green eyes as well, but with golden brown hair and a slight build that Alex judged he would retain even after he matured.

They were so precious. It was an obscenity to contemplate such a waste of their young lives.

It was Sam who regained her self-control first and pulled away, straightening her back in her own march of courage. "I keep reminding myself that it may not begin for years upon years. There has been dread of this for decades, and here it is, past the halfway mark of the century and no declaration of war has yet been made. Sanity may yet prevail."

Alex considered the continued bloodshed in Kansas and the huddled, threadbare fugitives who passed through Wild Swan, but she did not speak of them to Sam. We are all so busy reassuring each other, she thought, but in the end it will make no difference.

She found that her granddaughters were no less conscious of the changes war might make in their lives than were their male cousins.

Larissa, Phoebe, and Anthea at twenty, eighteen, and fifteen were well aware of the male population of the world.

As was her way, Anthea approached the subject and her grandmother directly: "Don't you think they'll wish they'd let lots of women be doctors if war comes?" she asked. "They'll need us then."

Despite her distaste for the subject, Alex almost smiled at Anthea's premature assumption of the mantle of trained physician. And she was coming to the realization that if she wanted to maintain her close ties with her grandchildren, she was going to have to accept their exploration of the ragged world they were facing.

"I expect you're right," she told Anthea, "but then, war changes everything and not always sensibly. It's perfectly possible that even a need for more physicians would not convince some people that women could do the job, particularly if the patients are men."

Anthea gave an exaggerated sigh of disgust. "I know you're right, Gran, but I wish you weren't."

Having progressed through a series of variations including "Gamma" and "Grandma," the grandchildren had, as if by committee, settled on "Gran." It was not new, but that summer the title took on a special poignancy. Alex was painfully aware of what she was doing; she was enjoying the last of their childhoods, storing up memories of carefree summer days and healthy, whole young bodies against the time when guns would shatter the stillness and the vulnerable flesh of the young.

Chapter

25

Alex had always welcomed the children's and grandchildren's young friends at Wild Swan, but now she was even more careful to make the outsiders feel welcome, for the more enjoyment they found at the farm, the more time the grandchildren would spend there. It was not really a problem, because all the grandchildren loved Wild Swan, particularly Larissa, Seth, and Gincie. And to Alex's relief, Gincie was always pleased when her cousins came out to the country; she spent a good deal of time with them when she was staying in the city for school, and she did not consider Wild Swan her exclusive property, though she had been raised there while the others had been more in Baltimore. Alex was especially pleased that Gincie got on well with her female relatives, as Alex hoped that exposure to them would somehow lighten the somber burden of responsibility Gincie felt regarding the Underground Railroad.

"I am glad there were witnesses to the girls' births," Philly had said. "Otherwise, there might be some doubt that I bore all three of them, they are so different from each other." And then with her usual quick humor, she had added, "And it's a good thing that Blaine trusts me."

The one subject Philly did not mention was the birth and death of a baby boy four years previously. Her pregnancy and the delivery had been normal, but the baby had been very small and frail, and after two weeks of struggling to breathe, he had died. It had been a hard time for Philly and Blaine, but they had sought comfort from each other and from their healthy daughters and had weathered the tragedy.

"I know it is a foolish thing to think," Philly had confided to Alex, "but it is almost as if Blaine and I were not intended to have a son because we have been so blessed in our daughters."

Alex had not disputed this idea, though she doubted that the pattern was so logically set, nor did she like the cruelty implicit in the theory. It seemed to her that nature was far more random, making mistakes no one had the knowledge to correct. But she agreed that the couple were blessed in their offspring.

The girls were lovely, each in her way, but as their mother noted, different in appearance from each other. Larissa was tall and willowy with a fine-boned face framed by a cloud of dark hair. Her eyes were a grayish blue that often appeared silver and gave her an ethereal look that belied her true nature. Like her cousin Gincie, Larissa was competent in whatever she put her hand or her mind to, so much so that boredom was her worst enemy. She could ride any horse in the stable as well as she could dispute with Horace Whittleby in Latin or Greek. She was nearly as skilled with herbs and simples as Gincie, despite having spent less time in the study of Alex's art. And best of all, she had a sense of humor that kept her from taking herself too seriously most of the time.

Phoebe and Anthea had also inherited the gift of laughter from their mother, though Phoebe's version of it tended to be sharp. Phoebe was short and slight with golden brown hair, dark blue eyes, an uptilted nose and a determined chin. Though it was Anthea who wanted to study medicine, Phoebe was a confirmed bluestocking. She cared nearly as much as her Aunt Flora about women's rights, and she wanted to be as good a teacher as Flora. She had begun teaching pupils the previous year, and Flora pronounced her a marvel of patience and enthusiasm with her students; her sharpness fled when she dealt with them.

Anthea had the same dark hair as her elder sister Larissa, but her eyes were a startlingly bright blue in her heart-shaped face, and she was of medium height and beginning to acquire a rounded figure.

"She is going to be just the sort of woman many men envision for their wives. And then heaven help them when they discover the crusader underneath," her father had remarked.

For the moment, Anthea had no interest in boys except as fellow adventurers in the woods or on horseback, and she and her youngest cousin, Nigel, got on particularly well due to their mutual interest in science. Though she was fifteen, she did not fault Nigel for being two years younger, and the rest of the brood were not nearly as interested in collecting jars of various bugs, frogs, and snakes. They had all learned a degree of tolerance from their grandmother and their parents, but it did not extend to the wholehearted enjoyment Anthea and Nigel got from the miniature zoos they maintained while at Wild Swan, always with the promise that everything was to be set free when they went back to the city. Nigel was a great admirer of his cousin and thought they should open a medical practice together when they were grown up. Alex reflected sadly that the prejudice against women in medicine was going to come as a shock to Nigel.

Though there were more than a few young men who came to call on Phoebe and Larissa, there were two in particular who were courting the sisters in earnest, and Alex considered the situation proof of the old adage that opposites attract. In spite of his rather somber name, Calvin Horner was anything but serious. He was likable enough and handsome in a smooth, brown-haired, brown-eyed way, but though he worked in his father's dry goods store, he didn't seem to have a sober thought in his head, and the unlikely object of his affections was Phoebe. She seemed to find him very amusing, but Alex doubted that she had any intention of accepting a marriage proposal from him.

The situation between Larissa and Luke Carstairs was more serious. Luke was a lawyer who already had a reputation for fair and even brilliant dealing with the law. Blaine respected him very much and had no objection to a marriage between Luke and Larissa. But whatever Luke's fire and grace in the courtroom, in his everyday life, he was quiet and unassuming to the point of being dull. Alex had discovered he was quite interesting to talk to if one took the time to draw him out, but it was work of great patience and only accomplished after annoying fits and starts.

He was a giant of a man, very tall and broadly muscular, and though he was fit, he was also just a trifle clumsy, so that the world around him always appeared to be too small to accommodate him easily. Doorways, chairs, and horses seemed to shrink when he was about, and dainty items such as cups and plates flew out of his hands of their own accord. His clothes were no kinder to him, for though they were made to fit him, they always appeared rumpled, even if he had put them on only moments before. In this he was much like Alastair, except that the doctor paid no mind to it, while Luke was painfully aware of his social shortcomings. He had sandy hair and kind, cinnamon eyes that were the outstanding feature of his rugged face.

He was surely strong enough to fight off any enemy, and yet he had the gentleness that often characterizes very large men, and he aroused deeply protective feelings in Alex. She couldn't help it. Every time she saw him, she had to suppress the urge to hug him as if he were a little boy and to warn him not to love Larissa so much.

It was not that she found her granddaughter unworthy of love; it was just that Larissa treated Luke too lightly, as if she didn't comprehend the depth of his devotion. Luke had first seen her when she was sixteen and he twenty, and it was doubtful that he had seen any girl clearly since. In his grave, shy way, he paid constant court to her, waiting for her to accept his proposal of marriage.

Lately Larissa appeared to be taking Luke for granted even more than before, and Alex lost her patience, as Larissa did, over a small but telling incident.

Luke was bringing Larissa a glass of cider, and he tripped. He managed to recover in time to prevent a complete disaster, but a little of the cider splattered on the hem of Larissa's dress.

"Honestly, I think you'd know where your own feet are by now!" she snapped, and then she accepted what remained of the cider and went on as if nothing had occurred.

But Alex saw the dull red flush of embarrassment stain Luke's neck, and she felt so sorry for him, tears burned her eyes. No one else seemed to have noticed, or if they had, they were pretending ignorance in deference to Luke.

Alex could not let it pass, and as soon as she could, she approached her granddaughter. "You were very harsh with Luke, and I don't think he deserves that sort of treatment," she said bluntly.

Larissa stared at her without comprehension. "Gran, I haven't the slightest idea what you're talking about."

"More's the pity, and that's the point!" Alex retorted. She made an effort to control her temper. "Luke didn't mean to spill the cider, but you treated him as if he were a misbehaving child. He's nothing of the kind. He's a grown man who loves you very much, and if you haven't any interest in him, I think you ought to set him free so he can find a woman who will appreciate him more."

Several emotions chased across Larissa's face. She had the grace to look abashed as she recalled how she had spoken to Luke; she was uncomfortable at being brought to task by her grandmother, who seldom had a sharp word for any of the grandchildren; and she was suddenly uneasy at the prospect of Luke ceasing his attentions in order to court some other woman.

"I don't mean to be cruel to him," she said in a small voice. "But he's so clumsy and uh . . . unsure. Sometimes I wish he would assert himself more."

"My dear child, a man of that size has the strength to cause damage without intending to; it is well for all concerned that Luke is so restrained. And as for his clumsiness, well, it is something he cannot help, and you make it worse. He wants to please you; he tries too hard and ties himself in knots. We're all apt to do that occasionally. Remember the tales of your father courting your mother. The first time he saw her, he did everything wrong. With Luke, there is more to control—longer arms, longer legs, bigger hands and feet, just more, the poor fellow."

Alex was pleased to see that Larissa's smile was tender, but she did not relent. "I don't think Luke is ever going to be a man of great social ease, though he will surely improve with age. If you are always going to feel embarrassed by him and want him to be different, it really would be better for both of you to break it off now."

"He's been nearby for so long, I've gotten used to him," Larissa confessed. "I haven't had to make up my mind about him because he hasn't demanded that I do. I'm not sure that I love him. There are other men I find more attractive, more exciting, but they don't make me feel cherished as he does. And I find I hate the idea of his being with another woman. Maybe that is love."

She scrubbed at her cheek in a childlike gesture. "Oh, Gran, sometimes I just don't know about myself. I know I am well educated; my mind works very well. And I can ride as well as anyone and cook and sew and lots of other things, but I feel so scattered! I can't seem to settle on one thing to do, and I don't want to be useless. Seth will be a fine lawyer or perhaps a writer; he's very good at putting his thoughts on paper, and he's very observant. And the others all have a plan, too; even Gincie has a purpose in her work with the fugitives, and she is only fifteen. I help at Aunt Flora's school, but I'm no born teacher; I'm too impatient. Most of the time, I just float along from one idea to the next, and things are too easy for me. This isn't a good family to belong to if one is so without direction," she observed with a rueful grimace. "And I have wondered if, when I think about marrying Luke, it is because that would at least be something to do, being his wife, rather than because I love him."

Alex was suddenly conscious of how she and the rest of the family depended on Larissa always to be carefree, laughing, and poised. It had never occurred to her that this grandchild could be so uncertain. She thought of how her own grandmother had always been so aware of her special needs, and she felt humbled.

"I owe you an apology," she said gently. "Lissa, you have always seemed so self-possessed and self-sufficient, I have overlooked the fact that you have doubts just like everyone else. I agree that you must find some way to challenge and channel your intelligence and energy, but do not be too fierce with yourself. There is still time for you to choose that direction you speak of. And don't let the rest of the family intimidate you. I don't think you would have to dig very deep to find that your cousins are not as sure of themselves as they appear. As for Luke, you are right to question your feelings about him, but you might also share your doubts with him, if you trust him enough."

Larissa was quiet, considering this proposal. Then her smile flashed, and she hugged Alex. "Thank you, Gran! Mind you, I'm still confused, but now I don't feel guilty for being confused."

Alex was satisfied with Larissa's response because she saw a visible change in the girl's treatment of Luke. Alex would not have wagered that the two would ever marry; rather she judged they would eventually drift apart, but at least she did not think Luke would be trampled in the meantime.

In the meantime. She prayed that this precious, shining generation would have time, time to make their decisions without the irrational pressures of war, time to find their work and their mates, time to savor life and grow through its seasons from youth to age.

She felt nearly as protective toward their friends as she did toward her grandchildren. And in addition to Luke, Calvin, and other familiar young people, including some female school friends of her granddaughters, in July there was another visitor.

Franklin Faber was a new friend of Seth's. His parents had immigrated from Germany when Frank was an infant, and his father owned and managed a German-language newspaper in Baltimore. At eighteen, two years older than Seth, Frank had an interestingly sculptured face with wide, flat cheekbones, and dark eyes in striking contrast to his flaxen hair. Though he spoke English without an accent, he was fluent in his parents' native language as well as in French, and he possessed a quaint old-world manner that mixed surprisingly well with a ready wit. Frank had made peace with the demands of his parents and with those of the more informal life of America. Mr. Faber, Seth reported, had an almost worshipful attitude toward education, and for that reason Frank would be attending Harvard beginning in the fall. Frank's only ambition was to write for a newspaper, either his father's or someone else's, as long as his words saw print, and he had tried to persuade his father that even manual labor at the presses would serve him better than days in academe, but his father was immovable, and Frank had finally decided that even Harvard could be used as experience for his pen.

Alex noticed that Seth asked Frank many questions regarding the subjects he would study and listened avidly to the answers, but as far as she knew, Seth had never mentioned that he himself might want to attend one of the prominent Northern universities.

When she asked him about it, he reacted in a very un-Seth-like way.

Sam had finally had her trip to China, sailing with Morgan in 1853 on a journey that had taken them to San Francisco, Canton, and London, where a cargo of tea had been sold for premium prices before the clipper returned to the United States. And during the months of the couple's absence, Alex had spent a lot of time with her grandsons. Because of that, she knew them better in some ways than she knew her granddaughters. She was accustomed to being able to sense Seth's moods before he spoke.

He could keep his own counsel, but at the same time, he was wont to be direct and articulate in his dealings with her. But when she questioned him about further schooling, his eyes shifted away from hers, and he mumbled, "I haven't really given it much thought."

"That lie is so transparent, I wonder you even bother to tell it," Alex said mildly. "And I cannot imagine why you would. Even if your parents could not afford to send you, there is no problem about the fees. Years ago Sinje and I decided that the income from a trust left to him by his grandmother would be used for our children's education. That fund still exists for your generation. So adequate funds are not the trouble, and I am sure you know that. The next consideration must be your level of academic achievement. I expect you could sit for the entrance examinations right now and do very well. And while you are not arrogant about your talents, you are also not so foolish as to deny them. So, would you please explain to me why you listen so eagerly to Frank, yet deny you have any interest in attending university?"

She spoke slowly, rationally, watching his face all the while, seeing the healthy color drain away. His hands were clenched so tightly together, his knuckles showed white. He drew a harsh breath, and when his eyes met hers again, the usually bright mix of green, gold, and brown was strangely muddied.

"Gran, there isn't time! I know it makes you sad, and you don't want to talk about it, but that doesn't change the truth. War is coming."

Alex closed her eyes against the pain, and then she heard the quavering tone of her own voice when she meant it to be strong. "It has not started yet, and even if it does, it is not certain that you would have to go."

It was as if she were the child, he the adult. His voice was at once gentle and firm. "When the war comes, I will go. I was born in this country, not in England, and the war will be here, not on foreign soil. I do not believe we can survive as a divided country. We would become colonies for Europe once again. Kansas is already being torn apart, and the South keeps threatening to leave the Union. Someday soon they will try it. Maryland may be part of the treason, but come what may, I will be for the Union."

Alex summoned her strength to combat their mutual despair. She thought of the brothers' conversation in the shadows of the barn, and she used the same argument Seth had employed to convince Adam to continue his study of mathematics.

"The war has not yet begun," she repeated, "despite Kansas. And until it does, your time is your own. If you waste it in waiting for the opening salvo, then you have already lost a major battle. And as they begin, so wars end. Unless you plan to become a professional soldier, you will need all the education you can acquire for whatever you choose to do with your life." Not for a moment would she admit the possibility to him that he might not survive. She realized that he believed war to be so imminent, he thought his younger brothers would have the time he himself lacked because the conflict would have come and gone before Adam or Nigel was old enough to participate. Above all else, Alex wanted him to consider himself young enough to learn and to hope.

"Promise me you will at least consider going on with your education," she urged. "You might even go to England, if you wish. With Hugh and Christopher there to sponsor you, I am sure you could attend Oxford or Cambridge."

"Trying to get me out of harm's way?" he asked. "It won't work, you know. And in any case, I would not feel comfortable in the country that gives so much support to the cotton interests in the South. I fear England would welcome the end of this republic."

Alex could not dispute his contention. The aristocracy was generally uneasy over the success of the American experiment and found more to admire and more profits to be made from the Southern way of life than from the Northern. It was an attitude that infuriated Gweneth, and with the support of her husband and her in-laws, she had more than once argued forcefully that England's ruling class must see the South for what it was—a system dependent on slavery and a culture growing more parochial and decadent by the year because of it.

When Gwenny had produced twin sons three years before, Alex had at last run out of excuses for not returning to England. She and Rane had gone and had been royally entertained by the Bettingdons, as well as warmly received by Rane's family in Clovelly.

For Alex, it had been a strange odyssey. She had been delighted with her new grandsons and with witnessing how happily settled in England Gwenny was. But a brief excursion to Gravesend had made her wish she hadn't bothered. She had not contacted her brothers because she had admitted to herself that she had no desire whatsoever to see them again and knew that they would feel the same. But she had seen the brush and small trees that now covered the land where the great oaks had once grown, the wood that had been sacrificed by her grandmother to finance

Alex's escape to America. And she had seen the farm, kept well enough by its tenants, but not at all the same vibrant place it had been when Virginia had owned it. Yet, for an instant, she had felt that if she turned around very quickly, she would see her grandmother in her gardening garb of straw hat and gloves. But the illusion was fleeting, and the headstone on Virginia's grave at Stone Church very real, as was that of Christiana, the little girl Alex and St. John had lost.

The West Country and Clovelly remained much as she remembered. But Rane's parents, Magnus and Gweneth, and his sister-in-law Barbary, were gone, and it was strange to find that Seadon and Elwyn, his brothers, Susannah, Elwyn's wife, and their children had all grown older, just as she and Rane and their family had. And with the lifting of duties, plus public outrage against the smugglers who had grown murderous in some parts of the country, free trading was no longer part of the Falconers' lives; fishing, coastal trading, and farming now provided their income.

"It sounds utterly fanciful, I know," she had confessed to Rane, "but somehow it seems as if all should have remained exactly as I left it."

Far from deriding her, Rane had agreed. "To be sure, it is a way of feeling one's mortality to see the companions of one's youth growing older."

In the end, she was not sorry she had made the trip to England—seeing the babies Gwenny and Christopher had produced was enough to make it worthwhile—but she was glad to return to Maryland. Though she would never be wholly American, she found England very foreign. It had ceased to be welcoming or familiar even before she had left it to journey to Maryland so many years ago.

And studying Seth's face now, she knew that England was no place for him either. He was an American to the depths of his soul, more profoundly so than she could ever be.

"Sethy, promise me you will at least consider going north to school," she urged, the pet name slipping out inadvertently, though no one had called him by it for years.

He did not take exception to it. "I promise," he said. He moved restlessly.

"Something else is troubling you?" Alex asked, and he sighed wearily, debating with himself a moment longer before he explained.

"It's really part of the same thing. I feel mean-spirited about it, but I hate going to Brookhaven. Grandfather Sheldon-Burke doesn't care about us anyway. He just needs Mother to make sure his bad managing doesn't ruin Brookhaven. And he rants on about how much better the South would be without the North. And he still owns slaves. It makes me sick to have a grandfather like him. It's awfully hard not to tell him what I think of him."

The worst of it was that Seth's assessment was accurate, and Alex sympathized with him completely. But she and Seth were not the important ones in this.

"If it becomes impossible for you to control your temper in his presence, then of course, you must stop visiting him," she said. "But I hope it will not come to that, for your mother's sake.

"You are very lucky. Your parents have adored you from the very beginning of your life. Your mother is not so fortunate. Her mother died long ago, and her father, your grandfather, has never loved her enough. I am sure he thinks he does, but in fact, though he expects a great deal from her, he gives little in return. It has been that way for a long time, and I doubt it will ever change. The tragedy is that your mother keeps expecting it will."

Seth's frown was like a spoken protest, and Alex answered it.

"I know, one expects one's parents to be invincible and wise in all things, but that is not possible. And in your mother's case, there is a part of her that is forever a little girl, hoping for the approval and the love she has never gotten and never will from her father."

"That makes me hate him even more!" Seth growled.

"He is not the point. Your mother is. And as long as it gives her some pleasure to have you and your brothers visit your grandfather at Brookhaven, I hope you will be able to tolerate him. You might take some comfort in the fact that he isn't any more cordial toward his other children and grandchildren."

Seth's smile emerged at her tart observation. "Mother doesn't make us go that often," he conceded. "I guess I can stand him in small doses." He paused, and then with emotion causing him to duck his head a little in embarrassment, he muttered, "I do love you, Gran. You always make things seem less worrisome."

A fleeting kiss on her cheek and he was off with the athletic grace he had possessed even as a young child. Seth had never had an awkward stage. If only it were true that she could ease his way through life. But all the problems she had ever solved for him were as dust in the wind compared to what lay ahead for his generation.

She had never felt so helpless in her life, and the phantoms followed her even when she slept. She dreamed of St. John for the first time in years, seeing him near death as they had amputated his arm after the last battle against Napoleon, and she saw him as he had been in death, honed to the cold perfection of a marble effigy. And in the nightmare, St. John's face changed and became their son Nigel's face and then Seth's. Even in the shifting, distorted images, there was no doubt that all life and laughter were forever gone.

Chapter

26

Rane was too attuned to Alex to overlook her agony or mistake its cause. Even when she cried out to St. John in the night, Rane understood, though that did not stop a brief stab of jealousy. But he felt as helpless as she and unable to offer any specific comfort. He noted the aching tenderness and fear in her expression as she regarded their grandchildren; in it he saw the mirror image of his own emotions.

He showed his affection for the children in the best ways he could, trying to be available when they wanted him to do something with them or help them with a project. But he could not be more open than that in his concern, because he lived in terror of breaking down and howling like a madman over the prospect of what carnage the war could cause to the young men of his family. It made him feel ancient and impotent, and if there was a more acute pain than this dread, he did not want to suffer it.

He turned most of his energy to work. He and Caleb had done very well over the years because, while they had taken risks, they had never aimed for the ultimate dollar or indulged in greedy speculation. Even the first clippers they had built had been based on their knowledge of what would best serve the traffic of the seas. Their success had been from the fruit of their own labors, not from some falsely gilded scheme. And they had adapted to changing conditions, building less extreme clippers, vessels with slightly more cargo space and more strength, as soon as they had determined that such would be safer in the pounding seas around

Cape Horn on the Western route to San Francisco and China. They had suffered some losses—unavoidable when dealing with a mistress as quixotic and demanding as the sea—but they had a wide reputation for safe, swift delivery of cargo and for some of the best ship's masters and crews anywhere. With Boston accurately judging the financial climate in San Francisco, they had anticipated the drastic fall in freight rates in 1854 which had caught so many other shipping lines unaware, and the Jennings-Falconer clippers sailed on, delivering flour and manufactured goods to South American ports when it was profitable, and competing for the best of the annual tea harvests in China. The tea had usually been delivered in time to collect prizes and premiums in England, as well as commanding high prices in New York and Baltimore. With smaller ships, the line had plied the coastal trade, too, bringing cotton, sugar, and rice from Southern ports in exchange for the output of Northern factories, finished goods from industries still sorely lacking in the South.

But if war came, and if it included naval action, no amount of care and planning could prevent the disruption of shipping. That knowledge drove Rane to work longer hours, trying to achieve enough so that at least he would have a solid legacy for the family to draw on. Caleb shared his view.

Now a youthful-looking sixty-three, Caleb was still lean and straight-shouldered, his dark eyes bright, his age betrayed only by the wealth of silver in his hair. He claimed that Flora kept him young.

But he looked every one of his years and more as he and Rane had dinner in a favorite Baltimore restaurant. It was a stifling August night without so much as a small breeze of relief from the bay, and both of the men missed their wives, who were at Wild Swan.

Caleb was uncharacteristically nervous, paying no attention to his food and continually losing track of the conversation, but Rane did not press his friend, waiting instead for Caleb to broach whatever subject was troubling him, hoping that it would not have anything to do with Flora.

Abruptly Caleb announced, "I've been thinking about a new direction for the shipyard, and I ask you to hear me out."

Rane nodded agreeably. "Of course," but he wondered why Caleb was so agitated; their minds worked along very similar lines in business matters. They had worked long years together without a major falling-out, and they were closer than most brothers. They were bound together by family ties of marriage, by time, by boundless mutual respect and friendship, and now by mutual apprehension about what war would do to the people they loved.

"We have done well, so well that we could stop working now, and we would not starve," Caleb said. "But we don't want to do that. We want the business to go on—for Morgan and for our grandchildren, too. But somewhere in the midst of this, the war is going to come."

His eyes met Rane's squarely, and without words each acknowledged how much he loathed the thought of the conflict, how much he feared it.

"Surely there will be a naval side to the conflict," Caleb continued. "And yet, the United States Navy is woefully short of ships. I propose that we finish the commissions we have for sail and begin to build medium-size steam and sail vessels, ships large enough to bear cannon. We do not sell shares in the ships; we hold them until the navy needs them, and use them for whatever coastal trading we can find in the meantime."

Too many things rushed in on Rane at once, and it was all he could do not to recoil openly from Caleb. They had always built sailing ships, and though they both knew that steam was destined to overtake the traffic, there were surely years of pure sail left, especially for the long voyages where refueling was such a problem for steamships. But far worse than destroying the purity of the sailing ships was Caleb's vision of the market created by war.

"To grow fat on war!" Rane spat the words out as if they had a foul taste.

Caleb winced but conceded, "In a way. But I do not intend that we reap inordinate profits. I intend that we sell the ships at fair market value. We build good ships; we can build as solidly for steam." He raked his hands through his hair. "God knows I have tried to pretend that the war won't happen. But it's no use. I would be willing to bet everything I own that it will begin within five or six years, if not much sooner—certainly no longer than that. And wars are fought by children; our children and grandchildren will be the ones. The least they should have is the best we can build."

His eyes shifted, and he gazed at his own thoughts. "It is a peculiar proposition. I propose that we risk our private fortunes on the public wreckage of war. If I am wrong, we could be left with a surfeit of ships without buyers or trade contracts, and yet that would delight me above all else. I fear that will not happen. Whatever else my failings, I am an astute businessman, and I don't think I have misjudged this time."

"Forgive me, old friend," Rane said, "for doubting your motives. I have had a lifetime to learn the depth of your integrity." He paused and then asked, "Will you give me time to consider this? I don't fault your reasoning, only my acceptance. I am playing the same game so many are. It is one thing to talk about war coming, to speak of it obliquely; it is quite another to turn the business around for it. It seems to give the nightmare substance."

"Just so," Caleb said. "For that reason, it has taken me weeks to summon the courage to speak to you. I don't expect your answer immediately. And whatever we decide, Morgan must be part of the decision. All our children will benefit in the future if we continue to do well, but Morgan is already vitally concerned."

If it had not been so late, Rane would have set out for Wild Swan. Death was in the air tonight. His death and Caleb's some day—and inheritance for the children and grandchildren only if the young survived.

He recognized that his first duty was to discuss the plan with Morgan, and he expected his own initial reaction to be his son's first reaction as well, but it was not so.

Morgan heard him out, and then he said, "My sons are going to fight this war. Seth, Adam, and Nigel—I would not change a single thing about any one of them. Sam nearly died giving birth to them, and she and I have celebrated the wonder of her survival and theirs every day of their lives. We have loved them, taught them, protected them, and yet this terrible, killing beast is stalking toward us, a little closer each day, and there is nothing we can do to stop it." His green eyes held his father's. "I would approve the building of a hundred gun ships that my sons might have even so little as one more day of life. Caleb is right, the time to begin preparing for the war is now."

Rane studied the lean face across from him and was awed anew that this forty-year-old man with the steady gaze and the enduring strength was his son.

"Will you tell Mother?" Morgan asked.

Rane shook his head slowly in negation. "Not unless she asks me directly."

"My thought exactly regarding Sam. It cannot help her to have the war given more substance by what we do at the shipyard."

They were in that instant bound not only by the ties of blood, but by their parallel determination to protect the women they loved.

And yet when Rane and Caleb arrived at the farm for the last week of August, Rane found that he ached to share the burden with Alex. But too often these days he saw the leap of fear in her eyes, and he knew it would be there again if she understood the import of Caleb's plan.

His own plan as well—day by day Rane had come to accept Caleb's idea as the best course they could follow. And larger events seemed, in a twisted way, to favor them, as the prices fell on the materials they required for shipbuilding. On August 24, the New York City branch of the Ohio Life Insurance Company failed. In the precarious world of current finance, with its shaky structure of doubtful and unenforced banking laws, the failure was enough to burst the bubble of prosperity. Speculation in land, railroad, manufacturing, wheat farming, and a host of other schemes had followed the acquisition of vast new territories at the close of the Mexican war. In the Northeast and West particularly, there had been a feeling that the possibilities for wealth were limitless. The rush for gold in California had added to the illusion. But as the last months of the year unraveled, businesses failed at an alarming rate, unemployment grew, people began to stand in line to be fed, and angry rumbles of dissatisfaction spread through the cities of the East. The wheat country of the West was equally troubled, and the middle western lands suffered bank failures along with the continuing problem of violence over the slavery issue.

When Alex went south with the horses, she discovered that Southerners were far less affected by the panic. Cotton prices had been good for some time and were high now. Unlike the industrial Northeast, the South did not face British competition but instead found a ready market in England for the cotton, and the low tariff policies legislated for Southern benefit allowed them to buy English goods at reasonable prices, again cutting into the industrial output of the North. And from Alex's viewpoint, the worst of it was that the South was actually gloating over the rest of the country's misfortune, as though it all went to prove that the Southern way of life was better and more prosperous.

She saw Allen Ralston at one of the race meetings, and at least with him she knew she could be honest. He inquired about Rane with real concern.

"He is very preoccupied these days," Alex admitted. "Every businessman in the North is. No matter how careful one has been, he is affected by what happens to the rest of the community. Oh, Allen, why can't people here see the truth of that? It is as if all the misfortune in the North is to their good!"

"Isn't it exactly the same in the North? Isn't there a cheer every time slaves are stolen?" Allen asked. "Slaves are legal property in the South, protected by law."

She felt the gulf opening between them, and she nearly cried aloud as she pictured the battered, frightened fugitives who had passed through Wild Swan. Only when Allen reached toward her in a placating gesture did she realize that his voice had been gentle.

"My dear Alex, please don't look at me like that! I am only stating the obvious, not endorsing it. We are in an awful mess in this country, and I don't see any way out. I still own slaves, though I know the institution is wrong. They are to be freed upon my death. But even that I wonder about. I cannot imagine my people fending for themselves."

This was indeed the unbridgeable distance between them. It had always been there, but now it mattered more than it ever had before.

"Can our friendship survive?" he asked softly.

"It must," she answered. As much as she despised slavery, if she and Allen could not continue as friends despite it, there was no hope at all for the country.

She told Rane about the encounter when she returned to Maryland, adding, "It has been like this since I first came to America. Always there is compromise over slavery, even though I believe it to be an unmitigated evil."

"Whenever and wherever people come together, there is compromise," Rane said, choosing his words carefully because he was thinking more of his own decision to compromise the truth between them in the matter of the shipyard, a course made more difficult by the memory of Alex's sacrificing the horses to save the yard. "That does not mean that the compromise is good or evil, only that it is made in order that people or governments can get on together without resorting to violence. Things cannot always be seen in black and white, no pun intended; gray is sometimes necessary for survival. Allen Ralston is a good man though he owns slaves; I believe he must be accepted on those terms."

Alex settled against him with a tired sigh. "You are a silver-tongued devil, for which I am grateful."

He hoped the flattery was true as he began to talk about the shipyard. "Caleb, Morgan, and I have decided to make a change in the ships we're building. We've decided to build ships with steam power as well as sail. I am reluctant to admit it, because sailing ships will always be closest to my heart, but steam is coming into its own, and we would be foolish to refuse change because of sentiment."

To his relief, he did not feel her stiffen in shock at the news, and her question was slow and sleepy. "I can see the practical aspects of it, and I know you must have thought this out very carefully, but isn't this a very unstable time to take such a risk? Businesses are still failing by the score every week. It must have affected the company's cargoes already."

"It has," Rane admitted. "But we have the capital to invest, and the time to wait until things are better, and there is the added advantage that the cost of materials has fallen of late. We will be prepared when the traffic improves again. The harsh fact is that current problems are working for us."

"Will you forsake the *Falcon?*"

The *Falcon* was a medium-size schooner with a black hull and lovely sleek lines. Rane had borne the total cost of her construction, and her house flag carried the golden falcon on crimson without the "J" of the Jennings-Falconer line. Though he did not get to sail on her as often as he liked, she gave him the feeling that he was still tied to sails and the sea. Even without steam, the *Falcon* was a swift, responsive ship. The captain and crew who took her on coastal trading runs were inordinately fond of her.

"I'm glad," Alex murmured and fell asleep. But Rane understood all that she had meant by those brief words. She knew how much a part of him sailing ships were, just as the horses were part of her, and she did not want him to lose the joy of them.

He wrapped her close in the darkness, and his guilt over not telling her the whole truth eased. It was as Morgan had observed after living with the reality of not telling Sam the whole truth. "We are not doing anything wrong. It's just that we know why we're building the ships. But there isn't any reason our wives should think anything amiss unless we behave like idiots. Lord, I sound like an erring husband!"

But the fact that Sam had accepted Morgan's explanation at face value and Flora Caleb's had made it easier for Rane to tell Alex. All the same, he was thankful that the task was done and had been done in the sleepy dark; in the bold light of day, with Alex's full concentration on him, he was certain he could not have managed it.

He thought of his employees and felt a little more justified. The men at the shipyard, though many of them were as addicted to sail as he, were grateful that they still had work while so many others were losing their jobs.

Christmas at Wild Swan this year was a time of special thanksgiving. The family was well, and all enterprises had survived, including Wild Swan West.

The name had stuck and was even more apt now than it had been in the beginning. With a decreased racing schedule in Maryland, the farm had been oversupplied with workers, particularly regarding the Barlow family. But now only Jim, his wife, their two sons Jimmy and Jackson, and the older Barlows, Jed and Mabel, remained. Georgie and Tad had gone with their wives and children to California and were working there for Boston. Billy and Bobbie, still bachelors, had gone to Chicago and Cincinnati, respectively, where racing was growing rather than declining. Della and Samson's oldest son Malachi was in California, having gone with Georgie and Tad. The state did not grant him citizenship rights, but at least there was no law against emigrating there.

Even wanting the best opportunities for them, it had been hard to see them leave, but it was not only the nature of the old way in which the children left when the land grew too crowded; in America there was the added attraction of the sheer vastness of the country, its offer of an infinite variety of living situations.

Boston was as content in San Francisco as he had ever been anywhere in his life. He had written to Alex that he didn't know whether it was because he was at an age where the wanderlust dimmed, or whether it was the basic fact of having run out of land on this continent, coming to rest on the edge of the Pacific; whatever the cause, he was home at last. And Rachel and their son Caton were happy, too, though Rachel would always have a feeling of being a part of two worlds without quite belonging to either.

Boston not only served as agent for the ships and for Alex's horses, but he owned the acres inland where the horses were kept until sale or for breeding and training. Quietly he had been buying city lots as well, investing in the future he foresaw for San Francisco, undismayed by the periodic fires and alarms that swept the still raw city.

If some had left Wild Swan, others were doing their best to increase the numbers there. Katy and Padraic had been longing for a child, and now Katy was pregnant for the first time, expecting the baby in June. Padraic was not reserved about the wonders of his impending fatherhood; it was as if such an event had never before occurred in the history of the world.

"Now you tell her what she's ta be doin' and what not, and I'll make certain she obeys," he said to Alex after announcing the cause of their joy. At his side, Katy made a face.

"As long as you feel well and don't overtire yourself, you needn't worry," Alex said to Katy, and then she addressed Padraic. "She is not ill, you know."

"I told you!" Katy chided her husband, but her eyes were alight with love. "If he fussed at one a' th' mares like this, he'd be gettin' a good swift kick, he would!"

Because she loved them so, Gincie was particularly pleased with the Joyces' news. Already she had great plans for helping to care for the baby. Alex was glad it was not due until June, since she feared Gincie would refuse to return to Baltimore were it due earlier.

As an added gift, Alex received news from Gweneth and Christopher that they were expecting another child, theirs in May.

"A healthy child is the first consideration," Christopher had written, "but I would very much like a little girl like Gwenny. She is not as sure, as she contends that I spoil our sons enough and would be impossible with a daughter."

Recalling the doubts she had had about the marriage, Alex hoped she would remember in regard to her granddaughters that the women in her family had a way of choosing good men, though there might be a false start, such as Flora's first marriage. And if any of the grandchildren, male or female, chose not to marry, she hoped she would accept that as well. In a way, that was a harder situation for her to imagine—as independent as she was, she could not divorce her own life from St. John and Rane; the men with whom she had shared her life had much to do with the person she was now. Not for the world would she have given up the time she'd had with either of them.

"What are you thinking of?" Rane asked softly as the festivities of New Year's Eve swirled about them.

"Of everything, of you," Alex replied, and she gestured with her hand, encompassing all the people in the room. "Of them, of how lucky we are. We are still here, healthy and together at the close of another year. I know it is only a day like any other, but this last one of the year always makes me nostalgic."

"I as well," Rane whispered, thrusting away the thought of ships large enough to carry cannon. "And every year when we wassail the orchard, I see you exactly as you were the first time you celebrated with us in Clovelly."

They managed to wait through the exchange of best wishes at midnight before they went off to their bedchamber. Rane made an elaborate show of yawning as he bade all good night, but Alex spoiled the effect by blushing when she caught the knowing smile Morgan exchanged with Sam.

And when they reached their room they discovered a chilled bottle of champagne and glasses waiting for them.

"I hope it was Della or Mavis who left this and not one of our children," Alex giggled.

The sound delighted Rane, and he pulled her close, inhaling the scent of her. "I regret to have to tell you this, but they know. They're very intelligent, and as I remember, their mother taught them quite openly about the basics."

With champagne and laughter and slow deliberation, they savored each other. Rane stroked the body he loved, the curve of waist to hip, the bend of her knees, the hollow of her neck, the curve of her breasts, the sleek thoroughbred lines of her. And when he was sheathed deep within her, he felt his age only in the control that allowed him to draw the pleasure out until it was unbearable, and he lost himself in the driving pulse of his need.

Alex felt the hot inner rhythm of her own response meeting his, but beyond that, she felt the absolute rightness of him—the shape, weight, scent, and texture of his body, and the essentials of the man inside. Even after so long, the fit of him around her body, inside her body, and in her heart, mind, and soul was splendid, and she cried his name aloud in celebration.

"Happy New Year, my only love," Rane murmured as they drifted into sleep.

Chapter

27

January might have been a bleak, lonely month at Wild Swan with the family back in Baltimore, but Alex did not feel that at all, for this was the beginning of the foaling season, and all her concentration was on the progress of the mares. With races in the Deep South, especially New Orleans, growing more prominent as those in the intermediate states declined, the early birth date conferred advantage, for the Deep South continued to use May 1 as the official birthday of all foals born in a given year.

The first two weeks of the month passed with no deliveries, but then Lucky Lady went into labor, and it was a tense time because the foal had one hoof back. The mare was eighteen, and this foal by Swan's Shadow would be her last. Alex stayed at her head, holding and soothing her, as Samson and Padraic worked together to pull the colt out after Padraic had reached inside the mare and maneuvered the errant leg until he could affix a rope around both of the baby's forelegs.

The foal, a chestnut colt, was weary from his ordeal, as was the mare, but neither seemed to have been injured, and the colt was soon nursing hungrily. Because he looked so much like his sire, and thus like his grandsire, Wild Swan, and because Lucky Lady was to be retired from her work as a brood mare, Alex named the colt "Swan's Legacy."

As if that was not enough excitement for the day, Temptress showed signs of going into labor, too. Her milk had been dripping for several days, and now she was moving restlessly in her stall, whinnying distractedly and kicking out clumsily at the barriers around her. But then she settled down again.

"This might be a long siege," Alex said later in the evening. "Please let me keep watch. If I need you, I will send for you. You did the hard work today, and I won't sleep anyway."

Reluctantly Samson and Padraic agreed. They knew how she was about the mares at foaling time, and Temptress was a special case, having lost her foal the year before. Temptress, a black eight-year-old, and Lady Sailaway, a chestnut nine-year-old, were horses Alex had purchased on her trip to England in order to provide more out-crosses for her stallions, and they were both valuable animals, having performed well at English race meetings as two- and three-year-olds. In addition, Temptress had been bred to Magic Swan for this foal. The stallion was thirty-one years old this year and had grown frail over the winter. He would not last much longer, and that made this foal that much more important.

Temptress went through another session of restlessness, but since she did not seem to be in acute distress, Alex did not summon the men.

"I don't blame you," she soothed the mare. "I remember quite well how uncomfortable it is to be so great with child that just getting up and down is major work."

Temptress settled down again. It was not a completely good sign, as the best deliveries began and ended quickly, but it would have to do until there was more evidence that intervention was needed.

Alex sank down on a pile of hay, thinking she would stay close for a while longer.

Katy's soft call kept her from being startled when the young woman appeared bearing a tray laden with a tea service and some of Della's gingerbread.

"I ought to scold you for being up so late," Alex said, "but I'm too grateful. Nothing could taste better right now than a cup of tea!"

"I was a wee bit wakeful," Katy said. "Padraic an' Fergus both are snorin' ta wake th' Divil. But Padraic won't be thankin' us if we let 'im sleep through needin' 'im," she added hastily.

"Temptress is quiet again," Alex told her. "I doubt she will foal tonight. I'd rather the men got their sleep; they put in a hard day."

Katy did not bother to point out that the same was true for Alex; she knew how involved her employer was with the beasts she raised, and she sympathized with her wish to be with the mare as long as there was the slightest chance the animal might need help. Though she didn't say it aloud, she also thought that Mrs. Falconer was going to be a comforting presence when her own time came to deliver Padraic's child, though Alex had assured her that a skilled midwife and Dr. Cameron would be there, too. Katy smiled to herself; as she had told Padraic, it was as if she were a lady born to have such attention focused on her.

Katy squealed, and Alex froze in terror at the bloody apparition that slipped through the half open barn door without warning. Then Alex recognized Thomas Whitmore, a young Quaker and an agent for the Underground Railroad.

"I'm sorry to burst in on thee like this, but the case is urgent! I have five passengers in sorry shape with slave catchers at their heels, and I couldn't think where else to take them." He was trying to be calm, but he was so frightened, his words ran together.

Alex understood enough. This was entirely out of the usual, no advance warning and in the dead of winter, an unlikely time for escapes because snow en route could make it too easy to track the runaways, and cold could well kill them even before they were caught. It was one thing to risk the weather in warmer states to the south; it was quite another this much further north. But these people had run because they were to be sold "down the river" to various owners, away from each other, from everyone and everything that was familiar. There was an older couple, their son and his wife, and the younger couple's eight-year-old boy. With the help of various people, they had made it from South Carolina all the way to Virginia, but when they had been ferried across the Potomac, Thomas having met them on the Virginia side, they discovered that the slave catchers had crossed ahead of them. They would have been captured right there except that, in the confusion, one of the pursuers' horses slammed into another, throwing his rider. Thomas and the slaves had scattered, regrouping when they heard the men ride off, searching in the wrong direction. They had not heard signs of pursuit since, but that was no guarantee of safety. Thomas would have preferred to take his charges on to a safe house in the District of Columbia, but they could go no further.

Thomas had been nicked in the ear by a bullet, which accounted for his bloody appearance, but the wound was not serious.

Alex's brain was beginning to function again. Mentally she reviewed all that had to be done as they moved toward the stud barn where the slaves huddled by the door. She saw the uneasy movement in the moonlight even before the lantern light touched them.

"Katy, go wake the men for guard duty, then get Della and the other women to help organize food and care."

A split second warning of hoofbeats, and the three men rode in. "They're here!" one of them yelled in triumph, spying the frozen figures by the barn.

Everything happened at once. One of the slave women began to scream, a high-pitched wail of terror. And Fergus, having awakened and found his mistress gone, burst out of the shadows in snarling fury, heading directly toward the men and causing their mounts to sidle and shy.

"Into th' barn!" Katy yelled at the slaves and without hesitation, she ran at the horsemen, screeching, "Git on, ye dirty divils!"

Shots rang out and both Katy and Fergus fell.

"Hell! Ya shot a white woman!" one of the men swore. It was the last thing he said. Other guns blazed in the moonlight, and all three men fell, their horses jumping away only to stop and mill in confusion not far away.

"Make sure they are all dead!" Alex did not recognize her own voice, but she had no reason to give the order in any case. Padraic had his own vengeance in mind. As he came up to the men, one of them moved, and Padraic shot him point-blank. Then he knelt beside Katy and touched her face as the last of life seeped from her body and from their unborn child in a bloody river that was black in the ghost light of the moon.

"Sweet Jesus." It was Samson's voice in a long whisper of pain, and then the two slave women were weeping, but Padraic made no sound.

Alex knew before she touched her that Katy was dead, and she wanted to crawl into a hole and grieve without ceasing, but the habit of protecting Wild Swan and everyone on it was too deeply ingrained.

The fugitives were secured in the secret room. Cold, footsore, hungry, and in shock from the bloody scene they had witnessed, they did as they were told, mumbling their thanks as if they feared blame would fall on them and violence, too.

"The slave catchers are to blame," Alex said flatly. "We will get you away as soon as we can. In the meantime, you are safe here, I promise it."

The older woman spoke softly, her dark face weeping without tears. "Neber did I s'pect no white woman be dyin' fo ma fambly. I prays t' de Lawd fo' her fo' all de res' a' ma days."

Alex carried on.

"Thomas, I want the horses taken as far from here as you can manage by dawn. Then tie them somewhere so they will not follow you and leave them. You must be careful that you are not seen. Can you do that?"

"Yes, ma'am," he answered, glad of something to do.

She had stopped the last of the bleeding from his wound with a lump of alum, and Della had given him clean clothes, but he still looked white-faced and worn. However, she needed her own men for the tasks still to be done at the farm, and she had to trust that Thomas could do as she asked. In his work on the Underground Railroad, he had lived with danger ever since he was very young, and that gave him an advantage.

There were stifled sobs from Della and the other women, and the men were no better off, but everyone did as Alex directed. The slave catchers' horses were stripped of all but their bridles so that identifying them would be more difficult, and no brands of ownership were found on the horses. When Thomas left with the animals, riding his own and leading the three, the men of Wild Swan were already beginning to dig a pit in the woods. When it was deep enough, the bodies of the three slave catchers and the saddles from their horses were dumped into it, minus only the papers Alex had had brought to her. The women were making Katy's body presentable for burial.

"What a peculiar ritual," Alex thought dazedly, "as if it makes any difference when one is dead."

At first Padraic had resisted their efforts to move Katy's body, but finally he relinquished it. Alex assumed he would follow them, but instead he was doing some grave-digging of his own, for Fergus, in the little patch where the children had buried dead pets over the years. He had still not spoken, and the image of him methodically digging a grave for the black and tan hound made Alex's throat burn with unshed tears.

No one had flinched from what she asked of him or her. She could not think of any other way out. The slaves were still hidden here, and even if they were not, to have any trouble with slave catchers was to attract undue attention to Wild Swan. The slave catchers had to disappear without a trace. There were many in Maryland who were sympathetic to the anger of slave owners over the escaped property and who would push hard for the arrest of anyone suspected of helping slaves elude capture. But at the same time, few liked those who were employed as slave catchers. Alex was counting on this distaste to make it unlikely that a general alarm would be sounded for their disappearance.

But the plan was by no means sure. For that reason she had given her employees the chance to refuse to take part. Not one person had.

When dawn broke, no sign remained of the slave catchers' coming except for Katy's shrouded corpse. Alex had even burned the papers the men had carried after she had read them. They, like the slaves, had been from South Carolina.

Jim Barlow took her message to Rane. It read:

Katy is dead. We will bury her in two days. We need the finest coffin available and a priest. Please have Caleb or one of the family arrange it. I need you now.

She dared not commit more details to paper, but Jim told him the rest, and Rane arrived late at night after Alastair, alerted by Thomas, had already come and departed with the fugitives.

The minute Rane put his arms around Alex, all the strength drained out of her, and she sagged against him, the full horror of Katy's death and the bloody reprisal finally registering. The anger and grief overwhelmed her, and all the tears she had not shed before seemed to pour forth at once, blinding and choking her.

Rane held her tightly, shaken by his own emotion. When Alex had quieted a little, he asked, "What of Padraic?"

She shook her head and wiped her eyes with the handkerchief he offered. "Samson is watching over him, but Padraic isn't really here. He's locked away somewhere inside himself. As far as I know, he hasn't said a word since it happened." She told him about Padraic burying the dog, and she started to cry again.

Rane realized that in addition to shock, Alex was suffering from lack of sleep and food. She could not remember when she had last eaten, and she had not slept since the tragedy had occurred.

"You have held everyone together for long enough," he said. "Now you will eat a little and then sleep. I promise to awaken you if anything needs your attention."

Alex surrendered gratefully, not stirring when Rane joined her in bed and sleeping through his rising the next morning as well.

He roused her in early afternoon. "I would like to let you sleep on, sweetling, but Temptress is foaling, and Samson insists you wanted to be there."

After all her nervous starts, Temptress now delivered her foal with such swift efficiency that Alex had barely arrived before the filly was slipping from her mother's body. She was a fine black with a curl of white on her forehead.

The sight of the foal was as bittersweet as anything Alex had ever experienced, because the picture of Katy bringing tea to the barn was so clear. The image of Katy was everywhere. She had become so much a part of Wild Swan; the love she had found with Padraic had spilled over to encompass everyone around her, including the fugitive slaves who passed through.

All of the family were fond of Katy, but Alex worried most of all about Gincie. In order to get to Alex as swiftly as possible, Rane had left the task of telling Gincie to Morgan, and as soon as Alex and Rane saw their granddaughter's face, they knew the blow had been severe, no matter how Morgan had tried to soften it. Katy's death was truth no one could mitigate.

Gincie looked years older than her tender age, and when Alex put her arms around her, she found the slender body unyielding. Though there was no sign of weeping, Gincie's face was porcelain-white.

The priest, located by Blaine, proved amenable to consecrating the ground so that Katy could be buried within her faith at Wild Swan, and the casket was, as Alex had requested, the best money could buy. But none of it really made any sense when they all gathered to bury the young Irishwoman and the baby she carried.

It was, Alex acknowledged to herself, the beginning of the war for Wild Swan. Whenever the guns began in the rest of the country, the firing had started here for them with Katy's death.

Alastair had returned with word that the slaves were safely away from the area, though what would happen to them on the rest of their journey, no one could judge. Alastair felt enormous guilt for what had happened.

"I involved you in it in the first place," he said to Alex. "Katy's death is at my door."

"Katy's death is the fault of the three men buried in the woods," Alex replied sharply. "And our involvement in helping the slaves has been voluntary." She paused, closing her eyes for a moment. "As it will continue to be."

"You can't mean to go on with it!"

"I can, and I do. Because if we stop now, then Katy's death has been in vain, and those brutes have won."

Alastair was clearly torn between his concern for her and the others at the farm, and the need of the fugitives for safe shelter.

"It is not your choice to make," Alex reminded him.

"Whatever possessed her to run at the men?" Alastair asked.

"We'll never know for certain, but I believe she somehow thought she could distract them long enough for the slaves to hide in the secret room or to run away. And there was surely anger in it, too. She was very protective of the runaways and of me. I read the slave catchers' papers; they were entitled to subdue the older man in any way they found necessary. He was labeled a troublemaker. I think they would have shot him down in front of his family had they not been killed first. They might have shot the rest of us, too. Again, we'll never know."

It was a true measure of the times that neither Alastair nor Rane nor anyone else suggested that burying the slave catchers in the woods had been a less wise course than reporting the incident to the authorities and claiming that an unprovoked attack by the three strangers had been countered by the guns of Wild Swan. The Compromise of 1850 had made the penalties for harboring fugitive slaves very clear.

"I'd keep a close watch on Padraic if I were you," the doctor said. "I know he won't hurt anyone else, but I wouldn't trust him to be so kind to himself."

"He hasn't eaten, or slept, or spoken since Katy was killed," Alex told Alastair.

Gincie was sitting a little apart from everyone else, her face blank, her eyes a muddy yellow-green, but she overheard the conversation about Padraic. She got up slowly and faced her grandmother. "I'll take him something to eat, and I'll see if I can make him rest," she said, and Alex was in immediate agreement with the plan; if anyone could reach Padraic, it was Gincie.

Gincie didn't want to go. After one quick glance, she had avoided even looking at Padraic since she had arrived. She was terrified of the pain and rage boiling inside her, terrified of loosing the tight rein she held. But tending to others was as essential as the beat of her heart, there by nature and nurtured by her grandmother.

When she took the food to the Joyces' little house, she found Samson sitting patiently outside.

"Dat's good," he said, rising to his great height and reaching out to touch her gently on the shoulder. "He listen to you. Go slow wid 'im. He waits, de light come back fo' him."

Samson's words heartened Gincie. He had been part of her life since she had first come to Wild Swan, and he had never lied to her. If he said Padraic would be all right, then it had to be true.

Nonetheless, her hands shook when she entered the little house, and she nearly dropped the food Della had sent. Everywhere there were signs of Katy—bright curtains, rag rugs, and pots of healthy plants, and everything meticulously clean and well cared for.

Worst of all was Padraic. She had never known him to be idle, but now he sat at the table where he and his wife had shared so many meals, and he was utterly still, his shoulders hunched as if he were an old man. He did not turn or give any sign he had heard her enter.

She put the covered platter on the table and twined her hands together, searching for the right words and giving up when he still did not acknowledge her presence.

"I was wrong! I'm not the one who should be here telling you to eat and sleep!" she declared passionately. "Katy was the only one who could do that, and Katy's gone!" She clapped her hands over her mouth, but it was no use, as soon as she said Katy's name, her control broke and she was swept by violent weeping coming from deep inside. "Padraic," she gasped, "not you, too; don't leave me! You're part of my family!"

He felt as if she saw the demons deep inside of him, saw his desire to end his life as if he had spoken aloud, and in that instant he knew he could not do it, not for a faith that said he would be damned for suicide, but simply for this young girl. He had felt responsible for Gincie since he had been witness to her mother's crime.

"Ah, lass, what'll we do without her?" He cradled Gincie as if she were a little girl again, and in comforting her, he was comforted.

"Katy wouldn't've liked all this weepin'. She was laughin' and livin'; dyin' has nuthin' ta do with me Katy."

They clung to each other until the sharpest pain had eased, and then, though he felt no hunger, Padraic docilely ate most of what Gincie had brought, just to please her.

He returned to his duties the next day. He said little and smiled less, but he worked with the same efficiency and care for the horses that he had always shown. And when Alex gently suggested that they forfeit the races for the season, he refused.

"Fer Katy and fer me, it's all ta go on, the racin' and all. Wild Swan's not ta be changed by such as those night creatures."

Even more immovable than Padraic was Gincie. Her first request was that Temptress's new foal be named "Irish Lass."

"Are you sure you can bear that?" Alex asked. 'She will remind you every day."

"I don't need anything to remind me. The name is a whim, nothing more. It would have amused Katy. And it is all right with Padraic, but if you prefer not, I won't press you."

"No, it is all right with me also. I hadn't thought what to name her yet, with all the sorrow and confusion." She heard her own voice growing thin and unsure; she could feel the force of Gincie's will despite her granddaughter's words. The name of the horse did matter to her; everything mattered to Gincie now.

"There is something more, Gran. I won't be going back to Baltimore. I want to stay here, and I want to be more active in helping the fugitives, not just here, but in getting from one safe place to another."

"Gincie, you are not yet sixteen years old!" Alex exclaimed.

"In a few weeks' time I will be," Gincie replied calmly. "And that has little to do with it. There are men, women, and children who help all along the line. I am no better or worse than they." She took a deep breath. "I hope you do not try to forbid me, because then I will have to disobey you. By my age, you were married and had children. And before that, you had aided free traders and helped to smuggle Uncle Caleb out of England. I love you very much, but this is work I must do. I promise I will take the utmost care not to increase the danger for Wild Swan, but if I cannot work from here, I will go elsewhere."

The memories rushed in on Alex—the nights of waiting for the cargo to come in and for Rane to return safely to Clovelly, the night she had gone with the men and the ponies to take the goods inland, and they had nearly run into a troop of dragoons; the stormy black sea she and Rane had braved to get Caleb aboard the Irish smuggler's ship.

She bowed under the weight of her own history and Gincie's formidable determination. As her own grandmother had accepted her womanhood when Alex had chosen St. John, so Alex now accepted Gincie's right to make her own choices.

"I ask one thing of you—that you always remember to consider the risk against the gain. Danger can be as strong as any potion I know; it can make one blind and foolish."

"I promise," Gincie said. "And I ask another favor. Do not cancel your attendance at the races. Padraic said you had suggested it, but you both need to go. With so many horse owners being slave owners too, nothing could be better to distract attention from the hiding of fugitives than for business to go on as usual. And Gran, there is so much I have to learn, nothing is going to happen immediately. The work will be random in any case."

Alex held up her hand. "Spare me, my dear. I have given my permission, but you must not ask me to believe in the absolute safety of this enterprise."

Gincie regarded her for a long moment, and then she threw her arms around her grandmother. "I do love you!"

Alex dreaded telling Rane of Gincie's plans, but strangely, his attitude was more resigned than angry. "It is far too late to ask Gincie to be a giddy, irresponsible girl. I don't like what she is planning to do, but I'd rather have her operating from Wild Swan then running away to be completely out of our lives." He was not about to explain to Alex that with the decision to build the steam and sail ships had come his realization that all, even those as young as Gincie, were preparing for war in their own ways, even if the action was not as conscious or deliberate as the building of vessels for war.

Alex told the rest of the family nothing about Gincie's new determination. They would undoubtedly find out little by little. In the meantime, there was no reason to worry them needlessly. She worried enough by herself for all of them combined.

Chapter

28

Gincie found little resistance among agents of the Underground Railroad to her request to be allowed increased participation in their activities; they needed all the competent help they could muster. And despite her youth, Gincie could treat the sick and injured; she could ride like the wind; she had a quick mind that could retain vital information without difficulty; and most important, her dedication to the cause of getting the fugitives to safety was profound. Even the most wary in the organization sensed that.

Thomas Whitmore and his parents were her principal tutors. They were a rather austere Quaker family, unshakable in carrying out the will of God as they interpreted it, but they were also loving and respectful of each other and of life. They, like Gincie, were leery of the rabid Abolitionists who seemed so casually willing to provoke violence. The Whitmores lived with danger and the threat of violence in their work for the escaped slaves, but they had no desire to instigate it, and none of them carried weapons.

Gincie would have worked unarmed, too, if not for her grandfather. Rane had given her a small pistol and had made sure she knew how to use it.

"If anything happens to you," he told her, "it also happens to me and to your grandmother."

His quietly spoken words had impressed her with the need to be careful far more than any amount of ranting would have done.

All the same, she hoped it would never be necessary to shoot someone; she was not sure she could. And all her training was to avoid such a possibility.

She memorized routes and stations that wandered all over Maryland as far north as Southern Pennsylvania and as far south as Northern Virginia. She studied maps of river crossings where ferries or other boats were necessary and others that could be forded unless heavy rains had swollen their waters. She learned to be alert for all signs that something might be amiss—a signal light not showing or burning in the wrong place, extra horses at a house or farm, the presence of strange dogs or the absence of familiar ones—a myriad of endless details that changed according to the station being used. Harriet Tubman, who went repeatedly south to lead slaves out, was the exception; more usual was the guiding of slaves from one refuge to the next by various conductors, black and white. And Gincie was determined to know enough so that she could choose alternate routes when necessary.

Though the purpose was deadly serious, Gincie could not help but be amused by the disguises she learned to adopt. She made a credible Quaker daughter, a self-effacing lady's maid, a young farm wife for Thomas, and a passable young man. This last was her favorite, because the boy's clothing and the slouch hat pulled down low over her eyes gave her the most freedom of movement and made her feel less vulnerable than she did as a female.

By the beginning of the summer, even Alastair Cameron, who had been very reluctant to have her expand her work because of his responsibility for involving Wild Swan in the first place, had to admit that Gincie was as effective as any agent he knew.

For her part, Gincie began to understand what her grandmother had meant about the seduction of danger. Try as she might, Gincie could not suppress the heady excitement that gripped her every time she helped move runaways. It was partially fear that something would go wrong and the slaves be captured or that she herself would be injured, but beyond that was pure exhilaration.

She felt it the day she and Mr. Whitmore smuggled a wagonload of slaves into the District of Columbia in the clear light of early morning, the slaves hidden under a load of vegetables. She felt it when she and Thomas crossed over the Potomac and escorted slaves from the Virginia side.

She began to feel it the minute she knew work was in the offing. Though she tried not to succumb to the heady rush of power it brought to blood and brain, everything else seemed dull in comparison. When her cousins came to Wild Swan to visit, she found she had to concentrate very hard in order to appear interested in what they said and did, but most of all, she did not want them to interfere with her work. She made it clear to the other conductors and to organizers such as Alastair that she did not want to do less just because Wild Swan had visitors.

It was inevitable that her relatives would grow suspicious of her absences, in spite of her excuses of visiting friends at neighboring farms or in Washington, but they were discreet. They knew of Wild Swan's involvement in the Underground Railroad, and none of them was really surprised at Gincie's new status in it—they had all seen the change in her after Katy's death.

But Philly told Blaine, "I would not be able to bear it if one of our daughters was taking such risks."

"Yes, you would," he corrected her. "If one of them was Gincie, you would. I'd say our girls have enough stubbornness, but Gincie is one of the most determined people I've ever known. It's rather terrifying in one so young, and yet you cannot fault her for it. She only plants her feet when it is to further someone else's good."

It never occurred to Gincie that interest in her comings and goings could come from other than her family. When she rode in at dawn one morning, at first she did not notice the man waiting for her. She was tired and depressed; last night's passengers had never arrived at the rendezvous. She hoped desperately that they had gone another way, but it was much too probable that they had been captured. The consequences of that did not bear thinking about, and yet she could not avoid it. For the slaves, it could mean anything from chains to mutilation or death when they were returned to their owners, and for the agents who had helped them, arrest at best or death for them, too, if they had not fled the scene.

"Gincie, whatever it is, I'll help you. Just tell me what to do!"

She wheeled around in fright from her task of unsaddling Brutus and found Seth's friend, Frank Faber, standing there. She stared at him blankly while her heart pounded violently. She was dressed as a boy, and he obviously knew she had not just ridden out for an early morning excursion. She couldn't think of what to say.

"I swear it doesn't matter what the trouble is. I know I can find a way to help. Please tell me!" he urged.

Finally she began to understand that he thought she was sneaking off to meet a lover, though why she should be dressed as a boy in that case must surely be puzzling him.

She had not paid much attention to him beyond acknowledging him as one of Seth's nice friends. Even a year at Harvard had not given Frank airs, and she did appreciate that, since Seth looked up to him and would be attending the school in the fall. But that Frank had been watching her movements so closely was an unsettling idea. He had been at Wild Swan on and off for quite a bit of the summer. Fear for everyone involved in the Underground Railroad stiffened her spine.

"You are assuming a great deal to interfere in what I do. I suggest you find a more interesting subject to absorb your energies."

Frank was taken aback by the rebuff. He really did want to aid her. He had been fascinated by her even during the previous summer but had kept his feelings strictly to himself because of her youth. But this summer she had seemed so much more mature. There was an intensity about her that attracted him like moth to flame, and though he was older than she, he felt green and awkward in her presence, more so now than ever. "I'm sorry," he mumbled. "I want only to help."

She believed him; he looked so miserable. But still she could not understand why he had singled her out for his special interest. "All right," she said, her voice kinder than before. "But it is none of your affair, though I thank you for your concern. I assure you my family knows what I am about."

She turned back to the horse, shutting Frank out so effectively that he didn't even dare to offer his help in unsaddling.

In his mind, the scene in the barn grew worse by the minute so that for the rest of the day he dreaded seeing Gincie. Supper was pure torture. By the next day he could keep it to himself no longer and went to Seth, blurting out his concern and suspicions.

Seth was stunned to see Frank so shaken when he was normally so collected and to witness the extent of his feeling for Gincie.

"We all know what she's doing," he hastened to explain, and then he gulped, wondering what to say next since his friend was clearly not reassured.

"Damn!" Seth swore. "I'd trust you with my life, but this isn't my secret to tell." He studied Frank's face. "But I'm going to, anyway, if you will give me your word that you will not do anything with the information."

"Of course," Frank agreed, his mind conjuring wildly improbable explanations, none of them correct.

"How do you feel about slavery?" Seth asked.

"You know I am against it," Frank replied, and a faint light began to dawn in his mind. "But I also believe in the law," he added slowly. "And slaves are property under the law."

"There are some who believe that slavery is so evil, it must not be protected by law or by anything else, and that slaves have a right to freedom. Gincie is a conductor on the Underground Railroad."

Frank was horrified to have it confirmed. "Is everyone insane to allow her to take such risks?"

"Quite the opposite. It is the height of sanity to accept what Gincie does because of what she is. She has always been special, more serious, more dedicated than the rest of us. And Katy's death has made her even more so. I worry about her, but I also admire her. I will fight when the war comes, but I would be no use at all in the clandestine business of smuggling slaves to freedom. Without a doubt, I would give the game away."

He regarded Frank with compassion. "I suggest you go carefully with her. It will do no good, and she will not thank you for harrying her about this." He wanted to warn him further that he doubted his cousin would welcome romantic attentions. It was not Gincie's age—many girls even younger than she were pleased to boast of beaux—it was her commitment to the fugitives. She had very little energy for or interest in anything else. But Seth decided he had said enough; further discoveries were for Frank to make.

Frank was sensible enough to know that he had already crowded Gincie too much. If he was not careful, she would take flight from him for good. So with all of the discipline instilled in him by his parents, he kept his speech to Gincie as short and to the point as he could.

"You were quite right. What you are doing is none of my business. I demanded the truth from Seth, and he told me only to prevent further trouble. I just want you to know that I respect you very much and will keep the secret."

Gincie had been wary when he approached her, but she relaxed with his words. Finally, she smiled at him. "You will make a very good newspaperman," she said. "You notice more than others do."

He restrained himself from telling her it was because he cared specifically about her and said instead, "Brutus gave you away. When you're here, you ride the racehorses most of the time. But Brutus is a half-bred gelding, not at all your usual style. More dependable than a stallion or a mare, I would guess. And less noticeable."

"You're even more astute than I thought!" Gincie exclaimed. "I have good cause to be thankful you are a friend." She regarded him with new respect. Everything he said about the big brown gelding was true. On close inspection, Brutus was a handsome animal, but he lacked the show of the purebreds, and as a gelding, he had no interest in fighting with stallions or mares. Prior to Gincie's appropriation of him, he had served mostly for young children or unskilled riders who visited Wild Swan. He had endurance and could muster good speed when necessary, but above all else, he was trustworthy.

"I am honored you call me a friend," Frank murmured. The timbre of his voice briefly revealed the depth of his feelings, but Gincie missed it, experiencing nothing more than relief that this potentially dangerous problem seemed to be solved. It did not occur to her that he had a romantic interest in her; very little outside of her work with the fugitives fixed Gincie's own interest.

In September Magic went down and could not get up again, thrashing in frustration at his failed strength. Though they had expected it, it was hard for Alex and Samson to destroy the old stallion who had been such a special animal in their lives.

"Dat's ma beautiful Magic, dat's ma beautiful boy," Samson crooned as he fired the shot that killed him.

In a strange way, Gincie was pleased to find she was moved to tears by the stallion's death. It was good to share the sorrow at Wild Swan. She had begun to feel that nothing was valid in her life except for her work on the Underground Railroad. Everything else seemed to be happening at a distance, and she recognized the danger of that and feared it. Unless she was careful, she would become a fanatic soldier of the night. She had met more than one such and had been chilled. They were dedicated to a good cause, but they were also curiously devoid of humanity, pursuing their mission no matter what the cost to others. Though she shied away from the thought, she knew her mother had been and probably still was just that sort of person, albeit without the excuse of a humanitarian goal.

Alex was as aware of the dilemma facing her granddaughter as Gincie herself was, but she schooled herself to patience, having to be content with the knowledge that she continually made her love for Gincie clear. And she had faith that Gincie was basically too warm and compassionate ever to turn too far from those who cared about her.

She thought of her new granddaughter, born to Gweneth and Christopher in England in May, and she very much hoped that little Eveline and her brothers would find life simpler than their American cousins. Gincie's situation was the most hazardous, but the others were facing the same complicated America. Seth was going to Harvard; Larissa seemed to be appreciating Luke more; Nigel and Anthea continued to talk of being doctors and Adam of following the sea; and Phoebe went on teaching. But Alex felt that they were all in some sense suspending their lives, tripping along busily on the surface while underneath they waited for the guns.

Selfishly, she welcomed the heart of winter because there was less traffic on the Underground Railroad; thus Gincie was in less danger. And when she and Padraic took the horses south for the 1859 spring racing season, Alex left detailed instructions on how to reach her should anything go wrong at home, by which she meant should anything happen to Gincie. She was immeasurably grateful to find her granddaughter in one piece on her return.

Alex considered how much her own expectations had lowered in recent years. In normal times, she would have expected Gincie to be not only unharmed, but joyful and thriving as well. Instead there was a fine-honed fever about the girl, as if she were only living from one adventure to the next, just as Alex had feared she would.

When Gincie announced she would be gone for as many as five days, it was all Alex could do to clamp back the words that would have forbidden it.

But Gincie saw the stark fear in her grandmother's eyes. "Don't worry. It has been very well planned, and there are many people besides me who are determined these passengers will go through."

Alex had to be satisfied with that. She did not ask Gincie her destination, for she knew it would only put her granddaughter in the position of having to refuse to divulge the information. It was a reasonable policy: what people did not know, they could not betray, even inadvertently.

But Alex could not forbear asking, "If you are going to be delayed more than five days, will you please try to send word? I know it might be difficult, but try."

Gincie nodded, hugged her grandmother, and rode away, looking for all the world like a slender young man in her disguising hat and clothes. A week later Alex still had no word of her.

Chapter

29

The plan was simple enough. Gincie and Thomas were to meet the passengers being ferried across the Potomac from a narrow point on the river above Mount Vernon. They were then to guide them across to the Western Shore where a boat would be waiting to take them to the Eastern Shore. There the slaves would be hidden for a few days of rest before they journeyed on to Philadelphia, where a ship would take them aboard for the trip to Canada. The complication was in the execution; there were many with proslavery views who lived between one point and the next.

Gincie and Thomas were halfway to their rendezvous point when Thomas's horse took fright at a bird that burst from cover when the horse was almost upon it. Thomas tumbled out of the saddle, and Gincie heard the sickening snap of bone.

"My leg," Thomas gasped.

Gincie knelt beside him, and gritting her teeth in sympathy, she pulled off his boot and rolled up his pant leg. The bone gleamed whitely through his flesh just above his ankle.

"Can't thee just bind it up? Then we could go on." His voice was so faint, Gincie had to strain to hear the words.

"I can put a rough splint on it, but the only place you're going is to the nearest farmhouse." She tried desperately to think rationally for both of them. They had been riding in broad daylight, maintaining the fiction of two young men going about their business, but now Gincie felt as if her disguise was very thin indeed.

"Listen carefully, Thomas. I am going to do what I can for you, and then I'm going to find help. And you are going to pretend that we just met on the journey. As soon as you can, send word to your family. And I will tell them, too, when I return home, so that a wagon can be sent for you. I'm going to go on. Someone has to be there to meet the passengers tonight."

"Thee can't go alone!" Worry for her made his voice strong.

"Yes, I can. I am as well trained now as you are. And that's why there are two of us—in case something happens to one. People see what they are expecting to see; if I'm careful they'll keep seeing a boy."

Thomas subsided helplessly, in too much pain and shock to argue further.

Aware of the time ticking away, Gincie splinted Thomas's leg as well as she could, sorry to have to hurt him, but glad that he felt a bit better when the task was done. She covered him with the blanket from his saddle roll, and she remembered to go through his possessions, transferring everything that might arouse suspicion—laudanum, bandages, and extra footstuffs carried for the slaves—to her own horse. And then she rode to a farm they had passed a short while before. It looked well kept, though small and rather poor.

She kept her hat on and her voice low as she spoke to the first person she found, a middle-aged white man with a weathered but not unkind face.

"Mister, I hope you can help. I was riding along with this other fellow, met him on the road a ways back, and he took a fall from his horse. The man broke his leg and needs care and shelter. I can't stay with him, but he can pay for his keep. He gave me these to prove it." She offered the coins in her hand, relieved when the man's eyes left her face to study the money.

"Confess we could use that money," the farmer said, "but we don't turn away nobody in need, able to pay or not. The Lord says to minister to the least of his brethren."

He said it nicely enough so that Gincie didn't worry that Thomas was going to end up with a family of fanatics, the past year having seen a rise of religious fervor that was not always kind. Quakers, or Friends as some still called them, weren't liked in every quarter. There was no sign of slaves here, but this was not a known safe station. That someone followed Christian tenets toward fellow whites was no guarantee of the same treatment for blacks or those who aided them.

Gincie reminded herself that she was doing the best she could under the circumstances.

The man summoned a younger version of himself and explained the situation to the faded woman who had come to stand at the doorway of the house. His wife nodded and promised she'd prepare a bed for the injured man.

Husband, wife, and son, no sign of a hired hand—it was appearing to be a less threatening situation by the minute.

The father and son drove their wagon with Gincie leading the way. She stayed long enough to see Thomas safely loaded in the back of the wagon and to hear the man assuring him that a doctor would be summoned as quickly as possible. She barely had time to whisper to Thomas, "They seem all right, but better not tell them anything." She was relieved to see that his eyes were alert, and he gave a slight nod.

Thomas's horse was tied to the back of the wagon, and Gincie remounted Brutus.

"Good luck, mister," she said, looking at Thomas as if he was indeed a stranger.

As she wheeled Brutus around, the farmer's voice stopped her. "You take care, young fella. You ain't built too sturdy, an' there's some on the road that ain't civilized folk."

For an instant the farmer's eyes were fixed on her in keen speculation, but Gincie didn't flinch. "Thanks for the warning," she said, and she rode away before the man could say anything more.

Only when she was out of sight of the little party did the enormity of what she was doing strike her. She had almost always worked with Thomas or someone else, and when she had worked alone, it had been closer to Wild Swan than this. But taking the time to summon aid would mean missing the meeting tonight. She went on.

She avoided close contact with everyone she saw on the road. She did not see that many people—only a few farmers and horsemen—and her aloofness quickly doused friendly overtures. The fact that she was carrying the little gun her grandfather had given her gave her an extra measure of confidence, though she was still not sure she would use it.

By pushing Brutus the last part of the journey, she arrived at her destination while there was enough twilight left to allow her to find the markers—a small cairn of stones in one place, a seemingly random slash on a tree a little distance away, and a piece of rag snagged on a bush. The area was wooded, deserted, on the edge of the Potomac. There were slave owners nearby, but not here. This land was owned by a man friendly to the cause, though he himself lived most of the time in Georgetown and was not an active conductor.

She kept in the shadow of the trees, watching the river, seeing the traffic passing to and fro on this major artery to Chesapeake Bay, traffic that had grown with the advent of steam on the river, though many of the boats still rode the wind and tide in the old way.

As the light faded, the night singing rose around Gincie, insects and nocturnal animals, each adding its own note to the chorus. She shivered though the air was warm, and she strained her ears, trying to hear anything untoward. The minutes seemed like hours, but at last she heard the faint scrape of a boat being pulled ashore.

"Sunrise," a male voice called softly, and for an awful moment, Gincie forgot what she was supposed to answer—Thomas was the one who was going to exchange passwords. But then she remembered and called back, "Tomorrow," as she advanced on the landing party.

By the shuttered ship's lantern, Gincie saw that there were three fairly young black men, two women, and three small children and their guide, a tall white man. And there was another passenger, a horse who coolly jumped from the flat deck on command.

"What—?" Gincie stammered, not understanding why the man would need a horse, since surely he was going back with the boat to Virginia.

"I want to see these people safely on their way. We've had some trouble—slave catchers a day back. I think we've lost them, but I'm not sure. They might telegraph ahead, or they might already have crossed the river at some other point." The voice had a slight drawl, but there was no doubt that the man was used to taking charge. He peered into the darkness and asked, "Where is the other man? Keepin' a lookout?"

"We had trouble, too," Gincie said. "He had a fall from his horse and broke his leg. I left him in the care of a farm family." Suddenly she was glad this man would be accompanying them, and she had a wild desire to laugh. He had called the horse "Clancy"; it was utterly incongruous to be standing on a beach with a group of fugitive slaves and a horse named Clancy who performed as if he were circus-trained.

Realizing the strains of the day were catching up with her, she made an effort to get control of herself.

"Travis," he said, offering his name.

"Gentry," she returned, having long since settled on a male name that sounded enough like her own name that she could answer to it without hesitation.

She learned the slaves' names and that Jubal, a large man in his mid-twenties, was the one the other slaves naturally deferred to. Jubal was calm and quiet spoken, and Gincie was glad he was there. August, another of the men, was not so amenable, glaring with general anger at all about him, but Gincie could hardly blame him—trusting white people under any circumstance must surely be difficult. The man had an ugly scar down one cheek, and she didn't want to know how he'd gotten it.

The boat slipped into the water and began its journey back to the Virginia shore. Under ideal conditions, the crews of the boats were sympathetic to the cause, but sometimes they were only exceedingly well paid to take the risk. Gincie hoped it was the former in this case. Anything that might thwart slave catchers was desirable. Gincie could not think of them without having Katy's death leap into her mind.

When she and Travis were mounted, they each took a child up before them on their saddles, the smallest child being carried by Jubal. Gincie often felt guilty about riding while the slaves walked, but it couldn't be helped. Most of them were not horsemen. And the horses made it possible for her and Travis to range slightly ahead of the group, checking for any signs of danger.

The little girl in front of Gincie could not be older than six, but she knew the hazards of the journey. She kept silent and sat very still, intent on causing as little trouble as possible.

Remembering her masculine role, Gincie whispered gruffly, "Lean back a little. You'll be more comfortable, and I won't let you fall."

The child obeyed with a grateful little sigh, and a wave of tenderness swept over Gincie. It was all worth it for the chance that this child would not grow up in bondage.

She concentrated all her senses on making sure they were not surprised by the enemy. And she decided that the fact of her true gender was just as well kept a secret. Travis obviously cared very much about getting the slaves to safety, and she did not think he would be reassured to know that a young woman was in charge of the Maryland crossing. Actually, she suspected that this Travis would be in charge wherever he was, and the change of command did not trouble her. As long as the job was done, she would be satisfied.

Dawn was just breaking when they reached the farm where they would spend the day. Everything appeared to be in order. There were no signs of extra visitors. Smoke wafted from the kitchen chimney and an oven had obviously been in use, too, because the air was redolent with the tantalizing smell of freshly baked bread. Gypsy, a collie kept by Mrs. Mills, rushed out barking, but quieted as soon as Gincie called to her.

Mrs. Mills was a round-faced, ample woman, a middle-aged widow and a devout Congregationalist. She and an older couple managed to tend the little place efficiently enough so that the land provided a comfortable life for them.

Gincie had been here previously, and she knew the slaves would be offered plenty of good food and other amenities, even though they would be hiding in the barn. Mrs. Mills's father had been a slave owner, and when Mrs. Mills was very young, she had seen a slave beaten to death by the overseer. The overseer's excuse had been spurious; the real cause had been the constant pride and attitude of defiance shown by the slave, though he had done the work assigned to him.

Mrs. Mills had never forgotten the brutal act, and her revulsion had grown into something more useful—a deep, smoldering rage against slavery and the commitment to foiling it at every opportunity. Her husband had shared her convictions, and she had not faltered in the work after his death. Her appearance of pleasant prosperity was a good disguise, and she was highly regarded by other agents.

Gincie handed her passenger down to the child's mother and rode in ahead of Travis and the others, a perfectly natural thing to do since she knew Mrs. Mills and the farm. But as soon as the woman greeted her, Gincie explained what had happened to Thomas and said, "I'm still 'Gentry' to the slaves and Travis, the man who brought them from Virginia. I would like to maintain that fiction, if you will oblige me. It's foolish, but all will feel more secure if they think I'm a boy."

Mrs. Mills regarded her skeptically. "A close look in broad daylight is likely to end the game, but as you will, child, and I'll do my best to help."

Mrs. Mills was as good as her word. She greeted the rest of her visitors and with ease managed all to her satisfaction.

She looked at Travis and then looked again, wondering if Gincie Carrington had gotten a clear view of him and doubting that she had, so intent was the girl on keeping her distance. Mrs. Mills guessed he was in his twenties and noted how tall and lean he was, though with enough breadth in his shoulders to please many a young lady. His hair was a deep honey brown, and Mrs. Mills liked the cut of his face because it was so male, almost harsh with a sharp blade of nose, the slash of cheekbones, the clear planes of brow and jaw. But his eyes were his most striking feature. They were a startling turquoise blue, and they were very observant.

Mrs. Mills had been blissfully content with Mr. Mills, who had been a squarely built man with simple tastes, but that did not make her blind to the charms of those around her. This Travis was a fine specimen of a man, and he was not likely to be fooled for long by Gincie's playacting, now that the sun was coming full up.

Mrs. Mills kept them apart for the day by having them take turns watching over their charges in the barn, the one not on duty being invited to sleep in her spare bedroom.

Gincie fell in gratefully with the plan, and Travis made no objection, though Mrs. Mills saw him eyeing Gincie curiously as she walked away to take the first turn at sleeping.

"He's hardly more than a stripling," Travis murmured. "Seems like the line is recruiting children."

"But he's a steady lad and good at his job," Mrs. Mills replied equably.

Travis nodded. "He is that. He hasn't put a foot wrong. I expect he wishes I'd minded my own business and gone back to Virginia."

"Quite the contrary, with Thomas left behind, I am sure Gentry welcomes your help."

Mrs. Mills bustled about, making sure everyone had water for washing and huge portions of food, and Travis smiled ruefully to himself —despite the gravity of the situation, Mrs. Mills had a distinct twinkle in her eye. Tired and worried as he was, he wished she'd share the jest. Though there had been no sign of pursuit in Maryland, that did not ease his tension. These were not broken-down old people they were bringing out, but workers in their prime and promising children, too. He willed himself the patience to take advantage of the rest and food offered at the farm.

They left as soon as it was dark. Storm clouds had boiled in the sky all afternoon and hung over them now in purple gloom. It was so humid, the air felt syrupy, but the rain held off. Gincie just hoped the boat would be able to negotiate the waters of the bay in spite of the weather.

Once a dog rushed out of the darkness to bark viciously, freezing them all in their tracks as a voice scolded and called the animal in from a distance.

"Good boy. Go home now," Gincie whispered, and after a whine of indecision the dog turned around and disappeared into the shadows once more.

Even with night-adjusted eyes, it was precarious going for both horses and people. They could not risk any kind of lantern, and so had to depend on the lamps of houses and small villages and had to slough across streams and a river in the dark. But they went on steadily, and there was not a single complaint from the slaves, not even the youngest of them. Their lives were at stake, and they were not going to whine about insect bites and tired feet.

As they neared the inlet of the bay, Gincie could feel Travis's heightened tension even when he was a good distance away, and she shared it. They were so close now. The wind was picking up, the scent of rain was strong over the salt water smell, but there was not yet a shrieking gale to prevent the boat from crossing the water.

Gincie nearly exclaimed aloud in gratitude when the boat turned out to be exactly where it was supposed to be, moored in the small inlet with the rowboat already ashore, waiting to take the passengers the short distance to the larger craft.

Passwords were exchanged. The slaves were rowed out in two groups to the waiting vessel. Gincie and Travis gave the slaves everything they could from laudanum, in case one of the children got too fussy after all on the journey and made dangerous noise, to money to help them on their way.

"God bless you bof," one of the women said softly, and Jubal offered his grave thanks before he stepped into the rowboat to go out with the second group.

Gincie and Travis were still standing there listening to the scrape of the oars growing fainter when other sounds intruded—the jingle of bridle bits, a man's voice saying, "I swear this is th' place! If they ain't here or ain't been here, I'll eat mah hat."

Another said, "If they ain't here, I'll have yer hide fer leadin' us on this chase!"

Still a third voice cut in with a low snarl, "Shut up! You wanna warn 'em?"

"Are you armed?" Travis hissed.

"Yes."

"Use it if you have to. Mount your horse. The way's too narrow to go around them."

"I know," she said as she scrambled up into her saddle. "Right through them." She knew Travis was sharing the same peculiar calm she felt. There was no time for fear, no time for anything except diverting the slave catchers long enough so that the boat could get underway without being sighted or hindered.

Though their horses tried to swerve out of the way, they rode them straight toward the voices, and Travis gave a great whooping yell just as they were upon the men, not three but at least four and maybe another. Gincie wasn't sure in the confusion.

"What th' hell!"

"God damn it!"

Other curses were lost in the uproar as the slave catchers' horses crashed into each other trying to shy out of the way of the mad riders coming upon them.

Gincie had the little pistol in her hand, but she didn't fire it. Travis did fire his larger weapon, pointing it skyward and achieving an extra measure of shock from the noise and flash.

A split second later there was an answering crack, but then one of the men bellowed, "Hold your fire, fool! You'll hit one of us!"

But the one shot had done its work. The ball hit Gincie's left shoulder, nearly knocking her from the saddle. The little pistol fell from a left hand gone suddenly numb, but her right hand held onto the reins. The first jolt of pain was lost in the pounding of her heart as all her energy was consumed by the need to stay on Brutus and keep riding. Brutus stumbled in the dark but righted himself and went on with brave speed, keeping up with Travis's horse.

There were more shots as their pursuers got their horses under control and came after them. And even with their lead, it came to Gincie that she and Travis could not win this blind race in the dark. If they weren't thrown and their necks broken, they were going to be finished off by the shots from the slave catchers. And with the same time-slowing, insistent logic, her mind also suggested that she might well be finished already; the warm river of blood was pouring down her torso, soaking her clothes.

The skies opened up, and it was as close to an act of God as anything Travis ever wanted to witness. The rain came down as if the bay were being upended on the land. Travis sensed their chance more than saw it in a split of lightning. Trusting that somehow Gentry would follow his lead, he plunged Clancy off the track and into dense brush. Brutus followed Clancy.

As they made their way deeper into the brush, they heard the other horses thunder by, the sound dying away in a wash of rain.

They stayed there for long moments, then again Travis led the way. There was no sign of the slave catchers backtracking yet, but Travis urged the pace, retracing part of their wild race until he found another road.

They kept riding through the rain, and Gincie lost all notion of where they were. Staying on Brutus became all. The pain in her shoulder was growing by the second, making it hard to draw breath. Hazily she set her mind on going home. If she could find the way to Wild Swan, everything would be all right.

After what seemed an eternity to Gincie, Travis reined his horse to a stop, and she halted, too.

"Well, Gentry, by now those men must've realized that the slaves were being loaded when we rode into them. With any luck, they'll go home, knowin' they've failed. Just the same, we're probably better off splittin' up. They're lookin' for two riders. I'm goin' to try to find my way back to the Potomac by mornin'. We'll take the risk if you want to travel with me, but I doubt your home lies that way."

"No, I go north," Gincie managed. "Thank you for your help." Dimly she perceived that she wanted him to go away. Her condition would make him vulnerable, and that would never do after all the assistance he had already given her. It also seemed very important that he not discover at this late date that she was female.

"Well, youngster, safe home. You've done well. I'd work with you any time." Travis put his hand out, and after a slight hesitation, Gentry shook with him, the damp hand slender and fine-boned for so good a rider.

"This murk and the rain are to our good, Travis. Safe journey to you too." The voice was low and tired sounding, and Travis hoped the boy would be warm at home before too long, though he had no idea how far away he lived.

They parted. Travis had gone quite a few paces before he wiped the rain splatters from his face and tasted blood. He put his hand to his mouth again in puzzlement. He thought he must have a nosebleed or a cut on his lip. Then he realized the blood was on his hand and was not his own. With a muttered curse, he wheeled Clancy around.

He found the other rider without difficulty, the horse was moving so slowly. In a flash of lightning, he saw Gentry swaying in the saddle.

"Why didn't you tell me you were hurt?" he demanded harshly as he came alongside.

The boy didn't check his horse. "It's nothing. I'll be fine." The words were so feeble, Travis could hardly decipher them. He saw him reel in the saddle and reached out instinctively, grabbing him by the shoulders before he fell.

The high-pitched scream nearly caused him to lose his own balance as both horses started nervously, and the boy went limp.

Cursing in earnest, Travis managed to dismount clumsily, keeping a hold on the reins of both horses and the sagging body. He had no choice but to lay the boy down on the wet ground while he tied the horses nearby.

The boy stirred and groaned under his hands as Travis opened the layers of clothing, the cloth more soaked with gore than with rain. By the time he got to flesh, the blood was flowing over his hands and over a last, unexpected garment. He froze and then used his knife to cut through the binding.

The storm no longer seemed a friend. More by touch than by sight, he determined two things—the wound was in the left shoulder and the shoulder belonged to a young woman. Her breasts, freed from the binding, left no doubt. Lightning briefly illuminated the dark blood on the white skin.

While he was still assimilating the appalling fact that she was female, her voice startled him. "If you'll help me tie something around it, I can go on."

"You can't," he snapped, too overwhelmed by the problems facing them to appreciate the gallantry of her offer.

He had to get her to shelter or at least to some place where he could light a fire. The region wasn't familiar to him, particularly after the disorienting chase; he had no knowledge of whom to trust. He wished they were in Virginia, North Carolina, or even Maryland closer to the Potomac—all areas he knew fairly well.

"Do you know any safe houses nearby?" he asked urgently.

"No, don't know exactly . . . where we are . . . too risky. The slave catchers might still be looking . . . maybe they know the places." Her voice was trailing off. He could hear the effort she put into the next words. "You must go. There are so few of us, can't afford to lose—"

He cut her off. "Would you leave me?"

"I don't know." The stubborn response drifted up to him.

"No more wasted talk. I'm goin' to bind your shoulder as tightly as I can, and then we're gettin' out of here." He hoped he sounded more confident than he felt. He tugged the breast wrap, which he had cut previously, out from under her and wadded it into a pad, and then he cut the bottom from his own shirt to use as strapping.

She tensed when he touched the wound, but beyond a rasping intake of breath, she made no sound. He willed his hands to steadiness. It was the best he could do for the time being. He closed her garments, wishing they were heavier as he felt her shivering with the damp and shock.

He led Clancy back and commanded him to stand. "I'm goin' to lift you onto my horse, but you'll have to hang on by yourself for a minute." He didn't ask whether or not she could do it; she had to.

She bit back a cry as he lifted her, but she stayed on the horse when he released her. He tied the reins of her gelding to his saddle, not liking the arrangement but glad the horse seemed as well-trained as Clancy. He swung up behind the girl, and they set off.

"Lean back against me," he ordered. "You're wastin' your strength sittin' like that."

She complied with relief and felt his arm go around her waist. She could not remember ever being so cold, as if ice were working from the inside out of her bones. The pain in her shoulder was erratic, fading one moment only to stab back in great spreading waves the next. She couldn't fix her mind on any one thought for more than an instant, and it bothered her. She felt as if brittle-winged creatures were darting around in her brain. She caught and held one of them long enough to examine it.

"You know I'm a woman."

"Yes."

Even in her befuddled state, she heard the grimness that shaped the small word. Doggedly she clung to the fluttering thought. "Peculiar, you see, man and a woman with a gunshot wound and good horses. Not sure where we are, can't risk . . ." Everything was slipping away again, but it was desperately important to her that he understand and not seek aid from the wrong people. She was still worried that he might do it for her sake. In the midst of all the confusion, the image of him being shot or hanged by the slave catchers was terrifying.

Everything was impossible, and Travis had never felt more helpless in his life, and yet he could not deny the sweet warmth he felt at the realization that her concern had been and continued to be for him. "Rest now, I'll be careful. We'll stop as soon as I find a safe place."

As the minutes ticked by into one hour and another, Travis was hard pressed to resist the despair that threatened to immobilize him. Once he thought he heard other riders, and twice the dense brush gave way to cleared land and the dangerous glow of light from dwellings that might harbor slave owners. The barking of dogs made him hurry the horses onward. The storm rolled over with gathering force, thunder rumbling and lightning splitting the sky while the rain poured down. The noise of it helped to cover their passage, but they were both soaked. The girl shivered against him, the tremors growing worse. He could feel her fading in and out of consciousness, rousing with a start when she felt herself slipping away until finally she slumped against him with a moan and remained so, kept in place only by his arms.

He found himself thinking of his grandmother Abigail and of her endless faith in the justness of their cause, her faith in God's mercy touching all who labored for it. He wished he was a believer in the same strong way she was, serenely convinced of God's presence in every life and instant of eternity. He began to speak in his mind as his grandmother had tried to teach him, asking for help without embarrassment or reluctance.

First the rain to shield them and then another miracle—a tumbledown shack limned by a shaft of lightning. He strained his eyes, unable to believe deliverance was at hand, but the rough-hewn, weathered boards remained as they were, sagging against each other in the rain—some tenant farmer's lost dream.

The girl hardly stirred in his arms when he lifted her down; even her shivering was growing weaker. He left the horses standing where they were, trusting they were too wet and weary to wander far.

There were dry islands on the damp, tamped earth floor. Travis used the flashes of lightning to get his bearings. He laid his burden down by the stone and mud hearth before he went back outside and brought in the saddles and supplies.

Fire. Heat and light. Fire was the first thing to seek. He set about the task grimly, finding leaves and twigs that had blown in over time, coaxing curls of smoke and then flame from them before adding the driest boards he was able to wrench free from the dilapidated cabin. Most of the wood was too thick and heavy, but lighter pieces had been used here and there to close gaps. The place obviously hadn't been prepossessing even when first built, but to Travis, it was infinitely welcoming compared to the wet and dark outside, and he blessed the man who had built the chimney, for, despite its crumbling state, it still drew the smoke away.

After he had piled their two blankets and every bit of spare clothing on the unconscious girl, he went out again, looking for water, hoping he wouldn't have to wait for rain to fill the two small cooking pans they had between them. He hobbled the horses in the best shelter he could find, regretting he couldn't provide better for them. He nearly stumbled into the little creek nearby in the woods. He felt a great surge of relief and gratitude. They had the essentials—shelter, fire, water, and enough food for a couple of days.

Everything except a doctor's skills, he thought as he unwrapped the wound and inspected it by the light of the fire and the candle stub he had placed beside her. Panic rose to obliterate the earlier feeling of satisfaction. She had lost so much blood, her clothing was soaked with it. Her skin had a grayish tinge and was ice cold to his touch. There was no exit wound.

He knew the rudiments of rough medicine; his grandmother and plantation life had taught him a variety of skills, but nothing had prepared him to do surgery on this delicate flesh. He sat back on his heels, sweat beading his skin. The wound might fester in any case; it surely would if the ball were left in. And he had no idea of a better place to take her in the next critical hours. They would be in as much, and probably more, danger with the coming of morning as they were now. It was just as she had said—a woman with a gunshot wound was suspicious.

He stuck his knife blade into the fire, and he tore a clean shirt and small clothes into manageable lengths.

She whimpered and came to, her body going rigid as he bathed the wound with water and brandy from his flask. Firelight and the flickering candle flame were reflected in her eyes, making them look an unearthly pale, shimmering green. No wonder she had kept her careful distance during the day. Now that he knew, he could scarcely credit that he had believed her a boy.

He raised her head a little and held his flask to her mouth. "Please drink. It's brandy. It ought to help." He kept his voice and hands steady with effort. She gagged and turned her head away after two small swallows, and he hadn't the heart to try to force more of the liquor down her, fearful that she would be sick if he did.

He knelt over her, a knee braced on either side of her. He washed his hands in water and a little of the precious brandy and waited until the glow had faded from the knife blade, trusting the fire had cleansed it.

The girl's eyes were open again, staring up at him.

"Go ahead and yell. I don't think anyone's close enough to hear. But hold yourself as still as you can. I don't want to hurt you any more than I have to."

Forcing himself to probe the ugly, swollen-edged hole was the hardest thing he had ever done. Her body jerked and shuddered beneath him and then stiffened as she struggled to do as he had bid her. Her breathing was reduced to harsh gasps.

He fished out a piece of shirt, but he was ready to cease the torture and admit failure when suddenly he felt the tip of his knife meeting metal. With the blade and his fingers, he dug until he could dislodge the bullet from its burrow of muscle and bone.

She screamed then, a keen of agony that ended abruptly as she fainted.

He kept working methodically, pouring brandy over the wound, cauterizing it deeply with the reheated knife, and then pressing a thick pad of cloth against it, holding it there until the bleeding stopped, and then wrapping a bandage in place.

He allowed himself to let go. He sat beside her, his bloody hands resting limply on his knees. He watched with detached interest as his hands started to tremble. He could smell the blood and the singed flesh. He could still feel the damaged tissues beneath his hands. He would hear the scream forever.

He roused himself to sort through their belongings, taking a more careful inventory than he had earlier. A little coffee, corn meal, salt, sugar, a bit of bacon, dried beans, and some bread and cheese—careful rations kept just in case there was a delay in getting to a safe house or home. The best of everything had gone with the slaves. If he could bag something on the morrow, broth from fresh meat would be just the thing for her. After all they had been through, he refused to consider the possibility that she might not survive.

He went back to the creek, ignoring the rain that soaked him anew. The water was muddy, but he washed the used bandages and the pans anyway, having no choice, and took a new supply of water back with him in one pan, leaving the other outside to catch the rain.

He had planned to make some coffee and eat something, but when he returned to the girl's side, thoughts of anything except her fled his mind. She was shivering again, so violently that it was as if she was in the grip of a seizure. Horrible whimpering sounds accompanied the chattering of her teeth.

He cursed himself for a fool. It had made a difference to him that she was female. He hadn't even considered taking off her wet clothing. In the unconsidered attempt to spare her modesty, he might well have further endangered her survival.

In swift, furious motions, he added more wood to the fire and stripped off her sodden garments, even to unpinning her hair, which had been tightly bound and hidden beneath her hat. He placed her on one blanket and covered her with the other while he undressed himself.

With the fire on one side of her and himself on the other, he sheltered her with his body, trying not to jar her as he pressed himself along the length of her to generate the most heat. He was shocked by the depth of the cold that gripped her flesh.

"I don't even know your name or where you come from. I'm not sure I'm takin' care of you the right way, but I don't know what else to do. You mustn't die, you mustn't! You're young, and there must be people waitin' for you to come home. You hang on, and I'll take you there as soon as I can." He continued to talk to the unconscious girl, needing his own voice to fight off fear and exhaustion. Not until he felt her warming in his arms did he succumb to the overwhelming need to sleep

Chapter

30

The slave catchers had her, and they were roasting her alive and stabbing at her flesh. Gincie fought to the surface of the fevered nightmare, terror giving her strength.

Travis came awake in the instant and held her tightly, pleading, "Please, quiet down, please! You're goin' to hurt yourself worse than you are already. Please! You're safe. It's Travis, and you're safe with me."

Travis, the man on the horse named Clancy. She ceased to struggle as she remembered, and the strength went out of her. "Hot," she murmured.

Travis let her go. She settled and gazed at him as he grabbed for his pants and pulled them on. That he was nude and she was, too, did not register as being out of the ordinary; her rising fever and the throbbing in her shoulder distorted everything. She tried to pull the blanket away from her skin.

Travis tucked it around her again. "Sorry, darlin', but you'll get a chill if you're not covered."

Gincie tried to focus on the face swimming out of focus above her. The only thing that really registered was the extraordinary color of his eyes. "Turquoise," she whispered, and then she added, "Name, Gincie Carrington," because it seemed important that he should know it, now that she was no longer Gentry to him.

"Travis Culhane," he said, but he doubted she heard him. Her eyes had closed again, and her good hand was plucking restlessly at the blanket. It worried him that her left arm hadn't moved at all. And then he grimly reminded himself that keeping her alive was his first priority; time enough later to assess the damage the bullet or his digging for it had done.

Travis had never experienced a more dreadful day. The fire had gone out while they slept, but he did not rekindle it. The storm had passed; the day promised to be very warm; and he did not want to risk the smoke being seen. He munched on hard bread and cheese without enthusiasm, eating only to maintain his strength. He took care of the horses as well as he could and periodically patrolled the area around the shack to make sure no one was advancing on it. But he resented every minute away from the girl. He was terrified she would die if he wasn't watching over her.

She was delirious throughout the day, alternating between periods of stupor and agitated babbling. Sometimes Travis could understand what she was saying—she was worried about Thomas and about her grandmother; she kept asking that someone tell her grandmother she was all right and would be home; and she fretted that the slaves had not gotten aboard the ship.

"She's coming to take me away from Wild Swan! She's coming! Keep her away from me! Keep my mother away!" It was a shrill wail of terror, and Travis had to hold her down as she tried to get her legs under her so she could run.

He didn't know why she feared her mother, but Wild Swan was a name he knew. He had once seen Alexandria Carrington Falconer at a horse race, and he knew the fame of her Thoroughbreds. He remembered the woman quite clearly because she was so striking. He remembered she had very green eyes. This Gincie had green eyes, too. It occurred to him that the grandmother Gincie referred to was none other than the formidable Alexandria.

"Oh, Lord!" he groaned, thinking how awful it would be if he had to tell her that this child had died.

No, not a child, not at all. Her body was slender and young, but the hips were gently curved, the breasts firmly rounded. He saw every inch of her as he bathed her repeatedly, trying to lower her fever. But he felt no desire for her, only the need to protect her.

He made her drink water; he tended to her needs; and he kept talking to her, as if his voice would serve to anchor her with the living.

It was nightfall before her fever fell enough so that she no longer radiated such fearsome heat. She opened her eyes as he cradled her head, urging her to drink for the countless time. Obediently she took a few sips. Her eyes closed and her jaw clenched until the worst of the pang in her shoulder eased. And then she gazed up at Travis and murmured his name as the fog cleared from her mind. "Thank you for taking care of me."

The faint words stabbed at Travis's heart, and tears burned his eyes. "I would give anything for a way to ease your pain," he said. "But I have nothing to offer."

"You could have left . . . didn't."

"No more talking now," he said, stroking her hair back from her face. It gave him an odd sensation as he realized that the color of his own hair was almost exactly the same as hers. He pulled his hand away and confined himself to practical matters. "It won't be very appetizing, but I'd like you to try to eat something a little later."

With the sun gone, he built a fire again, hoping that if anyone noticed the smoke, he would not track its source but assume it came from some farm in the region.

Travis's appetite had sharpened until he was hungry enough to eat anything, but Gincie only managed a little coffee and a bite or two of corn pone. Travis resolved to hunt in the morning.

He almost wished for her fever to rise again so that she could drift away from the pain in her wound. Though she did not complain, her face contorted with each wave of it, and her breathing was punctuated by little sighing cries.

He sponged her face and hands and then he took her right hand in his own. Her hand was clamped in a fist, and he carefully unfolded it and stroked the palm. "Why don't you hold on to me."

Gratefully she complied, her fingers curling around his and gripping with surprising strength when the pain was most acute.

Travis started talking again, as he had when she was unconscious, now hoping to distract her. "I know you'd like my grandmother Abigail. She's wonderful. Stubborn, but lovin' too. Though I'm supposed to be in charge, it's really Grandmother who runs Hawthorn. It's on the Rappahannock River east of Fredericksburg in Virginia. First part of the family that settled there way back named it for Hawthorn Manor, the home they'd left in England. Prettiest country you ever want to see. But my grandmother was a Philadelphia girl, a Quaker, when my grandfather Culhane met and courted her. She went south with him, and she changed his life. He owned slaves before, but not after she arrived. That was one of the conditions of the marriage. And he admitted to me before he died that he got the best of the exchange. He's been gone for ten years now, and Grandmother still misses him. My father was their only son, but he and my mother were killed in a steamboat accident when I was very young. I was at Hawthorn, and I really don't remember much about my parents, just the ghosts of a pretty woman and a man with a deep voice like my grandfather's."

He could see some of the tension easing from Gincie's face. Her hand wasn't gripping his so tightly now. He went on speaking, keeping his voice low and even. "My family has English, Irish, Scottish, and French blood, and there are cousins of every degree from my mother's side and from my grandfather Culhane, who had brothers and sisters both, cousins spread all over Virginia. Now, I like many of my kin, and even love some of them, but they weren't changed by Grandmother, so many of them still own slaves. But there sure aren't any at Hawthorn. Grandmother would smuggle slaves out herself if she was able, but she's been crippled by arthritis for a long time now, and she has to content herself with givin' refuge to the passengers when they come through our way."

Gincie smiled at that, but she hadn't the strength to explain. Travis's voice was acting like a lullaby, even though she was interested in what he was telling her.

Travis suspected, correctly, that she was thinking of her own grandmother, but he didn't ask, not wanting her to feel obliged to talk. "We raise a number of things at Hawthorn. Some grain, vegetables, and fruit and poultry, pork, and cattle for both meat and milk. No tobacco, thank God! My grandfather saw long ago that that was a crop that bled the land. I was tutored at home, and then I went off to Cambridge in England. My grandparents always intended I see a bit of the world. And I enjoyed it. But I'm a farmer and a Virginian at heart."

How odd, Gincie thought, Hawthorn sounds as if it is much like Wild Swan, and he even has a connection to England. She felt as if she had known him for a very long time, not a span measurable in mere hours. The peaceful dark enfolded her.

Travis waited until he was sure Gincie was sleeping soundly before he relinquished her hand and eased himself quietly out of the room in order to check on the horses and make a last patrol before he too slept.

In the morning, he risked the noise of a shot and got a fat rabbit. He had never taken more pleasure in his hunting skills. He roasted the rabbit over the fire, saving the drippings, and he coaxed Gincie to eat some meat and some of the juices on corn pone, feeding it to her in very small pieces over the whole day, his patience limitless. Her fever stayed within reasonable bounds, and she slept for most of the day, worn out by the ordeal. Though he was loath to cause her further hurt, he checked the wound in the evening when he could heat water. It was oozing and raw, but not dangerously inflamed. His sigh of relief was audible as he bound up her shoulder again.

"No smell of putrefaction," Gincie observed. "I am fortunate to have been shot in the company of a capable doctor."

Her voice was still thready, but her words were rational and even humorous. He grinned at her and shook his head. "My grandmother is the one with the skill; I know just bits and pieces. We're both fortunate they happened to fit here."

"My grandmother is very skilled at healing, too," she said.

"Your grandmother, would she be Alexandria Carrington Falconer?" he ventured, judging her recovered enough to answer.

"How did you know that?" she asked, though it didn't seem as peculiar as it should have.

"You spoke of Wild Swan when you were fevered. Your grandmother is a legend. People still talk about the match race she rode. Your eyes are very like hers. I saw her once at a race meeting; she's a strikingly beautiful woman." As you are, he nearly added, seeing clearly now that she was more conscious.

"She is," Gincie agreed. "I think you would like her very much." Then she frowned. "How long has it been? Gran will be frantic!"

"She shouldn't have let you get mixed up in this business in the first place!" he snapped without considering his words, his anger at her vulnerability surfacing.

"And your grandmother, could she prevent you from taking the risk?" Gincie asked shortly.

"That's different! You're a . . . ." he grinned ruefully. "Pray forget I even started to say that. In view of the women who work on the line and the female slaves who venture all to gain freedom, it is ridiculous to protest. And my grandmother couldn't even manage to make a Quaker of me." The humor left him. "It is just that it is hard to see you so hurt."

Gincie was suddenly overwhelmingly aware of him as a man—a big, strong, handsome, wondrously tender man.

There was no lack of presentable males in her life. From her grandfather to her uncles to her cousins and their friends, she was accustomed to vibrant, even dashing men. It was as if she were awakening from a long sleep of childhood and becoming a woman, because only that would match someone as splendidly masculine as Travis Culhane. She felt disoriented, and she closed her eyes so she would not have to look at him any more.

"I'm sorry, I've wearied you," Travis apologized.

"No, I was just thinking. The problem of getting home before my grandmother gives up all hope still remains." Anything to break the intimacy between them.

Travis was no less affected by the strange current running from one to the other than she, and he had to concentrate to discuss the problems facing them.

"I have been thinking, too. We still don't know how the slave catchers knew how to find the landing point. Sailors do talk, so perhaps it was just a matter of information overheard or sold. Or maybe someone has seen the boat taking on fugitives before. Unfortunately, as you know, it wouldn't be the first time the line has been compromised. We just don't know, and we don't know if any of the safe houses, few that there are, are being watched. It's probable that the slave catchers have given up and gone south again, but I wouldn't bet our lives on it. The safest place for you is Wild Swan, but you won't be able to ride there for a long time." He thought of the added handicap of her useless left arm but did not mention it. "The best course is for me to find a wagon somewhere. Can your horse pull in harness? Clancy can."

"Brutus can do almost anything except write his name," she answered, her smile drawing one from him. She did not bother to insist that she would soon be able to ride; the way she felt now, she would not be able to stay on a horse unless she was thrown over it like a sack of meal. She did not question how Travis would get the wagon; she felt as if he could do anything.

But Travis did not go in search of the vehicle for another four days. He would not consider leaving her alone before she was strong enough to walk out of the shack in an emergency and hide in the brush. And he left his heavy pistol with her, paying no heed to her contention that she could scarcely lift it with one hand.

"If you must, you'll manage," he said, his tone brusque because, as much as she did not want him to go unarmed, he could hardly bear to leave her alone, even for such a good reason.

"I'll be back as soon as I can," he said, and she nodded, her smile telling him it was all right. Making himself leave was physically wrenching, and he rode away with the image of her eyes, so green, wide, and trusting, haunting him.

Without him, Gincie felt completely vulnerable, helpless in a vast, unfriendly world. Tears of self-pity escaped before she got control of herself.

"If this is what falling in love does to people, it's a dangerous state!" she chided herself in disgust, and then she froze, hearing the words she had spoken aloud swirl around her.

It was preposterous, surely just an illusion of the proximity they had shared these past days and the intimate care he had given her. Her body warmed just thinking about it. Once she had become aware of him as a man, lying helpless under his ministrations had been at once a torment and a delight, not even the pain of the wound dimming the awareness. Not only had she blushed more than once, she had seen his hands tremble, his own color deepen. But she realized that might have been nothing more than his reaction to what he perceived as her embarrassment.

However, of all the strange new feelings swirling inside her, embarrassment was the least of them. He had stayed by her and saved her life; that had eclipsed all those intermediate and halting steps that usually accompanied the first meetings of a man and a woman.

Most terrifying was that he felt absolutely right in her life, as if there had never been a time without him and should never be. She thought of how resourceful he had been in providing rabbit and fowl and the tender shoots of edible plants for her to eat; how unfailingly patient and solicitous of every aspect of her welfare. She thought of all the stories he had told her to help pass the time and ease the hurt; his voice had acted like a drug, drawing her away from the pain and into his world.

She loved everything about him. The way he thought and laughed. The slight, soft drawl of his speech. The shape of his hands and the gentleness of his touch. The scent of him. The textures of his skin and hair. The fastidiousness that had driven him to stay clean shaven and washed under circumstances where less care could have been excused. And his eyes, his glorious turquoise eyes.

Loved him. It was the truth, whatever the circumstances that had thrown them together. She felt as if she would have loved him wherever and however they had met. She understood her grandparents better than she ever had before. Without knowing all the details, she knew that they had loved each other without ceasing in one way or another, even during all the years they had been married to other people. She remembered the vague sense of shock she had felt at the idea, though she had not been able to imagine either of them doing anything wrong. Now she knew that wherever she was and whomever she was with, Travis Culhane would be with her forever.

There was more shock than pleasure in the realization. She knew much about him and yet much was missing. He wasn't married, but that did not mean he had no special woman in his life. Too easily she could imagine a voluptuous creature awaiting his return to Virginia. And beyond that was another factor just as fundamental.

They had touched on the war; it was a subject they could not avoid, particularly given the clandestine work they did. They had acknowledged that it was coming, and very quietly Travis had said, "If Virginia sides with the South, and I fear she can do no other, I will fight for her. I sometimes wish I was a Quaker so I could refuse in good conscience to fight. But I am not."

"But you would be fighting for slavery!"

"No, I would not," Travis had replied, keeping his voice calm, not wanting her to grow too agitated, but still feeling the need to make his position clear. "If only slave owners were concerned, there would never be a battle. They do not number enough for even a small army. It is a wider matter than that. The North has come to view the Union as if it is a law of God, graven on sacred tablets. Many in the South do not see it that way at all. Many still believe that it was formed by a voluntary association that can be dissolved when that association no longer serves all equally. And it cannot serve equally when the needs of the regions are so diverse. States' rights must be considered, and that is something the federal government seems less and less willing to do."

"The claim of states' rights seems to have become synonymous with the justification of slavery," she said, and she could not disguise the anger in her voice.

"It has surely been used for that of late," Travis conceded, "but that makes it no less valid. If the population and factory growth of the North continues as it has been for decades, the South will have less and less voice in the government. She becomes more and more a despised stepchild. And that makes states' rights very important. I could never feel the same loyalty to Massachusetts or New York that I feel for Virginia."

Gincie had started to shiver violently, causing Travis to exclaim in remorse while he wrapped her in the blankets and held her until the trembling ceased. But deep inside, the cold persisted. As Travis was irrevocably committed to Virginia, so her own family would defend the Union no matter what decision Maryland made. Thinking back on the emotional chill, she acknowledged that even then the effect had come as much from the thought that his beliefs would separate him from her as from the idea that he and her family would be enemies.

She prowled the little shack on unsteady legs, cursing her weakness in very unladylike terms. She wished she had the strength to ride away from her troubled thoughts and from the complications of loving Travis. And she made herself face the fact that aside from little, involuntary signs which she might well have misinterpreted, Travis had given no evidence that he saw her as anything other than a fellow conductor on the Underground Railroad who was in need of help.

Before the day was half over, she had worn herself out worrying that something dreadful had befallen Travis, and she would never see him again. Brutus was there should she need to ride away; she had Travis's weapon; and she supposed she could make it, even with her left arm in a sling. But her own survival seemed insignificant without his. Angrily she reminded herself that her grandparents and the rest of the family deserved better than that from her.

She checked outside a couple of times, hearing the distant sound of a dog barking once and a stir in the brush later, but nothing came to threaten her. She meant to stay alert, but when Travis returned late in the afternoon, he found her sound asleep, not even awakened by the rattle of the wagon.

He stood over her, seeing the tear tracks on her face and noting how frail she looked. Tenderness welled in him, and he wanted to take her in his arms and assure her that nothing would ever harm her again. But he contented himself with waking her gently. He was more determined than ever to deliver her safely to Wild Swan.

"I got the wagon," he announced when she was alert. "Not a wonderful or handsome wagon, mind you, but good enough and filled with clean straw. And I know where we are." His face crinkled with laughter. "You'll have to forgive the story I told. I told the farmer that I'd gotten such a good deal on a load of pigs, though I'd meant to buy a milk cow, that I needed somethin' to put the pigs in, all trussed up, of course. Told him the pig man hadn't so much as a wheelbarrow to sell for transport."

Gincie giggled, all her earlier fear and despair vanquished because he was here. "As you say, a not very flattering description of me. A load of pigs indeed! Do you think he believed you?"

"I don't think he cared one way or another. He had a new wagon sittin' right there. I expect the one I bought was goin' to be allowed to fall into kindlin'." He had, in fact, been very relieved by the farmer's lack of interest in him; the man had been greedy, not talkative, and Travis had been able to maintain his own reserve without being rude.

"How did you pay for it?" she asked, remembering that they had given almost all the money they carried to the slaves. Travis must have had to pay quite a sum for a wagon and harness, no matter how worn they were.

"I used what money I had and my watch," he said without a trace of regret, but she did not feel so casual about it. She had seen him wind the pocket watch with loving care and had inquired about it; it was a heavy gold piece left to him by his grandfather.

"Oh, Travis, what a shame!"

"Not at all, darlin'. A watch won't get us any closer to Wild Swan, but the wagon will."

Though he called her darling as a casual term of endearment, as he would a child, she savored it. "A wagon it is, then. When do we leave?"

"Tomorrow mornin', if you think you're strong enough." His face sobered as he studied her anxiously.

"From your good care of me, I am."

They feasted that night on food Travis had wrangled from the farmer as part of his deal. Gincie thought eggs had never tasted so good, and the freshly baked bread with butter she pronounced fit for the gods.

Travis was simply grateful to see her eating well. She had lost weight she could ill afford in the past days, and that, coupled with the blood loss from the wound, had her looking waiflike. He kept having uncomfortable visions of Alexandria Carrington Falconer's reaction to her granddaughter's condition.

He was further heartened in the morning when Gincie carefully lifted her left hand with her right and put it in his hand. He looked at her inquiringly, but then he understood as he felt the small movement of her fingers.

"It's a start," she said proudly. "I woke up, and they worked! I can feel them quite well, and I know that I'm moving them. I expect before too long, my arm will be good as new."

Without hesitation, he gave her an exuberant kiss on the mouth. "Darlin', that's the best news I've heard in a long time!"

Only by an act of will did Gincie keep from touching her mouth. Though she knew it had only been a gesture of celebration, her reaction to it was not so simple. A warm ripple ran through her, quite unlike anything ever conjured by family gestures of affection. She felt gauche, and wished she had paid more attention to young men prior to this. She turned away hurriedly and began to gather up their few belongings, though she wasn't very efficient with only one arm.

As he moved to help her, Travis considered what an odd mix she was, capable of carrying out dangerous work as well as any, and yet, able to blush like a schoolgirl. It occurred to him that Gincie was in the habit of giving but was not adept at receiving from others. He wondered about her parents, particularly her mother. It was one subject he had not questioned her about, but he was curious; she obviously adored her grandmother and was generously loved in return, yet from the tenor of her fevered visions, her relationship with her mother was quite a different matter.

But as the day wore on, Travis hadn't a thought in his head beyond delivering Gincie into competent, caring hands. The trip had been unimpeded. Clancy and Brutus, albeit scarcely a matched pair, were both highly trained, willing animals and were pulling as a team far better than Travis had expected they would. Gincie was again disguised as a boy. She started out sitting beside Travis on the wagon seat, but before too long she was swaying unsteadily on her perch. Even leaning against Travis at his command did not provide enough support for long, and the effort of remaining upright caused a fine sheen of perspiration to gleam on Gincie's face.

When he suggested they need not go the whole way in a single day, she protested so vehemently he gave in, but she capitulated without a fight when he settled her on the straw in the back of the wagon. The jarring progress of the wagon was jolting her shoulder unmercifully. Travis tilted her hat over her face for shade from the sun, but even in the heat of the day, she needed the blankets because fever was making her alternately hot and cold.

To the few inquiries they received along the way, Travis answered curtly that his brother had a fever. It was enough to make people keep their distance.

Periodically he stopped to check on Gincie and to give her water.

"Don't look so worried," she pled. "It takes time to get one's strength back when there's been a blood loss; you know that."

Her practical assessment of her own condition did not comfort him.

"Just hang on, darlin'. By tonight you'll be in your own soft bed."

She closed her eyes with a little sigh and held her wounded shoulder with her good hand.

By the time he pulled the horses to a stop at Wild Swan, Travis would have braved the Devil to ease Gincie's hurt, and with cries and exclamations echoing around them, he picked her up from the wagon bed and cradled her in his arms.

He faced the green-eyed woman without a tremor. "Mrs. Falconer, you lead the way. Gincie needs quiet and care, but she's a stubborn little thing; she'll make it."

Not until much later did Alex realize she had taken orders from the tall young man as if he had a perfect right to give them.

Chapter

31

Though Travis had related their adventures in the calmest terms, Alex had grown more thankful by the minute that Gincie was still alive. The past days had been an agony of frustration and fear.

Thomas's message had come through, and his father and Dr. Cameron had gone to collect him. But Thomas had no idea what had befallen Gincie after she had ridden off to complete the mission.

The next piece of the puzzle had also been obtained by Alastair— the slaves had reached the Eastern Shore and had gone on to Philadelphia. The crew of the boat reported there had been shots on shore, but they knew no more than that. Gincie seemed to have been swallowed by the earth. The only encouraging thing had been the added bit of information that another conductor, a man from Virginia, had been with her. Mrs. Mills had confirmed it, and added that she thought him very trustworthy, though she had only seen him briefly.

Alastair had been in the process of trying to determine who the man was, where he came from, and whether or not he had returned home. But it was difficult to obtain such information outside of the immediate group of agents he worked with. Secrecy was what kept them safe, and secrecy was what hampered the search for Gincie. The men had continued their discreet inquiries, and Alex had waited at Wild Swan. And now Gincie was home in the company of the Virginian.

Travis had accepted a bath, food, and clean clothes from Rane's wardrobe with grave courtesy. But he was quietly insistent that he be allowed to sit beside Gincie's bed once she was settled there. "You see, ma'am, I've been takin' care of her since she was shot, and she just might be a little confused when she wakes up. I don't think she knows she's home yet."

Alex started to point out that Gincie was her granddaughter and hardly likely to feel disoriented in her presence, but studying Travis's face, she refrained. The same stubborn concern he was displaying now had undoubtedly kept Gincie alive. Nor did considerations of modesty have any place. He had ministered to Gincie for all these days, and there was surely little he had not seen.

Though she had not said anything, in deference to Alex's sensibilities, Travis stayed outside while Gincie was undressed, sponged down, and put to bed. But he was there when Alex, with Della's help, unwrapped the injured shoulder. The wound was ugly, and Alex flinched inwardly, thinking of the pain her granddaughter must have suffered, but there was no sign of inflammation beyond what would be expected from such a trauma, no ominous tentacles of red.

Gincie whimpered and her eyelids fluttered.

"It's all right, darlin', a minute more, and you'll be more comfortable. Just rest now." Travis took her good hand, and her fingers curled around his, though she did not rouse to full consciousness.

Alex and Della exchanged a glance, both hearing the deep tenderness in the man's voice and noting the absolute trust Gincie showed even in her exhausted state.

Alex handed Travis a cup. "It's a mixture of herbs and cordial, not as strong as opium, but it will deepen her sleep."

Not questioning Alex's action, Travis lifted Gincie's head and coaxed her to swallow.

Though he was ready to drop, he kept his vigil through the night, and his name was the first word Gincie said when she awakened in the morning.

"I'm here," he said, leaning over her. "And so is your grandmother. You're home at Wild Swan. And Thomas Whitmore is safely back with his family."

She turned her head and saw Alex. "Hello, Gran. I'm sorry I worried you."

Worried! Alex thought, fighting tears, and she spoke briskly to cover her emotions. "It's over now!"

Travis left Gincie to perform his own morning ablutions and to allow her the privacy of hers, but he returned to share breakfast with her. In a way, it was as intimate as if they had bathed together.

"Must be magic in this place; you've already got some color back in your cheeks," he remarked with obvious pleasure.

"While you will be pale as a ghost if you do not rest. Thank you for staying here last night; somehow I knew you were close by."

Their eyes caught and held for a moment, and Gincie's cheeks had even more color than before, but then Travis went on as if nothing had happened.

"You just might be right about that rest," he conceded with an elaborate yawn. "Suddenly I feel as if I could sleep for a week."

In the room assigned to him, he did sleep for most of the day, but he also thought a great deal. He missed Gincie even though she was only a small distance away. The realization made him very uneasy. He was twenty-four, and she was seventeen; they had been thrown together by the oddest circumstance, intimacy conjured by her helpless state.

She was beautiful and, he admitted now, desirable. But she belonged here, and he didn't. Time was out of joint for them. When the war came, her whole family would undoubtedly stand for the Union. And unless he was very mistaken, he would be on the other side.

Supper that night strengthened his resolve. Gincie insisted she was recovered enough to take the meal with everyone, and the gathering was raucous with the overflowing joy her relatives felt at having her back with them. And Travis was treated as a hero. It made him uncomfortable, though he understood the reason for it, and it made him draw back and observe the scene keenly.

Her aunts and cousins had already been at Wild Swan waiting for word, and her grandfather and uncles had arrived in time for the celebratory meal.

They were bright, handsome, loving people, and Travis could not imagine asking Gincie to forsake them to be with a man who might well shoot one of them before too long. For a moment, the delicious meal he had just consumed threatened to come back, and he swallowed desperately. He had never before seen the approaching carnage in such graphic terms.

"Are you all right?" Gincie asked him under cover of the noise around them.

"Fine," he lied, and looking into her green eyes, he thought he would like to watch them open to him every morning of his life. It was then he decided he had better leave as soon as possible. In spite of a fair amount of experience with women, nothing had prepared him for this feeling of cherishing that was as strong as desire.

He left in the morning. He explained that he had planned to visit friends in Georgetown after the business of the fugitives was concluded and that they must be wondering where he was by now. It was only partially the truth—it was an open invitation from his friends, and he had set no specific date for visiting.

"We could send word to your friends," Alex offered, but he shook his head.

"No, thank you all the same, ma'am, but I'd better be on my way." He did not think he had fooled her for a moment, but he was relieved that she did not press him further.

He took the money Rane offered only after making it clear to the older man that he considered it a loan.

"You do know there is nothing we have that we would not willingly give you for the care you have taken of our granddaughter?" Rane asked gruffly.

"I didn't bring her home for ransom, Mr. Falconer," Travis said, but his smile took the sting out of the words.

It was far more difficult to bid good-bye to Gincie, but he was aided by the fact that even after so short a time at home, she was looking so much better. It would take time, he knew, for her to regain her full strength and the use of her left arm, but he had no doubt of her full recovery. He was no longer responsible for her. He had a sudden, sharp recollection of how the young blond man named Frank had gazed at Gincie the night before; it was not only family who cared about her. Too easily he could picture Gincie and Frank together; grimly he reminded himself that it would be for the best.

Gincie felt like bursting into tears and begging him to stay; instead, she behaved with admirable reserve. She had felt him beginning to withdraw on the previous night. Now she could feel his impatience to be gone. Pride stiffened her spine. After all he had done for her, she was not going to make him feel uncomfortable now.

"Thank you for everything," she said with cool formality. "I hope I will see you again someday. I owe you my life. If there is ever anything I or my family can do for you, you only need ask."

Perversely he found himself wishing she were not quite so collected, and it was he rather than she who showed emotion. "Just get well and strong again, darlin'. I couldn't want anything more than that."

"Do you think my grandmother will allow anything less?" Gincie asked, and Travis left with the image of her rueful smile dancing before him. It was not until much later that he saw the sorrow in her eyes.

Alex had no such respite from Gincie's true feelings. As soon as she had seen Travis on his way, she went to her granddaughter and found her weeping.

"Oh, Gran, I don't even know what I want from him!" Gincie sobbed, struggling to get enough control to speak coherently. "I think I love him, but maybe it's just—just all we went through together. He—he's going to fight for Virginia." Her tears prevented any more words, but Alex understood, though she was stunned that anyone working for the Underground Railroad would fight for a slave state. Immediately she chided herself for her naiveté; nothing about the coming conflict was going to be simple.

"Hush now, my dear," Alex crooned, putting her arms around Gincie, taking care not to jar her shoulder. "If you weep so, you will make yourself ill."

But Gincie, having been so controlled in Travis's presence, hadn't the energy to maintain that control. She continued to weep so desolately that Alex finally gave her a dose of laudanum and stayed with her until the drug took effect and Gincie slept, her tear-stained face looking very young and vulnerable.

"Is she all right?" Sam asked anxiously, waylaying Alex as she left Gincie's room.

"As all right as I was when I thought I'd never see Rane again. As all right as you were when you thought Morgan would never love you as a woman." Alex sighed and explained where Travis's loyalties lay. "If it were another time, I would wager he would come back; he is no less smitten than she, if one judges by the look in his eyes when he was watching her. But things being as they are, I just don't know. Sir Galahad has ridden off to spare his fair lady, and he might just be strong and stubborn enough to keep to it."

"Damn this wicked threat that hangs over all of us!" Sam swore. "It taints everything!"

"It does indeed. I am not even sure I want him to come back for her, not if Virginia is to become the enemy. But for good or ill, we have a history of faithful and singular loving in this family, and I fear Gincie is cut of the same cloth."

She witnessed the truth of her assessment as the summer progressed. Gincie was young and resilient, and her general health improved rapidly. Regaining the full use of her left arm was another matter, and progress was slow in spite of the dogged exercises she forced herself to do. With one exception, she did not mention Travis, as if by refusing to speak of him, the pain of his absence would disappear. The exception was her insistence on a trip to Baltimore as soon as she was strong enough. Her sole purpose was to purchase a gold pocket watch, and when she explained that it was to replace the one Travis had sold for her sake, Alex offered to help pay for it. But Gincie wanted no assistance, and Alex suspected it cost much of what her granddaughter had. Gincie received an allowance in recognition of the help she gave at Wild Swan, and she was not lavish in her spending habits, but the watch was exquisite, wholly masculine and yet delicately wrought, made to be handed down from one generation to the next. Though the jeweler clearly thought the young woman a trifle unbalanced, he obeyed her request that he engrave a tiny outline of a wagon inside the watch cover.

Gincie did allow her grandfather to help by arranging delivery by one of the shipping line's agents.

"This is serious business, it seems," Rane said to Alex. "And yet, she never mentions the young hero."

"I refused to speak of you when I returned to Gravesend from Clovelly," Alex pointed out.

"My God! She's that serious?" He was only half joking; he was not quite ready to let Gincie go, having so nearly lost her. Alex decided not to mention where Travis's loyalties lay.

The money Rane had given Travis had long since been repaid, accompanied by a rather formal note extending good wishes to all. Alex wondered what Travis would say about the watch, but she did not press Gincie when the letter arrived from Virginia. She contented herself with being glad the timepiece had not been returned; she did not want Gincie hurt too much by this passage in her life, whether or not she ever saw Travis again.

Gincie found it difficult to think about anything else except that possibility. Travis's letter regarding the watch had been brief:

> *You should not have sent so handsome a gift, but I confess myself glad that you did. It is too fine to refuse. My thanks, and best wishes for your continued health.*

No mention of seeing her again, nothing very personal, but she clung to the hope that he might think of her whenever he consulted the watch.

She admitted to herself that as much as she wanted to help fugitive slaves, she also wanted to get back to work on the Underground Railroad for the chance that she would see Travis again through that connection, even though she knew the odds were against them. Routes were changed, and she worked almost all the time in Maryland, Travis further south. The leak in secrecy regarding the loading point of the boat on the Western Shore was judged to have come, as suspected, from a sailor who was overly talkative, but there was no clear proof, and extra precautions were being taken all along the line, precautions that might make it more unlikely that Gincie and Travis would see each other again as routes were shifted.

Gincie was rapidly discovering that pride had little to do with love. Whatever Travis felt for her, it was evident he had every intention of staying away from her and from Wild Swan. Pride would dictate that she accept the rejection and forget him; love dictated that he was constantly in her thoughts. Sometimes the shape of his face would blur, but his eyes remained as bright in memory as they had been in reality, and the soft drawl of his voice haunted her. And though she was often angry at him and at herself for the infatuation, it did not ease.

She had been so single-minded in her purpose before the advent of Travis in her life, she now felt cognizant of a multitude of things that had not registered before. Suddenly she was acutely aware of the relationships around her. Before, she had taken it for granted that her aunts and uncles and grandparents had good marriages; now she noticed the myriad signals —the words, looks, and touches—that passed continually between husbands and wives, binding them together in a constant flow of communication. Now she noticed the way Samson's face lit up when he caught sight of Della and how Della's rather severe beauty softened for him. And she was more conscious than ever of what Padraic had lost when Katy had been killed.

The loss had aged him and taken much of the joy from him, but it had not stolen the softness Katy had given him, and he talked openly to Gincie about Travis. "He's right, you know, ta want ta spare you from the trouble that's comin'. He's a good man fer that. But mind, he won't be able ta stay away foriver. Once a lass like you is in a man's heart, there she stays."

She knew Padraic was as fond of her as a father and that that might make him overly optimistic, but still his words were balm to her heart.

That her new awareness made her more sensitive to other people's feelings was not always comfortable. She came to realize that the way Frank Faber looked at her was exactly the way she would look at Travis were he before her. It made her treat Frank with careful kindness, even though she felt uneasy in his presence. She knew she was fortunate that he was such a well-mannered young man. Young—despite his time away at college, he seemed very young indeed compared to Travis.

It was September before she and Thomas were fit and working again, and in the middle of the next month, a fanatic named John Brown nearly started the war. Launching an attack on Harper's Ferry, Virginia, Brown and his small band of followers seized the town and the United States Armory there. But Brown was held at bay by the local militia until a troop of marines assaulted his position, killing ten of his men and taking the wounded Brown prisoner.

Brown's intention had been to establish a stronghold in the Appalachian Mountains for escaped slaves and freed blacks. From there they would launch an armed uprising to sweep the South. Brown had the backing of some leading Abolitionists, and had expected great local support at Harper's Ferry, but it had not materialized. Nonetheless, he had stabbed at the heart of the South by touching on the deepest fear. The specter of Nat Turner's Rebellion and every other slave uprising, no matter how small and no matter where in the world, rose up in the minds of Southerners and caused a common howl of outrage. And though Brown had been captured, and there was no sign of any slave uprising, many slave owners watched their slaves more closely than ever before.

In the North, many voices were raised in celebration of John Brown as savior and hero, the voice of the prophet crying in the wilderness, when he vowed that violence was necessary in expiation of the sin of slavery.

Alex was at a race meeting in South Carolina when news of the Harper's Ferry incident began to streak across the South. She was as stunned as everyone else. She was with Allen Ralston and Justin Sinclair when they heard the story, which, between newspapers and word of mouth, was fairly distorted, though the salient points remained the same from one account to the next. Alex found herself wishing the telegraph had never been invented; as it sped the transmission of good news, so it also allowed bad news to race swiftly and heedlessly about.

And then she realized that Allen and Justin were eyeing her, instinctively expecting her reaction to be different from theirs because she was so opposed to slavery.

She drew herself up to her full height and gazed at them levelly, though green fire was already dancing in her eyes. "Gentlemen, I counted you my friends. I was mistaken. No one who knows me well could ever think I would condone such bloodshed for any reason. John Brown is surely mad."

They both looked stricken, and then Allen said, "Forgive us! These times make everyone mad."

In fact, Alex knew the guilt was not all theirs. While she was vehemently protesting their unjust judgment, she was also praying that Gincie was all right. This latest development would make her work even more hazardous, work none of the family had been able to persuade her to give up despite her brush with death.

Gincie at that moment was riding south with Thomas to meet another group of slaves. And that night when the boat came the first person on shore was a tall white man who she knew was Travis even before he spoke or she saw him clearly.

She breathed his name and then stood frozen while joy rocketed through her. So often she had considered a meeting like this, but now she didn't know what to do. She wanted to run to him, throw her arms around him, and hear him call her darling with a new note in his voice. But she needed some sign from him.

The dream shattered from the moment he spoke in a hiss of anger. "Gincie! God damn it! I knew you'd be here. What in the hell are you doin'? Surely you've heard about John Brown?"

She would have backed away from him, but his hands came out

and gripped her arms so hard it hurt. She sensed rather than saw Thomas backing away—he had no confusion about who Travis was. But Gincie did. This was not the man she had dreamed about. This was a rough stranger. Even though she could not see his face clearly, she knew it was contorted with rage.

Embarrassment at how she had mooned over him swept through her, and her previously subdued pride rose like a banner. "I know about John Brown. But the only harm I've come to so far tonight is from the bruises you are inflicting." His hands loosened immediately, but she went on with the same cold precision. "You have no right to speak to me as if I'm a naughty child. I know the hazards better than most."

"Go home, Gincie, go home to Wild Swan and stay there! You don't belong here. And as you can see, there are no slaves tonight. They're hidden at Hawthorn and will stay there until I can get them safely away. This is no time for fugitives to be travelin'."

Only then did she notice that what he said was true; there were no passengers. She resented him even more for being so able to take her mind off even this vital work. Most of all she felt like a complete fool for harboring such tender thoughts of him when he clearly considered her no more than a troublesome child—a child he cared about, but child nonetheless.

The lapping of the river was the only sound as they stood facing each other, and then Gincie said, "Thomas, we might as well be on our way. There is nothing for us here." She turned her back on Travis and walked away. As the boat headed back toward the Virginia shore, Gincie and Thomas were riding away.

Thomas had a great deal of respect for Gincie and regarded her much like a sister, but he knew he was risking their easy relationship when he spoke. "I know he sounded angry, but I am sure it is because he cares for thee and fears thee will come to further hurt."

Gincie had to grit her teeth to bite back a sharp retort; at the moment, Thomas's soft words and his use of the informal "thee" of the Friends made her want to scream. Instead she spoke with studied patience. "Thomas, I know you mean well, but I don't want to talk about Travis Culhane, not now, not ever. The weather, our work, any other subject, but not another word about him."

Thomas subsided with a sigh, hoping that if he ever fell in love, it would go easier than this.

When her grandmother arrived home and was so obviously glad to find her unharmed, Gincie told her only that no slaves had come through on the last mission; she did not mention seeing Travis. She did her best to forget she had ever met him.

Alex might have suspected there was something more than Gincie was telling her, but she was going through a crisis of her own. Due to the storm over John Brown, she had forfeited races to come home early, and she was beginning to face the fact that the time for taking the horses to Southern races was truly coming to an end. She had accepted it on one level for a very long time, but to make the actual decision that this would be the last season for Wild Swan's horses was quite another matter.

She told Padraic and Samson before she told Rane. They stood before her, these two men so unlike in appearance, so similar in their dedication to the well-being of the horses.

"I want to finish with a flourish. I want a season that will make people remember the horses of Wild Swan. I propose to begin in New Orleans at the end of March and to finish in Lexington, Kentucky, at the end of May, with an appearance in Virginia in between. And by the end of summer next year, the horses will be on their way. I propose to send a few of the young ones to my brother in California, but the best of the young will go to Gwenny and Christopher in England. A few American horses have done quite well there lately. And the breeding stock will go to Canada. It is closer than California, and yet separate from this country which is so sadly racing toward war. I will not tell Rane until after Christmas, and I would prefer the rest of the family not know until they must. Are you with me?"

At that moment there was no difference in the men. They both had tears in their eyes, and they both nodded their acceptance of her will.

"Thank you, my friends," she said, and she turned away, fearing her own tears would overflow.

Samson's voice drifted back to her as the two men walked away together. "One mo' time peoples goin' to see dese de bes' hosses eber," he said.

Political developments in December strengthened Alex's determination. On December 2, John Brown was hanged in the public square of Charlestown, Virginia. Even knowing the full extent of his madness by then, many in the North still mourned his passing, while the South rejoiced in being rid of a criminal. Sectionalism had grown to such virulent proportions that the House of Representatives had taken two months to choose a Speaker. And Georgia passed laws in December that reflected feelings in much of the South. No longer could slaves be freed upon an owner's death by will or deed. And blacks charged with vagrancy were liable for sale. There were defiant demands in the South for reopening the foreign slave trade. While President Buchanan opposed such measures, in his annual message to Congress he also vowed to protect United States merchant ships against detention and search, an action specifically designed to thwart the British policy of waylaying suspected slave ships on the high seas. Though it could certainly be argued that the British had no right to stop American ships for any reason, it was also evident, and had been for the length of his term, that the President was sympathetic to the proslavery forces. His actions served to drive more men of free soil convictions from the more established parties to the Republican Party.

Alex threw herself into preparations for the holidays with great fervor, seeking not only to block out current tensions, but also to stop dwelling on her decision. Riding the horses, even just looking at them, was liable to bring a lump to her throat these days.

Rane observed her feverish pace and waited patiently for her to tell him exactly what was causing it. They had lived with the threat of war for so long now, he felt as if the edge of the sword was blunted. He, Caleb, and Morgan went on with the building of would-be warships, so it was not as if they thought war would not come, but they had learned to live day by day. He had thought Alex had learned the same lesson, but now he was not so sure. Gincie, too, was behaving much like her grandmother, and this he did mention to Alex. "She is working very, very hard to be joyful; it is painful to watch."

"I know," Alex agreed and suspected he was talking about her own behavior as well, but there was time enough to tell him her own news later. "It has to do with the Virginian, I'm sure. But I have no intention of questioning her. Travis Culhane is a forbidden topic."

Alex's back was to the door when Della escorted the unexpected visitor into the midst of the family on Christmas Eve, but she knew who it was because Gincie's face was instantly transfigured, shining with fear, hope, and wonder, and Sam muttered, "Oh, my! I do believe Father Christmas has just brought Gincie a special gift!"

Chapter

32

Travis noticed only peripherally that the room was crowded with people. All his attention was fixed on Gincie. It had been hard enough when he had left her at Wild Swan all those months ago; it had been far worse when he had driven her away with his anger on their last meeting.

He had felt possessed. When he slept, he dreamed of her, seductive dreams that turned into nightmares of parting and loss. During his waking hours, he was constantly distracted by thoughts of her so that he found himself drifting off in the middle of conversations. He kept the watch always with him, though it was a torment in itself. And finally his grandmother had told him to go away and solve his problem one way or another.

"But I would not be at Hawthorn for Christmas," he had protested.

"Thee's not here now," she had retorted, and then her voice had softened. "Can thee not guess that the return of thy joy, or at least of thy peace of mind, would be the best celebration for me?"

And so he had set out, but now that he had reached his goal, he had no idea what to say; he was not even sure what he wanted of Gincie. The problems he had seen before were no less valid now.

"Gincie, I'm sorry, and I love you," he blurted out.

He looked so anxious and vulnerable. He was shivering from the cold he had ridden through to come to her. His face was leaner, but his eyes, even across the distance separating them, were the same burning turquoise she remembered.

It did not occur to her to act coy or to pay him back for his harsh words at the river's edge. She went to him without knowing she had moved. "I love you too, Travis Culhane, now and for always." She took his cold hands and warmed them in hers, and only then did the two of them become aware of the silent attention from everyone around them.

"Dear God," Travis breathed, his face suddenly much ruddier than the cold had made it. And Gincie matched him in scarlet.

"Happy Christmas, Mr. Culhane, and welcome to Wild Swan," Alex said, taking pity on both of them. "Gincie, I expect he is weary and hungry. Why don't you show him where he may wash and then serve him some supper in the library?" The propriety of it did not trouble Alex; these two had their lives to settle and had already spent time together under the most intimate circumstances.

Travis ate what Gincie brought to him more because it gave him something to do than because he was hungry. He supposed he must be hungry, but he was too distracted by Gincie to focus on anything else. A fire crackled merrily on the hearth, and it was possible for him to imagine them as a married couple, happy and settled in the pattern of life together. He rubbed his face wearily, trying to temper the dreams with reality.

"Darlin', nothin's changed. War's still comin', and we're still goin' to be on opposite sides. But if I survive, and if you're still here, I'll come back to you. I don't mean for you to wait; I can't ask that of you. I just want you to know I won't ever love anyone as I love you. I had to come to tell you—" his voice trailed off as he watched anger leap to replace the tenderness in Gincie's eyes.

"How very noble of you!" she spat. "You have decided for both of us, and by your decision, we will perhaps be dead or at the very least much older before we may be together. And if I wish, I am to fall in love with someone more convenient, though the truth is that I cannot even see other men clearly because your image is before them all. I cannot hear another man's voice without listening for yours. When I sleep I dream of you; when I am awake I look for you everywhere."

Trembling with the force of her emotions, she leaned over him and gripped his shoulders. "Travis Culhane, I want it all, the good and the bad. I want to go on working to help the fugitives go north, but I want to work with you. I want it now so that we can be together before the war does its worst to us. You don't know any more than anyone else. You don't know whether it will start tomorrow or a year or ten years from now. You don't have any right to steal time from us! Life will do that as it wills."

It was hard enough to resist the physical reality of her after so many months of wanting to hold her in his arms, months that had begun the moment he left her at Wild Swan; it was impossible to resist her admission that she had yearned for him as much as he had for her.

"Gincie, I'm older, I ought to be wiser, but—" He tumbled her into his arms, holding her so close, for an instant she could scarcely breathe. She didn't care. Nothing on earth could be sweeter than this. She wanted to stay nestled against his heart forever.

He loosened his hold and tipped her head up. Gently, gently he kissed her brow and her eyelids, the curve of her cheeks and then her soft lips. He meant to go slowly, but the untutored eagerness of her response kindled his desire.

Gincie opened to the pressure of his demand and felt his tongue tasting and probing inside her mouth. She trembled with the strange ripples of warmth he was causing deep inside her, and she moved against him, wanting even more contact with his body, frustrated by the layers of clothing that separated them.

"Whoa, love, easy there," he commanded softly, stopping the kiss with an effort and taking deep breaths to steady himself. "I'm findin' I don't have much control where you're concerned. Some things had better wait until we're married." The image of her grandparents bursting in on them and discovering him in the midst of bedding their granddaughter after they had trusted him to be alone with her was enough to restore some of his sanity.

"Darlin' " and now "love"—Gincie wondered what other soft endearments he would use. He had strength and temper, but he was capable of an open, giving warmth as well.

"I don't want us to wait at all," she said. "I want to go back to Virginia with you, as your wife, as your mistress, as whatever, as long as we are together as man and woman."

He did not doubt the sincerity of her words, but he still questioned the motive. "Gincie, if there was no war ahead, are you sure you would rush so hastily into this? Would you not want time to think it over, time to be courted, time to plan your wedding?" He almost laughed at himself; he was the one playing the reluctant virgin.

"I don't know," she replied honestly. "I don't know at all what it would be to be alive in such a time. This is my time, and war is coming. But I cannot imagine wanting you any less."

She was wearing a deep green velvet dress with a froth of creamy lace at the bodice and cuffs. Her eyes looked as green as spring in the sun. Carefully he pushed the lace back from her shoulder until he could see the scar of her wound, and tenderly he kissed the ridged flesh that would forever mar her. She was right. She had already been bloodied in the war;

there was no way she could imagine a horizon of peace stretching on to infinity.

"Gincie Carrington, will you marry me on New Year's Eve? Is that soon enough?" he asked.

"Yes, and yes! I thought you would never ask! Aunt Philly and Uncle Blaine were married on New Year's Eve; it's an old family tradition." Gincie's laughter rang out, so young and joy-filled, Travis thought whatever was in store for them, he would remember the sound forever.

He put her away from him and stood up. "I think we had better see what your grandparents have to say about this."

"I'll ask them to come to us," Gincie said without the slightest trepidation.

Alex had surrendered the moment she saw the way Gincie and Travis looked at each other, though she was stunned that the marriage was to take place so soon. She started to raise objections and suggest some date in the coming summer, and then she stopped.

"Travis, you have already managed to keep her safe under trying conditions," she said, "and now I trust you will care well, each for the other."

Rane eyed Alex thoughtfully, wondering what was going on in her mind, but he did not gainsay the young couple. "Doing things in an orthodox manner has never been a measure of life in this family," he observed ruefully, and to put Travis at ease, he related the story of how Morgan had declared his intentions at the party celebrating Sam's engagement to another man. "That was surely more disruptive than your arrival here tonight, and yet, my son and his wife are still besotted with each other. The best I can wish for you is that you find the same contentment they have found and that Alex and I have enjoyed for so many years."

He and Travis shook hands, each pleased with what he saw in the other.

Travis felt a little overwhelmed by the rest of Gincie's family when the news was announced and congratulations rained down on them, but it was soon clear to him that, even in the midst of the confused babble and laughter, they all shared the single wish that Gincie be happy.

It was Gincie who suddenly remembered that, while she would be well represented at the wedding, Travis had hardly had time to summon any of his relatives or friends. "Have I pushed too hard?" she asked anxiously. "Truly, I will wait longer if you wish to have your family here."

"Too late," he replied, smiling down at her. "You've convinced me of the need for most unseemin' haste. The only relative who really matters to me is my grandmother Abigail, and she's the one who sent me to you, she got so tired of my mopin'." His face sobered. "She never complains, but her joints are so swollen, she can do very little and travels not at all. But you will love her and she you!"

Gincie wasn't so sure that Abigail Culhane would like sharing her domain with another woman, but she vowed to be patient and win her over one way or another, and she made sure that Travis sent word to her that he was to be married on New Year's Eve.

She was not the only one with questions about family. As soon as he could manage it without being overheard, Travis asked Alex about a subject that continued to bother him—Gincie's fear of her mother. "Gincie only mentioned her when she was ravin' with fever," he explained to Alex, "and she sounded so afraid of the woman, I haven't had the heart to press her for an explanation. She didn't say anythin' about her father."

He watched the face before him transformed into the Alexandria Carrington Falconer of legend, a formidable woman indeed. But just when he was going to apologize and beg her to forget he had ever broached the subject, she made her decision.

"Every family has its skeletons, and Piety is surely one of ours. But what Piety did is not even known by all of the family. I will tell you the whole of it because, as much as I have wished it otherwise, Piety has much to do with what Gincie is." With clipped precision, she proceeded to tell him everything about her son Nigel's unfortunate choice of a wife, including the fire and her final confrontation with Piety that had been overheard by Gincie.

"My poor darlin'," Travis murmured.

"She is like her mother, you know," Alex said gently, and inwardly she rejoiced at the fierce protective denial that rose instantly from him. "No, I don't mean that she is evil," she explained, "but she is single-minded in what she does. Her mother is like that, though Piety's only goal was her own gain. Gincie's has always been someone else's good, at least it has been so since she found out what her mother is really like. You have seen it; she would risk her life to prove she is not tainted by her mother's blood. Do not shut her out of your life; let her share it. You are the first thing she has ever wanted for herself."

"Ma'am, for better or for worse, she's got me," Travis said, and they understood each other perfectly, despite the years between them.

Alex thought of the events in her own life that had made it impossible for her to deny Gincie this chance for happiness in these treacherous times. Like Gincie, and indeed like Flora, too, she had not wanted to be like her mother once she had understood how cold and unloving the woman was. Like her grandmother, she would now allow her granddaughter her own life, no matter what the cost to herself. And most of all, she thought of herself and Rane; delay had cost them dearly. She would not give up the years she had had with St. John; they were part of her life, and Nigel and thus Gincie had come from them. Still, she hoped that Gincie's way would be easier, at least in this. It was hard, but Alex had to accept that the one gift the young couple needed most of all was beyond her power to give. Time, long days of peace to adjust to each other and to learn the ways of sharing one's life with another were not, barring a miracle, to be granted to them.

But when Gincie and Travis were wed at Wild Swan a week later, no shadow was allowed to touch the celebration. Despite the short notice, a few special friends, among them those who would have been there anyway for New Year's Eve, were at Wild Swan with the family. Frank Faber was one of them, there to wish Gincie happiness, though Seth had told him he didn't have to come if he thought it would be too hard.

By dint of generous payment to a noted Georgetown modiste and a small army of seamstresses, Gincie was dressed in a gown that could not have been more beautiful had it been months in the making, and the rest of her wardrobe had been expanded, too, though Travis had laughingly insisted he would be satisfied if she simply wore the green velvet gown of Christmas Eve from now on.

Travis saw very little of Gincie in the rushed week of preparation, and he began to resent all the fuss that took her away from him, until he saw her standing before him in her white satin wedding gown. The tulle edging around the neckline hid her scar. The fitted bodice showed off her slender figure, while the belled skirt, open over a tiered satin petticoat, swayed gracefully when she moved. And her face glowed with her love for him, her green eyes seeing only him as she firmly spoke her vows.

Travis had seen the yearning in Frank Faber's eyes when the man looked at Gincie, and suddenly he felt a great possessiveness and triumph, as well as love. Gincie was his, not any other man's, and to hell with caution and waiting. His voice was as sure as hers.

By midnight they were alone in Gincie's room, which was to serve as their bridal chamber. Gincie smiled mistily at the changes Della, Mavis, and her aunts had wrought while she and Travis were still downstairs.

Hothouse flowers scented the room, soft candlelight and a glowing fire warmed it, trinkets of childhood had been packed away, and champagne awaited their pleasure.

A new nightgown was beside Travis's robe, but Travis said, "You won't need that," as he carefully began to unfasten her gown, stopping to kiss the tender flesh slowly being revealed to him.

She shivered a little at the unfamiliar intimacy as his hands and then his mouth touched her breasts. She reminded herself that he had already seen her naked, but it was not the same. She was not afraid of what he would do to her; she was only uneasy that she might do the wrong thing.

"I know the general idea but not the details," she confessed in a small voice, and Travis's laughter was a warm ruffle of air against the slope of her shoulder.

"Darlin', I'll teach you all the details, just give me a little time. Of course, you've already given me time. I think the watch is enchanted; every time I look at it, I see you." His mouth captured hers for a long, sweet kiss that did peculiar things to her knees, and she gave up worrying about her possible inadequacies, finding it impossible to concentrate on anything except the delightful sensations Travis was causing.

It was as if she had developed a new set of nerves just to receive the sensations of his hands running over her flesh, the slightly rough pull in erotic contrast to the delicacy of his touch, strong skilled hands mapping the long line of her spine and the taut curve of her buttocks and dancing over her belly and down to tease the smoothness of her thighs while his mouth alternately plundered hers and tasted her skin. She leaned into him with a little sigh, and he swung her up in his arms and laid her down on the bed, stripping away his own clothes as he gazed down at her.

"There isn't a more exquisite woman in all creation," he said, and for him it was true. He saw her now as his love, his wife, and it was completely different from when he had tended to her wound.

Gincie drew a sharp breath at the lean horseman's length of him, the muscles not heavy, but flexible and well defined in his arms, chest, and legs. His belly was taut and his manhood was swelling from the golden-brown bush. But the expression on his strong-featured face and in his vivid eyes was most erotic of all. His concentration on her was as complete as if she had become his universe.

"I did not see you clearly before," she said, remembering the indistinct glimpse of his body she had had when he had gotten up from keeping her warm. "But I see you now. I never knew a man could be so beautiful." She opened her arms, and he lay down with her, his hands and mouth continuing to learn her body, circling and teasing until he stroked between her legs.

"No!" she gasped as she felt her control slipping away, her body writhing under the onslaught of new sensations.

"Don't fight it, love, let it happen," he crooned, and she surrendered to his will, feeling the tightening circles inside rush outward as if she were the coruscating center of an explosion.

Travis loomed over her, and though he had warmed and opened her with his love play, he was a man well endowed and fully erect with wanting when he began to ease into her virginal passage. She didn't cry out, but the discomfort showed on her face.

"Easy, darlin', easy. If I'm too much for you, I'll stop." He was trembling with the effort to control his passion, but he meant what he said.

"No, go on." Her voice sounded strange in her own ears. She was feeling too many things at once to explain coherently. The burning was acute as her tender flesh was stretched wide by his invasion, but at the same time, there was a deep flicker of pleasure growing inside her again and a need for more of him, not less. Though she cried out at the sharp tearing of the membrane, she still did not want him to stop. Instinctively she thrust her hips up, taking him deeper, clinging to him while her body adjusted to its new status.

And then when Travis thought he could control himself no longer, he felt her truly opening to him, sheathing him in rippling, silken heat. He repeated her name over and over again as he let the rhythm of his need take him, thrusting in and out of her until he lodged himself deep and poured the seed of his loving into her.

Even the weight of him when he collapsed on her for a moment before shifting to the side felt good. I have no words, she thought in wonder, no words to explain what just happened to me. What had begun as such a physical experience had finished by taking her out of her body completely and into his and beyond in a whirlwind of feeling so intense, it swept beyond the very nerve endings that had caused it.

Leaning over her, Travis smoothed the damp hair back from her brow and studied her face anxiously. "I promise it will get better for you."

She was so enervated, she wasn't sure her mouth had obeyed the impulse to smile. "Maybe easier, but better? I don't see how."

Travis started to laugh. "My own little voluptuary; who would have thought it?"

"No one, I hope!" Her attempt at propriety failed utterly because she still wore the lazy, satisfied look of a well-loved woman. "Happy New Year, my love, my husband." She savored her new right to use all the endearments.

His guilt eased. Virginia might soon be torn by war, but whatever the hazards, he and Gincie belonged together. He would give his life to keep her safe.

"I do love you so, Mrs. Culhane!" Just looking at her made his loins stir again, though an instant before he would have sworn she had wrung all from him.

With her new knowledge, Gincie correctly interpreted his look. "Is it possible to do it again so soon?"

"I've created a monster!" he exclaimed in mock terror. He nuzzled her neck, biting playfully at her earlobe. But the kiss he dropped on her cheek was quite chaste. "It is possible when a woman is as temptin' as you, and it is devoutly to be hoped for in other circumstances, but you, my sweet, will be sore enough as it is, and we have a long journey tomorrow. Your grandmother might change her mind about me if neither of us is able to leave this room in the morning."

"I don't think so," Gincie giggled. "After all, she is married to my grandfather. I understand them a lot better now."

She put an end to their nonsense by abruptly falling asleep, a small smile curving her mouth. But tired as he was, Travis stayed awake for long moments simply enjoying the feeling of her lying warm and relaxed along the length of his body.

Despite the bliss he had found there, Travis was not sorry to leave Wild Swan the next day. Everyone had been kind to him, and he knew it was because they liked him as well as for Gincie's sake, and yet, he had seen the shadows in their eyes. Not so far in actual miles, but he was taking their beloved a world away. He had thought he could not love Gincie more, but at the leave-taking, his love for her grew until it threatened to overcome him.

She shed no tears. She hugged everyone in turn, but she did not cast lingering looks behind her, and her joy at being with him shone in her eyes.

The weather held for them, clear and not too cold. They rode to Washington where they and their horses were loaded aboard a steamer along with Gincie's belongings that had been sent ahead. After an uneventful trip down the Potomac, they went ashore in Virginia and found people from Hawthorn, alerted by instructions Travis had sent ahead, waiting to load the baggage in wagons, while Travis and Gincie rode ahead, arriving before dark in spite of the shortness of the winter day.

Though she had made no complaint, Gincie had discovered she was, as Travis had predicted, sore from the previous night's initiation, and riding had not improved her state, so that by the time they reached Travis's home, she was so stiff and tired, her legs would not hold her when she dismounted.

Travis was beside her instantly, sweeping her into his arms. "Poor darlin', I was selfish, wantin' to get home so fast."

Ignoring her protests that it was an undignified way to meet his grandmother, Travis carried her into the house which was ablaze with lights of welcome. Even the first quick view of Hawthorn showed its beauty—airy rooms with intricate plasterwork scrolling across the ceilings and around mantelpieces. And the soft-voiced servants who greeted them made no attempt to hide their delight at seeing Travis's bride for the first time. She felt at home because she knew that these blacks were as free as those at Wild Swan, but the crucial reception would be the one from Abigail Culhane.

The room was white, trimmed with a vibrant shade of blue, and the old woman was a study in the same colors, her hair snow white and her eyes a little faded by age, but still a penetrating sky blue, not the same shade but the same shape as her grandson's. Gincie noticed other things, too—the walking stick beside the chair, the distorted joints of the old woman's hands, and the marks of suffering on the face that yet remained serene.

Travis set Gincie carefully on her feet. "I've worn her out in the rush to get home, Grandmother. Gincie Culhane, meet Abigail Culhane."

The two women surveyed each other for an instant and then smiled at the same time.

Abigail held out her hand, and Gincie took it as if it were of spun glass, being infinitely careful not to cause the old woman added pain. "I love him very, very much," she said, as if Travis wasn't standing beside her.

"I know, child. Nothing else could have made thee leave thy own fine home and the grandmother thee loves. I cannot and would not take her place, but I hope we will be friends. And mind, this house is thine now. Thee is mistress of it. Do not mistake me in this; I am glad to give thee the responsibility of it."

Gincie leaned down and kissed Abigail on the cheek. "Thank you. There is much I must learn from you."

Although Travis had constantly reassured her about the character of his grandmother, Gincie had nonetheless feared that the old woman would resent her. Now, the warmth of her welcome touched her deeply. Abigail was all her grandson had claimed. She dressed plainly and spoke as one of the Friends, but the house showed her tolerance for the life her husband had brought her to once she had settled the issue of slavery. And most of all, Travis showed her tolerance, for though he did not follow her faith, Abigail clearly adored and approved of him. Having already seen what a splendid man Travis was, Gincie chided herself for her prior reservations concerning his grandmother.

They shared supper with the old woman, and then the toll of the day caught up with Gincie again. She would have fallen asleep in her clothes had Travis not helped her to undress. Her last conscious thought was that it was lovely to hear him moving about the room and to know that soon, when he slept, it would be beside her.

Chapter 33

The fact that Alex missed Gincie dreadfully served one useful purpose. Rather than brooding over her granddaughter's absence, she threw herself into finalizing her own plans. Everything was changing, and she was determined to adapt and not be caught short. She wrote to Boston and Rachel in California, now connected to the East by a regular overland mail service, and to Gweneth and Christopher in England. And she told Rane about her intentions and asked for his help.

The major racing schedule did not surprise him. He agreed with Alex that they should not visit Gincie in Virginia until their granddaughter had had time to establish her own life there. As Alex pointed out, two grandmothers giving advice, even with the best intentions, might be a bit much for the young bride. And thus Rane could understand why Alex would want to keep busy with the horses at the spring meetings. But he was stunned by her announcement that this would be the last season and by her request that he help her make the arrangements to ship the horses out at the end of the summer.

"Are you very sure?" he asked. He could not imagine Wild Swan without the Thoroughbreds, and more, he could not imagine Alex without them as the focus of her energy. Somewhere inside, he had refused to admit it would ever really come to this, though he himself was building warships.

"Very sure," Alex said. "Oh, they are improving the courses here and there, and they will hold the dinners and the balls, celebrating lavishly right to the end, but it's already over. It is a dirge in silks. And you know how I feel about my horses being used for war. How ironic it is. I will not be able to protect my children and grandchildren, but I can send the horses out of harm's way." Her laugh was sharp, devoid of humor.

We are all doing what we can, Rane thought, considering again the ships the yard had been building these past years. The finished ones were useful enough, proving their seaworthiness in coastal trade and in runs to the West Indies and South America, but their real purpose lay ahead.

Suddenly he did not want her to make this final journey to the racecourses alone. "How would you like an aging lover to accompany you?" he asked, and after an incredulous hesitation, she realized he was serious and threw her arms around him. "I would like that above all things."

Caleb and Morgan did not question his reason for absenting himself from the shipyard; they knew how much Alex missed Gincie, and sympathized with Rane's need to give her the reassurance of his presence.

In New Orleans, he was as chilled as she by the mood underlying the outward appearance of a carefree life. There was a defiant conviction that, even if war came, this port was too deep in the South to be affected.

"They are arrogant fools," Rane observed harshly. "Any place with river and salt water touching it can be taken unless there are adequate defenses." He had a swift, clear vision of the ships of the Jennings-Falconer yard bombarding this lush place.

The horses had never been his life, but he found himself cheering them on with great fervor. When Lady Shadow, a chestnut filly out of Lady Sailaway by Swan's Shadow, won the two-mile-heats sweepstakes for three-year-olds, and when two days later Lady's Chance, a five-year-old son of Lucky Lady by Swan's Chance, stretched out to win the Jockey Club Purse of $1000 for three-mile heats, Rane felt a surge of pride and triumph nearly equal to Alex's. And he understood for the first time Alex's acceptance of loss as well as victory, as long as her horses had run clean, gallant races. He shared her admiration for the offspring of Lexington and Lecomte and cheered enthusiastically as Daniel Boone by Lexington won the Crescent Poststake for all ages. And finally, he understood the added tragedy the war would bring. All the years of careful breeding would be in jeopardy, and at the very least, the breeding years of some of the best stallions and mares would be interrupted. Alex's stallions had time and again been listed among the year's leading sires as their get appeared on the tracks and won. Now, by her own action, Alex was forgoing the glory.

At the Metairie Course, the spectator stands, including the special ones for the ladies and the barns and stalls around the track, were the finest in the land. The race crowds were brightly dressed, the air alive with the babble of the spectators and the cries of food vendors hawking their exotic dishes. The horses were among the finest in America. And yet Rane felt the sadness—as Alex had termed it, a dirge in silks.

In Virginia they saw Allen Ralston, Justin Sinclair, and other acquaintances, and though nothing was said about it, Rane sensed that old friends like Allen and Justin knew that Alex was saying good-bye. He stayed beside her day and night, lending his support by his mere presence.

When she told Allen, "You are always welcome at Wild Swan, no matter what the future brings," Rane added his own words of continued friendship. He knew exactly how Allen felt when the man turned away to hide his emotions.

It was no easier in Kentucky, for though there were not as many of their old friends attending the Lexington meeting, Alex still knew many of the leading horsemen. Most of all, this was the last time she would see her horses racing for who knew how long.

"It was Sinje's dream, and then it became mine. But still he began it, and now I am finishing it. I hope he would understand," she sobbed.

"He would understand better than most," Rane said. "He saw war at first hand. He no less than you would want to preserve so many years of work and care. And, sweetling, it is not over forever. You know what human nature is, people will look to their pleasures again someday."

His words sustained her when she announced her plans to the family on the return to Wild Swan.

They were, as she had known they would be, shocked. It was not because they were oblivious to the rising tension in the country, but because she had been the one who constantly encouraged them to live with hope.

"Christ, I feel as if war has been declared today," Morgan muttered to Sam, and Sam could not comfort him. She had her own burden to bear in her father's attitude. She dreaded going to Brookhaven these days. She wondered if her father had gone a little mad. He was actually looking forward to a separation of North and South, and was determined that Maryland would go with the South. She had stopped asking her sons to visit their grandfather; she felt as if the war had already begun in her own family.

"The oldest of the horses, the work teams, and a few of the half-breds for riding will remain here," Alex said calmly. "Gincie chose to take Brutus with her to Virginia. If any of you have a favorite you wish to keep here, I will, of course, agree, but eventually you may have to stable them in the city. Remounts are always necessary for armies, and if there is any action in this region, the animals will be at risk."

She could feel the painful realization flowing through her grandchildren, in particular, as they began to envision Wild Swan without its famous horses. But they shared her deep vein of practicality and were no less protective of the Thoroughbreds than she. Without protest, they agreed to her plan, saying they would ride the old racehorses and the half-breds when they were in need of a mount. Except for Seth—he made a specific request for Porthos, a half-bred chestnut gelding who carried the blood of Swan through Swan's Shadow and was, like Brutus, a horse of endurance and dependability.

"Porthos is yours, to go with you when you need him," Alex told Seth. Though neither of them said it outright, they knew she had just agreed that the horse would be taken into war. There was no reluctance in the decision. It was one thing to consider strangers confiscating her horses; it was quite another to make sure her grandson was provided with a good horse that might make the difference between life and death.

The summer drew the family closer together than they had ever been, even the youngest conscious now that time was running out, particularly because they witnessed much of the political agitation in Baltimore. The Constitutional Union Party, composed of former members of the American and the Whig parties, had met in the city in May, and the Democrats had two conventions there in June, one for the supporters of Stephen Douglas and the other evolving out of those who were dissatisfied with Douglas. These Southern Democrats favored Vice President John C. Breckinridge of Kentucky for president with a platform protecting the right to own slaves. The first of the year's Democratic Party conventions had been in Charleston, South Carolina, and when the proslavery platform was rejected, the delegates from the Southern states had departed, leaving the other delegates unable to agree on a candidate. The subsequent conventions had only proved what was already known—the Democrats were in serious disarray.

It was the perfect opening for the Republican Party, which had nominated Abraham Lincoln as its presidential candidate in Chicago in May.

Like most Easterners, Alex knew little about the man from Illinois except that his stand on slavery seemed moderate. He made it clear he would not oppose it in states where it already existed but only wished to prevent it from being established in new states and territories. While he did not condone slavery, neither did he feel he had anything in common with black men, and knowing them to be socially inferior, he did not expect other whites to mix with them, either.

It was hardly the stand of a Northern Abolitionist, but the South saw him as the enemy, the representative of free-soil advocates and everyone else opposed to the Southern way of life.

Day by day the Southerners grew more openly contemptuous of the system of government they no longer believed served them. Open threats of secession were made, should Lincoln be elected president. The promises of retribution if the election did not go their way made it only too evident that the fabric of the Union had worn very thin. And day by day, Alex grew more sure about her decision.

Wanting to tell her face to face, Alex waited until she and Rane visited Gincie at Hawthorn before she told her granddaughter about the horses.

There was no doubt that Gincie was sublimely happy as Travis's wife. The instant Alex met Abigail, she knew it had much to do with the old woman.

"I knew we would be friends," Abigail told her. "It could be no other way because we both love Gincie. What a fine job thee and thy husband did of raising her."

"I will return the compliment. Travis is a fine man."

And then Abigail said very softly, "They are not hiding from it. Gincie has taught Travis to live for the day, and with each other, they are sufficient."

Rane witnessed the truth of what the old woman had said to Alex when he went with Travis to see the various enterprises of Hawthorn. Nothing was neglected; the land, the crops, and the livestock were all cared for as if the golden days of summer would never end.

"This land has always mattered to me, Mr. Falconer. But since I brought Gincie here, it has become more precious. Gincie makes everything mean more."

This quiet admission impressed Rane, but he found he didn't need words at all to understand the depth of his granddaughter's relationship with her husband. The young couple were so aware of each other that it was as if they were bound together even when they were across the room from each other.

"I will send them to thee for Christmas," Abigail promised the Falconers. "It is only just, as I have the daily pleasure of their company."

Alex and Rane returned to Wild Swan with the conviction that, in spite of the haste with which the young couple had married, theirs was a bond that would endure.

That Gweneth and Christopher had the same kind of union had long been established, and having them at Wild Swan during August eased the pain of the final preparations for shipping the horses. They said they had come to serve as escorts for the animals going to England, but the real reason was that Gwenny wanted to see her old home once again before the hostilities commenced. And though she said she would bring the children to America when they were older, they all knew the visit was likely to be delayed.

It was hard for Alex not to smile when she heard her daughter speak. Though Alex had never really lost her native accent, Gwenny now sounded like an Englishwoman, her American accent having all but disappeared.

But there was nothing to smile about in the couple's report on the feelings in Britain regarding the situation in America.

"Father keeps trying to emphasize the folly of sympathizing with a power based on slavery, but England's ties are much stronger with the South than the North," Christopher said. "However, there are sane voices in addition to Father's, and I trust they will prevail."

"They will if I have anything to say about it," Gwenny declared staunchly, and her husband smiled. "She is one of the best advocates the United States has; Father says he would like to find a way to allow her to address the House of Lords."

Alex could not help envying Hugh and Angelica, at peace, with their grandchildren in their care, in a country that had only well-ordered days to look forward to now that its troubles with Russia in the Crimea were over. Alex had to remind herself that she had long ago cast her lot with America and would not, could not go back in time or experience.

And then, quite suddenly, it was time. In a short span of days, the horses left Wild Swan. Sleek from summer grazing and loving care, their coats glistening in a dark rainbow, they departed for California, Canada, and England. And with them went Padraic Joyce and Jackson Barlow, Jim Barlow's younger son.

"Samson and I, we've talked about it, and we've decided the horses deserve to have someone they know with them. Samson's life is here; he can't be goin' off like that. But I'm not so settled any more. And the Barlow boys, with their father's permission, drew lots ta decide which should go. The young horses, they need to know a foine rider's touch."

Padraic told her the plan matter-of-factly, and Alex was relieved of much worry. She trusted him absolutely, and knew that with him in charge of the horses in Canada, there would be no neglect of training. Breeding would be overseen, and the best of the youngsters would go to England on Padraic's recommendation. And at least one of the Barlow boys would be out of the danger of the battlefields.

But when the day of their departure came, Alex realized that, while Jackson Barlow might view the whole thing as an adventure, for Padraic it was as much of a sacrifice as it would have been for Samson.

"You'll be mindin' Katy's grave fer me?" he asked, his voice low and unsteady.

For a moment, Alex could not speak. Then she said, "Yes, I will, and Fergus's, too." She knew he tended the dog's grave as well as his wife's, and she understood it: Fergus had tried to protect Katy, and to Padraic that was cause for honor to be paid. "Padraic, it was a good day for Wild Swan when you arrived; it will be a better day when you return."

Beyond words, he nodded, and she wanted to hug him, but that was not the way of their relationship. They shook hands, and he was gone.

The long faces of Samson, the remaining Barlows, and the other workers at Wild Swan underlined the reality of the horses' absence. There was plenty of labor for the remaining staff with crops and livestock to care for, but the heart of the farm had been the Thoroughbreds and the work of preparing them for the races.

Swan's Chance, Swan's Shadow, Temptress, Lady Sailaway, Lady Shadow, Irish Lass, the list went on and on; of the stallions only the thirty-year-old Fortune remained, and of the mares, five who were past safe breeding age—Ember, Alchemy, Fairy Swan, Fortuna, and Lucky Lady—stayed at the farm.

In the sorrow of parting from the living, Alex thought of the legion of dead lying beneath the earth of Wild Swan. She could see all of them clearly as they had been in their prime: Sir Arthur, Leda, Mabbie, Wild Swan, Black Swan, Bay Swan, Oberon, Swan Song, Taney, Magic, Winter Swan, Dreamer, and Swan Princess. A few had died violently—Winter Swan who had been shot after the fall that had nearly killed Alex, Wild Swan who had been destroyed because of the fire, and Swan Princess whose heart had given out while she struggled to give birth to her last foal—but most had lived pampered lives and died of old age at Wild Swan where they belonged. To be shipping away the future seemed a negation of all Alex had worked for, however necessary for the preservation of that future. She had survived the sale of so many prize horses to save the shipyard twenty-two years before, and could survive this as well.

In some ways, the remaining task was the hardest because it formally marked the end of an era. After years of advertising which stallions would be available for breeding, Alex put a notice in the *Spirit of the Times:*

The stallions of Wild Swan will not be standing for the 1861 season. All breeding contracts are canceled until further notice.

Alexandria Carrington Falconer, Wild Swan,
Prince George's County, Maryland.

The responses from horse owners who had planned to send mares to the farm were swift. To each inquiry, Alex replied that the stallions were no longer at Wild Swan. She did not feel obliged to explain further; if they could not yet accept that war was coming to disrupt their lives, it was not her mission to convince them.

It was hard enough for her to get from one day to the next. She knew she would adjust because she had to, and she knew she had everything to be thankful for because her family was still whole. But she missed the horses so fiercely, it was as if the second children of her heart had departed. Caring for the horses and watching their progress had been so much a part of her life for so long, she felt as if she were without purpose.

She spent hours fussing over the old horses left behind, but she wanted Gincie, Padraic, Jackson Barlow, and all the Thoroughbreds back. She wanted the nation to turn away from its headlong flight toward disaster. She knew that Rane had his own burdens, and still she could not stop herself from clinging to him. She needed him to anchor her.

In those brief times when Alex had needed him beyond the daily interweaving of their lives, Rane had felt strong and protective. But now it unnerved him as if he could feel the beat of his own heart faltering. It was too much like the time after Nigel's death. She seemed like a frightened child, lethargically performing daily tasks by rote rather than with vitality and interest, waiting all the while for the night terrors to close around her. It made Rane aware of how much he depended on her strength and her ability to cope. He felt singularly helpless, but he did what he could, making sure he was there for her as much as possible.

On November 6, Abraham Lincoln was elected president, winning a majority of the electoral votes, but only a plurality of the popular vote. It did not matter that he had deliberately softened his words about slavery; his party's platform was not so tolerant of the peculiar institution, and the issues dividing the country had boiled down to sectional rivalry and slavery. Within days of Lincoln's election, Southern leaders began to speak of secession as the only course, though there were some who still insisted the Constitution must be upheld over states' rights.

In her current state of passive acceptance, Alex viewed the new president as inevitable, given the fumbling of the opposing parties, rather than as good or bad. By newspaper accounts, he seemed to her to be an American type she had never been comfortable with—the self-professed bumpkin whose outer appearance of rough dress and humble, self-deprecating manner hid a shrewd and coldly calculating intelligence. England was not without a counterpart, but Americans had raised the type to something approaching a national art. Alex thought Lincoln was hardly the sort of man a nation should choose in a time of such crisis, but then it occurred to her that perhaps things had reached such a point, it really made no difference who was president. The South might use Lincoln as an excuse, but the threat of secession had existed long before he came to the fore.

A few days after the election, Larissa and Luke announced their intention to marry, asking that they might have a family ceremony at Wild Swan on Christmas Day. Luke had no close living relatives, so there would be no complication of meshing two family groups.

Alex had long since assumed that Larissa would not marry Luke after all, that they had developed into dear friends rather than lovers. The news that they wanted to marry came as a shock and focused her attention far more than the election results had. She felt as if she were awakening from a long sleep, particularly when Philly sought her advice.

"I don't know what to do; I don't think there is anything to be done. But there is something very wrong with this marriage. I suppose one can't judge one's own children with any objectivity in such matters, but I don't think Lissa loves Luke enough," Philly confided. "And I can't for the life of me understand why she should decide to marry him now, after all this time. She has even seen several other young men this year. I've tried to talk to her, but it hasn't done a bit of good. And Blaine is no use at all! He keeps pointing out that she is twenty-four years old and capable of making her own decisions even if he doesn't agree with them. Damn his kind heart and his lawyer's logic!"

"Do you want me to speak to her?" Alex asked and hastened to add, "Though I can't see that it will do much good if she's not listening to you, to whom she is so close."

"Not as close as she is to you in some ways," Philly replied without a trace of jealousy. "You are special to all the girls, and I would truly appreciate it if you would at least try."

Larissa was neither defiant nor uncomfortable during the interview with her grandmother; rather, she was calm and set on her course.

"I will make him happy. It is the least he deserves after loving me so faithfully for so long."

"My dear child, that is a most generous sentiment, but where is your happiness in all of this? I know it is not a widely held opinion, but from experience I swear to you that, though a marriage may endure for many reasons, for it to endure with joy requires love on both sides. It is no small matter to share one's whole life with another human being. Your mind, your spirit, and your body will be entwined with his and his with yours by virtue of a few words. But those vows so simple in speaking are complicated in living. And I would not want to try to live them without love." She thought of the first days of her marriage to St. John, when the marriage had been in their hearts only because the law forbade sanction, and of how cruel it had been when St. John's heart had faltered in its commitment to her, and she had nearly ceased to love him as well.

"Gran, I know what you think we lack, and you are right. But don't you see, not everyone loves the same way. I cannot imagine feeling as deeply about anyone as you do about Grandfather, or even as my parents feel about each other. I am just not made that way. I know that Luke's love is deeper than mine, but I promise, he will not suffer for it. I want to have a husband, and I want him to be content before—"

"Before the war comes," Alex finished for her. "I cannot blame you for thinking that way; every generation that has ever faced battle has surely thought the same. But do consider, how will it be when peace comes? Your marriage should be made for all time, not just for the emergency of the moment."

"If Luke and I survive until then, there will be time enough to consider whatever adjustments we must make. Adjusting to peace—it is a task I look forward to. And in the meantime, I hope I can keep Luke safe."

Alex could think of nothing else to say.

On the twentieth of December, South Carolina, long the leading voice of rebellion, held a convention and voted to secede from the Union. President Buchanan in his final annual message to Congress at the beginning of the month had said that while the states had no right to secede, neither did the federal government have the legal means to prevent such an action. It was hardly a message designed to solve the crisis, and Congress was doing no better, desperately searching for compromises and solutions while events rolled on.

In this tense atmosphere, Larissa and Luke were married. Everyone tried to pretend that it was a completely joyful occasion, but even Larissa, lovely as she was, looked slightly removed from the proceedings. At least Luke was sublimely happy, and for once, he managed to move with a modicum of grace.

Alex was not worried about how Luke would treat her granddaughter; he would, she was sure, adore Larissa all the days of his life. Instead, she found herself praying that Larissa would not break his heart. She did not believe that her granddaughter was incapable of great passion, only that she had not found the man who could arouse it in her.

She glanced at Travis and Gincie. Abigail had sent them north as promised, and they had already been at Wild Swan when South Carolina had voted to secede. They gave every appearance of enjoying the festivities, but the news had obviously affected them. They behaved more like a newly wedded couple than Larissa and Luke. They were reluctant to let each other out of sight, and though they were discreet about it, Alex noted that they were almost always touching, holding hands or just sitting close enough for contact, as if by such means, they could keep at bay the forces gathering to separate them.

Alex looked away from them, but when the family saw the New Year of 1861 in together, she managed to remain dry-eyed, and her voice was steady when she bade Travis and Gincie a safe journey back to Virginia two days later.

"Remember, whatever Wild Swan can provide for you is yours, no matter what comes," Alex told Travis.

Travis leaned over and kissed her on the cheek. "Thank you for everythin'," he whispered, and Alex understood what he meant. Now everyone at Wild Swan knew that he would cast his fate with Virginia even if she left the Union, and though they had tried to hide their reactions because they liked him and knew how much Gincie loved him, it was clear they were very uneasy about his convictions. It had been particularly hard for Gincie to face Samson and Della. They had had much to do with raising her, and it was painful for them to know it was very likely that she would be living among those who would soon take up arms to defend slavery. To their minds, other issues had little to do with the trouble brewing.

They had said nothing; words had been unnecessary. And Gincie nearly lost control as she hugged first one and then the other in farewell.

But it was Samson who broke, shoulders heaving as he mumbled, "Take care, liddle Gincie, take care." He walked away, not even able to seek comfort from his prize horses, since the ones needing his skills for training were gone.

At the end of December, Robert Anderson, the major in command of the federal forts in Charleston's harbor, had moved his force to the biggest and most defensible, Fort Sumter. South Carolina state troops took over Fort Moultrie and Castle Pinckney, which had been under Anderson's command. Despite his Southern sympathies, President Buchanan did not agree to Southern demands that he remove federal troops from Charleston, and he warned the South Carolinians that Fort Sumter would be defended. Yet, in early January when an unarmed supply ship was sent by the president to Fort Sumter and had to retreat under fire from a battery in the harbor, no retribution was visited on the South Carolinians or on the Georgians, who had taken over another federal fort, Fort Pulaski, some days before.

Mississippi, Florida, Alabama, Georgia, Louisiana—one by one they slipped away from the Union during January, following South Carolina's example. Ironically, after so many years of bloodshed, Kansas was admitted to the Union as a free state.

In February, a provisional government was formed, and Jefferson Davis was inaugurated President of the Confederate States of America. Texas left the Union, but Virginia still held fast, and Alex clung to the slim hope that the state would not join the Confederacy. Gincie's letters expressed the same hope, but she added that Travis thought the situation would deteriorate as soon as the real firing began.

It was agonizing to wait for the first exchange of fire. The supply ship fired upon in Charleston harbor had been unarmed, and the incident had ended without bloodshed, but only an idiot could believe that that pattern would continue. Alex felt the volcano rumbling beneath them.

And yet, the normal cycles of existence went on. In February, both life and death came to Wild Swan. Samson and Della's son Jotham had married Jewel Hastings, a Baltimore-born daughter of free blacks, two years previously, and Jewel gave birth to a daughter they named Hope. Samson was so large, his newborn granddaughter could fit in one of his hands. To observe the huge man cradling the tiny baby was infinitely moving.

Two days after the new life had come, an old one ended. Horace Whittleby died with the same fastidiousness that had characterized his life. He had grown noticeably frail in the past year and had been plagued by a persistent cough through the winter. He had docilely swallowed Alex's potions and professed himself recovering nicely. But he had taken to his bed for the past month, and he died one winter afternoon. Alex was grateful that there was no sign of struggle or pain.

They buried him at Wild Swan, and they discovered without surprise that he had left his affairs in perfect order. There were special bequests of books to the children he had taught over the years; he had even specified the volumes to be sent to Samson and Della's son Malachi in

California and to the Barlow boys in their various locations. And because he had been a frugal man whose only indulgences had been his summer journeys and his books, he left a considerable sum to be used "as an endowment for the education of the children of Wild Swan, that my successor may be hired when there are again pupils in need of a tutor." He left behind his gratitude "for giving me the family I never thought to have."

He had had a long life, so his death could not be termed a tragedy, but that did not prevent Alex from mourning him fiercely. He had been part of life at Wild Swan for so long, it was hard to imagine being without his presence. But there was healing laughter mixed with the tears.

"I shall never forget Mr. Whittleby giving me dancing lessons," she told Rane. "Sinje couldn't, and Boston was no use—he and I were so awkward, the children fell about laughing—so Horace stepped into the breach. It was the first party Sinje and I attended at Caleb's parents' house in Annapolis."

"And I danced with you that night," Rane said softly.

Alex didn't have to ask why he remembered it; her memory of him was as vivid, all the small details of their entwined lives still sharp.

"Do you know," she said thoughtfully, "I think Mr. Whittleby just gave up. I realize he was old and not well, but I think most of all, he simply could not bear to see the children he had cared so much about march off to war."

They were both silent, considering the deep well of love the little man had contained behind his prim facade, showing it not in an effusive manner but in his endless patience with the children and his determination that learning should be a pleasure for them all of their lives. Though he would have a headstone at Wild Swan, his true monument was in the wide-ranging awareness he had nurtured in the minds of his pupils.

BOOK
FOUR

Chapter 34

~~~~~

Baltimore, Maryland, 1861

In his inaugural address on March 4, Abraham Lincoln said that he had no intention of interfering with slavery where it existed, and yet, "No State upon its own mere motion can lawfully get out of the Union." He wanted to make it clear that if war came, it would be over secession, not slavery. And he concluded, "The mystic chords of memory, stretching from every battlefield and patriot grave to every living heart and hearthstone all over this broad land, will yet swell the chorus of the Union when again touched, as surely they will be, by the better angels of our nature."

The "better angels" were not in evidence, Alex thought cynically. A far more accurate measure of the times than the new president's speech was the fact that he had had to travel to Washington secretly after being warned in Baltimore of a plot against his life. And he had become president of a much reduced United States of America.

And then when the green was so fresh, and the first flowers were opening to the sun, the waiting ended. On April 12, South Carolinian forces fired on Fort Sumter, and the fort surrendered the next day because there were no supplies to sustain a siege. On the fifteenth, President Lincoln declared a state of insurrection, a delicate distinction designed to prevent foreign powers from recognizing the Confederacy as a sovereign nation in the conflict. But the call for 75,000 volunteers to serve three months in the Union forces left no doubt that the war had begun. Two days after Lincoln's declaration, Virginia seceded from the Union.

Right until the news came to Hawthorn, Gincie had hoped and

prayed that Virginia would somehow stay in the Union. Now that hope was gone forever.

"You know I have to go," Travis said, and his voice was so gentle, Gincie bit the inside of her cheek to keep from breaking down entirely. "I know," she whispered.

"I will take you home to Wild Swan first if you want to go."

"This is my home. It has been since the day I married you." Gincie answered without hesitation, her voice gaining strength with each word.

Travis bowed his head, struggling with his emotions, and then he said, "Come with me," and they rode over Hawthorn together, drawing in the sight, the scent, and the song of spring, as if to fix forever the image of the last perfect day of the growing season before the killing began.

Abigail had withdrawn to her own rooms as soon as the news had come, but she was serene again when the young couple came to her.

She cradled Gincie's hand and Travis's in her own frail, twisted hands. "May God watch over thee who goes and thee who remains," she said, and both of them knew how much it had cost her to offer this blessing when the need for it arose from a war that was against her every belief.

For an instant, Gincie felt as if her own grandmother had reached out and touched her.

Even though Alex had expected Virginia's secession, she felt as if a wide ocean rather than the Potomac River divided Maryland from her sister state. Every protective impulse urged her to bid Gincie to come north, but she knew the futility of it. Gincie had traveled away not only in miles, but on the journey of her heart toward Travis, the new center of her universe.

Alex reminded herself constantly that she could not change Gincie's lot and that she had other people to worry about, people she would do her best to shelter.

She was in Baltimore with Rane and the rest of the family when rioting broke out on April 19. The Massachusetts Sixth Regiment arrived in the city on its way to Washington. Southern sympathizers barricaded the streets between the President Street Station and Camden Station to block the transit route of the troops. Despite the fact that Mayor George Brown walked at the head of the line of soldiers and Police Marshal Kane was at the rear, bystanders began throwing rocks. One shot was all it took to escalate the violence, and before it was contained, four soldiers and twelve Marylanders were dead, the first casualties of the war.

At the first hint that there might be trouble, Rane had ordered Alex to stay in the house while he, Caleb, and Morgan kept watch at the shipyard in case anyone had the notion of firing the waterfront.

"I'd rather be with you," Alex had protested.

"Please, don't argue! I am going to make sure Flora, Philly, Sam, and the children are with you, and I need you to hold things together here." He was certain that any trouble that arose would be directed toward commercial targets.

She could hardly refuse this arrangement, but it was a long, tense day, and all the women were relieved when Morgan came to report that the shipyard was still secure, though the men planned to spend the night there.

"We're not in any danger. Luke's with us, and he's so big, who would dare threaten him?" Morgan joked. Luke had brought Larissa by to stay at the house earlier in the day, and Alex was glad Rane had the imposing man at his side.

There was no way any of them could have expected the trouble that came the next day, directed not at the shipyard, but at the Kollers, the German couple who had taken care of the Falconers' Baltimore house for so many years.

There was little warning—the sudden sound of more than casual foot traffic outside and then the shout, "Damn Germans, mercenaries, bring 'em out!"

The initial feeling in the house was complete disbelief. "What in the world are they talking about?" Sam asked, more dazed than afraid.

Suddenly it dawned on Alex that this was simply part of the ugliness that had begun the day before. The great majority of German immigrants were in the North and were sympathetic to the Union. She saw the outrage growing on Adam's and Nigel's faces, and she feared that in another moment they would do something foolish in the cause of being the men of the family.

"All of you stay in the house," she ordered in a voice that brooked no refusal. She went outside so swiftly, none of them had time to consider what she was doing.

She was not afraid; she was furious that anyone would threaten the Kollers and her family.

"Shame on all of you!" she scolded, as if the crowd of fifteen or so were naughty children instead of potentially lethal adults. "How dare you come here so rudely! Is it not enough that there is trouble everywhere without making war on your neighbors?" She had caught sight of a man who lived down the street, and she fixed him with a steely glare, pleased to see his face color.

The men and a few women had come as a headless beast searching for trouble, more than a few of them already drunk in spite of the early hour, holdovers from the upheavals of the previous day. Someone had remembered an old German couple who lived in this house—a good target. None of the crowd had expected to face this enraged Englishwoman. The South needed English support, even the most ignorant in the crowd knew that, and it confused their will to hear Alex's accent.

"Just send out the Germans," a voice suggested, but now the belligerence was less than the nervousness.

"The people you are talking about are honest and hardworking. Not for the world would I turn them over to you. And to take them, you will have to come through me," Alex declared.

Absolute silence fell over them all. Then, one by one, the crowd drifted away, not meeting each other's eyes or hers.

Only when they had gone did reaction set in. Alex began to tremble so violently, she would not have been able to walk back into the house had not Flora and Sam helped her. And when Rane and Morgan came on the run, she knew her orders had not been completely obeyed, Adam having sneaked out the back to get word to the men.

Her family seemed to be making more noise than the attackers had, Alex noted vaguely. They were blaming themselves for letting her take the risk.

"No one says no to Gran," Anthea pointed out. "And besides, Aunt Sam had the gun and would have shot anyone who really made trouble; Aunt Sam's a great shot!"

Sam was looking as pale as Alex felt, so Alex thought it was probably true that her daughter-in-law had been prepared to shoot someone down.

"It's all over now, so do stop squabbling!" Alex meant to say the words in a firm voice, but they were so faint, no one heard her.

The Kollers' reserve had broken completely, and they were stammering their thanks, tears streaming down both old faces from the shock of finding that they could be attacked in their adopted country for no provocation other than that they were German born.

Alex gave up trying to restore order and concentrated instead on holding her teacup steady enough so she could drink from it.

Suddenly Rane was standing over her. "Are you all right?" When she nodded, and he saw no sign of a wound, his anxiety changed to anger. "Don't you ever, ever do anything like that again! You're an utter fool, and I am worse for having left you unprotected!"

"I am not a fool, and we were not unprotected. Sam had a weapon, and I had my accent." Again her voice failed her, emerging in a tremolo instead of with the strength she intended. And then the absurdity of what she had just said, the absurdity of everything that had just happened swept over her, and she barely managed to set her teacup aside before she started to laugh hysterically.

"Oh, sweetling, my God, you've frightened me out of years!" Rane exclaimed, and oblivious of onlookers, he swept her up into his arms and took her place in the chair, holding her so tightly against him, she stood in more risk from injury now than when she had faced the crowd.

"Mobs like that have no mind, no heart; they might have torn you to pieces!" Now it was he who was shaking.

By sheer effort of will, Alex got control of herself. "But they didn't. I'm quite all right, really I am." She managed to free one arm so that she could stroke his face, reassuring him by touch since he didn't seem capable of understanding her words.

Finally she felt his heart slow to a normal rhythm, and his hold loosened.

"I know you wanted me here because you thought the city would be safer than the country, but, my love, I far prefer Wild Swan," she told him wryly.

"I was blind. I did not believe that Southern sympathy would be so bold, but it doesn't matter; the government cannot allow Washington to be cut off from the rest of the Union. Virginia is lost, but Maryland will not be allowed to join the Confederacy."

The truth of his observation was borne out in the following days. Though some local authorities were so bold as to burn all the railroad bridges north of the city in response to word that additional troops were to be routed through Baltimore, on May 13, under the cover of a violent thunderstorm, one thousand troops commanded by Union General Benjamin Butler arrived in the city and, by the next morning, were encamped on Federal Hill, placing weapons that could physically enforce Baltimore's loyalty to the Union should it falter again. Pro-Union sentiment began to assert itself. Butler was shortly thereafter removed from his post for conducting his bold action without orders, but it was difficult to deny that he had subdued dangerous secessionist fervor.

While Alex and Rane deplored the need for such an occupation, they also admitted the necessity for it. There had been other German targets, among them *Sinai*, a German-Jewish monthly edited by an Abolitionist. The mob had destroyed the press. Windows had been broken at the Faber newspaper office, though Frank's parents were unhurt. Nothing could have been worse for Baltimore than had it resolved itself into different armed factions roaming the streets.

Alex discovered there was some advantage in having one shock piled on the next; numbness set in very quickly. Seth left Harvard and went to Washington to enlist before he visited his parents or grandparents; he had no intention of being dissuaded from his duty. Luke enlisted, too, and Larissa's face seemed permanently set in grim lines. President Lincoln declared a blockade of Southern ports, the Navy began a headlong race to acquire ships to do the job; and every ship Jennings-Falconer was willing to sell, the government purchased.

Rane and Caleb did not ask extravagant amounts for the ships, but they did make a good profit, vindicating the risk they had taken and still maintaining their merchant ships.

"What a bitter triumph," Caleb commented grimly.

"The navy is buying ships that scarcely float; at least ours are seaworthy, which is exactly what you had in mind," Rane reminded him.

But Rane did not feel so sensible when he discussed the sales with Alex. There was no way to avoid the subject, as the brisk business deal had been reported in Baltimore newspapers as an example of civic pride, not only for the enterprise of it, but also as proof of the existence of loyalty to the Union among leading citizens.

"This was the purpose of the new ships all along, wasn't it?" Alex asked Rane before he had a chance to make a full confession.

He nodded and waited for an explosion of temper that never came.

"Clearly you expect me to berate you," Alex said slowly. "But it really wasn't a secret. I never asked you because I didn't want to know. You, who have always loved sail, were suddenly building steamships; that should have told me enough. Should I now rage at you for my own cowardice? You aren't a warmonger for having ships to sell; you and Caleb simply accepted the truth in time to do something about it. You have not questioned my right to ship my horses out of harm's way; how could I then deny your right to do as you will with your ships?"

Rane stared at her incredulously, and then he said, "You will never know what agony I've endured. From the moment the decision was made to build those ships, I've felt criminal for not telling you, as if you would indeed think that somehow the ships would encourage war. Only now do I realize it had nothing to do with you but only with my own guilt. War is hellish on land or sea, but I have a seaman's nightmare of the latter. Ships catch fire and burn, and if sailors survive the flames, they drown. I never thought to be part of that."

Alex put her arms around him and rested her head against his chest. "My love, we all have our individual nightmares of what this war will bring." She felt the little tremor that ran through him before he surrendered to her comfort and let the tension flow out of his muscles.

She did not try to explain to him that lately to her everything had the altered aspect of a night phantom, making the worsening conditions seem commonplace.

First there had been the fear of Confederate troops taking the capital, and then Washington had become, overnight, a depot for thousands upon thousands of Union recruits. But there had been no shots fired since Fort Sumter. Arkansas left the Union on May 6, and North Carolina and Tennessee were sure to follow. Yet there was no way to predict when the first real battle would take place. The talk was all of how quickly the war would be over, how soon the Rebels returned to the fold. Few seemed to consider that surely the feeling in the South must be as blindly confident.

The Falconers had good reason to be aware of this. Letters from Gincie were still coming through because Alastair Cameron, with his wide network of contacts, made sure that they did. It was hard enough that Travis had joined the Confederate Army; it was an added burden that his relatives viewed this as an occasion to renew contacts with Travis and Abigail. Gincie wrote:

> *They had long considered his views on slavery suspect, and so had left him and Abigail alone. But now they feel he has vindicated the Culhane name. They are, as he warned me, difficult to like. Not only are they slave owners, but they see the South as some ancient kingdom of courtly mien, the North as the land of barbarians. It is wholly ridiculous. But I*

do not mistake them; they will fight to the bitter end to preserve this illusion.

Do not mistake me either. I detest slavery, as much as I ever did. And I feel far more Northern than Southern. But I will never regret a moment of my marriage to Travis. I would do it all again.

Because of her racing forays into the South, Alex had firsthand experience of how committed a Southerner could be to ideas, no matter how nebulous, of honor. Dueling had remained popular in the South long after it had ceased in the North; it was too easy to imagine Southerners seeing the war as just one more exercise on the field of honor, a challenge from which one did not retreat. Nor was there any lack of experienced military men in the South, as hundreds of regular army and navy men and officers resigned from Union forces in order to return to their home states to offer their services. And many upper-class Southerners, though not professional soldiers, were expert riders, deadly shots, and excellent swordsmen.

Seth's view of the Northern forces was quite different. His riding skill was providing him with rapid advancement. Many of the volunteer companies were allowed to choose their own officers, and the men had quickly seen that Seth Falconer could teach them what they needed to know to keep them from breaking their necks falling from their mounts long before they saw active duty.

"Good lord! Most of them are city boys, and even the farmers haven't known anything but plow horses," he told his grandmother. "Right now, if my men had to ride at faster than a walk or longer than a couple of hours, I wouldn't count their chances of staying in the saddle very high." He looked away and his voice was very low. "I fear President Lincoln is going to need an army for a lot longer than three months."

There were those in both the Confederate and Union governments who understood this, particularly as it related to the need for additional munitions and ships. Confederate agents were scouring England and the Continent for guns and for yards to build ships, as the South was lacking in manufacturing of all kinds. But Union agents were busy, too, not only trying to augment the federal supplies of armaments until factories at home could produce at the necessary rate, but also trying to block Confederate purchases, particularly of ships.

England declared her neutrality, thus dashing Southern hopes of recognition as a sovereign nation and of an active ally in the Crown. Though there were English regulations against the building of warships for either side, there were also ways around the laws—if the profits were high enough. The most obvious was to build the ships, but not arm them, in English ports, leaving the arming to be done elsewhere. The illicit construction was aided by sympathy for the Southern cause that prevailed among the aristocracy and in the mercantile class.

Alex deplored the British support for the South and was glad there were people like Hugh, Angelica, Christopher, and Gwenny doing their utmost to raise enthusiasm for the Union. But she had no inkling that those distant politics would change her life so radically by changing Rane's.

Rane felt he owed it to his son to speak to him even before he told Alex.

Morgan knew as well as Rane that the letters of marque and reprisal issued to private vessels by Jefferson Davis were an open invitation for Southern raids on Northern shipping, and he knew that Gideon Welles, Secretary of the Navy, had been in touch with Caleb, but still, he was stunned by his father's news.

"The Confederacy is hell-bent on building a navy in addition to the private raiders, and they're going to do that in England," Rane said. "We need all the voices we can muster to persuade England to cease giving any kind of aid, and that includes relinquishing the pretense that ships even now being planned will not be used in the war. Secretary Welles was impressed by the ships the navy bought from us through his brother-in-law Charles Morgan, and though Welles is from Connecticut, he knows about our company and about Caleb's family. It fits his plan that I am English-born and pro-Union. He has personally requested that Caleb and I go to England to plead the Union cause, to do what we can to block Confederate activities there, and to arrange for the purchase of certain firearms. Caleb and I need to know that you will be here to run the shipyard. It is important not only for us, but for the North. The need for commercial and military shipping will increase by the day."

Though Morgan listened with an outward show of patience, there was no patience in him. He felt as if sudden shackles bound every limb and his soul as well. Though he was forty-four this year, he was more fit than many men half his age, and he had long since decided that he could not stay safely home while his sons marched off to war. He had planned to enlist as soon as he had settled his own affairs and was sure that his father and Caleb could carry on without him. Instead, he was being asked to play the merchant.

At first Morgan did not trust himself to speak, and Rane watched him pace like a great lean cat confined in a space narrow beyond bearing.

The worst of it for Morgan was that Welles's choice of Rane and Caleb was indisputably a good one. Caleb had the background of a powerful American family of long standing, while Rane had the double view of being both English and American. And together, the two men were a powerful representation of American business and political interests. It would be difficult for English political figures to ignore the presence of the founders of the widely known and respected Jennings-Falconer shipping line.

Morgan ceased his pacing and stood before his father. "I will do as you ask." His voice was quiet, but his eyes were so full of angry frustration that Rane had to look away.

Morgan saw the pain he was causing his father, and recognizing the futility of it, he shifted the subject away from himself. "What of Mother? Does she know yet?"

"No, but when I tell her, I will ask her to accompany me. Flora is going to go with Caleb, and I would very much like to have Alex with me." In fact, he could hardly face the dread of leaving her behind.

Morgan kept his doubts to himself.

Rane explained it all very logically to Alex, and then he went through it again because she made no response but rather regarded him as if he were speaking a foreign tongue.

"I want you to go with me. It will be a chance for you to visit Gwenny and the Bettingdons again and to see our grandchildren there." He paused and then added, "Alex, I cannot refuse."

This time Alex understood every word he said. This was no nightmare, and the acceptance that had guided her response to everything lately was suddenly and savagely gone. Yet her voice was no more than a thread of sound. "I cannot go with you. I cannot leave Wild Swan."

Speaking out of his own dread of being without her, Rane used the cruelest tack. "You mean that Wild Swan is more important than I am to you."

"If you believe that, then we are lost." She looked so bereft, Rane would have given anything to take back his words.

"I love Wild Swan. I will not deny it. I have worked for most of my life to make this land provide." Her voice had more force now. "But that is not why I must stay. Samson and Della can run the farm as competently as I. I need to be here for the grandchildren and for the children. It is the only thing of value I can give them in this awful time— a place to come to and someone who loves them and will listen to their fears and encourage their dreams. It is dreadful to be so old and to have so little of use to give them! But this much I can offer."

"Forgive me! I didn't mean what I said! I am just miserable at the idea of being without you. And yet, I could not refuse this mission. I, like you, feel old and incapable of protecting the young. If Caleb and I can prevent even one ship from being built for the Confederacy, we might save lives."

She did not doubt his sincerity; his eyes were the mirror of her own agony. She did not resist when he drew her against him.

"You are wrong," he said. "Della and Samson could attend to the business if need be, but you are Wild Swan. It does not exist without you. And what you offer the young is no small thing; what could be of more value than a refuge in the midst of chaos? Who would know better than I? You are my safe harbor. But what would we be if we refused our separate duties when the young are being asked to give everything?"

Of all of the things Alex had thought she might have to face, having Rane so far away had not been one of them, and she moved through the next days in the grip of a growing panic she did her best to conceal. She kept remembering her grandmother saying, "What cannot be changed, must be accepted." Such a simple phrase, so hard to live by. But it was true. And Rane had to go to England while she stayed in Maryland.

Speed was essential, for there was no time to be lost in causing trouble for the Confederates in England. And the time was taken up in helping Rane and Flora pack for the journey.

Flora had not hesitated in agreeing to accompany Caleb. She turned the school over to Philly and Phoebe and knew that Sam and Larissa would help, too, when they were needed. The school was important to her, but nothing was more important than Caleb. Though she tried not to dwell on it, she was always conscious of the age gap between them, and she had no intention of being separated from him for any length of time. It gave Alex a measure of comfort to know Flora would be with the men.

"Do watch over them, particularly your father," Alex told her worriedly. "I fear he will do too much and not take care of himself. He is not that young any more, and I want him back safely."

"Mother, don't worry! I promise I'll make him behave." She paused and then added, "And the same goes for you. He'll want to find you healthy and happy when he comes home."

Alex could not imagine being happy while Rane was gone. It was not at all the same situation as when she had been away at the races or he had been away on business—this was a separation of thousands of miles and for an undetermined length of time. It reminded her too much of the time he had returned to England after Claire's suicide and Alex had wondered if she would ever see him again.

The men and Flora would go by train from Washington to New York, and from there they would take a steam packet to England. Rane spent the night before he left with Alex at Wild Swan. With the time for parting so close, they found it difficult to speak naturally, both of them fearful that their emotions would overcome them.

"If there is trouble in the countryside, you will stay in Baltimore, won't you?" Rane asked. "Martial law may not be the best of all circumstances, but it will keep you safe in the city."

"I am a very practical, sensible woman," she said. "And I will do the practical, sensible thing."

He realized she had not given him the promise he wanted, and he would not term facing a dangerous mob by herself a sensible action, but he was also aware that there was nothing to be gained by harsh words on their last night.

They lay together holding and touching each other, trying not to acknowledge that this would be the last time for months, but the reality of it intruded and altered the leisurely pace of their loving so that Rane took Alex with sudden quick ferocity that left them both feeling dissatisfied and yet too exhausted to make love again.

"Damn!" Rane swore.

"It is not us," Alex said. "The age is out of tune, and our days are discordant now." She lay against him, savoring the warm, hard length of his body. "It doesn't matter. Wherever you are, I am part of you; wherever I am, you are part of me."

She clung to that thought when she watched him ride away in the early June sunlight, but she felt as if too much of herself had gone with him—her heart, her soul, her youth.

She moved through the ensuing days with outward calm, fulfilling her various roles as mother, grandmother, and businesswoman, but inside she was dry and empty. Food had no taste. The days were too long and the nights longer. Her body decided to remember every tumble she had ever taken from a horse and to protest them all with stiff, painful joints when she awakened in the morning.

"Feeling sorry for yourself, aren't you?" Alastair accused her when he visited Wild Swan. But though his voice was gruff, his eyes were kind. "I can't promise it will be for the better, but I can offer you a change of scene. Come to Washington with me. The government is giving much thought to blowing holes in young men, but precious little consideration to the repair work that will be needed afterwards, let alone to the conditions necessary to keep soldiers healthy enough to fight in the first place. I am going to meet with other physicians and concerned citizens to see how we can improve the soldier's lot."

It was harsh but effective treatment, startling Alex out of her self-absorption. But her decision to go with Alastair was not without selfishness; in Washington she would be able to keep in closer contact with both Seth and Luke. And she would have work to do instead of spending her time in futile worry.

Chapter 35

Since the firing on Fort Sumter, Washington had been radically altered. As the main staging area for the army in the East, it had become a vast depot and training camp for troops, necessitating not only the sprawl of their encampments, but also the means to feed and transport them. Herds of cattle and mules were everywhere, including the Mall, and they kept the air churning with their dust and flies as they moved to the shouting and hooting of their drovers. Cannon being trundled about the city tore up what little pavement there was and added the noise of their creaking, rumbling progress to the general cacophony of a town filled to bursting.

And though the preparations were for war, or perhaps because they were, there was a frantic air of gaiety in the city, soirées and other entertainments abounded as if to deny the truth that the uniforms were for dying, not for dancing.

Beds were at a premium in the overtaxed hostelries, but Alastair and Alex had no difficulty, as they were welcomed into the home of mutual friends, Dr. and Mrs. Grover.

The idea of the Sanitary Commission had originated among the English during the Crimean War when far more men had died of disease than of wounds. In the United States, the first organization had taken place in New York City in April, but now in June, the government had shown an interest in it, though it was still to be supported mainly by private contributions. Churches and charitable foundations were already involved, and women were taking a leading role. The work was not limited to Washington, as help was needed wherever troops existed, but with the first Eastern theater of action bound to be close by in Virginia, it was certain that hospital facilities would need to be expanded in the capital. Measures must be instituted in the camps as well to control the outbreak of contagious diseases. Already measles and other infections were spreading among the farm boys, who, in the isolation of their homes, had not been hardened by previous exposure to various sicknesses.

Alex went with Alastair to inspect various hospitals and to the bivouacs to see what could be done to keep water and food supplies uncontaminated and living conditions fairly civilized, despite the press of men.

Boys, not men, Alex thought as she surveyed the endless sea of faces. There were older men among them, but for the most part, the soldiers looked scarcely old enough to have been breeched, many of them hardly needing a razor to keep their cheeks smooth.

"I suppose at my age, everyone under forty begins to look very young," Alex confided to Alastair, but he shook his head in angry denial. "No, they are young, mere infants! I doubt most have even tumbled their first woman, if you will excuse the bluntness, and yet they are judged old enough to be chewed up by musket and cannon."

When Seth and Luke dined with them that night, their views were no less chilling.

"There is tremendous pressure on us to engage the enemy; people are getting tired of waiting for the battle to begin, but the men aren't ready!" Seth said. "It's not that they won't make good soldiers in time. They're brave enough and willing. They simply don't have the skills yet."

"The three months of volunteer service are almost up, and that makes the call for battle even more anxious. What a pleasant idea—perhaps the time will run out and everyone can go home," Luke suggested with a wry smile.

Alex studied the face of her grandson-in-law with deep affection. This big, gentle man was not cut out to be a warrior, and yet he felt obliged to serve. He could, she suspected, become quite savage if need be to protect his men. He had his own company of infantry and was drilling them assiduously that they might acquit themselves well and remain alive when the time came.

There had been minor skirmishes in Virginia, including a loss on the Peninsula and a victory in Philippi, but nothing that could quiet the cries for action. And so, on July 16, despite continued protests of unreadiness from even the highest in command, the Union army marched off toward the enemy.

Alex had begun to divide her time between Baltimore, the farm, and Washington, and she was at Wild Swan when the army marched away, but she was in Washington on July 21, when the aftermath of the Battle of Bull Run hit the city.

General McDowell's Union troops had been routed by the Confederates led by Generals P. T. Beauregard and J. E. Johnston. The soldiers fleeing back toward the capital found their way impeded by the vehicles of senators, congressmen, and fools who had gone to witness the battle as if it were a picnic. Now, it was as if the demons of hell were swarming toward the capital on the heels of the defeated, and there was general alarm that the Confederates would pursue the vanquished right into the city, though now there was no sign of this.

For days the stragglers poured into Washington, and their faces were no longer young. Dirty, with blistered feet, and with rain adding to their misery, many soldiers dropped down and slept in doorways, seeking oblivion from the carnage they had witnessed. The talk of how easily and swiftly the South would be defeated was stilled.

The wounded poured in by the hundreds, and hundreds more were reported missing, presumed captured or dead. Alex went to help at the Armory Square Hospital.

A supply of chloroform eased the agony of surgery but little else.

Arm and leg wounds were treated by amputation; fine young bodies fit and strong such a short time before lay rotting with suppurating stumps; and only by a constant effort of will could Alex keep each face from turning into St. John's from so many years ago when he had suffered the amputation of his arm. While she went about her work, calmly, competently, inside, she recoiled in horror.

Men lay with head wounds that had stolen their sight or their senses; stomachs gaped open, bringing slow agonized death as the poisons of the gut spread. Piteous cries sounded a constant litany.

Alex focused on what she could do. She sent a messenger to Wild Swan with instructions that all available fresh fruit and vegetables be sent to her so that the wholesome food might be added to the diet of those soldiers well enough to eat. She bathed fevered skin and made sure her charges had cool, fresh water to drink. She wrote letters for those desperate to communicate with their families. She held the hands of the dying and answered as their mothers, or sweethearts, or whomever they needed her to be. And she refused to consider that Seth or Luke might be lying as helpless somewhere else in the city.

It was Seth himself who brought her the news, having located her through word she had left at Dr. Grover's house.

He was only twenty years old, but the last of his youth had ended at Bull Run. His face was gaunt, and his hazel eyes were sunken in dark shadows and nearly sightless with fatigue.

"We hesitated too long, and the day was lost," he murmured. "But many, so many tried to hold fast. It was impossible. Sometimes you couldn't even tell one side from the other, the uniforms and flags were so confused. The panic grew and swept all before it. They were not ready. They needed more time to be soldiers, more time." He rubbed his face wearily, and then he said very low, "Luke is dead," and the tears began to course down his stubbled cheeks.

She closed her eyes against the rush of pain, and then she breathed Larissa's name, but above all else, she wanted Rane beside her.

The wanting had not eased but had only grown stronger by the time they buried Luke at Wild Swan. Because Luke had no close family of his own, it was fitting that they bury him there. But nothing else was fitting. Luke's kind nature, his quick mind, his adoration of Larissa and his appreciation of her family, even his endearing clumsiness—everything about him was too precious to lose, and yet the newly turned earth was proof that they had.

Alex stared at the gaping hole in the ground and saw all the torn bodies that had been carried into Washington after Bull Run and all the youth that would continue to flow away in a river of blood until the war ended.

Most of the family were weeping unashamedly, but not Larissa. Alex studied her set face and wished Larissa could have the healing of tears. But when she tried to put her arms around her to comfort her after the ceremony, Larissa would have none of it.

"It was all for nothing. I did not love him enough. And I could not keep him from enlisting. So my grand gesture was for naught." Her eyes gazed into her own distance. "I told him how angry I was when he signed up, not how much I loved him. I did love him, just not enough. He deserved so much more."

The day was hot and muggy, but Larissa's voice was as cold as deep stone. Alex knew that platitudes would be offensive. She left her granddaughter alone and approached Philly instead.

Philly's eyes were red-rimmed from weeping; she had been very fond of her son-in-law, for all her doubts about the marriage. But she shook her head helplessly when Alex questioned her about Larissa.

"She's been like that since she heard about his death. The truth of the matter is that Luke knew exactly how much Lissa loved him, and it was sufficient for him. He told me once that he felt as if he had reached for a star and caught it. His dream of contentment was fulfilled in her. Going to war had nothing to do with that. He was a man of honor, and he believed in the Union. He did not feel it right to let others fight for him. But I cannot make Lissa believe any of this."

"We must be patient with her; there are many ways to adjust to death," Alex said, remembering how corrosive guilt could be. She still remembered how she had felt when her daughter Christiana had died in England of a sickness she had brought home to the child after caring for a stricken family. There had been guilt, too, when St. John had died, guilt because she had persuaded him to come to America; now she could see that the connection was tenuous, but at the time she had felt as if the immigration to a new life had directly caused his death.

She wanted to write to Rane and demand that he come home, to plead that she could not continue without him. But she suppressed the cowardly impulse and restricted herself to sending a brief notification of Luke's death and assurances of her continuing love to her husband.

She was glad of her restraint when she heard from Rane about the effect of the Battle of Bull Run on the English. She received letters from him and from Caleb and Flora through government channels, this having been arranged by one of Secretary Welles's minions in order that the communications be more protected than they would be through the regular mails. Rane wrote:

> *I would pay dearly to be home with you. But daily I see more reason to be here. The Union loss at Bull Run has grievously damaged our cause. Many now feel more emboldened to speak in favor of the Confederacy and to speculate on the eventual Southern victory or, at the very least, a settlement that will establish the South as a sovereign nation. That Congress has seen fit to resolve that the war is being fought to "preserve the Union" and not primarily to abolish slavery has not helped us here either. I understand that it was a conciliatory move toward the South, but whereas England is uncomfortable with the institution of slavery, she is only too willing to see the upstart nation of the United States perish. Such a dissolution would be to her gain.*
>
> *The work of building ships for the Confederacy goes on despite all efforts to stop it.*
>
> *My only consolation is that in seeing Gwenny, I see you. And our grandchildren are delightful. But this country is not mine any longer, and my spirit and my heart remain with you. Take good care of them and of yourself for me.*

He wrote again when word of Luke's death reached him: "I am so sad and so angry and so far away. It is more important than ever to me now that this war end as swiftly as possible and without foreign intervention."

Gincie also wrote, first to say that Travis had fought at Manassas, as the Southerners called Bull Run for the nearby town, and had come through safely. She sent her love and condolences to Larissa, and she admitted: "With Luke dead and Travis alive, I do truly feel like the enemy now." The sad words tore at Alex's heart, but there was nothing she could do to ease Gincie's feelings.

Conducting much of her life by letter had become a necessity, but that did not make it any easier, though she was grateful for the efforts Rane, Flora, Gwenny, Padraic, and Boston made to keep in touch with her. She suspected he hated the exercise, but nonetheless, Padraic had written detailed reports to her since his arrival in Nova Scotia. He wrote that while he was sure the horses would be happy to return to the milder climate of their own pastures in Maryland as soon as possible, they were flourishing in their temporary home, a farm in an interior valley where crops and livestock prospered. Though Alex trusted him absolutely and had not asked for an accounting, he also sent tidy columns of figures listing every expenditure. But most important of all were his reports on the progress of last year's colts and the ones born this year. It was serious business, making judgments about which should be sold, which sent to England to race, but it was a task for which Padraic had been trained his whole life, and Alex pointed this out both subtly and overtly in all her letters to him.

Irish Lass had done particularly well at English racecourses, and this did much to bolster Alex's confidence. Irish Lass had raced as a three-year-old, and in England, that was not young. Alex accepted that her horses would no longer be training for longer distances at older ages but would be competing in the dash races at two and three years old. She doubted that the long races would ever regain their popularity. Even in the South, the last stronghold of the great contests, there had been fewer and fewer of them in the past decade as races at shorter distances with younger horses had taken precedence.

The news from Boston regarding the horses in California was as encouraging as that from Padraic and from England, but the political news was not as good. There was constant fear of Confederate interception of gold shipments from California, as well as apprehension about raids for supplies and horses from enemy troops in the Southwest. The coastal valleys and much of the interior were protected by mountain ranges, but there were many Southern sympathizers in the state.

Alex was more sure by the day that shipping most of the horses to Canada and England had been the right decision. In the South, whole troops of cavalry were being privately equipped by wealthy gentlemen, and many of the horses were from the best Thoroughbred stables. It was a great relief to be able to say honestly that she had no horses to sell when the buyer came to Wild Swan to procure mounts for the Union army.

"Heard tell you had good stock here," the man protested.

"I did, but they are gone. They were raised to perform on racecourses and to be willing, intelligent beasts under saddle. But I never intended them to be blown to bits on battlefields," Alex replied.

He looked at Fortune and the old mares—the beauty of the animals still visible despite the toll of years—and then he said, "Mrs. Falconer, I don't blame you."

Alex clung to the image of the horses running free in their faraway pastures as she continued to spend as much time as she could in the grim task of nursing the wounded in Washington.

The war news in August was discouraging. Union forces were defeated at Wilson's Creek in Missouri where, despite a majority of Union sympathizers, there was strong Confederate sentiment, too. The Union general John C. Frémont imposed martial law in Missouri and declared the slaves of secessionists free, but by early September, the president, in yet another attempt at conciliation with the South, had reversed the action and transferred Frémont.

Congress instituted an income tax to help finance the war, and now the call was for more volunteers to enlist, this time for two years rather than three months. Seth reenlisted.

Confederate victories were not confined to the land. Though the navy was trying to extend its blockade of Southern ports according to the president's orders, Northern ship owners were beginning to call for help from some of the vessels to protect mercantile shipping as Confederate privateers prowled the sea and took prizes. But the navy stood firm in its appointed task. As a result, commercial shipping suffered.

Morgan understood the pressing need to cut off Southern trade, but that scarcely eased the pain when one of the Jennings-Falconer ships was taken and burned in the water after all valuable cargo aboard had been removed. The privateer had been too far north to have a friendly port to take the prize to, and so destruction had been the next choice.

"None of the crew was lost; in fact, they were released, and the ship was insured, but that doesn't make me feel much better," Morgan growled. "It's such a damn waste!"

He soon discovered it was more than a waste, for though the percentage of loss to Northern shipping was not that large, the insurance companies were quick to panic, and premiums began to climb so high that the cost of policies was liable to do more damage than the piracy of the Confederates.

Morgan felt as if he had failed his father and Caleb, though there was nothing he could have done to save the ship. His continued frustration at being away from the battle lines made it difficult for him to sustain a belief in what he was doing, albeit his rational mind knew the North's commercial shipping was vital.

Alex shared his distress over the loss of the ship, but she did not discern the depth of his feelings of inadequacy because he was as careful to conceal it from her as from Sam and the rest of the family. And these days, no one felt happy or settled for more than brief intervals stolen from the reality of the war.

In September, without consulting anyone, Larissa closed the little house she had shared with Luke in Baltimore and moved to Washington to join in the work of the Sanitary Commission. She rented a meager room in an overcrowded boarding house, not asking anyone's assistance in resettling.

When Alex learned of her granddaughter's action, she confronted her directly, thinking that Larissa, unlike Nigel and Anthea, had never shown any sign of wanting to minister to the sick, though she had learned the basic healing skills at Wild Swan. "Is this a form of martyrdom?" she asked her. "Because if it is, you had better not let the wounded know it. They have enough to bear."

"Whatever my reasons, I plan to ease the soldiers' lot, not make it worse," Larissa replied without rancor. She was as coldly self-contained as she had been at Luke's burial, but she was as good as her word. The patience she had declared herself incapable of in teaching, she now seemed to possess in abundance with the casualties of Bull Run and in the crowded camp conditions that, despite efforts to alleviate them, were still ideal for the spread of measles, typhoid fever, diarrhea, bronchitis, pneumonia, and various other complaints.

Logically Larissa knew there was very little one person could do, but that did not lessen her fierce determination that no more men would die, no more women be left to mourn them. Luke's absence was a dark void in her life. And in her rawest moments, she judged that it was because no one, not even her parents, loved her as unconditionally as Luke had. She had grown accustomed to his adoration and had taken it for granted until it was gone. Only in brief flashes did she know that she had given Luke all he had asked of her, that the element of aloofness in her had attracted him as much as anything else.

She did not, however, realize that this same aloofness was what made the patients she tended treat her with such respect. With her silvery eyes, her dark hair, and with her delicate features cast in high relief because of the weight she had lost since her husband's death, Larissa appeared ethereal to the men, though they quickly came to know that she did not flinch from even the most grotesque sights and smells. But there was some part of Larissa Carstairs that was locked deep inside, giving her an untouchable air of reserve.

The key to Larissa's iron resolve was that she saw none of the men clearly. She cared about them and their comfort, but she did not let any individual pierce her shell. She began working regularly at the Armory Square Hospital, and she watched her grandmother mourning each death as if it were one of her own children, and she did not envy her.

She gave no thought to pleasure or relaxation; those were things that had existed in a previous life. Graciously but firmly, she declined most of her grandmother's invitations to dine with the Grovers or in the company of other friends, though sometimes she agreed when Seth was going to be there. She was very fond of her cousin; in his company she sometimes felt a glimmer of the old joy they had all known together during summers at Wild Swan.

Frank Faber often joined them. He was now working as a war correspondent for a major Baltimore newspaper, and he was much in Washington. Larissa felt sorry for him, for in spite of his charm and good looks which could easily attract any number of women, he was obviously still in love with Gincie and asked about her at every opportunity, worrying about her fate in Virginia.

On October 21, the Union suffered another defeat, this time at Ball's Bluff, near Leesburg, Virginia, and in short order, the wounded began to pour into Washington. The toll of the battle was terrible: some nineteen hundred Union soldiers dead. But once again, Seth remained physically unscathed.

It was late November before Larissa felt she had time to take a deep breath, and then it was only because her grandmother threatened to drag her bodily from the hospital.

"You look like a ghost! It won't do anyone any good if you waste away," Alex pointed out. "You are coming home with me to Wild Swan for a few days." Indeed, Alex herself was gaunt and weary and longing for air untainted by blood, putrid flesh, and the pitiful sound of men crying out in intolerable pain.

Larissa acquiesced because she was too weary to refuse, and she had to admit she felt an instant lift of her spirits when they arrived at the farm. It looked so serene and prosperous, as if it had been caught in the amber of more peaceful days.

That the family came from Baltimore to visit added to the illusion. Seth managed a few days at Wild Swan, and his parents and his brothers didn't want to miss the chance to see him.

Seth brought not only Frank Faber with him but also a friend of Frank's, Reid Tratnor, a fellow newspaperman, though Reid was from New York. Just short of thirty years old, he was a tall, broad-shouldered man with thick black hair and blue eyes that missed little, eyes that were most often fixed on Larissa.

Finally Larissa grew uncomfortable under his bold stare, and deciding that anything less than a direct approach would be wasted on this man, she confronted him. "Mr. Tratnor, you make me feel like a prize horse. I would prefer that you turn your eye on someone else."

If he was taken aback by her indelicate speech, he did not show it. Instead, those blue eyes gleamed with amusement and purpose. "Not a prize horse, a prize woman—my prize. I know you are but recently widowed, but I tell you now that I intend to have you for my wife."

It took Larissa a moment to believe that he was serious, and then she said, "I have no idea whether or not you have used this approach before to women newly met; I would guess not, since you do not seem to have a wife. Or if you have used it, they have all had the sense to say no. But I tell *you* now you will not get a wife in this quarter either. I fear the war has damaged your sanity."

Reid laughed aloud. "You are the first sane thing to happen to me since I came south."

"I have not happened to you," Larissa countered coolly, and she walked away, taking care for the rest of his visit that she was never alone with him or close to him. She was not afraid of him; she just did not want to expend the energy to keep him at bay. He was brash and too forward. He stirred no special feelings other than annoyance in her. The romantic part of her life had belonged to Luke, and even for him there had been embers rather than flame. That part of her life was over.

Knowing the changes the war wrought would not be confined only to Gincie, Seth, and Larissa, Alex tried to prepare herself. And no matter how much she cared, she knew their mothers cared more. Sam and Philly, despite the differences in their appearances, now often wore the same expression, compounded of love, apprehension, and courage. Even though Philly's daughters were not likely to come under the gun, there were other ways to be at risk, including exposure to disease through contact with ailing soldiers.

Phoebe seemed satisfied for the moment in pursuing the work of Flora's school, but Anthea announced her intention to begin nursing the wounded in Washington in January. It was rather sly of her to do so in front of the rest of the family, but the ploy didn't work; her mother was not going to accept this plan without words.

"You are only nineteen!" Philly protested.

"I will be twenty in the new year," Anthea countered. "And soon enough I would have gone off to Europe to seek admittance to medical school, perhaps in Geneva as Elizabeth Blackwell did, or in this country in the rare instance that one of the colleges would have accepted me. That is all changed now. I have skills I can use to help the wounded, and if the war continues to go as it has, there will be more and more need of women like me." She emphasized the word "women."

"Mother, I can watch out for her, and Gran's often in the city," Larissa offered. She knew her sister well and doubted that anything could dissuade her.

By the normal measure of things, Anthea's plan was highly improper. She was not a widow like Larissa; she was a young, unmarried woman. But the war was changing all the rules. And there was a precedent, set by Florence Nightingale when she had organized a select group of women to go out to Turkey to nurse British soldiers during the Crimean War. Many might still condemn the impropriety of women nursing wounded men, but the fact was that they were needed.

Philly cast a despairing glance at her husband, who had offered her no support at all in this, and then reluctantly she nodded. "If you will promise, difficult as it may be, to defer to your sister and your grandmother, you may go."

This was no hardship for Anthea; she was not going to the capital to enjoy her youth, but to put it behind her in work that, while not exactly what she wanted, was as close as possible for the time being.

Later when they were alone, Philly complained to Blaine, "You could at least have checked her for a moment!"

"No, I couldn't," Blaine said. "You cannot have it both ways. We have raised our daughters to be thoughtful, rational human beings, not useless bits of muslin. I would not have them any other way. But there is a price to be paid for it, and letting them live their own lives is the greatest part of that cost."

"I cannot begin to tell you how annoying it is to be married to a man who is so consistently right," Philly said. She leaned her tiny form against him, drawing strength from his solid presence. She did not see the terrible fear in his eyes.

For Sam and Morgan, the threat of their children's involvement was even more acute, for with sons rather than daughters, death on the battlefield was only too possible. They had not gainsaid Seth's enlistment, not only because he had presented them with a fait accompli, but also because they had known for a long time that when war came, he would be part of it.

And now it appeared that the war would drag on long enough to involve their younger sons, too. Adam would be eighteen in the coming year and Nigel seventeen. Morgan was keeping Adam as busy as possible at the shipyard, but his son was talking openly of volunteering for the navy. And though Nigel made no announcement of his intentions, he was devouring medical texts at an even greater rate than before and getting as much practical experience as possible by continuing his apprenticeship with a Baltimore doctor, "young" Dr. Benjamin, the son of the man who had taken Gincie's father under his wing years before. Sam and Morgan had no doubt that before long, Nigel would make his own bid for service in the war effort.

As much as they confided in each other, Morgan and Sam had private dreads, and neither dared to confess the full force of the terror that arose from the parallel nightmarish vision of their sons maimed or dead. For Morgan, it made each safe day at the shipyard an agony.

For Sam, the inner conflict was quite different. She did not know the full extent of it, but she suspected more and more that her father was spying for the Confederacy. For years, he had rarely left Brookhaven; now, he was suddenly making frequent trips to Washington, which was known to be swarming with Confederate agents. And of late he had begun to speak often of her half brother. Though Sam had once been fond of her half brother and half sister, they had long since lost contact when the two had drifted away from Brookhaven, finding it an unwelcoming place under the auspices of Violet, their father's third wife and their stepmother. The last Sam had known of them, they were both married and were living in tidewater Virginia, which was where their mother Lydia had come from.

The possibility that her father was supplying information to the Confederacy through her half brother or other Southern connections was so chilling, Sam tried not to think about it at all. But it returned again and again to haunt her. That the father she had always tried so hard to please should do anything that would add to the danger threatening her sons was intolerable. She longed to confide in someone and dared not. Morgan was out of the question. He had never liked her father and might well do violence over this, and Alex shared his sentiments.

Sam still cared about the acres of Brookhaven. She had spent so many years seeing to their prosperity, she could not abandon them now. And the slaves there depended on her management. But she now confined her visits to business, making no attempt to linger with her father.

The year drew to a close with each of the family fighting his or her private war, and though they tried to celebrate a happy Christmas together, it was uphill going with Flora, Caleb, and Rane still far away in England and Larissa electing to remain in Washington, though she promised she would come to the farm for New Year's Eve.

"I just can't leave the men on Christmas, Gran. They're so sad, lonely, and ill, and Christmas will only make it worse," she explained, and Alex did not try to sway her because she herself felt guilty for seeking the comfort of the family celebration. But she reminded herself that she had a duty to her family that superseded all else.

Alex had missed Rane since the day he left, but the prospect of the holidays without him was excruciating, and there was Gincie as well, sending word that both Travis and Abigail had generously suggested she go north to be with her family. However, as much as she missed them all, she did not feel she could leave Hawthorn, especially because Abigail was growing so frail.

"She is such a gallant woman," Gincie wrote, "but the war is breaking her heart and her health. I fear that Travis and I will not have her with us for much longer."

There was nothing Alex could do to ease Gincie's lot or to hasten Rane home, but she did interfere on Larissa's behalf. She knew her granddaughter did intend to make her patients' holiday brighter, but she was sure that the memory of her Christmas wedding at Wild Swan was another factor in her decision to stay away.

Alex sent Larissa the best, though not the most comfortable, Christmas gift she could think of: she let Reid Tratnor know that her granddaughter was staying in the city.

Alex had read his work and was very impressed. He wrote with an understated eloquence and had a keen eye for detail that kept events on a human level. She had gathered some information about him from Frank

Faber. Reid's parents were both dead, having been quite old when he was born, and his closest kin was a sister some years older than he who had her own life in upstate New York. But most of all, Alex was relying on her own impression of him. Reid Tratnor was a magnificent male, virile and compelling in every strong, lean line.

"I trust you will not harm my granddaughter in any way," Alex wrote to him, but it occurred to her that her own grandmother had surely issued the same warning to Rane when he had come to Gravesend and found Alex committed to St. John. She touched the golden swan necklace that she wore so often these days to make Rane seem closer, and she thought that if Larissa could find even half the love and passion she and Rane had known, any risk would be well worth it.

Chapter

36

Larissa kept her self-pity under control until she left the hospital after midnight on Christmas Eve to walk to her boarding house. She had refused all offers of an escort, knowing her calm was held on a slender thread.

She missed Luke so keenly that she did not think she could bear it. He had been a man to grow more fond of by the year, a man to grow old with. He had been so kind and gentle, it was inconceivable that he had died such a violent death. She wished, as she had so many times, that she had been more openly appreciative of him.

She felt the ice that had allowed her to go on so rationally thawing around her heart. She put a hand to her mouth, trying to stifle the first sound. The force of the sobs struggling to break free nearly doubled her over, a strange, seizing pain as if a huge hand was clenching inside of her.

The man seemed to appear from nowhere, his arm going around her to steady her against his chest, his voice coming to her before she had time to be frightened. "It's Reid Tratnor. It's all right."

She collapsed against him, and then dimly she realized it was not all right. It was horrid to have him witness this, the tears beginning to flow in a great river, all the tears she had not shed since the day Luke had been killed. She tried to wrench away from him.

"No, dear heart, you're not in any condition to be alone," Reid said, holding her fast.

He had waited in the cold with the intention of waylaying her in order to wish her a merry Christmas, after which he would ask her to dine with him on Christmas Day. But now that was all changed. Thoughts of propriety fled before her need, and he steered her across the Mall toward his hotel on Pennsylvania Avenue. She walked blindly, trying to stem the tide of emotion sweeping through her. By the time they reached their destination, her violent sobbing had diminished to forlorn sniffles.

Reid arranged the hood of her cloak so that it obscured her face, as he led her into the Willard Hotel, trusting that the late hour would have vanquished even the hardiest of Christmas revelers. He breathed a sigh of relief when he found that even the night clerk was sound asleep. And when they passed two gentlemen who had obviously had more than a little strong punch, Reid ignored them, saying, "If our son wishes to join the army, there is not much we can do about it. He is of age." He doubted the two drunks would remember in the morning that the speaker had been too young to have a son of enlistment age.

But his words finally penetrated the fog enveloping Larissa, and she stood stock-still in his room as he closed the door behind them. "What in the world were you talking about, and where are we?"

"I was spinning tales to throw a couple of observers off the scent because you are in my hotel room." Seeing her expression of hurt betrayal, he hastened to add, "Please, don't look like that! I swear I have no designs on your virtue, at least not tonight. You need to be with someone who cares about you."

She believed him, and it was too much. The tears started again. "I'm sorry," she choked. "I don't usually cry, but I can't seem to stop."

He removed her cloak and her gloves and enfolded her tenderly in his arms, resting his chin on her dark hair. "It's all right. I think you've needed to weep for a very long time. It's all right, Lissa mine."

He settled in a chair with her on his lap, and she was too dazed and tired to fight against the comfort he offered. He felt so warm, solid, and male, different in scent and textures from Luke, yet like him in the shelter he was offering. Luke had always wanted to keep her safe and happy, as she had wanted to keep him—as she had failed to keep him.

The words came in broken phrases, but Reid understood her guilt, sorrow, and anger over her husband's death. He picked out the words as if he were listening to her thoughts instead of just her voice.

"He didn't have to go, he didn't!" she protested. "He was a fine lawyer. There were other things he could have done; like my father, he could have tried to keep civil life running as well as the military. If I had loved him more, if he had believed I loved him more, he would not have gone."

Reid waited until her voice had dropped away before he spoke gently but firmly, willing her to listen. "Do you think only men thwarted in love go to war? It's not true. The best loved are there among the despised. And I count your husband a lucky man. He had you for his wife, his lover, and his friend. I think you do yourself an injustice."

She was quiet for a very long time, considering what he had said, considering everything, including the peculiarity of being in a hotel room in Reid Tratnor's arms. It felt too comfortable, and suddenly she wanted to shift his concentration away from herself. She felt as fragile as glass and as transparent, as if this man had seen everything inside her. And the oddest thing of all was that she did not find that entirely displeasing.

"What do you think will happen in the war? Gran showed me some of your articles; you seem to have a very clear view of things."

He knew she was deliberately changing the subject, but he was pleased that she had been interested enough to read his work and pleased that she made no move to leave the circle of his arms; it felt utterly right to have her there, even though he knew her surrender was a matter of exhaustion rather than anything else. Someday that would change, but for now, this was enough.

"The outcome of this war is not foreordained, no matter what fanatics on either side might say. And the South has some decided advantages. The war is being pursued on her soil, and while that is hard on the land and the populace, it is also true that the Southerners are defending their homes and know every inch of ground. And the Confederacy has a host of fine army and naval officers, while the president has yet to find a suitable leader for the Union armies—I do not think that McClellan will prove much better than General Scott."

Reid went on talking, giving Larissa the safe harbor of words away from her own problems. He pointed out that the South was making her own mistakes. The South had judged that by withholding cotton from European markets, she could force foreign powers to take her side. But the years right before the war had provided a glut of the stuff, leaving warehouses full of it in England and on the Continent. And now the blockade was tightening the noose. Though no one seemed to be taking much comfort from it, the Union navy had not done badly. They had taken Port Royal in South Carolina, and from there they could extend the supply lines for the blockading forces. Already it was becoming difficult for raiders to bring prizes to safe harbor, and privateers were turning into blockade runners to supply the markets in the South.

"When the South is ready to ship massive amounts of cotton again, I think it will be very difficult to get it out. And I believe Europe will, in the end, find other sources of cotton rather than taking up arms here. I pray that is so. My calculations go all awry if England joins the Confederacy. The Trent affair has severely damaged our cause; Mason and Slidell must be released."

Larissa knew what he was talking about; she had read the newspaper coverage, and her grandfather had written to her grandmother from England about it. Mason and Slidell, Confederate commissioners, had been on their way to England aboard the British mail steamer *Trent* when the steamer was stopped by the Union warship *San Jacinto*. The commissioners had been removed from the ship and were being held in Boston. The incident had provoked renewed sympathy for the Confederacy and a bad case of war fever in England. The illegal stopping and searching of ships had been a cause of tension between the two countries for most of the century. In the past the British had been the offenders. Now England was making it clear that she did not like having the tables turned in this game.

Larissa felt Reid's body tense, betraying his emotional involvement in the subject, though his voice remained calm. "The South prattles about states' rights and economics, and it is true that the needs of a state like Massachusetts and one like Louisiana differ, but the real difference is slavery. The South wants to preserve an institution that has been abolished in the rest of the civilized world. They would be counted among the nations of darkness just to keep the ease of life they enjoy and to keep the black man from walking among them without chains. And I believe that will strangle the South.

"The North has more guns, more food, more of everything from nails to gunpowder, and most of all, more free men. The South is going to choke on its own irony. It has vast reserves of men, but they are slaves, and to allow them to fight would be to acknowledge that slaves are men, not beasts of burden or backward children. And the North must allow the blacks their share of the fighting, too."

"It seems so logical," Larissa ventured. "You can see it, and so can I. If only everyone else could, the war would end."

"Ah, but I have not mentioned the passion of men that will make them cast themselves into the pit even for a wrong idea," Reid said. "And on the other side, you know there are men in the president's own party who want him to sue for peace at any cost. In their arrogance, they thought the war would be short and easily won. If they grow loud enough, they could undermine the Union's advantages from the inside."

Larissa wanted him to go on speaking; she liked the deep timbre of his voice as much as the intelligence of what he was saying. For the moment, she was no longer embarrassed that he had seen her in such a wild state. It no longer seemed important. She felt comfortable in his presence.

The sleep of total exhaustion overwhelmed her. One moment she felt her eyes closing, and the next she was awakening to the tantalizing smell of food late on Christmas morning.

"Merry Christmas," Reid said.

"Oh, my heavens!" Larissa gasped, hating the missish sound of the words even as she said them. But she was lying on his bed with her clothing loosened and her shoes off, and all her embarrassment rushed back. She had never felt so off balance with a man before. Reid Tratnor made her feel as if she were a green girl who had never known intimacy with a man.

He did not tease her, and his grin was reassuring. "Nothing untoward happened, though it may ruin my reputation forever. I give you my word. You fell asleep, and no wonder! I simply put you to bed. I did loosen your clothing, but I took no other liberties. And now that that is settled, would you care for something to eat? If you will forgive my saying so, you are too thin."

Larissa's smile dawned slowly to answer his. "Mr. Tratnor, you are an exceedingly kind man. I would feel fortunate to count you among my friends."

He did not mistake her meaning. "It will do for the time being, but I want more than that, Larissa Carstairs, much more." He said it so matter-of-factly, she could not take offense, and in any case, she was suddenly very hungry. She seemed to exist on the most basic levels with Reid Tratnor.

The seemingly insurmountable problem of leaving the hotel discreetly was no problem at all as managed by Reid. He walked out confidently with Larissa on his arm, and anyone listening to the couple heard him assuring her that he would do his utmost to help increase subscriptions to the Sanitary Commission.

Only when they reached the entrance to her boardinghouse, did it occur to Larissa to ask Reid how he had known she would be at the hospital the previous night.

"I'm a newspaperman," he proclaimed in mock affront. "I have my sources of information, particularly when I am interested in the subject."

"I am going to Wild Swan for New Year's Eve. Would you like to come?" She suddenly very much wanted him to accept; he made her feel less lonely, something not even her family had been able to do since Luke's death.

"I would," he answered without hesitation. "But if you change your mind, I will not hold you to the invitation."

"I won't change my mind, but you may change yours without giving offense, should you decide you prefer livelier company."

"My, aren't we being polite," Reid observed. "Believe me, anything livelier than your family would try a stronger man than I."

As he had waited for her outside the hospital in order not to cause gossip, so he let her go inside the boarding house by herself, indicating that he was not going to presume on the lapse that had resulted in her spending the night in his hotel. But as she went inside, Larissa heard his voice following her. "Please, no more 'Mr. Tratnor'; my name is 'Reid.' "

Alex greeted Reid with visible pleasure when he arrived with Larissa at Wild Swan. But neither Reid nor Alex betrayed their conspiracy. Only later when they could not be overheard did Alex mention the subject.

"Young man, I congratulate and thank you. My granddaughter looks alive for the first time since her husband died."

He studied her for a long moment before he decided to confide in her. "It did not go quite as I hoped. I wished only to cheer her, deviously hoping she might think of me happily later on. Instead, I found her just as all the sorrow of the world caught up with her." He described the hopeless way Larissa had cried, his own voice not quite steady. "So now we are to be friends, she says, but I'm not certain of that. I know it is possible that she will remember her grief and loss of control every time she sees me."

"You know a good deal about people, Mr. Tratnor. It undoubtedly contributes much to the quality of your prose. While what you say *is* possible, I think it more probable that she will remember the ease and comfort there is in knowing someone has witnessed the worst and has not turned away. But I caution you to patience. Lissa mistrusts her own charm and is apt to think there is some subtle trickery involved when she attracts men."

"Ma'am, I don't need it to be easy, just possible somewhere down the road. I've never felt this way about a woman before, but I knew what I wanted the minute I saw her. I can't explain it; accepting it seems to be my only choice. And for her, I'll learn patience."

"Keep yourself alive as well. It would be too hard were she to lose you, too. And I would also miss you."

He raised her hand to his lips. "Thank you. I promise, the last thing I would ever do is hurt Lissa. I plan to live to a ripe old age with her beside me."

Alex watched him walk away, and she thought that in a sense, Larissa was right in her self-judgment—even though she saw herself as cool and unemotional, she could effortlessly attract even such a man as Reid Tratnor.

Alex wanted to urge Larissa not to waste time, to reach out and take what happiness she could find with Reid, but she knew that would be the worst thing she could do. Inwardly she sighed; here was her granddaughter keeping her distance from this attractive young man while she herself would have given almost anything to have Rane beside her. Christmas had been hard enough; beginning 1862 without him was worse. But she reminded herself again and again that he was safe in England, not facing death as so many of the young were.

Nothing marked the perversity of war more than its reaping of young lives while it left the old to continue. She considered the lives so long interwoven with her own; they were all old now.

For the first time, Mavis and Timothy Bates looked truly ancient to her, though they both still worked a full day. The tavern had a good reputation, and Annapolis was still capital of the state and the county seat of Anne Arundel County, but the war had drastically altered the little town. Annapolis was suspected of harboring even more secessionist sympathy than Baltimore, and the Federal presence was now a fact of life.

Several high state officials had been imprisoned, accused of seditious views, and more than one critic accused the president of being a tyrant for this action. The Naval Academy was gone, moved to Rhode Island for safety.

Alex thought that the last of the Bateses' youth had gone with the young cadets. Timothy and Mavis were now apprehensive instead of peaceful, as they had expected to be at this time in their lives. They had grown too old to adapt easily to all the changes.

The upheavals of war spared no one. Jed and Mabel Barlow had watched stoically as both their Jimmys, son and grandson, had gone off in the fall to enlist. Jim and his son had approached Alex diffidently, but their resolve was firm; there was no longer so much need of their skills at Wild Swan, while the Union army could use all the good horse handlers it could get. Both of them were farriers with the army now, making up for their lack of size with the skills Samson had taught them.

Alex would have liked to forbid all the young workers to leave Wild Swan, but she knew she could not stop them any more than she could her own grandsons. And she was in the odd position of being as torn for those who could not go as she was for those who went.

Though the navy had accepted blacks for years, albeit for the lowest positions in almost every case, the army would not enlist them at all. Alex sympathized with Della, who had put it very well when she said, "I do not want Jotham to go soldiering, but at the same time, I want him to have the right to go. That the Union army will not have him makes them no better than the Rebels."

It was an unanswerable indictment, and Alex believed that it would change before the war ended. She believed it because every communication from Rane stressed how important it was that the war be justified on the basis of abolishing slavery rather than on the issue of states' rights. Rane and Caleb were convinced that nothing less would prevent England's eventual support of the Confederacy. And if the official justification of the war changed, so surely would the status of blacks in regard to the army.

Others among the staff—Polly and Calvin, Cassie and Ned—so odd to find that they too had grown old, the women close in age to Alex, the men slightly older, too old for war. But Polly's two daughters were both married with children of their own, and Alex had no doubt that their husbands would be off with the army as soon as enlistment was open to them. They did not speak openly of it, but she knew they wanted the power of slave owners forever broken. She was glad that they, like Jotham, were not sailors, else they might otherwise be gone already.

The swans and geese were back on the Chesapeake, pursuing their own cycles apart from the violence of men, leery of the hunter's bullet. Often Alex watched the birds passing over Wild Swan and sometimes stopping to feed as they had for as long as she had been here and long before that. She wished winter could last forever. She would forgo even the flowers of spring and the plenty of summer to keep the cold upon the land. Armies seldom marched in winter, when bad weather could bog down everything from caissons to foot soldiers.

The wish was futile. The days went on; the seasons turned; and in February, the battles began to flower in malignant blossoms of a bloody spring.

Chapter

37

During January, Larissa found herself enjoying Reid's company more and more. He proved exceedingly helpful in such matters as finding more spacious quarters for them in the crowded city when Anthea joined her sister to work with the wounded. Reid would appear just when the sisters' spirits were at their lowest ebb and coax them to go out to supper or some other diversion, always making it clear that Anthea was welcome. And when Alex was in the city, she was included as well, Reid claiming that he would surely be arrested for monopolizing the company of no fewer than three of the most beautiful women in the capital.

Though Larissa wasn't conscious of it, having her grandmother so obviously charmed by Reid increased her own estimation of him.

And then, quite suddenly, he was gone, heading for the western theater of the war to cover it for his paper.

"I think it is going to prove the most important staging area of the war for some time," he said. "This idea of Richmond as the only prize worth taking is already changing. It may be the capital and heart of the

Confederacy, but it can't exist without the rest of the South, and cutting off the western part of the South will inflict a serious wound, isolating her from some of her richest acreage and foreign supplies."

It was only by chance that Reid had found Larissa alone, and she thought more of that than of what he was saying and felt angry, though she knew she had no right—it was she who had set the distance in their relationship, so she could hardly begrudge his failure to arrange a private meeting.

"Don't let anything happen to yourself," she said abruptly, and he smiled, thinking of her grandmother saying the same thing. "I'm a correspondent, remember, not a soldier. But I thank you for the concern. I'll write when I can. Please tell your sister and your grandmother good-bye for me."

He made no attempt to embrace or kiss her, but as he walked away, he turned and winked. "I haven't given up, you know, so don't marry anyone else while I'm gone."

Though she kept her observations to herself, Alex was pleased by the signs Larissa showed of missing Reid. Larissa suddenly had a keen interest in all the war news from the West.

On March 8, Washington was thrown into yet another panic when the Confederate ironclad *Merrimac*, which was called the *Virginia* by the Confederates though she had been built from the ruins of the U.S.S. *Merrimac*, steamed out against Union ships in Hampton Roads. This eight-mile-long channel where three Virginia rivers flow into the Chesapeake Bay was of importance to both sides and had been the site of a stalemate for ten months. But the *Merrimac* seemed destined to change all of that, as she easily destroyed two Union frigates, proving how vulnerable wooden ships were to ironclad vessels that could maneuver close while shot bounced off their metal shells.

In the capital many, including the president, some said, expected to see the *Merrimac* steaming up the Potomac. But by happy chance, the Union's own ironclad, the *Monitor*, having set out from New York on March 6, arrived in Hampton Roads the night of March 8 and the next day fought a four-hour duel with the *Merrimac*. The result was a draw, but the Confederate ship was compelled to head back to the Virginia shore, thus ceasing its sinking of Union vessels.

The *Merrimac* was described as a "barn roof belching smoke," and the *Monitor* as a "cheesebox on a raft," and from the engravings in the newspapers, Morgan judged both ships to be incredibly ugly, abortions of all the beauty of the shipwright's craft. But he did not mistake their importance—nearly impervious to shot and able to ram frailer ships, they surely signaled the beginning of the end of the wooden naval fleet.

But throughout March, most of the action of the war was on fresh water and in the West, as Union forces began a flanking movement, going against Southern strongholds in the Mississippi Valley. Fort Henry on the Tennessee River, Fort Donelson near Nashville, and then Nashville itself surrendered to the Union. Seen from Reid Tratnor's point of view, these victories engineered by General Ulysses S. Grant and Commodore Andrew J. Foot were of major importance, but in the East, the view continued to be that nothing could be as vital as taking Richmond.

President Lincoln, frustrated at McClellan's inaction, removed him as general in chief of the Union armies, though McClellan remained head of the Army of the Potomac. And early in April, the peninsular campaign against Richmond began, hampered by the activities of the Confederate General Thomas J. Jackson, nicknamed "Stonewall" for standing fast in the Battle of Bull Run. Toward the end of March, Jackson had begun his own campaign in the Shenandoah Valley of Virginia, thus pulling away Union forces needed for the peninsular campaign.

Still with Richmond as the goal, the Union Army of the Potomac advanced toward Yorktown, Virginia, early in April, but the fiercest action was still in the West where the Battle of Shiloh cost so many thousands dead on both sides that to call it a victory seemed obscene, and the Union troops had been too exhausted to chase the Confederates.

Larissa had come to depend on Reid's letters, and she read every one of his articles she could obtain, but all communication stopped after Shiloh. She knew she could write to his paper in New York and ask them what they knew, but she was too terrified of the answer. She kept trying to make herself believe that it was simply a matter of his being too busy in the aftermath of the battle to write to her, but that did not explain, as the days went by, why none of his crisp prose appeared in print.

Without consulting her granddaughter, Alex took the action Larissa would not, explaining in her letter to the paper that she and her family were close friends of the newspaperman. The answer was brief; the paper was sorry to confirm that Mr. Tratnor had, despite his status as a noncombatant, been seriously wounded at Shiloh. Reports were garbled, but they had every hope of his recovery.

For days Alex debated whether or not to show Larissa the reply—both of them knew only too well how many of the "seriously wounded" died—but finally she decided that her granddaughter could not suffer more than she was suffering now.

Larissa stared at the words for a long time, and then she said, "At least he is not listed among the dead. I will go on believing he is still alive." She paused, and then she snarled, "I could kill him for this! He promised he would take care."

Alex understood her anger perfectly and hoped it would sustain her until they knew for certain.

Toward the end of April, Union Admiral Farragut took New Orleans, and all Alex could think of was her last visit there when Rane had been with her and both of them had witnessed the arrogance of the city that felt itself so far away from Union power that it could never be captured.

She longed for Rane more than ever as the ripening season promised more and more damage. But with the death of the Prince Consort in December, the Union's cause had become even more difficult to argue in England. Prince Albert had been a strong voice for neutrality; a voice now silenced. The release of the Confederates, Mason and Slidell, in January had helped somewhat, but Rane still felt obliged to remain in England, though he wrote to Alex:

> *I cannot help but be struck by the absurdity of an old free*
> *trader dealing with England's high officials. Perhaps sitting*
> *through so many futile meetings and being so distant from*
> *you is my punishment for breaking the law so many years*
> *ago.*

For her birthday, he had had an exquisite pair of golden earrings made to match the swan necklace. On each earring, a swan bowed its head and dangled by a golden chain from a little flower. If the two earrings were held together, the curve of neck and bend of head formed a heart just as the swans of the necklace did, just as she and Rane together formed one heart, Alex thought.

Rane also sent some cuttings from choice English roses, as if to remind her that life did go on, no matter what.

She was touched and pleased by the gifts, but nothing could make up for his absence. She longed for a Union victory so decisive that England would lose all interest in helping the South, but shuddered at the probable cost of such a victory and thought of it in the very personal terms of Seth and Travis.

Seth had tried to reassure his family that the altered role of the cavalry would do much to increase his safety. Though many soldiers on both sides still used conventional muskets, the advent of the rifled musket and the rifle itself, as well as rifled barrels on cannon, had so increased the distance and accuracy of weaponry that it had proved suicidal for cavalry to advance boot to boot in the wake of the infantry or to launch daring head-on attacks, as they had in previous wars. The spiral grooves in the barrels of the guns sent their pointed lead missiles in a stabilizing spin of far greater velocity than the old musket balls could achieve. The cavalrymen might dismount and engage in hand-to-hand combat in heavy actions, but now their standard role was to scout for their armies, to screen their armies' movements, and to raid the communication and supply lines of the enemy. It was no guarantee of survival, but surely it was better than being uselessly mowed down in endless rows. Seth had found that he did not think much of his own survival day to day; it was the responsibility of keeping his men alive that rode him like a demon. A slight miscalculation this way or that, and it was only too easy to lead the men into a deadly hail of rifle or cannon fire. And though he did not like to consider it, it occurred to him too often that Travis and others like him on the other side were seeking to fight and yet protect their own men as well. Seth liked what he knew of Travis Culhane, and the fact that the man was now the enemy made the war seem like the distortions of a nightmare. There were days when Seth could make no sense of it at all, but he kept on with his duty because to do otherwise was unthinkable.

Reid was not even a soldier, and yet he had been hurt, and Alex thought of him often, as if he were another of her grandchildren. There was no word from him at all until Larissa received a message in mid-May, delivered to her at the hospital.

Alex saw her begin to tremble, a slip of paper clutched in her hand, and she immediately assumed that Reid was dead.

"My dear child," she said, putting her arm around her, but Larissa shook her head, tried to speak, and failing, handed her grandmother the note which read: "I am at Willard's Hotel once again and would appreciate a visit from you if you could manage the time. I've missed you."

Finally Larissa managed to speak. "How dare he! How dare he let me worry for so long and then send word only when he is back in the city!"

"There is some reasonable explanation," Alex insisted. "Above all things, Reid is a compassionate man, and he would not hurt you if he could prevent it. Perhaps he did send word, but it was not delivered. Perhaps many things. The only way to find out is to go to him. If you don't, I will. I've grown very fond of that young man."

When Larissa knocked on his hotel room door, she was so nervous, she could scarcely open the door at his bidding. At her first sight of him, all nervousness was eclipsed by her concern.

"Oh, Christ!" Reid groaned, and then he simply stared at her. She had not identified herself outside, and he had assumed she was one of the hotel staff or one of his newspaper cronies. He had expected her to send a written reply saying when she would come, if she would at all. He knew he had some explaining to do, but at the moment all he could think of was that he looked as unkempt as any drunk.

He needed a shave, and his hair was mussed. His face was gaunt, his eyes ringed by shadows and too bright. He was seated in a chair and wearing a dressing gown, and when he tried to struggle to his feet, Larissa flew to him.

"No, please, don't get up! I am sure you ought to be in bed, not sitting up at all." Her hand reached out to test the temperature of his skin, the same gesture she had used on countless patients at the hospital, but now it was Reid's flesh that radiated fever and sent a chill through her. "Where are you hurt? What did the doctors say?" It dawned on her abruptly that he had not warned her of his coming because he had not been sure he could make it. The handwriting on the note should have warned her; it had been far less boldly etched than his usual script.

She cradled his head against her breast as if such intimacy was perfectly normal between them. "My darling Reid, what would I have done had I lost you, too?"

The warm softness of her, the scent of her, and the fever of his illness swept away his control, and he heard himself babbling things he had never meant to tell her.

"I've seen battles before, but not like Shiloh. I lost my ability to function as an observer. The pain and screaming and death became my own. In the two days, there was heat and rain, dust and mud, blood ran in ribbons over the ground, and in some places the brush caught fire and burned the wounded to death. Children, so many just children, shot to pieces. Children from both sides clinging together through the night in some places. And most of the time, not even the location of the field hospital was safe, so the wounded carried in for aid were still in danger." Everyone has a job to do on a battlefield, Reid knew, and his was to observe and report what he saw. He had not done that. "I tried to help the wounded until I got hit myself. It was useless; I doubt I saved even one of them."

There was such despair in his voice, she could not bear it. "You're wrong! Sometimes it is the smallest difference that saves a life, a sip of water, bleeding stopped just in time, and most of all, hope given to the wounded by knowing someone is trying to help. The wonder is not that so many die, it is that any live in the midst of such destruction."

It was not only that she spoke with such conviction, it was also that hers was the voice of experience. He felt his anger and despair ease, but the sheer will that had sustained him in order to return to her faded as well. Against the doctors' advice, he had endured a jarring journey east by wagon and rail with the sole intention of seeing Larissa again. He had accomplished that. Even the fever and pain didn't matter now.

Larissa felt him slumping against her, felt the unhealthy heat increasing. She called his name urgently, and then coaxed, "Please, just hold on a moment more. I need your help to get you to bed. You'll feel better when you're lying down."

Anxious to please her, Reid roused himself, but it took all their combined strength to get him out of the chair. Larissa staggered and nearly went to her knees from the weight of him leaning on her as they moved toward the bed.

"Just a few more steps," she pled.

When they reached the bed, Reid sank down on it with a groan. His eyes closed, his skin gleamed with sweat. The fever spots on his cheekbones were the only color in his face.

"I'll be right back. I'm going to send for my grandmother," Larissa told him, but she wasn't sure he heard her. She went downstairs and dispatched a messenger. When she reentered Reid's room, he was murmuring her name.

"I'm here, my love, I'm here," she assured him, taking his hand. She found it very natural to call him her love.

"Thought I dreamed . . ." he began, but it took too much energy to talk.

He had been favoring his left side, and his dressing gown had gaped over his chest when he lay down, exposing dark whorls of hair and a bandage beginning above his waist, but she still didn't know the exact nature of his injury. She decided there was nothing she could or should do until her grandmother arrived.

Alex brought Dr. Grover with her, and it was all Larissa could do not to burst into tears of relief at the sight of them.

"Well, my boy, you didn't take very good care of yourself after all," Alex chided gently, but she was wholly professional as she assisted the doctor, and when they needed answers, she questioned Reid insistently until they got the information.

There was a burn on his left forearm, but it was healing well. The same could not be said for his side. He had been hit by a minié bullet from a muzzle-loading rifle. An army doctor had done his best in digging it out, the depth of the bullet's penetration having been somewhat deflected by a rib, but it had been some time before Reid had been treated, and by then the effects of exposure had set in. He'd suffered fever and chills that had impeded healing, and Dr. Grover diagnosed pus pockets as the cause for the extreme tenderness and jolts of pain Reid was still suffering.

"But he's strong," the doctor hastened to add. "He made it all this way."

"I want to take him home, to Wild Swan," Alex said. "Would that endanger him further?"

Dr. Grover glanced toward Larissa, who still stood beside the bed holding Reid's hand as she had all during the ordeal of the examination. "I think that with a night's rest he will be fit to make the journey, as long as your granddaughter is with him. You know as well as I that there is far more to healing than the few medicines and procedures we can offer."

There was nothing Larissa wanted more than to take Reid to the farm, but she was instantly stricken with guilt.

"Your sister will be perfectly all right without us," Alex told her firmly, "and we will be back here soon enough to help the wounded again. Reid is the only one who matters at the moment, selfish as that may be."

For Reid, the next days were physically agonizing, from the jolting wagon trip to the farm to the hot fomentations applied to his wound and the lancing of the infection, but it didn't matter; he had never been so cherished in his life, not even when he had been a small child. His elderly parents had been well-meaning but reserved, more interested in duty than in affection in all aspects of their lives, and his sister had been much the same when she had taken over responsibility for the boy who was already a

hell-raiser by her standards. She had done her best, but it had been difficult for her with a husband and her own family to begin. Reid had been
sent to good schools, and he had profited because his mind was quick and
curious, but part of him had been starved for affection and still was. At
Wild Swan, it was given to him constantly, effortlessly.

If Larissa wasn't there when he opened his eyes, then Alex was or
Della or even Larissa's mother, who he knew had come to take a closer
look at the man who meant something to her eldest daughter. He didn't
mind; he thought Philly was enchanting, so tiny compared to her tall
husband and daughter, and so full of life and laughter. And it was easy to
see that Larissa had derived her habit of directness as much from her
mother as from her grandmother.

He had still been very uncomfortable the first day Philly had sat
with him, and an unwise movement of his torso had brought an involuntary gasp of pain. Unlike the other women, Philly had panicked.

"Mr. Tratnor, should I summon someone else?" she asked anxiously.

"No, I'm okay," he managed.

"I am quite good at reading aloud or writing a letter if you wish,"
Philly said, "but I am no use at all in nursing the sick. I haven't the nerve
or the skill; I tried by volunteering at a hospital in Baltimore when some of
the wounded started being brought to the city. I disgraced myself by
fainting dead away the first day. My mother-in-law and my daughter are
terribly competent; I'm surprised they've allowed me to remain in the
family."

Reid smiled at her and assured her that he did not need anyone
else to minister to him. Indeed, he thought she was doing very well; her
bright chatter had diverted him until the pain eased.

He grew to be very comfortable with Philly in a short time, and he
thought he ought to be honest about his intentions regarding Larissa,
though her mother had not pressed him in any way on the subject.

"I do love your daughter very much," he began.

Philly smiled at him. "I know you do. It shows even in the way you
say her name."

"I want to marry her, but I've decided it oughtn't to be until the
war is over. It sounds hideously naive, as it is, but I didn't really have a
sense of my own mortality until Shiloh. And now it's not that I'm afraid to
die, though God knows I would rather put it off for fifty years or so, but I
am afraid of leaving Larissa widowed again and perhaps with a child."

Philly gazed at him thoughtfully. "As Larissa's mother, I am grateful for your concern for her as well as for your love, but I do not think my daughter will accept the delay easily. I swear to you she has kept her own counsel in this, but I would have to be blind to mistake her affection for you. It is quite, quite different from what she felt for Luke, and that is how it should be. She knew him for years before they married; I doubt she will have the same patience with you, and my daughter can be very stubborn." Philly's eyes sparkled. "She gets it from her father."

But Larissa did not react as Philly expected when Reid explained his position, adding, "I hope you understand that the most important thing in all of this is that I still love you, and I still intend to marry you. It is only a matter of timing."

"How very logical you sound," Larissa observed, but she showed no anger. Instead her eyes were veiled, an unfathomable silver, and a little smile played on her mouth, as if she knew a secret she had no intention of sharing. "And how much you take for granted. I do not remember saying I would marry you at all."

He looked so stricken, she could not tease him further. "But of course I will. I didn't intend to fall in love with you, but I have."

She leaned over him and very deliberately she began to kiss him, tracing the outline of his mouth with her tongue and pressing her lips against his, first softly and then more insistently. Luke had been an affectionate, considerate lover, and if she had not felt any great arousal with him, still she had learned from him to be at ease with a man's body. But already this was different; just touching Reid conjured warm currents deep inside her.

Reid was completely taken aback, not only by her action, but by his response to it—one moment he had been in control, and now it was all he could do not to tumble her on the bed and take her right there. He wrenched his mouth away from hers.

"Lissa! Good lord, your mother or your grandmother might come in at any moment!"

"Such a prude you are," she accused, laughing. "They would probably applaud. You've set your rules, but I shall play by my own."

In the ensuing days, he discovered what she meant. Every look and even the most casual touch signaled her desire. He was no boy; he was an experienced man, and outwardly he remained controlled and sure that his course was the only sensible one, but inwardly, he acknowledged that she was playing havoc with his senses. One part of him hated the idea of leaving Wild Swan, but another was anxious to get back to work, conceding that work was surely the only thing that might take his mind off the constant contemplation of what it would be like to make love to Larissa.

Though there would be some stiffness in the scar tissue of his wound for some time, he was feeling fit again, and he wanted to be there when the peninsular campaign was decided. The paper wanted him in the East again, and he had already missed the Battle of Seven Pines near Richmond, wherein only the arrival of reinforcements had saved the Union from another disastrous defeat, and the result had been inconclusive, with both sides suffering heavy losses. Before Seven Pines, the Army of the Potomac had taken both Yorktown and Williamsburg, Virginia, but Richmond was still the goal.

Larissa came to him on the warm June night that was to be his last at Wild Swan. She came to him when the household was settled and quiet. She came to him cloaked in a thin gown, candlelight, and her love.

"Marriage can wait, but this cannot," she whispered, and he saw that for all her seeming boldness, she was shivering at the risk of his rejection, her eyes huge and apprehensive. She put the candle down and very slowly she let her gown fall to the floor.

He could see the lovely young curves of her body and her trembling. He opened his arms, and she came to him, stretching her body the length of his with a little sigh, and he was lost.

Making love to her became an act of faith, faith that it was only the beginning and not the end. With his hands and his mouth, he learned her secret—the essential woman of her that would hold him in thrall until the day he died, whether that was to be tomorrow or years and years in the future.

With Luke, never for an instant had Larissa lost the consciousness of their separateness; she had always perceived their bodies as different territories coming together as well as they could. With Reid she felt as if she moved in the ebb and flow of a tide as great as the sea, one moment herself, the next indistinguishable from him, and all of it so exquisitely pleasurable that she cried his name over and over as he thrust high inside her.

"You win, dear heart," he said later as they lay at rest, their bodies still entwined. "We'll marry immediately."

"No, we won't," she countered calmly. "We will wait, just as you wished us to before I seduced you. I will not have you accusing me of entrapping you years from now when we are gray and discontented with each other."

"The gray will come, but not the discontent," he said, nuzzling her breasts, diverted by the image of their old age together. But then he realized that beneath her teasing manner, she was serious. "You must reconsider! For God's sake, you might well be with child from this night!"

"Nothing could delight me more," she replied. "But we can deal with that if and when it happens. In the meantime, I do not want to marry you until you can give me your full attention. I have come to understand what kind of man you are. For all your easy charm, you do not take anything lightly. And marriage least of all. It will be very important to you, but right now, the only thing I want you to concentrate on is your job and staying alive while you do it."

"Do you think I will not carry you in my heart and my mind simply because we have not exchanged formal vows?" he queried.

"I think you will. Indeed, I know you will, as I will carry you. But don't ask me how I know—it will not be the same distraction as a wife. I do not want you torn asunder by differing obligations. I want you to return to me in one piece inside and out."

He hated to admit it, but her reasoning was sound. To him, no matter how independent she was, marrying her would mean assuming responsibility for her, a responsibility impossible to fulfill from the battle-fields. And his prior reason for not wishing marriage was still valid; he did not want her to suffer widowhood again, or worse, to his mind, to be burdened with a cripple.

"You are as wise as you are beautiful," he conceded, "but I hope your grandmother never finds out about tonight."

"My grandmother would be the last one to condemn us," Larissa told him, and he listened in fascination to what she knew of Alex's history. "She is very brave. She misses my grandfather terribly, and it is horrid for her to have the horses gone, too, but she carries on. If she can do that with so much changed and missing in her life, I can wait for you."

They lay holding each other for a long time until reluctantly Larissa left him to go back to her own room. Reid stayed awake longer, savoring the scent and warmth of her that remained behind and thinking that he would very much like to survive to be part of her family and to create a family of their own with her.

Chapter

38

From June 25 to July 1, Reid covered the series of engagements in Virginia that at their end were deemed the Seven Days' Battles; Seth fought on one side, Travis on the other; and Alex, Larissa, Anthea, and countless other women and also men nursed the human wreckage that flooded into the capital from battles that raged through forests, fields, and fever-ridden swamps. Oak Grove, Mechanicsville, Gaines Mill, Garnett's and Golding's Farms, Savage's Station, and Allen's Farm, White Oak Swamp, Malvern Hill—Alex heard the names as an eerie litany of death destined to be written in the American heart as Edgehill, Turnham Green, and so many others were still inscribed in English hearts, though more than two hundred years had passed since England's civil war. And though she felt traitorous for thinking it, she could not help but admire J. E. B. "Jeb" Stuart's daring three-day ride around the Federal army, a feat which had given Lee a clear idea of where Union weaknesses lay. Travis had been with the dashing, plume-hatted Stuart.

When the battles were over, the Union forces pulled back to Harrison's landing on the James River while the Confederates withdrew to protect Richmond. The Confederate capital had not been taken; the peninsular campaign was over; and General Robert E. Lee, once superintendent of West Point and the man to whom President Lincoln had offered command of the Union armies at the outbreak of the war, began to acquire the stature of a legend as commander of the Confederate Armies of Northern Virginia.

Alex wondered if she would ever get the stench of this summer out of her nostrils. Blood, rotting flesh, sweat, human excrement, and the miasmal vapor of the polluted Potomac ripening in the heat combined in a hellish perfume that made her long for the sweet scents of the farm— even the sharp, ammoniacal fumes of mucking out a stall were preferable to this.

But like the others, she stayed, trying to make the wounded more comfortable, too often unable to do anything but hold the young, shattered bodies in her arms until they died.

Adam volunteered for the navy, and Alex tried to take comfort from the fact that it was likely that if he went to sea at all, it would be aboard one of the blockading ships along the Southern coast, and his worst enemy would be boredom. The Confederate navy did not have the strength to confront either squadron of the blockading fleet directly, and most of the Confederate energy at sea now went into raiding Northern commerce or running goods past the blockade.

Alex knew Morgan accepted Adam's relative safety, but neither one of them tried to convince Sam of it.

"I know there is nothing I can do about my sons marching off one by one, but I am not prepared to be reasonable about it!" Sam announced, and they took her at her word.

Though Nigel held off because he was only seventeen and because he truly did not want to break his mother's heart, it was increasingly evident that he had the skills to be of use in the war.

"He's as adept as many physicians twice his age," Dr. Cameron claimed, and Dr. Benjamin averred that the boy was nearly at the stage where the doctor would feel safe turning his practice over to him. "But don't tell him that," Dr. Benjamin added good-humoredly, "as I am not ready to step aside."

They all knew that Nigel's dedication, while in one sense typical of him, had been made more intense by the war, as if he felt unbearable pressure to learn everything he could in order to soon be able to treat the wounded more directly than he did now.

Anthea burned with the same fever to serve. The war had provided her with new heroines, including Dr. Mary Walker, who, though she held a degree in medicine, was working as a nurse for Union casualties. Dr. Walker was an ardent advocate of women's rights, and she shocked many by her habit of wearing male attire so that skirts would not encumber her work, but few disputed her skill.

Anthea was even more interested in Clara Barton, a Massachusetts-born woman who had worked in the Patent Office in the capital before the war but was now being called the "angel of the battlefield" because she had organized her nurses into efficient units that served right at the battlefields rather than in the safety of cities behind the lines. Miss Barton believed in treating the wounded of both sides without prejudice.

"I will wait until next year," Anthea announced to Alex and Larissa, "but if the war isn't over by then, I'm going to find work closer to the fighting."

Alex and Larissa exchanged a glance, both of them thinking that while Philly and Blaine were going to be appalled by this new plan, Anthea would undoubtedly hold to her course.

"The president would do well to appoint her commander of the Union armies," Larissa remarked to her grandmother. "She is surely more determined than the men he has appointed so far."

Harriet Tubman was another of the strong-willed women dedicated to alleviating the suffering of the wounded, and she had attached herself to the Union army. Alex believed the rumors of her leading Union expeditions into enemy territory; the woman knew the land well from her many trips to bring fugitive slaves to safety before the war. Alex encountered her once in Washington, and to her surprise, the rather dour little woman studied her closely for a moment and then smiled slightly, saying, "I 'members you, Miz Falconer. De Lord bless you."

The summer dragged on. General Henry W. Halleck was appointed general in chief of the Union armies by the president, and Ulysses S. Grant was left in command of the Army of West Tennessee, though Reid contended that from what he'd learned of Halleck and Grant when he was in the West, he thought Grant would be the better choice for supreme command.

Reid was in Washington briefly in August, but it was a frustrating visit for both him and Larissa. He was weary, preoccupied, and depressed.

"The war has only been going on for a little more than a year, and yet it seems as if it has been forever."

"It has," Larissa said. "It was so long in coming with so much bitterness on both sides before it began, and now there are so many dead and dying, no wonder it seems an eternity."

They had no time to be alone, and when he left again, Larissa felt even more empty than before. She was not pregnant, and though that was far better for the practical considerations of life, she did not feel practical about Reid and wished she were carrying his child.

August brought a Union defeat by Stonewall Jackson at Cedar Mountain, Virginia, and it also brought an outcry for emancipation spearheaded by an editorial written by Horace Greeley. The president responded by reiterating his belief that the war must be to save the Union and "and not either to save or to destroy slavery."

With the same slightly alien view she had had of her adopted country since the beginning, Alex could sympathize with both sides. On the one hand, the president continued to hope that some peace could be reached without total ruin on both sides, while on the other, the Abolitionists and many less radical felt a moral bankruptcy and needed the war to be put on a higher plane to justify the enormous suffering it was causing, to justify the continued fratricide.

And the outside consideration remained the need to keep England and other foreign powers from intervening on the Rebels' behalf.

Because of news from England, for several weeks during the summer Morgan lived with a new and wholly unexpected terror that made him more conscious of his mother as a woman than he had ever been before.

Trusting that he would keep the secret as Rane wished, Caleb wrote to tell Morgan that Rane was gravely ill with typhoid fever. In the starkest terms Caleb wrote that the crisis was fast approaching and that there was no time for Alex to rush to England. If Rane was going to die, it would surely be before Alex could reach him, and if he was going to survive, Rane did not want his wife to have what he considered the needless worry of knowing he was ill. It was all he talked about in his lucid moments. But Caleb felt that someone at home ought to know what was happening

As Morgan sweated out the days of waiting for further word, he wished fervently that he was not the one who knew. He could hardly face Sam, let alone his mother. But to share the news would accomplish nothing more than to make someone else as miserable as he was.

He began to have nightmares wherein he had to tell his mother that his father was dead; in the nightmares it was always the same: his mother's face froze in a rictus of agony, and then she simply ceased to exist, as if the earth had swallowed her.

He had always viewed his mother as being enormously strong and determined, and he did not see her as less now, but he did not want to find out how much of her strength came from having been loved so dearly for so long by Rane Falconer. And the threat of the death made Morgan more aware than he had ever been of the depth of his own love for his father; he hated the idea that that warm, wise presence might never grace his life again.

When he cried out at night, Sam assumed he was dreaming of

their sons in battle, as she too often did, and she held him closer in her arms, seeking to establish their own island of comfort in the troubled sea.

Morgan was desperately worried about his mother without being able to tell her why, and though he knew the wisest course was to avoid her as much as possible until he knew the outcome of Rane's illness, he found himself paying visits to her in Washington or at Wild Swan so frequently that finally she said, "Morgan, while I am always glad to see you, I do not understand why I have seen so much of you lately."

"I worry about you. I think you are doing too much," he replied, wishing his voice did not sound so harried.

"Truly that is not the case," Alex reassured him, and suddenly it occurred to her that Morgan was trying to fill his father's shoes, watching over her and caring for her in Rane's absence. "I really am all right," she said, "though I haven't heard from your father for quite some time now. I trust Gwenny and Flora are keeping an eye on him, but it troubles me that he is being kept so busy he hasn't time to write."

"I expect he's working hard that he may come home that much sooner," Morgan offered, and it took all his willpower to meet his mother's eyes—eyes like his father's, eyes like his own.

When word came from Caleb that Rane was very weak but recovering, Morgan's relief was so profound that he allowed himself to tell Sam, and she wept the tears he had not allowed himself.

"My poor love, having to keep it to yourself," she said, and she did not berate him for abiding by his father's wishes in keeping the secret. And even though Rane was recovering, neither Morgan nor Sam told anyone else in the family about his illness.

Though she was loath to abandon her duties at the hospital, in August Alex made more frequent trips to Wild Swan. The area had more than its share of Southern sympathizers, of which she counted Sam's father one, and marauders had made two lightning raids at night to run off stock. It was hard to determine which side the raiders were on, or if they had any interest beyond their own gain. In grim testimony to the baseness of too many people, there were roving gangs of robbers who preyed on the confusion of war.

The men at Wild Swan had clear instructions of what they were to do—they were to resort to violence only to defend lives at the farm.

"No property is worth a life," Alex had told them repeatedly, though she wasn't sure they agreed.

Steps had been taken to make Wild Swan a less tempting target. The best of the horses were long gone, and all the silver and gold trophies won over the long decades of racing were stored in Baltimore with other items of value. The men took turns standing watches at night, and the secret room beneath the stallion barn now served to hide food and supplies rather than fugitive slaves. In addition, Samson kept the finest of the half-bred horses hidden in the woods at night, though that practice would have to change with the onset of winter. Nonetheless, there was still much at the farm that lay open to raiders—poultry, cattle, the work teams, and the aging Thoroughbreds, these last left where they could be seen, a calculated risk to make marauders believe the only horses on the place were these.

In the two raids the farm had suffered, Wild Swan's losses had been costly—not so much in financial terms, but in sentiment. A few of the Devon red cattle had been run off, but far worse, Fortune had been taken. At thirty-two, the stallion had been growing feeble and probably hadn't much longer in any case, but it had finished him cruelly to be driven from his home at a pace he had not known for a long time. Jed Barlow had found him breathing his last by the roadside just a few miles from Wild Swan.

Alex was infuriated by the needless suffering the old horse had been put through. She could not imagine the kind of person who would be so stupid as to mistake the age and condition of the animal. But there was nothing to be done in retribution, no way to trace the culprits.

The end of August brought another Union defeat at the second Battle of Bull Run, and it began to seem more than possible that the Confederacy might triumph. There was no doubt that this news would fan the flames of support higher in England and on the Continent. Alex began to fear that Rane would not be home before the year was out, and she resolved that despite her obligations, she would go to him at Christmas if he was still in England because she simply could not bear to be without him any longer.

And then in the first week of September, Lee and his army crossed the Potomac into Maryland. His men were weary from the recent battle, thousands of them were without shoes, and their rations had not been as generous as those of the Union soldiers for a long time, but they were following a man they believed in, and they were taking the war to the enemy's ground to capture food, horses, and the hearts of Marylanders, who they hoped would rise to support them while the war-ravaged acres of Virginia had a respite.

Alex felt she had no choice; again, she went home to Wild Swan. Though Lee was advancing west of Washington, there was no guarantee that raiding parties would not move elsewhere. That the capital or Baltimore might be taken was an eventuality she did not even want to consider. Nor did she want Blaine or Morgan or anyone else in the family to stay out in the country with her.

"You have properties of your own to protect in the city, and if it gets very bad in Prince George's County, I will move everyone at Wild Swan into Baltimore—I do not intend that anyone should die for an orchard or a cow."

Her sons had to concede her point. If Baltimore was taken, there was every chance that the secessionists among her citizenry would exact their own price for the Federal occupation that had quenched their spirits at the beginning of the war. And after the sale of Jennings-Falconer ships to the navy, few would have any doubt where the family's sympathies lay.

Alex was at Wild Swan when the strangers rode in at dusk. The small but heavily armed band of men wore a motley of worn and faded uniforms of butternut and gray. They were, by all the news Alex had heard, clear across the state from the main body of the Confederate army, and even though she mistrusted everything about them, she was moved by their courage in being here and thought they must have enormous faith in the willingness of Marylanders to support the Confederate cause. To a man they were lean, and their eyes were wary, but they were taking the risk of riding in openly without drawing their weapons, as if in confirmation of the rumor that Lee had cautioned his troops to act the gentleman in Maryland.

Reminding herself that the regular army was far less dangerous than the wandering bands of faithless raiders, Alex, with Della and Samson beside her, met the men outside the house.

"Evenin', ma'am," the officer in command greeted her, and he didn't seem threatening, but then he added, "I'm Captain Blockett."

She knew it couldn't be, and yet it was, and she knew her expression had given her away. He was far better looking than the other Blockett, whom Alex remembered as a gross man with piggish eyes, but there was something of the same build in the wide set of the young man's shoulders and a frame that would carry more weight in more prosperous days, and the shape of his face was similar, though his eyes were large and intelligent.

"I see you remember my grandfather," Captain Blockett said with a pleased grin. "And I know you are Alexandria Carrington, and Falconer, too, though you weren't back then. And this is Wild Swan."

He surveyed the house and the outbuildings with an avid expression that chilled Alex; she wondered if he had come to avenge his grandfather after all these years.

"I'm sure we're being covered by your men; please tell them we mean no harm." He correctly read her skepticism and apprehension. "You have my word."

"I don't understand," Alex confessed; the whole situation was so odd, she was rapidly losing her bearings.

Captain Blockett dismounted and doffed his hat. "Of course you don't understand. But you see, you've been a family legend for so long, I wanted t' see you. I know my grandfather was mad as all get out when his horse lost to you an' Magic Swan, but by th' time I was old enough to hear th' story, he'd begun to think it was all ratha fine to be part a' th' legend, even a losin' part. 'Now that Englishwoman jus' brings her colt out cool as you please,' he'd begin, an' he'd tell anybody who'd listen th' story a' th' famous race, an' he'd go on an' on about how that colt ran th' second heat without a rider, just runnin' along straight an' fast as you please."

Alex started to laugh. She couldn't help it. Part of it was from sheer nervousness, but it was also true amusement as well at the idea that Mr. Blockett had turned an incident that at the time of its occurrence had filled him with murderous rage into a story that not only showed him in a better light, but reflected well on her, too, for her cleverness.

She gained control of herself and said, "Captain Blockett, if your grandfather could so change, then I must reconsider. Perhaps the earth is flat after all."

The captain's grin was really very engaging. "Don't change your mind about th' shape a' th' globe yet," he said in his soft drawl. "Everybody knew th' story anyway; it was betta for him t' spread his own version of it abroad. You needn't look so shocked; I was fond enough a' my grandfather 'til th' day he died, but I knew his shortcomin's from close hand experience."

And you aren't like him inside, thank God, Alex thought, feeling less worried about his intentions regarding Wild Swan.

"I am flattered that you have gone out of your way to see me, but I doubt very much that that is your sole purpose for being in this part of Maryland."

"Food, horses, volunteers," he answered promptly. "Virginia has supplied everything for too long."

"We will be glad to feed you," Alex said. "But as you can see for yourself, the only horses left here are too old for your purposes. The others I shipped away before the war began. And as for volunteers—those who believe in the Confederacy enough to fight for her are gone or are already in her service clandestinely. General Lee has made a mistake if he truly thinks this state will secede now."

"This whole war is a mistake," the captain said, but so softly, his soldiers could not hear him, and it struck Alex that he had a very clear view of the war and of all the destruction it was bringing, and yet he would go on fighting to the bitter end.

Though Samson remained on guard and Della's face continued withdrawn throughout, both of them detesting the presence of Confederates, Della cooked a good meal for the soldiers. "I don't want Wild Swan's standards to fall, even for them," she said, and then under her breath, she added, "And they're so young and hungry-looking," betraying a concern she didn't want to feel.

Captain Blockett did not ask that he and his men be allowed to stay at Wild Swan, and Alex suspected he had plans to seek shelter with known Confederate sympathizers; Brookhaven and Sam's father came to mind, but she thrust the thought away.

Nor had the captain asked, and she had not told him, that she had family fighting on both sides, but as he was preparing to depart, he looked around as if he could still see the farm in the dark. "I would have liked to've seen this land when all th' horses were here. It must've been a grand place for horses an' children both t' grow up. I hope they will all come home again soon."

"And you, Captain Blockett, travel safely until you are home again." She waited outside in the warm September night until the sound of the troop faded away.

"Doan make no sense to me why dey comes here," Samson said. "All dat talk 'bout Magic an' de race, jus' seems peculiar."

"Samson, this whole war is peculiar, and I think that young man just wanted a little time out of it, and perhaps a piece of his childhood made real. I believe in the Union and that it must prevail, but I hope he is not part of the cost."

The cost of Lee's invasion of Maryland was paid by both sides at Antietam where estimates of the dead and wounded ran to more than ten thousand for each side.

A copy of Lee's orders to one of his divisions had been found by Union soldiers who had understood its importance and rushed it to McClellan, but in his habitual way, McClellan vacillated instead of pushing through Lee's scattered forces. By the time the battle was formed, Lee, alerted to the lost order, had been able to retreat to Sharpsburg on Antietam Creek, where, with his regathered forces, he turned to fight.

The outcome of the battle was tactically a draw since McClellan had hesitated to use reserves at a crucial point and had thus missed the chance of crushing the Confederate army. He had also let Lee withdraw his Army of Northern Virginia across the Potomac.

But in a sense it was a Union victory, because Lee's Northern invasion was finished, and he was thrown back on the weary acres of Virginia. It was in the president's mind enough of a victory for him to issue his Emancipation Proclamation on September 22, to take effect January 1, 1863. It did not change the status of slaves in the border states, such as Maryland and Kentucky, which had stayed in the Union, but it declared all slaves in districts or states in rebellion against the United States would be forever free.

It could not make any real difference in the lives of Southern slaves as long as they were behind Confederate lines, though it was sure to enrage white Southerners. But it could achieve the president's other goals. It was clear that Lincoln had been planning it even when he had disavowed such a move. It put the war on a new moral footing—now the fight was to free slaves rather than to settle an argument over states' rights —and it put an end to England's interest in helping the Confederacy.

Of that, Alex had no doubt. It would not matter that some would still favor the South; the country would not go to war against a power that was fighting slavery. The middle class, growing ever stronger and more morally upright in England, would not stand for it. Nor would the laboring class, who in a vague way saw a parallel between their own working conditions and those of the slaves, though they hadn't any special feeling for blacks as fellow human beings. Nor did Alex think England would take particular note of the fact that slaves within the Union would still be slaves, though that seemed a terrible contradiction to her.

Rane would be home soon, she was certain of it. But she had no time for anticipation. As soon as news of the battle had come, she had gone back to Washington to await the flood of casualties. But she had scarcely begun to work at the hospital again before Frank Faber found her.

"It's Seth," he said, and seeing her immediate terror, he hastened to add, "No, he's alive, but he's wounded, a bad cut on his arm. But that's not the worst of it. Forgive me, I'm explaining this badly! But Seth seems to be in some kind of shock. He won't eat or drink. I don't think he's slept since the battle, and he was nearly violent when Reid and I tried to persuade him to come to the hospital. Reid's with him now at the hotel."

Alex went with him immediately, and after one look at Seth, she made her decision; she would take him home to Wild Swan, just as she had taken Reid. The remorse for leaving so many helpless men in need of attention in the city could come later; only Seth mattered now.

In the fashion of so many men these days, he now sported a beard, but she could see the hollows in his cheeks, and his eyes were so filled with confusion and hurt, she could hardly bear to look at them.

"I'm all right, Gran, compared to them I'm fine," he mumbled as if he were drunk.

"Seth, I've come to take you home," she said gently, and he stared at her blankly. "Home?"

"Yes, you'll know it when you see it," she assured him, as if being completely disoriented was perfectly normal.

Frank and Reid helped her get Seth to Wild Swan, and she asked a further favor of Frank. "You know Seth's parents well, and they are fond of you. Will you go to Baltimore and explain what has happened and take my note as well? If they can bear it, I would like them to give him a few days here before they come to see him."

Della nearly cried aloud at the sight of Seth, but she controlled herself and helped Alex put him to bed. They undressed him and sponged him down as if he were a child again, and he was docile under their ministrations, all his energy concentrated on keeping his eyes open.

"Sethy, you have to sleep. Close your eyes now. I'm here. You're at Wild Swan, and you're safe."

"Wild Swan?" He peered around as if the very familiar room was completely alien.

"Yes, child, Wild Swan." She thought she had won when he closed his eyes with a little sigh, but less than an hour passed before he was awake and violently ill. There was nothing for him to bring up except the bitter juices of his own body, and yet he kept retching.

At first she thought it was something to do with his wound, something she had not noticed, but though the cut was deep, raw, and undoubtedly painful, the army surgeon had treated it adequately, and there was no sign of spreading poison. In fact, Seth hardly seemed to notice it. Her next guess was that he had contracted one of the many infections that spread among the troops, but his symptoms didn't quite match any diseases she knew except perhaps severe food poisoning, and that made no sense because he had not eaten. And then she understood that his mind was making him ill, as if his body was trying to rid itself of the nightmarish vision lurking behind his haunted eyes.

But the physical signs were terrifyingly real with the risk of lethal dehydration and internal hemorrhaging, and for hours Alex and Della ministered to him, with Samson's help when Seth grew so violent that the two women were not strong enough to hold him. They sponged him down repeatedly to keep his skin moist, and Alex kept running a spoon with a few drops of water alternating with paregoric across his lips, trying to get enough of the drug to trickle down him without it all coming back up. It was a hazardous procedure, because the tincture of opium could itself be deadly in too large a dose, and yet it was hard to know how much was being absorbed by his body when his retching continued to rid his body of the liquid. When he started to vomit blood, Alex thought her heart would stop from the sheer terror of it, and when his involuntary moaning and retching stopped, she thought he had surely died. But then it dawned on her that he was still breathing, and his heart was beating strongly—the drug had taken hold.

She looked up to see that both Samson and Della had tears in their eyes. "I think he is going to be all right," she told them. "If the drug will allow him to sleep peacefully for a while, he will be worlds better for it."

The couple left her with him, Della saying that she would prepare a broth to be ready as soon as Seth was able to eat it.

Alex watched him sleep, willing him to feel the love enfolding him even in his unconscious state. He was such a perfect blend of Morgan and Sam, and so precious in his own right, Alex would have killed anyone who threatened him at that moment. But his enemy was within, and that was much more difficult.

When he awakened hours later, he was too weak to lift his head. He felt as if he'd been beaten inside and out; he was murderously thirsty, and his mouth tasted foul; but for the first time in days, he knew where he was. Wild Swan—all the good left in the world was at Wild Swan. "Gran," he rasped.

"Don't try to move or to speak for a while," she cautioned, and she wet his lips with water on a spoon, talking to him soothingly to take his mind off the fact he was swallowing while she waited anxiously to see if the deadly cycle of rejection would begin again. She did not allow herself to feel relief until an hour had passed and the water had stayed down.

Della came unbidden, wisely leaving the broth outside so that Seth would not smell it unless Alex thought it safe.

When he swallowed the broth and whispered his thanks, Della had to blink her eyes furiously to control the tears that had threatened ever since Seth had been brought in. She loved him nearly as much as she did her own sons and her grandchild.

Alex left him in Della's care long enough so that she herself could wash, eat, and write another note to be delivered to Sam and Morgan, this one saying Seth was much more himself and on the mend, though still very weak. She did not include the details of the past hours.

When she went back to Seth, she expected to find him sleeping, but he was lying there with his eyes open, staring at the ceiling. He lay like that for a long time. And then as abruptly as the vomiting had started, the words began to pour out of him, eerily powerful though they were only a low murmur because he was too weak and his throat too raw to allow more.

"It's not the dying, Gran, it's the how of it. At Antietam, I saw it too clearly. Todd Simkins, all he ever wanted was to survive and go back to his farm. But I saw him with his entrails hanging out of a hole in his belly. He was screaming that it felt like someone was cooking him alive, and all the time was trying to push the slimy ropes of his guts back into himself. And Carter Newley, he could make more music just by whistling than most musicians can play on an instrument. But he was lying there with half of his face blown away. Men I was responsible for and strangers, our soldiers and theirs, it didn't make any difference. I wanted time to go backwards so that guts and hands and feet and eyes and everything that had been shot or hacked off would go back to where they belonged, and men would be whole again. I felt like I was shrinking inside of myself until I was just this small cringing animal hiding in a man's body. But I went on fighting, went on doing the same damage I was hiding from. It felt good when my arm was cut. It reminded me I was still there. But after a while it stopped hurting, or I stopped knowing that it did. I saw Frank and recognized him, and after that all I saw were parts of bodies."

She had to bend close to hear his next words.

"Sometimes after a battle, it takes a long time to gather all the wounded in. The earth looks as though it's moving because so many men are trying to crawl for water, away from pain, to death, to a vision of Paradise for some, and for others, just home; like Todd Simkins, that's all he wanted, just to be home. I didn't know the world could hold so much pain.

"Gran, whatever happens to me, this is my homing place. I never told you, but I hope you know how much it's meant to me to have had so much time at Wild Swan. Most of my good memories of you and of the rest of the family are here. When I think I can't bear any more, I remember warm summer days with my brothers and my cousins. I think we were the luckiest children anywhere."

"Oh, Sethy, you told me, of course you did, you told me by being joyful here."

She doubted he knew tears were trickling down his face. She held him in her arms and wept with him, slow, healing tears for both of them.

This time when sleep claimed him, it was deep and natural.

Chapter 39

Alex would not have blamed Sam and Morgan had they been furious at her for requesting that they give Seth a little time before they came to see him. But if that had been their initial reaction, it was gone by the time they arrived at Wild Swan.

Leaving Morgan with their son, Sam confronted the problem directly by confessing to Alex, "When I most want to be helpful, I am the most helpless these days. I feel as if my control is slipping day by day. I dream of my sons at night, dream they are being mutilated or killed while I sleep—even Nigel, who is still in Baltimore. But he will be gone soon enough. When I am with them, I want to wrap my arms around them and beg the world to spare them. Frank described Seth's condition to us; if I had seen my son like that, I don't know what I might have done. Even now he is so frail and battered looking, it is hard not to smother him with my love." She shuddered, and then she put her arms around Alex. "Thank you for sheltering him as you sheltered me when I was a child in need."

Thinking of her own children she had lost, Alex understood Sam's feelings. She herself would have welcomed anyone who could have kept safe the babies or the marvelous man her own son Nigel had been.

Sam hugged herself against a sudden shiver. "Helpless and ineffectual, not at all what I had planned to be at this age. I work at the school, and I work for the . . ." her voice trailed off, and Alex supplied the words gently, "for the prisoners."

"Why did I think you wouldn't know? But you didn't say anything about it," Sam accused flatly.

"Only because you haven't mentioned it," Alex replied. "I assumed if you wanted to speak of it, you would. Surely you cannot feel guilty for trying to help those wretches?"

Agreements had been made between Union and Confederate governments regarding the exchange of prisoners-of-war, but the arrangements worked better on paper than in fact. Backlogs were created by battles, and though efforts were now being made to devise an overall plan, care and disposition of the prisoners were still piecemeal. Fort McHenry in Baltimore was one of the places where they were held, and many also passed through the city heading elsewhere. Many of them were poorly clad, hungry, weary, and ill, and yet adequate care was too often delayed or nonexistent.

Sam was one of those involved in trying to make things better for the captives, but she was not a Confederate sympathizer. The reason for her actions was simple: the dictates of humanity required kind treatment for anyone under one's power, even enemies. But her heart was torn. She was trying to aid those who would kill her sons if they had the chance, and yet, she wanted to believe that if she was kind to one of the enemy, some woman in the South might be kind to her son if one of them was ever taken prisoner. Complicating her emotions further was the fact of her father's loyalty to the Confederate cause. It had almost been enough to dissuade her from trying to help. But then she had angrily decided that to let her father's loyalties influence her own behavior would be to give him an undeserved victory.

Alex watched the conflicting feelings flicker across Sam's face. "You must remember that the first time I met Caleb, he was a prisoner-of-war, an enemy of England," she reminded her daughter-in-law.

Sam's eyes rounded in surprise. "No. I mean somewhere I knew, but it never occurred to me that it was the same." Her voice trembled as she added, "It makes me hope that there truly may be a long life after this war."

"If men and nations had not found ways to settle their hatreds by truce time and time again, mankind would have been extinguished long before this age," Alex pointed out, but neither of the women had to say aloud what both were thinking—that the tragedy was that the settlements were too often delayed until both sides were simply too bloody and exhausted to fight any more.

Alex's intention had been to return to the capital as soon as Seth was out of danger, but to her chagrin, she had to admit that her age was catching up with her. She was so tired, she finally had to give in and go to bed for a couple of days, a surrender made all the more galling by the way everyone hung over her, as watchfully as if she were an ailing child.

"Don't allow Seth to do too much," she ordered, "and stop acting as if I'm on my deathbed." But no one seemed to be heeding her. She was plied with tea and broth and dainty dishes that made her glad she had never been a woman to suffer from the "vapors;" the coddling invited by the condition would have driven her crazy.

"I swear on my honor that I do not want a cup of tea, a bite of toast or anything else," she said, not opening her eyes as she heard the bedroom door open, sure that Della or Sam was checking on her for the countless time.

"Not even your long-absent husband?" he asked softly, and Alex opened her eyes to see Rane standing beside the bed.

She stared at him, and then she cried his name aloud. He sat on the bed and pulled her into his arms, and they rocked against each other, incapable of speech.

Rane's heart was still pounding from the shock. He had come to Wild Swan expecting to find his grandson ill, having received the news in Baltimore, only to find instead that Seth was up and about, albeit moving gingerly, while Alex was in bed. Sam had not helped matters by bursting into tears and stammering that Rane would be the best medicine for Alex; nor had he been reassured by Della's insistence that Alex was just tired, because Della had started to cry as well.

Now he held Alex, relearning all that had been so familiar until he had been parted from her for a year and a half. She was more slender than he remembered, but then, so was he; their separate tasks had honed them fine.

He drew in her scent and murmured of how evocative it had been in his memory. "In crowded rooms reeking of cigar smoke and musty wool, your scent would come to me so clean and sweet that it was as if I held you in my arms like this. And I asked myself innumerable times what a retired free trader was doing bargaining with the British government while his life went on without him across the sea."

"It didn't go on without you," she whispered. "It only appeared to on the surface. Inside, I've felt as if everything stopped the day you left; I've just been waiting for you to come back to me."

She pulled away so that she could study him, and the changes in him registered far more clearly than they had at her first shocked sight of him. Surely he had not had as much exercise in England as he was accustomed to at home, and yet he had grown so much leaner. There was more silver in his dark hair than there had been; the lines in his face were deeply graven; and his skin was tinged with unhealthy gray.

She stroked his cheek. "My love, this is more than homesickness."

He caught her hand and pressed it to his lips. "Nothing could be more than the longing I suffered for you."

But she was not to be diverted. "The truth, please."

He hesitated a moment longer, and then he sighed. "I had a bout of typhoid this summer, but I'm well now."

Fear coursed through her in a huge wave. The Prince Consort had died of typhoid fever only last December. And Rane had surely come close to death, else he would not still be showing such clear signs of his battle against the disease. She thought of the long gaps there had been in his correspondence this summer.

"No one sent word to me—not Caleb or Flora or Gwenny or the Bettingdons!" Fury was mixed with the fear in her voice.

"I wanted it that way," Rane said. "It was the sensible way. The crisis of the disease passed very quickly; there was no time to summon you, and it would only have given you needless worry to tell you about it at all."

She had to admit she might have handled it the same way were their positions reversed, but she was unable to control the trembling that seized her at the knowledge that he could have died so far from her, and she would not have known until long days afterwards.

"Sweetling. it is over. I am here with you," he crooned. "We have been married thirty-one years this month; I would not let that end. I want thirty-one more years at least." With slow deliberation he kissed her, as she clung to him, and opening her mouth to the sweet invasion of his tongue, Alex felt her body quicken in response to his. The weakness of the past days vanished. She was shaken by the immediacy of contact with him. In all those long months of his absence, her flesh had been dry and dormant, the only ripples of sexual energy being those conjured by his letters.

Rane laughed aloud from sheer exuberance. After so many months of being offered sly glances, innuendos, and complicated ploys engineered for the most part by married women who wanted to sample the wares of the Englishman turned colonial, he had nearly forgotten Alex's honest sensuality. But now he was home, and they had time again, time for rediscovering each other.

He had scarcely spoken to anyone at the farm on his way to Alex. Now that he had determined she was all right, he knew he ought to return to the others, but for the moment he wanted nothing.

He gathered her close, cherishing her with the beat of his heart and soft words. "There wasn't anyone else, not in all the time I was gone."

Alex accepted the admission for the gift it was; she had already resolved she would not ask him, but she, better than anyone, knew he was a man of strong appetites, and that to be celibate for so long had been a true act of love.

"I haven't even thought of myself as a woman since you left," she said. "Welcome home, my heart."

They clung together quietly for a long space before they allowed the reality of the world to intrude on them, and they realized simultaneously that as much as they had longed for each other physically, even more had their hearts and minds been deprived by the separation.

Alex began by giving him an account of Seth and the rest of the family, and Rane in turn explained how he had left England by steamer as soon as word of Lincoln's Emancipation Proclamation had reached England.

"England will never come into the war on the South's side now," he told her triumphantly. "There are too many in England who are opposed to slavery. And cotton is being supplied from other sources—from warehouses filled before the war began and from other lands. Egypt may well supply all needs before long. Though we were more effective lately, it was still a near thing until the president acted. In the early days, Caleb and I were nearly insane with the knowledge that strong, fast vessels were being built there to prey on our own ships, and in the worst weeks, we feared to see troops leaving England to fight beside the Rebels. I am glad Caleb has Flora with him; it proved more difficult for him to be there than he had expected. He claims it has made him feel more American than ever before, and I know it reminded him more than a little of the days he had spent in terror as an escaping prisoner-of-war. He and Flora will be returning as soon as possible. Having each other, they understood my need to hasten home to you."

When Rane dutifully went out to be with the rest of the family, he dissuaded Alex from leaving her bed. "I would prefer you rest," he said, leaning over to kiss the soft hollow of her throat. "I will have need of your energy later." And then he laughed. "Alex Falconer, you are blushing most winsomely."

She was more than ready for him when he returned to their bed, and yet their first night together was strange, at once familiar and new. While Alex's mind remembered the planes and angles of Rane's body and the pleasure to be given and taken, her own body reacted with twinges that made her feel almost virginal again, so long had it been since her body had opened to his. But she gloried in every sensation that marked the renewal of their union.

Even when she closed her eyes, she could see the bright green of his, mirror of her own, as their bodies mirrored each other, his thrust met by her arch, his pounding heart answered by hers, voices blending, ancient notes of an ancient song.

The pleasure of having Rane home did not pale. In the next days, Alex had to fight to control the swell of emotion at every turn. Seeing Rane and Morgan together, so clearly father and son, so alike in the way they moved and laughed and myriad other ways, brought a lump to her throat, and Seth's delight in his grandfather's return played further havoc with her heart. Seth was rapidly regaining his strength, but his eyes were too old with the reflection of the horrors he had beheld, and too soon he would go forth to face them once again. Rane's eyes held a special tenderness when he looked at his grandson.

Because he had been away from them, Rane perceived the changes the war had made in his family more clearly than they did. He hated the fragile look it had given Alex, hated the toll it had taken on all of them, but the more he observed of Morgan, the more worried he was about him.

He had never known his son to be anything but forceful; even as a child he had been so. But now there was a hesitancy about him. Rane did not think the rest of the family was aware of it; the changes in them had come gradually, and they had adjusted day by day.

He noticed Morgan's new affliction even more keenly when he and his son began to talk about business.

"There've been losses to Northern shipping, including, as you know, one of ours," Morgan conceded. "But it is the insurance premiums that are ruining us. They've gone so high, few can afford to pay them any more."

"Which is why so many shippers are selling to neutral flags now," Rane finished for him. In past times, Morgan would have been angry, but now he sounded more baffled and tired than anything else.

Disdaining subtlety, Rane said, "It has been very hard, hasn't it, tending to business while the world has fallen apart around you and around your sons?"

Morgan started to deny it, but his father's face was so full of concern, he found himself telling the truth instead. "I feel like one of Mother's geldings—docile, well-behaved, castrated. And it has nothing to do with Sam. She is as loving as she's ever been, and what we have together is still as good as it ever was—it seems to be the only good, holding her at night, loving her; it's the only thing that makes me feel like a man these days. I meant to hold fast to the business, too; you and Caleb trusted me to do just that. But Jennings-Falconer is slowly dying; we're not equipped to build ironclads, and that's all the navy wants now. And there's no use in building wooden ships for commerce when we can't insure them. In any case, the men are leaving one by one to enlist; in no time, only the very old will be left.

"Blaine is steadily working to defend some semblance of democracy in the midst of martial law so that there will be a country worth living in when the war is over. All the women of the family are doing worthwhile work, whether it is nursing or teaching. And meanwhile, I am forty-five years old, and I feel more useless by the day. Now that you are home and Caleb will be soon, I want to enlist. I'm a good shot, a good rider, and a good sailor; surely there is something I can do in the army or the navy."

Rane wished he could forbid it as if Morgan were a little boy. He thought if something happened to this beloved son, his own heart would break. But Morgan was, as incredible as Rane found it to accept, a middle-aged man now, not a child. He remembered Morgan's restless pacing on the day he had told him about the English mission; now he was beginning to understand the full extent of his son's frustration at being kept from the action.

"I doubt that any words from me will convince you, but you have done a fine and necessary job at the shipyard. Despite the losses, we are in a far better position than most because you have kept the business going. And I want to ask one more favor," Rane said. "Wait just a little while. Your talents and knowledge could too easily be wasted if you simply enlist. Allow me to speak to Secretary Welles. If you're going to run the risk of being shot, I would just as soon it was for a good reason."

"I will do as you ask as long as you promise you will not try to get me stuck in an office in Washington," Morgan said, and Rane nodded and asked, "Have you discussed this with Sam?"

"Not yet," Morgan confessed. "There didn't seem to be any point in distressing her before it was necessary. But I will tell her now. I know it will be hard for her, but everything is hard these days."

Rane understood his protective attitude very well; so had he sought to spare Alex. "Thank you for keeping my illness from your mother," he said, knowing of Morgan's restraint because Caleb had admitted to having sent Morgan word.

"Not knowing for weeks whether you were dead or alive," the huskiness of Morgan's voice betrayed the extent of his caring, "I was terrified for Mother. It made me realize how much she loves you, how much she depends on you." He paused, swallowing hard before he went on. "And it made me realize how good a father you have been to me, to all of us, and how much I love you."

Moved beyond words, Rane reached out and gripped Morgan's shoulder tightly, and both pairs of green eyes were suspiciously bright.

Morgan admitted to himself that he was more willing to face Confederate guns than Sam's reaction. But he decided there was no sense in delaying. He trusted his father to keep his word without delay, and he wanted to tell Sam here at Wild Swan, as if the happiness she had known at the farm as a child would somehow sustain her now.

He told her as she sat brushing her long hair, and he watched the play of light in the shining brown shot with golden red and with the silver that had come with the war.

She went on brushing with long, slow strokes, and the room was so quiet, Morgan could hear the crackle of electricity in her hair.

"Sam, aren't you going to say anything?" he asked hesitantly.

Very carefully she put the brush down, and when she turned to face him, he saw the tears pouring down her cheeks, but her arms opened to him, and he went to her.

"I'm sorry," she sobbed, her face muffled against his chest.

"I believe that is what I am supposed to say," Morgan ventured.

"No. You're only doing what you need to do. I've been so busy fighting my own battles, I haven't noticed how you've been feeling for months. You've been weary and subdued, not like yourself at all, but all that mattered to me was that you were safe." She had heard the excitement that was even stronger than regret as he had told her this news he knew would devastate her, the first excitement he had shown in such a long time. She drew a deep shuddering breath. "I shall hate knowing you are in danger. But I understand why you must do this."

"Every time I think I know all the reasons I love you, I find there is yet another," Morgan murmured unsteadily, and he held her against his heart, wishing he could shield her from sorrow forever.

But sorrow continued to be the measure of the times. In November, President Lincoln replaced McClellan with Ambrose E. Burnside as commander of the Army of the Potomac. The horrific results of this decision were made clear at Fredericksburg on the thirteenth of December when the Federal troops were routed by Lee's Confederates, with the Union suffering more than double the Rebels' estimated five thousand casualties.

For Alex and the rest of the family, it was not enough to discover that Seth, Reid Tratnor, and Frank Faber had come through the battle unscathed; Gincie, living at Hawthorn, was too close to Fredericksburg.

The last letter from Gincie had been a sad account of the loss of Abigail in November, and now Alex wanted to go to Virginia to make sure her granddaughter was all right.

"Wait just a bit longer," Rane pled. "You might be able to get a pass to go through the lines, but you are not exactly an innocent civilian. I am an agent for the Federal government, and now Morgan is, too, and if that came to light, you might well be in danger."

She knew he was right. Christmas would be somber this year, dulled by worry for Gincie and fear for family and friends. Alex was further disappointed when Rane told her he would probably not be able to get to Wild Swan until late on Christmas Eve. In addition to sorting out their own business in concert with Morgan, Rane and Caleb were now working to coordinate the smooth supplying of army and navy with everything from rifles to hardtack. Their years in the shipping business had given them many contacts in the merchant community. But the greed involved in selling to the government was phenomenal and made it difficult to regulate the quality of goods shipped to various locations, particularly because little was done to merchants who were caught cheating.

"I trust the war will not last as long as it would take to devise an efficient system," Rane had told Alex with a wry grimace.

Mavis and Timothy, Alastair Cameron, Philly, Blaine, and Phoebe, Larissa and Reid, Sam, Morgan, Seth, and Nigel, Caleb and Flora home from England—they had all arrived before Rane. Anthea and Adam were not able to come, though Anthea planned on spending New Year's Eve there, and Adam would have some leave soon from his berth aboard one of the ships of the North Atlantic Blockading Squadron.

Alex knew she should be thankful for all those who were there, and she was, but she admitted the selfishness of her heart that would only be content with Rane.

The cold winter night at last yielded not only Rane, but Gincie and Travis, too.

There was dead silence as everyone stared at the young couple, and then Alex gave a cry and hugged first one and then the other, eyes bright with joyful tears. Travis had his right arm in a sling, but he managed to return her hug with his left.

"Happy Christmas, sweetling," Rane whispered under cover of the babble that followed the shock.

"How did you manage this; how did they?" Alex asked dazedly. "Is Travis's injury serious?"

"It took a little doing, but the gist of it is that Travis wanted Gincie to visit Wild Swan for the holidays, but she wouldn't come without him. And though his arm is healing nicely, he's little use to the cavalry at the moment. His horse was shot out from under him, and Travis broke his arm in the fall. So it seemed a good time for a family reunion."

"All of which means you are not going to tell me exactly how you accomplished it," Alex muttered, but she smiled at him—Rane was here, and Gincie and Travis, and that was all that mattered. And then a chill swept her. "My God, I seem to be thinking very slowly! Travis is out of uniform, but he is still a Rebel officer. It is very dangerous for him to be here."

"Very, for him and for us," Rane concurred. "But in this war, you can be sure it is happening in one way or another in countless homes and worth the risk."

Alex was more convinced of that with each passing moment. Her first euphoria at seeing the couple had blinded her to all but the obvious. Now she saw that Travis's wounds were far more extensive than the broken arm. He was so thin, she wanted to press every delicacy on him, but she saw that he ate sparingly even in the midst of plenty, his body conditioned to meager rations. And Gincie was as fined down as he, her grass-green eyes appearing huge in her pinched face.

As so often when events and emotions were overwhelming, Alex found herself focusing on one small thing—in this case, Travis's boots. No amount of polishing could hide how terribly worn they were. She gripped Rane's hand so tightly that he looked down questioningly.

"Is there time to buy a new pair of boots for Travis before he and Gincie leave?"

"They will be here through New Year's Eve; we'll get the boots," he assured her, not having to ask why that mattered so much to her.

Everyone was extremely glad to see Gincie and Travis, but still, Travis was the enemy, and no one wanted to betray anything to him. And he was under the same constraint regarding his own army's situation. The atmosphere began to feel uneasy because no one felt free to discuss the one subject they all had in common—the war.

Alex raised her voice so that all could hear. "We are surely civilized enough to keep to ourselves whatever is said or heard here. If we cannot do that, then this family gathering is a mockery."

There was silence, and then Seth offered Travis his hand, and Travis took it in his left. The two men shook, the two most likely to face each other on opposite sides of a battle.

There was still care taken in what was said, but the tension eased. Much was made of the nonpolitical aspects of the English sojourn, and Rane had ambrotypes of Gwenny and Christopher's children to show off in his role of proud grandfather.

"I would have brought photographs of Alex's horses, too, had we not decided that the animals would be too terrified by the process," he said, and there was laughter at the idea of the Thoroughbreds ever standing still long enough to be so captured.

"Gran's horses are obedient, but they aren't stuffed," Seth observed.

"Well, I am," Nigel said, patting his belly. "Della could cook me in place of a Christmas goose tomorrow."

It was Christmas morning before the party broke up, and Alex could scarcely keep her eyes open by the time she and Rane were in bed, but she wanted him to know how much the evening had meant to her. He had brought lavish gifts from abroad—books, exquisite fabrics, and a wonderful bonnet—but they were as nothing compared to having Gincie and Travis here. She tried to explain the depth of her gratitude, her face hidden against his neck, her tears dampening his skin.

"Hush, my love, I know. I too wanted her home, even if it was just for a little while. And I received all the thanks I could want when I saw the look on your face when the children walked in." He smiled in contentment as he felt her settle against him in sleep.

Caleb and Flora left early on Christmas morning in order to spend the day with his children and grandchildren in Baltimore, but they would return to Wild Swan for New Year's Eve. And Caleb was entrusted with the mission of bringing back the best boots available for Travis.

Alex's impulse was to load Gincie and Travis with all kinds of luxuries to take back with them to Virginia, but she soon learned from Gincie that the most practical items were far more needed.

"Even nails and pins, anything of metal—the government has begged for all of it so that the ironworks in Richmond can melt the metal down for arms and for armor for ships. And cloth, leather . . ." She gazed off into the distance. When she spoke again, her voice was very low. "Gran, it doesn't matter that the South seems to be winning now; in the end she will lose. There are shortages of everything. Even at Hawthorn we have been short of food because soldiers from both sides have come through and requisitioned supplies. How much worse it is in the cities, and how much worse it will become. Cotton fields are being replanted with cereal crops, but there isn't enough for everyone, and some plantation owners still insist that wealth lies in cotton, despite the difficulty of shipping it out now. And medical supplies—dear God, I helped with some of the wounded who were brought to Hawthorn after Fredericksburg; some are still there. Many had to endure surgery without anesthetic. They lay there staring at the beautifully decorated ceilings while their bodies were cut open, their arms and legs cut off." She covered her face for a moment, and then went on. "The blockade runners bring in brandy and silks, not drugs and surgical instruments. It's as if a large part of the South doesn't believe what is happening. The Confederate government is made up of states that care so much about their individual rights, they can't be trusted to act together, and yet people think that somehow General Lee will lead his army to victory, and everything will be as it was before the war began."

Her thin shoulders trembled. "I don't believe that. I am so tired of this war, so tired. And I miss Abigail. The war finished her."

Alex gathered her close, and Gincie did not resist. "I am so afraid Travis will be killed before it is over," she whispered. "He could so easily have been crushed when Clancy was shot out from under him. Gran, I've given him Brutus to ride when he goes back, as if Brutus can keep him any safer than Clancy did. Travis will go back; he will see it to the end because his honor demands it. Honor be damned! I'd sell my soul if it would keep my husband safe."

"I know you would, child, I know," Alex murmured, patting her back. "I assume you understand this, but there is shelter here for you and for Travis any time you need it, and I hope Brutus will carry Travis safely."

"Thank you, Gran," Gincie said, but Alex knew that as long as Travis's home was in Virginia, that was where Gincie would be.

"I want to have Travis's child, but I cannot conceive." Gincie's voice was toneless, as if this was the final insuperable insult of the war.

Alex just barely refrained from saying, "Thank God!", but chose instead a more tactful response. "This is not the best of times for you to bear a child. It will be far better when you are not so constantly upset, and when you are assured of enough food and good care. Your body has chosen the wisest course, even when you would not."

"What use will food or care or anything else be if Travis is not there?" Gincie asked. But Alex had no answer.

Chapter

40

Even as the family had voiced the wish for peace, and clung together as the last hours of 1862 gave way to 1863, the war was going on, as Federals and Rebels fought each other to a bloody draw in the West at Stone's River, Tennessee. But in cities all over the North, Abolitionists and black congregations waited for clocks and church bells to sound the turning of the year that marked the official confirmation of the Emancipation Proclamation.

Alex thought her heart would break when Travis and Gincie left Wild Swan on New Year's Day, Rane going with them to assure their safe passage through his connections, but at least the couple had been able to celebrate their third wedding anniversary at the farm. They could not take too much with them, but Alex had packed medical supplies, tea, coffee, salt, and various other essentials, and Travis had his new boots. He had been so touched by the gift that tears had glittered in his beautiful blue-green eyes, and Alex had understood all over again why Gincie found him so compelling. For the sake of Gincie's safety, Travis would have had her remain at Wild Swan; for the sake of her love, Gincie would not even consider it.

It was hard to face the new year with any hope. Two years of carnage leading into another that promised the same was a grim prospect. The president was assaulted by voices within and without his government demanding an end to the war. General Burnside tried to march his troops through treacherous mud in rainy Virginia to flank Lee's army and gained nothing for it; President Lincoln replaced Burnside with General Joseph Hooker as head of the Army of the Potomac.

Alex felt as if her family had become pieces of glass in a child's kaleidoscope, tumbling to and fro more rapidly than she could follow. Though Larissa remained at her post in Washington, Anthea went to join the battlefield nurses as she had planned, and Nigel, with his parents' grudging permission and Dr. Cameron's help, became a surgeon's assistant with the army. It meant he would be doing the lowest jobs most of the time, but he did not mind; he wanted to serve the wounded in whatever capacity, and he knew that in the heat of battle, his responsibilities were apt to expand rapidly.

But it was Phoebe's new venture that surprised them all. She announced that since Flora was back in charge of the Baltimore school, she felt free to pursue her own plan, which was to go south to join those at Port Royal in the Sea Islands who were engaged in teaching blacks. Prior to the Emancipation Proclamation, these blacks had been slaves left behind or escaped as their white owners had fled from the encroachment of Federal troops along the coast. Now they were free, but their new status was no cure for the ignorance that had come from generations of servitude.

In order to remedy this, a group of idealistic New Englanders had begun a teaching program among the blacks shortly after the capture of the Sea Islands off the South Carolina coast by Union Forces in November, 1861. It was this project that Phoebe proposed to join, having already corresponded with them and received an invitation to come to them.

She was nearly twenty-four years old and had the right and the intelligence to make her own decision—indeed, it was a mark of her high qualifications that she had been accepted by the very exclusive staff at Port Royal—but it was an odd group for her to join. The teachers were called Gideonites, or Gideon's Band, by their detractors who saw their mission as futile, and many of them were fanatical Abolitionists and evangelists, hardly compatible with Phoebe's moderate beliefs.

But when Alex pointed this out, Phoebe defended her determination fiercely. "I don't expect to like all of the staff or always to agree with them; I expect to teach, which is what I do best. And Port Royal is important. There are far too many in the North who do not believe a black man can ever be more than a beast; even people who oppose slavery continue to believe that. The only hope is to provide proof that blacks can manage their own lives, and they must be educated to do that."

There was no argument to counter such eloquent logic. As Philly ruefully admitted, "It is very difficult to try to dissuade one's children from doing what is right. I have the same problem with their father."

Even the reality of what she found there did not diminish Phoebe's enthusiasm, though she wrote a wry, clear-eyed account of her first weeks at Port Royal:

In truth, I find the New Englanders more peculiar than the blacks, undoubtedly because I am more familiar with the latter. The New Englanders are rather dour and overly pious, though well educated. Many of them knew little of the true condition of slaves before they arrived here. They seem to expect that the minute the people were away from their owners, they should have become dark versions of New England ladies and gentlemen: well-mannered, literate, quiet, pious, clean, et cetera. And of course, that is not at all the case. The blacks are exactly as anyone with sense ought to expect: confused, impoverished, accustomed to dire conditions of living, and clinging to the familiar patterns of their previous lives in the way they speak the dialect of the quarters and worship with a great noise of both exultation and grief. Nor is it amazing that with so little previous experience of education, they are like children in their span of concentration, apt to flutter off from one thought to the next.

There is no doubt that it is a difficult situation, and there is much to be done, but do not think I despair. There could be no better place for a teacher. With all the adjustments they must make, it is still abundantly clear that the blacks long to unlock the secret of the written word as other peoples long for gold.

One of my pupils is an elderly woman named Esther. When I showed her her name in the Bible, and she was able to recognize it in several places, she wept for joy, and I wept with her. And in that instant, there was no difference between us.

It was impossible to stop worrying entirely about Phoebe—Phoebe of the golden brown hair, dark blue eyes, and stubborn chin—but it was equally impossible to deny that she had found work that fulfilled her in a special way, demanding all her skill and dedication.

There were more faces missing at Wild Swan, too, as the year progressed. The first approved black regiments were being formed, and Samson's son Jotham, as well as Polly's and Calvin's two sons-in-law, joined the 54th Massachusetts, which was recruiting far beyond that state's borders.

In addition to the admission of blacks into the army, the first national Conscription Act passed in March, requiring enrollment in the army of all male citizens and aliens who had declared the intention to become citizens and who were between the ages of twenty and forty-five. However, conscripts could be exempted from military service by paying three hundred dollars or by providing a substitute, a practice that was already raising protests of special privilege for the rich.

In her darkest moments, Alex wished that her grandsons were the kind of men who would take advantage of these provisions rather than being as they were, men who had volunteered at the earliest opportunity. She was enormously grateful Rane was home. She needed the steady force of his love to anchor her in the swirling sea of change. It was not that he was always beside her, for he had to travel to various cities to make sure manufacturers and shippers were meeting the orders to supply the military, and she herself still spent as much time as she could nursing the wounded in Washington. But these separations were as nothing compared to having him thousands of miles away in England.

Though Grant was making some gains for the Union in the West, in the East Lee remained a terrifyingly formidable enemy, once again defeating the Union army, this time at Chancellorsville, Virginia, in early May. Casualties were heavy on both sides, and Caleb's eldest grandson, who bore his name, was listed among the missing. Men in his regiment believed he had been captured along with several others, but given the worsening conditions of Southern prisons, that news was only slightly better than finding him dead. Just determining where one's kin had been taken could be impossible, and the exchanges were still uncertain. But Caleb refused to be discouraged, and committed every moment he could to helping his son and daughter-in-law find young Caleb. He used every connection he had in the government, importuning people in a manner he would never have considered had it been for his own sake.

"He hardly eats or sleeps," Flora confided in mid-June. "But I can't convince him that exhausting himself won't help to bring his grandson back."

For the first time, Caleb looked like an old man. It was not the white in his hair, which had been eclipsing the darker shade of youth for years; that had made no difference when he had carried himself so straightly and his dark eyes had flashed with humor and intelligence. But now his shoulders were stooped, and his eyes too often had a glazed, faraway look over the deepening lines on his face.

Rane tried to ease Caleb's load by taking on more of the governmental work they were both doing, but Caleb was too conscientious to allow it when the help was too blatantly offered.

"I fear there is little any of us can do," Rane admitted to Flora, "but even though you may not feel it is so, believe that your husband needs you more now than ever before."

Flora squared her shoulders. "Though I profess to be an independent woman, the truth is that I depend a great deal on Caleb; it is only just that I have strength to offer him now."

Alex applauded her daughter's attitude, but inwardly she feared it would not be enough. She had noticed of late that Caleb ran out of breath too easily, and she had seen him surreptitiously rubbing his chest and his left arm more than once, ominous signs of a distressed heart. She did not share her observations with Flora, not wanting to add to her worry, but she did tell Rane.

He swallowed hard, and Alex saw the sheen of tears in his eyes as he spoke. "The reality is that we are all growing old, and life is not forever, but Caleb has been part of our lives for nearly fifty years; I do not like to consider the world without him."

Alex pressed his hand hard and then raised it to rub her cheek against it; there was no easy comfort to offer for this dread.

Rane had to go to New York on business, and he wished that Alex could accompany him, but he did not press her. Since he had returned to Maryland, he had become very aware of how central she was to the well-being of the family. They came to her in both joy and sorrow; she was their touchstone.

But he did not leave her without words of warning. "If there is any sign of danger in the countryside, I want you to seek shelter in Washington or Baltimore."

"My love, this is an old argument. I would remind you that I kept safe while you were in England. I value my skin more than you credit."

Rane didn't like her answer, but he had no choice except to accept it. He did not doubt that she had missed him as much as he had missed her while he was in England, but it was also true that in his view, she had managed very well in his absence.

He kissed her soundly and growled, "Remember, nothing is more important than staying alive for this."

As soon as he was gone, she went to Washington where the wounded from Chancellorsville were still crowding the hospitals. But she had scarcely settled in at Dr. Grover's house before word reached the capital that Lee had crossed the Potomac at Harper's Ferry on June 24, and was advancing north toward Pennsylvania. There were rumors that Jeb Stuart's cavalry was close enough to menace the capital. Alex returned immediately to Wild Swan. It didn't matter to her that Lee was west of Washington while the farm was east of it; when the Confederate army was loose in Maryland, she wanted to be home, though she continued to fear the vermin that traveled in the wake of the armies of both sides more than the regular soldiers. To make the situation worse, Hooker resigned his command, and General George G. Meade took over the Army of the Potomac and was in the desperate position of having to reorganize it immediately for imminent confrontation with the Confederates.

At first Alex did not recognize the bedraggled figure who rode in to Wild Swan on a disreputable-looking horse a few days after she had come home. The boy dismounted stiffly and leaned against the horse for support. There was no sign that anyone else was with him, and it was broad daylight, so Alex quickly discounted the idea of raiders and advanced on the slight figure.

"Are you hurt?" she called softly, and then she gasped as the boy turned, and she saw the bruised face.

"Gincie! Oh, my sweet child!" When Alex put her arms around her granddaughter she felt her wince.

"How badly are you hurt? Why are you here? Is it Travis?" Alex couldn't stop the questions.

Gincie slumped against her for a moment, then pulled away. "I'm bruised, that's all. Bess fell. Poor old horse, she's too stiff for such a journey. Travis—I'm going north to find him. There's going to be a battle, you see, and he's not fit. He caught a chill this spring, and it moved to his lungs, but he insisted on going back to Jeb Stuart after only a few days at Hawthorn. I'll find Travis, and he will be all right." The words came quickly in a strange, high-pitched voice, not at all like her own.

And then before Alex could say anything in reply, Gincie closed her eyes and sank toward the ground, caught by Samson, whom Alex had not even noticed. He swung Gincie up in his strong arms and carried her inside.

She was so exhausted that she didn't even awaken when Alex and Della stripped away her boy's clothing and gently bathed her. There were bloodstains on her undergarments, and she was bruised everywhere, some of the dark shadows quite clearly the work of large hands.

"She said her horse fell," Alex murmured grimly. "And until she tells us differently, that is what it will be."

Della nodded, her eyes bleak. It was as plain to her as it was to Alex that Gincie had been assaulted. But there were no signs of continued bleeding or of fever, and Alex did not try to rouse her granddaughter, judging that the respite from reality was the best medicine she could offer.

Gincie slept for hours, but then she began to move restlessly, becoming more and more agitated until she screamed in protest as she opened her eyes.

"It's all right, Gincie, you're home at Wild Swan," Alex crooned over and over until Gincie's eyes narrowed in recognition, and she stopped struggling.

"A bad dream," she muttered, looking away, but then her voice sharpened. "I have to go north. I have to find Travis."

"Child, that isn't sensible. You don't even know where Jeb Stuart's men are. You can hardly wander all over Maryland and Pennsylvania looking for them," Alex pointed out.

"There is going to be a major battle!" Gincie countered desperately. "Don't you understand? Lee is moving his whole army north, and the Union army is not going to let him go where he wills. A collision is inevitable."

"What do you intend to do if you do find Travis, forbid him to fight? You have known from the beginning that he would be a soldier for Virginia, and that is what he is." She could not imagine what had caused Gincie's sudden decision to become a camp follower, unless the attack she had suffered had happened at Hawthorn, driving her away. But Gincie's next words dispelled that idea; this was a purpose beyond whatever had been done to her.

"Gran, please try to understand. I don't know exactly why, but I know I have to find Travis. I just have to! I didn't mean to come here; I meant to go on my own, but I was so weary . . ." her voice trailed off, but her eyes pleaded for her grandmother's understanding.

With an eerie sense of foreboding, Alex did understand. There were bonds beyond normal reason between those who loved, communication that made spoken words seem clumsy. All those years ago, Rane had known she was in danger before Winter Swan had fallen on her.

"Rest now. We leave tomorrow," Alex said. Gincie stared at her, not expecting this early capitulation. "We?"

Alex nodded. "Yes, and we will take the wagon. If Travis is hurt or ill, we will need it to bring him back. If there is a big battle, vehicles of any sort will be difficult to purchase, and the railway will be useless."

Gincie closed her eyes and let sleep take her. For the first time since the degrading violence had been done to her—she wrenched her mind away from it; if she did not think about it, it was not true—she felt the tension leave her. Her grandmother had always been there for her, had always been able to make the world come right.

But Della and Samson were not as amenable to Alex's plan.

"You must be mad!" Della said bluntly. "Rane will be furious when he finds out."

"It's quite possible that he won't find out until we're back," Alex said. "He's in New York. Even if he suspects that I've returned to the farm because the Confederates are in Maryland, reports will tell him they are far west of here. It would be a very long chance that we would have visitors again, at least from the regular army like Captain Blockett. Morgan is also gone, on some business for the government. And I refuse to tell Blaine. Don't you see? If the rest of the family were to know, the best that could be expected would be a bumbling royal progress, confused and delayed. Gincie would not stand for it, and neither would I."

"Den I goes wid you," Samson announced. "Gincie be right an' sumpin bad happen to dat boy, you goin' need me to lift him up an' hep take care a' him."

Della was in complete agreement with her husband, and Alex swallowed her words of protest. What Samson said was true. A chill coursed through her. That was what Gincie was feeling, a threat to Travis strong enough to drive her from the comparative safety of Hawthorn, and with the armies on the move, it was far more likely that they would find him after the fact than in time to prevent harm to him. She could not, in any case, imagine Travis avoiding a battle because his wife appeared and asked it of him.

"We will be glad of your company," she said, and it suddenly occurred to her that the world had indeed changed. Samson was no longer liable to capture as a fugitive slave. The Emancipation Proclamation had superseded the fugitive slave laws, at least as far as slaves in Confederate states were concerned, and Samson had been a slave in Georgia. He had made no changes in his life prior to this; he was accustomed to the safety of Wild Swan, but now he had offered without hesitation to leave his sanctuary.

And though Della and Samson had protested her plan to go with Gincie, Alex realized that they had not, even for a moment, expressed any doubt about the validity of Gincie's intuition; they knew as much as any man and woman could hope to know about loving.

They stocked the wagon with fresh straw, bedding, food, and medical supplies, and they set out the next morning, taking an extra horse, one of the half-breds, so that they could take turns riding when the motion of the wagon became too tedious. Gincie was wearing one of her grandmother's riding habits, and at first glance looked like a respectable woman again rather than a tattered boy. But the bruises still showed on her face, and despite the sleep she had gotten, her eyes were glazed, her mouth set in a tight line as if she were already miles away from Wild Swan.

They kept to themselves on the journey, trying to make as good time as possible without overtaxing the team, but they did hear rumors, some so wild as to be wholly ridiculous, while others carried the stamp of truth. It seemed the armies had finally met at Gettysburg in Pennsylvania and had begun fighting on the first of July.

In Westminster, Maryland, they discovered that General Jeb Stuart, with three brigades of veteran Confederate cavalry, numbering approximately six thousand men, had encountered and routed a small unit of the 1st Delaware Cavalry, capturing many of the Union men in the fierce skirmish. But the town was now in Union hands, with lines of prisoners and the wounded moving through it, unwashed bodies stinking in the heat, and the surrounding farmland showed the ravages of trampling feet and wagon traffic.

To Gincie it meant only that Stuart's men, including Travis, must surely be at Gettysburg by now with Lee. Though she searched the drawn faces of prisoners being sent down from the battle, something inside her compelled her on: a certainty that Travis was at the battlefield.

Alex shut her ears to the cries of the wounded and resisted several efforts to commandeer her wagon, fixing the Union officers with a steely eye and telling them that her party was with the Sanitary Commission and was needed at the battlefield; it was hardly the time or place to admit that their interest was in a particular Confederate officer.

The weather was hot and humid, and the congestion on the road slowed their progress, adding further discomfort, but on the afternoon of July 3, they heard the distant rumble of the guns and then nothing. The rumor came down the line that the battle was over, the Confederates defeated, but the aftermath of it, the torn and hollow-eyed men, made it hard to believe that any victory was worth such suffering.

Late in the afternoon, Alex called a halt, paying well to shelter at a farm whose owner was not averse to a profit since he had seen much of his crops damaged by the overflow of armies in the past days. Alex didn't blame him for his attitude, but Samson didn't trust him and stood guard throughout the night.

Gincie was almost hysterical with the need to press on, but Alex overwhelmed her with cold logic. "We are not sure the battle is over. We cannot simply appear in the middle of it, for God's sake! And the horses are too tired to go on today. They must be kept healthy enough to make the trip back to Wild Swan. You have seen how it is. Do you think we would be able to buy another suitable team?"

Gincie subsided for the sake of the horses rather than her own exhaustion; only later did she realize that her grandmother and Samson must be the most tired of all. She was so accustomed to their strength, she too easily forgot that neither was young.

"I am so sorry, Gran," she apologized, not attempting to explain that she was feeling half mad with the need to get to Travis—one minute she could feel nothing but him, and in the next she could not sense him at all.

"There is no need for you to be sorry," Alex told her. "Do you think I would be any more patient than you if I were going in search of your grandfather on a battlefield?" Or Seth, she added to herself, more frightened than before now that she had seen the streams of wounded. Schooling herself to patience was no easy task. But she kept thinking that, having survived Antietam, Seth would survive this.

Clouds rolled over the sky the next day, but they could not soften the monstrosity that Gettysburg had become.

Nothing, not newspaper accounts of past battles, not the grim reflections in young men's eyes, not even Seth's graphic description of Antietam had prepared Alex for Gettysburg.

The smell of death came to them before they saw the bodies—a stench so strong it was an oily, metallic taste on the tongue. And then they began to see the corpses, acres and acres of men and horses and mules bloating in the summer heat.

Riding beside the wagon on the saddle horse, Gincie began to gag.

"Swallow hard and cover your nose and mouth; your sense of smell will soon dull." Alex's voice was harsh because she was having her own difficulty in keeping her stomach from revolting. Even the patient work team began to balk, and Alex was glad of Samson's firm control of them. But she could hear him murmuring under his breath, "Sweet Jesus, oh, my sweet Lord, all dem boys, all dem dead boys."

McPherson's Ridge, Oak Hill, Forney's Field, Cemetery Hill, Little Round Top, Devil's Den, the Wheatfield, Seminary Ridge—everywhere vegetation had been crushed by the armies and mowed down by volleys of shot as the men had been likewise harvested, and across the acres and acres of desolated farm and woodland, hill and valley, figures moved on the bleak land to pile the carcasses of animals together for burning and the bodies of men for trench burial. The workers were pathetically few for so vast a task. There were civilians as well as soldiers, people come to look for their men, for their dead or for those who still breathed but had not yet been sorted from the corpses. And some were undoubtedly there to loot the dead and dying. Blood had run in rivers; in too many places the earth was stained dark with it, and bits of flesh and cloth were obscene growths on what had been peaceful farmland only days before.

"See what a scourge is laid upon your hate!" Gincie's voice was high and grating as she quoted the lines, staring at a heap of bodies, hardly conscious of controlling the horse sidling beneath her.

"You have come this far!" Alex hissed. "Don't you dare give in now!"

Gincie clenched her hands on the reins until her fingers hurt, welcoming the focus of the pain because the grotesque landscape had begun to spin wildly in her vision. And then she felt it, a physical jolt that nearly threw her from the saddle, nearly as strong as when the slave catcher's bullet had hit her. "He's here, very close," she said with absolute certainty. "And he's hurt." And then her eyes clouded, and her voice rose in despair. "It's gone again. I can't feel him!"

"Gincie, it is enough! You know he's here, and now we'll find him," Alex assured her, but in the ensuing hours, the enormity of the task was made dreadfully clear.

The areas set aside for the care of the wounded were worse than the fields of dead. There was a constant chorus of moans punctuated by howls of agony. Everyone working there was splattered with blood and gore. Piles of arms and legs lay where they had been amputated, and many of the wounded lay out in the open because there were not enough tents to shelter them. Rain began to fall on them at midday, adding to their misery. Every available space in the homes and businesses of Gettysburg was being filled with the injured, and women of the town were trying to ease the suffering, but the carnage was so extensive as to make even the most heroic efforts appear puny.

Anthea and Nigel were surely here somewhere, Alex thought dazedly, and Seth, but repeated questions about their whereabouts yielded only the vaguest bits of information about where specific units were. And as for the Confederate wounded, the situation was even more confused. Some were with Union wounded, others were being held separately, but most were with their own army, which was still in the area.

Alex found that the most insane of all in the general madness— that the Confederate army was still there as well as the Union troops, and yet the battle was over, both armies apparently too weary to strike further at each other. It made the war seem more than ever a monstrous game.

The same eerie compulsion that had sent Gincie on her quest in the first place drove her to keep searching in the Union encampment, but Alex was beginning to think that they would have to go through the lines to the enemy and ask for news of Travis from his fellow officers. It was the reasonable thing to do, but she was torn, hesitating to act against Gincie's instincts.

"My God! How did you get here? How did you know?"

Gincie understood before Alex did, recognizing the man who was riding up to the wagon in the pelting rain, "Reid! You know where Travis is?"

There was a long, awful silence. Reid's blue eyes closed for an instant in his haggard face. "Of course, you can't know. Seth and Travis, they're together. Frank, Anthea, Nigel, and I, we've been taking turns sitting with them. Travis has a serious leg wound, but he's been conscious off and on. Seth was hit in the chest, and he—he hasn't been conscious since last night."

With detached interest, Alex watched Reid's throat working as he fought to control his voice. Nothing he was saying seemed to have anything to do with her. She heard Gincie sob and say something to Reid, and Samson seemed to be praying, and still she was removed from it all.

But when she stood with the others over the two pallets, the truth seared her.

Frank had his arm around Anthea, and they were both weeping. It was over. The pain and grief the war had caused him was gone from Seth's countenance; his face was younger and more peaceful than it had been since the day the war began, but his chest was swathed in a bloody mass of bandages.

"Sethy, my beautiful, beautiful boy," Alex sighed as she sank down beside him, but when she touched his hand, it was cold and resistant, nothing to do with the bright life that had been Seth. Surviving Antietam had been no talisman, but rather a step toward this death. She remembered her nightmare of his dying.

She heard Reid explaining to the others why Alex, Gincie, and Samson were here, his voice raw with the fresh grief of his discovery that Seth had died. She wanted to flee away from the sight, sound, and smell of dying men.

And then the selfishness of her own grief dawned on her as Travis groaned and opened his eyes to Gincie's soft pleading.

Seth was dead, but Travis still lived; Alex's energy flowed into the determination that he would survive.

He had a vicious saber cut running from his right hip bone to his knee, the blade having slashed through clothing, skin, and muscle, the deepest part being down his thigh. In a sense he was fortunate; he could have been sliced right across his belly or groin. But it was severe enough as it was. He had suffered a grievous loss of blood; he was feverish; and even with Anthea and Nigel trying to give him extra care, his chance of surviving the abysmal conditions of Gettysburg were slim.

"Stuart's cavalry got here late," Reid explained softly. "They didn't join Lee until the night of the second. And yesterday when they went into battle a couple of miles from here, they came on as if in review, close formation with sabers drawn, sunlight turning the blades to silver. Even our troops had to admire the sight. They were trying to protect their army's left flank and attack the Federal rear. But artillery fire and then a fierce saber melee took its toll and turned them back. Travis recognized Seth and saw him fall, shot out of the saddle, and then a little later, Travis was cut and his horse went down, too. Travis couldn't get up, but he crawled to Seth—I'll never understand how he managed that with his leg laid open. His own troops would have taken him with them, but he wouldn't leave Seth. He was still trying to cling to him when they brought both of them in. One of Seth's men saw it all. Travis tried so hard to keep Seth alive," he finished brokenly.

Alex could see Travis trying to fight his way through the confusion of pain, fever and the effects of the morphine he had been given.

"Travis, it's Alex. Gincie, Samson, and I are really here," she told him firmly. "We've come to take you home to Wild Swan." She made the decision in that instant; the journey would be painful and dangerous for him, but anything was better than having him remain here.

"Seth?" he croaked, finally summoning the energy to speak the single word.

Gincie put her cheek against his. "My love, you did the best you could, but Seth is gone."

Travis closed his eyes again, a shudder ran through him, and he lay still.

"I'm going to take Seth home, too," Alex announced. "I will not leave him here to be buried in the mud and blood of this place."

No one gainsaid her, and Alex never knew what it cost Frank and Reid to find the undertaker who prepared Seth's body that night for the trip. She and Gincie spent the time caring for Travis. And when the officer in charge protested his removal on the grounds that the man was a Rebel and therefore a prisoner-of-war, Alex stared at him in disdain.

"He tried to save my grandson's life, a Union officer's life. And he is my grandson by marriage. Do you think you or ten more like you are going to prevent me from taking him home? If you cause even the slightest delay, I will hold you personally responsible for any worsening in Travis's condition, or for his death."

The man was clearly taken aback by her outburst, but then he shrugged wearily. "All right, ma'am, but you'd better not be lettin' too many people on the road know you're transportin' a Johnny Reb. Some won't take kindly to that; a lot of our men were killed or taken prisoner by the Confederates here."

It took Alex a moment to realize that his advice was, in spite of the circumstances, well meant. "Thank you," she said. "We'll take care."

Nigel managed to seek them out during the night. His eyes were red from overwork and grief, but he tried to offer what comfort he could.

"Gran, I don't think he knew he was here most of the time. One of the last things he said was something about showing the swans to Jane. I think he believed he was at Wild Swan. And Jane must have been someone special to him, though he never spoke to me about her. Seth is— Seth was very private about such matters." His control broke, and he sobbed; his oldest brother had been very dear to him.

Alex embraced him, murmuring, "Take care of yourself, Nigel. We could not bear another loss." Inwardly, she was praying that what he had said was true, that Seth had envisioned Wild Swan in his last conscious moments.

In the morning, Alex discovered that news of Seth's death had spread among his men. Many of them, both the ambulatory wounded and those who had escaped injury, were there to honor him.

One of the men was holding the reins of Porthos. "The Capt'n set great store by his horse, Miz Falconer, an' we thought mebbe you'd like to take him home. He's been good an' steady in every battle. The Capt'n claimed you raised the best horses anywheres."

Alex observed the way the gelding stood quietly for the man, nuzzling him affectionately, and she swallowed the impulse to accept the soldier's offer. "You keep him. And when the war is over, if you have no further use for him, bring him to Wild Swan."

The soldier hesitated, and then nodded. "Yes, ma'am, thank you." He made no effort to wipe away the tears trickling down his weathered cheeks.

"The Reb's a good man, hope he makes it," one of the other troopers called softly as Travis was carried to the wagon and laid down beside Seth's coffin.

The soldiers stood at attention as the wagon rolled away from Gettysburg.

Chapter

41

When General Lee was convinced that Meade was not going to counterattack, he led his battered army and thousands of prisoners back to Virginia. The springless wagons carrying the wounded stretched for seventeen miles. And though there was some rearguard action, on July 14 Lee completed the crossing of the Potomac, whose rain-swollen waters had delayed him. He left behind him thousands of dead who had fallen in such gallant, futile actions as Pickett's charge, wherein the Confederates had flowed in a steady sea of grim determination into the murderous fire of Federal artillery.

In the West, the long siege of Vicksburg, Mississippi, had ended on July 4 with Grant getting the "unconditional surrender" he demanded. The Union now controlled the Mississippi River and had split the Confederacy north to south. Less than a week after Vicksburg, Port Hudson, the last major Confederate stronghold on the Mississippi, also surrendered, having been besieged for six weeks.

In New York, resentment of the Conscription Act flared into four days of riots that saw a mob, estimated to number as high as fifty thousand people, looting property and attacking the free blacks of the city. Federal troops had to be called in to stop the rioting, thus drawing valuable manpower away from the battlefields. But the Conscription Act was serving its purpose, despite the inequities and trouble it was causing, for many men were volunteering to avoid being labeled "conscripts."

Gettysburg, Vicksburg, and the continually replenished army of the Union—they were all signs that the South's cause was lost. "Stonewall" Jackson had died as a result of being mistakenly shot by his own men at Chancellorsville, and Lee had missed him sorely at Gettysburg. And Jeb Stuart, previously so vital in screening the movements of Lee's army and in lending swift support in battle, had failed to rendezvous with Lee when Lee most needed the cavalry right before and during the first days of Gettysburg. The slowing hindrance of captured supply wagons and a series of wrong guesses, rather than wrongdoings, had caused Stuart's delay, but the damage had been done.

Union soldiers had taken heart and fought valiantly at Gettysburg. Lee was not invincible after all. But though the legend was tarnished, Lee and his army had not surrendered, and showed every sign of being committed to fighting on.

In one part of her mind, Alex recognized that it all mattered, but she had little thought for anything or anyone outside the family.

The trip back to Wild Swan had been a nightmare of heat and suffering, with Travis crying aloud when the pain of having his wound jolted by the wagon's motion became intolerable. Safe doses of morphine or laudanum, both opium derivatives, gave no more than brief respites. He was more dead than alive when they arrived at the farm. And the odor of death had clung to them all, filling their nostrils from Gettysburg and underscored by the presence of death in the wagon with them. But at least no one had impeded their tortured progress; it was as if the misery contained in the wagon had served to ward off interference.

Rane had been waiting for her, having left New York because of the war news almost as soon as he had arrived there. Another day and he would have set out after her. But his fury was instantly transmuted into grief when he saw the human wreckage she had brought home. He had adored Seth, and he loved Travis, too.

They buried Seth at Wild Swan. Morgan had returned in time and was there beside Sam. Philly, Blaine, Flora, Caleb, the Bateses, and Dr. Cameron were there, as well as Della, Samson, and the others left at Wild Swan, but of Seth's own generation, only Larissa stood beside the grave. Gincie was not willing to leave Travis's side, and all the others were too far away in their war work.

Alex thought particularly of Adam, who had adored his older brother and who had not seen Seth near the end as Nigel had. Adam had been home briefly in the spring, but he was back with the North Atlantic Blockading Squadron, and she hoped he had good friends to help him bear the shock of the news about Seth.

She watched Sam and Morgan as they stood beside the grave, and she saw their hands entwine, saw Morgan's head bend to rest against Sam's as they both wept, and she was thankful that at least they were turning to each other, as she and Rane were turning to each other.

She glanced up at Rane's set face. Lean and lined with age and grief, it was very much the visage of a patriarch, but when he looked down at her, his expression softened instantly, and she knew that if he could take the pain of Seth's death from her, he would. She had thought that losing one's own children was as great a tragedy as anything could be; now she found that losing the next generation was easily a match for it.

She wanted to throw herself on the earth and shriek against the injustice of it. But there wasn't even time for grieving, not with Travis so close to death that he needed constant care.

He had been weakened by the illness Gincie had worried about, and then the long days of riding through Maryland toward Pennsylvania had taken their toll. The frail figure balanced on the edge of death had little resemblance to the robust young man he had been before the war began. Even his eyes were dimmed to a muddy gray-blue in a gaze that wandered feverishly without recognition.

If he lived, it was almost certain he would be lame, but at least he could still move his leg and his foot, proof that the major nerves had not been severed. Alex was determined he would keep the leg, though army surgeons would probably have amputated by now.

Not only the women, but Samson and Rane took their turns watching over Travis, helping to restrain him when he was violently delirious. But through it all, Gincie scarcely left her husband's side. Gincie still had not said anything about what had happened to her before she had gotten to Wild Swan, but the wounded look never left her eyes, and Alex found more concrete proof in the medicines missing from her store of curatives. Many of the substances were lethal if improperly used, and some had unpleasant effects even in proper dosage. Alex had never been lax in keeping track of them, training long ago instilled in her by her grandmother. She knew she was not mistaken about what was missing, and she knew why Gincie had appeared so ill for several days, though when questioned, Gincie had denied any specific symptoms.

Alex kept her knowledge to herself for the time being. The situation was dire enough without further complications, and she hoped that when Travis was better, the couple would work out their problems.

For days Travis's fever burned him, and he writhed mindlessly against the hands that held him down and changed the dressings on the roughly sutured wound that continued to seep and fester because his body was too weak to heal itself. Alex began to lose hope, but Gincie kept after Travis, talking to him until her voice was hoarse.

"Hang on, Travis Culhane. I love you, I need you, and I'm not going to let you go," she told him, and in his ramblings Travis called out to her and worried that he had lost the precious watch she had given him.

At three o'clock one morning, Gincie jolted awake in her chair by the bed. An ominous peace was creeping over Travis, smoothing out the lines of struggle on his face.

She grabbed his shoulders and shrieked, "No! No, God damn it! Travis, you can't die!"

Her scream brought Alex and Rane on the run. They found Gincie sobbing, her head resting against Travis's shoulder.

"He'll live now," she said, and they realized her tears were for relief. "He nearly left me."

She pulled back to study his face, and his eyelids fluttered until finally his eyes opened and focused on her. "Don't cry," he whispered, which made Gincie weep all the harder, but she was laughing too. "These are for joy," she assured him, and she rained tiny kisses on his bearded face.

In the days that followed, Travis began to slowly gain strength, though it would be a long road back. He was patient and enduring, and his eyes followed Gincie everywhere.

It was Gincie Alex worried about now. She seemed to be shrinking inside herself as Travis improved. Alex knew she had good cause to be exhausted, but it went beyond that. Gincie started at the slightest sound, and too often her eyes slid away from a direct look even at Travis. When Alex saw that Travis was becoming increasingly aware of the change in his wife and suffering because of it, she confided in Rane.

She explained about the bruises and bloodstains she and Della had seen and about the medicines now missing. Rane heard her out without a word, his face terrible to behold. And when she was finished, he grated, "I want to know who it was; I want to punish him myself."

"Rane, it doesn't matter who he was! Can't you see that? What matters now is Gincie and Travis! I don't know what to do. I had hoped that Gincie would tell Travis, but I know she hasn't."

Rane shook his head as if recovering from a physical blow, and then he said, "I'll speak to her."

Alex started to refuse his offer and then thought better of it. Gincie had adored and trusted Rane since she was a tiny child. And a man had caused her hurt; perhaps a man could help her heal.

Now that Alex had spoken to him, Rane became extremely sensitive to the changes in Gincie. He could feel the weight on her spirit, and anger and sorrow twisted through him to see this beloved child so diminished.

It took patience, but a few days later, he managed to speak to Gincie alone.

"Your grandmother and I know," he said softly.

Her head jerked up, eyes flaring wide. "You can't! I mean—there's nothing—"

"How could Alex not know? She is the one who taught you the use of herbs and drugs. Do you think she is so careless of her medicines that she wouldn't know what you had taken?"

The silence stretched between them until Gincie drew a long sighing breath. "I killed him, but it was too late. I—" She began to shake so hard, she clamped her teeth tight against their chattering.

Rane drew her into his arms. "Child, child, it's all right. You're safe now. Whatever happened, it has nothing to do with what you and

Travis share, nothing to do with that at all. Your grandmother and I, we're here for you, but it's Travis you must confide in. He loves you; you owe him your trust. And he knows something is wrong and fears he is the cause of it."

He continued to hold her, patting her back gently, willing her to feel all the love that was hers at Wild Swan. He hoped he had opened the way for her to go to Travis. But this was no child with scraped knees and questions about the stars above her small head. This was a woman more profoundly hurt than a child could ever be. But this was also the woman who had killed her attacker. That gave him hope for her strength.

Her shivering stopped, and she drew away from him. "Thank you." The words were barely audible, but he saw her shoulders lift and straighten as if she were physically accepting the task ahead.

"Please tell Gran that I will care for Travis alone this afternoon. I'll ask if I need help." New life was creeping into her voice.

Rane watched her walk away before he went to find Alex, who was preparing to relieve Della in the sickroom. He took the work bag and the books from her hands.

"Gincie has gone to him. What you suspected is true. She didn't tell me all; I didn't want her to. She must confide in Travis first." He forestalled the question in her eyes. "I don't know what will come of it. But they love each other very much, almost as much as we."

He felt his full age and hers in the horror of witnessing the war ravening on their young.

Suddenly Alex was clinging to him, wailing the echo of his thought. "This hellish war! It is taking them, all of our children, and spitting them back in bloody pieces! All the love, all the care, nothing stands against it! Nothing!"

"You are wrong, sweetling. We stand against it. Gincie and Travis stand against it. Wherever there is even the smallest shadow of love, there is hope against the war." The words were not empty. They rang with the growing conviction in his heart. Against all odds, Travis was alive for Gincie, and more, would surely help her to heal. And his Alex had so much to do with having helped to steal Travis's mangled body away from death, so much to do with having made Gincie the strong young woman she was.

"Come, you will lie down and rest," he commanded.

She went with him obediently, too tired to resist. He undressed her and himself and lay down with her in their wide bed, drawing her close. She sighed deeply, turned her head against his shoulder, and slept beneath his soothing hands.

He stroked the dark hair streaked with silver, feeling its heavy softness rippling against his skin. He studied the dark shadows of fatigue around her eyes and saw how her cheeks had hollowed and the line of her jaw had sharpened. Her body felt too light and bony against his. He saw it all, felt it all, knew how the passing years and now this war had marked them both, and yet, his mind tricked him with its own vast knowledge of her and gave her back to him as she had been when he first saw her, the grave child poised on the edge of womanhood. He fell asleep, his mouth curved in a smile at the memory.

Della left her post quietly at Gincie's bidding. Travis was sleeping, his face so lean and pale, it looked like carved alabaster. So close had death come to him, so close. Gincie shivered with the chill of it, only faintly reassured by the steady rise and fall of his chest.

His watch was on the table beside the bed where he could see it when he turned his head. Gincie kept it wound as if its ticking would keep his heart beating. For his sake, she was glad it had not been stolen or lost at Gettysburg.

Gincie checked the dressings on his hip and leg, her own heart jumping erratically until she was reassured that there was no extra seepage or bleeding.

"Must be mornin' or evenin', but doesn't seem so." His low voice startled her, but she was pleased that he had begun to keep track enough to know that the afternoon was usually the only time when she was absent from his sickroom.

She leaned down to drop a kiss on his forehead, noting automatically that the fever heat emanating from him was less. "You're right, it's neither one. I just got lonesome. Do you need anything?"

"No. Just you." His eyes closed, and she thought he was asleep again. "Gincie and Travis, fits, doesn't it?" His eyes were suddenly wide open, regarding her intently. "Doesn't it, darlin'? Or has this made it too hard? I know it should be Seth who came home alive."

The doubt and hesitancy tore at her heart, and she knew the truth of what Rane had told her. Even so weakened, Travis knew her too well to miss the change in her.

"No! It isn't your fault Seth died; you tried to save him! Oh, God, Travis, I love you! I love you so much, I wouldn't want to live without you!

But I . . . when I came north . . . I thought I could travel faster by myself . . . I was asleep one night by my fire and when . . . when I awakened, he . . . he was there. It didn't make a difference . . . that I was dressed . . . like a boy. He was a . . . big man and strong, so strong. I tried . . . but I couldn't . . . he raped me!" Her words shuddered out, and Travis was mesmerized by the rhythmic twisting of her taut-knuckled hands. "He hurt me . . . he . . . made me . . . feel . . . so dirty! Filthy . . . filthy . . . I still feel . . . that way. But I ki . . . ki-lled him. I don't know how . . . I hit him with my fists . . . and . . ."

The words continued to spill out, and Travis could see it all with brutal clarity, the blow landing just so, the ridge of the throat buckling in and blocking the windpipe. The same hands twisting in agony now, the same long, slender hands that did so many tasks so well, cared for him with such strong tenderness, had killed a man.

He was still so damnably weak, the mists swirled before his eyes and threatened to reclaim him. He concentrated on putting his hand out, reaching for hers.

At first Gincie didn't understand, sitting frozen beside his bed, reliving the horror, but then she gave him her cold hand, and he lifted it until he had it against his mouth.

His lips, dry from fever and pain-bitten, moved against her fingers, planting small, deliberate kisses. The dam crumbled inside her, and she put her head down beside his on the bed and sobbed.

This time, he didn't try to stem the flood. He put all his energy into moving his arms until he cradled her against him. "Love you, my brave Gincie, love always . . ."

She heard the evenly spaced words and felt his body relax as he drifted away. It didn't matter. When he awakened again, she knew the love would be unchanged in his eyes, in the curve of his mouth, in all of him that cherished her so deeply. She would not forget the rape; it was not possible to do so. But she felt washed clean, absolved of the connection. It was as Rane had said—the rape had nothing to do with the loving, physical and otherwise, she shared with Travis. And soon, if she awakened in the night terror of memory, Travis would be there to hold back the beasts. She refused to think of the day when he might be strong enough to return to the fighting. Surely the war would be over by then.

Having told Travis what had happened, she found she could discuss it honestly with her grandmother. "After wanting Travis's child for so long, I could not bear to think I might conceive by the man who attacked me," she explained. She did not know whether her body had simply adjusted itself or whether the draughts she had taken had worked, but in any case, the anxious moments were past; she was not pregnant.

"I do not blame you," Alex said, "but you know how dangerous those medicines are and that they are not always effective. Ergot can by itself make one dreadfully ill, and tansy can be poisonous to some."

"I know, but nothing could make me more ill than being forced by that man," Gincie replied grimly.

As the days of summer passed, Alex clung to the visible proof of Travis's recovery against the constant reminders that Seth would never grace Wild Swan again.

Adam came home for a brief visit, and while he was at the farm, he visited his brother's grave, spending a long afternoon there. When he came back to the house, his green eyes were still wet, his chestnut hair mussed as if he had repeatedly run his fingers through it.

"I tried to convince myself that he was really there, dead and buried beneath the earth, and I know it is the truth, but everything inside me wants it to be a lie, wants Seth to come riding in and make everything as it was before." He paused, unconsciously rumpling his hair further. "It's as if part of my own memory, my own body, died with my brother."

Adam was only nineteen years old, but there was nothing of the child left in him, and Alex could not ease his grief.

Letters of condolence came from Padraic, from the Bettingdons and Christopher and Gweneth, and from friends everywhere, as soon as they received news of Seth's death, and each message was a clear indication of how deeply the young man had touched the lives of those who had known him, though his time had been so short. Alex was particularly touched by a letter that came through the lines from Allen Ralston in Virginia. She guessed that he must have heard directly from someone in the Confederate army. And he had his own sad news to impart:

> *Justin and Maddy Sinclair have lost their fine son. He was only eighteen. I think of him and of Seth, and I think I have lived too long.*

But of all the communications, the most valuable came from Jane Winthrop:

Dear Mrs. Falconer,

I saw Seth's name among those listed dead at Gettysburg. Even with death from so many quarters, it seems as if men like Seth ought to be spared so that our sad world can find a way to go on more sanely. He was strong and bright and tender. He was the most courageous man I have ever known. He was so clear-sighted, and yet he carried on. This is a darker earth without him.

Surely you know, but I shall write it anyway. Seth was very fond of you. He spoke of you often and referred to you in his letters. I feel as if I have seen Wild Swan and the fine racehorses you raise there. Seth saw everything vividly. Nothing is enough in such a case as this, but he died knowing he was beloved of you and the rest of his family, and that must be the best any of us ever take away from this life. I loved him too, very much, though our time together was brief, and Seth was always careful to treat me as a friend, not a lover. Now I will never know what might have been. Even in mourning, there is selfishness.

I met your grandson while he was at Harvard, where my brother was also a student. I saw Seth again while I was serving in the field with Miss Barton's nurses. But I had to return to Boston because my brother was severely wounded and will need care for some time to come. But he is alive; I give thanks every day for that.

These journals were sent to me only for safekeeping. I have not read them. They were sealed by Seth. He left instructions that they were to be sent to you in the event of his death. I trust that in the days to come, they will give you comfort.

Alex thought of how generous it was of Jane Winthrop to have carried out Seth's wishes, and for a moment she contemplated inviting her to visit the farm. And then she realized how futile and cruel it would be.

Seth had been the reason this Jane might someday have come to Wild Swan, and Seth was gone.

Seth's letter to Alex was to the point:

Dear Gran,

I hope you will never read this, as it would mean that I shall never be home again. Though I consider the possibility as directly as I am able, I find that believing in one's own death is nearly impossible, even when death is all around. But if it should come for me, I want to leave some legacy, hence the journals. They are a meager record, but the best I can offer. You have seen much of life and death, so I would have you decide whether or not my father and mother should see these pages. Not for a single day of my life have I doubted their love for me; I know how they will grieve. Please give them the journals only if you think it will ease rather than add to their burden.

If I were to have my choice of Wild Swan or Paradise after I die, I would choose Wild Swan.

I love you dearly.

At first Alex did not think she could bear to read the pages of Seth's strong, even script, but once she began, she found them a gift beyond price.

He had begun to keep the journals when he was sixteen, and even then he had possessed an observant eye that astounded Alex. She had always known he was articulate, but that was a pale word for his writing. With humor, intelligence, and love, Seth had charted the passage of his days at Wild Swan, in Baltimore, and at Harvard. People and places jumped vividly to life from the pages—his family, friends, and Jane Winthrop, whom he had had every intention of marrying if the war spared him.

He had known the war was coming; he had met it head-on. He had written of the cruelty and waste of it, but he had also recorded the camaraderie and the humorous incidents. Sometimes his humor had deserted him; sometimes he had doubted his own courage, but his humanity had never failed him.

The last entry of the last journal had been made some days before Gettysburg:

> *Unmistakably a summer night with air I can feel, so humid and rich, and the press of men and horses cannot smother the scent of the lush growth that has come on the land. Marsh and Jacobs are playing their harmonicas, and their efforts blend with the night music of the creatures who love the dark. There have been nights when Rebs nearby have joined the concert. Strange that we soldiers want the sentimental songs, "Home Sweet Home" and the like, while ordinary citizens prefer the martial air of Mrs. Howe's "Battle Hymn of the Republic" and such. Yet another of the war's imponderables. More easily solved is my urge to sleep. I am grateful that when I dream, it is most often of Wild Swan, not of battles past or still to come. Wild Swan, so long the sweet center of my earth. And in another world and time, I will take Jane there.*

If he had begun another journal, it was lost. Alex was unutterably grateful that the last words were not a premonition of violent death, but rather a celebration of the immediacy of his situation and thoughts of a time when the war would be over.

That he had died when he was only twenty-two was a monumental tragedy, but now wonder overrode it; wonder that he had managed to appreciate life so fully before he died.

Alex wrote to thank Miss Winthrop for carrying out Seth's wishes. After careful deliberation, she added:

> *You were, indeed, very dear to my grandson. The last thing anyone heard him say had to do with showing you the wild swans that so often fly overhead at the farm during the winter.*

She resisted the temptation to tell the girl that Seth had planned to marry her; Jane Winthrop already had enough to mourn.

Alex did not hesitate to give the journals to Morgan and Sam. She was certain that they would find the same comfort there that she had.

Sam's reaction to the mere existence of the journals, before having even opened one, confirmed the rightness of the decision. She touched first one and then another of the books with reverence.

"Thank God," she breathed. "Too often I cannot even see him clearly, and not even photographs help. They are so stiff and flat, not at all like Seth."

"My dear, the journals will not give him back to you, but I promise you that even without them, you will come in time to see him as clearly as you ever did while he lived, and he will be forever young in your heart." She did not have to explain to Sam that her own loss of a son had taught her that.

Grief had marked both Sam and Morgan, but they did not falter. True to his promise, Rane had secured a special assignment for his son. Morgan's work for the navy was clandestine and hazardous as he slipped in and out of Southern ports, seeking information about how they might be taken from the Confederacy, looking for weaknesses in their defenses or new developments in their equipment. As much as the South suffered from shortages, she was proving adept at dedicating much of what she had to the war effort. Morgan knew the risks he ran every time he went on a mission, but he thrived on the work, feeling truly useful at last.

Sam accepted the fact that Morgan could not tell her where he was going on his assignments. She made the most of the time she had with him and did her best to conceal her terror when he was gone. And she continued her own work, trying to alleviate the sufferings of the Confederate prisoners, who now numbered more than ever in the aftermath of Gettysburg. She had also helped to nurse Travis in the first crucial days, never betraying with the slightest hint that she wished Seth had survived instead. It was not an exchange she allowed herself to consider.

Caleb and Flora were not faring so well. The Jenningses had at last received word that young Caleb had died in Libby Prison in Richmond. Weakened by a head wound, he had contracted a fatal fever.

While Flora mourned the loss of her grandson by marriage, she was frantic about the deteriorating condition of her husband's health. He was beginning to look as if a slight breeze would carry him away. And though his family and friends could not slow him down, his own body finally did.

Caleb suffered a heart seizure and was confined to bed by an angry

Dr. Benjamin, who maintained that his patient had been keeping a pace that would have felled an eighteen-year-old, let alone a man of his advanced age. Dr. Benjamin judged Caleb to be of basically sound constitution, though his heart was obviously not completely sound, and the doctor disliked contemplating the loss of such a good man. Like everyone else, Dr. Benjamin had had his fill of wasted lives since the war had begun.

Alex meant to be patient when she visited Caleb, but Flora looked so strained and Caleb so pale and ill, she felt more angry and afraid than patient.

"Tell Rane I'll work on the new contracts very soon," Caleb began, but there was a note of hopelessness in his reedy voice, a subtle admission that he did not expect to recover.

"You are taking the coward's way, Caleb," Alex said. "You cannot say I don't understand, because I do. We have both lost grandsons who were immeasurably precious to us. But that is no reason to feel guilty that we still live, though I have felt it, indeed, I have. Dying won't bring them back. It will only hurt everyone further. And most of all, your death would wound Flora terribly. She has always known the chance is that you will predecease her, but you have no right to deprive her of your presence before it is necessary."

"She is young and beautiful; there is time for her to have a second life," Caleb countered without heat, but with utter conviction.

Alex stared at him for a moment, and then she laughed in genuine amusement. "Oh, you are a dear; no wonder Flora adores you so! You haven't learned yet that years have passed for her, too. You still speak as if she is twenty because you see her thus. I remind you, she is forty-eight, not twenty! And she has spent most of her adult life as your wife. She has grown in your love and care and has given you hers. Do you think her so faithless and fickle that she would replace you like an old bonnet?"

Caleb was astonished by Alex's outburst, and then he smiled, as amused as she. "It is true. Though you tried to make me see her clearly once before, I dote on her as much as I did the day I married her, and I will never see her as other than young and shining."

Sobering, Alex took one of his thin, veined hands in both of hers. "I know it will not be easy, but promise me you will try to treat yourself more kindly, that you may treat your wife more kindly, too. There has been so much weeping already, and the war goes on; I would prefer not to shed tears over you, too."

"I promise," he said, and there was a spark more life in his voice than there had been before.

She stooped down and kissed him on the cheek, and then she sought her daughter.

"I know he requires quiet and care, but don't be too brave for him. He needs to know that he can still offer you support."

Flora sniffed and rubbed her eyes before she spoke. "That won't be hard to do; I don't feel in the least bit brave."

Alex had her own cowardice to bear. She knew that Travis and Gincie would go back to Virginia soon, and she dreaded the day. But Travis was beginning to move about quite handily with the aid of a walking stick, though his leg was stiff and tender and likely to remain so for some time to come. Deep inside Alex hoped it would last long enough to keep him from returning to his regiment. Jeb Stuart, with his flowing sorrel hair and beard, his plumed hat, his love of a good song and of the ladies, provided colorful material for tall tales, but his flamboyance was no shield for himself or his men against sabers and shot.

Frank Faber precipitated the Culhanes' departure. He came to Wild Swan and told Alex bluntly, "Too many people know now that Travis Culhane is here. Your taking him from Gettysburg was no secret. And he has quite a reputation for daring horsemanship. There are those who think capturing him would be a coup. A lot of people know I'm friendly with your family. I was asked outright about Travis, and I lied. I said he'd long since gone south, but I doubt the lie was enough to keep the hounds at bay for long."

"It will be the truth shortly," Alex replied, and then she added, "You are a very generous man."

He did not try to deny that he loved Gincie still; he knew it showed every time he said her name or looked at her. "Part of loving is wanting the other person's happiness at least as much as you desire your own; I would have to be blind to mistake the joy Gincie has found with her husband."

He tarried only long enough to exchange brief greetings with the couple before he was on his way again, leaving Alex to relay the news he had brought. There was a limit to what Frank could bear of Gincie's presence with Travis beside her.

"Rane is due back in a day or so; I will trust him to arrange your safe passage back to Hawthorn," Alex said. She was proud of the steadiness of her voice. They had to leave; it was far too dangerous for them to stay.

But that night, Travis tried to make Gincie see reason. "They aren't after you. You could stay here in perfect safety. And I would know you were safe."

"No," she said, and she refused to elaborate.

Travis sighed; it was obviously a subject she was not even willing to discuss. And he was not strong enough to press the issue. The thought of being apart from her until the war ended sometime in the uncertain future was appalling. Even if he went back to his regiment, at least Gincie would be in Virginia where he could go to her. No Union soldiers could keep him away from land he knew better than his own face.

Gincie had begun to sleep beside him as soon as he could bear the movement and weight of another body in the bed, and she had held him and talked to him when the pain of his wound had made it impossible for him to sleep. She was far better medicine than the opium extracts that gave distorted dreams and made him feel dizzy and sick while they eased the pain. But he had made no overtures of love to her, not even in these past days when he had felt strong enough and desire had started to reawaken.

He was afraid of how she would react to renewed intimacy. He could not fathom how it must feel to have been raped. He had been big and strong for a long time; fear of being overpowered and abused was not part of his nature. But now he realized that for a woman, it was something that must always be considered. It made his guts twist to think of his brave Gincie being so vulnerable, being so hurt. Nothing could mitigate the rage he felt against the man responsible. He wished it had been left to him to kill the beast.

Seeking a more comfortable position, Gincie rubbed against him as he lay on his good side, and her warm curves stirred his blood. She stiffened instinctively as she felt the rise of his manhood, and he started to shift away from her onto his back. But her arms came up to hold his shoulders in place.

"Make love to me, Travis. If that—that man—if he killed this between us, he won after all." Her voice shook, and her grip on his shoulders was convulsive. She wanted to prove the truth of what her grandfather had said about the rape having nothing to do with what she and Travis shared.

The importance of the moment nearly unmanned Travis. He was, in any case, still forced to move carefully due to the tight pull of the long scar, and he thought in some desperation that they were a matched pair—she damaged on the inside, he on the outside.

But he was wrong. The slow, gentle rising of passion between them was exactly what both of them needed. At first she trembled like a wild bird, but she tamed under the gentle persuasion of his hands and mouth. He touched and tasted her everywhere, reclaiming her body for his own, giving pleasure where her attacker had given pain, and when she began to tremble anew, it was from passion, not fear. And she in turn offered her own healing, tracing the hard ridge of scar tissue that marred his body, telling him without words that she still found him pleasing to her senses and her heart.

There was no resistance when he eased into her; her body sheathed him in liquid heat, and she arched her hips against him to take him deeper, calling his name.

Travis lay awake long after Gincie slept. His wound ached from the exertion. But it didn't matter, nothing mattered except having Gincie in his arms.

Only now did he see how fitting it was that they had renewed their loving here. Their marriage had begun at Wild Swan, and no matter how loyal she had become to Hawthorn, Gincie's strength had come from this place. He lay listening to the even rhythm of her breathing as he waited patiently for the pain to ease enough for him to sleep. And he admitted to himself that despite the danger, he was very, very glad that his wife was going to return to Virginia with him.

Chapter

42

The day after Gincie and Travis left, soldiers rode in to demand that Travis Culhane surrender to them.

Alex took pleasure in telling the officer in command that he would not find his quarry at Wild Swan. She did not volunteer any additional information, and after a desultory search, the soldiers left. Alex suspected that though they were looking for a Confederate, they had also been told something about the Falconers' connections to high officials in the government. The confusion of family loyalties was not new in the war, particularly in the border states.

Alex had bidden farewell to Travis and Gincie with a minimal display of emotion. She trusted Rane to find a way to deliver them safely to Hawthorn. And beyond that, she had suffered so many emotional ups and downs in the past months, she felt rather numb. She suspected her face wore the same grimly enduring expression she saw on Della's.

Jotham and his compatriots from Wild Swan had so far managed to serve bravely and to stay alive in the 54th Massachusetts, not a small feat considering that their involvement in the July attack on Fort Wagner, Morris Island, South Carolina, had resulted in the death of their colonel R. G. Shaw and a casualty rate of forty percent. The Union forces had been driven out and had then laid a formal siege that ended when the Confederates abandoned the island during the night of September 6. Shaw had been a white man devoted to his black troops, and the Confederates had mutilated his body and thrown it into a trench with the dead blacks to demonstrate their fury at the very idea of black soldiers.

The reservations so many had held about the ability of black soldiers to fight were beginning to ease, but there were as yet very few black officers, and as an added insult, black soldiers were paid at a lower rate than white. The men of the 54th Massachusetts were among those who were protesting this practice by refusing any pay until they were paid equally. It was a gesture of courageous defiance, but it was also an action liable to punishment under the strict code of military regulations.

Jotham was a well-educated and dignified young man, and though they seldom discussed it with her, Alex knew his parents worried constantly that he might end up in as much danger from Union military discipline as he was from Rebel guns.

As the autumn drew on, Alex discovered there were other things Della and Samson were not discussing with her.

When Frank Faber sought her out once again at Wild Swan, Alex's first thought was that he had come for news of Gincie and Travis. Alex had been in Washington for the first days of October but had seen neither of the newspapermen—Reid was in the West again, and she hadn't known where Frank was—so her assumption had some merit until she got a closer look at Frank's face.

He was obviously troubled and very ill at ease, and they exchanged only the briefest of greetings before she asked, "What is it? What's wrong? Is it Reid or Larissa?"

Frank shook his head and then asked bluntly, "Do you know where Mr. Falconer is?"

She saw his skin flush darkly as he asked. The question took her completely by surprise. "I expect he's in Philadelphia, or he might even now be arriving back in Baltimore or Washington," she said slowly, watching Frank all the while. "You know the problems of supplying the army and the navy are never ending, and there is still a little business to do for Jennings-Falconer, even though fewer ships are sailing for the line. Caleb is not yet fit for much, and Morgan is busy with governmental work." (Alex was no more privy to the details of Morgan's missions than the rest of the family.) "Rane is due here any day now. This month marks the thirty-second year of our marriage; we plan to spend a few days here together." The cold sharpness of her voice contrasted with the innocuous explanation as fear crept over her. Frank was shifting from one foot to the other, as if he were a small boy caught in some mischief. "Why are you here?" she demanded.

"There's talk that the *Falcon* is being used to trade with the blockade runners and that Mr. Falconer is captaining her," Frank blurted out. Though Gincie was beyond his reach now, he cared deeply for this family. He hated the errand he had set himself this day.

"Have you lost your reason?" The question was not asked kindly. "You know where Rane's sympathies lie, you know how he has supported the Union! How dare you suggest such a thing!"

"I'm not the one who suggested it," he protested miserably. "I only heard it and came to warn you. It did not seem to be idle rumor. The man who told me knows I am fond of your family. I think he was trying both to find out if I knew anything about it and to warn me if I didn't. I feel like the messenger doomed to beheading for bearing bad news."

She was instantly contrite. "I'm sorry, Frank, and I promise to be more reasonable."

She led him to the library and sent for tea to give herself time to collect her wits. Cassie brought the tea and left them alone, and only after Alex had poured two cups with a nearly steady hand did she broach the subject again. "Now, tell me exactly what you know."

"It isn't much, but enough, I believe, for worry. A fellow reporter has a brother in the navy, and this sailor swears that his ship gave chase to the *Falcon* and that he is sure Mr. Falconer was on board. The light was dim, the figurehead was shrouded, and the name covered, but he's sure. Before the war, he worked at a shipyard in Philadelphia, and he knew and admired the Jennings-Falconer vessels. Mrs. Falconer, he didn't betray his knowledge to his captain, but it's only a matter of time before your husband is caught. My friend's brother is sure this isn't the first time; a ship matching the same description has been sighted a few times before."

For a moment she hid her face in her hands, willing calm to quiet the furious gallop of her pulse, unable to think clearly beyond the pounding in her head.

Frank watched her, terrified she was going to faint, but his feeling of inadequacy ebbed when she raised her head and squared her shoulders, visibly becoming the commanding woman he knew Alexandria Carrington Falconer to be.

"I honestly do not know a thing about this," she confessed. "But I do know he is loyal to the Union. And I'm sure it does not concern Gincie. I would know if it did. The way to her is not by sea." She answered his unspoken torment. "Whatever Rane is involved in, there must be a good reason. He is a rational man and no traitor."

She could see how anxious Frank was to escape. She rose from her chair and extended her hand. "Thank you for coming to me. This wretched war has tested all our loyalties in one way or another. And you have aided and protected us at every turn. Were it not for you, the patrol that came looking for Travis might well have taken him prisoner. Take very good care of yourself."

She stayed where she was for long moments, looking inward, recalling all the times in the past weeks when she had not known exactly where Rane was but had assumed his absences were all part of his work for the government. And then she began to recall the whispered conversations between Della and Samson, always when Rane had been gone, and always stopped when she drew near, and the anxious expressions they had both worn lately—she had assumed all of it had stemmed from their worry about Jotham. Now she doubted that.

She maintained her air of calm until she found Samson, but he took one look at her face and braced himself for the onslaught.

"You know where Rane is, what he's doing! You know, don't you!" she shrieked, and then her face crumpled, and her tears overflowed. "I can't bear it! If something happens to him, I—" Her sobs choked off the rest of the words.

Samson could withstand her anger, but he was helpless in the face of her grief. He took her hand and patted it awkwardly. "Easy now. Dat man, he de smartest man I knows, he be back. Quick as lightnin', him an' dat boat, nobody catches 'em."

Several things penetrated her misery at once. This wild tale Frank had reported was true, and Samson had indeed known all along what Rane was up to, but even though he had revealed much in his effort to comfort her, he was going to do his best to keep the final truth from her. She knew she could force him to tell her everything; she could feel his vulnerability to her distress. And she knew she would not make him further betray Rane's trust.

She drew away from him. "He is in more danger here than he is on that blasted boat! I may strangle him with my bare hands when I see him!" She summoned every bit of anger to reassure Samson and strode away swiftly, not wanting to test her nerve. Samson watched her go, heart aching for her.

The following days passed in a haze of terror for Alex, as one grim possibility after another occurred to her, the worst being that the *Falcon* would be fired upon and sunk by the same ship Adam was on. And with that vision came a renewed burst of fury that Rane would risk putting his grandson in that position, let alone risking his own life.

And over it all was her utter confusion about what dealings he could possibly have with the Confederate blockade runners. She could not imagine any reason the government would have assigned him such a mission; Rane and his ship were too well known in Southern ports to pass for Confederate sympathizers. And in any case, the *Falcon* was a sailing ship, hardly a match for the steam-powered vessels that were now the rule for both sides. However, the idea of Rane having private business was no less baffling. She was well aware of the huge profits being made by those running cargoes into the South past the Union blockade. That Rane might be tempted to share in those profits was incredible. Yet, in her darkest moments, she considered that he had simply succumbed to the temptation to experience once again the excitement of smuggling.

The worst of it was that there was nothing for her to do except wait for his return; any attempt she might make to locate him and his ship could well put him in added danger.

When Rane finally rode into Wild Swan one afternoon, the relief of seeing him alive overwhelmed every other emotion in Alex in the first moments, and she threw her arms around him with a glad cry.

He gave a grunt of discomfort. "Careful, love, my ribs are a bit tender."

She stepped back from him, and he saw that she knew about the smuggling.

"How did you find out?" he asked, accepting that denial would be fruitless.

Her rage flooded back. "I seem to have been the last to know!" she snapped. "Frank Faber brought a warning; you and the *Falcon* have been sighted and identified. What in God's name have you been doing? Did the old game tempt you so sorely, you could not resist?" She was sorry as soon as she said it, for she was suddenly conscious of how gray and weary he looked. "Never mind, you can tell me while I see to your hurt." Alex was feeling so many things—anger, relief, joy, and curiosity—she needed the pause more than Rane did.

He had a deep runnel across the chest where a bullet had creased his flesh. It was raw, and the area beside it was bruised and angry looking. Though it was in no way life-threatening, her hands shook as she cleaned and dressed the wound. So close—he had come so close; he might have taken the bullet in his heart.

"I was smuggling," he said abruptly, "not free trading, smuggling. I had to do it. I watched Travis writhing in pain even with drugs to ease him, and I thought of all the young men in the South who are suffering and dying for the lack of the most basic medicines. I believe in the Union and in the necessity of blockading the South to help the war effort. But I don't believe in withholding medical aid. Surely everyone has a point of barbarity beyond which he will not go, not even to win a war. I reached that point over the medicines. The Confederates lack quinine, morphine, chloroform, surgical instruments, and everything else. You know better than most that those basic drugs cannot be duplicated, no matter how skilled one is in brewing simples. It is surely the most damning thing of all that the citizenry of the South continue to buy silks, lace, and French wines instead of insisting on goods to help their soldiers." He sighed wearily and closed his eyes for a moment before he continued.

"I could find only one major Southern shipping company, Fraser, Trenholm, and Company, that was patriotic enough to think of something other than greed, and the irony is that they are surely reaping vast profits, though they concentrate on such necessities as munitions, weapons, salt, coal, and the like. My risk was not as great as theirs; we met their ships outside the blockading fleet, and they ran the medical supplies through the blockade. On this last trip, we were intercepted and fired upon before we could lose ourselves in the dark. I hope the runner got through; the medicines were already on board. I knew it was the last trip even without the word you received from Frank. I picked my crew carefully. They're all good men who have seen the suffering, and I don't want them to die needlessly for their compassion.''

She wanted to tell him that what he had done was brave and splendid, but she couldn't. Her sense of betrayal was at the moment greater than her admiration. "Why did you tell Della and Samson but not me?"

"To spare you. They love me, but not so much as you do," he pointed out. "And beyond that, I wanted them to know, in case anything did happen to me, that there had been a good reason for what I was doing. I didn't want them to believe I had suddenly become a Confederate sympathizer."

"Rest now. I'll have Cassie bring you a tray." She did not meet his eyes. "I need some time alone." She stalked out of the room before he could react.

When she was outside, she took a few deep breaths to calm down, and then she went to saddle a horse. Samson found her there. He looked so worried, she said, "He's back in more or less one piece; he's not going on any more secret voyages, and I didn't strangle him. But I am not yet prepared to be civil about this."

She rode the autumn-hued acres of Wild Swan and tried to consider everything logically. Rane had not allowed her to be notified when he had had typhoid fever in England, and now she had again learned only after the fact that his life had been in danger. It made her feel shut out when she most needed to be close to him.

Though Wild Swan still prospered with various crops and livestock, it felt empty to her with the prize horses away. There had been some losses—two of this year's foals had sickened and died in Nova Scotia, to Padraic's sorrow, and one racing prospect had to be destroyed in England because of a broken leg—but the news was generally good from Padraic, from the Bettingdons, and from Boston in California. It was a particularly heady triumph for the horses of Wild Swan to be acquiring such a good reputation under the exacting standards of dash racing in England. And yet, Alex found it harder and harder to generate any enthusiasm for her absent champions. They no longer seemed to be connected to her.

Though she tried to flinch away from the knowledge, it came to her that her own trip to Gettysburg, the times she had stayed at Wild Swan despite the threat of raiders, and even the nursing of the sick and wounded in the capital, had carried their own elements of risk, risk she knew Rane would rather she had not taken.

The sorrow of it settled on her heart. Even after so many years together, they still had lives and obligations apart from each other, these not by choice but as the war dictated them.

She did not arrive back at the house until the sun was nearly gone. Rane was waiting for her, curbing the impatience that would have sent him in search of her.

She approached him directly. "What you have done is valid and brave. And you are perfectly correct—each one of us must make a decision about what we can and cannot tolerate. But in risking your life, you also risked mine, because you are so much a part of me. I do not ask that you cease to do what you must, only that you cease to keep it secret from me. I have a dread so terrible you cannot imagine the force of it. I dread having someone come to me with news of your death. And it is made a thousand times worse when I think that with that news I will learn that I have had no knowledge of where you were or what you were doing. I am not sure you can understand this, but it is the way I feel."

In the strange mirror imaging that had been so much a part of their lives together, Rane did understand. He suddenly knew how he would feel if he was told that Alex had been killed racing one of the horses while he had thought her forever safe from that danger because she had promised him she would never race again.

He reached out and touched her face, gently tracing the strong contours. "I do understand. And I have a confession to make—my motives may have been of the highest order, but I also enjoyed the smuggling, shades of my youth." He raised his right hand. "I solemnly swear that I will henceforth behave as a sober citizen."

"Sober citizen, never that!" She tried to smile, but the effort failed in tears. "Oh, Rane, stay by me! The world doesn't make sense to me any more."

Heedless of his sore chest, Rane drew her against him. "We make sense, and that's all that matters," he murmured.

It was still disconcerting to feel such uncertainty in her. Seth's death above all else had changed them. And his own recent activities had added to her burden. He was not sorry for the smuggling, only for the fact that Alex had found out about it. He could not bring Seth back, nor could he banish the frantic worry Alex had suffered these past days. But he could give her more of his attention.

They rode over Wild Swan together; they spoke of the children and the grandchildren; and they made slow love before the fires lighted against the autumnal chill.

"Are you courting me, Mr. Falconer?" Alex asked one afternoon, feeling warm and sheltered by his love.

"Today and every day of my life, even when I seem remiss," he answered, and Alex could see his heart in his eyes.

"And every day my answer will be the same—yes, and yes, and yes," Alex whispered.

In November, he accompanied her to the races in Baltimore, but the outing wasn't very successful. An attempt was being made to reinstitute the sport in the capital and Baltimore, but there were scarcely more than half a dozen weary horses available to race in both places, and they were not of the best quality.

"You were very wise to send the horses away," Rane told Alex after watching a mediocre heat.

"I doubted that at first," she admitted, "but no longer. It's common knowledge that remounts are becoming one of the Confederacy's most pressing problems. Wild Swan is a tempting enough target as it is; if the horses were still there, the raids would undoubtedly be much worse." She thought of all the Southern breeding and racing stock that had already gone onto the battlefields and all that would follow, and she mourned the loss of generations of care and hope that had gone into improving the Thoroughbreds. The best of the breeds—man and horse— seemed to be doing most of the dying. She knew she would never forget the sight of the acres of corpses at Gettysburg.

The round of entertainments continued in the cities, particularly the capital, but no number of horse races or soirées could soften the grim fact that the war continued.

Grant had been made supreme commander of the Federal forces in the West, and most of the fighting was once again in that theater. President Lincoln had declared the last Thursday of November as Thanksgiving Day, but Alex thought privately that it was going to take her a while to be thankful for anything without thinking of Luke and Seth lying beneath the earth of Wild Swan. She thought the address the president gave to dedicate the new National Cemetery at Gettysburg was more to the point. Many complained about the brevity of his speech, but Alex had a sense of hearing the eloquent lines through Seth's ears: ". . . government of the people, by the people, and for the people, shall not perish from the earth." Seth had so believed, and he had believed in the beauty and power of language. But his voice, like those of so many other young men, had been stilled, and it was for others to speak for him. The president had done the job well. Less easy to consider was the fact that the work at the cemetery was only partially done; thousands of bodies were yet to be exhumed from hasty graves and reburied. So many thousands had died there.

Grant's forces drove the Confederates away from Chattanooga toward the end of November, and by early December, Tennessee was under Union control. President Lincoln, with firm hope for the war's end, issued a Proclamation of Amnesty and Reconstruction, which offered pardon to Confederates in return for a loyalty oath.

Alex read about and heard of these developments from her bed at Wild Swan. To her disgust, she had scarcely returned to her nursing duties in Washington before she succumbed to a putrid sore throat which rendered her useless to her patients and everyone else. Rane ordered her home to recuperate, reinforcing his edict by telling the children so that he had what seemed to Alex a veritable army instantly summoned to smother her with concern. It was particularly hard to be incapacitated when she felt that her family needed her to be a source of comfort, not an invalid.

All her children and their spouses appeared worn and blue-deviled to her. Morgan, Sam, Philly, and Blaine could not help but worry constantly about their children, and Flora and Caleb worried not only about her nieces and nephews, but about his grandchildren, too. And anything Flora gained by not having children of her own, she lost in her fear of Caleb suffering a fatal heart seizure, and she had difficulty finding reassurance, though her husband looked better now than he had in months.

"Gran, you just want to be the chief worrier and mother hen," Larissa teased when she came to visit. "But you might as well resign yourself to being coddled for a while. Grandfather is not going to relent until he sees that you are healthy again."

"Make sure you take care of yourself," Alex retorted. "You look decidedly wan to me."

"I am lonesome for Reid," Larissa confessed. "But in his last letter, he said he would be coming east soon. Honestly, he has the worst effect on me; I think of him all the time now, as if I were a mere girl mooning over her first love."

He is your first love, Alex thought, but she didn't say it. Larissa had enough guilt about Luke. Instead she made an admission of her own. "Even after all these years, I still spend an inordinate amount of time dreaming over Rane. I am convinced that marriage scarcely has a chance unless that kind of involvement is part of it. You do plan to marry Reid, don't you?"

Larissa nodded, but her expression was suddenly sad and austere.

"The war cannot last much longer," Alex said with as much conviction as she could muster, but her voice sounded hollow in her own ears, and as she bade her granddaughter once again to take care, she hoped Reid would return very soon to raise Larissa's spirits.

Indeed, Reid was on his way back even as Larissa left Wild Swan, and when he arrived in Washington several days later, he paused barely long enough to unpack and clean up before he went in search of Larissa.

He went to the hospital first, so anxious to see her that he was prepared to ride immediately for Wild Swan if she were not with the wounded or at her boarding house. But at the hospital he was told that Larissa had taken a chill and had been ordered to rest for a few days.

"She works too hard, and there was the matter of Private Simkins. He was so very young, only seventeen. You see, he lied when he volunteered at fifteen. Just a farm boy, he was, and so homesick. He seemed to be recovering nicely, and then, two days ago he died. Larissa took it very hard; she had become much like an older sister to the boy."

Mrs. Watson was a middle-aged, motherly sort whose husband and four sons were fighting in the Union army. She had always wanted a daughter and had taken a great liking to Larissa Carstairs. She did not believe for a moment that this tall, blue-eyed man was no more than a friend of the family. She had seen Larissa with him on several occasions, and she thought the sight of him now would be good for the young woman.

Reid was too worried to perceive her kind intentions. "Is there anyone with her, her grandmother or someone else?" he asked sharply.

"Mrs. Falconer is at her home recovering from a bad throat. And as I'm sure you know, we can ill afford to spare good nurses from this place," she reminded him gently. "Don't worry so; Larissa is a sensible girl, she'll take care of herself."

Reid did not believe that. It was beginning to dawn on him that everyone, including himself, expected Larissa to be always self-sufficient, as if her usual air of calm collectedness and slight remove was the whole of her. And because he had seen her weeping so helplessly, he was doubly guilty for expecting so much from her. He knew, perhaps better than her family, how Luke's death and each of the hurts and sorrows of the war had wounded her, and yet, it had suited him to consider only her strength.

He was shaking by the time he got to her boarding house. Having helped her to find the room when Anthea had joined her in Washington, he knew where it was and slipped into the house and up the stairs without encountering the landlady.

He knocked on the door and was not reassured by the muffled sound of Larissa's voice when it bade him enter.

Her dark hair was matted to her head by the fever sweat; her gray eyes were red-rimmed and ringed with shadows; and she was huddled under the covers of a bed that had obviously been the scene of an unsuccessful battle for comfort. She looked so woebegone that his heart turned over, and before Larissa could utter more than a shocked cry at the sight of him, he sat on the bed and swept her into his arms.

"My poor love, you've been so busy taking care of everyone else, you've forgotten all about yourself."

"I didn't expect you so soon. Truly, I will be fine by tomorrow," she murmured. In fact, she could not remember feeling worse in her life, low in both spirit and body, and even his very solid presence was blurred by the fever haze, but she was conscious that she looked terrible, and she didn't want him to see her like this. "Why don't you go away and come back later?" she suggested weakly.

"As you did when I needed help? No, I think I'll stay here and take care of you instead," he answered cheerfully, and he proceeded to do just that with admirable skill.

There was little evidence that Larissa's landlady had expended any energy on her plight, and when Reid spoke to the woman, he realized it was not only from a reluctance to add to her work, but also because she was afraid of what she might catch—everybody knew that all sorts of fevers were rife among the wounded. Reid used this to his advantage, requesting clean linens, warm water, hot broth, and a few other items while he assured the woman that she would not be required to do anything except supply these essentials.

"I am going to marry her as soon as she is well again," he announced to ease any qualms the woman might have about the propriety of his actions. "And I want that to be as soon as possible."

He wrote a message to Dr. Grover and requested that the landlady have someone deliver it. He gave the woman a generous gratuity, which brightened her tired eyes enough so that he knew he would have her continued cooperation.

"Reid, you can't—" Larissa protested when Reid started to remove her bedgown.

"Of course I can. I've seen you before, and you'll feel much more comfortable in a moment," he assured her.

She ceased to protest because she was too stunned by this turn of events and too weak to fight him.

Taking care not to let her grow chilled, he gave her a thorough bed bath before dressing her in a clean gown, wrapping her warmly, and depositing her in a chair while he changed the bed linens. Larissa watched this with bleary-eyed wonder.

"Where did you learn how to do all this?" she finally asked, the effort setting off a coughing spell.

"Hush, Lissa mine." He patted her back gently and waited until the cough had quieted before he put her back in bed. "I'm a man of many talents," he said, not wanting to discuss the fact that the war had taught him the basic skills of ministering to the sick and dying.

But he was relieved when Dr. Grover arrived to examine Larissa. "Overworked, overtired, undernourished," the doctor pronounced out of Larissa's hearing, "and heading for pneumonia. It's a good thing you came back, Mr. Tratnor. With rest and care, she should be fine."

"Should I send word to her family, even though she told us not to?" Reid asked.

Dr. Grover studied Reid's anxious face closely. "If you think you can't cope, then do send for someone. But I think you're the best medicine she could have." The doctor was impressed by the easy command Reid had already taken of the situation, and he had seen these two before —Larissa had been good for Reid when he had been ill; surely the reverse would be equally true.

Reid had every confidence in his ability to care for Larissa for the simple reason that he was certain that no one, not even her family, loved her as much as he did. In the next days, he fed and bathed her, read to her and often just sat quietly beside the bed while she slept. All the lives he could not protect, all the lives he could not change for the better became focused in her. This small part of the world he would save for himself.

And when Larissa's fever was down, and she was feeling far better than she had when he found her, he told her his plans for them.

"I did not consider before that I might lose you, only that you might lose me. I know better now. We are going to be married as soon as possible." He anticipated and forestalled her protest. "It is, as you once said, a matter of responsibility, but now I am changing the rules. I think you will behave more responsibly in the care of my wife than of yourself, and I intend to stay in one piece to see that you do.

"You have a right to know about my prospects, a subject we've never really discussed," he went on. "I am a good newspaperman, and I intend to continue in my job, but even were I to lose it, we would not starve. My parents left goodly sums to my sister and to me. I have no particular affinity for New York, albeit I was raised there. I am sure I could find work closer to your home. It would be no hardship; I like your family very much."

Larissa felt him sweeping all her uncertainties away, and she was both touched and amused by his presentation of his "prospects," but she still felt obliged to be cautious for both of them. "Don't you think the war is dictating this just as it has kept us apart before? We have gotten this far; should we not wait until the war is over to be sure of how we feel?"

"I love you," Reid said. "I can not imagine not loving you, war or no war. And it is not just your being sick. I dream of you. I wake up reaching for you. I have not been very successful of late in tempering my desire for you. Finding you so ill was just the final straw. Tell me honestly, do you have doubts about your love for me?"

She looked at his strong face and the dark cap of hair and the blue eyes watching her so anxiously, and she surrendered. "I have no doubts. I love you, Reid Tratnor, forever." And then she added with a spark of mischief, "I probably love you too much. At first I didn't even know I was really ill. I thought I was just pining for you."

He put his arms around her and kissed her soundly. "I will wait if a wedding at Wild Swan is something you want, but I would rather marry as soon as possible."

Now that he was sure of his course, he could hardly bear the idea of delay, and he thought her family would forgive him, considering how long he and Larissa had waited. Or almost waited; he remembered how it had been the night she had come to him, and he was amazed at the restraint that had governed them since.

"I had a wedding at Wild Swan long ago," Larissa said, the ghost of sorrow still there for Luke. "Once was enough." But then the joy she knew in loving Reid reasserted itself along with her own memories of their lovemaking. "However, I will be glad to find you in bed at Wild Swan without having to travel as far as I did last time."

"Lissa mine, we are going to be very, very happy together," Reid murmured as he drew her close.

Chapter

43

Christmas at Wild Swan was both bitter and sweet this year. It was always a time of heightened emotions, and with Seth gone, that was more true than ever. The smallest things brought memories of him, from the delicacies that had been his favorites to the absence of packages for him. Alex thought of how easy he had been to please—books, a fishing pole, a new bridle for his horse, she could see his expression of delight as he had received each gift. He had been the best of all combinations—fit in mind and body, steadfast of heart.

Alex reflected that Death was grotesquely inharmonious in its predations. Even when there was sorrow for the passing of an elder such as her grandmother or Horace Whittleby, there was also a feeling of pieces fitting, of orderly seasons. But with Luke, with Caleb's grandson, and most of all with Seth, because she had known and loved him more, there was a terrible discord. It was as if a killing frost had come at the height of spring. And the worst of it was that it would never have any rightness. Time would dull the pain, but the sense of outrage and loss would never vanish.

There was emptiness, too, where Gincie and Travis ought to have been. The risk of another visit by the Culhanes to Wild Swan was too high. Alex and Rane had made sure that a supply of necessities had been delivered to Hawthorn, and gold coins as well; prices in the Confederacy were soaring as the value of Confederate currency fell. And Hawthorn suffered the added problem of being in an area that had seen both armies coming and going. But Alex had made sure that a new dress for Gincie and a new suit for Travis, as well as shoes for both of them, had been included in the otherwise dull offerings. At least they were still alive and faring well enough, given the difficult circumstances of the times.

But despite all the tensions, the pulse of life and joy went on. Larissa and Reid arrived at Wild Swan with their marriage a fait accompli, and even Philly and Blaine accepted the news without rebuke. It was impossible to do less, because Larissa was more radiant than they had ever seen her. And Alex had a lump in her throat when she saw the way Reid's tall body curved protectively toward Larissa when he stood beside her.

The marriage was not the only surprise. Though Phoebe and Adam were unable to come home for the festivities, Nigel and Anthea were there, and Anthea had brought a friend with her.

Alex's first impression of Dr. Maxwell Kingston was that he looked distressingly like a frog. Though only in his mid-thirties, he was already nearly bald, left with only a thinning brown fringe around his pate. His brow was high and round over protruding blue eyes; his nose was too big for his face; and his mouth was too wide.

Yet, in a very short time, Alex understood entirely why Anthea was so captivated. Dr. Kingston possessed a tangible warmth. Humorous and erudite, he was interested in everything and everyone. His personality was so compelling that his appearance suddenly had an attraction of its own, and Alex knew she would never again see him as she had at first.

A final mark in his favor was that he clearly adored and admired Anthea. He was from Pennsylvania, but had taken his medical training in Edinburgh, a fact that endeared him to Alastair Cameron, and he was prepared to return to Europe—though probably Geneva rather than Edinburgh—with Anthea so that she might receive the medical training she so desired.

"She's already as skilled as any physician I know," he declared, "but the diploma might ease the prejudice she is sure to face."

Alex drew a good measure of comfort from the fact that Anthea and Max, as he bade everyone call him, were looking forward to a future, even though their daily lives were so bound to the suffering and death caused by the war.

Larissa observed Anthea with wonder, having never seen her practical sister behaving in such a giddy fashion as she did with Max. Larissa had actually heard Anthea giggle at something the doctor had said.

"She's always had a good sense of humor, but she's never been the sort to giggle, not even when she was quite young," Larissa told Reid later. "I think it's splendid that she's found someone who appreciates and amuses her."

"Just as you have," Reid said, nibbling at her ear and nuzzling the hollow of her throat until he felt her shiver of response as she laughed in the darkness.

They were legally married. Her family had accepted her change in status gracefully, and he had written to his sister to tell her the news. But still every minute he was with Larissa felt miraculous, and he found it hard to believe that the soft, slender body that opened so eagerly to his invasion was no dream of illicit comfort in the midst of war, but the new reality of his life.

While his mouth paid tribute to her breasts, coaxing her nipples into hard peaks, his hand traced the curve of waist to hip until his fingers delved between her legs to stroke the center of heat until she moaned and moved against him.

But she was not content to receive all the pleasure, and with one lithe movement, she pushed him to his back and hovered over him.

"Ummm, all mine," she murmured in mock greed, and she proceeded to claim him, tonguing his flat male nipples until they responded as her own had to his ministrations. And then her mouth wandered downward with delicate, agonizing leisure.

He felt each butterfly kiss as if it were a brand, the trail of fire searing the definition of his ribs and the hard muscled plane of his stomach and flickering over his thighs. She teased his staff with her mouth, and the pleasure-pain made him tremble until he could bear no more. He pulled her up the length of his body and kissed her mouth, tasting himself as she guided him inside her and began to ride him.

When they lay spent in each other's arms, Larissa whispered, "I want to be like them; I want the time to be like them."

"Like whom?" Reid asked sleepily.

"Like my grandparents, like the Bateses, the Kollers, and Samson and Della. Each couple has been together for so long, even when they disagree over something, it is like a dance, both of them knowing the steps long before the music begins. Timothy and Mavis, they're both looking so frail now, but still they go on, sharing the work a little more, doing it more slowly, but still managing each day with their own kind of grace. The Kollers are the same. It's the same with all of them, but most of all with my grandparents. They are both so fiercely independent, but they're like pieces of the same puzzle, only complete together. That's how I want to be with you."

To Reid, it was a measure of the war's effect on them that the frailty of old age should seem so blessed. Too moved to speak, he simply held her closer.

The days of the new year passed too quickly for all of them. They all shared the same thought—when the winter chill left the land, the spring campaign would begin.

On February 17, the Federal sloop *Housatonic*, which had been blockading Charleston Harbor, was torpedoed and sunk by the Confederate *Hunley*. The *Hunley* was a tiny semisubmersible, and it sank with all hands aboard, death by suffocation and drowning, which somehow seemed infinitely worse than dying on the surface.

Because Adam was not on the sloop, Alex had no sense of personal tragedy until Rane found her in Washington, where she had returned to work at the hospital. But the instant she saw his face, she knew something dreadful had happened.

"Morgan was on the *Housatonic*," he told her bluntly, "though he wasn't on the official roster. All but five of the men and Morgan were taken aboard another Union naval vessel. His body wasn't found, but Morgan is missing."

"First Seth, and now this; Sam will go mad," Alex whispered, not willing to face her own pain in the first moments of shock.

"Sam will do what all of us will do. We will find out what happened to Morgan. We have no proof that he is dead. He may well have been picked up by a Confederate ship in the area. Enemies or no, sailors mind their own."

Though his voice was even, Alex saw the torment in his eyes, and it steadied her against her rising panic. Rane loved all his children, blood related or not, but Morgan was the child of his heart, born of the brief and desperate days when he had come to Alex at Gravesend. And he had waited so long to be acknowledged by Morgan, never begrudging the bond his son had had with St. John Carrington.

By the time she saw Sam, Alex knew more about Morgan's latest mission, but found no comfort in the information. The Union blockade had gradually tightened the noose so that Wilmington, North Carolina, and Charleston, South Carolina, remained the two principal ports for the blockade runners, and if those ports could be closed, the South would suffer accordingly. In addition, the Union navy had had reports of a strange new Confederate vessel, and Morgan had been there to try to ascertain what this ship was. It was a matter of the worst timing that the vessel in question, the *Hunley*, had attacked before the Union vessels had determined what they would be facing.

Morgan had disappeared in one of the most zealously guarded Southern ports. With her own control threatening to crumble, Alex wondered how Sam could bear it.

But Sam was made of strong metal. Rane had been right about her reaction. "I knew he was taking terrible risks," she said, "but he believes in the work, and so do I. Now I want to find out where he is." She refused to speak of him in the past tense.

It was a question of how to proceed. Additional details of Morgan's disappearance came through Rane's naval contacts and complicated the situation a thousandfold. The *Housatonic* had been attacked by the *Hunley* at about nine o'clock at night, but Morgan had already left the ship, having rowed away in a small boat to reconnoiter Rebel defenses. He had not been seen again. It was probable that he had been captured, but there was also the possibility that he had seen the attack, had been unable to reach another Union ship, and had gone to ground somewhere in Charleston or outside of the city. And if that was true, then any inquiries about him would put the hounds on his scent. It was doubly dangerous that he had been in civilian clothes; that made him liable to execution as a spy if he were caught. His face was also well known in Charleston— another hazard. That he had somehow been killed in the harbor was a consideration of no use to anyone.

Daily they hoped for word to come from him. Morgan was a resourceful man; if he was not a prisoner, he would manage to get a message through. Yet, no news came.

But they also began to pursue news of him through the various governmental and civilian connections available to them, always making it clear that they did not want him endangered by the search.

Rane used his shipping and naval contacts; Alex sought the advice of the volunteer medical community, many of whom had treated soldiers from both armies; Philly and Blaine sorted through the list of his clients; Caleb painfully retraced all the steps he had taken when he had been trying to locate his grandson; and Flora asked for help and advice from everyone she could think of, including Anna Ella Carroll, daughter of a former Maryland governor, and an influential speaker and writer in her own right. Miss Carroll was not only a staunch supporter of the Union, she was an unofficial and unacknowledged member of the president's cabinet. The strategy in the western theater of the war had been largely hers, and she had traveled to various military encampments in order to report conditions to the president. But even she had no solutions to offer because the situation was so confusing. As the weeks passed and March moved toward April, the family was forced to accept the fact that Morgan was so incapacitated that he could not speak on his own behalf, or he was a prisoner, or he was dead.

The situation regarding prisoners-of-war was far worse than it had been earlier in the war. Much of the abuse was in the South where the number of prisoners had grown far beyond the Confederacy's ability to cope humanely, and the widespread shortage of supplies left the prisoners the most deprived of all. But in some prisons in the North, conditions were scarcely better. Sam had seen the conditions firsthand. Fort McHenry was bad enough, but the prison at Point Lookout, where the Potomac flows into Chesapeake Bay, was a disgrace, a filthy tent city where the inmates suffered dreadfully from exposure to the elements and overcrowding. It was the cruelest irony that Sam's knowledge, gained because she had acted out of charity, should now be the very thing that haunted her as she imagined her husband being held in even more trying circumstances than those she had witnessed.

The exchange system, never efficient, had, in past months, begun to break down entirely. Without notification that Morgan was in one camp or another, the situation was impossible. In the past, had he been treated as a Union officer, he probably would have been held in Libby Prison in Richmond. But that had changed in February after a large number of the Federals had escaped. Libby was now only a temporary clearing house from which prisoners were sent to other facilities. And the record-keeping was degenerating with everything else. Requesting information about a prisoner named Morgan Falconer among the many thousands being held offered slim hope, but they did it anyway, having no other choice now that so much time had passed without word.

The news came finally, from a Union army captain named Blaker who sought Sam out in Baltimore. He had been exchanged from Andersonville in Georgia, and he had brought word of as many of his fellow prisoners as he could remember, as well as personal messages.

"He wanted me to tell you where he was and that he was all right," Captain Blaker told Sam.

Sam looked at the tall soldier. He was so thin that his new clothing hung on him as if on a scarecrow. "Captain, I appreciate the trouble you have taken to come to me, but I would like the truth. You appear to have been close to starvation short days ago; how then can my husband be 'all right'?"

Captain Blaker bowed his head for a moment. Then he said, "He isn't, ma'am. He's ill, as so many of the men are. He couldn't get very far even if he escaped. He has a badly cut foot; his shoes were stolen shortly after he was recognized and taken prisoner in Charleston. I can't go to every family individually—most of them I'll write to and trust the army to contact as well—but I wanted to come here because your husband is a special man. He is older than most of the prisoners, and he is steady and courageous. He has been a great help in keeping spirits up and in maintaining order under appalling circumstances." He swallowed hard, and his hands clenched into fists. "The conditions at Andersonville are hellish. Shelter, water, food—everything is in short supply or contaminated. You must get your husband out as quickly as you can. There is a rumor that General Grant is going to stop exchanges entirely in order that the Rebels be even harder-pressed for men."

Sam managed to thank the captain with a semblance of calm, but as soon as he had left, her heart started to pound frantically. She took deep breaths and repeated over and over, "He's alive, and I know where he is."

But Sam and the rest of the family quickly discovered how little use that information was. They had all felt that the recent appointment of General Ulysses S. Grant to replace Halleck as commander in chief of the Federal armies was a positive step in the president's seemingly endless search for a competent man to lead the Union forces, but now Grant became part of their nightmare. Scarcely had Sam gotten the news of Morgan's whereabouts to Alex and Rane than they learned that on April 17, Grant had indeed discontinued the prisoner exchange. And to add to the horror of the situation, it was being said that rations of Confederate prisoners were to be reduced by the War Department in retaliation for mistreatment of Union prisoners, as if one inhumanity could be countered by another. It was only too possible that this would further worsen the lot of those in Southern prisons.

They started retracing all the steps they had followed before in the quest for aid, but the added advantage of knowing where Morgan was was negated by the new policy. Sam had spared no detail of what Captain Blaker had said about Morgan's condition, and they all had a terrible sense of time running out.

Sheer numbers worked against them. It was not only Morgan who was a prisoner of war. A multitude of men were in the same category, and the majority of them had families who wanted them back just as much as the Carringtons and Falconers wanted Morgan home.

Alex did not tell anyone that she was going to see the president. Even Flora, who loved Morgan dearly, quickly discarded the idea of asking Miss Carroll to intercede with the president on their behalf under the new circumstances. But Alex decided she would simply go as Morgan's mother to plead his cause. Did not Americans have access to their highest officials? Alex felt she had given enough of her heart's blood to be considered as American as the native born.

She was shocked at her own naiveté when she saw the other petitioners waiting to see the president. She had told herself repeatedly that Morgan was not the only prisoner, yet somehow she had not expected this importunate horde.

There were many women in the crowd, and it seemed to Alex that they were vying with each other in the comparison of their tragedies, though she believed their stories were essentially true. A son, a husband, a brother was missing, and the mother, wife, or sister could not manage without the man's help on the farm or in the city. The man had to be found, else all was lost. Or a pension was needed to help ease the loss of this or that relative. And there were those who knew very well where their men were, since the men were in trouble with the military or the law for various reasons—all of which was denied by the petitioners. Many were dressed in black as if to emphasize the weight and dignity of their needs. Even though Alex was dressed in deep rose, she suddenly felt as if she was one of a flock of vultures come to pick the president's bones; she felt so because she caught a glimpse of Lincoln's face as he moved through the crowd.

He had been a homely, spare man when he had taken office, but now he looked as if the trials of the past three years had worn him away. His skin was gray and lined, his eyes sunken in dark sockets, and he moved as if all the sorrows of the world were on his shoulders. Alex thought of all he had borne in these past years: the death of his beloved son Willie; the rumors that his wife, with all of her Southern relatives, was a spy for the Confederacy, the dissension in his cabinet, his difficulty in finding a commander in chief for the armies, the voices in the North that accused him of prolonging the war, and most of all, the thousands of his young countrymen who had died on both sides in a war he could not prevent.

People were beginning to be admitted to his office to plead their cases. Alex stole away, shaken to the bone, but she found Sam immediately and confessed her failure.

"I couldn't do it, not even for Morgan. There were so many there to beg favors; it is impossible that he could grant even a small fraction of them. My courage and my hope failed me. But I will go back and try again if you think it will do any good."

Sam's face had worn a look of unrelieved tension ever since she had heard that Morgan was missing, but now there was a feverish brightness in her eyes. "I need to go to Wild Swan for a few days," she said, and though it was not the reaction Alex expected, she agreed readily. If there was a more frustrating city than the capital at the moment, Alex did not want to be there; she thought it would do both of them good to spend a few days at the farm. She felt badly leaving the men in the city, but Rane also thought the time away would be beneficial for her and Sam.

"I think you were very brave to think of petitioning the president," Rane told her. "I could not do it."

"As it was, I could not either," Alex said sorrowfully.

It seemed perfectly normal to Alex that Sam wanted to ride out alone once they were settled at Wild Swan, and Sam was grateful that Alex left her to her own devices. She felt like thin glass, liable to shatter at the slightest pressure. But she knew what she had to do.

She had been at Brookhaven infrequently since Seth's death, going there only to keep the ledgers current and to make sure work went on as usual on the land. She had been careful to see her father as little as possible. For a long time her suspicion and rage had grown apace in her mind, lurking in the dark shadows there, but growing, and now it lurched forward into the light, an ugly twisted creature but worth facing for the small chance that it might save Morgan.

All her life, Sam had tried to please her father. All her life she had waited for him to show that he loved her and judged her important in his world. For years she had managed the practical affairs of Brookhaven, allowing him to lead his life of country gentleman with little real work. And she loved the acres of Brookhaven for the beauty she had found there ever since she could remember.

Whether she succeeded or failed, it would all end today. The love would never be offered, and the acres would pass from her care. That she knew without doubt. She clung to the thought of Morgan.

When she was face to face with her father, her strongest feeling was revulsion. He looked years younger than his age, his eyes bright, his movements energetic, and she was more sure than ever that she knew why.

"Morgan has been taken prisoner," she announced without preamble. "He's in Andersonville prison in Georgia. I want him back. Will you help?"

"General Grant has forbidden prisoner exchanges," her father pointed out. As she saw his eyes slide away from hers, she relinquished her last hope that this meeting would be civilized. She had no time and no skill to charm this favor from him.

"I am not speaking of an exchange. I want him back. Call him a gift to me if you will. Or a bribe—a bribe for my silence. If you do not arrange to have him released immediately, I will turn you in for spying and sedition. And what is more, I will report the names of those you meet in Washington. I know who they are. I have seen you, and I have had you followed." It was a fabric of lies; she had no proof of anything. But she spoke with absolute conviction, and when his eyes focused on hers in shock, she did not flinch from his gaze. His guilt was clear.

"Never think I won't do it. I would kill for Morgan. This is far easier. I have lost a son. I will not lose my husband."

Obviously he believed her story; he did not even bother to protest that he did not have the power to gain Morgan's release. "You'll have him back." His voice was devoid of emotion. "And I presume you will not come here again."

"A fair bargain," she said, and she was proud that her voice was as steady as his.

She did not look back as she rode away from Brookhaven. When she arrived at Wild Swan, she went to Alex. "I have something to tell you, but you must swear you and all the family will abide by the terms. Morgan is coming home," Sam said, and she told her mother-in-law what had transpired at Brookhaven. She made it almost to the end of the story before she began to shake as if she had ague.

"Damn your father to hell!" Alex swore as she put her arms around Sam. "Oh, my dear, I do understand. Until the day I learned of her death, I hoped a miracle would happen and my mother would love me. But she never did. I still regret it. I have learned ever so slowly that it is no use to look for love where there is none. One cannot force love from another. Far better to appreciate it where we find it. Never forget that we have loved you very much for a very long time."

Alex held her while Sam sobbed, her control broken now that she believed she would see her husband again. "It was so easy to destroy everything between us. It was so quickly done."

But at least Sam's father kept the bargain. In a surprisingly short time, Morgan was in Washington, shipped north through the lines under a white flag and in the company of another Union prisoner released to care for him.

Sam made the decision to take Morgan to Wild Swan immediately. "It is where we take all our wounded and our dead," she stated flatly. "When he opens his eyes, I want him to know he is home."

Morgan was in no condition to make the decision himself. He was so emaciated, his lips were drawn back from his teeth in his sunken, bearded face. His right ankle and foot were wrapped in filthy bandages; he had boils and open sores wherever his filthy clothing had chafed; and he was out of his head with the chill and fever cycle of malaria.

Short days after Morgan's return it was reported that on April 12, when the Confederates took Fort Pillow on the Mississippi River, they had massacred a number of black soldiers there, and the outcry in the North was fierce. And in early May, Grant and Meade, with an army of 100,000 men, crossed the Rapidan River in Virginia, marching toward General Lee and Richmond. The savage fighting on Virginia's soil resumed with days of bloody battle in the thick woods of the Wilderness, where many of the wounded burned to death, and at Spotsylvania where five days of killing ended with exhaustion on both sides and wounded left to die between the two armies' positions. In the Shenandoah Valley of Virginia, the Confederate Jubal Early defeated Federal forces who were trying to clear the valley of Rebels. And in the West, General Sherman marched from Tennessee toward Georgia, intent on capturing Atlanta.

It was all vital war news. Nigel, Anthea, and Dr. Kingston were treating the wounded just behind the Union lines in Virginia; Reid was writing reports from the battlefields; Larissa was seeing the pathetic casualties pouring into the capital; and Gincie and Travis were only short miles from the scene of some of the worst fighting, if indeed Travis had not rejoined the Confederate army and was thus even closer.

It was all vital, but those at Wild Swan were engaged in their own battle to save Morgan's life. The threat of a fresh grave beside Seth's haunted them all.

Chapter

44

Morgan had the kind of malaria that some called "tertian" fever because attacks came at forty-eight-hour intervals. First he shook violently with the chill, then his fever soared, and his head pounded so unmercifully that the pain made him moan even in his delirium. Next sweat poured from him, his fever fell to normal, and the headache disappeared until the next attack. But he was so debilitated that, even when his temperature dropped, he was not lucid.

They dosed him with quinine and dressed the body sores and the cut on his foot. They kept him clean, dry, and warm except when he was in the grip of the fever and needed to be cooled down. They gave him water and broth constantly to replace the fluids in his dehydrated body. But most of all, they counted on his normally strong constitution to reassert itself and win the battle for him.

And through it all, they listened to his disjointed ravings. He railed at invisible enemies to increase the rations of water and food for the men. "They're so young, so young," he repeated over and over. And maggots—he saw legions of them crawling over everything and eating the living and the dead, eating his own flesh. Alex shuddered when she realized at one point that he was surely talking about leaving the maggots on wounds, that in the absence of medical attention or supplies, the men had deliberately introduced maggots to wounds to allow the loathsome creatures to clean away putrid flesh. But now Morgan thought they had gotten inside him and were boring their way out.

Alex glanced across the bed at Sam, hoping she hadn't understood, but she had. Her face was green-tinged. "They couldn't have done that, could they?" she asked faintly.

"As horrid as it sounds, it has been known to work," Alex answered. "It may well be the reason the infection in Morgan's foot isn't worse."

As the days passed, they began to worry that the fever had damaged Morgan's brain, but nearly two weeks after they had brought him home, he finally knew where he was, though at first he did not believe it, having no idea of how he had gotten there.

He saw Sam first as she bent over him, bathing away the sweat of the latest attack. He blinked, closed his eyes for a long moment, and then opened them again.

Sam felt the change in him before she saw the question in his eyes. She dropped a light kiss on his forehead, restrained her impulse to overwhelm him with her relief and love. "You really are at Wild Swan, sweetheart. And I am not a hallucination. You were released and shipped north." She decided details of his release could wait.

But possessed of sudden urgency, he caught her hand in his own skeletal fingers. "Others?" he grated, and she nodded, not trusting herself to speak the lie. She understood that he wanted to know if other prisoners had been freed with him.

His hand dropped away, and his eyes closed again, but for the time being, he had accepted her gesture as confirmation; time enough when he was stronger to tell him the truth.

Having seen Morgan so close to death just days before, to Sam, Alex, and the rest of the family, it appeared that he was recovering rapidly now that the chill and fever cycle was being subdued by quinine and care. But to Morgan, the rate was intolerably slow. He had always been able to rely on the strength and quickness of his body, and aside from childhood illnesses that passed swiftly, he had had no previous experience of real illness. Now his body seemed a treacherous thing trapping him inside. He ached all over and felt as if he were nailed to the bed. He would think about getting up and walking about, but in actuality, even lifting a spoon to feed himself required great effort. Being cared for as if he were an infant was embarrassing, making him short-tempered, and it did not improve his mood to be treated with endless patience and good humor. He had been surviving day to day in Andersonville, but he had never let himself doubt that he would make it. He did not share his family's vision of how close he had come to dying, nor had he seen how thin and ravaged his own face looked, and so he felt smothered by the love they showered on him. Even his father wore an expression of enormous tenderness when he sat with him.

Though he didn't know it, Morgan was spoiling for a fight, a way out of the velvet enwrapping him. And Sam, closest to his heart, was the target.

The pillows were too high, too low. The food was too hot or too cold when she served it. The bandage on his foot was too tight or too loose. The list of petty complaints went on and on, and there was no truth to any of them; Sam was an excellent nurse.

He demanded that she read the war news to him.

"Wouldn't you rather wait until you're stronger?" she asked gently.

"No, I wouldn't!" he snapped, and she gave in. It made him angrier still that her reluctance had been sensible; there was nothing he could do to change the course of the war, and hearing the news was depressing, but he was too stubborn to admit his mistake.

"Is it true that prisoner exchanges have been stopped?" he asked one day, and though Sam had expected eventual questions about his release, he took her by surprise.

"Yes," she admitted, and she explained why General Grant had made the decision.

"The others, the men who were in my shelter, they weren't released, were they?"

She shook her head helplessly. "We didn't even know about them. How could we do anything for them?"

Morgan was not appeased. "How did you arrange my release?"

He was growing so agitated, Sam felt trapped. She meant to maintain the fiction that they had managed it through various governmental channels, but instead she heard herself blurting out the truth. "My father did it. I went to him, and he arranged it."

Morgan's eyes glittered as if the fever had returned. "Your traitorous bastard of a father arranged it! A favor to a high-ranking Confederate agent was done and here I am while my friends are still rotting in Andersonville! How in the hell do you think that makes me feel? How do you like your pet gelding?"

Sam stared at him in mounting disbelief. She had expected some anger, but not this howling. And she had not known he suspected her father's activities. "You were dying there. Don't you understand? Soon you would have been no use to those men or to anyone else!"

Too vividly he could see the faces of the young men who had lost their commanding officer and had looked to him for guidance. All his frustration, guilt, and rage at being so cosseted while the others were left to suffer boiled over onto Sam. "Always back to your father, even though he hasn't given a damn about you since you were born! Did he enjoy showing off his power? Who knows, information he passed along could be responsible for the deaths of many young men like Seth. Did you think of that when you went to lick his boots? Get out of here! I can't bear the sight of you!"

He was panting hard, and Sam backed away from the bed, staring at him in wordless supplication. The long days and nights of worry, and now his complete rejection of her sacrifice, added its crushing weight to her spirit. His face was unrelenting, and suddenly she wanted to be miles and miles away from him. She left his room without another word.

And she left Wild Swan within the hour. She refused to give details of what had passed between her and her husband, saying only that they had had a disagreement and it would be better for them to be apart for a while.

Alex hated the dead look in Sam's eyes. "My dear, pray reconsider! He is feeling better now, and he is not the sort of man to be a good patient. But I'll wager that by tomorrow the storm will be over."

"No, it won't," Sam said quietly. Nothing Alex or anyone else could say to her could make her stay.

In the days that followed, no one mentioned Sam to Morgan, and he refused to ask about her. Let her sulk. What she had done was wrong. He felt a deep twist of pain every time he thought of his friends left behind. Sam had betrayed his honor and his duty when he was helpless to prevent it.

Sam with the gold and green lights dancing in her eyes. Sam who had had his heart for so many years. Sam who had loved him faithfully since childhood and had borne his sons at the risk of her own life. Sam with the boyish name and the woman's body, who had learned to please him so well and to take pleasure from him.

Suddenly he wanted her beside him, not his mother, his sister, Della, or anyone else, just Sam, who knew what he needed without being told. He could almost feel her cool touch, soothing him as it had when his fever was highest.

He shifted restlessly, and Alex leaned forward in her chair. "May I do anything for you?"

He held onto his pride and outrage for one more moment and then let them go. "Where is Sam? Get Sam for me."

"I fear your change of heart is a little late. Sam isn't here. She left the day you argued. She did not tell me what passed between the two of you, but I suspect you told her to go."

His mother's voice was calm, and he could read sorrow but not condemnation in her eyes. His impatience to see Sam grew with his unease. "I did. I was very angry, and I still don't think she ought to have interfered, but I need to see her. I need her. Please send someone to Brookhaven for her."

"Morgan, she is not at Brookhaven or in Baltimore either, at least not at your house. We've had people looking for her, but we haven't located her yet. I should have tied her down rather than let her leave when she was so upset. I thought she'd stay in Baltimore, but she only stopped there briefly to gather a few things to take with her."

Now he could hear the fear beneath her calm. "Not at Brookhaven, you're sure?" he asked.

"My God, don't you understand?" Alex got control of the rising note in her voice. "She can't ever go back there. She blackmailed her father into arranging your release. She went to him, and she told him she would inform the Federal authorities of his work on behalf of the Confederacy. She had no proof, but she has suspected his involvement from the beginning of the war, and he believed her threat."

Alex took a deep breath. "Sam managed your release when none of the rest of us could. I even intended to ask the president to aid us, but when I saw how weary he looked and how many petitioners crowded the corridors waiting to beg a favor of him, I could not do it." She closed her eyes, trying to block out the memory of Lincoln's gaunt, suffering face.

The silence stretched between them until Morgan could hear too clearly his own voice ranting at his wife.

Alex reached out and ruffled Morgan's thick dark hair as if he were a child again, though the first hints of silver were there at his temples. "I don't want to take sides in this. I love you dearly, and Sam as well. But though I had something to do with raising Sam, you are my son, blood of my blood, part of my soul. I can understand what a nightmare it is for you to know your friends are still in that unspeakable prison. But Morgan, you would have died. A little longer without care, and you would have died." She didn't know she was echoing Sam's words.

"I don't know if there is always a difference in the ways men and women think of honor and duty, but I know for a certainty that I would not let Rane perish for either one if I could prevent it. I think you must ask yourself that if the situation were reversed, if Sam were being held in such a place, would you leave her there?"

"It's not the same—" he began and then stopped abruptly. It was exactly the same, and nothing on earth could make him abandon Sam to the prison—the heat, the cold, the damp, the short rations of slimy water and rotting food, the maggots in wounds, the stench of disease and offal—he shuddered at the thought of Sam in such conditions, and he wondered if the day would ever come when his mind would no longer conjure the degradations of body, mind, and spirit that he had endured there.

He faced what Sam had given up when she had gone to Brookhaven. For her husband, Sam had sacrificed her father and the acres she had loved and nurtured for so long.

He had trained himself not to think of Seth; the pain was too raw. But it burst on him because he could feel how it must haunt Sam, cut off as she was from everyone now. "Seth," he moaned, but it was Sam's face he was seeing—Sam cradling her newborn son, her face radiant with love, and Sam on the day they had buried Seth, her face terrible in its white stillness; Sam turning to him and acknowledging that the loss and grief were shared between them.

Alex reached for Morgan's big hand and cradled it against her cheek. "I feel so helpless! When you were young, I could solve problems for you and ease trouble. But now you and the world have grown too old and complicated for me to be of any use," she said, and Morgan could hardly bear the sorrow in his mother's face.

As the days passed, they ran out of places to look. Even Morgan's suggestions proved fruitless in the search for his wife. Alex was relieved to find that he was recovering his strength rapidly rather than buckling under the added pressure of having Sam missing, but her unease over Sam's continued absence grew. She kept reminding herself that Sam had not been stolen away but had left on her own power. Alex was sure Sam would not take her own life—whatever the estrangement between Sam and Morgan, she still had two living sons to worry about—but these were dangerous times, and Sam's safety depended on where she had gone.

Rane was no less concerned than she, and when he returned from following yet another useless lead about a woman who had not, it transpired, resembled Sam very closely after all, he announced, "I am forced to believe that Sam truly did want to disappear. Lord, I hope it is all on purpose! There seems to be no trace of her."

"We know she is not working at any of the prisoner-of-war camps nor any of the hospitals in Maryland or Delaware; I think we've checked them all," Alex said. She was, however, still convinced that Sam was using her nursing skills somewhere. Casualties from Virginia were flooding north, and she could not imagine Sam, even in her saddened state, ignoring their plight.

The third of June had seen a futile encounter at Cold Harbor, Virginia, where Union soldiers had fallen by the thousands in attacks on unbreachable Confederate defenses, and now, in mid June, by all accounts, Grant was being beaten back in his attempt to take Petersburg, Virginia. The dead and wounded from these engagements ran to astronomical numbers, and far more for the Union than the Confederacy. But the South had fewer men to conscript and had recently extended the army age limits to include white men seventeen to fifty.

Contemplating the grim statistics, Alex's spirits sank lower. "Rane, she could be anywhere! The wounded are filling hospitals far north of here."

He nodded in grim agreement. "And she might be working at a private facility, which will make it even more difficult to locate her."

They were contemplating placing personal advertisements in major papers of Northern cities when Flora brought them the letter from Sam.

"She will probably never speak to me again, but, poor darling, by the tone of this letter she really doesn't expect to be missed." Flora shot a murderous look at Morgan, hesitated a moment, and then handed the letter to him.

In the letter, Sam assured Flora that she was perfectly all right and being kept busy with hospital work, and she gave her leave to tell the family not to worry. But her principal reason for writing had been to ask her sister-in-law to let her know immediately if Morgan had a relapse or if anything happened to Adam or Nigel or one of her nieces. Beyond that, she requested that her whereabouts be kept secret:

> I don't expect there will be much of a fuss. Morgan can't stand the sight of me right now, and I need a little time to sort things out. But in any case, please don't tell anyone where I am unless there is an emergency. And forgive me for involving you in this.

She was in Boston, Massachusetts.

"Boston," Morgan said. "Why Boston?" He was dazed by the relief of knowing where she was, but he also felt as if he'd been punched hard; the letter was final proof of the terrible damage he had done with his angry words. He was so accustomed to Sam being competent and assured, he had forgotten that the neglected little girl he had first met nearly forty years ago still existed in the woman Sam had become. And suddenly it came to him why she had gone to Boston.

"Harvard. Cambridge and Boston. Seth was so happy there before the war," he said, and a wave of sadness passed through all of them.

Morgan had been up and about for some time now, but he still tired easily, and Alex was desperately afraid that a trip to Boston would bring on another malaria attack. But Morgan was a man, and the only concession he would make was a promise to take quinine and rest if he suffered symptoms of the disease.

But as he traveled north by train, the only thing he felt was an overpowering anxiety to reach Sam. He made himself eat, drink, and rest as much as he could on the journey only because it was necessary; his energy was consumed by memories of Sam, years of memories. And overlaying all was the sound of his own voice berating her and the look of pleading in her eyes that he had only recognized long after she had left.

He found her at the hospital where she had volunteered. She was giving a young man a drink, cradling his head gently, and in the mist of the stench and sound and sight of suffering and death, she looked so young and slender to Morgan that he wondered if he was hallucinating again, but as he drew closer, the illusion was gone, and he saw that she was thin and worn, her face etched by fatigue and sorrow.

She did not hear him approach; all her concentration was fixed on her patient, who could not have been more than twenty years old, and she could not have treated him more tenderly had he been one of her own sons.

Morgan could see the effect she was having on the youth, who, weak and sick as he was, smiled as he whispered, "Thank you, ma'am."

"Sleep now," Sam said. "I promise the letter to your family is on its way; very soon they'll know where you are, and that you're getting well."

Only when Sam patted the boy's left hand did Morgan realize that the right arm was missing, the stump swathed in bandages. He swallowed hard and waited until the boy's eyes closed and Sam turned.

He said her name very softly, and he watched the swiftly changing expressions in her eyes. Shock that he had found her, followed by weary sorrow, and then a blank, waiting stillness. He saw the full depth of the wound he had dealt her. As surely as the young soldier had lost his arm, Sam had lost a part of her heart and soul when he had lashed out at her, and he wondered if she would ever heal.

"Sam, I—" His throat tightened, threatening to close off his power of speech and his air as well. He swallowed hard, searching desperately for words, forgetting entirely that they were surrounded by beds of wounded men, many of whom had suddenly found great interest in the little drama unfolding between one of their favorite nurses and the stranger.

"Sam, I love you. I always have. I always will. I know I can't make up what you have lost for my sake, but I'll try."

Short of sleep and food, moving from one broken body to the next, Sam had ceased to have any sense of herself. Losing Seth had been terrible, but having Morgan turn on her with such grim fury and disgust had been worse than anything she could have imagined. She worried about Adam and Nigel, but she trusted Flora to tell her if anything happened to either of them, as she had trusted her to keep the secret of her whereabouts. But even her concern for her remaining sons was at a distance from the center of herself because that center belonged to Morgan. Only when he had rejected her had she understood how little of herself she had kept to herself—everything of value that she was had long since been given into Morgan's keeping. She had sensed this when he had sailed away on the *Liza Gwen*, but now, nearly twenty years later, the loss of self was even more grievous.

For an instant she was tempted to send him away. Perhaps there was yet time for her to reclaim herself so that she would never be so vulnerable again. But then she saw his vulnerability was no less than hers.

"It is too late," she murmured, and Morgan's shoulders slumped in defeat. "No, you mistake me!" She closed the small distance between them and reached out to touch his cheek, as if to erase the pain in his face. "I meant it is too late for me to be separate from you. I believe it has been too late since the day I met you when I was eight years old."

He drew her against him with an unsteady breath. "Oh, Sam, do you remember that dress you wore when Mother took us all to the races in Washington? It fit you so badly and was a dreadful mustard color. Even then, I wanted you to have something better. And instead, I've—"

"Never say it!" she ordered fiercely. "Your family, our sons," there was only the slightest tremor in her voice, "and most of all your love, so many gifts." It was she who initiated the kiss, and she who stopped it as the intensity of many staring eyes finally penetrated her consciousness.

She blushed to the roots of her hair and instinctively hid her face against Morgan's chest. This was too much for the men, who joined in a ragged cheer. Morgan ducked his head in a mock bow and then grinned in acknowledgment.

"Better take her with you before we change our minds about letting her go," one of the men called cheerfully, and Morgan complied, laughing aloud when he heard Sam mutter, "He's my husband."

Sam didn't have a clear idea of where she was until they arrived in Morgan's room at the Parker House.

"Confident, weren't you?" she observed without rancor when she saw the well-appointed suite that was far too large for one person.

"No, scared to death, but hopeful, and feeling my age," he confessed. "I thought that even were I to be miserable, I wanted a good bed and clean room to be miserable in."

She knew what an admission it was; this was not the man who wanted to be so invincible that he had damned her for her efforts on his behalf. He looked much better than he had when she had left Wild Swan, but he was still much too lean, and his skin had yet to regain its healthy color. And she knew the threat of further sieges of malaria would hang over him for the rest of his life.

"I am weary now," she said. She felt strangely shy with him, but she wanted him to rest.

She had chosen the easiest course, for as they lay holding each other without urgency, drifting in and out of sleep, the awkwardness between them eased.

They went out for a sumptuous meal in the evening, and on their way back to the hotel, they gathered up Sam's belongings from the boarding house where she had been staying.

"It looks like a nun's cell!" Morgan exclaimed when he saw the starkness of her room, and he regretted anew the rift that had caused her to live like this.

But Sam refused to dim the joy of their reunion. "How would you know that?" she teased.

"Speculation, mere speculation," he said with a grin.

"You have been without me for too long!" She laughed, and when they left, she did not look back at the room where she had spent too many lonely hours.

With undisguised pleasure, Morgan watched the familiar rituals as Sam prepared for bed; even the sound of the brush sliding through her hair brought its own enjoyment, both of them willing to let the time unfold slowly now that they were together again. And when she slipped into his arms and he into her body, she whispered, "Welcome, my love, welcome."

Chapter

45

Rane cheered the news of the sinking of the Confederate raider *Alabama* by the U.S.S. *Kearsarge* off Cherbourg, France. The British-built *Alabama* had wreaked havoc on Union shipping since her launching in 1862, and even now the Union government was claiming damages from England for allowing the raider to be built there.

Alex, seeing the savage gleam of triumph in her husband's eyes, wondered if any of them would ever recover from the skewed vision brought on by the war. Before the war, it would have been unthinkable for Rane to approve the loss of any ship, involving as it did the loss of sailors' lives.

Samson and Della were triumphant over the action Congress had taken not only to equalize the pay of black soldiers, but also to grant back pay due them. It was, on the surface, reason to rejoice, but Alex thought how odd it was that there had ever been any argument over equal pay for dying.

Wanting a little more time away from outside pressures, Sam and Morgan had returned to Wild Swan from Boston, and Alex found it easy to confide in her daughter-in-law. "You are so kind, I doubt you would tell me were it true, but of late, I've begun to wonder if I might not be a bit unbalanced. Nothing seems straightforward any more, no matter how I try to make it so."

Sam's laughter was perilously close to tears. "You are the sanest person I know! I have come to the conclusion that anyone who views things in simple terms nowadays is truly mad. I thought about it while I was in Boston. The city should have seemed very alien to me. But it didn't. Before the war, Maryland and Massachusetts had little in common, but now states everywhere, North and South, have a horrible sameness in the wards of maimed young men. What an awful, twisted way to discover how much we have in common!" She dabbed at her eyes. "Before we came home, Morgan insisted on taking gifts to the ward—razors and soap, books and fruit, those sorts of things. He made it easy for the men to accept the offerings by telling them it was bribery for letting him take me home. But his purpose was really quite different. Though Morgan's gesture was appreciated, those men in Boston are fairly well provided for; in spirit, he was giving those gifts to the men left in Andersonville."

Sam gave up trying to control her tears and let them roll down her cheeks. "He has nightmares about it. It's not the fear of dying that haunts him, it's the feeling of being so helpless, of being so incapable of aiding the others. And often one of the men he is trying to help is Seth. And he blames himself for being captured in Charleston in the first place. When I hold him and talk to him, he quiets down after a while. Please understand, I am glad to be there for him. It is just that it breaks my heart to know such fear lives inside of him now. It makes him seem so—so fragile, even more than the malaria does."

"I can't promise it will make any difference," Alex said. "But it might make you feel better to talk to Caleb. One of the worst things about wars is that they are all the same in the damage they do. I expect Caleb's nightmares were fierce for some time after he returned home. I know that when I first found him in the cave, he was desperate for light and human company."

She was glad she had thought of it because she could see Sam mulling it over, considering the strong, steady man Caleb was despite his experience as a prisoner-of-war.

And then suddenly there was no time to think about anything except the security of Wild Swan. The Confederate Jubal Early had crossed the Potomac into Maryland and on July 9 had reached Frederick, Maryland, and had won a victory against the Federals at Monocacy, southeast of Frederick. By July 11, reinforcements from the Army of the Potomac were pouring into Washington to defend the capital, and the city was in an uproar.

At Wild Swan, it was still not the regular Confederate troops they feared, but the marauders who were without political allegiance and were growing more bold as the war went on, more adept at judging where the countryside was most vulnerable. And Wild Swan was indeed vulnerable with all Federal forces scrambling to protect the capital from the incursion of Early's troops from the west. Farms east of the city did not enter the official calculations.

Though they were still desperately shorthanded, at least this time Morgan and Rane were there to guard the farm; with the business so quiet now, they had little left to protect at the shipyard.

As Early penetrated the District of Columbia, the raiders struck Wild Swan. A ragged, hard-faced band of ten men rode in boldly, clearly expecting to find no more than a few women and old men.

There was no time to resolve it peacefully; the raiders had guns drawn and were barking orders before they had reined in their horses.

The memory of Katy Joyce shot dead at Wild Swan was with Rane as he calmly gave the order to fire. Three of the men fell from their saddles, and though the others started firing, the defenders of Wild Swan were all behind cover and provided difficult targets. Alex, Rane, Sam, Morgan, Della, Samson, and Jed were all armed. In the next barrage, two more men fell. Alex was sure she had hit one of them, but she was curiously numb, taking aim automatically and feeling as if she were watching it all from a little distance away.

The raiders had had enough. There was a shout of surrender and their guns clattered to the ground. Rane ordered them to get off their horses one by one and lie flat on the ground. Morgan and Samson quickly trussed each one.

They loaded the living and the dead into a wagon, and Jed and Morgan took them to Washington to turn them over to the authorities. And they penned the raiders' horses in order that they could be turned over to the Union army.

Aside from a few bloodstains on the ground, it was all over.

"It was too simple," Alex murmured. "I killed one of them, and it was too simple."

"It is no stretch of the imagination to say that they came here to loot, rape, kill, and to burn Wild Swan to the ground," Rane said. "Our response was swift; it was not simple. Everything that has occurred in the past three years has something to do with what just happened. And that is damned complicated!"

He was relieved to see the glassy look in her eyes ease, but she was still very pale, and he stood over her anxiously as she drank strong tea.

"I'm sorry," she said finally. "I think it got all confused with the night Katy was shot."

"For me too, though I wasn't even here when she was killed," he replied, and the knowledge that he shared at least part of her reaction to the violence comforted her.

The tension eased when Morgan brought the news that reinforcements had reached the capital in time, causing Jubal Early to withdraw to the Shenandoah Valley without a fight.

But efforts to take Petersburg continued to fail, sometimes spectacularly, as in the case of the attempt to gain a way in with a tremendous explosion through the defenses, an attack which resulted in thousands of Union casualties but few Confederate losses. For a second time, General Burnside was dismissed for incompetence. Even with Grant now in charge, the Union army still had its share of unfit officers.

In early August, Admiral David Farragut led his flagship into Mobile Bay, Alabama, and toward the end of the month, the port was taken and thus closed to blockade runners.

At the beginning of September, Sherman took Atlanta. As well as being a terrible blow to the Confederacy, it was a prize guaranteed to help Lincoln in his bid for reelection.

Alex received a letter from Gincie after a long silence. In spite of her granddaughter's attempt to sound optimistic, it was a sad missive. Travis was again with the cavalry, though his leg made him very clumsy and slow whenever he was not in the saddle. Jeb Stuart had been mortally wounded in May, another flamboyant Southern leader gone, but the men kept on.

It was all Alex could do not to order Gincie to come home, but she reminded herself that she had no authority to do that and that, for better or for worse, Gincie's home was now Hawthorn.

The South was short of everything from men, to horses, to shoes for both of them. Food prices had soared. A barrel of flour brought anywhere from $300 to $500 in Richmond, a Confederate dollar now being worth less than a nickel in comparison to Federal currency. There was no longer any chance of foreign intervention on behalf of the Confederacy. But the Rebels did not lay down their arms.

"It is suicidal, not honorable!" Alex raged.

"I agree," Rane said. "But remember, it is not only that

Southerners do not believe they are wrong, they know that their old way of life will be over forever when they lose. Apparently enough of them dread that more than dying."

They were all grateful for a brief respite from the war when Anthea and Max came home to be married at Wild Swan in October.

"Gran, you married Grandfather in October; it seems a lucky month," Anthea said with a smile.

It was a small wedding, but Anthea was particularly pleased that both of her sisters were there. Larissa attended alone because Reid was traveling with the Union army in Virginia, but Phoebe had come north with a fellow teacher, Aubrey Edwards.

At twenty-eight, a few years older than Phoebe, Mr. Edwards was a rather cadaverous man of bony features at odds with bountiful dark hair and large brown eyes. Phoebe was obviously very fond of him, but Alex quickly discovered she did not share her granddaughter's enthusiasm.

Aubrey was the sort of man who thought in broad causes while noticing little of what happened around him. Life had no immediacy for him. Alex noticed that already he and Phoebe had established a relationship wherein Phoebe was in charge of practical matters. It was she who knew where he had left his reading spectacles, his pocket watch, and anything else he misplaced. It was she who coaxed him to eat a bit more when he got caught up in one dissertation or another, she who made his days run smoothly in many small ways.

"Well, what do you think of him?" Philly asked.

"I think it won't make much difference what any of us decides about him," Alex replied. "But I judge him to be the kind of man who will always need and expect to be taken care of. It is not that I object to his ideas about the betterment of mankind; it's just that I think he ought to know where he is as well as where he wants to go. If Phoebe marries him, she will acquire a large child rather than a husband. Some women like that in a man, but I couldn't bear it. Sometimes I need Rane, and sometimes he needs me; it would be very hard if I always had to be strong."

"I wish I didn't agree with you," Philly said, wrinkling her nose. "I keep wanting to ask Aubrey if he knows the price of bacon while he's rambling on about the basic goodness of man. But then, Phoebe has a certain officiousness about her; perhaps she needs a man she can manage." She glanced across the room at Blaine, and her look softened. "I, on the other hand, am, like you, very glad I married a man and not a child."

It was a true measure of the times that Anthea and Max departed

Wild Swan after their wedding bound not for a honeymoon, but to return to duty at a battlefield hospital.

And there was need of their skills, for the war went on to a relentless cadence that had nothing in common with the jaunty step that had sent men hastening to the first Battle of Bull Run. All the rules were changed now; the South would not surrender, therefore, the South would be destroyed in a total war.

General Sheridan drove Early's Confederates from the Shenandoah Valley and laid waste what had been a major source of food for the Rebels.

In November, President Lincoln was reelected, and General Sherman began to march across Georgia to Savannah, destroying everything in reach and giving orders to his men to forage the countryside widely for food. He entered Savannah on December 22, after the Confederates had withdrawn two days previously, and he sent a telegram to the president, presenting the city as a Christmas gift. Even the weather had favored the Yankees, with scarcely a drop of rain to slow them down. The South had been cut horizontally, west to east, and the Union would go on hacking it to bits until it surrendered, though for the time being the armies of Grant and Lee had gone into winter quarters.

The Christmas gift most precious to Alex was Gincie's presence at Wild Swan, but in reality, it was another proof of the war's dislocation.

Gincie was three months pregnant, and Travis had sent her to Wild Swan. She had had no choice; Travis had ruthlessly used the excuse of the baby to force Gincie out of harm's way. He no longer wanted his wife in Virginia, not even for his own comfort. Despite knowing what he was doing, Gincie had not been able to refuse now that there was another life involved. She had not even had the option of withholding the fact of her pregnancy from him because he had stolen home to visit her, had found her in the grip of a particularly violent bout of morning sickness, and had instantly recognized it for what it was.

Travis had had the devastation of Hawthorn on the side of his argument. The lovely house had been burned to the ground months before by drunken Union soldiers. Travis had not been there, and Gincie and the others at Hawthorn had been lucky to escape by hiding in the woods until the looters left. All the able-bodied men were gone from Hawthorn, black and white men who had worked together for years, but the blacks had joined the Union army, while some of the whites, even though they were antislavery like Travis, had, like him, joined the Rebels.

Gincie, the women, the old men, and the small children who were left at Hawthorn had been living in various outbuildings since the fire.

"Why didn't you send word to us when the house was burned?" Alex demanded.

"So you could worry more?" Gincie replied. "There was nothing to be done." She glanced down at her still flat stomach. "Just as there is nothing to be done now except wait for the child to be born. Strange how much I wanted a child, and now it is only keeping me from Travis."

"How wrong you are! The child binds you closer to him than you have ever been before," Alex corrected. "Do be sensible; Travis isn't at Hawthorn, and knowing that you are safe here will do much for his peace of mind."

Gincie was silent for a long time, and then she managed a smile. "Here I am, eating well, while most of the South is starving. I'm carrying my husband's child, and I am safe. And as far as I know, Travis is also still safe. I think carrying the child must have addled my wits. Gran, I promise I shall cease to be so gloomy."

She was as good as her word, making every effort not to let her desperation affect the holiday, and she found if she took each day as it came, not thinking beyond it, it was possible to share the joy that still existed at Wild Swan. She savored the cold winter beauty of the farm and the strong wing beats of the swans and geese passing overhead, pretending for sweet stretches of time that no war existed. And she let the love of her family warm her.

Of her generation, not only Larissa and Reid were there, but Adam too. The long sea duty had darkened his skin, making his green eyes appear jewel bright, and his chestnut hair had light streaks as if he carried the sun with him. He was so broadly built, he tended to dwarf those around him, and when he entered a room, it was impossible not to feel the jolt of his physical presence.

Once Gincie made him understand that she was not going to wince every time he mentioned something connected with the Union navy, they returned to their old ease with each other. Adam was three years younger than she, which had meant a recognizable gap when they were children, but now he seemed a great deal older than his twenty years, and the difference no longer existed. Gincie certainly didn't feel that she had to watch over him as she had when he was small.

For Rane and Alex, there was pleasure beyond having a beloved grandson home because Adam looked so much like his great-grandfather

Magnus, Rane's father. And the likeness went far deeper than the surface, for, in spite of the general boredom of the blockading squadron, Adam was still enamored of ships and the sea.

There was a formula for the distribution of prize money awarded for the capture of Southern blockade-runners, and because his ship had been active and lucky in captures, Adam had amassed a small fortune.

"I'll warrant you've planned quite a celebration ashore when the war ends," Morgan teased his son.

Adam looked faintly shocked. "I plan to buy a ship, not waste the money," he said, but then he added with a grin, "Of course, a small celebration might be in order."

Rane and Alex exchanged a look, both of them seeing the ghost of Magnus before them. And Alex felt an additional pull on her heart when she saw Rane, Morgan, and Adam together as they conferred about rebuilding the shipping business, which had been much diminished as they sold off ships to buyers from neutral countries as insurance rates climbed too high for vessels of United States registry.

"It gives me hope when they speak of the future," Sam said, and Alex realized that the certainty was stealing through all of them that the war could not last much longer. And Alex had her own gift of the future from Hugh Bettingdon. He had kept a year-long record of her horses' wins and losses, of the progress of their training, and even of their individual peculiarities, and sent it to her. He had always had a keen eye for fine horseflesh, and he had applied his wit as well for entries such as "an impudent colonial who will race just as he pleases." More than Padraic's meticulous accountings, Hugh's vivid record made it possible for Alex to imagine Wild Swan's paddocks and pasture once again alive with the flash and fire of the Thoroughbreds.

And it gladdened her heart to hear Larissa, Gincie, and even Adam the sailor describing the horses to Reid in glowing terms.

"They make fine saddle horses look as if they belong behind a plow," Adam claimed.

"Samson speaks to them as if they are his children," Larissa said, "and I swear they answer back."

The baby had taken on a new reality and power for Gincie since she had returned to Wild Swan. "I want my child to learn everything he or she can from Samson and Gran, even if it means talking to horses." Her hand rested in an instinctively protective gesture over her abdomen, and her smile was radiant as she pictured another tiny child trailing after Samson as they had each done in turn.

It was stealing over all of them—a feeling of renewal implicit in a new generation.

"I wrote to Boston and Rachel, and I expect they will write to tell me before too long that they are to become grandparents," Alex told Rane.

Boston and Rachel's son Caton had recently married an Irish girl whose parents had promptly disowned her. It was already a family joke that when Boston had angrily accused them of prejudice against Indians, he had been informed that they had no objection to Rachel's Cherokee blood, it was his own English heritage they despised in his son. Even Rachel, who had good reason to despise bigotry, found this irresistibly amusing.

"Fortunately, Caton's wife Muirne does not share her parents' views," Rachel had written. "She is blessed with good sense and good humor, and she adores my son, so I cannot help but love her."

"What are you doing?" Alex asked with a gurgle of laughter, her wandering thoughts abruptly recalled from California by Rane's suddenly insistent hands. His touch was more in the nature of inventory-taking than erotic, and his own laughter joined hers. "I am discovering what a great-grandmother feels like."

He sobered, and the rhythm of his hands changed, stroking her with his finely tuned knowledge of how to bring her pleasure. "You feel as you did when I first loved you, as you did when you became the mother of my children, as you did when they in turn had children of their own. My Alex, always my Alex."

They had just seen another new year in together; it had been more than fifty years since they had first set eyes on each other; and their love was stronger now than it had ever been, binding them one to the other in a silken net of shared memories, triumphs, and tragedies. For an instant, Alex felt as if she were in sight of an overall plan as carefully drawn as a ship's navigational chart of reefs, shoals, and currents, but then it dissolved into what it had always been—a gamble of events, a reckless race with the winds of chance and change. And she would not have had it any other way.

She wanted to tell him how much she loved him, but her throat was swollen with the force of her emotions, and she knew if she tried to speak, she would weep. She let her body speak for her, paying tribute to his flesh until he cried his pleasure aloud.

Chapter

46

The cold and rain that had held off for Sherman's advance on Savannah came on the land in January, slowing the renewal of troop movements.

At Wild Swan, January had for decades been an exciting time, heralding the onset of the foaling season. The war had changed it into a sad month, for Alex and Samson felt the absence of the horses keenly then, left as they were with only the aging Thoroughbreds, dying off one by one.

But this year the conviction that the war could not last much longer possessed both Alex and Samson to such a degree that they began to plan the practical aspects of the horses' return. Though there had been a careful sell-off by both Padraic in Nova Scotia and the Bettingdons in England over the years, with only the finest kept for Wild Swan, there would still be a considerable number of offspring born abroad coming home with the original breeding stock. And since Wild Swan had been shorthanded for quite a while, barns, paddocks, and fencing had not been kept as well repaired as in the past. It was all they could do to keep up with the remaining livestock and get the crops planted and harvested.

But now Samson seemed determined to single-handedly return everything to perfect order, hammering away even in the rain.

Alex stood beside him, peering through the rain that ran off her heavy cloak. "Samson, we will surely have workers aplenty before the horses come back. I have no intention of having the animals shipped home before the war is truly over, and once it is over, there will be many who need employment, even if our former workers want to go elsewhere. You don't have to do it all yourself, especially in this weather."

"I doan be meltin' in de rain," Samson replied peaceably. "And dere be no lightnin' to strike me down. Trufe be dat I'se powaful lonesome fo' dem hosses, an' dis makes 'em feel closer."

"I can't argue with that," Alex conceded. "Perhaps I ought to get a hammer and join you, except that I would undoubtedly pound my fingers flat in this slippery wet without ever hitting a nail."

Samson's low rumble of laughter was a comforting counterpoint to the patter of the rain, and Alex leaned against the fence, ignoring the water that soaked into her clothing.

"You know," she said, "I have a theory that whatever one doesn't use for a time, whether it be a house or a fence, begins to destroy itself. Houses shed their windowpanes, and fences sag to the ground as if they know they've been forsaken."

Samson turned his head to regard her as indulgently as if she were one of the children. "Mebbe, Miz Alex, mebbe. Dey's mo' magic in dis worl' dan anybuddy know." He concentrated on his work once again, muttering, "Doan want dat liddle Irish tellin' me nuthin' be fixed while he gone."

The anticipation and affection in his tone belied the words; clearly Samson could hardly wait until Padraic came home. The friendship between the two men, begun on such shaky ground, had grown to a bond of great strength, and the separation brought on by the war had been hard on both of them.

Beginning to feel chilled, Alex started back toward the house, a smile curving her mouth as she imagined how the rough reunion would take place between Padraic and Samson, both hiding the vulnerability of their feelings.

Her smile vanished abruptly as she froze in shock. It was happening very quickly, but Alex saw it very slowly. Under cover of the rain, the men had ridden unopposed right into the heart of Wild Swan.

There had been no trouble in the area since the raiders had come in July in the wake of Jubal Early's invasion of Maryland, but now Alex saw how unwise their growing complacency had been. Even through the rain, she saw it in the avaricious eyes of the strangers. They were dressed in a motley of Confederate gray and butternut and Union blue—scavengers of both armies.

It fluttered through Alex's mind how few there were at Wild Swan to withstand an attack. Except for Gincie, the family had returned to their own homes. And Rane had ridden to Washington two days previously.

"I told you, Captain, Wild Swan is a place that has much we can use."

Someone who knew Wild Swan had led the raiders here. Someone who spoke with a fairly educated voice. Alex peered at him through the rain, but did not recognize him.

But he recognized her. "Well, old woman, didn't think you'd see me again, did you?" He pointed his long pistol at her with casual contempt.

Samson had been moving slowly toward Alex, but now with a bellow of rage he sprang forward to place himself between her and the gunman.

Alex felt the bullet's impact as if it had hit her own chest, but it was Samson who fell to the ground.

"God damn it!" the leader snarled, and then there was an eerie silence louder than the rain.

She knew that by now there were guns of Wild Swan trained on the men, but she was in too vulnerable a position for them to fire. None of it mattered.

Her hood had fallen away from her head, and her eyes were a wild, glittering green visible in the storm's dimness, but her words were deadly calm, carrying to every man. "It will not help you to kill me. I would follow you from the grave. This is your one chance to go. Stay, and I will pluck your eyes and your hearts from your bodies to feed the foxes. I will throw your bones to the night scavengers. You who would make beasts of men, I will feed to the beasts."

Her voice seemed to roll and reverberate around everyone even after she had finished speaking. The "captain" was overwhelmed by a superstitious dread alien to his nature and more compelling because of that. He felt the hairs rise on his neck and arms, and a cold current rippled over his spine and pooled in his groin. Not all the battles he had seen in this long and hopeless war had caused this. It only deepened the haunting when he heard the woman murmur, "He has been my friend for longer than most of you have lived. Go home, beastly children, go home."

He looked at his men, and though other guns were at the ready, he saw that he was not alone in his apprehension. And though he registered the fact that it was ludicrous for his hardened followers to be held off by one crazy white woman and a black woman who was beginning to howl as she crouched over the fallen man, still he wanted to tell the women that he had not meant for this to happen, that he had not known the man's purpose was so personal and violent. He wanted to tell them that he had had a family and loyalties at the beginning, all lost now, all dead. And he knew that none of it would make any difference.

Very soft and far away, Alex heard Samson sigh, "Goin' nor . . . you . . ." the words stopped in the harsh rattle of blood drowning his lungs. There was no more sound from him, and Alex felt his spirit brush the air as it fled.

Della's keening wail rose to rend the air, but Alex could not make another sound. She knelt in the mud, and the truth bowed her down.

It was Mark, Piety's eldest son, one of Gincie's stepbrothers, who had brought the beasts to Wild Swan, who had killed Samson. His face was not so much changed from the way it had been that day when he had glared his hatred from the carriage before Piety had left Wild Swan for the last time.

She looked up at him, and he nodded, pleased at the recognition he saw in her eyes. "Yes, I'm Mark," he said, as if she had asked. "You should not have turned us away that day, Mrs. Carrington Falconer." He made her name sound like an insult. He looked past her. "Is that my sweet stepsister, Virginia?"

Gincie was frozen in place. "Mark?" she whispered, and then she shrieked his name.

"One more mistake from you, and I'll blow your brains out!" the leader snarled as he saw Mark's hand twitch nervously on the pistol. He had had more than enough of the madness the man had ignited. "Ride out!" he commanded, and he was almost sorry when he was obeyed; he could not be able to trust this man again, and he had a primitive urge to finish him here, to give him to the women as a sacrifice.

Alex closed her eyes, and when she opened them again, the men were fading out of sight, riding away as quietly as they had come.

None of the livestock had been taken, none of the buildings had been damaged, but the guiding, protective spirit of Wild Swan lay dead.

Della's face was stark, awash with tears and rain as she stared at Alex. "I always knew he would die for you. And at the last, he thought of her, his first wife, of going north with her."

Alex reached for her, shaking her head in wordless denial, but Della was too locked away in shock and grief to respond to the gesture. Alex's hand dropped back to her side. "Old friend, old friend," she whispered, not aware she had given sound to the words as she gazed down at Samson's still body.

Gincie was bone-white, and she began to shake violently as she approached the two women and Samson's prone body. The depth of her distress registered with Alex, and Alex began to function again, though everything had to be held at a distance, else she would surely break. Even her bones felt brittle.

"Gincie, go into the house. Get warm and go to bed," she ordered.

Gincie stared at her blankly.

"Go inside now!" Alex snapped, and she turned her toward the house and gave her a little push. "Remember, you are carrying Travis's baby."

Gincie moved jerkily, as if she herself were a child not yet sure of how to walk.

From the oldest to the youngest, black and white, the expressions were the same as the people of Wild Swan gathered around Samson's body—disbelief and horror were equally mirrored in their eyes.

They took Samson's body into the house he and Della had shared for the long years of their marriage, and Alex helped to make him fit for burial. She wanted to take Della in her arms and comfort her, but the black woman's face forbade it. There was an awful stillness in her, though tears continued to flow down her cheeks.

Alex wanted to scream and go on screaming, but she kept her mouth clamped tightly against any sound. She could not stop the images crowding her brain. They whirled faster and faster until, by the time she was alone, they were bursting on her in a continuous stream.

The first time she had seen Samson—a huge black man in tattered clothes blocking her path to ask for a job, frightening her until she noticed that the skittish mare she rode had quieted at his touch. His killing of his owner. His despair when he had learned of the death of his first wife and his sons. His marriage to Della. His endless patience with the children and the horses, with all creatures young and vulnerable. Samson leaving the sanctuary of Wild Swan to guard the journey to Gettysburg.

Alex thought of all her children and grandchildren had learned from Samson, thought of all Samson had taught everyone who knew him about the dignity and grace of spirit that could reside in one man. All of it ended by one jealous, twisted soul, a random murder among the hundreds of thousands slaughtered in these past three years.

The tears came then in a hot flood, and even when her sides hurt and her body heaved, she could not stop weeping.

Summoned from Washington by Jed Barlow, Rane found Alex

curled in a tight ball on their bed. Her cries were reduced to whimpers from a raw throat; her face was ravaged; her eyes nearly swollen shut; and still the tears flowed.

He gathered her into his arms, and his own harsh sobs filled the room. They clung to each other until exhaustion overcame them, but in the morning, they faced the same dreadful truth. And when the children came from Baltimore and Larissa and Reid from Washington, they were all stunned not only by what had happened, but by how old and fragile Alex and Rane suddenly appeared. Della had become a dark effigy, as if her spirit had departed with her husband's.

It was beginning to rain again when they buried Samson at Wild Swan.

"It's as if the whole world is weeping," Morgan murmured to Sam, his voice breaking.

Sam gripped his hand hard but said nothing. She listened to Alastair Cameron reading the burial service as he had before at the farm, and she watched Tim and Mavis Bates clinging to each other as they wept. She thought of her father. He would be the first to claim that he treated his slaves humanely, and while she had been in charge of Brookhaven, she had been very careful to make sure it was true. But he would never be able to understand this depth of mourning for a servant. His heart would never have room for a black man as a friend, nor even for such whites as Mavis and Timothy. And she herself might never have learned there was a saner way of life than her father's, had she not wandered one day into Wild Swan after the Carringtons had arrived. She felt a deeper kinship with Samson than she had ever recognized before: they had both come as strangers in need to this place, and they had both given something back in return. And now Samson had given his life and was being buried in the same ground as Seth. "Wherever you are, take care of each other," she thought.

They all had separate and shared memories of Samson, and they all listened to their inner voices more than to the traditional words of the service. And Gincie most of all, but there was no softness in her mind, only sharp, stabbing guilt, guilt Alex understood only too well, though she knew it was as useless in her own case as in her granddaughter's.

"I think you're being too easy on Gincie," Sam told Alex before she returned to Baltimore. "She has too much time to brood."

"I expect I am, but I do worry about her. She was doing so well, and now this. She needs Travis."

"Well, she can't have him. She needs you to speak sensibly to her and give her responsibilities here. You can use the help. Philly, Flora, and I will come out as often as we can. Be sure you send word if you have special need of us."

Alex knew that Sam was right, and she approached Gincie after the others, with the exception of Rane, had left.

"It is utterly foolish for you to blame yourself for Samson's death," she told her bluntly.

"But it was Mark; it was my stepbrother! He must have known I was here!"

"Listen to yourself! You sound as if you are the center of the storm this war has brought. It is highly unlikely that Mark knew you were here. What is plain is that he remembered this place clearly and with envy for all these years. If anyone is at fault, it is I. I know how miserable those two boys were, but they were wholly Piety's; only fleetingly did I consider trying to wrest them away from her. Can't you understand how common this sort of revenge must be in any civil war? It is what civil war is about! It is a perfect opportunity for the mean and envious to take what they have long wanted from their neighbors. But those men were no part of either army, for all the title of 'captain.' They were scavengers, probably deserters from both armies, the lowest dregs. Can't you believe that?"

She cupped Gincie's face in her hands, looking into her eyes, willing the frightened child to disappear.

Gincie blinked her eyes as if awakening from sleep. "I'll try," she promised.

Alex employed the rest of Sam's suggestion, too, giving Gincie all manner of tasks, for, indeed, she did need her granddaughter's help. With Samson gone, the chain of command at Wild Swan was broken. Jed Barlow was, as always, willing to do any work assigned to him, but he had never been a leader.

Phoebe, Anthea, Nigel, and Adam would be informed by their parents, but Alex had to write to Gwenny in England and Padraic in Nova Scotia about Samson's death. Rane, seeking to spare her, offered to do it, but she refused, feeling it was her duty. The lines to Padraic were hardest of all because she kept thinking of Samson's anticipation of his friend's return.

She had thought she could shed no more tears, but as she labored over the letter, the tears trickled down her cheeks. She heard the library door open and looked up, expecting to see Rane in her blurred vision, but it was Della.

Alex suffered a fresh wave of despair, sure that Della had come to tell her she was leaving. They had scarcely exchanged a word since Della had made her angry charges over Samson's body. Alex wiped at her eyes and tried to keep her expression impassive as she invited Della to sit down.

Della's eyes met hers for a minute, and then she looked down at her folded hands. "I apologize for speaking as I did. It is true that Samson loved you enough to die for you, but you took great risks for him, too. And more than that, you gave him a new life here. I would never have been his wife or borne his children had it not been for you. This was his home, and it is mine."

Alex let her breath out in a long sigh of relief. "Thank God! I thought you were going to leave Wild Swan, and I couldn't bear it!"

Della said softly, "No, you are wrong; you can bear anything. I have seen you do it. And now I have to learn how to do the same." Her hands were clenched so tightly, her knuckles gleamed palely in the brown skin.

"You are wrong, too," Alex said. "You believe he thought of his first wife as he died. I know he spoke of going north, but I think it was not so much a specific place he meant any more, but a dream of life where slavery does not exist nor war either. He knew and loved you for far longer than he did his first wife. You gave him life when he would have perished for sorrow. I swear to you he could not have seen any other woman except you before his eyes as he died."

Alex had to strain to hear the soft litany that began to pour from Della.

"I keep looking for him. He filled my world; even when I didn't want to fall in love with him, he was all I could see. So big and tender. The scars of slavery—I could touch them on his skin, but his heart was whole and unmarked. I never knew him to do an unkind thing, not even when he feared Irish was going to take his job. He could have made it very hard for Padraic, but instead, he let him prove that he was competent with the horses. Samson made my heart, my soul, and my body sing. No more music, no more music ever again." Her voice wavered, and she covered her face with her hands.

Alex went to her and held her, weeping with her, but later Alex had Rane to comfort her when he saw she had been crying again, and he was there to awaken her gently and assure her of his presence when she dreamed that he, not Samson, had been murdered. And all the while, she knew that Della was alone. Despite having her daughter-in-law Jewel and her granddaughter Hope with her at Wild Swan, without Samson, Della was alone.

When Alex diffidently suggested that Della might like a rest from her duties for a time, Della regarded her in panic. "What would I do with all the hours of the day?"

Alex conceded the point with the admission that she had already begun to worry about how she would manage without Della's contribution to the daily routine.

The work necessary to keep Wild Swan running smoothly in spite of everything kept them all busy and sane. Alex understood better than ever how her grandmother had depended on the land for sustenance. The earth demanded dedication but gave back in full measure, each season yielding its own reassurance and bounty.

As Sam had predicted, Gincie was far better off with her time better employed, and as the days passed, Della's inner strength also reasserted itself so that she began to lose the desperate look she had worn immediately after Samson's death.

Though Alex was torn as she had been since early in the war between duties at the farm and the help she could offer the sick and wounded in Washington, she had come to terms with the fact that she was needed at Wild Swan more than ever now. And she had to accept as well that Rane still had work to do for the government, though he had put aside everything to be beside her since Samson's death.

"I know you feel some responsibility for not being here when Samson was shot," she told him, "but that makes no more sense than Gincie's idea that it was all her fault. None of us could have anticipated it. And staying beside me to the neglect of your other duties will not serve. We have been apart before; we led quite separate lives before the war ever began. Though, mind you, I will not tolerate it if you steam off to England again."

Rane was grateful for the smile she offered, for as reluctant as he was to leave her side, it was true that he was needed elsewhere; the war effort still required massive amounts of supplies to keep the forces fed, clothed, and fighting.

In February, Sherman began his northward invasion of the Carolinas, again laying waste to the land. The reports of waves of soldiers singing "John Brown's Body" and "The Battle Hymn of the Republic" as they took the cities and towns was enough to give Alex chills even at a distance. Columbia, the South Carolinian capital, was occupied and destroyed by fire, though there was confusion as to which side had started the blaze. Charleston was taken by the Federals, and then Wilmington in North Carolina, one of the last havens of the blockade-runners, surrendered to Union troops. The night songs shared, as Seth had written, by soldiers of both armies were too gentle for this new and final phase of the war.

On March 2, Sheridan vanquished Early's remaining troops in the Shenandoah Valley at Waynesboro, Virginia. And two days later Lincoln was inaugurated for his second term.

Alex went with Rane to hear the president's inaugural address. She could not explain it adequately even to herself, but she felt as if she needed to hear what he would say at this time when the grinding struggle of the past four years was surely nearing its end, and she needed to be there for him, though she would be only one among many who now could not imagine any other man who would have been strong and wise enough to bring the Union through such terror.

It was worth the effort to be there. There were many black faces in the crowd and in the celebration, including delegations from various organizations of free blacks, and a black brass band from the army, unthinkable before the war. The Thirteenth Amendment to the Constitution, which would abolish slavery in the United States, had passed the House of Representatives on January 31, and though it now faced ratification by the states, it must become law before long. And however Lincoln had felt about slavery at the beginning of the war, even his nasal, twangy voice could not impair the eloquence he brought to the subject this day:

> *Fondly do we hope, fervently do we pray, that this mighty scourge of war may speedily pass away. Yet, if God wills that it continue until all the wealth piled by the bondsman's two hundred and fifty years of unrequited toil shall be sunk, and until every drop of blood drawn with the lash shall be paid by another drawn with the sword, as was said three thousand years ago, so still it must be said, "The judgments of the Lord are true and righteous altogether."*

> *With malice toward none, with charity for all, with firmness in the right as God gives us to see the right, let us strive on to finish the work we are in, to bind up the nation's wounds,*

*to care for him who shall have borne the battle and for his
widow and his orphan, to do all which may achieve and
cherish a just and lasting peace among ourselves and with
all nations.*

For an instant, Alex felt as if Samson were standing beside her and
Rane. "Not in time for you, old friend, but for your sons and their children, this war has changed our world forever," she whispered.

Despite the noise of the crowd, Rane heard her, and his green eyes
were as tear-bright as hers.

Chapter

47

In mid-March, the Confederate Congress authorized the use of
slaves as troops. It was a last desperate effort to replace the legions of men
lost by wounds, disease, and by a high desertion rate caused in large part
by pleas from destitute families that their men come home to save them
from starvation. The change of policy regarding slaves as soldiers came far
too late.

Sherman's troops continued through North Carolina, and Sheridan's men rejoined the Army of the Potomac and turned Lee's flank at
Petersburg on April 1 in a battle with Major General George Pickett at
Five Forks, Virginia. At long last, Grant broke through Lee's lines at
Petersburg, and Lee began to retreat westward. The Confederate government fled from Richmond, Federal troops marched in, and on April 4,
Lincoln visited there while the North went wild with the news of the
city's capture. Lee's retreat was harried and cut by Federal troops, and on
April 9, he surrendered the Army of Northern Virginia to Grant at Appomattox Court House, Virginia.

It would take time for all the forces on the far perimeters to receive the news and cease the struggle, but the war was over. And because
of Lincoln's and General Grant's generous spirit, the Confederates were

free to ride home on their own horses, and the officers were allowed to keep their sidearms.

The news was telegraphed throughout the North, and Rane was the first to bring it to Wild Swan. He swept Alex into his arms, and she could feel him trembling as he said, "It's over! My God, it's finally over!"

Within twenty-four hours, Flora and Caleb, Philly and Blaine, Morgan and Sam, the Bateses, and Alastair Cameron were at Wild Swan. As they had been drawn together for all the tragedies of the war, so they wanted to be together to mark its end.

The celebration was not without sorrow. Everyone at Wild Swan gathered together, the adults supplied with wine or whiskey, the children with milder drink, and Rane, at Alex's request because she did not trust her voice, proposed the toast.

He raised his glass and his voice was steady. "To those we will not see again at Wild Swan—to Katy, Luke, young Caleb, Seth, and Samson—we will remember you. And to the living, our family and friends who can now come safely home from their battlefields. May this be the beginning of a long and lasting peace." His eyes sought Gincie's; he wanted her to know he spoke of Travis no less than of those who had fought for the Union, and she smiled at him, starry-eyed with her faith that she would see her husband soon.

Less than a week later, Morgan returned to Wild Swan, knowing that both of his parents were still there.

When she saw Morgan's drawn face, Alex's first thought was that something dreadful had befallen one of her grandsons or Sam.

"The president was shot last night; he died this morning," Morgan said, and then his shoulders heaved, and he wept like a child.

Rane put one arm around Morgan, the other around Alex, and they stood huddled together.

Gincie found them like that, and when she heard the news, she cried, "North and South, we are all lost now!"

Alex shivered with the force of the prophecy.

Secretary of State Seward, confined to his house by illness, had been attacked there, stabbed with a knife. It was surely part of the same madness that had slain Lincoln, and first rumors pronounced Seward dead, though this was not the case.

In fact, the only things wilder than the grief and shock that struck the capital and the North were rumors that blamed everyone from Jefferson Davis, President of the Confederacy, to members of Lincoln's own cabinet. Many people did not want to believe that a small group of fanatical Southern sympathizers and Lincoln-haters could have created such havoc.

On April 18, Alex, Rane, and the family from Baltimore were all in Washington that they might attend the president's funeral on the following day. Gincie did not accompany them. She was as sorry as anyone, but she was also keenly aware of being a Confederate's wife, and under the circumstances, the capital did not seem a safe place to be. Southern sympathizers who lived there were said to be cowering in their houses in fear of reprisals.

The city was festooned with black in token of mourning. And the faces of the citizenry wore expressions of deeply personal grief and anger. However he had been regarded and often mocked when he first became president, to many Lincoln had become the embodiment of enduring wisdom and leadership during the war years. This was particularly true of the former slaves who had flooded the city as the Union armies advanced into the South, automatically putting the Emancipation Proclamation into effect.

A twenty-one-gun salute awakened the capital at sunrise, and all morning people scurried to find places to view the funeral procession. The sea of humanity was an awesome sight on its own, and many faces were wet with tears.

The procession moved from the White House to the Capitol where a funeral sermon was preached and a closing prayer offered. The body was to remain in the Capitol for two days before being loaded on a funeral train for the seventeen-hundred-mile journey to Springfield, Illinois. Along the route, the president's body would lie in state in various cities in order that people might pay their last respects.

Alex felt curiously numb. Too much had happened too quickly. She had felt the tragedy of Lincoln's death more keenly when she had seen Morgan crying than she did now. Today, Morgan, like her, stood stony-faced, locked away in his own thoughts.

It came to her suddenly—the image of the president's worn face as she had seen it when she had thought of petitioning him for help to bring Morgan home. It seemed as if the mark of death had already been visible on him.

She had had enough of death, enough of the sight and feel, enough of the sound and smell, and even the taste of it. The horrific sensations of all-encompassing death as she had experienced it at Gettysburg washed over her, and for a dizzying instant, she had to fight to keep from being physically sick.

Rane saw all the color drain from her face and perspiration bead her skin. He put his arm around her, fearing she was fainting in the close press of bodies.

"What is it?" he asked urgently, and she looked up into his anxious eyes. "I want to go home. As soon as possible."

They had planned to stay another night in Washington, but Rane did not question this change. He simply let the family know, and as soon as the crowd had thinned enough, he led Alex away.

On the journey home, he deliberately steered their conversation away from the sorrow of the day, asking Alex about her plans for the horses.

Her face began to brighten. "It's hard to believe that they can truly come home. I'd like them to be in the barns and paddocks right now, but it will take time for the Bettingdons and Padraic to arrange everything, and it will be better for the horses to come back in July or August. That way the new foals will be better able to withstand the journey."

"Morgan and I can arrange the shipping for you," Rane offered, and Alex beamed at him. "That would be wonderful!"

Gincie was alarmed to see them a day early, but Alex hastened to reassure her. "There is anger about Lincoln's assassination," she told her, "but they aren't lynching Southern sympathizers in the capital. The war is over, and the Confederate soldiers are going home."

Her slender body swollen with the seven months of her pregnancy, Gincie was doing her best to maintain a brave facade, but the president's murder had given her nightmares of revenge exacted in various horrible ways from Rebels, mainly Travis.

A few days later he rode in to Wild Swan. He was thin and bone weary, and his face was oddly marked from long days outside, his skin paler where his hat had shaded his forehead and where a beard had, until recently, shadowed his cheeks and chin. He limped horribly when he got off his horse, but he was alive. And when he heard Gincie cry his name as she started to run toward him, her gait ungainly due to her pregnancy, his face lit up, and he hobbled toward her as fast as he was able, swinging her up in his arms as soon as he reached her.

They both started to laugh. "My God, what a pair! That has to be the most awkward reunion seen anywhere," he gasped, and they both struggled to control the hysteria of relief and love that washed over them.

Travis's laughter was close to tears as he felt the swell of his child, and his mouth trembled as he kissed his wife. "Darlin', you are far more beautiful than my dreams of you," he murmured huskily.

It was balm to Gincie's heart. For though she had known it was foolish, among all the other things she had worried about had been the fear that Travis would find her unappealing in her obviously pregnant state.

She looked up into the shining turquoise eyes. "I love you, Travis Culhane, then, now, every day of my life."

She had gone with him to live among the enemy; she had supported him while he fought against her own family; she had journeyed to find him when Death would have taken him; she had waited for him, her body growing great with child while he fought the last battles of a lost cause; and her words were a benison, telling him that she regretted nothing.

In that instant, Travis's inner desolation began to ease, and a future with his wife and child began to seem possible.

It was not only Gincie who welcomed him; everyone at Wild Swan treated him with such warmth, even Della who had lost so much, that sometimes he had to remind himself that he was not dreaming. To have enough to eat and a comfortable bed with his wife in it were incredible luxuries after the deprivations of the war.

"If you can bear some advice from a meddlesome old man," Rane said, "I would suggest that you tell Gincie about the bad times as well as the good. I have learned that the women of this family do not appreciate being shielded from the truth."

Travis was relieved to take him at his word; he had experienced so much, he needed to confide in Gincie. He told her of the hopeless last months, of the endless losses, and of Robert E. Lee's final moments as commander in chief of the Confederate army, a title he had, ironically, held officially only since February.

"He was so dignified and so sad. The war has aged him terribly. I think he feels responsible for every casualty. He praised us and thanked us, and the ranks stacked their guns, furled the Stars and Bars, and it was time to go home. I won't ever forget the sight of General Lee ridin' away on his horse Traveller."

Gincie listened to all of it without flinching, but she was as aware of the gaps as she was of what he told her, proving the truth of what Rane had told him.

"You speak of everything except Hawthorn," she pointed out gently. "I know there is much to rebuild, but I am ready to go back whenever you wish."

He hesitated a long time before he answered. "In the first place, you will stay right here until our child is safely delivered. And in the second," his voice faltered, and she could feel the effort he made to continue, "I am no longer sure I want to rebuild Hawthorn. The South lost more than the North did when Lincoln was shot. I believe he meant the peace to be firm, justly administered, and he meant the blacks to have a better life than they had before. Now only God knows what is goin' to happen. But if my relatives are any measure, it won't be good. Cousin Lucinda and her brood are at Hawthorn now; they left Richmond with the government. I found them at Hawthorn on my way to you."

Gincie bit back an exclamation; she loathed Cousin Lucinda, her husband Floyd, and the rest of them. They were to her mind the worst the South had to offer—lazy, useless human beings, accustomed to being waited on every waking minute by a host of slaves.

"They've lost a great deal in Richmond," Travis continued, "and I must feel sorry for them for that, though I know they made a good profit by financin' blockade-runners. But the terrifyin' thing is that the war hasn't changed anythin' except their place of residence. They hate Yankees more than ever; they hold to a fanciful image of the South as the last bastion of civilization; and they cannot imagine payin' a black a fair day's wages for a fair day's work. And I fear they are not a minority. I fought for Virginia; I did not fight to perpetuate all the old injustices and intolerance." He covered his face with his hands. "I've survived the war, but I don't think I can bear the peace."

Gincie wrapped her arms around him and held him close. "We can stay here," she said. "Gran could use both of us. There will be much to do with the horses coming back." Her heart beat faster as she considered the bliss of settling at Wild Swan again, but then she felt his body stiffen in protest as he spoke.

"I can't live off of your grandparents! And this is not far enough away."

She knew she had a chance to press her suit to live here; despite his words, he was so grateful to be with her again, he would do anything to make her happy. To make *her* happy—but what of him? For an instant more she clung to the idea of living here, and then she relinquished it. "Where do you want to go?" she asked.

"Out west, all the way to California," he answered, and he waited for her protest, but it did not come.

"When the baby is old enough to travel, if you still want to go, then we will," she said.

"Just like that?" He could not credit her lack of resistance.

"Just like that."

"I could go ahead, and send for you when everythin' is settled, or return if I do not think we will find a good life there."

This time she did protest. "No. When you go, your child and I go with you. I know you will have to leave me to check on things at Hawthorn in the next weeks and months, but that is as far as you go without me. Understood, Mr. Culhane?"

"Understood, darlin'." He felt a surge of hope as he considered a new life far from the scene of four years of unspeakable carnage. He was resolved that they would go and that one day Gincie would have as good a life there as she had enjoyed at Wild Swan and at Hawthorn before the war.

"Do you mind if we wait a while to tell my grandparents?" she asked softly. "They have had so much to adjust to, and I think it would be better for them if things were a bit more settled before they have to adjust to this, too."

Travis agreed readily; he wanted to have his plans firmly and sensibly enough made so that Alex and Rane would not fear that he couldn't provide for their granddaughter. Events were occurring too erratically, and everything was too unsettled at the present to make the final decision seem sane.

On April 26, John Wilkes Booth, an actor and Lincoln's assassin, was cornered and shot to death near Bowling Green, Virginia. Other conspirators had also been apprehended, but despite mounting evidence that they had acted on their own, the belief persisted that Jefferson Davis was responsible. The fact that he had gone into hiding did not help his cause. President Johnson offered a huge reward for his apprehension.

Davis was captured on May 10, and though there were those who wanted him hanged, saner heads prevailed in the demand for a trial for his part in leading the rebellion of the Confederate states, not for any connection to Lincoln's murder. There was little doubt that imprisonment would follow the trial.

On May 23 and 24, Alex, Rane, and the family, except for Gincie and Travis, were once again in Washington, this time to see the Union Army march down Pennsylvania Avenue in the Grand Review.

Alex, so thoroughly sick of war, was not sure why she felt compelled to attend this final spectacle, particularly when she considered how she had reacted to Lincoln's funeral.

"If we are not witnesses to our own times, then who will be?" Rane asked, and it was enough for Alex.

And the Grand Review was a sight not to be forgotten. For two days, row on row of soldiers marched or rode past the reviewing stand containing President Andrew Johnson, General Grant, Secretary of War Stanton, and other dignitaries. The various divisions brought with them their mascots, animals ranging from dogs, cats, and cows to the more exotic owls, eagles, and monkeys. And small mishaps added their own humanity to the proceedings, such as the sight of General Custer being dumped ignominiously in the dust by his big black horse when an admirer miscalculated her aim and hit the horse right in the face with a wreath of flowers. All the officers' horses were festooned with blossoms, strange ornaments for beasts who had recently charged into battle.

Nigel, Anthea, Max, Larissa, and Reid were all there, as well as Frank Faber, whom Alex had invited repeatedly to visit Wild Swan whenever he wished. But though he smiled and thanked her each time, she doubted he would avail himself of the hospitality as long as Gincie and Travis were there.

When Alex had first seen the capital nearly fifty years before, it had been more a matter of hope than of reality, and during the war the city that was supposed to be a symbol of the freest and most justly governed people had been the most fortified capital in the world, with the campfires of soldiers ringing it all around. But now this vast army that had risen to defend it was marching together in a last display before disbanding to resume or begin their lives as farmers, shopkeepers, clerks, factory workers, doctors, lawyers, architects, westward wanderers, or whatever else they had been, or planned to be before the war, or wished to be now. It was a fitting resolution for a nation where the power was vested in the people, not in the standing armies of a monarch.

"I am very glad I have witnessed this," Alex told Rane, using his word, and he nodded. "It is going to take a long time to heal all of the wounds, longer because President Lincoln is gone. But slavery will be ended forever, and now this country has at least a chance to live up to its promise."

And as the soldiers and sailors of the Union and the Confederacy made their way home, so the grandchildren came home to Wild Swan.

Nigel, Anthea, Max, and Larissa still had patients to care for in the capital, but they were rearranging their lives. Anthea and Max would go to the Continent in the fall so that she might attend medical school in Switzerland. Nigel, with glowing recommendations from Dr. Cameron, from both old and young Drs. Benjamin, and from the army surgeons he had assisted, would go to Philadelphia for medical school there and perhaps to Europe for further training in a few years.

True to his word, Reid had already secured a job with a prominent Washington newspaper, and he would enjoy the best of two worlds, since his old paper in New York was prepared to contract for periodic reports from him about the political happenings in the capital.

"Someday, when I can think about it clearly, I want to write a book about the war," he confided to Larissa, "a book that will record at least part of the uncommon valor of men like Seth, Travis, and Samson and women like you and your grandmother, all of you. I want future generations to know that, even in the darkest times, people are capable of behaving with humanity."

They would live in Georgetown, and had already found a house to rent there, but they both looked forward to being at Wild Swan as much as possible.

Adam came home from the sea, and he still wanted nothing so much as a life bound to it. His enthusiasm gave new spirit to Rane, Caleb, and Morgan, though none of them was unaware of how difficult it was going to be to rebuild a shipping line now that the British and other foreign powers had taken over most trade while Union shipping had declined.

Phoebe evinced every sign of being completely dedicated to furthering the education of the freed slaves in the South and to staying with Aubrey Edwards, whom she planned to marry in September.

Philly continued to view the matter philosophically. "Perhaps they won't do so badly. He is well educated, and she is practical enough to make sure that what they both know will be put to good use. She makes it very clear in her letters that she expects their way will be difficult; already slave owners who fled their lands along the coast are coming back, and Phoebe does not think the former slaves will be the winners when it comes to land disputes."

The secret of Philly's equanimity was that she was prepared to accept almost anything as long as her daughters were alive and reasonably happy. It had not been quite the same as with Sam's boys, but Larissa, Anthea, and Phoebe had all been exposed to grave danger during the war. And she had learned just how terrified Blaine had been that one or more of his girls would not survive. He was reading the latest letter from Phoebe when suddenly his face contorted, and he bowed his head and wept.

"What is it?" Philly asked in alarm, certain she had not read anything of such a disastrous nature in her daughter's letter.

"It is nothing out of the ordinary. absolutely nothing, and that is everything. At first I thought the girls would not cause the same amount of worry as boys in the war, but our daughters went off as bravely as any sons. All these years I've feared to hear that one of them has contracted a deadly disease from an ailing soldier or been hit by a stray shot. And now it is finally dawning on me that all three of them have prevailed and are getting on with their lives."

"I am so sorry, my love," Philly said. "You are so blessedly calm and rational, I forget that you can be as terrified as the rest of us. But you were right to gift me with your silence; I kept thinking, 'Blaine is not so worried; therefore, I need not be either.' "

She held him close to her heart and felt him tremble for a long time.

And then they talked for hours about their plans, both of them taking growing delight in the realization that it was now possible to consider what they wanted to do rather than what they had to do for the war effort. Blaine looked forward most of all to a return of normalcy to the law. He had understood the president's need to suspend certain rights, but it had never settled easily with him. In the ordered world Blaine wished to inhabit, the law would be the law not less but more in times of emergency.

Philly's dream was part of Flora's, but no less her own for that. She and Flora had discussed the new purpose for the school along with the old. They had admitted to each other that there were decided advantages to being married to successful men who did not need their wives' wages to put bread on the table.

"Lord knows, it will be a miracle if we ever make a profit again," Flora said cheerfully, "but none need education more than freed slaves and women, both black and white."

Flora's fervor for the cause of women had not died during the war, and she saw very clearly that with so many men coming out of the army and needing jobs, many of the jobs women had done for the past four years would be taken away from them. She understood that she could not change the inevitable, but she wanted women to have at least a basic education in order that they might have a chance to make something of their lives. Philly shared her enthusiasm, though both of them had to accept that their work would be only a tiny flicker in the vast darkness of need.

Watching his wife's animated face as she described plans for the school, Blaine smiled and then laughed aloud. "I have no doubt where Phoebe comes from! But I am glad you have better taste in men."

Abandoning seriousness for the play that had been too long lacking in the stress of their lives, Philly brazenly licked at his ears and then nibbled his mouth. "Ummmm, I have very good taste in men."

"And I have superb taste in women," Blaine countered, and he proceeded to show her how delicious he found her.

Flora and Philly approached Sam about teaching with them as she had in the past, and though she didn't refuse, neither did she agree to it. They did not press her, accepting that her adjustment was more difficult than theirs.

Sam and Morgan were unendingly grateful that Nigel and Adam had survived the war, but Seth's absence continued to be a raw wound. Both of them had read his journals until they knew them nearly by heart, but nothing could replace his living presence. And Sam had come so close to losing Morgan as well, she still had a tendency to become panicky when he was away from her for too long. Though he said nothing about it, Morgan eased her anxiety by staying close to her when he could and by telling her exactly where he was going and when he planned to return if it was necessary for him to be away from her.

When Sam's father died in early June in a fall from a horse, Morgan was far more angry than sorry. There was no deathbed reconciliation, just a slave coming to Wild Swan to ask that the news be conveyed to "Miss Sam" in Baltimore.

When Sam received the news, her only reaction was, "Well, so there's an end to it." And she betrayed no surprise when she learned that she had been deliberately disinherited in her father's will and that Brookhaven had been left to her half brother by her father's second wife Lydia. The only concern she showed was for the slaves at Brookhaven, left as part of the property to her half brother.

"Slavery has been abolished in the South, and it will be here soon; I am sure of it," Morgan told her. "At least there is no market for the people at Brookhaven; I expect the new owner will let them stay." He could not bring himself to call the man her brother, nor could he let the matter remain as it was, but he did not tell Sam about his plans. He spent as much time with her as he could and hoped that she would not keep the hurt her father had caused her locked inside forever.

Alex felt no more regret over Mr. Sheldon-Burke's death than Morgan did, but that was not her reaction to the letter from Maddy Sinclair.

With the birth of Gincie's first child drawing near, Rane was staying at the farm as much as possible, not so much for the women in this case, as for Travis, who, though he was doing his best to hide it, was growing more fearful for his wife by the day. Rane drew his own peace from the land that reflected so much of Alex's spirit, an·d he wanted Travis to share in it, too.

This day Rane felt pleasantly tired, after lending a hand at various tasks, but he tensed at Della's words.

"She's just sitting in the library. She doesn't want tea or anything else, she says, just wants to be alone for a while. But I don't think she ought to be, she looks so . . . so little and lost."

Rane saw what she meant as soon as he went to Alex.

"Sweetling, what is it?" he asked softly.

Disoriented, she blinked at him for a moment, and then she handed him the letter.

Maddy Sinclair had not written to place blame or seek aid; she simply wanted to let Alex know that Justin Sinclair and Allen Ralston were dead. "They both considered you a special friend and a great horse-woman," Maddy wrote, "and I know you will share my grief in their passing."

Allen had died months before, shot down when he tried to defend Windower from raiders—Maddy did not specify whether they had been Confederate, Union, or renegades—and Justin had died of wounds received while serving with Lee's army in the last days of the war.

"God damn it!" Rane swore, and then he added a string of oaths that would have done any sailor proud. "It never ends!"

His cursing was more healing to Alex than gentle sympathy would have been, because he reflected her dawning rage, rage that the war had not spared those two old friends, though under the fury moved a vast current of sorrow for all the losses.

Rane picked her up, and then he settled down with her in his lap, and they remained like that for long minutes, until Alex finally said, "I have reminded myself again and again of what my grandmother told me—that people devise all sorts of spells and prayers for births and deaths because they are the two most important events in life, but that in truth we have no power over either. That seems a simple fact, but I think we still go on believing we have some control. The war and its aftermath have made me feel adrift, more at the mercy of the currents than ever before. Life and death are so tangled, I don't have any idea how I will react from one moment to the next—joy, sorrow, and anger seem to be the same these days. Right now, part of me accepts that Allen and Justin are dead, but another part is certain that I will see them riding into Wild Swan one day or that I will meet them at a racecourse somewhere. They were both good men. And poor Maddy, she has lost her son and her husband."

There was no easy comfort for Rane to offer, but he refrained from adding to her burden by speaking his thoughts aloud; he was sure that Allen Ralston had never ceased loving Alex, though outwardly he had confined himself to friendship once he had understood that Alex and Rane were in love.

Sam showed more reaction to Justin's death than she had to her father's, and before he could stop himself, Morgan snapped, "You would not have been in Maddy Sinclair's place! There is no way on earth I would have let you get away from me, not even if you had married Justin."

Sam regarded him in amazement. "Even after all these years, you are still jealous! I ought to think that is foolish, yet I find I am very flattered. But I wasn't considering that I might have been Justin's wife—I can no longer imagine being with anyone but you; even back then I didn't imagine it for long—I was thinking about how young we were and how carefree."

Mollified by her avowal of love, Morgan said, "Young, yes, we were that, but carefree, not entirely. We knew even then that terrible trouble would come if slavery did not end."

Sam nestled wearily against him. "Just hold me, please, just hold me."

The birth of Gincie's baby in mid-June heartened them all. Gincie went into labor early in the morning, and late that night produced a lively baby girl whom she and Travis named Alexandria Abigail Culhane, quickly nicknamed "Lexy," as Alex's brother Boston had called her in childhood.

Gincie did her work with enduring patience, but by the time the baby arrived, Travis was near collapse, and Alex sent him to Rane to be dosed with brandy.

"Going into battle didn't scare me as much as this," Travis confessed.

Rane nodded in sympathy. "Even though it's been over thirty years since Alex bore her last child, I can still remember the terror of it all too well. It is not the same as being in danger yourself; it's much, much worse to see someone you love in danger and to be unable to help."

Travis went back to Gincie, and finding her sleeping, he drew Alex and Dr. Cameron aside, the midwife who had assisted having already left the room. "Gincie looks so white and still, are you sure she's all right?" Travis asked.

Alex smiled at him. "I'm absolutely sure! She's done a hard day's work, and she needs a rest, but that's all."

When he looked back at Gincie, her eyes were open, her mouth curved in a smile. "Don't worry, darlin'," she said, mimicking his drawl perfectly, "you'll feel better tomorrow."

Travis had to laugh at that, and his tension eased enough so that he could enjoy the sight of his tiny newborn daughter lying close to her mother. "You're beautiful, both of you," he whispered in awe, and he did not notice that Alex and Alastair had left the room.

"Another generation at Wild Swan—I find that idea very pleasing," Alastair said, and he, Alex, and Rane toasted Alexandria Abigail Culhane, wishing her a long, healthy, and interesting life.

"Named as she is for her two formidable great-grandmothers, I don't see how she could possibly become less than a fascinating woman," Rane said, and his eyes as well as his words paid tribute to Alex.

Epilogue

Wild Swan, Prince George's County, Maryland, July, 1865

The first horse to return to Wild Swan was not one of the Thoroughbreds.

Alex recognized the animal before she recognized the man who was riding another horse and leading the half-bred gelding.

"Porthos!" Alex cried, and it all came back to her—the trooper at Gettysburg offering her Seth's horse to take back and her bidding him keep the animal until the war was over. She had not really believed she would ever see either of them again.

"Welcome to Wild Swan," she said as the man dismounted.

"Miz Falconer." He touched his hat in greeting. He was no longer in Union blue, but he still carried himself with easy confidence. He looked around and then nodded. "Yep, it's no wonder Capt'n Falconer cared for this place." He held Porthos's reins toward her. "I brung the horse back, jus' like we said."

"I am very, very glad you got through the war and Porthos, too." She made a swift decision. "You have come so far together, please keep the horse if you have use for him."

"Thank you all the same, ma'am, but I made a promise—if Porthos'd carry me safely, I'd bring 'im home. He kept his side of it, now I'm keepin' mine." He evinced not the slightest embarrassment at confessing to having struck a bargain with a horse, and Alex felt a swell of liking for the man.

He refused all rewards except a meal, paid a visit to Seth's grave, and went on his way.

"A lot of men died, ma'am, but none finer than your grandson. Me an' the rest of the men that came through it won't forget 'im.'"

His parting words had brought tears to her eyes, but Alex was also comforted; as young as he had been, Seth had earned his own kind of immortality.

Polly and Calvin's sons-in-law and Jotham had returned from their regiment, and Jimmy Barlow and other workers had also come back. Alex welcomed them all, but she did not press them about their plans. She realized that their years in the army might have changed their goals, but one by one they came to her and told her that they would like to stay on at Wild Swan. She was touched most of all by Jotham.

"I'm not the man my father was," he told her bluntly. "No one can take his place. But he taught me how to train a horse without breaking its heart, and I can work fine with Padraic and with the Barlows." He paused, and then he added in a low voice, "Sometimes thinking about Wild Swan and the horses was all that kept me going."

"I am very pleased that you will be staying," Alex said gently. "You have your father's job. I leave it to you and Padraic to work out the details." She did not fear a problem there; Jotham had a wife and child while Padraic had had nothing but the horses since Katy's death. Alex was quite sure that Padraic and Jotham would divide the work by choice as Padraic and Samson had by necessity, with Padraic going to the race-courses, and Jotham managing the farm in his absence.

At last Alex could see Wild Swan coming to life again, and her excitement began to build in anticipation of the horses' return. But she tried to be practical as well.

"No one can predict what turn racing will take. The best of it was vested in the South, and now nothing is left there."

Rane refused to share her doubts. "People are desperate for pleasure, and watching fine horses run and wagering on the outcome is the preferred pastime of more than a few in this country. The racing may be done in the North and the West now instead of the South, but it will be done. In a few years, there will be more race meetings than you can attend."

Alex was grateful for his reassurance, but she did not fool herself. In one sense, racing as she had known it for most of her life was over. When she and St. John had arrived in America, they had had to learn the ways of American long-distance racing, and now she was to relearn the English style, because the longer races were, she was certain, a thing of the past. The four-mile-heat races had been grueling contests, difficult to watch to the finish. Yet at the same time, a part of her acknowledged the loss, knowing that the gallantry of horses such as American Eclipse, John Bascombe, Fashion, Boston, Swan, and a host of others would not be seen again.

They began to arrive at the end of July, first Padraic, Jackson Barlow, and the horses from Nova Scotia, and then the animals shipped from England, minus the few Alex had decided to leave there for the rest of this year's racing schedule and the yearlings who would race as two-year-olds next year.

Chestnuts, bays, browns, blacks—even after the rigors of travel, the Thoroughbreds were exquisite to Alex. Their coats shot rainbows in the sun; their voices filled the air from stallion scream to the endearing whicker of foals investigating new territory at their mothers' sides; and their long legs flashed as they thundered around the pastures, running swiftly and surely for sheer joy, impelled by centuries of careful breeding.

Alex existed in a haze of joy for days, greeting old friends—among them Swan's Chance, Swan's Shadow, Fire Dancer, Lady Sailaway, and Irish Lass—and making the acquaintance of young stallions and mares she had previously only read about in letters. Swan's Chance in particular seemed to recognize her, and even if he didn't, the illusion was pleasing. His name meant more to her now than when he had been given it—the horses, the farm, and all of the survivors had another chance to prosper after the killing years.

There was sorrow, too. Padraic had had time to adjust to the loss of Samson, but still Alex saw him look around in the first moments of his arrival as if he expected Samson to greet him. And she saw the little shake of his head he gave, as if to remind himself that it was not to be. She did not say anything about it, leaving it up to him to discuss Samson's death if he wished. His answer was in the small bouquets of flowers that appeared not only on Katy's and Fergus's graves, but also on Samson's, Seth's, and Luke's within days of Padraic's arrival.

Alex was not so reticent about what he had done for her. "Never has trust been better placed," she told him. "I sent you away with the dreams and work of years, and you have brought back far more. I will always be grateful."

"No need fer that. This is my home, fer all that I was born across the sea." Emotion made his voice gruff, but the Irish lilt was sweet music to Alex after so many years of not hearing it. She had further cause for gratitude when she noted that he, Jotham, and Jed Barlow quickly found a smooth way to work together, none of them indulging in petty jealousy or stratagems to acquire more power.

"Your other children are finally home," Rane teased Alex as they stood outside in the summer dusk one evening with no other purpose in mind except to listen to the last sounds of the day on the farm and to observe the horses before the light failed.

Alex breathed a sigh of utter contentment. "See that three-year-old colt, the black with the white snip on his nose? He looks so much like Swan's Chance, and that chestnut filly is a lovely feminine throwback to Swan."

Rane chuckled as he observed Gincie and Travis walking along one of the fences, Travis carrying their infant daughter in his arms. "I think Lexy is being introduced to her equine relatives."

"It's lovely having them here, isn't it?" Alex said. "Travis has been back to Hawthorn so seldom, only two times, and he stayed such a short time while there, I've begun to think perhaps they will stay here. Oh, how much I would like that!"

Rane turned her to face him and took both of her hands in his, and his expression was very serious in the fading light. "Sweetling, enjoy them while they're here, but don't set your heart on their staying. Remember, lives are still being sorted out, and you and Wild Swan give the family the strength to do that, but that does not mean the choices will be as you wish."

"Have Gincie and Travis spoken to you?" she asked suspiciously, a chill snaking through her veins.

"No," he answered honestly, "and I have not asked them what their plans are. They will tell us when they are ready. I just do not want you to be too disappointed if their plans do not fit with yours."

Alex reminded herself that if the young couple did return to Virginia, it would not be the same as it had been during the war; Virginia would once more be part of the United States. Provisions and requirements were already being set forth for the Confederate states to be readmitted to the Union. And yet it was difficult not to dwell on the delight it would be were the Culhanes to settle at Wild Swan with the baby. Alex had an endless list of things she wanted to teach and show her great-granddaughter.

It was a summer of family, and Alex loved having the house full of children, grandchildren, their spouses, and their friends. Even Frank Faber came visiting again. Larissa reported that he had begun to see a young woman in Georgetown and that that must be making it easier for him to be around Gincie.

"I'm feeling very grandmotherly these days," Alex told Rane, "and I find I enjoy it more than ever before. It has an ease and privilege not granted to mere parents."

"I quite agree," Rane said. "I find my words accepted as if spoken by a sage, even when I have been discussing the most mundane subjects." He pulled a very dignified face for a moment, and then he grinned. "Wouldn't they all be shocked if they knew what we still do in bed?"

"We may be a bit slower, but we are very, very thorough and very, very skillful," Alex purred wickedly, and then she giggled, beguiling Rane with the decidedly youthful sound that belied her claim of feeling like a grandmother. But they both knew the truth that lay beneath their new levity—during the war, their role as elders in the family had been more pain than pleasure, making them witnesses to the depredations of the war without giving them the power to protect the younger generations. In the far more ordered world of peacetime, they both felt they had much more to offer each other and the family.

Though Alex had to admit that her joints tended to creak a bit, even her body felt younger these days from the vigorous riding she was doing. With the racing stock needing exercise, there was an overabundance of fine, fast horses to ride, and the family, good riders all, enjoyed helping with the task when they were at the farm.

Morgan chose such an excursion early one summer morning to give his gift to Sam.

"I am surprised at you," she teased. "Whatever possessed you to want to be out so early? The sun is barely rising!" But she hadn't tarried in donning her riding habit, and she looked bright-eyed in the pale light.

He kissed the tip of her nose. "You possessed me. I want to see the world at dawn with you."

They rode out, but when Sam realized Morgan was leading her toward the boundary of Brookhaven, she balked. "I don't want to go there," she said with quiet intensity.

"I can't ever make up for my cruelty that drove you away," Morgan said, "but I hope this will soften the memory of it."

Sam took the paper he handed her, and when she had read it, she stammered, "I don't—I don't understand."

"Brookhaven is yours to do with as you will, keep it or sell it, it is no matter to me. But I could not bear the injustice of your losing it for my sake. I bought it from your half brother. I am willing to admit that relationship now because he was quite decent about Brookhaven. He didn't want it, and he did not think it right, either, that he should inherit after your years of work. He sold it for a fair price. He came to Baltimore for the final transfer, but before that, Blaine helped with the correspondence and legalities. There is no way your ownership can be disputed now."

She had not said a word to him about her longing to return to Brookhaven, but sometimes she had felt the pull of the land as if it were a physical force, and it had been all she could do not to ride over the beloved acres. She had accepted the severance of contact with her father, but the land was innocent and called out for the nurturing she had given it for so long. That Morgan had not only felt her longing but had acted upon it was a fine measure of the depth of his love.

She leaned from the saddle to hug him, and then they rode in to Brookhaven together, the sunrise turning the tears rolling down Sam's cheeks to living crystal. Tears of joy and of sorrow, too, for the final acceptance that her relationship with her father had never been and would never be touched by the love she had needed from him.

Brookhaven was shabbier than it had been, but there was nothing that could not be repaired. The slaves, grown fearful and apathetic in the absence of a master and not sure of what would become of them, had nonetheless stayed because they did not know what else to do.

One by one they wandered out as word of Sam's presence spread, and as they saw that it was really she, they began to smile.

"My husband has purchased Brookhaven for me," she announced in a clear voice, her tears under control. "And I intend to keep it. As of this moment, you are all free. I will see that the papers are properly drawn. You may go or stay, as you wish. But I will welcome any of you who would like to remain and work for me for wages."

Morgan and Sam rode back to Wild Swan with the joyful words of the ex-slaves still ringing in their ears, and there was no lack of rejoicing at Wild Swan either, for neither Rane nor Alex had known of Morgan's scheme.

Rane was enormously proud of his son for choosing such a direct way to ease the hurt he had caused Sam. Alex shared this pride, but she was also looking ahead. The renewal of Sam's ties to Brookhaven meant not only justice, but with Brookhaven and Wild Swan both in the family, she could envision her grandsons spending that much more time in the country in the future and bringing their future wives and children to enjoy it. And though she tried to heed Rane's warning not to count too much on Gincie's and Travis's remaining at Wild Swan, it was impossible to prevent herself from imagining little Lexy and any brothers or sisters she might have playing with Adam's or Nigel's children or perhaps Larissa's. It was not altogether impossible that Anthea and Phoebe might also bring their children to Wild Swan and Brookhaven one day.

Inwardly she laughed at her own folly in giving her grandchildren imaginary offspring, but the charming pictures remained clear in her mind, particularly because Lexy was coming into her own as an individual by the day, losing the commonality of the newborn. She was a long, elegant baby with slender hands and feet, sure to take after both of her tall parents, and though she was lively, she was easily contented by being within the sound of human voices. Alex doted on her and maintained that it was simply impossible to spoil a baby by loving it too much.

"It's called the great-grandmother law," Travis muttered darkly, but he was remarkably adept himself at spending absorbed hours with his daughter. And the sight of Lexy at Gincie's breast never failed to move him, evoking a response so deep and primitive that he continued to be awed by it. It was as if the three of them were bound together by an invisible cord as strong as time.

And with the tenderness and the protectiveness he felt came the desire to be settled and providing well for his family.

"Are you very sure?" Gincie asked him when he prepared to go to Virginia. "For the moment don't think about me and Lexy, think about yourself. You will be surrendering your past to relatives you don't even like; can you bear that?"

"You are my past, my present, my future," he answered, echoing Gincie's declaration, and her doubts eased. She did not accompany him on his final visit to Hawthorn, nor did she tell her grandparents the purpose of it until Travis returned.

They approached Alex and Rane together. Very directly Travis explained what he had done and why.

"I have sold Hawthorn to my cousins. They are foolish and self-indulgent in many ways, but they possess the basic knowledge to be good farmers. And if they fail, it will be on their own heads. Most of the people who worked for me are gone; those who remain are strong and educated enough to demand fair wages and to leave if they do not get them. My cousins made a good profit on blockade runners during the war, and they did not trust Confederate dollars." He grimaced in distaste. "And at least I got a good price from them for Hawthorn. Gincie and I will be able to start a new life in reasonable comfort." He took a deep breath and persevered, trying to ignore the stricken look in Alex's eyes. "We have decided to go to California."

California. Boston and his family and Samson and Della's son Malachi lived there; horses from Wild Swan had been sent there for years; Jennings-Falconer ships had traded along its coast; and yet, to Alex California remained a mythical place a vast world distant.

"I want to run away," Travis said. "I know that is what I am doin', and I thank God that Gincie is willin' to go with me. It is impossible to know exactly what President Lincoln would have done, but he meant the civil rights of blacks to be part of his 'reconstruction.' President Johnson calls his own plan 'restoration,' and I dislike the man and the term because I don't believe either is strong enough to rebuild a reasonable South. There are voices in the North clamorin' for severe punishment of the Southern states and voices in the South demandin' that all former rights and privileges be reinstated as if the war never happened. And no matter what happens, I foresee only sorrow for the freedmen in the next years. They are not like most people displaced by war. They have no lands or villages of their own to return to. Already it begins—endless schemin' to cheat the blacks of their new free status. And there are evil whispers; even my idiot relatives have heard them. Whispers of organizations being formed in the Deep South to defend the 'sacred rights' of white Southerners against Yankee barbarians and black savages. This despite the fact that the freedmen have not risen up to kill their former owners, but have instead, in more than a few cases, sheltered them and taught them the skills necessary for survival."

Travis reached out and took Gincie's hand in his own, needing the contact. "Some sort of justice and equilibrium will surely prevail one day, but I do not have the patience to wait for it to be done, nor the courage to help establish it."

His voice died away. The room was utterly still.

Alex wanted to cry out in protest, but she was mesmerized by the sight of Gincie's fingers curled trustingly in Travis's hand, and she could feel Rane willing her to caution.

Finally she said, "You have obviously been thinking about this for some time. I hope you will allow me time to consider your plan." It was the best she could do. She left them without another word.

"Give her that time, children," Rane said. "She loves you and Lexy very much, and the idea of your going so far away is a shock. But she will adjust; she always does. She cares too much about other people's feelings not to."

In the next days, he wondered if he was expecting too much of her. She would not discuss Gincie and Travis at all, and she spent long hours riding alone, as she had always done when she was troubled. He held her at night, but even though she did not move away from him, he felt her distance.

At first Alex managed to keep her mind quite blank, working at it by exhausting her body, but then she was sabotaged by the relentless honesty of her nature, and the thoughts she had tried to hold back flooded through her.

She had thought that seeing Gincie leave for Virginia on the eve of war had been the hardest thing she would face with this treasured granddaughter, but now she knew the fallacy of that. California was not only a river away in a bordering state; California was thousands of miles away. And she would never go there. She knew it as absolutely as her own grandmother had known she would never see Maryland. It was possible that the Culhanes might come back to visit Wild Swan one day, but there was no guarantee of that, and at best, rare visitors were all they would be henceforth in her life.

Everything Travis had said about the current situation in the South was true. And beyond that, the young woman she had been when she had emigrated to America and the man Travis was now were very much the same. She had wanted to leave behind all the sorrow and injustice she had known in England, and St. John had changed the shape of his dreams for her, just as Gincie was doing for Travis.

But Alex was no longer in Travis's position; she was now where her own grandmother had been forty-five years ago when Virginia had watched the departure of the ship carrying Alex, St. John, and their children away from her to the New World.

Alex had taken all the love, kindness, and wisdom her grandmother Virginia had offered. And she had tried to give the same gifts in her turn to Gincie. But to close the circle of her grandmother's life and her own demanded that the last gift given to her by Virginia be passed in turn to

Gincie. Virginia had given her benediction for the journey to America; Alex could give no less to Gincie for her own journey. Now she understood that Gincie's years at Hawthorn had been only a beginning.

She bowed her head under the onslaught of pain at the vision of a future without Gincie, Travis, and Lexy.

She had lost children as her grandmother had; she was bound to a particular piece of earth as her grandmother had been; she had been shaped heart, soul, and mind by her grandmother, but all was not the same.

Her grandmother had lost her husband Trahern decades before she herself had died. As far as Alex knew, her grandmother had never again known the love of a man after Trahern had perished at sea.

Alex's situation was profoundly different for one reason: she had Rane beside her. Rane, still fit and strong and handsome in her eyes in his seventy-first year. Rane, still shielding her when he could and accepting when the battles were her own. Rane, still mirror of her life as she was of his. She thought of all the lives cut short by the war, and she was humbled by the gift of time she and Rane shared.

The children and grandchildren, including Gincie, had their own lives to lead, their own paths to follow. Someday one of them might want to take over Wild Swan and the Thoroughbreds, perhaps Larissa and Reid, who showed more and more interest in the day-to-day running of the farm. And Sam, trained by Alex, was already competent from her years of overseeing Brookhaven. Sam was also determined that Morgan would spend more time in the country in order that a slower pace of life might prevent future attacks of malaria.

But Alex understood now that it did not matter if no one carried on after she was gone. Wild Swan was part of her dreams. Hers to cherish while she lived, hers to relinquish when she died. And Rane was the greater part of all the dreams she had ever had.

Except for Larissa and Reid, the grandchildren were scattering to the four winds, perhaps to return to Maryland or the District of Columbia, perhaps never to live close by again. For the first time, Alex was able to face it all without fear, without regret.

She went to Rane. "You can cease worrying about me. I did a very foolish thing. I began taking you for granted."

He regarded her in puzzlement, not sure what connection this had with the recent turmoil.

She reached up and framed his face in her hands. "I have you.

With the world torn to pieces, and widows weeping everywhere, I have you. Let the grandchildren pursue their own dreams; you are mine. I swear to you I will not only let them go from me, I will celebrate their leaving. Because of you, I know joy; I can wish no less for them."

Rane felt the slender length of her hands against his skin; he felt the warmth of her body touching his; he breathed in the scent of her and drowned in the clear, deep green of her eyes. The silver in her dark hair, the faint tracery around her eyes and mouth, lines left from years of laughter and weeping, made her even more beautiful to him now than she had been in the smooth perfection of youth. And yet, he perceived that the same spirit that had captured him then still held him fast. The same steadfast courage, the same gallantry, the same loving heart were there to enchant him as they had from the very first day.

His throat tightened, tears gleamed in his eyes, and with infinite gentleness he drew her to him and cradled her against him. He noticed then that she was wearing the swan necklace clasped around her neck, just as he had imagined it when he had purchased it for her on a free trading run more than half a century before.

She was as good as her word. In September she watched Phoebe marry Aubrey Edwards and return to the South. She saw Nigel, Anthea, and Max off to their medical schools. And she wished each of them joy and meant it. In November she greeted the news of Larissa's pregnancy with a glad heart. And when the winter was giving way to the first hint of spring, when the wild swans were leaving and new foals were still being born, Alex bade good-bye to Gincie, Travis, and Lexy with an unfaltering smile, sending with them a fine young Thoroughbred mare and a stallion.

"You may keep or sell them," she had told Gincie and Travis. "Either way, Wild Swan will be part of your new life."

And just when she thought she could not bear it after all, because Lexy was reaching for her with a little cry, the baby's green eyes filling with tears, Rane gripped Alex's hand tightly, whispering, "I will love you forever."

As much as she heard the husky words, she felt them in the lean strength of him, in the solid pulse of life she could feel in his hand. And in a strange way, she felt as if they, like Gincie and Travis, were starting out together all over again instead of coming to the end of their lives. Full circle.